All Who Are Lost

LINDSEY FORREST

All Who Are Lost

Ashmore's Folly Trilogy: Book One

St. John Publishing Group, Inc.
Plano, TX

St. John Publishing Group, Inc.
P.O. Box 250774
Plano, TX 75025-0774
www.stjohnpub.com

First St. John Publishing Group e-book edition, October 2014.
First St. John Publishing Group paperback edition, October 2014.

The characters and events, except for those of obvious historical
importance, are fictitious. Any similarity to real persons,
living or dead, is coincidental and not intended by the author.

Library of Congress Cataloging-in-Publication Data.

Forrest, Lindsey.
All Who Are Lost / Lindsey Forrest – 1st ed.
ISBN-10 (print): 1941521020
ISBN-13 (print): 978-1-941521-01-4
1. Contemporary Family – Fiction. 2. Contemporary Romance – Fiction.
3. September 11, 2001 – Fiction. 4. Forbidden Romance – Fiction.
5. Virginia – Fiction. I. Title

Cover Design by Robin Ludwig Design Inc.
(www.gobookcoverdesign.com)
Book Design by St. John Publishing Group, Inc.

Dedication

To Elizabeth and Lucas
lights of my life

Table of Contents

All Who Are Lost

Yes: I have re-entered your olden haunts at last;
Through the years, through the dead scenes I have tracked you;
What have you now found to say of our past—
    Scanned across the dark space wherein I have lacked you?

("After a Journey," Thomas Hardy)

Act One:
If All Else Perished

If all else perished,
and he remained,
I should still continue to be;

and if all else remained,
and he were annihilated,
the universe would turn to a mighty stranger:
I should not seem a part of it.

(Wuthering Heights, Emily Bronte)

1

Ghost of a Girl

I KNOW YOU'RE OUT there somewhere....

She stared out across a crowded London square, unknowing, unseeing, the serenity of her face captured in the flat surface of the theatrical poster. The light noon rain ran down in small diagonal rivers across her, crinkling the smooth plain of her forehead and the gentle cut of her jaw. She wept, large, abandoned tears that warred with the lovely turn of her mouth.

The Great Cat, they called her.

Many of those who had come to Leicester Square, hunting for half-price theater tickets, gravitated to her, beckoned by her eyes, lured on by the legend of mist and mystery that surrounded her. A few balked at the price of "An Intimate Evening with Cat Courtney." Others realized to their sorrow that they had conflicting tickets, meals planned with in-laws, flights to catch. Three nights only, announced the poster, and this, unfortunately, was the last night.

She smiled out at them all, oblivious to their concerns, uncaring of the rain wetting her face.

The American tourist who came walking into the square, his daughter by his side, did not notice her at first. The rain had stopped for a few minutes, and other matters engaged him: folding up a handy umbrella, glancing at his watch, reading a guide book over his daughter's shoulder. For one minute longer, he remained merely a tourist on a much-needed vacation. For one minute longer, the Great Cat never crossed his mind.

But the Great Cat could wait, and for this man she would wait forever.

She had left him a decade before, both of them reeling from the blood of their folly, in a deserted cottage on a desolate shore on the other side of the world. Had she eyes to see, she would know him instantly.

Eventually, respite ended. Eventually, Richard Ashmore lifted his head, his eyes scanning across the theatrical posters, in search of an evening's entertainment suitable for a young girl. The titles made little impression – *Les Miserables*, *The Graduate*, *Noises Off* – until he saw her and everything around her blurred into oblivion.

He knew her too, instantly.

Laura.

His worst mistake.

"Dad?" Julie touched her hand to his. "Do you think we can get tickets?"

"We can try." Richard closed his fingers around hers, a talisman to ward memory off. "Don't get your hopes up, Julie. Her concerts usually sell out."

"Let's ask over there," suggested his daughter, pointing across the square to the ticket kiosk. "Maybe someone bought tickets and can't go. Maybe someone dropped their tickets, and someone turned them in. Maybe—"

"Maybe, maybe, maybe," he teased, but already he was allowing her to drag him across the stones towards the waiting queue.

They took their places in line. Julie was glowing with excitement, the happiest Richard had seen her since the morning before her grandparents had died. He was less optimistic. Others ahead of them had requested tickets, and the possibility of stray tickets lessened as they moved up the line. He sought to cushion her against disappointment by letting her plan the afternoon. They were only a couple of blocks from the National Gallery, or would she prefer to hop the tube for Harrods?

"Harrods," said Julie immediately. "And tea, Dad." She leaned in against him to look at his guidebook. "I have my birthday money from Lucy. I want to get something to wear to the concert."

"Keep your money, kitten." He wished that they had never seen the poster. Selfish, yes, but if meeting her eyes in a poster disturbed him, how would he feel to see her again, even in the black anonymity of an audience? Better not to know, better to go back to an occasional evening of listening to her songs in the dark and trying to make some sense of what had happened.

And Julie had endured enough recently.

They were second in line now, behind a couple attempting to get tickets to the latest Andrew Lloyd Webber. *Good luck*, thought Richard, who had tried for three months. They bought him a few minutes of reprieve while they settled for a sex comedy instead.

"Two for Cat Courtney," he said, and if the gods had been with him, just this once, he would have been told in that inimitable British way, *Sorry, sir, but that show has just sold out….*

"Yes, a few tickets have been turned in," and his fate was sealed. He and Julie looked at the seating chart. She sparkled as she so seldom did, and as he paid for the tickets he thought that he would bear any pain, any guilt, to see that look on her face.

"Those are good seats," said the man behind him, another American from the sound of him. "I've seen her before, and she's worth twice the price."

Julie forgot her usual shyness with strangers. "I can't wait! I've wanted to see her for so long—"

A woman with a Southern accent said kindly, "You know, darlin', you're just the picture of her."

"Thank you," said Julie. "I'm glad I am. She's my aunt."

And Richard Ashmore looked at the tickets and realized, with a shock, that it was June 9, and he had been married for seventeen years.

In his life, Richard Ashmore had made three mistakes with women. Not that three was so unusual; no man reached his thirties without suffering the particular pain that women could inflict and without inflicting it in return. He was luckier than most men, perhaps, for he had erred early and grievously, and caution had been driven into him like a bullet. He carried with him permanent reminders of his follies: a marriage gone disastrously wrong, the painful conscience that he had not always been the upright man his daughter loved, a shoulder that ached in cold weather.

Ah, Diana, unattainable once attained, a monumental mistake made in all the first flush of adolescent desire and pride. Too young to marry, too blindly in love to recognize the ice behind her eyes, he had turned a deaf ear to his father's warning that his princess was hollow at her core.

Francie, silver-quick smile and hungry eyes, and his own need for the warmth of a woman's arms. The dangerous combination of a magnum of champagne on New Year's Eve and three years of exile from his marriage bed had erupted into a springtime of madness. The gods had demanded their due: a marriage wrecked beyond salvage, a family foundered, two young women cast adrift.

And the third…. Oh, but even now, all these years later, he stood before her picture, and he still did not understand. She watched him from the poster, more animated in flat gray and white than he had ever known her. But he knew those eyes. He knew how they adored him, how they burned in fever and desire, how they haunted odd moments of the day and dark pockets of the night.

Diana. Francie. Laura the Cat.

He supposed he had a special weakness for shuttered eyes that invited a man in with promises implied and unkept, for wild autumn hair spread gloriously across a pillow, for tall, elegant figures and clear, sweet voices and beguiling, destructive ways. They all three had this and more in common, and why not? They were sisters, after all.

Julie tried hard to contain her enthusiasm all afternoon, first at Harrods, then at the V&A. She tagged along quietly while Richard sketched the woodwork, and he explored the bookstore while she toured the Worth collection. Later, they walked through the Pleasure Gardens in Battersea, where, so long ago, a young Air Force pilot attending the Festival of Britain had met a lively Irish nurse and fallen in love forever.

"Grandma knows we're here," whispered Julie, and was not old enough yet to hide the trembling of her lips.

He cradled his daughter against his chest and let her weep. Fifty years, he thought, a love affair that had spread across decades and formed the bedrock of his childhood. Even the horror of their deaths six weeks before, at the hands of a bourbon-soaked driver, lessened in the soul-felt knowledge that they would have preferred to die together than ever live one without the other.

He and Diana, married thirty-three years later, had scarcely lasted one summer.

Julie lifted her tear-streaked face from his jacket. "Dad?"

He stroked her hair. "Yes?"

"Grandma always loved Laura—" Julie drew a quivering breath. "Do you think she knows?"

In the days of grief, in the knowledge that he now stood alone, the last of his blood, he had never thought to wonder if Laura Abbott had learned of his parents' deaths. He considered the possibility and rejected it swiftly. Surely, surely, if she knew, she would have broken her years of silence.

"No," he said. "No, she doesn't know."

For, if she knew, her silence might be the one thing that he could not forgive her.

"Come on, kitten." He kissed his daughter's forehead. "Time for tea. Mom told me about a place she and Dad found when they were here last year."

Grief could not be buried, but they could put it aside for an hour, stepping out of time in a Knightsbridge tea shop, accepting scones and fresh cream from a Victorian maid. Peace and healing lay in sharing the tea Philip and Peggy Ashmore had described so enthusiastically. He could enjoy the quiet, the lack of hurry, the sight of Julie's lovely face across the table.

A perfect afternoon.

If only the gods had not decreed that his path would cross the trail of Cat Courtney....

"Do you think we can talk to her?" asked Julie.

"No." Richard reached for the strawberry jam. "She'll have security backstage."

At least, he hoped she did. He had good reason to believe that Cat Courtney was more insulated backstage than most performers. Three years before, her sisters had tried to call her during a live guest appearance on television and found it impossible to penetrate the wall around her.

"She might talk to me," Julie said hopefully. "She can't be mad at me, can she, Dad? I was only two when she ran away."

"Julie," he sighed, and put his hand over hers. "Don't count on it."

"But *why*? Why won't she talk to any of us?"

What could he say? He had kept her safe from the bitterness and guilt running like a cleft through the family. She might wonder occasionally why he refused to live with her mother, why he so carefully kept her away from his father-in-law, but she never asked and he never volunteered. Not that any of that mattered here and now.

Nothing explained why Laura Abbott, at seventeen, had left her father's house one summer day and walked away forever.

"She was very unhappy at home."

"But you didn't make her unhappy," Julie pointed out logically. "Grandma said Laura liked you. She might like to see you again, don't you think?"

No, I don't think, Julie. I think Laura would go to the ends of the earth not to see me again. I think I hurt her worse than anyone else ever did, including Dominic. You see, she thought she loved me. Then one day, and dear God, I do not know when or how, I taught her to hate me....

He took refuge in fatherhood. "Ready? I want to call Lucy before she goes to lunch."

"Okay," Julie said meekly, and bit into her scone.

She made one detour on the way back. They passed a florist, and Julie asked if they could send her aunt flowers. He endured one momentary vision of Laura throwing the flowers against her dressing room wall, but he looked at that young, beseeching face and wondered if this, after all, might be the best solution to Julie's need to reach out to her own flesh and blood. So they went in and ordered white roses sent to Miss Cat Courtney at the Eldin Theatre, and Julie signed the card: *Love to Laura, from Julie and Richard Ashmore.*

"Should I put my mother's name too?"

"No." He remembered again that it was his wedding anniversary.

Seventeen years, and on this day he was sending flowers not to his wife, but to her younger sister. Diana, lovely, lost Diana.... If he sent her roses now, would she even remember what day it was? Would she rub a petal against that exquisite face and remember the flowers he had sent her during their courtship?

Probably not. She had left off wearing his ring years before.

He still wore his wedding band – burnished gold, worn and shiny from years against his skin, with its faint memory of the spring afternoon when he and Diana had selected their rings. He supposed that most men were not that sentimental about their rings, and he was sentimental about little else, but he still cherished the ring Diana had placed on his finger. He had broken his marriage vows eventually, in the most spectacular fashion, and he had continued to break them sporadically after she left. He would break them in the future. He did not think that he loved his wife anymore or could ever love her again. But he was not ready to remove his ring.

He wondered how she was celebrating their anniversary, half a world away. He wondered who was keeping her company in that pale blue bedroom where he had been most manifestly unwelcome.

No roses. A futile gesture at best, and Diana might not be alone to receive them. He shuttered himself against the old anguish and bought a rose, not for Diana, but for her daughter.

The overseas operator connected Richard with Lucy just before she left for lunch.

"Well, this is a pleasant surprise," greeted the second of Dominic Abbott's daughters, and the only one who did not scourge his conscience. "What's up?"

He told her. She fell silent for a long, expensive moment, and his mind's eye saw her staring out her office window over the colonial rooftops of Williamsburg and into the past, a past made painful by the shadows of the two sisters who had left her and the one who had not.

"I can't promise we'll go backstage," he finished. "Julie wants to, but I don't think it's a good idea. I don't want her hurt. She's been through enough."

Lucy sounded subdued, a sure sign, for those who knew her, that she was fighting off her own ghosts. "Can you at least send a message? Laurie will talk to you, Richard. She doesn't have any quarrel with you."

Loyal and straightforward, Lucy did not suspect that Laura Abbott's quarrel ran more deeply with him than with anyone else in the family. But how could she? Now that his father was dead, that remained a blackness only he knew.

"I'll try," he promised, because she was his dear friend and he knew how badly Laura's silence had hurt her. "I'll report in tomorrow."

"We need to talk anyway. Listen, when you get back, I need some help with Di. I can't deal with her anymore."

He squelched the instant irritation. Oh, the damnable obligations and burdens of once-spoken vows: *For better or for worse.* "Now what?"

She hesitated. "Same old thing, I'm afraid. She hasn't been sober one day since you left." Her voice faded for a moment. "Please. I know you hate this, and I don't blame you, but you're the only one she'll listen to."

"I doubt that," he said flatly. "How bad is it this time?"

"She passed out at the Tavern last night."

"God!" *What's happened to you, Diana? Where have you gone?* "Where is she? At her place?"

Alone?

"I haven't heard from her today. She's probably still asleep." Her tone changed; she had finished with Diana. "Richard, if you do go backstage – even if you don't see Laurie – listen around, okay? People talk. I just need a name. If I can get that, I might be able to find her through Social Security."

He let her talk on, about checking with UK Immigration and trying again with Cat Courtney's record company and following up on the leads that had the Cat variously glimpsed in Seattle, Boston, Dallas, Miami. He summoned Julie in to talk to her aunt, and they did not speak of Laura again until he brought the transatlantic call to a close.

Lucy had one last instruction. "If you see her, give her a hug for me, will you? Then turn her over your knee and paddle the hell out of her for doing this to us!"

He felt on edge now. Julie had lent him her excitement, Lucy her hope and anxiety, but his own feelings encompassed so much more than anticipation of a gala evening on the town. It took him three attempts to knot his tie acceptably, and his fingers were so tensed that he could not insert his cuff links. Diana had performed that for him during their first year, when she still liked being his wife, before Julie was conceived and the world fell apart.

But his thoughts did not linger on Diana, sleeping off her excesses in her secluded chambers. He was keyed up because in an hour he would see *her*, she who had haunted him for ten years. He would be in the same room with her, he would hear her voice, he would look at that familiar, once-loving face. He did not feel like a husband seeking out an errant young sister-in-law, and he knew it.

"Oh, Dad, you look so handsome," said Julie, when he knocked on her door to escort him. "Too bad you can't have a real date tonight, instead of just me."

"And give up taking the prettiest girl in London to the theater?" He smiled down at her. At fifteen, she had all the promise of Diana's great beauty.

"Well," Julie pursued, as they took the lift down to the ground floor, "you shouldn't be with just a kid. You should be going with – with – someone sophisticated and beautiful – someone like Laura. That's the sort of woman you should date."

He looked at her sharply – he had a longstanding policy of not discussing his private life with anyone, including his daughter – but Julie had inherited the Abbott acting ability, and she was looking particularly innocent right now. He wondered if Lucy had said anything to her and rejected that thought out of hand. Little in life could be counted on, but Lucy's discretion was solid. Perhaps this was only another manifestation of Julie's natural longing for a mother, and so he said nothing to her.

Cat Courtney.

The Great Cat, a reporter had dubbed her, linking her to that other beauty whose passion for privacy had become the stuff of legend. A merry chase she had led the media these last years, a Cat-and-mouse game played from the safety of a wall of managers and shell corporations. Her New York address was empty, her biography patently false.

Her fans did not care. She drew them from all walks of life, young, old, her own tired contemporaries. Men sensed that she had long since lost all innocence; women recognized her pain. Cat Courtney knew all the anguish of loving a man who looked right through her.

You never saw, you never knew, I drifted by, a ghost of a girl....

She had loved him once. She had followed him around, baked his favorite cookies, defended his wilder ideas, smiled bravely when he married her older sister. He stood before the giant lobby poster of her incredible, lost face, and on cue his shoulder began to ache.

Thank heavens for Julie. She exclaimed over the ornate settings of the old theater, begged him to buy her the Cat Courtney bear (long curls, provocative outfit, two emerald glass eyes), speculated on the shadowy figures in the boxes, swore she saw Royalty, and fell into blissfully silent worship when the current James Bond took his seat three rows ahead. He retreated from her raptures by reading Laura's official biography in the glossy program.

Julie read along. "Is this true, Dad? She's married to some professor at Harvard?"

"No." Lucy had checked that out and found it as false as Cat Courtney's Foreign Service father or her Juilliard education.

"Then why—"

"She doesn't want us to know, Julie."

Indeed, Laura plainly did not. Her manager had so routinely met Lucy's calls with the statement that Cat Courtney had no living relatives that Lucy had long since abandoned that avenue.

"I wonder what she'll sing," mused Julie, flipping through her program. She sent him a sidelong glance. "Maybe 'Francie'?"

"Maybe," he said with gentle finality. He had no intention of discussing Francie Abbott with his daughter.

Not that Laura's first single had anything at all to do with the mercurial girl who had illuminated a long-ago spring. "Francie" had been a shining light, a beacon of conscience, and no one who had known the real Francie had ever misread her as Laura so plainly had. Wishful thinking on Laurie's part, Lucy had said, after they listened in disbelief. Francie brainwashing Laura as usual, Diana had snapped. Dominic Abbott had walked out of the room rather than hear one missing daughter sing the praises of another.

But not even "Francie" had prepared them for the devastation of Cat Courtney's second single, one of the most heavily promoted releases of the decade: "Persephone," a song of such startling contrast, such galvanizing energy and passion, underlaced with a strong dance rhythm, that it had promptly sailed above "Francie" on the charts and gone platinum. Critics had enjoyed a field day, speculating about the identity of the dark god and the unexpectedly masculine Demeter locked in mortal combat over the soul of their ultimate prize. Richard Ashmore had heard it first in public and struggled to control his shock at the unerring exactness with which Cat Courtney had dissected his marriage. From then on, he listened to it only under the protective cover of night, away from prying eyes.

One interviewer, at the beginning of her career, had made the mistake of asking her to explain "Persephone" and refused to take "I don't discuss that" for an answer. Cat Courtney had clammed up and refused to answer any more questions, a move that won her a place on every reporter's worst interview list. She obviously did not care. Her private life was her own business; her refusal to talk only added to her growing mystique. No one wanted her reality; her fans wanted Cat Courtney, clothed in lace and secrets.

Only her critics, hearing the occasional keen blade of her lyrics, carped that she wasted her talent in fantasy. Only her family, listening in anger and anguish, wondered if Cat Courtney was the reality after all, Laura Abbott the fraud.

"Maybe she'll see us out here in the audience?"

"No." He heard the edge in his voice and softened his tone. "She'll have the footlights in her eyes."

The second warning bell had sounded. And now the lights were dimming, the humming of the crowd was dying down, the stage was blackening. The first notes of the anthem song from "Persephone" drifted out from the string section, and the percussionists started their slow, steady underbeat.

A slow small light, the blackness breaking.

She stood stage center, a solitary figure against a background of shifting lights. She wore a trademark Cat Courtney costume, a confection of lace and pearls and glittering gold fabric, and the lights caught the sparkle of heavily made-up eyes and the graceful lift of her chin. Her hair, that incredible hair, glistened with interwoven pearls.

He remembered losing his soul in that hair.

> "Come home with me,
> Down to the deep,
> Where heaven and hell meet...."

Her voice seduced and charmed, beckoned and invited, implored and remembered and wept. She lifted her voice in entreaty and need, reached out her hand, asking for love, willing to settle for so much less, as she had always settled. But perhaps, he thought, now she was merely acting, perhaps she had finally found someone to love her.

As he never had.

> "Remember
> Remember
> Remember me for the dreams
> I lost in the dark of your heart...."

Memories glimmered of a long-vanished afternoon on the other side of the world: Laura, reaching out in welcome, all her secrets and schemes hidden behind a mouth that answered his own needs, behind a body that ached and melted and echoed his loneliness.

And Diana, he thought as Cat Courtney shook out her great mane, Diana as she had stood before him a few weeks before, offering, yielding, finally granting the desire long ago extinguished in the cold nights when he had reached for her and she had not been there.

> "My wish to love you
> My wish to seek you
> In the silk of warm summer winds...."

Cat Courtney looked pale, he noticed, tired beneath her stage smile. A few months before, ill health had forced her to cancel a concert tour, and a photo of the Great Cat in silhouette at a New York ballet had given rise to a rumor of a possible pregnancy. A false rumor, certainly. Her gown clung to the slender figure she had bewailed as a young girl.

"I like her dress," Julie whispered. "Is she as pretty as you remember?"

"Prettier," he whispered back, and looked through the autumnal goddess to the child twenty years gone, a child who had cheerfully given up her Saturday mornings to fly model planes with him, a child who had unabashedly loved him and trusted him never to break her heart.

He glanced at his watch.

> "Across the earth,
> Across the heavens
> I will seek you with my heart...."

Cat Courtney sang for two and a half hours with only one break. By the clock, she gave a satisfying performance; by his heart, it lasted interminably. For the better part of an hour, she accompanied herself on the grand piano for a set of throbbing ballads, one of which summoned such arousing images to mind that he forced himself to think hasty thoughts about his income tax. That song, thank God, sailed right over Julie's head.

"That was awfully sad, don't you think, Dad?"

After an intermission, Cat Courtney turned from goddess into glamor queen, in an abbreviated black dress that showed off her long legs and most of her bosom. Maybe she changed to keep cool under the hot lights of the stage, but not a single male in the audience failed to appreciate the cleavage appearing centimeter by centimeter. Cat seemed not to notice. She switched from songs of love lost and never found to celebrations of love grabbed with both hands, pulsing music meant to stir every blood cell in every man in the theater. By the end of her second encore, he suspected that he was not the only hormonal basket case present.

Julie revealed an unexpected strain of her Aunt Lucy's bossiness as the audience started to file out. "Down that aisle, Dad. That's how you get to the back."

He had to exert pressure to keep her still. "Hold on, Julie." He did not often talk to her in that tone of voice, and she stopped in her tracks. "Look, I'm serious that this might not be a good idea. I don't think Laura wants to see us—"

"Let's *try*, Dad, please."

"Or anyone else," he continued inexorably. "She was a very unhappy girl when she left. Don't you think she would have gotten in touch with someone – maybe not me, but at least Lucy – if she wanted to see us again?"

The crowd eddied out around them, but he heard none of them, he felt none of the jostling. The world had narrowed down to his daughter absorbing the bitter taste of the tragedy that had torn the family apart. He had protected her from the folly of his marriage for the whole of her life, but he could not protect her forever.

She laid her other hand on top of his. "We have to try," she said. "I know what you're saying, really I do. You mean that I shouldn't get my hopes up because maybe she'll refuse to see us, right? But it's okay, Dad, honest. It doesn't matter if she doesn't want to see us. She'll know we came, and maybe someday – well, someday she might be lonely or sick or she'll need us for something, and she'll know we still love her. She'll know it's okay to come home."

The lights overhead caught shadows on her face, and he saw again the splendid young beauty her mother had once been. But it had been a long time since Diana had looked that innocent.

Diana's heart had never been that loving.

So they went backstage, too easily, for all the security guards standing around. His architectural knowledge of theatrical structure guided them down one passageway and up a flight of stairs through a morass of props and pianos and musical instruments, and when one attendant finally stopped him for identification, he said merely that he was Cat Courtney's brother-in-law and he wanted to talk to her.

The guard took one look at Julie and made the obvious mistake.

"Ah, this must be Meg. To the left, Mr. St. Bride, and up those stairs." He obligingly pointed the way. "You look just like your mother."

Julie did her best to look like a Meg.

St. Bride. A name for Lucy. As easily learned as that, after all the years of silence. And Laura had a child. He had known that; it should not come as such a shock, that she had become a mother.

Meg. Margaret. She had named her daughter for his mother.

St. Bride. In memory, he saw a card, one among many that had arrived after the funeral. Lucy had handed it to him, asking if he knew who had sent it. *Peggy, Philip, I shall miss you forever, L. St. Bride,* in handwriting unremembered across the years.

She had known. And, dear God, she had reached out.

Where had that card gone? Had they kept the envelope?

"I can't believe it," Julie whispered, as they started to ascend the stairs against the wall. "We're really going to see her. Let's ask her out to dinner. I'll bet she's starving."

But more security guards milled about upstairs at the entrance to the green room. A champagne reception with Miss Courtney was about to begin, and their tickets were not enough to admit them. "I'm her brother-in-law" did not work this time, and a careful match of his passport against a list produced only a shake of the head. Julie was not as prepared as he was for the polite statement, "I'm sorry, sir, but Miss Courtney did not put your name on her list. I cannot allow you through." She was tired from the day and the high of anticipation, and she looked devastated.

He thought for a moment, then pulled out a business card and wrote *Call us* on the back. A long shot, but Julie was right. Laura might need them someday. He nudged Julie, who obediently signed her name, and he turned back to the guard.

A gamble on the name. "Could you please see that this gets to Ms. St. Bride?" he asked formally, and knew victory when the guard nodded and took the card. "She didn't know that her niece and I were going to be in London."

Another nod, a flicker of irritation in the guard's eyes, a dismissing "I'll deliver it to Miss Courtney. Please move along, sir."

So easy now, a simple way out. He had tried; he had made the effort.

Richard Ashmore stood there for a second, while his daughter's face saddened with the failure of their mission, and knew, to his relief and regret, that he could still reach Laura.

He need only wait for her and then raise his voice. The old theater walls echoed back at them murmurings from the departing audience, an inefficient sound muffler. At most, she sat scant yards away, behind one of those wooden doors, waiting for the arrival of the ticket holders who had paid a premium to meet her, summoning up energy to bury Laura Abbott in Cat Courtney for one more hour. But she would enter that room he saw over the man's shoulder, and she'd hear him, he'd make sure of that.

And then, perhaps, she would take the bait, turn around and step into the corridor, come face to face with him, acknowledge the blood on their hands.

"Move along, sir," an edge to the guard's politeness.

But she might not care. The need to know might not gnaw at her as it gnawed at him. He was only, after all, a small, dark part of her past.

"Dad?" Julie whispered.

Richard Ashmore looked down at his daughter's beseeching face, and chose to walk away.

"Come on, kitten," he said gently, and prompted her back towards the narrow stairs. "Let's go on back to the hotel. We've got a busy day tomorrow."

Months were to pass, and mountains were to fall, and the world would change, before he understood what happened next.

A man taking the narrow stairs two at a time, head down, blocked their path down. He clearly did not see them, and Richard pulled Julie back out of the way as the man brushed past them and came into the light. The newcomer was nearly as tall as he was, a Viking giant of a man wearing the familiar CAF bomber jacket.

An American.

Richard instinctively halted Julie's downward movement with a hand on her shoulder.

"Where is my wife?"

No imperious American intimidated this guard. He requested identification impassively while the man searched through his jacket. "I'm her husband, for God's sake! Here's my passport—"

"I'm sorry, Mr. St. Bride, your name—"

But the guard was cut off mid-word by the quiet intensity of the man's voice. "I've flown clear across the Atlantic to speak to her.

Don't give me that crap about her list! *Now, I want to see my wife.* Where is she?"

The low murmur of the guard's voice masked the reply. Cat Courtney's husband pocketed his passport and started down the hall, to be halted by another low comment from the guard. "Her brother-in-law… not on the list, so I didn't—"

"Brother-in-law?" repeated St. Bride, and his voice rose. "My brother isn't here. Who the hell—"

And then he glanced down at the card proffered by the guard, and he stiffened, this man whose existence had mattered one terrible afternoon. He straightened, and he turned slowly, too slowly, until he met Richard Ashmore's eyes.

Then, deliberately, St. Bride crumpled the card in his hand. "My wife," he said distinctly, "has no family. They died long ago. I am all the family she needs."

Richard expected tears from Julie, some depression or hurt, but she surprised him. She remained quiet on the way back to their hotel, and she acknowledged his suggestion that she get ready for bed with only a small nod. He loosened his tie and rang the concierge for coffee before he went in to check on her.

She was already sitting in bed, her arms curled around her knees, not far removed from the child she had been until his mother's death had made her the lady of the house. Her new Cat Courtney bear sat on the nightstand beside her. He sat down by her side and touched her shoulder, and she turned her cheek to his hand. Her lashes swept down over her eyes.

"Thanks for taking me anyway, Dad. I'm glad we went, aren't you? I'm glad we tried."

"Yes," because he was glad too. He had precious few memories of the woman Laura for the dark spaces of his mental lock box. "We needed to go."

She slumped down against the pillows at her back and stared away from him. "Dad?"

"Yes?"

"Did you remember that today was your anniversary?"

He was silent for a moment, and then he said gently, "How could I forget something like that? Of course, I remembered."

"Oh." She turned so that one eye could peer at him through the dusk. She reached out like the adult she would be in too few years, and she touched his hand. "Are you sorry about my mother? I mean, do you wish you hadn't married her?"

Diana, drifting down the garden path towards him, glorious, not of this world…. Diana, looking him coldly in the eye, with her unspeakable infidelity…. Diana, distant and awkward with the baby she had not meant to give birth to…. He said, and hoped that his voice did not catch, "No, Julie. Without her, I wouldn't have you."

She said nothing more. He dropped a kiss on her forehead and went to retrieve his coffee.

Seventeen years.

Who would share Diana's bed this night, seventeen years after their wedding night?

Did he care?

He sipped his coffee, blessedly hot for once, and stretched out in the chair by the window overlooking the rooftops of central London. Across the ocean, his wife was entering her office at her club, chatting on the telephone, reaching for the oblivion of a shot of whiskey. He cherished no illusions that she thought of him or the daughter she had given him.

On his hand, his wedding ring weighed heavily.

He set his coffee down, carefully, bracing himself against the ancient pain. The fingers of his right hand paused seconds, almost a minute, against the worn florentined gold. Then slowly, deliberately, he slid the ring off.

He waited for the pain to descend, but it hovered, a dark presence, just out of reach.

The ring lay against his palm, a mere whisper, a fleeting memory of a sunlit afternoon seventeen summers ago. Diana nervously forgetting her vows and having to be prompted by the judge; Diana's sisters in their rainbow dresses, catching his eye as he glanced over the veil of his bride. Lucy winking, Francie pasting a smile on her face, Laura staring sadly until Diana finally got her vows right.

And the rest of the world disappearing, as Diana put the ring on his finger and lifted her eyes to him in relief.

He slipped the ring into his pocket and settled back again.

The dark presence over his shoulder vanished.

As simply as that, then, he was no longer Diana's husband. No longer the cherished husband of one brief summer, no longer the betrayed and betraying husband of all the seasons after.

And his heart did not ache.

Oh, but his shoulder did, as it always ached in the cold or damp. He moved it restlessly. That one mistake, at least, would never let him go.

I will seek you with my heart….

Laura. Quiet, shy, sweet. On the surface, the image of her sisters, but paler, self-effacing, less interesting. A kind heart. A boundless generosity and loyalty that he'd enjoyed and exploited. A surprisingly fierce temper….

Come home with me….

And now mouse into Cat. A mysterious stranger who wooed audiences and broke hearts with that sensuous voice that bespoke a lifetime of experience. Not Diana. Not Francesca. Laura….

She stayed with him now, her voice coaxing him home with her, her eyes watching him as if he were the only man in her world. He thought how anxiously she had once awaited his approval, when she was young and had just baked him a batch of cookies. He remembered teasing her, baiting her hook, teaching her to dance, helping her with her math homework. He remembered trying uselessly to give her some small comfort after her father had destroyed her stray cats.

And his shoulder ached with an old wound, as he remembered a hidden afternoon many years before, the utter beauty of her skin beneath his hand, the glory of her hair spread across the pillow, the hatred and fear brimming in her eyes in those seconds before she tried to kill him.

2

What Goes Around

FROM ASSOCIATED PRESS:

Dominic Abbott, the central figure in one of Ireland's most celebrated trials, was found murdered in his home early Tuesday morning.

Mr. Abbott's daughter, Diana Ashmore, discovered her father's body when she returned from a business trip. Police investigators believe an intruder broke in while Mr. Abbott was working at his piano and attacked him with a blunt instrument. Results from an autopsy will be available Wednesday morning.

Mr. Abbott was known as a composer of minor operatic scores such as "Renata" and "Serenissima." He was better known as the defendant in the trial for the 1970s murder of his long-time mistress, Renée Dane, mother of his three daughters. The two lovers caused an international scandal in the music world when Mr. Abbott, then a monk, directed the American Ms. Dane in "Medea," then left the monastery to live with Ms. Dane, who remained married to the Irish Earl of Shilleen until her death. The often stormy affair, played out on the stage of the opera houses of Europe, was punctuated by numerous breakups between the lovers and the Catholic earl's refusal to grant Ms. Dane a divorce.

On October 2, 1970, three weeks after their last child was born, Ms. Dane disappeared under suspicious circumstances off the coast of Ireland and was never seen again. Mr. Abbott was tried for her murder, but a jury refused to convict on the circumstantial evidence amassed against him. The closed-courtroom testimony of his eldest daughter, Diana, 5 at the time of the alleged murder, was cited as the turning point in the defense case. After his acquittal, he returned to his native America with his children and settled near Jamestown, Virginia, where his daughter by a brief marriage lived with friends.

When Ms. Dane was declared dead and her will was probated,

Mr. Abbott inherited her estate, including an irrevocable marriage settlement given to her by the earl. With this inheritance, he devoted himself to his music and the cultivation of the musical talent in his children. He developed a minor directing career and wrote for several musical publications. He never remarried.

Mr. Abbott is survived by his daughters, Diana and Lucia, and one granddaughter, Julia Ashmore. The whereabouts of his other two daughters, Francesca and Laura, have been unknown since the late 1980s.

A funeral Mass is set for....

From Associated Press:

The mystery surrounding the murder of Maestro Dominic Abbott deepened Wednesday evening when police sources identified Abbott's oldest daughter, Diana Abbott Ashmore, as a person of interest in her father's death.... Ms. Ashmore was interviewed about inconsistencies in her claim that she discovered the body upon returning from a business trip.... Police say that Ms. Ashmore has cooperated with the investigation....

From Associated Press:

Diana Ashmore was arrested this morning on first-degree murder charges stemming from the death of Maestro Dominic Abbott last week....

From Associated Press:

A grand jury today declined to indict Diana Ashmore, daughter of murdered composer Dominic Abbott, for the death of her father two weeks ago. Police indicated that investigation is continuing into inconsistencies in the story she told police concerning the discovery of her father's body.... A source close to the case said that all evidence at the crime scene pointing to her can be explained by her frequent residence at the house....

From Associated Press:

Police revealed the results of the autopsy performed on Maestro Dominic Abbott, found murdered in his home two weeks ago in what police now indicate may have been a home invasion. The composer and conductor, best known for his avant-garde works in the field of Italian opera, died as a result of a single brutal blow to the skull with a blunt instrument. He suffered a cerebral hemorrhage from the blow and died within minutes.

The murder weapon has not been located….

Because Mr. Abbott was found slumped at his piano over his sheet music, police believe that he may not have seen his attacker….

Police have interviewed his daughter, Diana Ashmore, who told police that she discovered her father's body when she returned home from a business trip at noon on Tuesday. However, investigators say that Ms. Ashmore had changed her travel arrangements to return on Monday evening. The coroner placed the time of death between 8 p.m. Monday evening and 8 a.m. Tuesday morning.

Police have interviewed other family members, including Mr. Abbott's daughter, Lucia, and his son-in-law, architect Richard Ashmore, but say that neither had seen Mr. Abbott for several weeks. Police sources say that neither is considered a suspect.

Mr. Abbott was known as a recluse who preferred his music to company….

Robert Marlowe, Earl of Shilleen, nephew of the earl whose refusal to grant a divorce to his wife placed Mr. Abbott and his mistress, Renée Dane, Countess of Shilleen, in the center of a long-running international soap opera, forwarded his condolences to Mr. Abbott's daughters but said that the families have had no contact since Mr. Abbott's 1972 acquittal in Ireland for the presumed murder of Ms. Dane.

ASHMORE & McINTIRE

Architects and Designers

RICHARD P. ASHMORE, AIA
SCOTT N. McINTIRE, AIA

FAX TRANSMITTAL SHEET

TO: Mr. Cameron St. Bride
FROM: Julia Ashmore
DATE: 9/7/2001

Dear Mr. St. Bride:

I am trying to find my aunt, Laura Abbott. I know she is married to a man with your last name. We saw him in London on June 9. He was tall and blond, and he was wearing a CAF leather jacket with "St. Bride" mono-grammed on it.

It's taken me all summer to track you down. I've been searching the Internet to find CAF members. I sent emails to people in all the chapters, and one person emailed me back from the Dallas chapter and said to contact you. So I looked up your company's web site to see if it had a picture of the man I saw, and it looks like you could be him. I tried to send you an email, but it got answered by the marketing department, so I'm trying a fax.

My father doesn't know I'm doing this. If you are the man I saw, I think that is important to you.

If you are my aunt's husband, please don't be angry about my contacting you. I know my aunt has not seen us for a long time, but I really want to find her. Please tell my aunt that I would like to talk to her. My mother is her sister Diana, and right now she needs help. I think my aunt may want to know that her sisters really miss her.

Julia Ashmore

3

The Day

SHE STOPPED RUNNING the day the world changed.

Nothing in the late summer standards of the morning heralded the close of the long, icy years of her exile. She and her daughter shared a birthday week, and Meg woke her late with a steaming cup of mint tea and an enthusiastic kiss. They exchanged presents and talked about her newest song and Meg's ballet class, and Laura St. Bride tried hard not to think about lost Francie, who too had shared this birthday.

Meg was in top form, flitting around, laughing, and her graceful arm in extension turned Laura's heart over. Thirteen in just a few days, growing up fast, tossing childhood away, reaching eagerly towards independence and maturity. So tempting it was, so easy to hang on, to keep her forever, the two of them in their own cocoon, safe....

When the man who had kept them safe called to say that he had flown over during the night to see them, that he had important news, she thought nothing of it. He had a right to celebrate his daughter's birthday, after all. Indeed, when he arrived, he spent a few minutes hugging Meg and presenting her with another hopelessly extravagant gift. "My two birthday girls," he said fondly, and above his daughter's head he smiled at the woman he had won and lost and never explored in all the years of their marriage.

She waited until he extricated himself.

"Terrible timing, but I wanted to be here when you found out," he said gently, and handed her the news clippings of her father's death.

Daddy dead.... She pulled away from Cam's enveloping concern and wandered over to the teapot. Dead, gone, buried, never again a malevolent force to be eluded. They no longer walked in the same world. The pale sun shone on her face alone. No more need she wonder if somewhere her father heard her voice and cursed the misfortune that had left her alive.

She stood beside this man who had protected her and watched Meg happily winding up the antique music box. Through this child, this fortuitous gift of the gods, that dim time still claimed her. For how long had she used Meg as her shield, her excuse to run to earth?

Daddy was dead.

"This came Friday." He drew a folded paper from his breast pocket. "I'll hand it to your niece, she's clever.... Don't worry. It came in on my private fax line."

She saw the letterhead, and the handwritten letter below, and she went cold with shock.

"Read it." He lifted her hand and put the paper on her unresisting palm. "You'll want this." And, with a sensitivity seldom shown in all their long history, he said to their daughter, "Go get dressed, Meg. I'm taking you and your mother to brunch."

Laura was left alone in the sun-dappled kitchen, with a letter and the ghosts she had left behind.

Not Richard, she thought finally, when she could bring herself to think. In the midst of the move after the separation, she had come across a saved scrap from the past: a mass of trigonometric problems, printed in his precise architect's hand, from the last time he had helped her with high school math. No, not Richard; this handwriting was young, feminine, unweighted with knowledge.

Wrapped in the warmth of her home, she shivered, and then she read it through twice, quickly.

Cameron St. Bride found her there, standing in her kitchen, the letter lying at her feet.

"Laura."

She heard his voice through the storm in her mind, and thought in wonder that only now, too late to salvage their marriage, did he finally attempt to reach her. She felt him allow himself the small luxury of touching her hair. "Laura. Darling. Tell me what you're thinking?"

She said nothing, for how could she tell this man what Julie Ashmore, who scarcely remembered her, had known? That he and Meg were still not enough, that she needed to be whole again? Julie, part of the world left behind when she had torn her life apart, at seventeen, too young to know how heavily the destruction would weigh upon her – Julie was the first person in thirteen years to recognize her as Laura Abbott. Daughter of Dominic. Sister of Diana and Lucy and Francie. Not Laura St. Bride, that invented woman whose life had begun, full-blown, at eighteen, with a wedding ring and a brief ceremony at City Hall in San Francisco.

"What are you going to do?" he asked now, in the dead space of her silence, and she heard his dread then, the presentiment that he had finally lost.

She turned then towards him, and she was gone, she was already changing from the Laura Rose St. Bride he had sheltered and stifled and finally, gracefully, relinquished.

"I'm going home."

She couldn't go right away, and she knew it. She had a contract; the producers had waited a year to stage *Rochester* with her, saying that only Cat Courtney could bring the right emotional depth to their vision of Jane Eyre. People depended on her. She could not pull out and leave the other actors, everyone else associated with the production, high and dry and out of work. She had worked hard for this opportunity; she had the chance to prove that her father had been cruelly wrong all the years of her exile, and the years before that.

Cameron St. Bride knew it too, and he spent the remainder of the weekend cajoling, reasoning, persuading. He enlisted her manager, who argued that she could not walk away. This was her moment, he said, her time to step into the first ranks of musical artists. Jane was a plum role, a chance to dazzle the critics with all the passion and light that Cat Courtney was capable of. If she blew this, she'd never get another chance. Her co-star, normally an unlikely ally for the resolutely conservative Cam, echoed their arguments and added with wry humor that he promised not to bore her with football scores if she would stay on. His partner, a Cordon Bleu chef, dangled the prospect of private cooking lessons in front of her.

Primed by her father, Meg pitched a fit at the idea of leaving her ballet master and an even bigger fit at the idea that her mother might go to Virginia without her.

As the weekend wore on, Cam fought more desperately, the ferocity of his struggle increasing as he saw Laura slipping away, eventually abandoning gentleness and persuasion for all the tried-and-true methods that had worked for so long.

"I thought you left all that behind you," he said icily. "This niece – this child you haven't seen since she was a baby – writes this note, and you want to throw everything away to run back to people who hurt and mistreated you? What's wrong with you? You've got a damn good life. You have what you wanted." And then, because his fear rode too high to keep his pain inside, "Is it him? Is that why? Damn it, haven't you suffered enough at Richard Ashmore's hands? Haven't we all?"

Laura heard them all – soon-to-be-ex-husband, child, manager, friends – during those late summer days, and she even said the right things, promised she'd stay through her contract, made all the soothing sounds they wanted to hear. Those who knew only Laura St. Bride accepted her promises with relief and understanding. Just stage fright, they said, understandable for an artist who had never faced the prospect of a six-month run in the West End, eight performances a week – eight chances to succeed beyond her wildest dreams, eight chances to fall flat on her face. They had confidence in her. Cat Courtney was a professional who showed up on time, learned her lines, and did what her husband, manager, and director told her to do. She wouldn't cause trouble now.

Crisis abated, Meg rolled her eyes, opined, "Whatever," and went off to play a video game.

But he who had known Laura Abbott saw the end of the painful splintering that had begun so many years before, and he finally faced the real possibility of defeat.

"I can't stay," he said Monday evening, after Terry outdid himself with a splendid feast. "I rescheduled the BankKorea people for breakfast at Windows to sign a new agreement. I can't reschedule again. How about—" he consulted his Blackberry— "next weekend. I can clear my schedule. We'll talk then." He paused. "Among other things."

Laura nodded acquiescence. She had learned during their marriage to go with the flow and keep her own counsel. Still, he looked worried, so she whispered as she kissed his cheek, "We'll talk."

He studied her for a moment, this master of the universe who could fly through the night on his Gulfstream, negotiate with other merchant kings at the top of the world, rule his empire of bits and routers, and never fathom the heart of the woman who had shared his bed for so many years. He pulled her against him, and she felt the intensity of his feelings for her. But then passion had never been their problem. "I still want you, Laura. That hasn't changed. I'm sending the lawyers an email – I'm putting this thing on hold. We'll work something out – we'll revisit the idea of adoption, if you want."

She knew then that he still did not understand. She said only, as she had earlier, "Time – please give me time."

He said only, "Time isn't infinite," and in the veiled threat she heard his underlying frustration. But she saw, too, as he smoothed back her hair, that he wore his wedding ring again, the ring that he had taken off in fury the night she had left him over a year before.

Meg, seeing her parents wrapped in each other's arms, said exuberantly, "Come back, Dad! You should take Mom on a *date!*"

"Good idea," said Cameron St. Bride with a last hug for his daughter and a last searching glance at Laura, and boarded his private chariot for the other side of the world.

Email from Cameron St. Bride to Jean McKenzie, executive administrative assistant

TO: Jean McKenzie
FROM: Cameron St. Bride
SUBJECT: Tuesday To-Do

HIGHLY CONFIDENTIAL

Jean,

Print the attached – do not read – and place in an envelope in my safe.

Meeting should be over by 8:30. I'll have the BK agreement faxed to you ASAP. Take to Contracts immediately for processing.

I've instructed Johnson to withdraw the divorce petition. Follow up with him this morning to make sure he understands I want it done TODAY. Tell him to confirm. I'll call him once we're airborne with further instructions.

My gray pinstripe is at the cleaner's. Have it delivered this afternoon.

Clear my schedule on the 14th and 17th. I'm spending the weekend in London with my girls.

See you this PM.

CDSB

Attachment: Letter_to_MSB.doc

Email from Cameron St. Bride to Laura St. Bride

TO: Laura
FROM: Cam

I hope you are as frustrated as I am. This damn meeting! There you are, in London, still asleep, I hope, and here I am, six miles over the Atlantic in the dark.

How about this – before the play starts, we'll take a few days alone, without the munchkin, and really talk. How about Provence? The worst of the heat will be over soon. You can indulge your passion for antiquities while I plead my case.

If you want an abject apology, you'll get it. I want you back, Laura. I screwed up last year, and I'll cheerfully spend the rest of my life making it up to you. I promise you this. I have learned my lesson, and I don't repeat my mistakes. But you have to give me a chance.

I found this online – you know I must be desperate if I'm sending you poetry! I'll call you later today. Tell the kid I'll call her after school, and not to get too full of herself now that she's 13. My God! I remember when she fit in my two hands. Time's gone too fast.

Love,
Cam

When he finished his emails, he put his laptop in his briefcase and stretched out on the cabin sofa. Beneath him, the dark expanse of the sea; ahead of him, a city of shining towers; behind him, the only two people in the world who mattered.

He slept. He had all the time in the world.

Then a handful of men with dark eyes and dark hearts boarded four airliners, and time ran out.

Laura and Roger escaped to a late lunch at Terry's restaurant after a morning of working with the director to block out the second act. He took one look at their exhausted faces – blocking was tedious, tiring work – ushered them to the chef's table in the kitchen, and concocted a tender chicken and grape salad in a delicate vinaigrette so *nouveau*, a bouquet of herbs so *piquant*, he said as he placed their artistically arranged plates before them, that even the chickens were swooning in appreciation.

"Yes," said Laura, "but are they *free-range* chickens?"

"Darling girl," said Terry, "have you forgotten where you are? We feed our chickens only the finest of English cuisine. Why, these birds dined on scrap scrod and chips only last week."

Roger said, "Let me scrape the grease off my arteries. At least, we can be sure that the grapes are free-range… and speaking of ranges, Laura love, did your Texan give up and go back to the colonies?"

"Last night." She took a bite of the salad. "But he's coming back next weekend."

"A dictatorial gentleman. One would think he wasn't divorcing you," said Roger, whose matinee-idol looks and Caruso voice belied his equal passion for Manchester United and juicy gossip. "Now, tell all. I'll pay for this magnificent spread if you'll 'fess up. Why are you so hell-bent to go to Virginia? I thought you hailed from the Emerald Isle."

"I was born in Ireland. My mother was married to an Irishman. She and my father were American, though." During the years of working in Europe, Laura had met people who remembered the scandal of her mother's death and her father's trial, and she had become adept at denying any connection with Dominic Abbott and Renée Dane. How strange it felt to talk about them now, to admit to the world that she had family of her own blood. For more than ten years, she'd had no roots beside Meg and Cam. "I grew up outside Williamsburg. My sisters still live there."

"One gathers there's some estrangement?" One of the things Laura enjoyed most about her co-star was his bombastic phrasing; he liked to pontificate like the professor of literature he had set out to be before acting got into his blood. Terry teased him that he used twice his fair share of words. "How long since you've graced the Old Dominion?"

"A long time."

"How long?" Terry passed her a bowl of strawberries. "Inquiring minds, you know."

Laura took a deep breath. "Thirteen years and three months."

For all their levity, both were intelligent men, and it took them only seconds to do the math. She saw them exchange glances across the table. "*So*," said Terry, "a love affair gone sour, a broken heart, and you left holding the baby?"

"And, to spare your family the terrible disgrace, you ran away from home, gave birth in dreadful poverty." Beneath his melodrama, Roger's eyes showed understanding. They knew all about unforgiving families, her friends. "Shivered through that first winter when all seemed lost and you thought you might have to sell your body to keep your child in nappies, then you pluckily pulled yourself up by your bootstraps and began your meteoric rise to stardom in triumphant single motherhood fashion?"

His nonsense sliced too close to the bone. Her heart picked up a beat, but she was well-schooled in masking her emotions. She looked at her two friends steadily and helped herself to gorgeous strawberries. "Something like that."

"And that," said Terry, "showed *him*. Well, darling, you should return in glory and take every opportunity to show this cad, this scoundrel, this heartless fiend —"

Terry could be just as ridiculous as Roger.

"—Exactly what he so carelessly tossed away when he broke the tender heart of an innocent maiden. And don't go forgiving and forgetting, either. When I get tired of Sam Superstar here, I'm switching teams, and I want first dibs on you."

Roger cocked a beautifully shaped eyebrow at her. "But then it wasn't single motherhood, was it? You married your cyber-cowboy and lived – well, ever after, at least."

Even in fun, they were heading down a path best not taken. She said lightly, "You are making the huge assumption that Cam is not the heartless fiend who abandoned me in my hour of need."

"Oh, please, were we born yesterday?" said Roger. "The Viking and that little minx with the map of Ireland on her face? Don't try to scam us. No, I'll wager the progenitor of the delectable Meg is to be found in your dark, hidden past, Cat Courtney. And where does the mysterious fax from your long-lost niece enter in?" At her look, he shrugged. "The delectable Meg is a blabbermouth."

"Well, my sister seems to have helped my father along to the grave." Beneath her careless words, she felt a dark red anger welling up. This was not Diana's first kill, not at all, even if she'd been pushed into this as she had into that other death of long ago. "Except a grand jury has no-billed her – I think that means they don't have the evidence to indict her. And my niece wants me to contact Di – that's her mother. She tracked me down through Cam."

For the first time since Cam had handed her the fax, she thought of Julie's extraordinary detective work. Her niece had seen Cam wearing his CAF jacket – it must have been on the last night of her concert series in June, when he had flown across the Atlantic to tell her that he wanted a divorce. She remembered sitting across from him in the intimate restaurant where he had taken her after her concert, staring fixedly at a stray thread coming loose from the *B* of the embroidered name on his jacket, while he methodically laid out all the reasons for throwing in the towel on their marriage. Julie had come close enough to see the St. Bride name. *We saw him in London…* who was *we*? Who had been with Julie?

Please let it have been Di, please not Richard. She couldn't bear to think that he had sat out in the great dark unknown audience, listening to her sing of love lost and mourned.

Maybe Julie had been on a school trip. She was old enough.

Roger's fork clattered to the table.

"What in the name of God is that?"

At his abrupt change of tone, sharp disbelief wiping out the foppish banter, Laura looked up and saw that he was staring transfixed at something beyond Terry's shoulder. She followed his line of sight to the group gathering around the television screen on one of the shelves in the great kitchen, all staring at the picture on the screen. A picture that made no sense, since it showed a – smokestack? – against the Manhattan skyline.

Their exquisite lunch lay forgotten on the table. They joined the group around the television, and soon diners from the main room clustered around, all staring at the unthinkable live broadcast from CNN, the great glass-and-steel mountain breaking the New York skyline, the opaque black veils of smoke flooding upward against the morning sky. Roger held up his hand to quiet the chatter, and they heard news anchors reporting the inconceivable – that, on a severe blue morning, an airplane had run into one of the towers of the World Trade Center.

"How does a plane run into a building?" Terry's boss said. "It's perfect weather there."

"A bloody big plane," said one of Terry's fellow chefs. "Look at the size of that hole."

The news camera zoomed in on the gaping black wound in the side of the building, outlining the remnants of an enormous wingspan. Above the impact zone, ripples appeared next to the steel beams, and seconds passed before she realized what she was seeing – people leaning out broken windows, trapped as the fire climbed higher.

Impossible to shield the mind against that horror; impossible not to imagine that hell raging inside. Impossible not to put herself at a window, begging for air that did not fog the eyes and sear the lungs.

Cam had taken her to the World Trade Center the year before, the week before Christmas, when they still thought they might have a chance. *Nutcracker* at Lincoln Center, Meg thrilled to be wearing her first evening dress and heels, she in the loose black silk dress that she had been superstitiously afraid to buy, the photographer snapping her in silhouette while Cam and Meg went off during the entr'acte, then the surprise of dinner in the sky—

No.

She pulled Terry's sleeve. "Terry?" He glanced at her almost without recognition, and she was shocked to see tears in his eyes. "What's the restaurant at the top of the towers?"

"Windows on the World," he said tersely.

"Which one is it in?"

"That one," he said, and his shoulders began to shake. "The one that's burning all to hell."

Her heart leaped into her throat. *"Are you sure?"*

"Yes, I'm sure," and now tears were spilling down his face. "I worked there for a couple of years before I came back to London."

"Oh, no." Panic bubbled up inside her, sending fear to her throat and a hideous adrenaline spilling throughout her body. *No, think, think, think! Focus!* A breakfast meeting – it was straight up two now, and New York was five hours behind. Nine o'clock – was his meeting over? *Where was Cam?*

Oh, please God, I'll never ask for another thing. Let him be all right. I'll be his wife again. This time, I'll love him. Please let him—

She fumbled in her bag for her satellite phone. Then, for the rest of her life, she remembered that second as she turned back, her hand rising to her mouth in horror as her eyes processed the unimaginable. She heard the wordless shouts of the others, coming from a distance, as the world watched the great silver bird fly gracefully, mercilessly, into the other tower.

Billowing fire, and a second great mountain erupted into the sky.

She numbly pressed the speed dial over and over, unable to break through the busy signal, hoping against hope that Cameron St. Bride would answer and tell her she was worrying for nothing. He had not signed the check for breakfast at 8:35 a.m. He had not waited, staring out over the vast expanse of the river flowing into the Atlantic, while the concierge faxed the signed agreement to the Plano office. He had not received a call from his brother at 8:43 a.m. as he and his group waited for the express elevator. He had not handed his briefcase to his corporate counsel, waving away the last elevator ever to descend from the sky – all because he did not want to cut off the call.

He had not stood at the northern window three minutes later, talking to his brother, witness to the 767 aimed like a dagger at the heart of the building.

If God were merciful, he had not sent a text message to her phone: *Fire trapped love you.* He had not called her flat because he did not know that rehearsal had run late and she had lingered at lunch. He had not fought to control the fear and panic in his voice as he told her, *I am so sorry for everything, Laura. Forgive me. I did love you. I never stopped. I can't tell you how much I regret – I'm sorry about Francie. I should never have—*

He had not then choked from the smoke. The screams and cries of those trapped with him had not transmitted in perfect digital fidelity. The sound as he collapsed to the floor had not clearly bounced off the satellite and come to rest forever on her voice mail.

On their daughter's birthday, their time ran out.

Amid the snowstorm of free-floating paper, the cameras caught people falling from the sky, limbs held tightly against their bodies, arms and legs splayed out to brace against the approaching ground, hands clasped on their last journey. Men and women whose only crime had been to go to work, keep an appointment, attend a meeting – lost souls who preferred a last rush of cool, clear air against their faces to the flames of hell.

Not Cam, though, not Cam. For all his faults, *not Cam. Please, please, please, not Cam.*

Then the explosive clouds, cries of disbelief because they could not trust their eyes. *Though mountains may fall….* Buildings did not fall; they stood forever, urban peaks against the heavens. But now a mountain fell, the second tower hit, buckling from its mortal wound, in a mushroom cloud that foreshadowed the end of the world. She stood between her two friends, their arms wrapped around her, her fingers endlessly working the redial – *your call cannot be completed* – and she sent up mindless prayers to the God she had neglected too often in the years since she had last seen Richard Ashmore. *Oh, please, please, please, please….*

For twenty-nine minutes, she lived beyond hope, beyond despair. That second mountain could not, would not, fall. That pledge to love again could not, would not, go unheard. That man who had held her only a few hours ago could not—

For twenty-nine minutes, fate tossed her that rope.

Then the north tower fell to its knees and began to slide into the abyss, the great antenna descending into the obscuring ash of history.

And hills turn to dust....

It fell, eleven inexorable seconds of descent from the sky it had once conquered, the last act in a day that had redefined horror. Captains and kings, bond traders and secretaries and waiters, all fell from the sky in the merciless and egalitarian obliteration of millions of tons of stone and steel.

Across a vast sea, under a peaceful sky, Laura St. Bride watched as the man she had married and never loved enough, all his creativity and power, his charm and his infidelities, his kindness and generosity and manipulation – all that he had been, all that he would ever be – ceased to exist.

From dust we came, to dust we shall return.

Only his wedding ring survived, found in the rubble months later.

As so many other women did that day, Laura kept on breathing, kept on putting one foot in front of the other, for the sake of her child. The man in the tower was not only a husband but a father; she was not only his wife but the mother of his child. She dug deep inside herself to find the strength to tell Meg that her adored father was missing, presumed dead at the hands of men unknown for a cause he abhorred. In the flat that still held his presence, the day did not seem quite real to her, like one of those violent action movies that he so enjoyed and she took pains to avoid.

Impossible that he would never come back for the shirt he had overlooked, unbelievable that he would never again fiddle with the temperamental thermostat. Unthinkable, and not to be accepted, that he would never again take her in his arms and ask for another chance.

She wrapped herself in his shirt and knew that she was alone, as alone as the night she had met him.

And, in the middle of one of the great cities of the world, isolated. The international telephone lines were all jammed, and her computer kept losing its Internet connection. Her satellite phone became her only lifeline to the United States.

It rang all evening as she fielded frantic calls from Texas, as Cam's brother Mark tried to find out if he had made it out alive and was now wandering the New York war zone, dazed and hurt. The St. Bride Data counsel, who had escaped down seventy-eight flights of stairs from the sky lobby, searched the hospitals and kept her updated through Mark. The corporate pilot, marooned at Teterboro by the ground stop of all aviation, called her to ask if she had heard from Cam.

They had only his text message: *Fire trapped love you.*

Her manager reported that the producers of the show had offered to delay the opening a month, at considerable cost, to give her time. Roger and Terry stayed with her until finally she sent them home, telling them she and Meg were all right.

She held together, existing beyond thought in a day beyond belief.

More than anything, she wanted desperately to be alone with her living and her dead.

She held her daughter in her arms all evening, as she had from the precarious beginning of Meg's life. For all her new teenage status, Meg was a child who had lost her father in an act of unspeakable evil, and she needed her mother. There was purpose in that, Laura acknowledged to herself, terrible as it was to find any relief at all on this day of days, she found it in being a mother. She cradled Meg in her arms, rocking her, until Cam's little girl sobbed herself to sleep.

Then, for hours, she sat in bed beside her sleeping daughter, unable to close her eyes, watching as CNN relentlessly replayed the images – the smoke, the airliner, the fireball, the Pentagon, the falling bodies, the south tower, the rural field, the north tower. She saw the second plane dive to its doom again and again and again; she saw the towers, in their death throes, fall again and again and again. She could not summon the wherewithal to stop watching, even when the small part of her mind that hadn't succumbed to shock told her to stop torturing herself.

When CNN reported that a man had been pulled alive from the rubble, she allowed herself to hope until the reports came that the survivor was one of the missing police officers.

Towards dawn, pictures of the prominent among the missing and the dead began to flash on the screen, and she saw the studio portrait that Cam had used in the last annual report. She stared at him as if at a stranger, not the man she had slept beside for so long. A summary of a life – founder and CEO of St. Bride Data, former Marine pilot, engineering doctorate, inventor, programmer, one of the few cyber-space masters who had flourished throughout the dot-com collapse. Husband. Father. The only member of his party who had not taken the last elevator to safety and a chance to see sunset.

No one picked up on the newly filed, newly rescinded divorce pe-tition. No one knew that the glamorous Cat Courtney was now a widow. In the enormity of September 11, no one cared.

The London night had started to lighten, a sliver of light against the horizon, when she heard the line engage – not her satellite phone, recharging on the nightstand, but the data line for her laptop and printer. She trailed through the darkened flat – the flat that Cam's mother had left her, an unexpected bequest from someone who hadn't accepted her for years – and found paper lying in the top printer tray. Through the shadows, she saw the blinking light signal-ing a voice message.

She forgot to breathe.

She had checked her voice mail when she had come home, in one last bid for hope. The message, among so many thousands from Manhattan that day, had been delayed in transmission.

She pressed a button, and her husband spoke from the grave, what some were already calling Ground Zero. Paralyzed, she lis-tened for minutes – ages – eternity – while around him people gasped for breath and begged for help that would never come.

I did love you, I never stopped....

The message ended abruptly, long after he had last spoken and the phone had fallen to the floor. It ended with the most ungodly sound that had ever existed on earth – the death cry of a mountain that could no longer stand tall against the heavens, surrendering to the dust from whence it had come.

The absence of hope, she discovered, lay beyond hell in a vast, icy void.

After a long time, she switched on the reading light and reached for the fax. The cover sheet showed that someone at Cam's office, where his admin and senior executives were keeping vigil through the night, had looked up her private number and forwarded the message.

She looked at the next page.

ASHMORE & McINTIRE

Architects and Designers

RICHARD P. ASHMORE, AIA
SCOTT N. McINTIRE, AIA

FAX TRANSMITTAL SHEET

TO: Whoever is in charge at St. Bride Data
FROM: Richard Ashmore
DATE: 9/11/2001
NOTE: URGENT! Please transmit to Laura St. Bride ASAP

Laura—

I just saw your husband's picture on CNN – like so many Americans to-night, I cannot sleep, I cannot tear myself away from the TV. I have no words to express my grief for you. I cannot imagine what you are enduring right now. We'll continue to pray that your husband has survived.

Don't feel you need to respond – you have enough to deal with right now. If you need anything, call me. It doesn't matter what time of day or night. If you need me, I will come to you.

For the time being, I will not tell your sisters that your husband is missing. Lucy is in the hospital and Diana is falling apart. I will leave it to you to contact them – or me – if and when you feel like it.

Remember that you have a family here that loves and misses you.

Always know that you can come home.

Richard

She sank to the floor, her legs no longer able to hold her up. She traced her finger across his scrawled name, and then she buried her face in her hands and went far, far away.

As she had for so long, Laura St. Bride did what she had to do. With air traffic grounded in the United States and British flights under restriction, she and Meg waited in limbo for the first transatlantic flight out. Cam's final message to her had dashed any hope that he might be found alive. They could take comfort from that, his brother Mark said, he had not lived to know the final moments of the tower.

Five days after a group of fanatics had decreed that their cause trumped his right to live, Laura and Meg arrived at the house in the exclusive community in Collin County, Texas.

There she found an awkward welcome. Cam's siblings were unsure how to deal with a widow whose husband had been divorcing her. They didn't dislike her, but they had never understood her; she did not share their business interests, and her career as Cat Courtney had only placed more distance between them. Only her position as the mother of his only child and her status as his best investment smoothed the way for her. No one wanted to traumatize Meg further or antagonize Cat Courtney by suggesting that Laura not stay at Cam's house or attend the memorial services.

Cam had left complicated legal issues. He had not changed his will after he had filed for divorce, and she remained the beneficiary on his considerable life insurance policies. He had named Mark, now CEO of the St. Bride Data companies, as executor, and it was Mark, finally, who assessed her obvious grief at the memorial service, along with Meg's heartbroken declaration that her parents had been reconciling and the confirmation from the attorneys that Cam had indeed ordered the divorce petition withdrawn, and decided that everything should stand as Cam had originally intended.

"Look, you were married for – what? Twelve years?" he said, and she nodded. "I know that Cam was no picnic to live with. Believe me, when you see this will, you may wish he'd changed it."

Their sister Emma, who had never forgotten that her mother had left the London and New York residences to Laura, objected, "But they were getting divorced. Ex-wives don't inherit—"

Mark seemed very much like Cam as he wheeled on her. "He's provided for all of us. No one's going to suffer if Laura's place in the estate stands. And she wasn't his ex-wife."

"I really don't care. I have enough money," Laura said wearily. She loathed all this discussion of wills and inheritances; it seemed surreal and venal when bodies were still surfacing at Ground Zero. When she had finally fallen asleep from sheer exhaustion on the night of September 12, she had suffered nightmares of Cam trapped alive beneath the collapsed mountain of steel and rubble.

Then, in the midst of the haunting images she could not scrub from her mind, a practical thought occurred to her. She didn't care about the St. Bride fortune, but she did care about her own creations. Cam had owned the Cat Courtney trademark and the copyrights to her songs. "I still have the rights to Cat Courtney, don't I?"

Yes and no, she learned. Cat Courtney, Inc., one of Cam's privately-held companies, indeed owned all that – but under the terms of the will, all intellectual property went into a special trust to be run by his brother. He had intended to protect his own patents and trademarks, Mark explained, never considering how it would affect her. He had probably thought she would tire of being Cat Courtney long before he died, so it would never be an issue.

"Oh, my God." Laura sat down and stared at her new boss. "Do I have anything?"

"Of course," Mark said immediately. "You own half right now – you always have. This is a community property state. And the rest of it – well, come on, Laura, I'm not going to interfere with a successful property like Cat Courtney. I do have some ideas that we can talk about when you feel like it."

He outlined the rest of Cam's will to her – a third to Meg in trust until she turned 35, a third to her in trust until she turned 35 or remarried, a third to be split among Mark, Emma, and various charities and minor beneficiaries. She and Mark were co-trustees, but he held the controlling vote. The total of Cam's holdings in his privately-held companies and his portfolio gave the trusts astounding capital, but she had made her own money as Cat Courtney – that, thankfully, had already been in her name, along with the shares of stock Cam had given her and the investments he had made for her.

The money didn't concern her. She could take care of Meg by herself.

The setup of the trusts bothered her. *Typical Cam*, she thought, and then felt guilty. Leaving Mark in charge showed his complete lack of faith in her. He had never quite grasped that she was no longer the frightened teenager he had met in San Francisco. His child bride had grown up, raised a daughter, made a success of herself, and still he had never trusted her to come in out of the rain.

She felt uneasy about Mark's intentions. Cam had certainly trusted him, and she had no reason not to. Still, he now had the power literally to sell her songs out from under her. If the Beatles could lose control of their catalog, then who was she to stop Mark from licensing "Persephone" for antihistamine commercials? With his majority vote, she could not stop him from doing anything.

That was brought home to her several days after the memorial service, when Mark explained gently that, since Cam had bought the house in the corporation's name, she had no real rights to it, although he wanted her and Meg always to think of it as their home. Except for her flat in London and the brownstone in New York – and she was not going there, not for a long time – she was now homeless.

"Are you moving in?" she asked.

"When it's convenient for you," said Mark. "When are you going back to London? You still have that contract to fulfill, don't you?"

Laura made up her mind on the spot. She had never been so grateful to her mother-in-law for leaving her the London flat; it was hers outright, and Mark had no say about it. "I want Meg back in a normal routine. She needs to get back to school as soon as possible, and I want to return to work."

"I agree," Mark said, and his casual assumption that he now exercised any control at all over her child shocked her. She had not felt her rights to Meg so in jeopardy since San Francisco. "Don't worry about anything, Laura. You take care of Meg and write your songs. I'll take care of everything else."

That was what she was afraid of. Whether intentionally or not – and probably not, since Cam had never planned to die in his early 40s – her control freak of a husband had substituted for himself a new protector, one equally prone to think he knew best how she should live her life, and one without his vested interest in her happiness.

She immediately felt guilty for thinking of Cam as a control freak.

The headaches began that were to plague her for several months.

It was a relief to return to London, away from Mark and his helpful suggestions, away from Emma and her uneasy jealousy, away from all the talk of Cam's estate when no one had officially declared him dead. Away from the fog of fear that hung over her country. People knew fear in London, but they'd had decades of experience dealing with the IRA, and they had learned to live with terror. No one, Terry pointed out, was going to blow up Knightsbridge. "They *like* to shop at Harrods."

Laura settled Meg back into her school and ballet and reported back to *Rochester*. Her manager had been in touch with her director and voice coach, and they did their best to help by working her to the point of collapse. She had just enough energy left over to be a mother. She couldn't write or compose – the music that had flowed through her for so long had dried up. For the first time in her life, she experienced writer's block, and she panicked.

"It will pass," said Roger. "Indeed it will, my girl. Give yourself time. You're processing a jumble of emotions right now – you can't write with all that chaos inside."

Her manager said the same thing, but he must have told Mark, who called within the hour. "You know, Laura, all things come to an end. Have you thought of retiring?"

The fax from Richard Ashmore was never far from her thoughts, but she pushed it away into a compartment to take out later when she and Meg had begun to recover. Right now, Meg had to be her top priority. Terry gave her the name of a grief counselor, and she left the card on her desk until the night Meg threw her father's birthday gift at the wall and crumpled in a sobbing heap. The next morning, shopping for groceries, Laura found herself gasping for breath in a full-fledged panic attack. As soon as she stumbled into the flat, she called for an appointment.

After several sessions, Meg began to regain some of her sunny nature, remembering her father without obsessing about his death. One day in late October, she found enough of her old self to talk back to her mother, and Laura had never been so glad to see her daughter serving up attitude. *You just don't get it, what's the BFD*, were welcome, familiar words.

Laura spent several hours putting Meg's music box back together, her head aching, wishing she could piece their lives back together as easily.

Meg mourned honestly, and so she recovered faster. She joined a group of teens who had also lost parents in the attacks – nearly a hundred Brits had been among the victims – and she had friends to talk with, email, and IM about her feelings. Her friends from home rallied around her; she spent the greater part of each evening on the computer chatting with them. Learning to use her position as Cameron St. Bride's only child, she insisted on being included in the engineering chair that St. Bride Data endowed in Cam's name, and she asked to participate as a full donor when the family created a relief fund. Before Laura's eyes, the willful, demanding child of September 10 began to mature into a more sensitive and thoughtful young woman – but, more than once as the autumn wore on, Laura woke up to find that Meg had crawled into bed with her.

September 11 was a terrible way to grow up.

Meg, at least, had her peers to talk to. Laura found herself isolated, her anxiety only increasing over time. The wall she and Cam had erected between Cat Courtney and Laura St. Bride meant that few people in London knew that she had lost her husband, and the people she had known in Texas did not know where Laura St. Bride had gone. Both Roger and Terry had told her to call any time she needed them, but they were busy and she shrank from the idea of burdening them with her grief.

This was the time, if ever, that a woman needed her sisters.

But the sister she'd been closest to had been gone for ten years. She'd never been that close to Lucy and Diana.

Cam's sister Emma didn't even want to acknowledge that Laura had a right to grieve.

She told the counselor about her headaches and the panic attack, only to hear that her reactions were normal. Many of his American clients were suffering from sleeplessness and anxiety. It would pass, he said, gradually the shock of seeing her husband die before her eyes would fade, and she would think more about the good days of her marriage than about its end. She couldn't admit the truth, that mixed in with all her grief and horror was relief that the marriage, with all its heartache and failure, was over.

She couldn't tell him her conviction that the headaches were God's way of punishing her for never loving Cam enough.

The Atlantic shielded them after the *Wall Street Journal* ran an article on the financial holdings of the wealthier victims. Cam, it turned out, had the unenviable distinction of being the richest man to die in the attacks, and since most of his holdings except for St. Bride Data had been private, the appetite of the financial reporters was only whetted for the probate proceedings. To buy time and privacy, Mark held off filing the inventory that could expose Cam's 100% ownership of Cat Courtney, Inc.

"I can't delay this forever," he said in one of his daily calls. "I filed a preliminary inventory, but eventually I'll have to file the full document, and the press will be all over it. The company gets calls every day about his will."

"I know," Laura said wearily. Did it really matter now if anyone knew who Cat Courtney was? Did anyone care? Daddy was dead. Richard knew, and by now he had certainly told Diana and Lucy. The years of running had ended the moment the airliner had slammed into the north tower. "Just – please keep them out of my hair as long as you can. I don't want Meg exposed to that. She's been through so much – she's doing so much better."

"I'll do my best," he said. "How are rehearsals going?"

On opening night, Mark crossed the Atlantic to accompany Meg to the theater. As Cam had predicted, Laura dazzled as Jane, stunning even those critics who had carped that Cat Courtney never quite connected emotionally. She reached deep down inside herself to illuminate Jane's wretched childhood, bringing up chilling memories of Dominic Abbott at the piano for her lessons. She fueled the adult Jane's attraction to Rochester by remembering her own reaction to Cam in San Francisco. In Jane's passion, she mirrored that long-lost afternoon – she didn't want to think about that.

She knew the source of Jane's grief. *That* was all too easy to bring to the surface.

That night, a new problem reared its head.

At the opening night party, Mark stood at her side, his arm around Meg's shoulders, beaming at all the praise showered upon Laura – for all the world as if he had the right to share in Cat Courtney's night of triumph. The next evening, as Cam had after her first concert, he hosted an intimate late dinner for the cast at an exclusive restaurant. When he raised a toast to "our glorious leading lady – Miss Cat Courtney!" Laura felt the elves in her head start their enthusiastic banging behind her eyes.

Roger, no one's fool, looked at her quizzically and kept his own judgment.

Over the next few months, Mark crisscrossed the Atlantic to check for himself how she and Meg were coping with Cam's loss. He now had the corporate jet at his disposal, and he made use of it so often that Laura wondered how he got any work done. He flew over in the middle of the week for Meg's ballet recital. He brought papers dealing with the various trusts so that he could explain them to Laura before she signed them. He hired Terry to prepare a traditional American Thanksgiving dinner at the flat and dragged Emma along so that Meg would have her family together for the holiday.

He hand-delivered the death certificate from New York.

He brought over her collection of blown glass Christmas ornaments and stayed to trim the tree with Meg. He took Meg shopping for presents. He hung around in the kitchen while Laura and Meg made their traditional Christmas cookies. Then he announced his intention to fly back to spend the last two weeks of the year with them, obviously hoping that Laura would invite him to stay in the guest bedroom.

"*Guest* bedroom?" said Roger. "Right. And I'm jolly St. Nick."

Laura fiddled around with her tea and felt the stirrings of another headache. "He's taking a suite at the Kildare."

"How happy you must be. A hop and a skip away."

She started to retreat – when she was tired, she was no match for Roger's sarcasm. But then she remembered the email Mark had sent that morning, and she burst out, "Oh, my God, he is such a pest!" She took a deep breath. "He emails me every morning! He forwards me jokes and links all day long. When I get home at night, I've usually got at least five messages from him. He put me on speed dial. He calls me at least once a day. He wants Meg's grades sent to him—"

"And how is she doing?"

"Badly. She's barely passing math, so of course he has all kinds of helpful suggestions about that." She looked at her friends. "Last weekend, he got worried because the heating is so temperamental in the flat, so he called a contractor to repair it. *It's my flat!* And then this morning – he called to find out what I'm doing for New Year's Eve after the show."

Roger and Terry looked at her.

She calmed down. "Okay. I know what I think. What do *you* think he's up to?"

"Terry, can I have more wine? Thanks, love," said Roger. "Laura, I don't think you see this as Mark does. He doesn't see that he's being a pest. He sees his brother's beautiful young widow who will someday remarry. He sees that aura of vulnerability that he fears will attract the wrong sort of man. He sees that trust that will dissolve the moment you say 'I do' to another man, with all that lovely money flying out of the St. Bride family. And he sees – forgive me, Laura, but this is true – that Meg misses her father. And he is thinking to himself, she needs a husband, her child needs a father – why not me?"

The elves began to pound.

"He's also thinking that he may have inherited Cam's toys, but he inherited a lot less than you. Didn't you say that he and his sister had to split the remaining one-third with other beneficiaries? If he heroically steps in and marries his brother's widow, becomes a father to her poor fatherless child, then he controls more than two-thirds of the estate."

"And," added Terry, "he's thinking that you may start dating again—"

"I'm not interested in a relationship with another man. In fact," she hesitated, and then said before she lost her courage, "I think that's dead and gone in me."

"No, it's not," Roger said. "You've had an *annus horribilis*. You lost a baby, your husband told you he wanted a divorce, and then you watched him die in the most horrific way imaginable. Of course, you're not interested, but you will be again, and Mark knows it. He is thinking logically that he needs to stake his claim before you meet someone else. If he marries you, it solves a whole host of problems – a win-win situation. I detect some sibling one-upmanship at work here also. Mark knows that you weren't happy with Cam. If he succeeds where his brother failed, doesn't he prove himself the better man?"

Terry watched as she rubbed her temples, and, without a word, fetched her some aspirin. She gave him a grateful smile and drank the tablets down with the herbal tea he placed in front of her.

"I don't get it. Mark is a fundamentalist." She saw their blank looks and explained, "He takes the Bible literally. Isn't there somewhere – Leviticus – where it forbids a man marrying his brother's wife?"

"Leviticus 20. You are grasping at straws," said Roger. "Keeping the money in the family with a second marriage is a time-honored tradition, and don't think that Moses & Co. didn't do it when they thought they might lose a flock of sheep. You haven't been upper crust your whole life or you would have expected this. You won't even have to change your monograms. And, Laura sweetie, don't talk to us about Leviticus – it forbids certain other things too." He settled back, and the light in his eyes warned her of his change of mood. "Of course, you have another solution to your problem."

When was the aspirin going to take effect? "What's that?"

"Marry one of us. We'll help you break that trust."

For a moment, Laura and Terry both sat in shocked silence. Then he started laughing, and Roger laughed, and Laura felt the elves put down their hammers. She didn't think she had laughed since the moment she had first seen the burning tower. "You know, I might take you up on that. So who gets me? I'm a wealthy widow. Make your case."

Terry pointed a finger across the table at Roger. "Back off! I called dibs on her months ago."

"Forget it. You have a steady paycheck. I, on the other hand, survive at the whim of the audience. I need that trust more than you do. Besides, I'm better-looking." He dropped to one knee and kissed her hand. "Laura, will you marry me? I won't hound you for sex, I won't spend all your money, and I wear a smashing tux if you want arm candy. And, if you ever want out of the marriage, trust me, I'll supply you with plenty of grounds."

"Unfair!" Terry took her other hand. "I cook like a dream, I *will* hound you for sex now and again – not that you have to feel under any obligation – I *will* spend your money on the kitchen of my dreams, and I at least own a pair of jeans. You don't go to parties anyway. *Plus,* I won't declaim to the rafters when I ask you to pass the salt and pepper."

She looked at her two dear friends – she didn't care what Leviticus said, these were the most wonderful men in the world. "How can I choose? Can't I marry you both?"

They flipped a coin for her, but they wouldn't let her see who won.

Christmas was salvaged when a sinus infection kept Mark from flying. She and Meg spent their first Christmas without Cam quietly, attending the liturgy at Westminster Cathedral, sleeping late, exchanging presents by their pretty tree, cooking their traditional dinner. After cleanup, Meg vanished into her room to work out at her barre, and Laura curled up by her bedroom window, sipping hot chocolate and staring out at the snow-topped roofs of her neighbors.

She had not spent such a solitary Christmas in her entire life.

The Christmases of her childhood – she leaned back and closed her eyes. The sisters in their winter finery, much of it hand-me-down because money was always tight. When one outgrew the teal winter coat with the fake fur collar, the next in line inherited it. Midnight Mass, their voices singing out in the choir, Diana's dramatic coloratura, Francie's pretty lyric tones, her own coloratura mezzo. All of them with carefully trained vibrato. Lucy, under the protection of the Ashmores, lucky enough to escape the command performance. Dominic, in his severe black suit, reminiscent of the monk he had once been, critiquing their performances.

Christmas dinner at Ashmore Park, all of them on their best behavior. Awed not only by the magnificence of the house, its shining elegance in sharp contrast to the genteel poverty of their own, but also by the son of the house, with his confident manner, secure in his place in the universe. Warmed by the welcoming smiles of Philip and Peggy Ashmore. Envious of Lucy, who enjoyed this every day.

That last Christmas at home, when she was seventeen – Richard and Diana with Julie, their eyes sliding past each other, the emotional distance yawning between them. Francie watching, waiting, planning. Richard coming to Laura after dinner as she watched the lights on the tree from the loveseat, pulling over the ottoman to sit opposite her, the light from the fireplace casting a glow across his dark hair. He had been wearing a beautiful blue ski sweater that his mother had given him.

Laurie, I need to ask a really big favor.

Sure, Richard. What do you need?

Across the years, Laura remembered him taking her hands in his.

I'm finishing up my thesis. Can I hire you to type it for me this week? I really need an expert – it's full of footnotes and equations. You're the best typist around.

The thrill that he was entrusting her with something so important to his future. Through the vicious headache from the cold she'd had all week, her eager agreement. *Of course! You don't have to pay me, Richard. I'll be glad to do it.*

Great! Why don't you come back with us tonight? And of course I'll pay you. I know how you like to save up. No knowledge of what she was saving up for. *You're not my slave.*

But, in her heart of hearts, she was. She would do whatever Richard Ashmore wanted her to do.

Fast forward thirteen years to last Christmas, she and Cam circling each other gingerly, wondering if the pregnancy that had resulted from a post-separation night of passion could herald another chance for them. This pregnancy had seemed different from the others. The first trimester had passed uneventfully; she felt pregnant, she was even beginning to show. So far, everything looked good. They had agreed to tell Meg that evening. Then, as she prepared Christmas dinner, the excruciating cramps, the blood, the heartsick feeling of loss, because this time she had dared to hope….

Her doctor telling Cam forcefully, *For God's sake, man, get yourself fixed! You can't put her through this again.* His desolate eyes, as they looked at each other wearily and knew that their dying marriage had run out of hope….

Laura buried her face in her hands.

Two Christmases. Each, in its own way, the end of the line.

Pain began to flicker behind her eyes.

She rose from the window seat and went to the dresser where she had put Richard's fax. It was folded tightly, hidden beneath her hosiery where no one would ever look. She spread it out beside her on the window seat and read it again and again.

Looking for – what? What was she going to find there that she hadn't seen before?

For the first time, in her mind's eye, she imagined Richard writing the note to her that terrible night. Unable to sleep on his side of the Atlantic, as she had been on hers, watching CNN as obsessively as she had. Recognizing Cam's picture (*How had he known? Had he been at the concert with Julie?*). Pondering the best course of action, finding the fax number on the St. Bride Data web site, bending his dark head over the paper as he wrote to her, choosing his words carefully so as not to frighten her with this intrusion from the past, but opening the door in case she ever wanted to come home.

He must never have found her out. It seemed impossible, after all these years, that her cover still held strong, but it had to be true. No man could write such words to a woman who had—

No. There be dragons....

She ran her fingers lightly over his handwritten words, touching him. His words, his signature, his telephone numbers scrawled beneath his name.

His telephone numbers.

She stared at them a long time before she reached for her satellite phone. Her fingers shook as she dialed the number he'd marked with (W) – then hit *End*. Of course, he wasn't at work today. It was early afternoon in Virginia. He and Diana were hosting the annual dinner in the great ballroom of Ashmore Magna, the first Christmas since Peggy and Philip had died and they had become lord and lady of the manor. The long table was gleaming with luminous china, polished silver, sparkling crystal that picked up the lights from the twenty-foot tree. The chandelier was reflecting back the flames in the fireplace in a waterfall of light, and Diana was escaping her hostess duties by playing carols on the grand piano.

If her sister wasn't spending Christmas in jail. In the crush of dealing with Cam's death, she had forgotten her father's death three weeks before September 11. In the face of great evil, Dominic Abbott's petty malevolence had slipped into insignificance. She had no idea what had really happened to Dominic, but whatever Diana had done, it probably hadn't been painful or bloody enough.

Forget Daddy. He doesn't matter anymore.

And Francie – she would not remember Francie, nor think of Richard's part in Francie's loss, or Diana's. She would not remember what had happened within minutes after she had agreed to type his thesis, Francie moving in for the kill, seizing the opportunity to take her revenge against Diana for the jealousies and rivalries of their childhood.

She started to dial the (H) number beneath his name, then hit *End* again. She had to mask her number; she wasn't ready to come in from the cold.

She dialed the St. Bride Data voice mail system, put in the code for an outside line, and listened while the signal winged its way into space, bounced off the satellite, and then flew back through the atmosphere to Texas, to speed through the phone lines to the great house outside Williamsburg. One ring, two... how long would she give it? Not long... three, four....

"Hello?" A young, sweet voice. Julie? Or did Richard and Diana have other children?

She was surprised to find her voice calm, collected, with a hint of the British clip she tended to pick up in London. Despite the chilly room, she felt feverish in her sweater and jeans and wool socks. She pressed her cold hand against her heated cheek. "May I speak to Richard Ashmore, please?"

What would she say if the girl asked who was calling? But her niece, it seemed, was a typical teenager, oblivious to such niceties. "Dad! Phone for you!"

She counted off the seconds by her heartbeat, breathing in and out to keep from hyperventilating. She heard music, footsteps approaching, a masculine laugh, a "Don't be such a sore loser, Luce." She heard him picking up the phone. "Hello?"

She clutched the phone. She couldn't speak. His voice… he sounded just like Richard. *Hello, what have we here, Laurie?* Her hero, the prince of her childhood, always out of her reach.

A wave of such intense longing swept through her that she felt sick.

"Hello?" Sharper, slightly irritated. Her chest and throat tightened. "This is Richard Ashmore."

She hit *End* in a panic.

At that moment, the little elves that had knocked around playfully behind her eyes all day attacked with a vengeance, with the most appalling headache she had experienced yet. She stumbled, her phone falling to the floor, afraid that she might throw up, and managed to make it over to her bed before she collapsed. She had just enough strength left to crawl under the duvet.

She was shivering in reaction, overheated and chilled at the same time. *I am desolate and sick of an old passion….* Well, she had proved one thing, at least. For all her brave words to Cam – *I'm going home* – she was not ready to face Richard.

She lay there for a long time, until her heart rate slowed and the shivering stopped. Inside the cocoon of the duvet, warmth and peace seeped into her through the December dusk. The house was silent except for the faint strains of hip-hop coming from Meg's room. Gradually, she relaxed into the mattress, and the elves muted their hammering in response to the echo, *This is Richard Ashmore, this is Richard Ashmore….*

Eventually, she fell asleep, a deep, dreamless sleep.

When she awoke, she felt more rested than she had in months.

Cat Courtney gave the show her all for six months, but told the producers regretfully at the four-month mark that she did not want to renew her contract. Almost everyone – her manager, Meg, Roger – argued with Laura. The show was a success; *she* was a success. She had proved the doubters wrong. Why turn her back on that now?

"Big mistake," said Roger. "Do *not* leave me to the mercy of that understudy of yours, I beg you! The woman *cannot* carry a tune. Who do you think she's shagging?"

"Are you sure?" Dell, her manager, said. "We don't have anything scheduled until fall. What are you going to do with yourself?"

"Don't I have another album on my contract?"

"Yes, but there's no time limit. I thought you weren't writing."

"I'm working on something."

"Mind telling me about it?"

"Not yet. I'm not ready. And – by the way – please don't tell Mark about all this just yet."

A long silence across the Atlantic. "Laura, I don't have a choice. I work for Cat Courtney, Inc. He's my boss."

She could not tell anyone that Laura St. Bride, the woman they knew, was spending long hours alone groping her way back to Laura Abbott, wrenching lyrics so painful from a heart so rent that she put them away until she could gain some distance from them. The first song she wrote burned with images of smoking candles, the second with mountains crumbling to dust, the third with the longing of a woman lying on a shore. In the fourth, a woman called an old lover just to hear his voice.

Her performance took on a new depth. One critic, coming back to see if she had sustained her initial performances, wrote that she brought a new prism to one of literature's great heroines.

In the mornings, after Meg went off to school, she wrote, gradually regaining confidence in her creative abilities. In the early afternoons before she had to report to the theater, she took a leaf from Cam's book and brainstormed strategy, thinking hard about what she wanted to do with the rest of her life. First priority was to get Mark off her back. Then – where to live? Where to raise Meg? Where to take Cat Courtney next? Hard to look to the future yet, she acknowledged, while the past still wrapped its tendrils around her. Somehow, somewhere, she had to find the strength to move beyond Virginia.

Beyond Dominic. Beyond Francie. Beyond… *him*.

Finally, one afternoon, she took a deep breath, sat down at her laptop, and typed *Richard Patrick Ashmore* into the search engine. She pressed *Enter* and knit her fingers tightly together as the search criteria went out across the world.

Thank heavens for the global desire to put everything online! His firm's web site immediately popped up at the head of the list. A picture showed him on site, conferring with another man over a blueprint, wearing a hardhat. Terrible picture – it showed him only in profile, obscuring his face. He was wearing glasses – had he finally stopped fighting his far-sightedness? The *About the Principals* page linked to a book he had written on Palladian architecture in Virginia. She ordered ten copies air-shipped to her. He had been one of several architects profiled in another book about restoration architecture. She ordered only one copy. He wasn't getting royalties from that one.

The profile said that he had one child. So that *had* been Julie on the phone.

Interesting, she thought, no mention that he was married.

She methodically went through the other hits, filtering out those that didn't apply, printing those that did. He had amassed a considerable portfolio of accomplishments – restoration projects involving museums, churches, theaters, plantation homes, and even a century-old winery. He had rebuilt the Folly at Ashmore Park and allowed photographs of the exterior to be published in an historic preservation magazine. He had won an award from the Virginia Historical Society. He belonged to the local Chamber of Commerce. He served on the governing board for the private school she and he had attended – now Julie's? – and the finance committee of the Episcopal church Philip had attended. (Richard had been critical of organized religion – this couldn't be the same man.) He belonged to a local RC club and owned a share in a co-op airfield. He had attended a fund-raiser for a local Republican Congressional candidate. He was an adjunct instructor in architecture at the University of Virginia. He and his partner had gone down to defeat last spring in a local tennis tournament. He had served as executor of his parents' wills.

He was leading exactly the life he had been destined from birth to lead. Francie had not made any difference.

She found no hits on Julie other than a listing for Junior Cotillion and a brief description of a piano recital at Bruton Parish. So Julie played the piano – a true Abbott. Other than the news reports after their father's death, Diana showed up only in a report (as *Diana*

Abbott) on a Canadian opera production a few years before and – startlingly – a DUI arrest the previous April. *Diana Ashmore* and *Mrs. Richard Ashmore* yielded nothing, and, surprisingly, *Lucia Abbott* and *Lucy Abbott* came up empty too. Lucy had been in law school when she'd left home. She had expected to find some trace of her sister's career.

In the late evenings, after the show, she pored over her printouts. They told her everything but what she wanted to know – had he and Diana stayed together? What had happened to their marriage after Francie? Did he ever think of her?

Did he ever remember…. *There be dragons.*

She combed back through the descriptions of his projects, and a hyperlink caught her eye – Edwards Lake. The name seemed familiar. She logged onto the Ashmore & McIntire web site and searched through the site for the exact page with the link.

Edwards Lake had its own small web site, advertising itself as a luxury vacation hideaway in the heart of the Tidewater. She mapped it, and then it came back to her exactly what and where Edwards Lake was. A lovely old home, Ashmore Park's neighbor, whose long-ago owner had refused to sell to Richard's great-grandfather in the early 1900s when the fortune of the trophy wife, the Great Lakes shipping heiress, was fueling the expansion of Ashmore Park. She took the virtual tour of the beautifully restored interiors, the graceful back terrace overlooking the pool, the quiet, secluded surroundings behind a tall gate – and then she saw the link to the property management company.

Laura printed the page and sent an email.

She did not intend Mark to know anything until it was too late. She wanted all her plans in place before she broke the news to him that she was leaving the show.

Richard's book arrived, and Laura pulled a copy from the box and immediately turned to the back flap. She had braced herself for the best and the worst – he was either completely unchanged, or he had gone to seed. What she had not allowed herself to anticipate was that Richard, in his late thirties, might be more devastating than when she had known him.

Something deep inside – an appreciation for a frankly gorgeous man – stirred to life.

She'd had publicity photos done, so it took no imagination to know how this photograph had ended up on the book. The publisher had told him to submit a few pictures – a studio portrait, a few casual photographs – and he had thrown this one in because his mother had taken it. *Photograph by Margaret Ashmore.* Some female book designer had seen the photo of him leaning against a pillar on the great portico of Ashmore Magna, his hands in his pockets, giving his mother a humoring smile – all 6'5" of him echoing the long, lean lines of the pillar – and said, "That one."

He had dedicated the book to Julie. *To my daughter, light of my life.*

The rest of the photographs in the book, attributed to the author, featured Palladian architecture. Laura read it cover to cover and learned more than she had ever wanted to know about Jefferson's interest in Andrea Palladio and the five-part Palladian plan he had adapted for Monticello. *Monticello.* Richard had promised to take her there once, but it had been Francie instead who had gone up the mountain with Richard that snowy day, while Laura covered for her at school. Later that night, she'd listened, anguished, as Francie made a long, emotional tape for Richard about the way she had felt when he had made love to her in the Monticello forest.

February. She held up her fingers and counted. That fit.

For the first time in her life, she desecrated a book. She carefully cut the picture of the author from the back flap and placed it inside the engagement book she always carried with her. Then she hid the books underneath her bed where Meg couldn't see them.

In March, Laura took a few days off from *Rochester*, and she and Meg met Mark and Emma in Manhattan to view Ground Zero on the six-month anniversary. By now, they had accepted that Cam's body would never be found; the DNA samples they had provided had failed to match so far. This was their pilgrimage to his gravesite.

The St. Brides were a VIP family. The four heirs had set up a relief fund for families in the north tower, and St. Bride Data had donated services and consultants to restore data lines around Ground Zero. The mayor met them in the private viewing suite to shake hands with Mark and convey his condolences to the family. Because they had requested privacy, they did not encounter any press.

They were left alone to view the devastation.

From twenty stories above, Laura looked down into hell. Impossible to believe that mountains had stood here, reaching to the heavens. The hole in the earth was filled with absence.

To an unknowing eye, Ground Zero resembled an ordinary construction site, with trailers on the site, cranes lifting huge pieces of steel, heavy equipment beeping as it backed up, and workers shouting to each other. But, even after the concerted cleanup and recovery effort of six months, rubble and burned steel lay in organized, twisted mounds in the crater. Front-end loaders cleared debris from a small hill of ash and broken stone, spreading it thin on the ground. Rescue workers in bright orange vests, bundled against the early spring chill, raked through the material. It took her a while to realize what the men, who seemed to sift through even the smallest particles, were looking for.

That Cam might still be down there was too terrible to contemplate.

They had no words. Mark kept his arm around Meg's shoulders, and Emma, animosity briefly laid aside, clung to Laura. No one wanted to stay; no one wanted to leave. They owed it to Cam. They could escape this. He could not.

The chill wind was whipping around the streets when they descended to walk around the chain link fences. They stopped to look at the makeshift memorials, flowers and teddy bears and hand-lettered signs each mourning a loss. Handbills with faces – *Missing! Last Seen 78th Floor, 2 World Trade Center* – still papered every available surface. Nearby, street vendors hawked flag pins and World Trade Center pictures. People were even taking pictures, but in silence, as if at a sacred ground.

They had not posted a picture of Cam. He had been one of the confirmed victims from the first night. Maybe they had been lucky in that, Laura thought, and heard her thoughts echoed when Mark said quietly beside her, "At least we didn't have to wait. We knew."

Later that evening in Laura's brownstone, Emma settled down to paint Meg's nails, and Mark asked Laura to go for a walk. The evening was clear and cold, and here on the Upper West Side, life went on as it did not at Ground Zero. People hurried by, taxis honked, the sounds of urban life filled the air. Even here, though, the great city seemed muted, remembering.

Two rays of light, representing the lost towers, speared the night sky, bouncing off the heavens.

Bundled against the cold, Mark and Laura turned in silent agreement towards the park, walking towards the lake. Among the trees, they lost sight of the rays of lights, and Laura sensed that Mark relaxed once the trees obscured their view of lower Manhattan. Street lights shed a wintry glow on the park paths, and remnants of a days-old snow provided some light. Very few people were venturing out in the park tonight.

Silence surrounded them, a glissando sliding from peace to the underlying sounds of the night.

They had walked for almost twenty minutes when Mark spoke. "I'm parting company with everyone else. I think it's an excellent idea to leave the show."

Laura looked at him, startled. She hadn't planned to tell him yet, but, of course, Dell had reported to him. "You do?"

"Sure. Are you warm enough?" He moved a little closer to her as they walked. "You've been working hard, Laura, too hard. Although I must say you've lost that brittle look that you had last fall – you don't seem quite so fragile now." She hadn't thought of herself as fragile, and her heart sank. She'd called on all her reserves of strength, and the remaining St. Bride male still thought she might fall apart at any minute. "When does this tour start?"

"September 15 in Copenhagen. Two shows every week, a couple of hard weeks with three, and there's a really bad week in Australia and South Africa." She concentrated on keeping pace with him. "Finish up New Year's Eve in London."

"And nothing else planned?"

"No." She felt uneasy about where this might be heading. "I want to do some writing – not just songs, either. I have a book idea I want to develop."

"Are you going to stay in London?"

Oh, now they were getting down to it. She stopped and forced him to stop too. "What are you getting at, Mark?" And when he said nothing, she said urgently, "I don't want to dance around with you. What do you want?"

"I want you and Meg to come home."

Silence between them. She saw in his face not Cam's handsome, broad features, not Richard's Black Irish splendor, but a plain man used to playing second fiddle, forced by circumstance to step into his legendary older brother's boots. She saw weary resolution, and she realized in that moment that Mark was far more serious than either she or Roger had thought.

She had to tread with care. "I never planned to make London my permanent home. This is my country – I don't want to be an expatriate, and I know Meg wants to go to high school here. I don't think she likes this ballet master that much; she wants to go back to her old teacher. I may contact a broker, see what's on the market."

"You don't have to do that," he said before she could finish speaking. "You can move back home."

She forced cheerfulness into her voice. "We can't impose on you, Mark. You don't want your widowed sister-in-law living with you, cramping your style! And Emma runs that house better than I ever did, she has the knack – believe me, it won't work for two adult women to live under the same roof! She has her own ways of doing things, and I'd just get in the way. No, I'd prefer to have my own place."

That ought to be well-nigh unanswerable. He looked uncomfortable. "Em doesn't dislike you."

"No. But I'm not her favorite person." He started to say something, and she shook her head. "It's all right, Mark. She and I are very different, and I know she thinks I could have been a better wife to Cam. She's loyal to both of you. No, I'll look in one of the gated communities, find a house where I can have a studio. We won't be that far away." And it would be *hers*.

"We can talk about that later." So Mark was going to shelve it until he could marshal arguments against it, humor her until he judged the moment right. She suspected he had a timetable all worked out; she probably had six months of respite until the first anniversary. "To get back to your plans after the tour – you've had a good run as Cat Courtney. You've proved what you set out to prove, and you certainly don't need to work. Have you thought about retiring to family life and leaving it all behind?"

Oh, dear Lord, was he going to accelerate the timetable? She decided to answer him at face value. "Well, I think staying home to be with Meg qualifies as family life. Plus—" he deserved this, the idea Cam had finally been willing to consider— "she's going to be fourteen, she's growing up – I may adopt a couple of kids."

The shock on his face showed that he hadn't seen that one coming. He stared at her, and she thought how strange it seemed to look at Cam's eyes in Mark's face on her own level. Cam had been much taller – *almost as tall as Richard*, though she mustn't think of that – but Mark was her height. Mark couldn't dominate her with his height as Cam had.

"I'd counsel you not to rush into anything," he said finally. "You may want to marry again, and that might stand in your way. No," he held up his hand against her automatic protest, "it's true. Not many men care to deal with children who aren't their own."

She kept silent, thinking of the man who had given the lie to that.

"Besides," he said, "if you want more children, Laura – you can have your own."

She had walked right into this. She cursed herself even as they looked at each other, and she knew that now she couldn't stop him. Her show of independence had alarmed him. He was moving up his timetable, and she was going to have to tell him what she had planned, and this day that had already been difficult enough was about to turn brutal – all because she'd blurted out her splendid idea prematurely.

He put his gloved hand on her shoulder, and through the layers of coat and sweater, she felt his touch. It brought him close to her, and she had to fight the instinct to retreat. "I'm not my brother, Laura. I don't have his problems. If you want more children – that would not be an issue."

She felt the blood drain from her face.

Cam had told him. Cam had told him the secret that they had agreed must always remain between them. Cam had jeopardized – but no, he had adored Meg, he would never have done that. Mark couldn't have meant what she thought he'd said. It was impossible.

Mark saw in her face the shock, fear, doubt, and in the next second, he dashed her brief hope. "He told me some of it years ago," he said. "And he left a long letter for me with his will."

"Oh, my God." She lifted her hand to her mouth, and, despite the cold air, she felt hot tears filling her eyes. She remembered Cam smiling with pride at the adoption hearing, Cam carrying Meg around on his shoulders at her first birthday party, Cam and Meg waving on their way to a baseball game, Cam never indicating in any way that he didn't think of Meg as his own.

Why would he have ever told anyone?

Laura forced herself to look at her brother-in-law, this man who now held frightening power that had nothing to do with trusts or Cat Courtney, Inc. "What do you want, Mark?"

But she had misread him; he wasn't thinking of Meg at all. He said gently, "I want you, Laura. I know it's too soon, but I thought you should know." He gave a small laugh. "I want to be first in line."

Oh, no. The words were out in the open now, where they had a life of their own. Her third proposal in three months, and as loveless as the other two. Perhaps more so – Roger and Terry at least had her best interests at heart. She turned away abruptly and walked over to a bench.

Mark followed her. "This can't come as a surprise to you, Laura."

Her head started to ache. "No. No, it doesn't."

"I know you don't love me." She sensed he was choosing his words carefully. "Until Cam died, you and I never really talked or spent much time together. He liked to keep you to himself – he never was one to let anyone else play with his toys. Frankly, I always thought that was going to backfire on him, but when it came to you, no one could tell him anything. When Cat Courtney took off – well, you know how he reacted. It was fine for you to have a little success, but only a little. I know," he stopped for a moment, "I know you re-sent the trust setup. It wasn't my idea, believe me. I have enough to do running the companies without having to shepherd these trusts around."

She looked at him, surprised at the sharp tone in his voice.

"And I know you've chafed at the idea that I control so much of the money, but my brother wanted it that way, and I'm not going against his wishes. I'm a better choice to run those trusts than you. I'm interested in money. I know how it works, how to invest it and make it grow and work for you – and, face it, Laura, you aren't inter-ested. I've seen your eyes glaze over when I show you the financial statements. I can do a lot more with your money for you than you ever could for yourself or Meg."

"I know." Laura felt herself relaxing. He was looking at her straight now, and his voice had changed. He no longer seemed pa-tronizing or controlling; he was a man talking about his expertise, and he spoke with authority.

"And, for the record, I haven't flown back and forth across the Atlantic to harass you. I wanted to be with you and Meg. I have enough to do. I've done nothing but work the last six months – nights, weekends, all night flying there and back. I've got big shoes to fill. I don't have Cam's vision and imagination, he could see possi-bilities where I don't, and I have to scramble every minute to figure out where he wanted to take the company next. It's not my natural bent. But I have to keep things going." He gave her a grin, unexpect-edly attractive in his ordinary face. "I'm more comfortable with my spreadsheets."

"You're a numbers person." She found herself smiling back. "He was – I don't know, connections. He knew how to connect ideas. I used to see him working on his process charts, and I never could get it, how he could take ones and zeroes and make them do what he drew on those charts."

"The same way you take notes and words and make music," he said, and smiled at her astonishment. "What, you think I can't recognize a genuine artist when I see one? The night I saw you in *Rochester* blew me away. It was the first time I ever knew what Cam saw in you besides a pretty girl. You were like him, you could take random elements and make a coherent whole. And it got me thinking about him and you, how he could be smart enough to make you his wife and then be such a moron when it came to being your husband. Oh, yes, I knew about his girls. I used to wonder why you didn't take Meg and leave – then," he paused, "one night he told me about your family. About San Francisco."

Her heart stopped. "What did he tell you?"

"About Francie. Your father. The other sister – what is her name? Diana? And the husband. He most definitely did not like your sister's husband." She sensed him looking at her hard. "I'd always wondered why you never saw your family. Why Meg didn't know anything about them. After he told me, I understood that Cam and Meg were all you had. You really hadn't anywhere else to go."

She thought, a wisp of a thought, of Richard's fax: *Remember that you have a family here.*

Mark said, "But you do have a family here. I can promise you one thing. I'm not my brother. I may not have his imagination and drive, but you can be damn sure that I'll be a faithful husband. I don't want to push you, Laura. I know you haven't had enough time yet. It's all still so raw. You're still dealing with the aftermath – see, you're rubbing your forehead. I know about your headaches."

"That kid has the biggest mouth."

He smiled. "She sure does. By the way, what are you going to do with her this fall while you're on tour? Can Em and I have her?"

"Absolutely. That solves a huge problem for me." She thought of telling him about her plans, and then stopped, because he was moving over on the bench to sit close beside her, and his hands were sliding up her arms, and he was pulling her gently, inexorably towards him.

Oh no, oh no, oh no. What do I do?

His kiss was gentle, tentative, the kiss of a man trying not to scare a woman off. It wasn't unpleasant, she thought as he tried to coax a reaction out of her, it was – *nice*. Diffident. Polite. Comfortable. Just – *nice*.

She'd been kissed passionately in her life, kisses that had made her forget who she was and everything she believed in – hard, uncomfortable, world-destroying kisses. She wasn't in danger of losing her soul in Mark's arms. She felt no stirrings of old feelings, no resurrection of the joy of being a woman held by a man. She felt less than she did during Rochester and Jane's last embrace on stage, when Roger would clasp her masterfully in his arms and whisper off-color jokes in her ear.

"My God," he whispered, nibbling at her lower lip, "you are so beautiful."

She didn't want tentative, she didn't want pleasant. Her sisters had known passion. One had married for love; the other had risked all for the love of her life. She'd seen so many other people heart and soul in love. Was she destined never to know that? Was she always to do the dutiful, *right* thing?

Just once in her life, couldn't she have what her sisters had?

No, I can't, I can't....

She pulled herself away gently with a heavy breath. Maybe he would put her reluctance down to mourning Cam, or observing the proprieties, or not wanting a public display of affection – not that anyone was around to see them – anything except a panicky feeling of being trapped in a predestined future. "Mark." She managed a shaky laugh. "I'm – I'm not ready. I'm so sorry."

"It's all right." He was breathing a little harder himself; she saw his breath in the chill air. "We can wait. We have plenty of time." He leaned back against the bench, and she felt his hand against her hair at the back of her neck. "Maybe – this summer, when you're done with the show – come on back to Texas, Laura. Don't wait until fall to bring Meg back."

"Actually—"

He overrode her. "I'd like for us to spend some time together, see where this goes. I think," he picked up her hand, "if you'll give me a chance, you'll see this is the best solution."

If only he had not said that, if only he had stopped a few seconds earlier. She might have acted like a proper upper crust widow, looking to the preservation of capital, reclaiming her place at the side of the master of the St. Bride universe. Mistress of the St. Bride house, mother of future St. Bride children. The St. Bride heiress, keeping the St. Bride money in the family.

The best solution. Problem, solved. Bloodless, rational, head over heart. No explosion of heaven and hell, no blood between them. No world lost for love. No man leaning against a pillar. And every minute, her very self vanishing deep inside, until one day she might awake and find that Laura Abbott had disappeared forever.

Two men, united by blood, divided by death, touching her hair, trying to touch her heart.

Always know that you can come home.

I need to ask a really big favor.

Laura Abbott straightened and looked over at her brother-in-law. Her headache had subsided. "About this summer, Mark – I need to ask a really big favor."

He let his arm drift around her shoulders. "Sure." Kind, indulgent. Confident that she would come around. He was going to have all of Cameron St. Bride's toys. "What do you need?"

"I need you to take Meg earlier – June, when her term is up."

He shrugged. "No problem. Why? Are you taking a trip?"

She looked around her – the darkened park, illuminated only by lamplight, the melting snow, their breath hanging in the chilly air. Far from her September kitchen, wrapped in warmth, reading a message from the past. Six months ago, a lifetime ago, a vast chasm like the darkness between the ghost towers shining up to the heavens.

"I'm going home."

5

The Journey Home

FOURTEEN YEARS AFTER SHE WALKED AWAY from her father's house, nine months after she saw her life broken apart, three months after she stared into the abyss of a frightening past and an unwanted future, Laura Abbott turned her car towards the East Coast and started on the journey home.

She drove for three days, fueled by determination and anxiety, each passing mile sweeping her away from her life as Laura St. Bride. Away from the man who wanted her, the daughter she could not take with her, the life she had known for so many years. Closer to the Laura Abbott she had struggled so hard to find again during the last months in London.

Months of hope and grief and anticipation that finally telescoped down to a moment when Laura Abbott drove through familiar ornamented iron gates, followed a winding road through a forest of ancient oak and hickory trees, and mounted the steps to the resurrected Folly to knock on the door.

But now her courage failed her.

She stared at her hand, wavering in mid-air, and all her fine resolutions died a quick and shameful death. She pictured Richard hearing her knock, coming to the door, staring, speaking her name. Finally seeing through her mask to the truth. Slamming the door in her face.

Her hand dropped.

She heard a noise inside, the ringing of a telephone, and her breath caught. The ringing stopped abruptly in mid-ring, as if he answered, and she put her hand against the great door for support, sick with relief at the reprieve.

A minute, that's all, just a minute, give him time to get off the phone....

She leaned her forehead against the door and waited for him. She even thought that she could hear him faintly, a voice talking, laughing. How many feet separated them – ten? Twenty? He was here now, within her reach. After all these years, with one knock at the door, with one ring of the bell, she could come face to face with the prince of her childhood.

She could, if she wanted, if she dared, reach out to touch his face.

As she had once reached....

She was shaking so violently that she scarcely knew when her feet began to carry her back down the stone steps. Fear, a nasty, tight fear, rode high in her throat as she glanced, once, over her shoulder and stumbled in her haste to escape before he came and found her.

She had parked hundreds of yards away near the oval lake, hidden by the thicket of trees at the turnoff of the main Ashmore Park road to the Folly. Parking there brought her into sight of Ashmore Magna, but she had taken one look at the windows, drapes drawn, and known that it now stood empty. She had seen that a car sat in the circular drive before the Folly – Richard's car? – and she remembered from an article she'd downloaded that he lived there.

Some instinct of self-preservation had told her not to drive up right up to the Folly. Better to stay out of sight, better to keep their first meeting on her terms, not his. So she had lingered behind the comforting curtain of forest, promising herself small rewards if only she would take the first step toward coming home. Think of it like falling off a horse, finding the nerve to ride again – but then, once she'd fallen off in front of Cam, and she had never ridden again. Scratch that. Think of it like that first concert, walking out to face an audience, unknown, unconvinced, but predisposed to like her.

Remember that Richard had told her to come home.

No, he'd said that she could always come home. He hadn't promised open arms waiting for her.

She headed back through the trees to the car, its silver lines concealed by the copse, walking faster and faster until she broke into a run to reach its safety.

She collapsed against the car door and waited for her heart to slow down and her nerves to stop jumping. She waited there, how long she did not know, and finally the warmth of the afternoon soothed her and lent her the courage to look back through the trees.

The Folly. Richard's old dream....

He had made good on that, at least. It stood there now, an incongruous piece of the Gilded Age set against a Virginia hill, limestone-walled and slate-roofed and multiple-chimneyed. His plans to restore the rain-shattered wreck of the Great Lakes shipping heiress's brainstorm, dismantled stone by stone from a Beaux Arts mansion in Newport because she insisted on living in a bigger house than her mother-in-law, had run like a thread throughout childhood.

"We'll live here someday, Di," he'd told her sister, who had glanced at his sketches as if they had nothing to do with the future he wanted with her. Lucy had stomped on the idea with all the confident supremacy of one who hadn't thought of it first, and Francie had looked pityingly at Diana because, after all, who wanted to live in a hovel – a very big hovel, a very fancy hovel, but still? He'd said nothing, only surveyed his small harem until his gaze rested on the youngest of them all. *Well?* his eyes challenged, and so Laura chimed in her enthusiastic support, because he was the center of her limited universe and she was his devoted handmaiden. He'd rewarded her well for her loyalty. He had given the others his most superior, aloof smile, and bestowed upon her the honor of a lift home on horseback.

She had nestled against him, his arms reaching around her to hold the reins, while the three traitors trudged beside them, complaining step by step.

Laura shielded her eyes from the sun beating down and peered through the trees, branches waving in the breeze. But she had parked too far away to pick out details easily, and the thicket lived up to its name. She hesitated only a minute before she reached into the passenger seat for the binoculars she had packed for use in the mountains. She was not, she thought ruefully, strong enough to resist the temptation to use them.

But first she needed a safer perch. She started the engine and headed for the house at the end of the wooded road. The great house of Ashmore Park, Ashmore Magna, situated on the highest point of the estate. Five minutes, and she threaded her way up through the front gardens to the portico. And she settled down to watch.

For years she had struggled not to remember. Once, a face in the crowd had caught her eye, and she had turned wildly to stare at an elusive resemblance – the frame of an eyebrow, the cut of the jaw, the set of the shoulders. All too often, his eyes as she had last seen them, blazing, furious, filled with hatred, had haunted her as she slept.

But oh, that shouldn't matter now! She was an adult. She was Cat Courtney, toast of the West End, with three pending proposals to her credit. She wasn't his handmaiden anymore. He meant nothing to her, nothing at all, that wasn't why she was coming home, no matter how he looked leaning against a pillar. Julie had said it best in her message – she wanted only to find her sisters again. She had only come to Ashmore Park first because Diana and Julie lived here with him, and she still hadn't found any trace of Lucy.

In her hotel room the night before, she had rehearsed it all in front of the mirror. She would drive the remembered path to his home. She would walk bravely to the door, and when he answered, she would be the one to smile, to put him gently at his ease, to gloss over the raw awkwardness of the long-lost runaway turning up on his doorstep.

She would thank him for his note to her. She would tell him she was sorry she hadn't responded before this. She would tell him of her sorrow at his parents' death. She would visit prettily, catch up on old times. She would be poised, polished, sophisticated, Laura St. Bride at her Plano matron best.

She would never, ever let him know that she had called him just to hear his voice. That she had tucked away the picture of him leaning against the pillar. Or that she waited here, courage extinguished, binoculars in hand, spying on him for all the world like a teenage girl with her first crush.

She waited over an hour in the shimmering heat, leaning against the same pillar on the portico of the great house, feeling the same warm stone against her back, before she saw him, riding over the rise behind the Folly.

The glasses brought him close to her, so close that surely he saw her…. Oh, but he didn't, he couldn't. He sat astride an enormous gray hunter, a tall man silhouetted briefly against the bright morning horizon before he blended into the trees and the glasses blurred.

She knew him at once.

Her heart skipped. She adjusted the glasses to bring him back into focus, starved for all the signs of the years' passing, starved for the sight of him.

He pulled the reins up quickly and looked back over his shoulder, and did she imagine it or did she hear him call to someone? Diana? Julie? He turned back, and she saw his hand reach to the pocket of his shirt, as if he wanted…. Oh, no. The impatient movement of his hand as it came away empty brought a warm tide of memory. So many times she had chided him about his smoking; so many times he had tried to quit. "For me?" she'd wheedle, and with a quick smile, he'd promise to try again....

Did he still devour homemade cookies to chase away the craving? He had liked hers best.

He cantered the hunter around, still waiting for his companion, and now she saw the full range of him. Still lean, despite all those cookies (*don't look, don't remember*), but his shoulders had filled out. He had needed that, he had needed to leave that boy's lankiness behind, gain the stature of a man. She looked at him as he waited on the great horse, and he was perfect.

Nothing had changed, nothing....

I am sick with old longings.

She lowered the binoculars to dash her hand across her eyes, and when she looked again, she saw the girl riding over the rise, approaching him.

Enormous sunglasses and a riding helmet hid the girl's face, but even so, this must be Julie. Her body was too young, her movements too lithe, her clothes too ragtag, to belong to Diana, and Richard leaned in towards her with the universal protective stance of a father towards a daughter.

Julia Ashmore. Sixteen now, not the newborn who had won Laura's heart through the nursery glass or the toddler who liked the songs her aunt made up for her. In her infant innocence, clearly the center of Richard's life, even as Diana receded in importance. No one watching Richard and Diana that last Christmas had missed the obvious deterioration of their marriage, the careful politeness, the contempt coiled beneath the surface. Francie had seen, had moved in swiftly to strike. *He just wants to keep Julie,* she'd whispered fiercely later, in the shadows of night, *or he'd get rid of Di. She doesn't deserve him, she doesn't know how to make him happy.*

Oh, but Francie had known. By then, she and Richard had become lovers....

While her mind wandered, she had stopped paying attention. She refocused on the pair and saw, in horror, that Julie had bolted upright on her horse and was pointing straight in her direction. Dear God, not like this, she hadn't thought they could see her! She didn't have to hear Julie's words to catch the girl's urgency. Richard looked at his daughter, his brow creasing in consternation – and then – no, no, *no!* – he turned and stared in the direction of her arm until he stared right at Laura.

And then he forgot Laura completely, as Julie's mare reared up and dumped her unceremoniously onto the ground.

Laura's breath froze.

For one terrible moment, Julie lay motionless. Richard reached out quickly to catch the mare's reins and failed as the mare shied away from him. Laura watched him dig his heel into the hunter's flank to urge it on after the fleeing horse, and she released a breath she hadn't even known she held when he caught up with the mare, grabbed the reins, and yanked them sharply to bring the horse under control and away from the girl lying on the grass.

A second after the horses stopped, he was sliding off his saddle and running across the grass to Julie. Oh, dear Lord, what had she done, was Julie hurt or worse…. She tasted blood where she had bitten into her lip, but she never felt the pain until she saw Julie sit up, shaking her head.

Richard leaned forward, his arms slipping around his daughter, and then he stopped.

In one terrible glance, across hundreds of yards, he looked straight at Laura.

She lowered the glasses and found herself shaking. Oh, what had she done, why hadn't she waited for him to open the door….

She went running for her car, slamming open the door, fumbling for the ignition, desperate to leave before Richard Ashmore decided to come find the woman who had nearly killed his daughter.

She drove restlessly all morning, relearning the roads of her younger life, marking the changes of her lost years. Her old school, the park where she had received her first kiss, the bookstore where she had worked…. She stored up her mental snapshots to mull over the lunch she ate out at the James.

There, Mark found her. Well, it was her fault, she shouldn't have answered the call. She listened patiently to his tale of woe. Meg had talked back to Emma again, and Mark, who had already discovered that it was easier to master the universe than to referee between two strong-willed females, wanted her to fix it all. Not now, she thought, not now, but she was inured to responsibility, so she chastised Meg and commiserated with Mark about the trials of living with a rambunctious teenager. While she talked and listened, she looked out over the waters of childhood and let herself bathe in the soft airs of Virginia, and she did not easily remember all the years of exile.

Finally, she disentangled herself from her two master manipulators and told them in no uncertain terms to work it out and not to call her for the rest of the day. She needed to be alone, to remember that once she had been Laura Abbott, and she had loved the man who had married her sister.

After a while, she headed west, following the bends of the river, and with one hand on the steering wheel, she fished around in her shoulder bag with the other for the key she had found in her jewelry case.

Not that it would fit now. Surely her father had changed the locks at some time in the last fourteen years; if not, then Lucy or Diana must have changed them after his death.... She hadn't a hope that the key still opened the front door of the house where she had grown up, but maybe they had never fixed the window in Diana's old bedroom, the one with the broken latch and the strong branch a foot away.

Her father's house looked cared for, for all that the sign in the front lawn read FOR SALE BY OWNER, with *Call D. Ashmore* and a phone number below it. Not the number at Ashmore Park, so that must be Diana's work number. The grass was mowed, the bushes trimmed, the windows clean, and someone had watered the roses Lucy had planted when she was fifteen.

No hint of death or violence here.

She parked the Jaguar in the drive, unworried that someone might see her. Even now, the nearest neighbors were at least a mile away. No unwelcome company had disturbed the silence that Dominic Abbott demanded. And such silence! She was used to the muted rush of London traffic, but she heard nothing now but the engine cooling down and a far-away plane trailing above.

Dominic's piano had fallen silent forever.

She stared at the front door, and she felt sick.

He was dead. They had buried him, his remaining daughters, in some unknown grave that she intended never to visit. She need not worry that he would appear at the dining room window, his cold, remote eyes watching her turn the key over and over in her hand. The sound of the key in the lock could not disturb his reverie, could not wreck whatever strange, atonal chord occupied his mind, could not summon him into the front hall to confront the daughter whose key still worked.

Someone had seen to that.

So you're back, he might have said, if a person unknown had not swung at his head with tremendous force. *I'm working, don't disturb me now....* She walked into the music room, just off the main hall, and the strain in her fingers eased ever so slightly around the key. She slipped it into the pocket of her jeans.

Oh, this room! Dominic's refuge from the world, where he mapped out his conducting strategies and wrote that unworldly music that no one wanted to hear. He had replaced his old stereo system, and the musician in her was absurdly pleased to see that. She stepped around his reading chair to the shelves that held his vast music collection, and she was startled to see that he even had bought one of her own CDs. She lifted it out, with shaking fingers, and she saw his jottings among the liner notes.

Well, she could imagine what he had written; she remembered very well his comments in that unspeakable review. She tucked the CD back into its place.

She wandered around the room, avoiding the piano where he had died as long as possible, letting her fingers trail over his desk, his reading chair, his stack of once-read *Opera News*. She stopped at the desk where he had spent so many solitary evenings, planning the next step in his vagabond career, and she picked up the photograph – the only sign that the man who had dominated this room had any human ties.

Diana, on that unforgettable night when he had conducted her in concert. She had worn her elegant satin wedding dress a second time, and Dominic had paid tribute with the string of pearls he placed around her neck. Richard had taken the picture, probably gritting his teeth as his father-in-law monopolized his bride – or perhaps not. He and Diana had still been happy, still laughing in the glow of their summer honeymoon.

Just off camera, Francie had been ready to spit nails.

She put the picture down and sat down at the piano.

No trace of blood, no lingering remembrance of life seeping away....

For a moment, she was afraid to touch the keys. What might she not hear – *Sit up straight, keep your fingers curved, how many times do I have to tell you, child?* Or, more likely, *Again! Again! Pay attention! Higher! Higher!*

Everyone in the family knew what Dominic said to his daughters at the piano. Anyone could stand outside the door and know instantly who sat beside him at the keyboard, just from the tone of his voice. For Diana, lovely, blessed Diana, all gentleness and awe; for Lucy, a certain guarded respect – if he ripped up at her, she might just rip right back, and Lucy always had the option of leaving. For Francie, laughter and flirtation; Francie had known from birth how to charm him. But for Laura—

She leaned over and ran her left hand along the piano leg. There, right there it was – he'd never had it repaired, that gash left when one of her kittens decided that a Bösendorfer made the perfect scratching post. Dominic had been stopped in the midst of his tirade, and she thought he had let the subject drop, but the kittens she had rescued from starvation and nurtured back to health disappeared, and later she found them in the back fields down near the James. Their necks had been twisted, their bodies thrown away.

Violence to violence, from a woman flung into the sea to kittens flung into the James, to a man's life blood spilling away.

She straightened up now, and assumed the posture that he'd drilled into her. Her hands curved over the keys. She closed her eyes against the memories and played the opening chords of her first hit, the song that Dominic, in his infinite malice, had deemed trite, sentimental, and vastly overrated.

She played through the entire song, three times, on this piano that someone kept regularly tuned, and several things didn't happen. No keyboard melted; no laughter rang out in mocking applause; no voice cut through the silence and ordered her to stop.

The steel metronome that Renée Dane, Countess of Shilleen, had given her lover kept no time.

His ghost wrapped itself in silence.

When she finished, she carefully folded the cover over the keys, rose, and went upstairs to her old bedroom.

Not just hers alone. She lingered in the doorway, and nothing had changed. The bulletin board where she and Francie had tracked their lives had gone, and the desk where she had written her first lyrics was swept clean, but nothing else seemed changed from her last summer morning in this house. The same gingham bedspreads – not her taste, but she had given in to Francie – the same knitted afghan, the same toss pillows that she had hugged night after night, muffling her anguish as Francie confessed the harrowing details of her revenge on Diana.

He had left the one picture she hadn't taken with her: the four sisters on that last Christmas, Laura and Francie standing together in matching sweaters, high school seniors on the brink of their lives. She had come to hate that picture; it had marked the breakdown of their lifetime of solidarity. A few days later, Francie had begun her revenge against Diana, effectively isolating her twin in the process.

Twins, they'd called themselves, she and Francie, after someone referred to them as Irish twins. They were a year less a day apart, but they passed for twins, and a childhood bout of rheumatic fever had kept Francie in class with her. They'd behaved as twins, too, dependent on each other, confiding in each other, each living in the other's life. A year less a day, only that separated them, but it had been enough. Enough that Dominic Abbott treated Francie with loving indulgence, the child of his reconciliation with his great love, enough that he looked upon his fourth daughter as an encumbrance whose birth destroyed the fragile bonds between her parents and who was, after all, another mouth to feed. Enough that Richard Ashmore submerged his deep unhappiness in Francie and still treated Laura as his adoring young slave. Enough that Cameron St. Bride knew right away who would make him a malleable, submissive wife—

Enough! She brushed her hand across her eyes. She had no business crying. If tears were going to loom every time she remembered Francie, she had best go back to London immediately. She couldn't spend the summer weeping at every turn.

She turned away from the door and ran her hand along the fabric-covered wall towards the staircase. Then, of course, she stopped at one door, because she couldn't resist; she had to see if he had changed this room too, if he had kept it as much a shrine as he had Francie's.

Unbelievable! The man must have spent these last years living in the past. He'd decreed early on that Diana, as the oldest daughter, was entitled to the bedroom suite with the private bathroom and the fireplace and the window seat, and Francie would inherit the room when Diana left for school. But Francie had elected to stay in the back of the house out of Dominic's hearing, so Diana's room had been left inviolate.

Except that someone had been dusting it. She traced a finger across the dressing table and came away clean. Come to think of it, the piano had looked pristine, and the entire house lacked that dusty smell of abandonment. She'd seen no sign that anyone was living here – still, if someone came in….

She turned around and looked into Richard Ashmore's eyes.

Not really, of course. Just another picture (and, she hoped, the last one – it was more upsetting than she had anticipated, glimpsing the past in unexpected corners like this), but this picture was special. Richard and Diana at their engagement dinner, young and glorious, laughing at each other with the familiarity of long-time lovers, never doubting for a second that they would look at each other with the same passion in fifty years.

Laura Abbott took the picture in her hand and sat down at the dressing table and let her dreams slide into her thoughts.

Richard. Richard….

Still learning to handle that incredible height. Thick dark hair that he had worn short enough (barely) to please his father and long enough to infuriate hers. Slate blue eyes and lashes that any girl would have killed to possess, and an easy smile in evidence all the time. A kindness that rescued Laura from Dominic more than once, and a blind infatuation that kept his heart trained on Diana, lovely, lucky Diana, and blinkered his eyes against the one who really loved him.

He'd known all about that broken window latch. He had broken it himself when Dominic became aware that his crown princess had come home once too often with her blouse buttoned wrong. For the first and only time, Dominic disciplined Diana, grounding her for two weeks, and that only motivated the two lovers to circumvent that restriction with a vengeance. Diana locked her door, Richard climbed the tree, and Dominic composed in oblivious peace at his piano, unaware that his fast dominion over his best-loved daughter was nightly broken by the ardent worship of a young man's body.

Diana's sisters kept her secret for her, Lucy because she despised Dominic, Laura because she thought it thrillingly romantic, Francie because she liked having something to hold over Diana's head.

Richard had been seventeen, Diana six months younger. Two years later, one June afternoon, Dominic had conceded defeat and reluctantly handed over his darling to the usurper. How perfect they had seemed, Richard and Diana, he so tall and tanned and laughing, and she shining and sweet and frail in her wedding gown! Prince Charming and the princess he had awakened to life, the perfect ending to a perfect fairy tale.

Oh, but the prince never saw the lady in waiting; the currents of time that decreed that six years would always separate them had swept him out of Laura's reach. So she accepted coming in last, she was used to it, and she settled for his affectionate hug as he took his turn dancing with his new sisters-in-law.

Diana smiled graciously in her indubitable triumph; Francie sulked bitterly in a defeat she clearly considered temporary. Honestly, Lucy snapped after being shoved out of the bridal bouquet's path, Francie seemed not to comprehend that the battle was finished. Richard was *gone*. He had taken himself out of circulation the first time he met Diana, when he was eight. Of course, she said, ignoring Francie's glower, he ought to have put an end to this long ago, but he was so head-over-heels with Diana that he didn't realize that he had ever served as a battleground.

By that last afternoon, though, he knew. By that last afternoon, he bore the scars of the war, he knew the guilt of being the prize in a contest of blood, and he was not inclined to give quarter to any daughter with Dominic Abbott's eyes.

By that last afternoon, he had declared his own war.

The last time she saw him…. *No. There be dragons….*

She placed the frame gently on the table and looked around one last time, and she wondered again about the lack of dust and the sign out front. Was Diana living here? But no, Richard still lived at Ashmore Park, she'd seen that clearly…. Were he and Diana still together? She didn't know. All her research hadn't told her if their marriage had survived. She knew nothing about them at all.

She gave Diana's royal bedchamber one last look and headed downstairs.

She was at the door when one thought stopped her.

When she'd made the decision to come home, she'd blithely assumed that she'd have no trouble contacting her sisters. Of course, she could always return to Ashmore Park, but she'd already fizzled at that, and she hadn't the courage for a repeat performance, at least not today. She had Diana's number now from the sign, and she had all of Richard's numbers from his fax, carefully tucked away in her shoulder bag. Lucy, though, elusive Lucy – she'd found no listing for Lucia Abbott, and it hit her then, only then, that of course Lucy had married and changed her name.

Of everyone, she preferred to face Lucy.

She gave herself no time to think. She marched back into Dominic's music room and straight over to his desk, where surely he must have kept an address book or a telephone list or *something* that could help her find Lucy. She laid her purse and keys down on the blotter, and two things happened.

The telephone rang, for one.

The noise startled her, and her heart began to beat faster. Absurd, of course, as if a telephone could hurt her, and she knew that even as she counted off the rings and waited for it to stop. Strange, that no one had disconnected the phone, but then – and the answering machine switched on, and her father's cold, remote voice, dead these last months, advised that he could not answer the call and issued a completely insincere invitation to leave a message.

Terrible enough to hear her father's voice, but that was not the worst of it.

"Diana." She had never forgotten that voice, clipped and cool and very angry. She would remember the sound of it in her last thoughts. "If you're there, pick up the phone."

She didn't, of course. She stood there and listened.

"I don't know what the hell you were playing at this morning, spying on us, but you scared the devil out of your daughter. If you have something to say to me, call me, and we'll talk. Otherwise," he paused, and his voice lost a little of the edge, "don't pull a stunt like that again." Another pause. "I assume that you've bought yourself a Jaguar. You'd better call me, Di, that's a hell of a car to take care of. And, for God's sake, change the message on the phone."

He hung up.

How long she stood there, staring down at the offending machine, she couldn't have guessed. The tape whirred on for a few seconds, and then disconnected, and a red light flashed at her. That woke her up, and she reached for the erase button, because Diana must never hear that message. Her fingers hovered over the unfamiliar buttons, and she depressed one to erase just as the man spoke.

"A Jaguar. Are you the guilty party?"

The man spoke quietly, gently, as if he did not want to frighten her, but the effect on her already stretched nerves was inevitable. She jerked around, one hand sweeping her keys to the floor, the other hand going instinctively to her throat.

He didn't look threatening, certainly, standing there in the hall doorway. He looked like any nice, quiet man with graying brown hair, a conservative suit, and a hand that still bore the imprint of a recently removed wedding ring, and he didn't have an ax on him. He didn't leer, he didn't look dangerous – but, nonetheless, she was a woman confronted by a strange man in a deserted and isolated house where her father had been murdered, and she reacted accordingly.

"Stay where you are." Thank heavens for Cat Courtney's cool under pressure; Laura St. Bride certainly needed her now. "Don't you move one step closer."

Too bad her voice squeaked on that last word.

"I wouldn't dream of it," he assured her, and held up his hands to show that he was harmless. "It's all right, I promise you."

Her heart was pumping blood wildly below her throat. "How did you get in here?" And, when he forgot and shifted from the door, she said sharply, "Stand right there! I don't know who you are, and until I do, you stay put."

God, what could she use as a weapon? Was the metronome close enough?

"Okay." He leaned back against the door jamb, and then she felt foolish. Whoever he was, he *did* look harmless, and she could see perfectly well that he had a key in his hand. He probably had more right to be here than she did.

She saw, too, that he had recognized her.

"Relax, Miss Courtney," he said, after an agonizing moment of silence during which she realized that he blocked the only exit. "I'm not going to hurt you."

She could think of nothing to say but a futile "Don't call me that, please. That's not my name."

He looked surprised. "Whatever you like. I'm just pleased to meet you." He held out his hand. "Kevin Stone. I've been a fan for a long time."

Now she felt more than foolish. "You've got a key. How did you get it?"

Did she imagine it, or did he hesitate there, just for a second, before his hand dropped? "The owner gave it to me. I'm her lawyer."

"Oh." Worse than foolish, downright humiliated. Diana's attorney, so he probably knew Richard, and wouldn't he have an interesting story to tell? She hadn't a hope now that Richard wouldn't find out who had spied on him, unless Kevin Stone forgot what he had overheard.

Vain hope, indeed. "I take it," he said, fighting off an amused smile with little success, "that you've been out to Ashmore Park? What did you do to put our good friend Richard in such an uproar?"

If she had learned one thing from Cam during their marriage, it was the fine art of brazening it out when you got caught. She took her time answering, first relaxing the fine tension between them by leaning back against Dominic's desk and scuffing her shoe against her keys. She pitched her voice to a low, confiding tone and looked him straight in the eye.

"I spied on him."

"Really?" He didn't bother to hide his surprise. "And why, may I ask? Richard wouldn't let you in? Or is something wrong with the doorbell?"

"No, with my courage." She straightened up. "Let's not play games, Mr. Stone—"

"Kevin, please."

"If you're Diana's lawyer, you know who I am."

He straightened up too, and she did not resist or order him back when he entered the room. He kept his distance still, walking around the other side of the room, leaning casually against the shelves on the far wall. His manner, respectful, almost diffident, encouraged her to relax. She knew from experience that he was assessing her against some mental checklist – could ordinary Laura Abbott in her Old Navy jeans really be Cat Courtney, she of mist and mystery? – but he kept his conclusions off his face.

"I believe," he said, "that you're the runaway. Or one of them, I keep forgetting there were two of you—"

"Laura."

"The mezzo soprano." He smiled. "Francie was the lyric soprano." Unusual knowledge for a lawyer to have about his client's family. "So is this a homecoming? Or are you just passing through?"

"I – I don't know." Her uneasiness returned. She stooped to pick up her keys, buying time, keeping her eyes on him, but her hand shook, and they crashed to the floor again. Oh, dear heavens, what more could she do to disgrace herself in front of this man who knew Diana and Richard and probably Lucy too?

"Laura." She opened her eyes, and he was down there beside her, opening her hand and placing the keys in her palm. "It's all right, you know," his voice, deep, low. "You've got a right to be nervous."

He drew her to her feet, steadied her, before he reached around her to open a desk drawer. She stiffened at his unexpected closeness, and wondered, too, at his familiarity in this house. Who was he, that he so matter-of-factly pulled out Dominic's strong box and removed a key? Diana's lawyer? Or a thief with a ready story and the confidence that she had no more business here than he did?

Just my luck. I come back and get attacked by an intruder.

But he had a key to the house.

"Who are you?" she asked, before she lost her nerve. "And what are you doing here?"

He looked amused. "I'm getting the safe deposit box key for Diana." He nodded towards the telephone. "Do you want to call her? She'll verify my right to be here."

She bit her lip. She could imagine the call: Diana in shock, she herself unable to contain her emotion.... No, she wanted to see the surprise of her return in Diana's eyes.

If she could still keep it a surprise, after blowing it at Ashmore Park and running into Kevin Stone.

"Will you—" Damn it, her voice squeaked again. "Will you tell her about seeing me here?"

He glanced over at her wryly. "I was just wondering that myself," he said. "I should. She's my client, and I just caught someone breaking and entering on her property, except—" He gestured towards her keys. "You're not the usual intruder. Tell me, Laura. What do you think I should do?"

She sagged against the desk in relief. "Forget you saw me."

He shook his head. "Sorry," and her heart sank.

"Please," she said, "*please*," and she forced herself to touch his arm. "Don't – don't tell her. I've spent a lot of time – I've given up a lot to come here. Let me contact my sisters in my own time, my own way, please. It's better that I do it, truly it is."

She sensed his intensity as he listened to her, and the frisson of unease returned.

"You won't leave without calling them?" he said. "Or will you say anything to get rid of me?"

She lifted her head sharply. "No! I want to see them. Except—" She looked at him. A lawyer. "Do you know my sister Lucy? Or maybe she goes by Lucia now."

In some strange fashion, the mention of Lucy tipped the balance of power in her favor. She sensed that the question left him nonplussed, uncertain how to answer.

She pressed him before she lost her advantage. "I can't find a listing for her. She was going to be a lawyer—"

He said slowly, "She is. In fact, I'm supposed to call her later. Are you going to contact her at home?"

"Wherever I can reach her, Mr. Stone."

"I'll give you her number." He pulled out a business card and a pen and wrote on the back, and during the few seconds it took him to write the number, he seemed to come to some conclusion. He held the card out, but when she reached for it, he held it just out of her grasp.

"Oh, no, you don't, Cat Courtney. I've promised you silence and collusion against my client's better interest. I want a couple of things in return."

"What?" she asked warily.

He held the pen out to her.

She laughed then, in relief. For the first time in her life, she laughed in Dominic Abbott's music room, and the phantom of that sad little girl at the piano slipped away. "I can do better than that," she said, and she took her CD from Dominic's collection and signed an extravagant autograph. Kevin promised never to read any of the liner notes.

"What's the second?" she asked, at her car door.

"Dinner some evening," he said, and held up his hand at the instant response in her eyes. "Please, consider it before you say no."

"I'm sorry," she said. "I'm recently widowed."

He nodded at her left hand. "That doesn't look like a wedding ring."

She glanced down, startled at his perception. "It isn't. I'm not ready to date."

In the face of that, he visibly retreated. A tactician, then – but why? Surely he'd been turned down before, and surely he didn't expect to meet Cat Courtney in a deserted house and have her fall into his arms. She'd been approached over the years by charming men desiring her time and attention, but those men had wanted Cat Courtney. Not so with Kevin Stone. This man's interest lay, not in Cat Courtney, but in the depths of Laura Abbott.

He said, "Think about it. I won't alert the media. Believe me, if Cat Courtney will have dinner with me, I'm not about to share her with anyone." He smiled, the gray of his eyes not quite masking that curious intensity. "You've got my card – or will you let me call you?"

All those years of Cam protecting her, and she had never appreciated any of it until this moment. She shook her head. "I don't think so."

Something moved behind Kevin Stone's eyes then, some hard emotion she couldn't read. Laura sank against the warm metal of her car door, anxious to escape the uncomfortable weight of this man's eyes upon her, wishing she'd listened to Mark's lectures and laid Laura Abbott to rest and never come back to Virginia in her lifetime.

"You know, Laura," his voice had a new edge, "I want to get to know you better. We'll be seeing a lot of each other in the future—"

She found courage then, irritated with his shadowed words and ungrounded certainty. "I doubt it, Mr. Stone. If you don't mind—"

"We'll see each other." And then he paused, hooking her with that flat assurance; she wanted to turn away from him before he said another word, but he'd baited her well.

She waited, fatally curious.

He saw that, damn him, and smiled.

"You see," Kevin Stone said, "I'm going to marry your sister."

Of all the things he could have said, she did not expect that. She found herself gaping at him, trying to imagine the blunt, straightforward Lucy she remembered with this intense man and his damn-your-eyes stare. Either Lucy had changed all out of proportion, or she had lost her mind.

"Lucy? You're going to marry Lucy?"

She had startled him again. "Lucy? Good God, no!" He reached past her, as she stood there, stunned, and opened her car door for her. "A Jaguar for a Cat! No, Laura Abbott," and she scarcely noticed that she obeyed the sweep of his hand and climbed into her car, "I'm going to marry Diana."

And he walked away.

As an exit line, it was superb. Seconds before, she had wanted nothing so much as to flee the subtle menace of his presence; now she stared after him, fighting down the urge to run after him, grab his arm, demand an explanation for words that, on their face, made no sense at all.

Marry Diana? Didn't Diana already have a husband?

But – a husband who did not know what sort of car his wife drove.

She inserted her key into the ignition and noticed that her fingers trembled.

He's crazy, Laura told herself, finding a small comfort in the ritual of fastening her seat belt, checking the mirror, shifting into reverse. *A little off. Like that reporter who kept trying to get into the suite in Rome. He didn't hurt you. He didn't threaten you. He just wanted to have dinner with you.*

It's Diana he wants.

And Diana, after all, was scarcely defenseless. She had family, she had a husband, and she could always fire a lawyer who overstepped his bounds.

Or, if he really pushed her, she could always cut his throat.

Kevin Stone had parked behind her, blocking her escape. He politely backed out to make way for her and waited, as if – oh, no – he planned to follow her.

She wondered sickly if he might seek her out at her hotel, but common sense asserted itself. She hadn't told him where she was staying; he probably assumed that she'd found a hotel here on the Peninsula. He would never look for her in the glittering anonymity of Virginia Beach.

She could lose him easily on the bridge-tunnel, if she kept her head and remembered that, after all, she wasn't Laura Abbott any-more. She was Cat Courtney, supremely sure and self-confident, and one slightly crazy man wasn't going to get the best of her.

She made it a game, to calm herself down. He followed her for a couple of miles down the country road, and remained on her trail until she reached Jamestown. It didn't do any good to call him every name she could think of, he certainly couldn't hear her… but it made her feel better, more in control, while she waited for the chance to lose him.

When the opportunity came, it was straight out of the security lectures Cam had made her attend. She waited at a green light, counted off the seconds after it turned yellow, and then floored the accelerator and shot across the intersection as the light turned red.

She heard Cam, or was it Mark? *What's wrong with you? You've got the phone. Use it!*

But the police…. She bit her lip and winced. Police… reports, unwelcome attention—

And Mark finding out. Mark saying the night before she left, *This is a very bad idea, Laura.*

She played it safe at the interstate, just in case he had found her again. She headed away from Virginia Beach, away from the hotel she'd registered in under – oh, no! – Laura Rose St. Bride. Away from Ashmore Park, where Kevin Stone might well expect her to run.

So Laura Rose St. Bride ran west in search of a place to hide.

Williamsburg made a splendid sanctuary and provided a certain ironic closure, Laura acknowledged, as she locked the car in the parking lot and fell into step behind a group of French tourists head-ing for the old city.

Fourteen years ago, in the bright heat of a June afternoon, she and Francie had left their father's house and vanished into Williamsburg forever. A waitress at one of the restaurants later recalled the two look-alikes for the police, the last time anyone in Virginia ever saw the younger Abbott girls together. After that lunch, they had separated, Francie boarding a tourist bus bound back to Washington, Laura driving to Richmond and catching a bus to Chicago. Weeks later, reading the papers in the Palo Alto branch library, they had been astonished to learn that the police had found their car, completely stripped, in Baltimore.

Some anonymous soul, more faceless than Laura and Francie Abbott that day, had helped himself to their beloved car.

"Stripped?" Francie had cried, as if that minor tragedy overshadowed all else. "Honestly! The nerve of some people!"

Williamsburg beckoned now, a sanctuary of peace and charming quiet, where Richard Ashmore did not issue cool, clipped words to a wife whose life he apparently did not share, where Kevin Stone did not menace her with unsettling emotions and bizarre statements.

Off his rocker, she repeated to herself like a talisman. *I'll tell Lucy, when I see her. Or even Richard. They'll know what to do.*

The serenity of the old city touched her, soothed away the last vestiges of the distasteful encounter at her father's house. Laura lost herself in the masses of travelers, wandering around, stopping for tea at a tavern, browsing for antique lace to trim a shirt for Meg. No one looked twice at the woman in jeans and cotton blouse; no one nudged a companion and remarked that Cat Courtney was there in the next aisle, examining a handmade quilt.

Kevin Stone certainly never found her there.

By five, the tourists had thinned out, and the weariness in her muscles told Laura to head back. She gathered up her packages, boarded the bus back to the tourist center, and followed a crowd out to the parking lot, grateful again, as she had been fourteen years before, for her invisibility.

Then she saw her fatal mistake, as she inserted her keys into the Jaguar trunk.

She drew her breath in, as the truth sank its teeth into her.

The keys, the damned keys! She saw herself dropping them at his feet, saw Kevin Stone picking them up and putting them in her hand. The keys, and the attached hotel key card for anyone to see.

And, thrown carelessly on the passenger seat of her car, the hotel brochure.

She might as well have issued an invitation.

When Karen first started work as administrative assistant to the senior partner at Ashmore & McIntire, Architects and Designers, she figured that there had to be some catch to her new boss. No one could be that easy on the eyes and not harbor some grave personal flaw. A total lack of organization, an awesome temper, an unreasonable libido – sooner or later, Richard Ashmore would drop those perfect manners and show the true man underneath. It was a matter of time.

She was still waiting. He wasn't a perfect boss; he worked long hours and expected her to work them too, but he always followed an all-nighter with a paid day off. He offset the precision he brought to his architectural practice by the regularity with which he mislaid his Blackberry. He had never lost his temper with her, but she had heard him lay with devastating sharpness into the wife he had forgotten to divorce. She was attractive, but he had never made a pass at her; presumably, his libido was being cared for by the sporadic soft-spoken woman who called the office.

Not perfect, then, but an easy man to work for, as long as she kept his practice running smoothly, made sure that the coffee pot was never empty, and ignored his occasional dark moods.

Like the one he was obviously nursing when he came in after spending the morning with his daughter. *Diana*, judged Karen with the expertise of years. She placed a cup of freshly brewed coffee and five sharpened pencils on his desk and closed the glass door so he could fight with his wife in private.

Stupid bitch, she thought, and turned her attention to her computer and the proposal he wanted to get out by five.

When she took the proposal in, he had cheered up; he even complimented her on her speed. They talked through various revisions, and he looked through a stack of correspondence she had left on his desk earlier. "I hate to ask this," he said, as he started signing some letters, marking revisions on others, "but can you come in tomorrow for a few hours? We need to work on the Charleston specs."

"Sure," said Karen, and mentally figured the overtime.

The light on his phone blinked, and Karen reached over to catch the incoming call. "Tom," she said warmly, at the first sound of the caller's voice, and Richard looked up. She liked Tom Maitland; he was a good friend to her boss, and an even better lawyer.

"I'll be with him in a second," said Richard, eyes racing through the rest of his correspondence. "Tell him I reserved the courts for Sunday."

Karen relayed the message, and was a little surprised when Tom Maitland, normally the most genial of men, said brusquely, "This is urgent. I just got a call from Kevin Stone. Whatever he's doing can wait."

She lowered the phone and hit the hold button.

"You'd better take this. He says it's urgent. Kevin again."

Richard glanced up warily. Kevin's name meant only one thing: Diana must have something new up her sleeve. Her demands had escalated over the months since her father had died: an increase in her support, a share of his royalties, his mother's jewelry, a renewal of visitation rights. Karen had typed the first replies to Diana and her attorney, and her dislike of them both had grown with every measured response Richard Ashmore made to his wife's demands. No, Diana wasn't getting any more money; he refused to contribute further to her problems. No, she wasn't entitled to any of the royalties from his architecture book; he had invested that money for Julie's education. When he received the next demand, Richard had thrown the letter down on his desk and asked Tom Maitland to step in.

"All right." Richard handed her the finished letters. "Send these out."

She left the office and shut his door, honoring his unspoken need for privacy. *Damn that woman*, she thought, and slapped the letters down on her desk with unnecessary force. If Diana Ashmore needed money so badly, why didn't she get a real job?

Except, of course, that Diana didn't want money. What she wanted, as far as anyone could tell, was to make Richard Ashmore's life hell.

Scott McIntire's admin nodded at the hapless letters. "What's that all about?"

"Diana," said Karen.

"Maybe she's been arrested again." The office consensus, kept carefully from the senior partner's ears, was that Diana was getting away with murder.

"No such luck," said Karen, and then heard a sharp noise and glanced up through the glass walls.

She saw it all in an instant, but she never understood what she saw.

Her boss was staring at the opposite wall, phone still clutched in his hand, coffee spilling over the proposal draft and dripping off the side of the desk onto the muted gray carpet.

Richard Ashmore looked like a man whose world had just turned upside down.

Not Julie, she thought, and she remembered the day his parents had died. She started to rise to her feet, but no, he was moving, he was putting the receiver down, he was putting his hands to his face. She saw shock, disbelief, yes – but did she see, for a second, hope, anticipation, a brief flare of happiness?

She had never seen Richard Ashmore happy.

The next moment, his door opened, and he stopped at her desk, his blazer slung over his shoulder. "I'm gone for the day," he said abruptly. "We'll do the proposal in the morning."

And he vanished out the door.

Karen sank back into her chair and stared after him. Now what on earth had Tom Maitland said to bring that look of disbelief to his face? And what had happened to make Richard Ashmore abandon his work on a busy Friday afternoon?

Not Diana, she thought. *He doesn't care enough about Diana for this.*

Laura walked off the elevator on the concierge floor and saw him, waiting, staring out the windows at the Atlantic.

He heard her, and he turned. Across thirty feet, his eyes stopped her, and she stood there, breathless, her blood pounding in her ears, as he came to her.

Across space, across the years, they stared at each other, survivors of that late bloody afternoon.

Then he took that last step, and she felt his arms close around her, and he was gathering her in, and for all his calm, his heart was hammering against hers.

"Oh, Laura," said Richard Ashmore, her brother-in-law, her childhood hero, her first love. "My dearest girl, welcome home."

Act Two:
Not All That is Past is Over

There's blood between us, love, my love…
And blood's a bar I cannot pass.

("The Convent Threshold," Christina Rossetti)

6

Blue Eyes, Dark Heart

"LAURA." HIS VOICE SURROUNDED HER; his hand held her against his shoulder in sanctuary. She had known this, she had dreamed this through the years, to stand in the circle of Richard Ashmore's arms, safe, home. They stood there together, without words, with only warmth and comfort.

If you need me, I will come to you.

In time, he gently held her ever so slightly away.

"I can't believe it," he said, and she saw in his eyes an echo of her shock. "It really *is* you—"

She opened her mouth and could not speak.

"After all this time – my God, Laurie, you've served up a hell of a surprise—" and then he smiled. Behind him the concierge, openly eavesdropping, watched warily this disturbance of a prize guest's privacy. How could the woman know that, for a few seconds, the warmth of his smile wrapped around her, cherishing her as if she had been loved and missed? "And that was you this morning—"

She felt herself start to shatter.

"No, no, no, don't cry," he said, and brushed a tear from her cheek. "It's all right – everything's all right now—"

"I didn't want you to find me," she managed. "I'm not ready yet."

Do you know? Do you sense it was me?

He shook his head, and his eyes upon her were tender and indulgent. "Then you went about it the wrong way, Miss Jaguar. I'm at least the third person to find out." He put his arm around her shoulders and hugged her against his side. "Let me have your key."

Wordlessly, she held it out to him. The concierge was still watching them, looking concerned and uncertain, but she was only human, and she melted when Richard turned his smile on her. "Could we trouble you to ring for tea?" he asked, with that exquisite courtesy he'd abandoned only once. "In Mrs.–" he looked around at Laura for confirmation – "St. Bride's room?"

Of course, she agreed instantly to do his bidding. "I'll have it sent right up, Mrs. St. Bride."

The silly girl was blushing as she picked up the phone. Females had never been proof against that smile and that rich voice. Only Diana, for her own unfathomable reasons, had finally resisted him. And here she herself was melting, letting him take over and orchestrate a scene that should have been hers to direct. How could she be losing control, after all the months of rehearsing this moment? Laura started to dig in her heels, even as he led her down the hall to her suite. "Maybe I don't want to go to my room."

Oh, that was stupid, childish. That wasn't what she meant. *Maybe I don't want you to hold me, maybe I don't want you to look in my eyes as if you missed me, maybe I don't want to know that my blood still can leap at your merest touch....*

Maybe I don't want to face that I still need you and you've come to me.

He inserted the key card in the slot and looked at her sidelong, and now the gentleness had given way to a quelling look. "And maybe you want to continue this out there where anyone can come trooping by. I thought you'd appreciate the privacy. We can talk in the lobby if you'd prefer."

Those words, from an adult to a fractious child, shriveled all resistance. He was acting for her protection, after all. Laura Abbott was probably going to make a fool of herself; Cat Courtney did not need to account for it. She preceded him into the suite, aware of his every movement as he searched out the lights, and stood still for his inspection.

He was here, really here, standing before her, his eyes traveling over her, gauging the changes of the years. She had grown accustomed to the looks men gave Cat Courtney, but this man had never known her as a woman. Her crush on him had been a family joke. Diana and Francie had never considered her a serious rival, and he, unaware that such a rivalry existed, had treated her only as a younger sister to be placated with some occasional attention.

He stirred at last. "What happened to your hair?"

"My lioness mane?" She smiled. "That's a wig."

"Say it ain't so!" He was reaching out, touching one of her curls. "Legions of males will be cast into deep mourning, Laurie. A great fantasy shattered."

Cat Courtney had so often been her shield, and she stepped behind Cat now, to hide her own terrifying vulnerability. She moved away, past him, towards the French doors to the balcony, so she could breathe. "Legions of males don't have to spend hours drying their hair, either."

He laughed. "Now that *really* shatters the fantasy, Cat Courtney. You're supposed to exist on a plane above such mundane matters."

Cat Courtney, all that she had become, shimmered between them. Laura Abbott could think of nothing to say.

"Laura?" He had come up behind her, and his hands had closed around her shoulders. "I'm sorry. Don't mind my teasing – I'm thrown for a loop. I didn't expect this when Tom called. I don't know," he drew in a deep breath and allowed a small ruefulness into his voice, "the right protocol for this."

"I – I don't know, either." She felt the palms of his hands through her shirt. "I guess that's why I've botched this so badly."

He was speaking again, quiet, gentle. "You haven't botched anything. You're here. That's all that matters." He drew her back against him, and she was weak, so she let herself rest against him. "Couldn't you have come to me, Laurie? Or let me come to you?"

"I tried. I did, really, but you can't go up to the door after fourteen years and say, 'Hi, here I am, and, by the way, I'd like some tea.'"

"Of course you can," he said, "you could have always come to me, I would never shut you out, but you didn't believe that, did you? Although it would have been a shock, if I'd answered the door and found you standing there. When Tom said that Kevin had caught an intruder at Dominic's and it was Cat Courtney, I spilled coffee all over a proposal I was reading. My admin will be furious."

"Tom?" Who in the world was Tom? "I thought – Kevin Stone."

"News travels fast." He went to the door to answer the knock. "You ran into Kevin, didn't you?"

"Yes." His voice had been neutral, unthreatened by Kevin's interest in Diana. Either he felt confident of Diana, or he didn't care.... She ventured, "Richard, who *is* that man? Is he really Di's lawyer? He had a key to the house."

"He's helping her sell it." He slid a bill into the waiter's hand and closed the door, and Laura had the sudden unsettling thought that he seized the opportunity to keep his face averted from her.

She said experimentally, "He said he was going to marry Di."

Silence. She waited.

Then Richard laughed. She watched the relaxed body language of his shoulders as he said pleasantly, "I don't doubt that for a minute. That he said it, that is, not that it's going to happen. Kevin is a strange bird, Laura. I hope he didn't upset you."

So Kevin Stone was crazy. Richard apparently took this threat to his marriage in stride – if he cared at all, after the sharpness of his words that afternoon. She watched him as he unwrapped the tray of scones the concierge had thoughtfully added. "He said he wouldn't tell Lucy and Di. Do you—" she hesitated— "do you think he meant it?"

He reached for the pitcher of tea and poured her a glass. "Don't worry about that. Tom talked to him. We agreed that I'd tell Lucy after I had the chance to talk to you." He glanced at her. "To be honest, Laurie, it's not a good idea to surprise her right now."

But still no mention of Diana. "Did you tell Di you were coming here to see me?"

"No. I haven't talked to her since Tom called."

Diana stood there then, listening, her lashes hooding her eyes where a light shone that had never seemed quite right. Strange, lost Diana…. What would she think of this scene, her husband approaching Francie's twin in a hotel suite?

Richard touched his glass to hers. "To homecomings."

She inclined her head and sipped the tea, enjoying the coolness in her throat. He moved past her to the French doors, and she had the chance now to look at him all she wanted, to measure the changes in him. The photograph on the book jacket, in black and white, hadn't captured the mark that time had left on him. He had been a handsome young man, sure that life would always smile on him, carelessly confident that he could handle anything fate chose to throw at him. His mother's camera had only hinted that life and time had matured that surface beauty, silvered his temples, chiseled those cheekbones. He wore glasses now, and surely she wasn't the first woman to notice that they gave character and gravitas to that face and defined that strong jawline even more sharply.

No longer merely handsome, he was devastating now, all Black Irish and Virginia class.

His face so wondrous fair…. The purest eyes and the strongest hands….

And she was not immune. Her eyes welcomed the maturity of his older face, the cool assessment of his slate blue eyes, the repose of his once-laughing mouth. Her pulse remembered how he had held her against that body that had finally adapted to its great height.

Deep inside, she felt a small blade of desire, trying to break through the snows of grief into life.

Black is the color of my true love's hair....

Oh, but for all the changes, for the shadows that shielded his heart from his eyes, he was still Richard. Still her knight protector, her best friend, the all-knowing hero she had worshiped with all her heart. She had stopped confiding in him only when Francie confessed one winter night that she and Richard had become lovers....

I love the ground on where he stands....

He was still Richard, and she had loved him.

He put down his glass, took hers from her, and for a moment, they were back on that long-ago Christmas. *Laurie, I need a really big favor*.... But his eyes were gentle on her, and she knew what was coming.

"Laurie, your husband—"

"I got your fax," she interrupted in a rush. "They – they forwarded it to me that night. I saw it – I don't know, maybe an hour or so after you sent it, I couldn't sleep and there it was. Richard, I'm so sorry I didn't get in touch, I just had so much to do—"

"No!" He forestalled her with a quick lift of his hand. "I said not to feel that you had to respond, and I meant it. It's just – when I saw his picture, I recognized him right away. Julie and I saw him backstage in London last year, and I heard the name. All I could think was that you had to be going through hell. I didn't know what support you had, if you had any at all. I wanted you to know that you didn't have to be alone." He gathered her hands between his. "Have they found—"

"No." She shook her head. "We submitted the – DNA, but nothing so far. They – they did find his wedding ring a couple of months ago, so we got that back."

"The things that survive us." He fell silent for a moment. "Does it bother you, talking about it?"

She shook her head again. "No. You get used to a lot in nine months."

"That's true," Richard said, and she saw a brief shadow in his eyes. She opened her mouth to ask him about his parents, but he anticipated her with a quick movement that told her to wait. "Do you know how he got caught there? Don't answer if you don't want to, but Lucy's going to ask, you know that."

"She knows?" But of course Lucy knew. Lucy would make it her mission to know everything.

"I told her a few months later when she recovered – what I knew about him, what your name was – and we agreed we'd wait for you to contact us, although," he showed a glint of humor, "you know Lucy, she wanted to get on the next plane. I have to tell you that your timing is perfect, because she has run out of patience. She set up news alerts on you – she found out that you left your show, and she was hot to go track you down. So brace yourself. I understand if you don't want to talk to me about it, but you're going to have to tell your sister."

His sensitivity touched her. A memory touched her briefly, Richard finding her weeping near the bodies of her kittens, comforting her with a boy's awkwardness. *Tell me, Laurie, I'll do whatever I can.* In all these months, she had talked only to the counselor in London, and he had not been interested in what had happened so much as how she was dealing with it.

She met his eyes. "He had a meeting in the restaurant at the top of the north tower."

"Oh, dear God." He closed his eyes for a few seconds as he absorbed the significance of that. She heard him keep his voice deliberate and flat. "Then you know he never had a chance."

"No." She looked down at their joined hands and thought how beautifully shaped his fingers were. "There was no way out – it was hit first – they say all the stairs were blocked. His group had left, but Mark – his brother – called him, and he missed the last elevator."

"So you must have known pretty quickly." Quiet, matter-of-fact.

"Yes. He'd been with us the night before – I was rehearsing in London, and he flew over for the weekend because—"

He finished for her, "Because your birthday is September 9."

She nodded, surprised that he remembered. "We knew he was supposed to be there, in the restaurant. And then," she swallowed hard, "I saw CNN, right before the second plane, and I knew – I was afraid he was in danger."

His stillness told her, as clearly as if he had said the words aloud, that he would wait for her to tell her story. The tension in her shoulders seeped away. Even now, after all these years, this was vintage Richard, kind, considerate, taking the time to listen to a small girl's problems.

Except that now it was one of the biggest cataclysms of a woman's life, and in all these months no one had asked her to tell her story. No one had asked, *What did you know? What did you see?* So many people had told her how *they* had felt watching the tragedy unfold, but no one had asked – had wanted to know – how she had felt watching the man she had married burn to death.

Not even Mark, who avoided talking about that morning. She suspected he was still carrying guilt for the call that had kept Cam off that elevator.

"He left a call for me." She hadn't planned to tell him that.

"You spoke to him?"

"No. I found it on the voice mail that night." She saw the compassion in his eyes, and now she felt like a fraud. She bowed her head so that she didn't have to look at him. "We were talking about divorce," she said, and didn't know why she had admitted it. "We'd been separated for over a year. It – it was a lot worse for other people."

Other survivors had actually loved those they had lost. She had steadily deflected all suggestions that she join a survivors' support group for that very reason.

Richard spoke over her head. "I'm sorry to hear that," he said. "It must have made things even more difficult for you. Did you and he – do you have children?"

Her heartbeat picked up. She looked up; she couldn't keep staring at the floor. "A daughter."

"How is she doing?"

Of course, he'd consider the impact on a child; Julie was not much older than Meg. "Okay. Better than last fall," Laura said. "She had some rough moments. It's gotten easier, but she misses him terribly. We've included her in all the decisions, like the memorial service and the marker, and that helped her, I think."

Richard glanced around the suite. "Where is she?"

"She's spending the summer with Cam's brother and sister. I thought—" she hesitated and then said truthfully, "I thought it would be better if she stayed in Texas. I knew this would be stressful – I didn't want her to have to deal with it on top of everything else."

And you can't meet her, not ever.

He lowered their joined hands, and it startled her. It had seemed natural for her hands to nestle in his, and Laura missed the touch with a physical intensity as he walked over to pour himself a fresh iced tea. She couldn't help her eyes following him. "Last year," he said, and his tone had changed, stepping back from the morass of grief to a place of objectivity, "was a terrible year for this family. Do you know about Dominic?"

Thank God, this she felt honest about. "Oh, yes," she said, and matched his tone. "Cam showed me the news clippings that last weekend. He had just found out himself."

"Is that—" he gestured loosely— "is that why you've come home?"

She nodded. She could not lie to him. Too often, he had rescued her from Dominic with a well-timed *Come riding, Laurie* or *Mom wants you to come over and help her.* Once, he had stopped Dominic in the middle of a punishing tirade. *You hit her again, I hit you. Then I call the police.* "It helped. It wasn't all of it, but – it helped. It would be much harder to have to see him."

He came back towards her and stood against the wall by the French doors. "Laura," he said, "Dominic should never have mattered. This was your home, and God knows you showed him up. If it's any consolation, he never got over the shock of Cat Courtney. Lucy is going to wring your neck and then forget you were ever gone. She's missed you terribly. Diana—" He stopped then, seemed to keep his own counsel. "I don't know how Diana will react."

She felt herself relaxing. "I thought she liked me when we were growing up."

"She liked you just fine." *You weren't Francie* hung between them. His manner, abruptly cool and remote, shut down that line of discussion. A moment of silence, and then, unexpectedly, "Did you send a note after my parents died?"

"Yes." The shadow had returned to his eyes, and she saw that this man still grieved. The Ashmores had died in an auto accident four months after the Christmas miscarriage. It had indeed been a terrible year. "Cam told me. I made him promise to tell me if anything happened to any of you. He probably had news alerts too – he didn't tell me much, he tried to keep all that away from me. Richard—"

"I know," and she heard the quiet sorrow in his voice. "It's been over a year, and I still find myself thinking I'll see Mom out in her garden or pick up the phone and hear Dad's voice." He gave her a small smile. "I didn't put two and two together until later. It meant something that you wrote, Laura, indeed it did. Thank you."

She had thought about going to the funeral incognito, but she had still felt shaky from the miscarriage and hadn't been sure if she could pull it off. "I couldn't *not* do something. Your mother was the closest I ever came to a mother, and – I always envied you your father."

He nodded. The silence lay there between them. The room, she thought, had shrunk on them. She felt wound up, almost ready to fly apart, with the emotional probing of wounds not yet healed. Did he feel the tension? She thought that he did, as he wandered around the room, looking at the framed prints on the wall, rifling through the stacks of books on the desk. She hoped she didn't have anything too lightweight in the stack; he used to read books like *Atlas Shrugged* while she read *The Thorn Birds*.

"Richard?" The question in her voice brought his quick glance at her. "You said that you told Lucy about – about Cam after she recovered. What was she recovering from?"

Her question visibly caught him off guard. For the first time, he seemed at a loss for words.

Laura pressed on, "In your fax, you said she was ill."

He put the fourth Harry Potter down and picked up *The Lovely Bones*, buying time, she thought. "Let her tell you about it. Do you know what this book is about? The subject matter's pretty gruesome. It might upset you to read it."

Of all the paternalistic deflections. "I've already read it, and I'm not that fragile. Is Lucy all right?"

"She's fine now." He put the book down and walked towards the open door into the bedroom of the suite, and she had a sudden, un-asked-for appreciation of the lines of his long body. "I'd wait for her to tell you – is that your daughter?"

Her heart leaped. "What?" She followed his line of sight, and she saw it then, on the nightstand, Meg's picture, the picture she had taken out that morning, to remind herself what was truly important. She held her breath as he picked it up and looked hard at it, and surely he heard the pounding of her heart, the knell of guilt and fear.

Why, *why* hadn't she put that picture away?

But she had never expected that Richard Ashmore would stand in her hotel suite to see it.

"What a beautiful girl." He sounded merely like an interested uncle. "She has your eyes."

"Margaret." She forced herself to speak. "We call her Meg."

"Margaret." His voice dropped, and her heart stopped. *Oh, no, no, no....* But his tone was pure pleasure. "For Mom. She'd have loved that, Laura. Thank you."

He turned around, and through the shadows of the room, she saw no latent recognition in his eyes. Blood had not called to blood.... He came back out into the living area with the picture still in his hand, looking at it – *why?* He reached into his breast pocket and pulled out a cigarette case, and Laura, who despised smoking, forgot her alarm long enough to shake her head at him. He promptly put it back. "Sorry, I forgot what a stickler you are."

"My voice is my trade," she reminded him. "I take care of it."

He was instantly penitent. "And you should. It's an awful habit. I'll give them up again, if—" and he smiled at her— "if you'll make me some of your wonderful cookies. I've missed them. No one else made them like you."

Now how could she resist such a charming request? "I'll have Meg send up a batch. I passed along your mother's recipe."

Richard's manner changed then, ever so slightly; she went back on guard and cursed herself for mentioning Meg again. His eyes traveled over her curiously. "Just the one?"

"Just the one." She made her voice light, as though four miscarriages and a marriage of desolate infertility had never happened. "And if you knew Meg at her best – or worst, however you want to look at it, you'd think one was enough."

Damn those eyes of his. He saw right through her. "Going to make it without her?"

"No."

"Bring her here. Julie would love to meet her cousin. I know you want to protect her, but this – your coming back – isn't going to be as hard as you think."

She had foreseen this, and she dealt with it calmly. "No, she's enjoying being back with her friends in Plano. She's discovered boys. I couldn't resist the temptation to run away from that."

He laughed. "How well I know! I've felt like running away a time or two myself, and Julie doesn't have much of a social life." He came back around to her. "Strange, you having a daughter old enough to be thinking about boys. How long were you married?"

"Twelve years."

What was he thinking behind those unfathomable eyes? "You must have met him soon after you left, then."

Perilous territory, this. That active mind of his might start fitting the timeline together. As much as Cam, Richard had always excelled at puzzles and patterns. "A year or so."

Did she imagine the fine sharp edge to his gaze?

"You were still very young then. You must have married him very quickly." She stared at him in horror, unsure how to deflect this dangerous train of thought. "No wonder he wanted to protect you."

As he had, many times in the past. She had the unnerving feeling that he had forgotten Cam, that his mind had flown straight back to his wife. Had he failed to protect Diana? Against himself? Had they inflicted wounds on each other too deep for healing?

Of course they had. Had the fissures of that marriage ever sealed?

He had accused Diana of spying on him – not the reaction of a loving husband to a wife, nor even of a man to a woman he lived with, no matter what the state of their marriage.

And he had accused Diana of scaring her own daughter.

She said softly, "I'm sorry about this morning, Richard. I never meant to alarm Julie. Did the fall hurt her?"

He looked at her sharply at the change in subject. "No, it just knocked the breath out of her. You weren't at fault, Julie was, and she knows it. That mare is skittish, and Julie spooked her." None of the clipped anger of his call to Diana. "Of course, it never occurred to me it was you, not until Tom's call."

So Julie was safe. A small burden wafted off her shoulders. "You keep mentioning Tom. Should I know him?"

A startled pause, and then he smiled. "That answers one question. Your husband really didn't tell you much, did he? Tom Maitland. You'll like him. He's my lawyer, my tennis partner, my closest friend, and, not least of all, Lucy's husband."

"Lucy's married." That small puzzle piece set her at ease. No wonder Kevin Stone had looked so disconcerted. "Are they happy?"

If he thought that a strange question, he still answered gently. "Yes. Mom and Dad thought him perfect for her. It's one of the best marriages I've seen. She's still as bossy as ever, but Tom just ignores her." His grin invited her to join in. They both knew that the only defense against Lucy was passive resistance. "She's mellowed a lot. He's very good for her."

"So she doesn't try to run everyone's life anymore?"

"Of course she does! I'm a continual source of frustration to her." Richard took the glass from her hand. "I know today's been tough on you," he said, "but we need to talk. Let me take you to dinner."

And not a word about his wife. She tried again, half-heartedly, "What about Di?"

He smiled, and now he looked more like the old Richard. "I'm not accountable to Diana. And I want to take Cat Courtney, or Laura St. Bride, or Laura Abbott, or even all three of you to dinner."

Laura flew around the bedroom, getting ready, while he waited in the living area. Nothing too fancy, he had said, an intimate piano bar with seafood, and she shucked her jeans and shirt and dove into her suitcase. Some of her prettiest clothes were stored back in London, and she wasted a small regret before she reminded herself sternly that this was not a date.

But the admiration in his eyes fed her imagination.

"Look at you," he said, and touched the hair that she had managed to tame. "Is this the girl whose ponytail was always falling down and who was always losing a lens out of her glasses?"

"No glasses," Laura said lightly. "Contacts. I've grown up."

Richard summoned the elevator and turned back to her. "Oh, that you have," he said, "you certainly have."

But if his eyes were admiring, his words became casual, matter-of-fact, a brother talking to a much younger sister. The trip to the restaurant blurred before the panoply of family events that he described: Lucy's wedding, Julie's first day at school, the opening of his practice, the rebuilding of the Folly…. So much she had missed. She soaked it up like a parched flower. Julie, he admitted readily, was the center of his life, and he handed over his wallet to show her snapshots of her niece. "Trusting soul," she teased, and was stunned to see that Julie, sans obscuring sunglasses, was Diana reborn, lovely and luminous at sixteen.

No pictures of Diana. He never mentioned her, as though she had no place in his life. Anyone listening to him could be forgiven for assuming that she was dead, that he was well past the shock of loss, content to be a widower.

And no mention of Francie, as though no other sister-in-law had ever existed.

By his silence, Francie and Diana joined them; Laura could not shake the feeling that they watched her and, worse, read her fantasies. She basked in his attention, letting him order her wine, indulging her daydream that they were just another couple on a first date, enjoying the stirring of attraction, feeling out each other's terrain – and Diana sat there between them, watching with cool contempt. She answered his questions about her career – her stage work, her songwriting – and Francie, frozen at eighteen, hung all over him and tried to distract his attention.

Even Cam intruded.

"Was it your career?" Richard asked.

Laura had heard that assumption plenty from her in-laws. Success gone to her head, they'd said. Ingratitude. Ambition. Another man (and Cam had verbally shredded Emma when she suggested that). "Part of it, I guess. I wasn't the wife he wanted anymore. He – oh, I don't know, he wanted to keep me all to himself, and I grew up, I outgrew that. I worked, I worked a lot, and I've been successful in Europe – more so than here – and I started spending more time over there." She hesitated. "Neither of us was happy. We'd had problems for a long time."

Then that final Christmas, when they lost their last best hope….

"Some marriages don't work," he observed flatly. "For what it's worth, when we saw him in London, he seemed very married – he made it clear that he didn't want anyone trying to hurt you."

Laura came to attention. "You *talked* to him?"

"Well," and she heard a wry note in his voice, "it wasn't exactly a conversation. But he knew who Julie and I were, no doubt about that."

In all these months, she hadn't thought to wonder about that cryptic statement in Julie's note: *My father doesn't know I'm doing this. If you are the man I saw, I think that is important to you.* Richard and Cam had come face to face. She tucked away the thought to mull over later.

"It worked as a business. Cat Courtney makes plenty of money for St. Bride." She wondered at his look, that a dysfunctional but civilized marriage seemed so foreign to him. Had he divorced Diana, or she him? What had happened after Francie? "But – over time – *we* stopped working. I knew for a long time that we weren't going to make it. I knew that I could live to be ninety and be happy if I never won a Grammy, or I never had a – another child, but I just couldn't see being ninety and still being married to Cam."

Serves you right, said Francie. *I told you not to marry him.*

She thought she heard, "Oh, dear God," but his face told her nothing.

"It was actually a relief once we admitted everything was over." She drew a breath. "I think we dealt better with each other those last few months – especially after Meg and I moved to London – than we had in years."

Richard said slowly, "I hoped you were happy, wherever you were."

She smiled. "Oh, but I was. I had Meg." She saw an opening. "We weren't fated to go the distance, I guess, not like you and Di. What has it been now, twenty years?"

He took his time answering, his body extraordinarily still, his eyes not betraying his thoughts by a flicker. "Something like that."

Actually, it had been eighteen years and five days; she knew his anniversary as well as her own. Laura felt a shadow of unease. Reticence she could understand, but he avoided mentioning Diana, she thought, the way someone might avoid touching a still painful wound.

Maybe he cared about Kevin Stone more than he wanted to admit.

Before she could regroup, he turned the tables on her. "How about you? Are you seeing anyone?"

"What?" So much for basking in her fantasy date. "No. No, I'm not. I – I'm not ready." That seemed inadequate. "I've been busy. Working in a production six nights a week doesn't leave a lot of spare time."

He said nothing. She hurried on against his gaze, "It was – good to be busy. It helped."

Richard sat back, and his voice turned musing. "I went for a run that night. I had to take a break from watching – the same pictures, again and again—" She caught her breath, and he looked at her swiftly. "*You* know. That endless replay, and each time it seemed more and more like one of those high-tech action movies, disaster averted at the last second, but this time," he shook his head, "no one to the rescue. I stood out there at Ashmore Park, everything quiet and at peace, a world removed from the hell in New York, and I looked up, and it hit me, it had even come to us here. Usually, I see the flight patterns from the west, the lights of the planes on approach into Norfolk, but—" he paused— "not that night. The sky was empty. There were only stars. And I thought, it's happened, someone has finally stopped the engine of the world."

He leaned forward and took her hand, and she felt the warmth of his long fingers on hers. "Everything's changed," he said. "You know better than most. We won't go back to September 10. Just – don't let those bastards stop anything for you, Laurie. Don't *not* live because the stairs were blocked."

He released her hand, and sat back again.

She kept her eyes on him, and the silence lay between them.

He must have felt the heavy intensity, known that he had to break through it. He picked up his wine and smiled at her, and his voice lightened deliberately. He was once again the big brother. "You have to get back in the game sometime. You are still very young—"

Just how young did he think she was? She matched his tone. "I'm thirty-one, O ancient one."

Her retort – or her age – seemed to take him aback, but he recovered quickly. "Too young for the cloisters. Time to spread your wings, little butterfly. Besides," and he flashed her a grin that said, as much as anything, that he had shifted into teasing mode, "you need to get your defenses up in quick order before Lucy gets hold of you. Be prepared to be fixed up."

Laura spared a second of sheer horror at that thought. "I don't want to be fixed up. That's not even on my radar."

"Understandable." He waved the waiter off. "But that will change. This will – recede in time."

He sounded just like Roger, but, she saw, he had left her an opening. "Right now – I don't want to date just to date. It's not worth it. If it's not going to be," she gestured, "the world lost for love – what's the point?" She hesitated, unsure of her way. "You had that, Richard, you of all people should understand how I wouldn't want anything less."

She'd said the wrong thing, she knew that instantly. He fingered the goblet of candle-lit wine, but somewhere behind his eyes, he shut down and went away from her. Tension flooded her limbs; she found herself clutching the linen of her skirt. She had gone too far, probed into a wound too fresh or too deep for healing. She scrambled for a light-hearted remark to gloss over the awkwardness, lift that darkness from his eyes, anything, and then lost her train of thought when he turned back to her and put his wine down. "Let's see if you still know how to dance."

She rose uncertainly, her blood still trembling from this brush with his unknown pain. The dance floor shimmered before her, a small square of space before a great open hearth, flanked by large floor candles and an anonymous piano swathed in shadows. He drew her into the shelter of one arm.

His free hand raised hers to heart level, and she found only one thought in the warmth of his fingers closing around hers. *I have wanted you across these years, I have waited to step into your arms. Now here you're holding me, and what do I feel? What do I say?*

He had taught her to dance after she had stepped on his toes at his wedding. "You need to know this," he had lectured, "you and Francie will have all the boys after you in a few years." So he had mercilessly drilled her that summer until she could acquit herself honorably, and Diana, still a laughing new wife, played the piano patiently for those lessons. *And I didn't mind at all,* said Diana. *You were moonstruck over him, but so what? He was mine then, all mine.*

"Relax." Richard's voice ruffled her hair.

She stared hard at his shoulder. "I'm afraid I'll step on your feet."

And I don't want you to feel how hard my heart is beating.

Oh, if only her fantasy had been real, if they'd been just another man and another woman, with no history and no blood between them, no wife and no mistress and no lost afternoon forever staining them. She might then have relaxed against him and enjoyed the heat that began to seep down her back; he might not have held her so carefully, befitting a man with his wife's sister. She might have whispered her thoughts for the night ahead, and he might have suggested that dinner was an option best left untaken. And when the inevitable happened and she dug her heel into his shoe, they might have tossed it off with a silly lover's joke.

"Sorry," she mumbled.

Richard's voice sounded measured in the extreme. "Stop acting as if you're dancing with a serial killer."

She laughed at that, and he took advantage of her momentary looseness to draw her closer against him. "Much better," he said. "Didn't you ever dance with your husband?"

She shook her head. "Cam was Baptist. He didn't drink, dance, or play cards."

He just slept with other women when he got mad at me.

But she didn't want to think about Cam, not now, not ever while she was dancing with Richard. *This* was how it felt to dance with him now, not a child seeking comfort, but a grown woman held against him, with his arm around her waist and his hand sheltering hers. *This* was how his pulse accelerated, just for a moment, when she turned her head. *This* was the way his hand slipped gently up her back, and his fingers touched her nape…. She thought for a moment that his lips brushed her hair.

She closed her eyes and leaned against his shoulder, and she willed the music on and on, until the mellow voice of the piano intertwined with the steady tide of Richard's breathing. She moved her cheek against the fine weave of his lapel, closer to the heat of his skin, and she heard the catch of his breath, the tightening of his hand on her back, the echoing song of his heartbeat against hers.

She drifted into a dream: the two of them alone, in a darkened room, moving inexorably towards their doom, like dancers, like lovers, and all the time his hand in her hair, his fingers trembling with passion against her skin.

She moved her hand against his and realized, with a shock, that his fingers did tremble.

He held her away abruptly, and she swayed against his arm. The piano still showered them in lush romance, but for them, one look at his face told her, the dance was over.

"Laura." His voice was neutral. "It's warm in here. Let's get some air before dinner."

The room wasn't warm. The heat still clung to their bodies, though, and a flush colored his face. Thank God for the candles, and their gentle, forgiving light; she thought that she might brazen this out in the dusk, just as long as he couldn't look at her face and know what she had been thinking.

Let me die, right now, before he says anything.

His hand behind her waist, guiding her towards the doors of the veranda, was light and impersonal, and he said nothing as he escorted her out into the night. The evening enveloped them and masked her embarrassment. She felt all the disturbed balance of someone ripped rudely awake from a wonderful dream.

If Richard felt awkward, if he tamped down the just-lit flames of arousal, he disguised it well. He pulled out a chair for her at the table closest to the railing, in the deepest shadows, and she sank into it warily, eying the chair across from her. But he did not join her. He strolled to the railing and, without speaking, pulled his cigarette case from his breast pocket. She watched the brief light and followed the burning point through the air as he smoked.

No words, still. The warm silence wrapped around her, and she leaned back against the chair, aware of exhaustion creeping through her blood as desire fled. It had been a long day, a long journey to this silence between two people who had just stepped back from a precipice. Or rather, she thought in shame, remembering how she had cuddled into his body like a small kitten, a man who had just yanked a woman back from the edge before she pulled him over with her.

She couldn't believe she had behaved so thoughtlessly. She was not an innocent; she had lived twelve years in a marriage that, for all its problems, had worked in the bedroom. But, oh, how wonderful it had felt to be held again by a man who cared about *her*, not Cat Courtney, not Laura St. Bride. Any man might have done.

Not that any man had ever cared about Laura Abbott. Not Cam, who had wanted to stamp Laura Abbott out. Not Mark, who didn't even want to acknowledge that Laura Abbott existed. Not Richard, who hadn't seen Laura Abbott when she was right under his nose.

And might any woman have done for him? Had he closed his eyes and imagined Francie in his arms again, warm and giving? Had he even known who had danced against his heart?

He had not known once.

She could not bear the silence any longer. "Richard," she said into the night, "sit down."

He glanced around at her, amusement cracking the darkness of his expression, and she realized how she must sound, Cat Courtney giving an order to an underling. She swallowed her nerves. "Please," she added gently, waving her hand at the seat across from her. *Now what can I say?*

He came back towards her but ignored the seat, choosing instead to lean against the railing and enjoy his cigarette. He made a point of keeping the smoke away from her, and she didn't doubt for a moment that he used that cigarette as an excuse not to sit close to her. It also gave him a splendid reason to stand over her and use his height to put her at a disadvantage.

She wasn't embarrassed now; she was irritated. She was coming close to grabbing his cigarette and demanding his attention when he broke the silence, and then she wished that he had never spoken.

"How long are you in town?"

Whatever she had expected – an apology, a lecture, a proposition – this wasn't it. She drew a breath for courage. "A couple of months."

Richard's hand paused in mid-air. "Months?" he echoed, and she thought that he looked dismayed. *"Where?"*

"I've leased a house." She didn't look at him, but concentrated hard on adjusting her ring. "Outside Williamsburg."

He said nothing.

She said in a rush, "Edwards Lake."

He stubbed out his cigarette carefully. "You remember that it borders Ashmore Park."

Apprehension curled up in her stomach. "Of course I do." *What a stupid idea. He doesn't want me there.* "I have a lot of work to do – I'm under contract for a new album, and I have to get ready for a tour this fall, and I thought it would be quiet out in the country—"

He probably thinks I want to be near him —

"Privacy," she said firmly. "I need the privacy."

"What Lucy allows you," said Richard. His eyes, when they met hers, were expressionless, and that worried her, that he deliberately shielded his thoughts from her. "I hadn't heard that the Careys had a new tenant. Julie will be excited to hear about this." He smiled, and the sick fear inside her started to subside. "Your niece is one of your biggest fans."

"I can't wait to meet her." She watched him. Julie, at least, seemed a safe topic. "Do you mind, Richard? Is it all right if I meet her?"

"Of course it is. She's very proud of you."

She groped for something to say. Julie, how much she wanted to get to know her niece – and then he spoke again, and she discovered that Julie was not safe after all.

"Before you meet Julie, we need to get a few things straight." His voice had lost his neutrality; she sensed a wall thrown up against her. "She doesn't know much about what happened when you left – no one does. She doesn't know why you ran off or why you never got in touch with anyone. No one's ever had an answer to give her. I don't know if she'll ask you. She's a polite girl, and I want to think she won't come right out and ask, but she'll want to know."

She reached for breath, and found herself too tense to breathe.

"Julie lives with me." Richard straightened from the railing. "I've had custody of her since she was five. For reasons I won't go into right now, she doesn't see her mother very often—" He must have seen the shock on her face; his voice gentled, just for a moment. "Sorry. I've no way of knowing what you know and what you don't. Lucy will tell you soon enough anyway. Diana and I haven't lived together in over ten years."

Francie? Or the unknown devastation that had opened the door to Francie?

"I'm sorry," she said into the appalled silence.

Liar. You're not sorry. You're not sorry at all.

"Don't be," Richard said briefly. "We aren't. You've been through it. You know what it's like when a marriage is dead."

So the damage had run so deeply that there had been no salvaging the wreck. "Why?" she asked helplessly, a stupid question, but all that she could muster.

But her grief was lost on him. He leaned forward, across the table towards her, his hands on the glass top on either side of hers. "You know why." His voice was calm, flat. "You know better than the rest of them. What I don't know is what it had to do with you."

He was closer than she'd thought. She had to school her eyes to keep from sidling away from the chill of his look; she had to still herself to keep from jumping when he brought one hand up and lifted her chin with one long finger.

"Why did you run away?"

She couldn't think. She stared at him, and panic started down in her stomach and fought its way up. He watched her now with eyes that betrayed no trace of affection, and she heard the questions shouting in his mind: *Why did she die? Why did Diana live?*

"You were very clever," he said, and when she tried to avert her head, his fingers kept her chin rigid. She closed her eyes against the hardness of his face. "You must have planned it for some time. Telling your father that you wanted to visit us, and Francie planning to see her friends in Baltimore. It took him a week to realize that you were missing."

"That was the plan," she whispered. "We had a better chance of getting away if we split up."

"Do you know you devastated my parents? My mother *wept* for you, as if she'd lost her own child. Dad blamed himself till the day he died. He felt he should have known you were planning to run. Two girls out there somewhere – dear God, we thought you must have been kidnapped or killed!" She flinched at the coldness of his voice, no longer a grown-up, but a scared girl shying away from an adult's fury. "We couldn't even be sure you were alive until the police found that you'd withdrawn all your savings. Where the hell did you go, anyway?"

He let her go then, as if afraid of the remembered anger sweeping through him. She swayed away from him.

"San Francisco," she said, grasping at the least painful of his questions. "I thought I could find a job and a place to stay out there. I worked and sang in clubs, until I met Cam."

"Is that why you married him?" A cool note to his words. "You needed money?"

"Yes." She looked straight ahead beyond his shoulder. "Don't worry, I didn't cheat Cam. He got his money's worth. I tried to be a good wife."

He ran his fingers through his hair, calmer now. "You still haven't told me *why* you left," he reminded her. "And where is Francie?"

Earlier that spring, she had tried to write down what she remembered of the great break in her life. She had consciously tried not to remember for the first few years; she had kept memory at arm's length through her child and her music. So successfully had she blocked out that time that several painful afternoons had produced only a couple of pages, filled mostly with bits and pieces of conversations.

Dominic Abbott, the summer before her senior year: *You are not to see that boy again, do you understand?*

Dominic, later: *I have decided that you will not go away to school.*

Francie, hysterical after Diana's attack: *I can't tell Daddy, Laurie, I swear I can't. What am I going to do? I'm past three months already.*

Laura, staring in despair down at her desk: *Does he know?*

Francie's unexpected reaction, as she grabbed her twin's arm: *No! And don't you tell him either! He'll never leave her. He'll never risk losing Julie.*

It's okay, Francie. Laura, assessing the panic in her twin's eyes and making the decision to alter her life, opening her desk drawer to pull out the notebook where she had outlined her escape. *I'm leaving, I'm going away from here forever. Do you want to come?*

Her savings had not gone far in those last few months before Meg's birth. Francie, usually the picture of health, had endured a difficult pregnancy, culminating in enforced bed rest, and Laura kept them afloat through a succession of transient jobs that she obtained by lying through her teeth about her age and being willing to take less than minimum wage. Her carefully planned budget had disintegrated under the weight of care that Francie needed; she had been forced to learn early the reality of public clinics and charity hospitals. Faced with the true cost of Francie's spring idyll, she had found herself unable to sleep, unable to eat, unable to shed the terror of adult responsibility.

She had tried hard not to let Francie see her fear, but Francie knew. *Go home, Laurie,* Francie's voice echoed in memory, *I'll be okay. Get back to your own life.* After all, Laura had nothing to hide, no pain-filled memories to confront, none of Diana's insane jealousy to face. But why go home? She had no one left. She had said her goodbyes. She'd never had anyone but Francie, and Francie could not return, heavy with a child who should not exist.

She and Francie would survive. They had survived Dominic Abbott. They could survive anything.

Then – near-tragedy. Francie went into labor eleven weeks early, right after their birthdays, and delivered a two-pound daughter. While physically she bounced back with the resilience of youth, mentally she was a mess. She didn't want to see the baby, hold her – she flatly refused to nurse her, and she cried almost every waking hour. Laura found herself sitting by the incubator that held Francie's baby, hour after hour, watching, praying, seeing nothing but a spiraling nightmare of worry and debt.

She worried about Francie. She had never seen her sister so depressed. Neither of them had ever heard of postpartum depression; they had no idea that help existed for the condition.

The bills for the baby were so staggering, even at the county hospital, that she had no choice but to risk disclosing their location. One day, she gathered up all the jewelry that she had stolen from her father's house – much of it costly jewelry given to the Countess of Shilleen by the husband who had refused to divorce her – and she started hocking it methodically all over the Bay area. A tiara here, a matching necklace and ring there – she didn't receive even a tenth of their value, but what she did get helped to whittle down the frightening numbers that she faced. She lived in fear that someone would report her to the police – what was a young girl doing with such expensive jewelry? it had to be stolen – and that Dominic would come roaring out to San Francisco to find them.

After eight weeks, the staff doctors told Laura that she could take the baby home in another two weeks. Against the odds, Francie's baby had lived, breathed on her own, grown and gained weight. She no longer looked like a little human scrap but more like a real baby, her skin filling out to be pretty and pink and plump. Francie still refused to see her or even give her a name. Laura started to tell the doctors that they couldn't release to her, she wasn't the baby's mother, and then fell silent. Of course, they thought she was the mother. She was the only one they ever saw.

On the way back to the garage apartment – despite the postage-stamp dimensions, she didn't miss Dominic's house – she stopped at a consignment store and found a bassinet that she could afford. She brought it up the stairs with her and then heard in horror Francie's reaction. *I can't – I can't – I'm too young to be a mother – I can't take care of her – let them keep her – someone else can take her—*

You can't. Laura grasped at the one certainty. *You can't give away his child. He has rights too. You need to tell him. He'll take her.*

She would never see the baby again if the child went to Richard and Diana – oh, dear God, if Diana *would* take her. She could not go home. She could not go back to Dominic after her taste of freedom.

Francie stopped crying long enough to yell back at her, *Richard, Richard, Richard! Is that all you think about? She's my baby. She's not his. I didn't even put him on the birth certificate.* And then, later, when she calmed down, *I looked up the laws in this state. If I give her up for adoption, he'd have to sign away his rights, and face it, can you imagine him doing that? And if he takes her, then she's still there, she's still in my life, I have to see her! I won't ever be free!*

But you can't give her away, Francie, you can't—

Francie had rounded on her swiftly. *What do you mean, I can't? You don't get a say in this! I'm the one who was pregnant. I'm the one who had to be fat and sick. I'm the one who had to go through labor – you try it and see how you like it!* Then she broke down. *I didn't think it would be so awful. I thought it would be so romantic to give him a child. I thought it would make him love me.*

She would have given anything in the world to trade places with Francie. Richard should have turned to her – but no, she wouldn't think that, there lay madness.

So she outwitted Francie, who still spent most of each day lying around the apartment, sobbing her eyes out. When the doctors said the baby could go home, Laura combed her hair to match Francie's – a center part instead of a side part – and dressed in the loose jumper Francie had worn most of the summer. She wore heeled sandals to match Francie's two extra inches. She slipped the hospital ID that Francie had thrown down on the cheap kitchen table onto her wrist and took her Virginia driver's license. At the hospital, she gambled on the constant personnel turnover in the three months since the baby's birth, and later that day, "Francesca Dane" brought Baby Girl Dane home.

Get her out! Out! Take her away! I don't want to see her!

No. Laura stood her ground, even as her heart crumbled at the agony on her twin's face. *She stays. You don't want to be around her – then you leave.*

They had stared at each other across that tiny body, and Francie, older by a year less a day, used to getting her way with her sparkle and vivacity, never thwarted until she had run into the wall of implacable biology, finally faced with a *No* she couldn't charm her way around – Francie backed down.

She calmed down and apologized. She promised to do better. She had been cooped up for months, she said, and the enforced bed rest had depressed her. She had to get back out in the world before she went crazy. *Okay, you win. She can stay here till I decide what to do.*

She has to have a name, Laura had pointed out. *What do you want to call her?*

I don't care. You pick.

Laura named Richard's daughter after his mother – the closest to a real mother that she herself had ever known. Being with baby Margaret – soon Meg – let her feel closer to Peggy.

Fine with me, Francie said. *I'm going to go find a job. You stay with her during the day, okay? I'll babysit at night when you're out singing.*

So Laura had time during long autumn days to continue making Meg's acquaintance. At first, she loved taking care of Meg because the baby belonged to the two people she loved best in the world. Then – she carefully never examined her feelings to know when they changed – Meg began to belong to her. When she took the baby out, people complimented her on her baby, and only the first time did she put anyone right. The second time, she smiled and said thanks. Meg *should* have been hers. She sang to Meg, she rocked her, she soothed her to sleep, and she cringed every time Francie talked about adoption.

But babies took money, and their cash situation was critical. The little money they saved had to be kept in case Meg got sick, and the bills for the baby's care continued to arrive. Francie, exclaiming in despair: *I can't take this anymore! Something's got to give! I'm going to talk to that counselor at the hospital tomorrow. She said it would be easy to place a white baby girl for adoption.*

Somehow, each time Francie made the threat, Laura was able to soothe her, extract a promise to think on it, wait until after the new year, things were sure to get better…. Then came the December night when she walked home from the club to save bus fare, exhausted, wondering how she was going to pay the heating bill – and there Francie had sat at their little table, sopping wet on a dry night, Meg in her little carrier beside her. Francie, with haunted eyes and flotsam in her hair. Meg, dry, but with a trace of sand on her delicate skin.

She knew then that she had to run again. This time with Meg, this time from Francie.

She had $33 to her name, and one last piece of jewelry.

She waited and watched, and over the next few nights, as she sang her smoky songs and gazed out alluringly at her small audience, she felt only the dread of coming home to an empty apartment. The police knocking on her door. *Could you come with us to identify….* The darkness that hung over the apartment, the unspoken remnant of that night. The look in Francie's eyes that never warmed, that iced her every time she saw her sister look at Meg.

And then – salvation.

A Stanford doctoral student escaped from a downpour into the lounge and lingered for her act. At the end of her set, he bought her a drink. The songs she sang and the dress she wore made her seem much older; Cameron St. Bride could not know that the siren he watched with such hungry eyes masked a scared girl in search of a rescuer. He danced with her, he sat through two more sets, and when she got off duty, he kissed her for what seemed like hours. She had been kissed before, but never like this. She had never been held against a man's demanding body, and she responded eagerly.

"I want you," he had whispered finally, his hand on her breast, "come with me." Laura made the second fateful decision of her life and went. She craved the warmth his body offered; she was dazed and aroused by his assault on her senses, and she had already noticed the money in his wallet when he paid for their drinks. Virginity and virtue seemed trifling matters next to the cold hard cash she needed to take Meg and run.

Less than twenty minutes later, a stunned Cameron St. Bride got the truth out of her, and what began as a diversion for him and an act of desperation for her changed as he heard her stammer out the story of that terrified dash across the continent and the agonizing months of her break with the past. His first, instinctive opinion that she should go right back home died seconds after she began talking about Dominic, about Francie, about Richard. About Meg.

He took her home that night, claiming that he always saw a lady home from a date, and at the door he had pressed two hundred dollars into her hand. "Buy the baby some milk," he had said, and vanished into the night. She thought never to see him again. She *hoped* not to see him again. She had, after all, sunk to a level she had never imagined all those months when she had plotted her escape in the safety of her father's house. She had sold herself. She was no better than the girls who walked the street down the block from the club.

But she had enough for a bus ticket. Enough to take Meg and run, at least as far as the next state.

Then, the next day – he came back. He admitted later that he had asked himself why even as he mounted the stairs to her apartment, wondering if he truly wanted to get involved with a girl barely of age, a girl caring for a frail baby, a girl who had suffered a dark history of emotional abuse and whose sister remained a burden she could scarcely manage. He even turned away once. But finally he knocked, and she answered the door holding Meg in her arms. He looked at them both and fell in love.

His presence that weekend, larger than life in their tiny room, made all the difference in the world. Meg, too quiet for a baby, brightened when he picked her up. Francie's eyes lost that cold, dead look. Laura slept soundly for the first time in weeks.

"I'd like to see you next weekend," he said Sunday night, before starting the trip back to Stanford, and she who had loved another for the whole of her life said, "Come back."

"Wolf in wolf's clothing," Francie speculated after he left, and shot a suspicious look Laura's way. "Something happen you didn't tell me about?"

"No," said Laura.

Francie stared at her intently. Laura kept her face still while those all-too-knowing eyes tried to pierce her calm. The unspoken tension that neither wanted to acknowledge grew until Francie shrugged and buried it all. "Suit yourself. All I can say is, he looked like he wanted to eat you up."

"You're imagining things."

"Richard used to look at me that way," said Francie, and burst into tears.

No, he didn't, thought Laura, who was finally learning skepticism.

The next weekend, Cam returned, and the weekend after that. Over the next month, he wooed and courted and cosseted Laura. She finally came first with someone. She grew to depend on him; she confided in him her terrible fear of the Bay. *I have to take her away.... If I go to Texas, will you ask your father to help me find a job?*

I can do better than that, he said, and touched her face tenderly. *Oh, God, Laura, you are so young to deal with this. I'll take care of you. You don't have to live like this....*

But I have to keep Meg, she said, knowing that he wanted her to live with him. He had not made any advances since that first, terrible night, but she knew that he still wanted her. His eyes told her that.

At night, huddled under a blanket in her narrow bed, listening for Meg in the darkness, she could even contemplate going to bed with him, just to have him hold her afterwards and tell her that everything would be all right. *Do you really want to live with a baby, Cam? She has to come first. And she's a lot of hard work. She's not a toy I can put in the closet when I'm tired of playing with her.*

We could adopt her.

She couldn't have heard him correctly. *Adopt her? But they won't allow that, we're not—*

Marry me, Laura, and he framed her face with his hands. *Marry me, and I promise you'll never have to worry about losing Meg again. Besides,* and he smiled down at Meg, sleeping on a blanket, *she grows on you, doesn't she? I don't know anything about being a father, but I'll be the best you could ever want for her.*

No! Francie's response to the first tentative question echoed down the years. *Oh, my God, I just want to forget! How can you even think – I'll see her and I'll never stop remembering—*

And Cam's quiet voice: *Francesca, let's you and I go somewhere and talk this out.*

Later, Francie returning from that private dinner, subdued and thoughtful, and for the first time in months, not shadowed in pain. Her only reaction, when Laura asked her hesitantly what Cam had said: *Don't marry that man just to have a roof over your head, Laurie. You'll survive. We'll all survive. I won't take Meg away from you. But – just don't marry him.*

For the first time in her life, she ignored Francie.

She was grateful to him, of course, and it was the worst possible basis for marriage. Passion existed between them, and their devotion to Meg bound them together, but she never loved him, and for that she felt inordinately guilty. She *should* have loved him. He was generous with himself, his time and money. Better than that, he showed her a gentleness that went a long way towards destroying the insecurity Dominic Abbott had built in her. When he took her to bed the night she agreed to marry him, his loving patience allayed her fears and did much to erase the emotional damage of that first night.

He never mentioned that night again.

He determined, too, to erase another memory. Sight unseen, he despised Meg's biological father, and his distrust of Meg's birth mother, now living next door to them in the rental house at Stanford, did not abate over the year they spent in California. For Cam, the year was a necessary waiting period for the adoption, a time to finish his dissertation and plan the future. For Laura, the year became a co-coon of healing from the past, a year in which she existed contented-ly as a wife and mother, a year in which her first pregnancy, un-planned but welcomed, ended in pain and blood one Saturday afternoon. For Francie, the year imprisoned her in a boring job as a bank teller and a restricted social life under the conservative eye of a brother-in-law she despised.

But then the year ended. Cam received his doctorate; a judge signed the final adoption papers and sealed the records; Francie, de-claring passionately that she never wished to set foot in California again, decided to move to Texas with them.

There, Francie cut her ties. *I'm afraid I'll try to be Meg's mother if I live with you, Laurie. I know myself too well. You need to take care of your marriage and your baby without me hanging around. Don't worry, darling.* She laughed and hugged Laura. *I've already talked it over with Cam, and he agrees. You'll see me all too often anyway!*

Laura, still recovering from her second miscarriage: *Oh, Fran, no. Stay a while. I need you.*

No, you don't, said Francie flatly. *And I don't need to be around Cam or Meg. I can't stand him, and it hurts to see her. But, Laurie, you call me whenever you want, okay? We're still twins. We're twins forever.*

So Francie left her twin to a marriage far from her dreams. The marriage that had worked well on a college campus changed charac-ter in the real world. Laura Abbott melted into Laura St. Bride, the wife of a man coming up fast on his own in a new industry, the mother of a child determined to work her way through every entry in the behavioral textbooks. She had a baby to take care of, a hus-band to please, and a household to run, and Cam left no room in their marriage for the girl who stayed up late at nights writing poet-ry and finding music in old romantic myths. A few hours at the pia-no during the week ought to satisfy her. Her time belonged to him. *She* belonged to him. Laura Abbott had gone forever, she was Mrs. Cameron St. Bride....

Resentment began to rage below the surface of her Cinderella marriage. (And how *had* Cinderella liked marrying up the social lad-der, anyway? Had she wearied of remembering how much she owed her prince?) Oh, how often did she wish that Cam had taken a shine to Francie instead? Francie had her own apartment and a job at the St. Bride family investment bank; she had resumed her voice lessons. She dated; she went to college classes; she even cajoled Cam into fly-ing lessons. On the weekends, she crewed on the local lakes with

Cam's parents. Dallas blessed her. She was coming into her own, her natural allure deepened by her thwarted love affair; she seemed happy again.

Only once, when Laura found her crying over an architectural magazine, did Francie admit that Richard had not vanished into the past. *I want to see him. I try and try to forget, and it's no good. Every time I look at Meg—*

Then go back, said her disillusioned twin, certain that, for someone, the world must still be well lost for love. *To hell with Daddy. To hell with Diana. If you still love him – there's divorce. Even Richard has his breaking point.*

Francie shut the magazine wearily. *He asked her once,* and that startled Laura. *Do you know what she said? She told him to go ahead if he wanted to lose Julie. How that bitch uses that child – Richard loves Julie. I think he'd do anything to keep her. He won't risk a divorce, not now.*

What are you going to do?

I'll go back eventually. When Diana is gone and Richard is free.

But she'd not paid attention to that, the first clue that Francie had her own master plan. She'd not seen that in her twin's eyes seethed the birth of a long-awaited revenge. Swamped in her own unhappiness, falling out of love with a husband she wasn't sure she had ever been in love with, resolving to keep her third pregnancy to herself until she got beyond the danger stage – oh, with all that baggage, she thought later, no wonder that she'd not divined that Francie had reached Richard again.

Then one day, fresh from a quarrel with Cam, she had sought refuge at Francie's apartment. She had her own key, and she let herself in quietly. And she heard Francie talking wildly, passionately: *Get her out of the way, everyone will just forget about her. Oh, dear God, I am so sick of losing to her, that bitch, that two-faced bitch – and I want my family back, I want my place back, I do, I do....*

Confronted, Francie confessed. Diana had denied Richard a divorce. They had one option left.

We're going to kill her.

His voice called her back. "Laura?"

When she looked at him, all the attraction that had shimmered between them earlier had gone. (And it had shimmered, no use denying that now.) She saw him, this man who had struck back using sister against sister, and the ice that had protected her for so long closed around her again. She was no longer as vulnerable as she once had been.

"You know why Francie left," she said. "What did you expect, after Di caught you together that day? Francie was devastated, she was humiliated beyond belief. She wanted to leave, and – and I went with her because—" She grasped at control of her voice. "I loved her. She needed me, and you and Di were so caught up with each other – you didn't give a damn about her."

Her words hit home, hard. She saw a flash of pain in his eyes, the knowledge of an old guilt, before he retreated behind his shield.

"I cared," every word deliberate. "Diana was brutal to her. I'm glad Francie had you to go to. I'm sorry—" he stopped, and he straightened up. "I'm sorry that you got mixed up in that. It must have come as a shock—"

Her voice was calm, Cat Courtney's voice. "I'd known for months," she said, "Francie told me as soon as she got back after New Year's. She couldn't wait to tell me."

"Of course not." He sounded tired, strange. "It wasn't any good if she couldn't tell you."

"Yes." Why did she hate hearing him so unhappy? What was wrong with her? She had to get her feelings for him in order. "I was the only safe one to tell."

"I'm sorry you ever had to know. You cared about me, and it was hard to lose that." He sounded weary, like someone who has watched a favorite keepsake slip away forever. Without warning, he held out his hand. "Come, I'll take you back to your hotel. I don't see any point in dinner."

She nodded. Better to leave now, better to savor her anger away from him, away from the scent of his skin and the timber of his voice. He had done her a favor; he had reminded her of all the reasons she had to despise him, and maybe, away from him, she would not forget.

Black is the color of my true love's heart….

She waited quietly while he settled the bill for their wine and assured the waiter that, no, there was nothing wrong, they had merely discovered that they were not hungry…. The waiter was suitably discreet, but he cast her an appraising glance, as if to judge her not worth the loss of a dinner. She was furious to remember that her own thoughts had run in that channel earlier, and she spared the waiter a scathing look before she obeyed Richard's subtle, guiding pressure out to his car.

"Laura."

She stopped at the passenger door and stared down at his hand.

"Where is Francie now? Did she come with you?"

All the pain she'd held inside for eleven years hit her then in a flood. Its passage was instant and splintering, and she looked at this man who had killed Francie as surely as if he had cut her throat himself.

"She's dead."

"Dead!" His fingers bit her arm. "When? What happened?"

And then she took her revenge. She remembered the horror and humiliation of that bloody afternoon, she imagined the terror of Francie's last moment on earth, and she lifted her chin and looked straight into those lying eyes, alive now and full of remembered anguish. She said softly, "She bled to death, Richard. Eleven years ago. Right here in Virginia." And then, "After you left her."

Later, much later, Richard Ashmore sat in his darkened home, while his daughter slept upstairs. He treasured these pockets of night, his only refuge from the privileges and burdens of his life; he sought these moments to regain those parts of himself that the day had chipped away.

Most nights, he listened to music, to relax himself for sleep. He'd learned to love Chopin and Rachmaninoff during his years with Diana, and Francie had taught him Verdi; he often intermixed a symphony with the rock of his youth.

But tonight only the music of Cat Courtney would suit, and he was not a masochist.

Most nights, too, he fixed himself a cup of coffee. Years of watching Diana drink herself down the drain had given him a healthy dislike for the oblivion of the bottle.

Tonight, he granted himself one small glass of wine.

Tonight he faced the fact that he might not be a masochist, but when it came to women, he was certainly a fool.

Three mistakes….

Diana, Francie, Laura.

And the least memorable had just caught up with him with a vengeance.

He did not often think of Francie, lovely, seductive, scheming Francie. The guilt he had carried after her disappearance had given way to quiet regret and then to a more adult acceptance of a young man's follies. He had yielded to temptation one New Year's Eve; he had broken an unspoken code; he had hurt his unfaithful wife terribly. He wished he had never stayed home with Francie that evening, and he certainly wished he had never touched a drop of the champagne she had so thoughtfully brought with her. But wishing changed nothing. He could only live with the past, and live his life.

He looked down through the dark at the photo album. He had pulled it down from the shelf after Julie had gone to bed, knowing what he would find. His trained eye saw shape and line, and Laura must have forgotten that or she would never have left that picture of her daughter where he could see it.

His mother, Margaret Ashmore, at ten, in a shot taken over sixty years before; Margaret St. Bride, in the photo he had phone-mailed to himself while Laura dressed for dinner. Nearly twins. Oh, he saw some subtle differences. Meg St. Bride beamed in jeans and T-shirt; Peggy had been wearing her Sunday best. The older picture was in black and white, Meg's in full color, so no casual viewer would know that Peggy's eyes were the Irish blue that she had passed to her son. But anyone could see the forest green eyes that Francesca Abbott had given her daughter.

His daughter, too.

Meg St. Bride, of course, had to be more than ten.

He leaned back and tried to figure just when she might have been born. After fourteen years, a few isolated sexual incidents (and he refused to dignify them as anything more) were difficult to date. The only one he knew for a certainty was New Year's Eve, and it did not seem possible that Francie had conceived then.

Easter break…. The timing worked out, so Meg would have been born after Christmas. He thought in horror of the hardship Laura and Francie must have known, while he enjoyed his first holiday out of college.

It did not bear thinking of.

He had scarcely remembered how to think in those few seconds after he'd seen her picture and realized that he had fathered a child. How he'd managed…. And Laura had instantly gone on edge. Even through his shock, he had sensed her fear, and every instinct had warned him that he must not alarm her. Betray once that he recognized his own blood in her daughter, and she might well vanish back into Laura St. Bride's life.

She had only the one child.

How had she ended up with Meg? Ah, Cameron St. Bride. He'd forgotten the reclusive computer genius, although he certainly had never forgotten the utter hatred that St. Bride had turned on him in London. Of course, and he understood now. Not because Laura's husband had ever learned of that hidden afternoon – not unless Laura had suffered a fit of conscience and confessed – but because St. Bride had loved his daughter.

He understood that. He would fight to the death to protect Julie.

And Laura, he suspected, could kill like a tigress for her cub.

He sipped his wine and wondered what primeval fear underlay that incredible hostility she had turned on him. He'd expected her to be nervous, secretive, even defiant. Returning home after fourteen years, blood on her hands, she risked rejection on a scale he'd never known. He'd expected that she would never relax until he forgave her.

The moment he'd seen her, those wide green eyes panicked at the sight of him, forgiveness had become moot. Best instead to bury that hour forever.

She had followed his lead. No apologies, no explanations – maybe… and he turned his head towards the window, a thought breaking through the wine. Maybe she honestly believed her cover still held. Only if a woman believed that the man on whom she'd turned fury and violence did not know who she was could she go to dinner with him, dance with him, ask to meet his daughter.

Certainly, that last vicious remark, born of the pain and horror he'd seen in her eyes, made sense only if she still felt herself shielded from discovery by Francie.

In that, hope might wait for them yet. He had lost his wife, the only woman he had ever loved, in the dreadful aftermath of their mutual betrayal; he had lost a daughter he'd never known he had; he had lost confidence in his own honor and integrity.

He hated to think that he had also lost his friend.

He finished off his wine and contemplated a cigarette, and Laura's laughing, disapproving gaze settled around him.

She had come home. She had come to him. She might not want to see him again – she'd told him so when he took her back to her hotel, in a burst of adolescent melodrama – and at the moment, he was of a mind to grant her wish.

Not because of what she'd said. But because the curve of her throat caught his breath – and her sidelong glance roused his heart from long anesthesia —

And because he'd learned not to be a fool.

He had not forgotten, God help him, that she was his sister-in-law.

7

Upon That Shore

ON A DAY SUCH AS THIS, Laura had last seen the ancient Chesapeake sands. The high afternoon sun had bathed her then, laying a light blanket of humidity over the landscape, and surely those gulls were descendants to those that had circled over Francie's death bed.

On such a day, she had come to this remote shore, a mother and sister, desperate to prevent the bloodshed she saw coming.

She had never remembered leaving, sick, betrayed, a mother and sister no longer.

She parked the Jaguar close to the cottage, far beyond the gates that locked the bridge and barred access to the spit of land, and pocketed the keys she had filched from Dominic's desk this morning.

On such a day....

But the day had changed. She felt that change, standing there on the shore, listening to the squish of the wet lands beneath her sandals. Eleven years had come and gone, the signs of their passing even in the changeless scene before her. Dominic's hideaway, that old guest cottage where he had gone to compose his unearthly music, bore a fresh coat of paint. Hundreds of yards away, the Ashmore summer cottage, its proximity symbol of the intermingling of the two families, stood guarded by a new fence. The seascape itself had shifted infinitesimally; the crescent of the cove where Francie had lived her last minutes had widened and deepened.

And the greatest change, she knew, lay deep within herself.

She forced herself to unlock the door of her father's cottage. The sunlight from the east spilled into the room, and old dusty air flooded out around her. No one had come here in a long time. The one main room held the few essentials of the solitary composer's life – the piano (not the best, for the salt air), the kitchenette where Francie had prepared that treacherous cup of tea, the double bed where (family legend had it) Dominic had brought an end to Renée Dane's career by impregnating her with Francie. The bed—

She swallowed the sickness in her throat and touched the bed.

The bed, ancient site of her greatest shame.

Oh, God! She battled down her nausea. She felt as frozen as she had on her rare occasions of stage fright, as terrified as if the curtain were about to rise on an unfamiliar act. She shut her eyes to block out the image of those younger players, trapped in their cross-dramas, clashing in one terrible moment.

I can't think about that....

But you will. You're here, aren't you? And it's time the dreams stopped.

When she forced her eyes open, the phantoms had fled. Before her stood merely an old, dusty bed, sagging, nondescript, where heaven and hell had never met in supreme explosion. Beyond it, Francie had never stood at the stove, brewing her beguiling ticket to oblivion, ensuring her own death on the Chesapeake shore. And Laura herself had never fled this room, destroyer of her own dreams.

The musician in her could not resist testing the keys of the piano. She winced at their sound, discordant, neglected, ruined by the rich air of the bay, untouched for how many months before Dominic's death. Had he still sought refuge here, after the trauma of Francie's death?

For surely he had known.

Francie had never been found. When Laura had first awakened in a Newport News hospital, disoriented, empty and sick from convulsions, Cam had soothed her with the promise to search for Francie's body. And he had tried. But two days had passed, and the evening tide had claimed Francie. Days melted away, Laura grew stronger, Cam searched, but Francie never washed up, mute witness to her own killing.

But not the only victim.

Another life had vanished that day, at Francie's hands. And Cam, suffering from his own loss, had expressed the savage regret that sharks did not hunt the Chesapeake.

"Bitch."

Her voice startled her in the claustrophobic silence of the room. She said it again, enjoying the strength of the word, and it occurred to her that she had not dared before to acknowledge her fury. And she had a right to her fury! Forget what she herself had done in this very room, forget that she had put herself beyond the pale in one ill-thought moment, forget that she had brought all this upon herself (as Cam had justly told her) by attempting to deal with Francie and her murderous ideas alone. Fate – or Diana – had denied her the chance to exact her vengeance.

She opened the cabinet above the stove and found it empty. Dominic must have cleaned it out years ago, tossing away the tea, thinking it a leftover from the times he had brought the twins out with him while he worked. He didn't like tea; he claimed that aged Scotch better oiled his muse.

So only she and her baby had tasted Francie's fine poisonous brew.

And her baby had not survived.

On such a day had Francie merrily prepared tea for her twin, a task threading together all the events of their lives: *Oh, for God's sake, Laurie, have some tea! You're so on edge! And trust me, okay? I'll behave, I promise. I'll be so sweet and penitent, Di will hardly believe it's me.* And later, brushing her hair, carefully putting on her lipstick: *Let me borrow your dress – red for courage!* Admitting: *I'm scared, Laurie. I've never been so scared of anything in my life.*

But, on such a day, not so scared that she hadn't thought to poison Laura into inaction, so that she could destroy Diana once and for all.

I never want to come here again.

Laura locked the door behind her – no sense advertising her visit – and faced west, away from the cottage. The sunlight invaded her sight; beneath her eyelids danced a thousand sunbursts. She dug into her bag for her sunglasses.

A lone gull, attracted by the movement, uttered an ungodly cry and careened in closely. Probably looking for food, she thought, and remembered abruptly that she hadn't eaten since last night. But her hunger faded before the pull of this panorama of remembered death. She walked down into the breeze and the shifting sands at the edge of the Chesapeake, and in a few minutes the crescent of the cove yawned before her.

She descended into the abyss and sat down near the tide.

Innocent enough, that cove. She and Francie had often gone down there to sunbathe while Dominic wrote, untying their bikini tops safe from all prying eyes, giggling, half-hoping that someone would come along and startle them. And, oh, the confidences flying between them there, on those very sands! Francie planning to study in

New York after graduation, sight-reading Laura's first forays into songwriting, speculating what life would *really* be like once they were out of school and out from under Dominic's thumb. Laura never mentioning, not then, not until later, her own plans for escape, with her secret savings account and her mother's filched social security number and her squirreled-away birth certificate and passport.

She scooped up a handful of sand and let it drift down through her loosely-laced fingers. The grains clouded the stones in her mother's ring and dulled the gleam of the gold, and she scooped it up and sifted it over and over, while day and time slid away and Francie reappeared there on the sand beside her, talking and singing and laughing. Always laughing.

Meg, too, laughed. She had envied her twin that, and she envied Meg now, for that insouciant giggle and that slapdash confidence. She herself had been too serious a child, too quiet a teenager, too solemn a wife. ("For God's sake, lighten up," Cam had complained so often, and maybe his other women had provided him the laughter he missed from her.) Whether her fear of Dominic had stilled her laughter, or whether she simply had never learned how (for in that house only Francie had laughed, and usually at someone), she knew that she had never approached life as a game but as a deadly serious obstacle course.

Any gift she'd had for laughter had died with Francie.

And so here – on Francie's deathbed, scene of who only knew what pain and terror in those last terrible minutes – Laura forgot Francie's betrayal, her selfish disregard of everything blocking her destruction of Diana (and if that had included Laura's unseen child, what of it?). She cast away the anger and shame she had carried across the years that separated her from Francie's death. She let the waters wash over her toes and watched the gulls screeching overhead, and she thought that she would forgive Francie anything, if only she could hear her twin laugh again.

Later, she did not remember falling asleep.

The rush of the waters rocked her to sleep, and the sun laid its healing cover over her. She slept away her grief, and when she awoke, the afternoon had begun to wane.

She had buried her dead. Francie and her unknown baby both – they had deserved her mourning, and she had finally given it. She stopped at her car, brushed the sand off as best she could, and looked back towards the bay in farewell.

I will never come here again.

8

Three Little Maids Are We

LUCY MAITLAND HAD NEVER STOPPED looking for her missing sisters. A waste of time, her husband told her after it became apparent that they weren't to be found. "Give it up, don't break your heart over this," Tom advised. "They'll turn up when they feel like it."

Her brother-in-law counseled her to save her energy and money. All the ads in the world wouldn't help, Richard said, Laura would never come back.

Her sister Diana cut to the heart of the matter. Francie, she announced, had damn well better not return, not while she was still drawing breath.

But still Lucy searched. Newspaper and Internet ads, news alerts, calls to Cat Courtney's management, a PI once when her Christmas bonus permitted – anything that might work, anything that might bring her sisters home again.

Because, no matter what, they were still a family. She believed that, she had taken on the responsibility of keeping the family together, she had willingly served as its core all these years. And she knew that, until she had all her sisters back, the family would never be complete.

So why, on a morning when she should have been ecstatic, when half of her search had come to an end – why did she feel nothing so much as hurt and resentful and not really sure that she wanted her prodigal sister back after all?

She slammed down the phone and glared at her brother-in-law. "Where is she?"

"How would I know?" Richard snapped back. "I'm not her keeper."

"Well, you saw her last." Lucy buried her face in her hands for a moment and told her stomach to settle down. She didn't need this excitement; nausea had haunted her all morning, and Richard's terrible mood only made it worse. "Didn't she say anything? Shopping, swimming, *anything*?"

"Not a thing." Richard leaned back. She peeked through her fingers and noticed that, although his voice had gentled, his expression seemed just as moody. "Maybe she went to visit some old friends."

"I don't remember that she had any friends," said Lucy. "Of course, we were away at school those last years, but she always seemed to be such a loner. Did she mention anyone that she might want to look up, places to visit for old time's sake?"

He shook his head. A gauzy curtain of dust motes floating on the plane of sunlight softened the lines of exhaustion around his eyes; Lucy thought that he had not slept well and noticed, irrelevantly, that he needed a haircut. "She really didn't say much. She was fairly close-mouthed about her plans—" this from the man who posted *No Trespassing* signs all over his personal life— "except that she's staying at Edwards Lake for a couple of months. Something about needing privacy to write some songs."

You're lying through your teeth.

That bothered her. He usually told her everything (well, almost everything – he maintained an admirable if maddening silence about the women inhabiting the fringes of his life). That he chose to cast a fine reticent shade over the previous evening drew her suspicions. Something had disturbed Richard's generally even temperament; something had dampened the enthusiasm she'd thought he'd show over Laura's return.

She realized, with a start, that he had not mentioned Francie.

Even as she formed the question, he scraped back the chair. "Good luck, Luce. I've got to run."

"You're leaving?" She hadn't counted on this.

He touched her cheek. "I'm in Charleston next week. I need to get some work done. You don't want me here anyway. The Abbott girls need to spend some time together without the rest of us."

A convenient excuse, but he was right. Time enough for a grand family reunion when Laura showed up – *if* she showed up – and she and Diana had time to absorb this shock to their lives. Lucy pretended reluctance as she gave in. "Okay. Call me later, will you? And, Richard – you never said—"

"Hmmm?" He shrugged on his leather jacket.

She pondered how to ask. He'd proved himself a slippery customer when it came to eluding subjects he didn't want to discuss. "Did Francie come with her?"

His eyes shuttered instantly. "No."

He meant that cool retreat to intimidate. Lucy was made of stronger stuff. "So what did she say?"

"Ask her. Maybe she'll tell you the truth."

Lord! No mistaking the bitterness now. She certainly *would* ask. "Have you told Di yet?"

"No," he said briefly. "She must have left early. I tried calling, and I went by her place before I came over here."

Oh, no. No use making excuses. He knew that Diana was a late sleeper, that if she had deserted her bed at that hour, she must be sleeping in someone else's.

"I didn't leave a message." He looked at her directly. "This isn't something to hear on voice mail. And I'm out of pocket until evening, so—"

"I'll tell her." The less Richard and Diana had to deal with each other, the better. "She's on tonight, so she'll be in by four."

"Thanks." He gave her an unexpected hug. "Sorry I've been such a grouch, Luce. I've got a lot on my mind, and Diana being missing in action this morning didn't help. Plus—"

She accepted his hesitation, because she had fears of her own, and she thought she understood his. "Plus, this changes everything. I don't know if I'm ready. Are you?"

"Ready has nothing to do with it." She sensed him stepping away mentally, even as he headed out. "Laura picked a bad time to come home, but then she didn't consult us. Considering what happened to her, she didn't need to."

A sad commentary, thought Lucy, shutting the door, how little they had known Laura, how cheaply they had valued her, that her return loomed mostly as an inconvenience. Small wonder that she had so easily walked away. She must have vanished in spirit long before she vanished in body.

But not this time, thought Lucy. *When I find you, you're staying put.*

She still could not fathom Richard's anger (anger? yes, he *had* been angry), but she was honest enough to admit that Laura's return disturbed her. She cherished being the family center. It was her right. She had kept the family together, and that gave her a certain dominance that she did not want to yield. Laura was no longer the mouse to do as she was told; she might well upset the balance of power.

Lucy retrieved her family scrapbook. Tom often joked that they would have to pry it from her on her deathbed, that she would still be rearranging the pictures and press clippings that documented the Abbott family. All fine and good for him to say! He came from a large, secure family with parents married for over forty years and siblings who all came home for Christmas. The Maitlands *worked*, and Lucy, whose mother had deserted her, whose father had left her stashed with the Ashmores so that he could junket around Europe with another man's wife, whose sisters had walked away without a backward glance, valued the genuine love so lacking in her own family. The Abbotts had not worked. She saw the debris in Diana's glazed eyes, in Julie's immaturity, in the loneliness of Richard's heart, in the missing places at Thanksgiving dinner – but that was no reason to pretend that the Abbotts had never existed.

She flipped over a few pages to a picture of the adult Laura. She had one photo among all the clippings, sent to her in response to one of her letters to Laura's record company. ("Miss Courtney appreciates your interest and support of her music and hopes that you will enjoy her new album, *Waterfalls*, available in record stores everywhere.") She'd nearly torn it up in anger, and one corner was still rumpled from its sojourn in the waste basket before she'd rescued it.

Cat Courtney. No doubt ever that Cat was Laura, not Francie in some elaborate charade. That voice identified her anywhere, low, huskier now, undeniably Laura's. Other physical distinctions marked her too, things only her family would notice. The way she parted her hair, Diana thought. The needy look in those eyes, the legacy of never enough attention, Lucy said. Her damned ungrateful silence, snapped Dominic, nicely overlooking that his pet Francie had remained just as silent.

I don't know you, Lucy thought. *I used to* – and she flipped hastily back to a picture of the younger Laura, excited at wearing her first long dress at Diana's wedding. *I didn't pay as much attention to you as I should have, and I'm sorry about that, I'm so sorry. You were still at home, and I had to stay away so he wouldn't suck me into that whole dark sickness of his. And I left you there with Francie, and of course you got the short end of the stick.*

I don't know you now. I've wanted to see you for so long, and now you're here, and I don't know what to say to you. You sit in that photo, in all that mist and mystery, and you have nothing to do with the Laura I knew. And I don't know if I want you back. I don't want you disturbing everything I've worked for. I can take care of Di, now that Dominic's gone.

Richard's way past everything that happened, and Julie is almost grown. They don't need you.

But you need us, and, oh, I need you, said Lucy Maitland silently. *You left such a hole in my heart. I'm damned if you're walking away from me again.*

She spent the afternoon moodily staring out the window, waiting for vendor deliveries, waiting for Diana to show up with some implausible excuse, waiting for Laura so that she could wring her neck.

Julie called, wanting to share her excitement. Funny, thought Lucy, listening to her niece bubble on, paging through her memories, but Laura might find that only Julie truly welcomed her back into the fold. Laura had disappeared shortly after Julie's second birthday, so Julie had no real memories of the young Laura; she knew only the glamor and mystery of Cat Courtney. The years of Laura's silence had never hurt or infuriated or drained her.

Probably because only Julie, of all of them, suffered no guilt.

"The only strange thing," Julie babbled on, and Lucy wrenched her attention back to her niece. "I asked Dad about inviting her over for dinner – I mean, she's going to live near us, so I thought it might be a – a *welcoming* thing to do."

"It would," concurred Lucy, and stopped at a photo of Laura Abbott on the steps of Ashmore Magna at fourteen, gazing adoringly at her oblivious brother-in-law. "She has a daughter a few years younger than you. She'd probably enjoy talking with you."

"I don't think he wants to," said Julie. "He got really quiet and said that he'd have to check, he wasn't sure she would be available. But of course she will be, that's the whole point of her coming home, isn't it, to see all of us? Do you think it's because of 9/11? What should we say to her about that? Do you think she's still in mourning?"

"I'd wait for her to bring the subject up," said Lucy, who had no intention of waiting. "People do get over things, even as terrible as that. Your dad said she seemed to be doing pretty well."

"Well," said Julie, going into confidante mode, "it's almost like he doesn't want to see her again. What do you think that's all about? I always thought they were friends, but then, I remember, I really had to pester him in London to get him to go backstage."

Lucy murmured something soothing and noncommittal, she wasn't sure what the moment the words left her mouth, but mentally, she started rearranging the jigsaw pieces. So Richard *didn't* want to see Laura. She cast her mind back over their talk that morning,

and in retrospect, his reticence loomed larger, darker, louder in its silence. What had happened the night before that Richard wanted to
conceal?

She disentangled herself from the call. "Forget your father, Julie. I
promise you'll get to meet her." *Oh, famous last words, you can't even
find her yourself.*

The bartender intruded upon her thoughts; deliveries and
invoices demanded her attention. The afternoon had worn away; the
staff would be trooping in soon, and she hadn't accomplished anything on her to-do list.

She blamed that, with great pleasure, on Laura.

And where the hell was Diana?

"Ms. Maitland?" The bartender stuck his head around the door into
the middle of a discussion with a supplier. "Your sister's here for
you."

"Fine," said Lucy absently, jotting down notes and figures. "Tell
her I'm on my way out. No, no, tell her to get back here, she needs to
take care of this."

He disappeared, and Lucy turned back to wrangling a better net-
10 discount. She enjoyed this; she was an excellent negotiator, and
she liked the give-and-take of bargaining. Diana hated it, so Lucy
wasn't surprised that her sister dragged her feet joining them. No
doubt Diana, Scotch in hand, was rehearsing an elaborate excuse to
explain away her tardiness. Lucy had grown used to such stories;
she'd listened to Diana lying her way out of trouble most of her life.
So she was caught unawares when the supplier, in the midst of a cal-
culation, looked beyond her shoulder and froze silent.

She knew, she knew from the first flare of consternation in the
man's eyes, and for a moment she fought turning around. Anyone
else, she thought wildly, she wasn't ready for this, she didn't know
what to say, what could she say, what should she do—

"Lucy?" And there was no hiding now from the lilt of that voice,
rich in all its history and longing and fear. Lucy drew in a shuddering breath and turned around.

Her first thought, absurdly, was that this was not Laura at all, but
Francie.

Oh, Laura had changed. She cataloged all the changes in those
first few seconds: Laura was taller now, a little curvier, infinitely

more polished. Her perfectly tailored slacks were Bond Street chic, her blouse must have cost a thousand dollars, her shoes and shoulder bag whispered that she never consulted a budget. And her hair – Lucy frankly stared. Shorter than she'd expected, but beautifully cut and as far from the ponytail of old as she could imagine.

And Laura, unnervingly, returned her silence.

"Ms. Maitland?" the rep reminded her.

"I'm sorry. Excuse us, please," said Lucy, without breaking the stare-down, and decisively shoved her errant sister out into the hall.

Her action broke the spell. She shut the door quickly and whipped around to see Laura wincing.

"You have a hell of a nerve showing up here." She marveled at the icy control of her voice; she felt anything but cold. Such a cauldron of emotions boiled inside – rage, shock, heartsick relief that Laura had not run away again – that she felt herself teetering on the edge of explosion. Laura's eyes widened at her tone, but she did not retreat in the face of her fury. Lucy, perversely, was glad of that.

"Yes." Laura did not flinch. "I do have a hell of a nerve."

That cool agreement knocked the wind out of Lucy's sails. She preferred a fight. "Where have you been? I've been calling around all day, looking for you."

"I'm sorry." Laura's voice offered conciliation. "I went out to the Eastern Shore, and I got lost coming back—"

"Not that," Lucy said furiously. "Although you could have called, damn it, Richard said he gave you the number." Her voice slipped into a tremble and betrayed her. "Damn you, Laurie, I've been worried sick about you! I *looked* for you! I *wanted* to know how you were, I wanted to make sure you were safe and happy, and you never even wrote me – or called me – or acted like you remembered us – you never answered Richard's note – I couldn't believe it when he told me—"

She caught her breath, and then Laura moved towards her, and she felt her sister's arms closing around her, hugging her in closely. Her resistance lasted a second, maybe two; she was starved for this warmth, she treasured the tears that dropped onto her shoulder. Lucy clung to her fiercely. "Damn it, baby, I missed you! Don't you even *think* of running away again! Ever!"

"Oh, Lucy," and Laura laughed shakily, tears and laughter bubbling up together. "I don't think I'd dare."

✐

"So why did you go to Richard first, brat?"

"I didn't. He found me." Laura leaned towards the mirror and attempted to repair her face. "Don't ask how, either. I'm not sure myself."

"A secret, huh?" The mirror reflected Lucy's speculative glance at her. "He's playing mystery man about last night. What happened?"

Thank heavens. That had worried her, not knowing what Richard might have told her sisters. She ducked her head and pretended to search for a comb. "Nothing. We talked for a while, then he had to leave to pick Julie up from babysitting." Time to change the subject. "I'm really thirsty. Can we get something to drink?"

"Sure." Lucy opened the door to the dressing room. "We have a whole bar at your command."

Laura asked for a Perrier, and what might have been approval and might have been relief flashed across her sister's face before Lucy waved her over to a side table and called out an order to the bartender. Coming here to the club might not have been the wisest thing to do. The room that had first appeared deserted, empty enough for a reunion that promised pain at worst and awkwardness at best, now seemed filled with people. Word had gotten around quickly that the missing Cat Courtney had walked in the door.

She waited until Lucy had collapsed into a chair to ask, "Where's Di?"

"I haven't the faintest idea." She picked up on the sharpness of Lucy's voice, but maybe she was hypersensitive, too much on edge. "She should be in soon. She's supposed to work tonight."

A waiter approached and set their drinks on the table; Laura carefully did not meet his eyes. Oh, she *had* made a mistake, coming here to the club. She hadn't considered that her sisters' employees might witness this first meeting; no one could blame them for their curiosity. She could only hope that no one had called the press. *Mystery Cat reunites with long-lost sisters....*

"Richard says you have a daughter," Lucy broke into her thoughts. "How old is she?"

The first of many such questions she'd have to dodge. "Twelve. Going on thirty."

"Twelve? You didn't waste any time, did you?" Lucy sounded envious. She sipped her mineral water and reached for the photos Laura held out. "Laurie – first off – what can I say? I am so sorry, I cannot even imagine what it was like to lose your husband like that, and Richard said you watched it all as it was happening. I hear you were getting divorced, but still it must have been – well, I don't have any words. How are you doing?"

"Okay," Laura said when Lucy stopped for breath. "It helped when they stopped showing everything on TV so we didn't have to see it over and over again. Last fall was pretty grim."

"And your daughter?" Lucy looked at Meg's picture. "Good heavens, Laurie, what a beauty. Is she coping all right? I looked up some articles this morning on helping kids deal with 9/11 if you want to see them. Here, write down your email address. I'll send you the links when I get home."

She had forgotten – or had she just not wanted to remember? – Lucy's essential goodness. "We went to a counselor for a few months. Meg is – she has a very strong character. She finally decided that she was going to go on, and she resolutely set her sights on the future. But she misses him so much. I am dreading the first anniversary."

"Oh, I am all for counseling," said Lucy. "And thank goodness you took her, what a smart thing to do. So many people try to tough it out, and this is too big for that. I read an article on how there are going to be terrible mental health issues in a couple of years when we have a chance to catch our breath. But, anyway, back to Meg – when do I get to meet her? You're bringing her up here, aren't you?"

She also should have remembered Lucy's ability to bore in on a subject. She remained silent.

Lucy leaned forward. "Don't give me that song and dance you gave Richard about having to shield her. I want to meet my niece. Ask Julie, she will tell you I am the world's best aunt."

"Lucy," she hesitated, "let's just see how it goes, okay?"

"It's going to go fine," said Lucy. "Bring her up here."

"We'll see," Laura murmured, and prayed that Lucy would find something else to talk about.

Her older sister settled back in her chair and looked at her with a speculation that reminded Laura to pay attention. "I understand your husband was a computer genius," she said. "I never heard of St. Bride Data until – well, you know, but my husband was very impressed. You'll have to meet Tom, he's a fan of yours, he's the most wonderful man—"

She had married Tom Maitland eight years ago, she told Laura. They'd met at an RC competition when he approached Richard ostensibly to compliment him on a model, really to meet her. "And I only went because Richard wanted me to watch Julie, and I thought, well, here goes two hours out of my life I'll never get back. And then

I met Tom!" Their personal alliance had become professional as well; they had started their own law practice a few years before. They lived in one of the newer suburbs and raised African violets, "real suburbanites – me! the rebel!"; they had no children. "Yet," added Lucy, and Laura noticed that her hand stole to her stomach. Aha!

"So how about you?" Lucy slouched down and propped her feet up on the next chair. "So why were you getting divorced? Tell me all about it."

Laura had started to relax, falling prey to Lucy's artless confidences. She should have remembered how Lucy soothed her prey to the kill. "Just like that? You haven't seen me for years, and that's the first thing you want to know?"

"Sure." Lucy shrugged and finished off her water. "Why not? If you'd been here, I'd know all the whys and wherefores. I'm your sister, remember? Sisters tell each other these things." No better way to start than to go for the jugular. Laura reminded herself to stay alert. "So? What happened?"

"We just didn't want to be married," Laura said blandly. "Most amicable split in history."

Lucy said shrewdly, "I doubt it was as easy as that. He looked like he had an ego, in fact he looked to me like he wrote the book on ego, and you're certainly not as meek and mild as you used to be." She fiddled with her swizzle stick. "How did he get along with Francie?"

Oh, clever Lucy. How could she have forgotten the Byzantine paths of Lucy's mind, her subtle means of extracting information? She decided to stick with a modicum of the truth. "Not well. She thought he was stuffy, and he thought she was a spoiled brat."

Lucy said softly, "Past tense? For him or for her?"

She had seen this coming, but, oh, how it hurt, after her grieving on the Chesapeake, to say it, as if the saying made it real.

"She's dead."

Lucy's shock filled a long silence. She broke it finally with a whisper. "Poor little Francie. Dead. How strange. I never *felt* it, and I thought I would have known.... I wasn't surprised when Di found Dominic dead, I just felt the *absence* of him, but Francie – oh, Laurie, how awful for you. You were so close to her. When?"

The lie fell easily from her lips. "A plane crash. In the Panhandle. She went skiing with some friends, and they went down coming back from Angelfire. It – it was quick, Lucy. She didn't suffer."

"Oh, Laurie." Lucy touched her shoulder, the warmth of her fingers through the cotton gentle and comforting. "Oh, baby, I'm so sorry. She and I didn't get along, that was no secret, but I was always glad that you two had each other. I don't like to think of you being alone all this time."

She repeated, like a talisman, "She didn't suffer."

"Maybe she didn't," said Lucy, and this time it was she who held out her arms, like a mother, like a sister, like the guardian angel she had once been, "but, oh, Laurie, *you* did."

Their tears required another repair job at the mirror. When they returned back to the table, they ordered more mineral water and agreed that they needed privacy. "Not that I don't want to show you off," said Lucy, ushering Laura to her office, "but we may get soggy again, and it's bad for morale to see the boss crying."

Laura glanced at the time. "I'm keeping you, aren't I? Do you have plans for the evening?"

Lucy grimaced and settled down behind the desk. "Yes, we're entertaining one of Tom's clients. I never entertain mine, I just tell him to get what he wants out of the fridge—" She caught Laura's mystified look. "Richard. I do his legal work. He has his own practice too, did he tell you?"

"Yes." Lucy had handed her the perfect opening. "He said that he and Di broke up."

"He did!" Lucy nearly dropped her Perrier. "That's incredible! He *never* talks about her to outsiders. Well, I mean, you're not an outsider, but—"

"I'm an outsider," Laura finished. "That's okay. When did they get divorced?"

"Divorced? They're not divorced."

"What?" She let her astonishment show. What *had* he said about Diana? Not enough, obviously. "I could swear – he said the marriage was dead, he got Julie—"

Lucy laughed shortly. "Dear Richard! Ever tactful. He threw her out years ago."

Laura sat up straight. "Why?"

"A lot of reasons. He was right to do it. She wasn't fit to be around Julie, and he couldn't take it anymore. She pushed him too far."

Richard had thrown Diana out? But it was Richard who had strayed…. It glimmered again, the great unknown, the hidden fissure in the marriage that had led to Francie's triumph over Diana that spring. The affair with Francie had not blown in out of nowhere. Something, sometime, somewhere, had broken the bonds holding Richard and Diana together.

Or maybe you hope that because it's the only way to salvage him.

She asked, "Why aren't they divorced?"

"They're legally separated." Lucy had relaxed again. "It's called divorce from bed and board here in Virginia – they just can't re-marry. Not that Di ever would, but Richard should have remarried years ago. And Julie lives with him. No joint custody."

"Why not?"

"Oh, Lord." Lucy sighed and fiddled with her bottle. "I was hoping to avoid this for a while longer, but I guess you'll find out sooner or later. Di has some very serious problems, and – and she's not always dealt with them well. Plus, Julie is a sweet, darling girl – we do a lot together, we're very close – but she *defines* daddy's girl. It used to be Richard protecting his little girl, but she's sixteen now, and it's more Julie than Richard saying she won't see Di out of loyalty to her father."

She couldn't imagine letting a child, even one nearly grown, making such a decision. One possibility occurred to her; she picked her words cautiously. "Does Di see other men?"

"Good heavens!" Lucy finally relinquished her drink before she dropped it once and for all. "Have you been a fly on the wall all these years?"

"They're separated. It's a logical assumption."

"I guess so. Yes, Di dates around." Lucy wet her finger and drew circles on the desktop. "Not that Richard can throw stones. He's no monk. Oh, don't look so shocked. He's had women. I don't blame him. Why shouldn't he date? He's an attractive man, and for most purposes he's single. He's not treated like a husband, so why should he act like one?"

She remembered – oh, God, how memory betrayed her, that it chose now to thrust upon her the feeling of his arms around her, his hand against her back, the harmony of their bodies. She didn't care how priggish she sounded. "Because he is one, that's why."

Lucy said reflectively, "I think he stopped feeling married after Mom and Dad died. He came back from a trip, and he'd stopped wearing his ring, and to me, that marked the end. Besides," she shrugged, "he's had a hard time with Di, but he hasn't abandoned her, and for that, I'll forgive him anything. She doesn't really want a divorce, you know. She knows she'd lose Julie forever. Did you and your husband fight over Meg?"

"No. There was never any question that Meg stayed with me."

"I've seen custody fights," Lucy said, "and I never saw anything as vicious as the way Di and Richard went after each other when they separated. My God, it was bloody! She started it, Dominic got involved, Mom and Dad filed affidavits against her, I got subpoenaed – and then one day she dropped it. Just dropped it. No explanation, just threw up her hands and said *I surrender* and went her merry way. I'll give Richard credit, he fought for Julie tooth and nail, and he takes good care of her. He's a good father. He may not have been the best of husbands, but then Di hasn't been a sterling wife either."

All this history, all this pain, had lain behind his eyes the night before. And she, absorbed in her own anguish, had not seen it. She drew in a deep breath. "Maybe not, but even if Julie is a daddy's girl, she needs her mother."

"I try," said Lucy. "Richard tries to be all things to Julie, but even he knows that she needs a woman's guidance. Not that it really helps. Julie is sweet and intelligent – with that gene pool, how could she miss – but she's isolated after school hours, living out there in the country. So she's comfortable with adults – you'll find that you can talk to her about anything – but, Lord, is she *young*."

"Meg's just the opposite," said Laura, and silently blessed her daughter. "I'd like her to stay a little girl a while longer, but I think that's a lost cause."

"You're so lucky." Lucy sounded wistful. "What's she like?"

"A miniature Bette Davis." Laura eyed her sister surreptitiously. Her own doomed pregnancies had always glowed in her skin and shone in her hair, but maybe Lucy was different. Or maybe her suspicions were off base. "She's grown up so much in the last year. She used to be very willful and demanding, but now she – well, sometimes, she tries to take care of *me—*"

But any other maternal musings were swallowed up then, by Lucy's sudden lack of attention as her eyes swiveled to the closed door behind Laura, by the faint sound of a pretty voice talking, by the faint squeak of the knob turning and that same sweet voice saying breathlessly, "Okay, Luce, I know you're upset, you're right to be, I'm sorry—"

Then shocked silence, and a scream.

The sound shattered the air. And now she had to move, break the paralysis of this moment, confront the architect of her nightmares.

She had to, because Diana still stood behind her and Lucy sat across from her, stunned frozen, and she could not endure another second waiting for someone to speak.

Laura stood up and looked into the eyes of Francie's killer.

Oh, she had wondered about this, the moment when she would recognize the guilt in Diana's eyes. Eleven years did not suffice to wash away the blood shed by Diana's hands. But she had not known, she had never dreamed, how the shadows had touched Diana, how empty her glittering eyes had become, how old she would look, how sick.

Di, Di! What have you done? Where are you?

She should never have shown her shock, she should have controlled herself better, for Diana's eyes flamed in acknowledgment of that shock, and that pretty voice spat, "You *bitch!* How dare you—"

Laura drew in a breath that rasped her throat, a sound covered by Lucy's quick, "No, no, Di! It's not her, it's Laurie!"

"What?" Diana's attention was arrested. Her forward movement stopped as she snapped around to face Lucy, and just as quickly she swung around to Laura.

And she changed, in the moment of that turn. Laura watched in astonishment, her horror forgotten, as Diana's face lightened and the harsh hatred drained from her eyes. And then Diana moved towards her, and, back against the wall, she felt herself forced into her oldest sister's embrace.

"Laurie!" The old, alluring music had returned to Diana's voice. "Oh, honey! I didn't recognize you, I thought you were Francie!" Laura felt herself snap rigid; she felt the warmth of Diana's breath, the icy condensation of Diana's drink against her blouse, between them. "It's so good to see you! What a shock, I had no idea – when did you get here?"

"Yesterday. I'm glad to be back." She had lost control of her tone. She sounded too effusive, too placating. Too much the younger sister, needing her elders' approval, not enough the survivor of Diana's war with Francie.

"You've grown." Diana held her at arm's length and eyed her critically. "And you dress so much better. I don't remember you wearing anything but jeans. And your hair—"

Of all the things she had thought to discuss with Francie's killer, clothes had not ranked high. Had Diana forgotten that Francie was dead? Sickening thought. "Well, what did you expect?" She laughed shakily. "I'm thirty-one. I couldn't stay a teenager forever."

Wrong thing to say! She'd reminded them that, if their baby sister was thirty-one, they were closer to forty. Annoyance flashed across Diana's face, and Lucy, sitting still across the room, had uncharacteristically drawn into herself.

"You look so grown-up now," Diana recovered gracefully. And before Laura could retort that she *was* grown-up now, a full-fledged adult, her sister moved to the phone. "And I think all this calls for a drink! We need to celebrate your coming home. What will you have, Laurie?"

"Tea?" She couldn't identify the amber drink in Diana's glass.

Lucy came back to life and waved her Perrier bottle at Diana. "Order some food too, Di. You look hungry."

"Oh, I don't need anything, really, I'm not hungry." She sparkled a smile at Laura. "I'm too excited to eat! I'll just have my drink."

"Order something," Lucy repeated, and did not clothe the steel in her voice.

Diana did look hungry. The freshness of skin had given way to a thinness that made her cheekbones stick up unattractively and her eyes sink into her face. Even her hair seemed dull now. Her pupils were dilated; she kept sniffing as if she had a bad cold. *He threw her out…. He was right to do it.*

So one of Diana's "very serious" problems lay in the bottom of a tumbler of Scotch. She had forgotten the DUI arrest report. And the other…. *I've seen this, I know this. Oh, Di, no….*

Lucy ended up ordering for them all. Laura paid her little attention, her eyes fixed on the wraith who perched on the side of the desk and proceeded to launch into an interrogation that even Lucy had not had the nerve to attempt. And, as she asked, as she probed, as her eyes unflinchingly never left Laura, she drained her tumbler.

No *where-have-you-been.* No *why-are-you-here.* No *why-didn't-you-call-us.* And no *where's-Francie.*

Because Diana knew. For all that drama, Diana knew that Francie could never walk in the door.

"*I* want to know about your singing. Daddy almost had a heart attack the first time he heard you. What possessed you? I thought you were training for opera."

"No," said Laura. "Daddy thought I was training for opera."

Diana raised an eyebrow in acknowledgment and nodded; her nod, a shade too deep and quick, almost threw her off balance. Laura was astounded at Lucy's cool indifference – didn't she see how stoned Diana was? "I hear you there. Daddy was always after me about my voice, when all I really wanted to do was study piano. But this techno rock mysticism whatever? You can't imagine what he had to say about that."

Oh, yes, she could. She had read his review. She said carefully, "I know Daddy looked down on classical crossover. I can give you all the usual arguments – I use tried and true compositional patterns, I draw on folklore and mythology for my source material, I'm in the vein of the Romantics – but the truth is I like telling stories through music. I feel lucky that others like it too."

"What are your demographics?" Diana leaned back on one hand and twisted herself around to open a desk drawer with the other, a contortionist's trick that somehow didn't topple her over. "I can't imagine that you really fly with Gen-X or Y or whatever the new Gen is right now."

"Well – no." Laura watched, appalled, as she pulled out a bottle and refilled her glass. "I sell best to baby boomers, especially men. I do very well, don't ask me why, in Scandinavia and Canada and Russia. The fastest I ever sold out was in Iceland. I guess it's all those dark nights."

My God, Di, you keep Scotch in your desk?

Lucy, now off the phone, looked impassively at Laura. "Sure," she said, "they need something to listen to while they're drowning their sorrows over the short days."

She's trying to live with the memory of Francie. And you let it happen.

"But your voice," Diana continued, without missing a beat. "You never sing anything but mezzo now, and you had such a sweet soprano when you were younger! I was shocked the first time I heard you. And Daddy was so mad! He said he'd wasted all that time working on your range—"

"I sing mezzo because that's what I am. I had problems with my voice about ten years ago, and the doctors said I had been straining my vocal cords trying to sing out of my *tessitura*." She did not add, because she did not have to, that she had only attempted coloratura soprano because Dominic had forced her to.

Silence greeted that. Diana looked deep into her glass, and Lucy looked down at the blotter on the desk, not quickly enough to hide the sheen of tears.

"How do you deal with it?" Diana finally broke the stillness, restlessly, rhythmically tapping her shoe against the desk front.

"Deal with what?" Diana's abrupt switches in topic confused her.

"Daddy," said Diana flatly. "What he did. To you. To all of us."

She hadn't prepared for that. Maybe she hadn't really prepared for any of this, or else why did she feel so disoriented? She bit off the instinctive answer, *I don't keep a bottle handy, for starters.* Diana hadn't been joking. "I went to counseling for a few years. I learned a little about myself, that there wasn't anything inherently wrong or – or bad about me, it was him and his obsessions. And – and I just put him out of my mind, as much as I could. I was pretty busy when Meg was little, and by the time she was older – it didn't hurt as much to think about him."

"Meg?" Diana turned back to Lucy with her question.

"Laurie's daughter. Doesn't look like her at all."

"Oh, we have a niece?" Diana refilled her tumbler. "What's her voice?"

"She's in ballet." Laura wondered where the food was; Diana's eyes were glazing over. "She started when she was four. She went *en pointe* last year."

"Ballet!" Lucy leaned forward. "Di – didn't your grandmother do some time in the corps?"

"No." Diana dabbed at her nose with a lace handkerchief. "You're thinking of our great-grandma. She danced in Paris *fin de siècle* – mostly with her clothes off. You probably never heard, Laurie, you know how Daddy was. Mama used to tell me the stories."

Laura knew almost nothing about her mother or her mother's family, since Renée Dane had disappeared into the sea three weeks after her birth. Francie had not remembered her, and the Ashmores had never known her, so Laura had only glimpsed the woman who had given her life through Diana's few memories. She hadn't seen a picture of her mother until she was an adult (Dominic had destroyed all photographs), so she never expected Lucy's next question.

"Have you ever heard from my mother, Laurie?"

"Me?" She didn't bother to hide her surprise. "No. Why would I?"

"We thought you might." Lucy sounded matter-of-fact. "Sometimes, when people become rich and famous, they start hearing from all kinds of forgotten relatives."

"I didn't." She was still stunned from the unexpected broadside. "Maybe she did contact someone, I don't know. If she asked for money – it's entirely possible that Cam got rid of her and never told me. And I don't get my Cat Courtney mail. It goes to an outside firm for scanning."

"Yes, we know," said Lucy dryly. "I have conducted quite a correspondence with them. Did it never occur to you that we might like to hear from you?"

"It was thoughtless, not to say rude, to ignore us," added Diana. "We missed you."

The force of their accusing stares drove her back against her chair. "I wasn't sure I'd be welcome." She wanted to wince at her defensiveness; she had nothing to excuse. "I wasn't before."

And no way on earth was I going to bring Meg back here.

Lucy's head shot up.

"How dare you? Did we ever, either one of us, make you feel unwelcome? Don't you confuse either of us with Dominic – *you* never had *any* reason to think we didn't want you to come home—" And she left her words dangling, weighted with the burden of that unspoken name.

Diana had gone pale, but she managed to whisper through dry lips, "You should have known better. You were silly to think that we would throw you out. Remember that poem Philip always used to recite? Something about home is where when you go there, they have to take you in?"

"Frost," said Lucy. "His favorite. I'm sorry, Laurie. I didn't mean to snap at you, but I don't understand why you ran off like that. I wish you'd tell us."

The invitation hung in the air.

Laura looked at them both. "No."

She'd thrown down the gauntlet, she knew that. She could not gauge how they would react – Diana, clearly stoned, clearly drunk and getting drunker, and Lucy, flexing some familial muscle to see how malleable Laura still was. She sensed a battle of wills even between the two of them, a hint that Diana had not totally surrendered to Lucy.

But Lucy surprised her. "Okay," she said, "you'll tell us in your own good time."

The atmosphere, tense enough at that moment, lightened with a discreet knock and the arrival of a plate of crudités. Lucy abandoned the power struggle and kept a light conversation going. Laura told them about the show in London and life as a working actress; Diana gave her a quick turn around the club that they had bought two years before and remodeled from a bankrupt gentlemen's club, gambling that adult piano bars would come back into fashion. "Maybe we'll turn a profit soon," said Diana hopefully when they returned, and managed to eat an orange slice before she helped herself to another drink.

"We'd better," Lucy sighed. "I'm getting tired of Tom's lectures about cash flow."

"Do you enjoy it, Di?" Laura could not imagine Diana running a business.

Diana shrugged. "Most of the time. It's a good place to meet people." Lucy shot her a curious glance under her lashes, and Laura noticed the coldness Diana volleyed in return. "I handle the entertainment side – you know, line up the acts – and Lucy does the books. I hate that sort of thing."

She had no problem believing that. "Do you ever play here?"

She saw the idea dawning in Lucy's eyes even as Diana shrugged again and said that, no, she wasn't much interested in playing for the clientele. She said, "No, Lucy!" but Lucy paid her no heed.

"Of course! It would be perfect. You're our sister, after all, the one who made it big. Why shouldn't you come and sing for us one night? My God, think of it—"

"No, no, *no*—"

"Cat Courtney herself appearing at the Tavern – we'd make it into the black for sure!" She turned sparkling eyes to her victim. "Come on, you know you'll do it. It doesn't have to be a big deal. You can do the playlist from *Waterfalls*. Di could play for you. Your songs are all arranged for piano."

Still running everyone's lives, Richard had said. "No. I'm on vacation. My manager would have a fit."

"Doesn't he work for you? Or do you work for him?"

"Well, I wonder sometimes. I don't—"

Lucy dismissed all that. "Just one night – that shouldn't interfere with your vacation that much. We'll make it for a charity, sell tables, have a reception and auction afterwards... people love that sort of thing. My God, what a coup!" She pulled a sheet of paper towards her and started writing. "The neonatal wing at the hospital, they're always looking for money. I'll contact them... and I'll work things out with your manager. Give me his number."

She'd argue better with a tank. "But I don't want to."

"Just one performance, Laurie, that's all," Lucy coaxed. "You can't believe how much it would help us. You're big time now, even if this isn't the North Pole. Besides," and she smiled sweetly, "you're our sister. You've cut us out of half your life. Are you really going to turn us down?"

"Lucy—"

"And think of those poor kids – all those crack babies, and the preemies – it'll just break your heart—"

Had Lucy always been such an accomplished blackmailer? Laura turned to Diana for salvation. "Surely you don't want this?"

"Why not?" said Diana, and finished her drink. "It would help the club. I don't mind playing for you, if we can get some decent rehearsal time in."

"Of course." Oh, dear heavens, she was agreeing to this nonsense. They obviously had no idea that Cat Courtney sang with a full orchestra behind her, not one drunk piano player. "No, no, I mean – my manager won't approve it – *Lucy*—"

Lucy lurched to her feet, stumbled across the room to the adjoining bathroom, slammed the door, and audibly threw up.

"What the hell?" Diana began, and started to put down her glass.

Laura didn't wait for her. She thrust past Diana to the closed door and raised her hand to knock, then hesitated until she heard running water and Lucy saying faintly in protest, "I'm all right. Go away."

"Open the door, Lucy."

"What in the world—" Diana swayed behind her, and fell silent when Lucy peeked out again.

If she'd had any doubts about her informal diagnosis, the sight of Lucy, pale, trembling, and too sick to be humiliated, dispelled them. She ignored Lucy's protest and hooked her arm around her sister's waist. "She's okay. Get her a damp cloth, all right? And get out of the way." Lucy was no lightweight. One foot, two – it couldn't really be such a trek back to the desk, but Lucy had gone limp against her, and it took ages to cross the floor.

She managed to deposit her sister back in her chair. Lucy moaned, a quiet little moan with no real backbone, and slumped forward onto folded arms on the desktop. Cool to the touch, Laura noted. She smoothed back Lucy's dark hair and took a dripping cloth from Diana's outstretched hand.

"Here. Raise your head."

Diana hovered while Laura squeezed the cloth into a glass. "I'm almost afraid to ask." The alcohol had fled from her voice. "Are you pregnant again?"

"Again?" Laura looked up in surprise, and barely caught Lucy's weak assent.

"Lucy?" Diana reached over to touch her arm. "How far along?"

They had to strain to hear, "Two months."

"Oh, honestly!" Whatever Laura had expected to hear, it was not such an indignant response. Diana's eyes had lost their dullness and were shining with all the animation of – what *was* she sniffing? Not cocaine, surely, not from a handkerchief, unless she was really extravagant. "Didn't your doctor tell you to wait six months before you tried again? What is the matter with you, are you determined to have a baby or die trying?"

"That's enough." Laura hadn't meant to sound so sharp. "If you're not going to help, sit down and be quiet. Lucy," she bent over her sister, "are you okay now?"

Lucy lifted her head slowly. Laura saw that a little color had begun to stain her sister's face again, and automatically her hand went out again to smooth back the hair from Lucy's forehead. "I'm fine." Lucy's voice gathered strength. "Something just hit me wrong all of a sudden. Maybe it was the fruit."

"More likely, all the tension," Laura said gently. "I know my stomach's been tied in knots all day, and I'm *not* pregnant. Look, should we call Tom and have him come get you? Or I'll run you home, if that's more convenient."

Diana had slumped down into Laura's chair, her arms crossed across her chest. "Yes, call Tom, why don't you? He's going to get a piece of my mind, getting you pregnant so soon—"

"Shut up, Di." Lucy definitely felt better now. She was strong enough to scowl ferociously across the table. "Don't blame Tom. He was just as upset as you when we found out."

"Why should anyone be upset?" Diana and Lucy stopped glaring at each other long enough to turn startled eyes in Laura's direction. She couldn't fathom Diana's antagonism – surely a childless married woman was entitled to get pregnant without her family acting as if she had done something criminal? "I think it's wonderful. When are you due?"

"January," Lucy started, and Diana interrupted.

"It *isn't* wonderful! It's damn dumb, is what it is! January – oh, my God, that'll make it just a year—"

Lucy said quietly to Laura, "All this ranting and raving is because I had a stillbirth last September. The – the baby did live for a few minutes. We named him John for Tom's dad. Then I had another miscarriage in January."

"Oh, Lucy." She hurt for her sister. Her own miscarriages, except for the last, had been fairly early; she had mourned terribly, had blamed herself for her inability to sustain life for those poor flawed embryos. But to lose a baby that you could actually hold in your arms – *oh, Lucy, how do you stand it? I couldn't bear the loss.* She said carefully, "Do they know what happened?"

Diana still sparked angrily. "Yes. Premature labor syndrome. Incompetent cervix. And only a certified idiot would get pregnant again after that, particularly after having three – *three!* – miscarriages in the two years before *that—*"

"All right, so I'm an idiot," Lucy yelled back. "We can't all be Miss Fertility—"

"Cut!" Incredible! She couldn't believe her sisters, spitting and clawing at each other, two mother cats each clawing the other's maternity. "I don't see the point in this," she said more calmly, as Lucy subsided back onto the desktop and Diana slouched down into her chair. "I, for one, am excited, Lucy, being a mom is – it's just the best thing in life."

This is what Richard wouldn't tell me. This is why Lucy was in the hospital. Diana continued to glower, even though deep down she had to be scared stiff. The stillbirth must have been harrowing. No wonder he had written that Diana was falling apart – forget al Qaeda, she had been worried about Lucy.

Hers had not been the only September 11 loss, or the greatest.

She drew in a deep breath and held out her hands to both her sisters. Lucy didn't hesitate but slid her hand under Laura's fingers; she was shocked to feel how fragile Lucy's capable hand felt in her own. Diana wasn't as easy to win over. She pointedly looked beyond Laura's shoulders, and after a few moments, Laura let her hand drop.

Fine. If Diana wanted to sulk, she wouldn't stop her.

She stood up and summoned Cat Courtney's command. "You need to get on home, Lucy. I'll follow you home, if you're up to driving." Lucy nodded, subdued. Laura looked over at Diana, who had reached for her not-quite-empty tumbler. "Give me a call, Di. Here's my cell number. I'll be out at Edwards Lake for a while."

"Edwards Lake?" Diana's head jerked up. "Out near Richard?"

"Right." Storm warnings flew in Diana's eyes again, but she'd had quite enough. "Come on, Lucy, let's go."

Her firmness had thrown her sisters. They were eying her cautiously, unsure how to take a baby sister who had seized the moment. The balance of power had shifted again. Lucy obviously still felt unwell; her protestations were mild, and she put up little resistance as Laura packed her into her car. Diana, trailing behind them, kept a strange silence while Lucy settled herself.

"I'll be right behind you," Laura said, and Lucy nodded tiredly as she pulled the seat belt around her. "I'm in the silver Jag. Keep me in the mirror."

"Before you go," Diana's voice cut through hers, "I want to know something. Where's Francie?"

That nailed the coffin of Laura's patience.

"Diana," she said clearly, and didn't care whether her voice carried, whether the patrons now arriving for cocktail hour heard her or recognized her, "this isn't the time or place to discuss Francie. We'll talk later."

She thought she heard "Thank God" from inside the car, but she ignored Lucy. She felt in control now, fixing Diana with all the strength of her stage presence and watching as Diana straightened up and visibly fought her way past the alcoholic mists. She was angry, angry that Diana dared bring Francie up, angry that she had forgotten that Francie could never laugh and argue with them again. Angry because, for this hour, she had not remembered how Diana had won the war.

"No, I want to know now," Diana persisted. "You don't want to talk about you, fine, don't! But I want to know. Where is she? Why did she run away?"

If she hadn't spent that wild hour mourning on the sands of the Chesapeake, she might have forgiven her. She might have listened to Diana and wondered, she might have seen the questioning in Diana's face, but she never would have turned on her.

But she had mourned, and now she lost her temper.

"How dare you! Why do you think she ran away? You caught her with Richard that day, you screamed at her like a fishwife, you damn near gave her a concussion, and all this when he'd already broken it off, so you had what you wanted anyway! You tell me, Di, why do you *think* she ran away?"

Impossible to catch those words back, impossible not to see the horror and pain draining her older sister, impossible not to realize, too late, the slamming impact of her anger in the pallor that spread across Diana.

"At long last," Lucy murmured, almost to herself, but Laura could not turn to her.

"Di?"

She moved towards Diana, but it was Diana's turn now to retreat, to avoid her touch. She would have given anything at that moment, anything, to draw the pain from her sister's eyes. Diana said nothing. She only backed up, and backed up, until she stumbled. Then, with what might have been a sob, she turned and ran back into the club.

"Oh, my God." Laura sagged against the car. "What did I say?"

Lucy said slowly, "Only what no one else has."

"I don't understand." She was shaking in reaction. Somewhere in Diana's shock and Lucy's calm acceptance lay some key whose existence she hadn't suspected.

Lucy drummed her fingers against the wheel. The sound, slight as it was, slivered Laura's already fragmenting nerves.

"Francie slept with Richard the spring before you ran away, right?"

She hadn't thought that anyone would doubt that. But the last few seconds had taught her a tardy caution. "I can't say—"

"Oh, yes, you can," Lucy interrupted. "You knew if anyone did, and I don't think they were particularly discreet. Francie wanted Di to find out, and Richard no longer cared. Oh, he was a damn fool, he never could see that Francie meant trouble, but I will give him credit. He kept his mouth shut. We've all suspected, and Di's asked, and I've asked, but Richard has never said anything. Not a word. Ever."

"No. *No*—"

"That's right." Lucy let her absorb the impact. "Di's never known for sure."

"Until now." The thought made her ill.

"Until now," Lucy agreed.

The sun set as Laura walked along the far side of the ornamental lake towards Ashmore Magna, out of sight of the Folly. This time, she did not worry that he might catch sight of the silver car from the glints of the dying sun; she had parked the Jaguar out on the public road half a mile down and hacked her way through the gate passwords with only two tries. Why she was behaving like a lovesick girl, she did not begin to justify to herself.

She just wanted to be near him.

This is called stalking, my girl.

The binocular bag bumped along her hip as she skirted the north end of the lake and briefly came into view of the Folly. His car was parked in the front circular drive, and windows shone on the first story, so she had to be careful that he didn't look out and catch sight of her. She walked rapidly through the front gardens – hard to tell, in the gathering shadows, if Richard was keeping up his mother's pride and joy – and mounted the steps to the front portico of Ashmore Magna.

The front door was locked, and she had long since lost the key Peggy had once given her. *Take this, Laurie. If you ever need to come over here – for any reason at all – you come. If we're not home, wait for us.* Peggy putting the key into her palm, and closing her hand around it. *There's no need to tell your da about this, do you agree?*

She wondered where the key had gone. She'd worn it on a chain around her neck, hidden beneath her blouse, for several years.

She did not spare any time for the famous pillar tonight. Instead, she walked to the end of the portico, then walked down two steps and up three to the southern Venetian porch at the side of the house. At some time – probably during the reign of the Great Lakes shipping heiress, the Edwardian trophy wife whose fortune had kept Ashmore Park going for the last century – the Ashmore family had added an enclosed piazza off the master suite, and *that* she remembered how to get into. Richard had showed her one day when it was pouring down rain.

She lifted the handle to the French doors and carefully shifted it slightly to the right, and success! The door swung open. She stepped inside.

Breaking and entering. How many more crimes are you going to commit tonight?

She sat down on a cushioned bench beneath one of Peggy's hanging baskets and drew a deep breath.

Ashmore Magna. Sanctuary. House of light and laughter and love and safety.

A home built on Philip's quiet strength and Peggy's warm Irish lilt and open arms.

She had so many memories here, and across the years, they still warmed her.

When she was ten, Peggy had brought her out here one afternoon and explained to her the changes that would soon happen to her body. Always the nurse, she had taken a down-to-earth approach that Laura had tried to emulate when it came time to tell Meg. A year later, Peggy had judged it time to tell her about sex before she heard the wrong thing from her classmates, and Laura had listened with eagerness and horror – surely no one really *liked* doing that? It was, said Peggy reassuringly, the grandest thing in the world when you were in love beyond all thought. It had occurred to her later, going home, that Richard and Diana must be having sex when he climbed the tree to her bedroom at night.

No doubt that Richard and Diana were in love beyond all thought. But she knew better than to ask Peggy, who would not, Laura thought, have liked hearing that her son was engaging in behavior so risky to his future.

In that master bedroom on the other side of the inner French doors, Diana had dressed for her wedding, her sisters fluttering around her. With the mother of the bride dead, the mother of the groom had drawn double duty, and Peggy had done her part, even though, in retrospect, Laura remembered, her lips had been uncharacteristically tight. That hadn't kept her from crying when her son walked her to her seat in the front row and then took his place to wait for his bride.

Laura crossed her arms on the window rail and looked out towards Richard's house.

A few years later, in front of the same mirror, Peggy had hemmed one of Diana's dance dresses for her so that she had something to wear to her junior prom. She hadn't planned to go – she had been so shy that boys tended to overlook her – but at the last moment, the equally shy Neil Redmond had asked her out. His mother was one of Peggy's garden club friends, and the moms had cooked it up between them. Peggy had helped her get ready, showing her how to put her hair up in a French twist, and Philip had taken her picture, knowing that Dominic would never think to do so.

When she and Neil had continued to date that summer, Peggy had taken her aside to remind her that premarital sex was a sin and she should wait for her husband on her wedding night when it would be right in the eyes of God. *Oh, Peggy, what a total hash I made of that.* She had been mortified; the weekend before, she had let Neil slip his hand inside her bra. And she had felt put upon. Her sisters hadn't obeyed the rules, so why should she?

Two days before she left home, she had come to see Peggy for the last time. Philip had been on rounds at the hospital, so she had missed him, but at least she and Peggy had shared one last cup of tea.

She wished – oh, how she wished – that her last words to Peggy had not been a lie. *I'll be over next week to help you plant the hyacinths.* Knowing that, by that time, she would be a continent away.

I miss you, Peggy. I wish – I wish you could know your granddaughter.

Richard ran across her line of sight, about fifty feet away.

She pulled back into the shadows, although of course he couldn't see her. It was too dark in the piazza, and he wasn't paying attention anyway. She trained the binoculars on him. He was jogging, judging from the running shoes and headphones, following the drive around the lake. And, the wicked part of her couldn't help noticing, he looked just as good from the back as he did from the front.

So he still ran. He had run track in high school. The basketball team had tried to recruit him, but Richard had preferred a more solitary sport that did not interfere with his studies.

He disappeared around the curve of the lake.

The stars began to appear in the indigo of the twilight.

She still remembered all the constellations. Long ago midnights, she and Richard had accompanied Philip down to the James for stargazing; Diana, refusing to face the mosquitoes, had gladly ceded her place to Laura, and Francie had not been invited. Through the lens of the telescope he and his father had built, Richard had shown her worlds – lunar craters, rings of Saturn, sister stars of the Pleiades, galaxies pin wheeling through space….

Such a rich texture he had, even as a boy. Whether it came from a youth steeped in the history of a family living on the same land for three hundred years, or from the books that he read so passionately, he had grown up like no other young man she had ever known. The social recognition his looks and intelligence might have won for him from his peers, he had shrugged away; he had devoted himself to Diana early on, and the time he spared from her and his studies, he spent in developing a rich inner life. He'd bypassed normal teenage activities to build his telescope, learn to fly, sketch the old houses to determine the secrets of their structures.

He'd developed ideas that did not always sit well with his elders. Early in his teens, the erstwhile altar boy had stopped accompanying his parents to church, declaring that God had walked away from the universe. Peggy had been horrified for fear that her boy was going to hell; Philip, amused, said it was mild for teenage rebellion; Dominic had said darkly that godlessness was no more than he had expected of *that boy*. Later, a brief infatuation with the philosophies of Ayn Rand had provoked outright laughter from Philip. His plan to take

Diana backpacking in the Smokies before he left for college had caused such uproar from all the parents, who were afraid that they would run off and get married, that Diana, no athlete, had happily waved her boyfriend off on his adventure and stayed home.

An explorer of worlds, of the inner universe. Once, fresh from reading *The Fountainhead*, she'd told Richard that she fancied him as Roark. Richard, always the straight arrow, had laughed and said that he hoped she didn't think he had a superman complex. Of course, she never told him that she saw herself as Dominique. What if he'd laughed? Worse, what if he'd remembered the famous bedroom scene that had so thrilled her that she could practically recite it word for word?

She would have been humiliated beyond salvage.

She waited a long time before he ran by again.

By the time he emerged from the trees and paused on the steps to the Folly, fingers against his jaw to measure his heartbeat, it was completely dark. She saw light when the front door opened briefly, and knew that there was little chance he would see her the rest of the evening. It was safe to go closer.

Stalking, Laura. Stalking. How would you like it if someone did this to you?

She ignored her inner voice.

She followed his path around the lake, walked through the grove lining the road to the Folly, and settled down against a tree at the end of the drive. From here, she could see two sides of the house – the front and the western side, dominated by an enormous bank of windows that took up most of the surface of the wall. She trained the binoculars on the window, lit by a diffuse light from somewhere beyond her sight in the house, but nothing happened for a long time. He was probably showering after his run.

She would *not* think about Richard in the shower.

Determined to discipline her mind, she made it a game to name the stars showing up in the June evening sky. She had just found brilliant Vega in the Summer Triangle when a movement at the window caught her attention.

She saw him pass by, turn on a desk lamp, lean over a computer screen that instantly flashed up colored graphics. A slanting board – a drafting table? – cut off part of her view. He appeared over the board, his shoulders moving; he must be working on a design.

And, oh, he looked so good, looking down intently at his work, reaching up to adjust his glasses, taking a sip from a mug. She shouldn't be thinking that. She shouldn't be thinking how her heart had tripped at the sight of him jogging by. She should be thinking of the pain in Diana's eyes, her utter hopelessness as she had run back into the club. She should be thinking of Francie sleeping forever in the depths of the Chesapeake. But here, now, watching him, seeing his concentration, watching him lift his head and stare off in thought, seeing the satisfaction of a solution flash across his face, she could only think how much she had loved him.

Remember Francie, remember Di, remember….

I must be the wickedest, most perverse woman in the world.

His concentration broke at one point. He turned his head and said something, and Laura leaned sideways to see if she could catch sight of Julie. But Julie, just out of sight, frustrated her; Laura glimpsed only the hint of a radiant ponytail and the blue-jeaned curve of a pretty teenage figure.

Reward! Richard laughed, and all stress fled his face. He reached out. Julie moved in towards him, into the curve of his waiting arm, and he hugged her in close.

She barely saw his loving, teasing smile, for the tears misting her eyes.

He's a good father.

Dominic had never smiled at her with such love.

Julie said something and motioned towards the desk. He turned then, and his back masked his movements from Laura, until he lifted something to his ear and she saw that he was using the telephone. After a minute, he shook his head and replaced the receiver. She wasn't home, Laura surmised, and did not want to face her jealousy.

He's not treated like a husband, so why should he act like one?

Julie pointed back at the drafting table, as if to say, *Get back to work, Dad,* and Laura noticed in amusement that Richard did just that. Julie herself disappeared, then reappeared at the front side of the house, opening double glass doors into an atrium to expose a room with a baby grand in front of a wall of etched glass. For a moment she stood there, not more than a few yards away, and then she turned and sat down at the piano, her back to Laura.

Laura had to strain to hear the music through the open doors of the atrium. Something classical, she thought, and she appreciated the depth of her niece's skill; Julie's hands flew over the keyboard surely, knowingly. She switched her binoculars back to Richard and caught him watching Julie, with a look that battered at her defenses.

Later, Richard made another phone call; again, he was out of luck. He shrugged and buckled down to work, and Laura began to hate the woman occupying his thoughts.

But impossible to resent Julie, playing her heart out. She finally heard enough to identify the *Pathetique*, third movement, and knew that Julie had inherited Diana's great skill. She wished she dared to move closer, dared to walk through the open doors and request entrance, dared to hear for herself if Julie had inherited Richard's great passion.

But she had locked herself out fourteen years before.

She brushed at her eyes and lifted the glasses again. She watched as Julie played, as Richard's pencil stopped moving, as he turned his head to smile at his daughter.

Lucky, lucky Julie. A beloved daughter of a loving father. Like Meg; like Diana and Francie. Only she had known the cold whip of a father's voice.

She couldn't stand any more. It hurt too much, reminded her of too many past rejections, too many times when Dominic had given his attention to Francie. She had only been Francie's shadow, after all.

For Dominic, for Richard, for them all.

As she turned to leave, she saw Richard lifting the phone.

Later, Laura sat out on the balcony and stared out over the lights on the Atlantic. Rachmaninoff poured through her headphones, shutting out the gaiety of Saturday night. It did not quite shut out the ringing of the telephone behind her.

Mark, she supposed. He had told her to check in, and she had forgotten. In the depths and heights of this incredible day, Mark had slipped away from her memory. The life she had built with his brother, and now had to build without him, his own power over her present and his plan for the future he wanted with her, seemed like the remnants of an unremarkable dream.

She thought about Diana.

She wondered where her sad, lost sister was tonight. Still at the club, most likely. She crossed her arms on the balcony railing and wondered how Diana, once-lovely Diana, was coping with the day's revelations, shut away from that circle of love Richard had built for himself across the river.

He threw her out.

We're going to kill her.

Lucy, left to deal with the wreckage of Francie's revenge, unaware of the true demons from which Diana fled…. She thought of Lucy's careful neutrality about her pregnancy, about John who had died and Meg who had lived, and it came to her then that she would do anything for her sisters.

If it meant giving a concert, so be it.

If it meant not seeing Richard…. She'd told him she didn't want to see him, and she had meant it for at least ten minutes after she'd stalked away from him in the lobby last night. She thought of Diana's dazed eyes and Francie's spilled blood, and she hardened her heart against him. She thought of Julie smiling at him, and she wanted nothing so much as to walk again into his arms.

She sat late into the night, listening to her music, ignoring the telephone that continued to ring until eleven. Only then did she remember that it couldn't have been Mark; he had taken Meg to a baseball game.

She rang voice mail for her messages, and then she knew who had not answered her phone.

9

Diana, Beginning

I STOPPED KEEPING A JOURNAL years ago.

I don't like to write things down. Once it's in writing, it's real somehow; it has an existence that can't be denied. It becomes truth. And I'm no good with the truth, never have been.

My lawyer gave me a yellow pad last night and told me to start making notes on everything that happened between Richard and me, to help us build our case for getting what I want out of him. I asked why, and Kevin said I was going to need something more than Francie.

I asked if I could use a recorder. I'm used to recording thanks to Daddy. So Kevin gave me this digital recorder.

I much prefer recording. If I say the wrong thing, or I decide I don't feel like Kevin hearing the deepest, darkest secrets of my soul, I can just hit that delete button, and poof! The file is erased from the memory card, and it's like I never said it. If I never said it, then it didn't happen. Isn't technology wonderful?

So now I have this dilemma that's a long time coming. What's truth, and what's a lie? What really happened, and what did I fib about to get out of a jam?

Perhaps I should write down the lies to keep them straight. I actually do a pretty good job, but sometimes it gets to be such a strain, trying to remember which story I told Daddy and which one I told Richard, not to mention the thousands of lies I've told Lucy.

The more I think about this, the more I think I'll do it just for myself. Seeing Laura again has brought back a flood of memories. Since Francie appears to be among the missing – wonder what happened there, note to self, ask Lucy – Laurie is now the only other person on earth who knows how it was to grow up in that house. From her words – *no, Daddy thought I was training for opera!* – her memories are as dark as mine. But she'll never say anything. You can bet that Miss Cat Courtney doesn't want the world to know that, for all intents and purposes, she grew up as an abused child. She'll take that to her grave.

But I don't want to take it all to my grave. I want the truth to come out someday – Mama's death, Daddy's obsession, my marriage. There's definitely one truth that should come out, but I want to control the timing on that, to minimize the fallout. Maybe I should start trying to remember everything, so that someday when I'm old and gray, I can write my memoirs and set the record straight.

I can see it now.
Memoirs of a Golden Girl Gone Bad?
The Broken Bride?
Two Men Too Many?
Just Leave Me Alone?

So where should I start?

I'll start with me, Diana.

My name is Diana Renée Dane-Abbott Ashmore. I am the oldest daughter of Dominic Abbott, ex-monk, and Renée Dane Marlowe, Countess of Shilleen, and when I was five years old, I watched as my father let my mother drown off the coast of Ireland.

Maybe not a good place to start… okay, let's try this. I am the wife of Richard Patrick Ashmore, master of Ashmore Park, God's gift to architecture, and all-around Mr. Perfect. I married him eighteen long, long years ago, and for the last seventeen, we've hardly spoken to each other.

Oops! Well, that's laying it on the line. But is being Mrs. Richard Ashmore me? Isn't that the problem, that it never has been me?

So who am I? Let's see….

I really like this wine. This is fun. I should have done this years ago.

I've always thought I'd make a good hermit.

I read somewhere that women are never hermits because they have an enduring need for companionship and bonding. Nonsense! I could be perfectly happy with my piano, my house, my own company. If I could do anything in the world, anything at all, I'd escape to a desert island and lie in the sun staring at the clouds.

Or go live in a nice little place in Paris. Sleep with a man now and then. Drink some wine (okay, so I do that already, probably a lot more than I should, and truth to tell, I sleep with a man now and then too – also probably more than I should). Play the piano! And never sing another note as long as I live.

The sleeping with a man is important, and so is the "now and then." I do like men, and I do like snuggling up to a warm male body on occasion. Despite what Mr. Perfect believes, because his entire world view is founded on thinking the worst of me, I am *not* a sex-crazed slut stumbling from bed to bed in search of the perfect orgasm. I've had some good lovers in my life, one more than a little good, but I can take or leave sex. Mostly leave it.

Well, that's not the only thing Richard is wrong about, is it?

So where are we? Oh, yes, I am a musician! A *pianist*. Mark that, because it is important. I am not the second coming of Renée Dane, soprano. My mother was one of the great Medeas in opera history, and from the time Daddy retrieved me from the foster home where my sisters and I lived while he was on trial for her murder, he intended me to wipe her memory out. Diana Abbott would take Renée Dane's place on the opera stage, his own created star. From that moment, everything in my life, every waking moment of every day, was orchestrated to bring about the desired result. I learned languages. I worked on posture and breathing. I followed a prescribed regimen of exercises every day, because a good singer stays in shape (contrary to all that you hear about heavy-chested sopranos). I practiced two hours on the piano and endured two hours of voice lessons – and that was on school days! You can imagine how hellish weekends and holidays were.

And everything went according to plan, until the usual happened. Girl met boy, and….

That's true on the surface. But I don't think it's the true me. Why doesn't it feel true?

Probably because truth is not what my life is about.

All right, here's truth for you.

My life has revolved around two men.

My father. I think of him, and all I remember is: *I want.*

I want you to practice more.

I want that perfect high E.

I want my star.

I want her back.

He never stopped wanting from me. My voice, my talent, my soul. And I never satisfied him. How could I? I wasn't my mother, not by a long shot. I just looked like her. I didn't sing like her, I didn't have her ambition. I just knew how to please men in bed, like her. Face it, in the end, isn't that all she was really known for?

Well, that and getting killed.

And my second male nexus. Richard. Did I love him ever? I certainly had every reason to, and he had every reason to expect that I did. He was my escape, my savior, and who wouldn't love a savior? Especially one who looked (*looks*) like that.

But I think of Richard, and all I remember is: *I want.* He never stopped wanting either – not for a long time. Jailers don't always carry keys, or even chain you to an operatic score and make you practice until you're so tired you can't even remember what language you're singing in. Sometimes they place the bars of expectation around you. Sometimes they jail you with a wedding ring and "wife." Or, worse, with a baby in your belly, when all you want is to be young.

I want you to love me.

I want you to be my wife.

I want you to be the mother of my children.

I want you to be satisfied with our life together.

Did I love my father, tyrannical, charming, manipulative, utterly and completely selfish? Oh, yes. I was my mother's daughter. No matter what he did, I feared him, I adored him.

Did I love Richard, handsome, intelligent, courteous, the answer to a maiden's prayer? No. I was my father's daughter. Most of the time, I just wanted to smash his face in.

10

Blood Between Us, Love

SHE'D SAID THAT SHE NEVER wanted to see him again.

And how often had she told Meg to be careful what she asked for?

Monday saw Laura moved into Edwards Lake. Her clothes were stored in the armoire, her linens put away in a lovely cedar-lined closet, her Kurzweil and laptop plugged in, her music set out on the piano. Tuesday, she had one expected delivery – Max, her cat, whose indignation at his flight from Texas she assuaged with generous helpings of tuna – and one unexpected delivery – a bouquet of daisies and baby's breath left at her back door. *Can't wait to meet you, Aunt Laura! You're the best! Love, Julie.* Wednesday, she welcomed two expected guests, Lucy and Tom, for dinner – and one unexpected guest, Diana, who showed up in time for dessert.

"The club can spare me for an hour," Diana said defensively to Lucy's pointed look.

Dinner might have been fun, if only Diana hadn't morosely withdrawn into herself. Laura kept no liquor on hand, so Diana substituted numerous trips to the powder room and kept quiet the rest of the time. If she seemed subdued, Laura thought, it was because Tom Maitland had very little use for her, and she knew it.

Laura liked Tom on sight. He hadn't the charm Cam had turned on and off at will, and next to Richard he suffered both in height and devastating good looks. He looked what he was – a lawyer sliding towards forty, a middle-of-the-road citizen with sandy hair, conservative clothing, and a kind manner. Kind above all. He didn't wait for Lucy to perform introductions; he came towards Laura, took her in his arms, and kissed her cheek. "Welcome home, Laura. You've been missed." Then a grin. "Can I have your autograph?"

"As many as you want."

Tom adored Lucy. How nice to see after eight years of marriage, Laura thought wistfully, watching him reach for his wife's hand. She and Cam had *never* looked so at each other, had never talked and touched and so eagerly bonded together. Not for Lucy and Tom, the long awkward silences at dinner, the welcome relief of the phone ringing or a child's intrusion. Lucky Lucy. She'd found a man to laugh with.

"Now about the benefit," Lucy interrupted her thoughts, and enthusiastically dug into her mint chocolate chip ice cream as if she hadn't spent the day laid out by morning sickness.

"Okay." Lucy didn't want her just to write a check; her sister wanted her to actually invest herself, to atone for the fourteen years of silence. "I'll do it."

"Great," said Lucy. "Let's start making plans. How long are you here for?"

They settled on a date a week before Laura's expected return to London to prepare for the tour ("Maybe if I'm really good," said Lucy, "I'll still fit into my evening clothes," and Tom pretended to miss the disgusted look Diana roused herself enough to send his way). Laura handed her a proposed playlist, as close to the tour program as she could legally get, and offered to polish up a new song for a world premiere. They discussed financing, publicity, logistics – matters Cat Courtney never dealt with herself – and, as they talked, Laura noticed that Diana's interest slipped away by the minute.

"Do you still want to do this?" she finally asked her sister.

"What?" Diana woke up. "Oh, sure. Just get me the music so I can start work."

Less than a whole-hearted endorsement, but Diana didn't seem prepared to offer more. Laura gave them her standard contract; she wanted protection against the vagaries of an owner whose mood depended on the contents of a bottle and her ubiquitous handkerchief. Maybe Diana divined her reasoning, for she insisted on writing her accompaniment into the contract, and Lucy said, "Good. Now you can't bail out of this."

Whether she meant Diana or Laura, she didn't specify.

By the time the evening wrapped up, Lucy and Tom had hammered out a proposal to submit to Laura's manager, Diana had made two more trips to the powder room that had cheered her up considerably but induced another attack of the sniffles, and Laura felt torn between fury and fear of what she would find once they left.

Diana came to life only at the door, with a shriek. "What's that?"

"That" weighed fourteen pounds and was waving the plumed tail he was so proud of. Laura laughed and scooped him up. "This is Max, my best friend and soul mate. Max, meet family."

But Diana was backing away, real panic in her face. "My God, it's a cat."

Out of some recess of her mind came a picture: Diana, stranded on a chair, hysterically crying, while below her a wide-eyed calico sat and washed its paws. "Oh, Di, I'm sorry, I forgot. Here, Lucy, take him—"

Diana was wheezing now, hyperventilating, eyes fixed on Max in fear, even as Lucy bundled the miscreant, over vociferous protests, into the drawing room. Laura ignored Tom rolling his eyes and drew Diana out onto the veranda. "Come on, Di, he's in the house, he can't get to you—"

She spent a lot of time nursing her sisters, she thought, even as she smoothed Diana's damp forehead and patted her back.

Her words must have penetrated Diana's haze, for her sister came to herself once she realized they were outside, that a solid oak door stood between her and Max. Her gasps slowed down. "I'm sorry," she managed between hard breaths. "Of course you have a cat. I know it's stupid—"

"Not everyone likes cats," Laura said soothingly. "It's all right."

A trace of moonlight glimmered through the trees and washed out the lines of fear. With her breathing returning to normal, Diana looked more alert than she had all evening. "Julie will like him. She loves animals."

Had she screamed out an obscenity, she couldn't have startled Laura more, and she saw it. A measuring look came into her eyes. "Haven't you met Julie yet? Lucy said you'd talked to Richard."

"No," said Laura, thinking rapidly. She sensed danger in admitting to that evening with Richard; she wanted to head Diana off as quickly as possible. "I called over there, and no one answered."

"Oh, they're not there. Richard's out of town." They turned around at Lucy's voice from the open door. "Julie's staying with the McIntires until he gets back."

"Why isn't she with you?" Diana said sharply.

"She has a cold. I couldn't afford the risk at this stage."

So no use looking for him, no use hoping that he would turn up at the door. At the moment, Laura would have liked him to materialize, so that he could look into Diana's devastated eyes and see the damage he and Julie had done.

She said flatly, "Why isn't she with *you*, Di?"

Out of the corner of her eye, she saw Lucy frown and shake her head.

"Oh, God forbid!" Diana showed surprising animation. "I might corrupt her – I'm certainly not the parent Mr. God Almighty Perfect Ashmore is. Just ask him! My God, she's sixteen, what does he think I'll do to her—"

"Di," Lucy's voice cut right through her words. "Come on now, we've been over this time after time. Laurie, don't start anything with her. She knows better. Richard's within his rights, and the courts back him up. Until you straighten up," she punctuated her words with a sharp glance at Diana's handkerchief, "he's not going to change his mind."

So Richard and Diana had already been to court. But, of course, she remembered Lucy talking about a long-ago custody battle. *My God, it was bloody! I never saw anything as vicious....*

Diana said bitterly, "Julie is nowhere near as innocent as everyone thinks. And she needs her mother. Oh, I know," she gestured towards Lucy, "you do everything you can, Luce, but you've got your own baby to think about now. Richard can't rely on you to mother Julie forever. Honestly, what does he think I'll do, hand her a bottle of Scotch and tell her bottoms up?"

So Diana understood her own terrible problems. Laura thought of asking if she might expose Julie to the fine white grains that no doubt now decorated the downstairs powder room, and then stopped before she could voice the thought. She saw the bravado on Diana's face; she heard the tremor in her voice that admitted that she did not stand on the moral high ground that she would have preferred. She saw, too, the desolate chill in Diana's eyes; she heard the real grief underlying her words.

How much had Diana's loneliness, child of Richard's separation of mother from daughter, brought her to this sorry pass?

"How long has it been since – no," Laura held up her hand as she saw Lucy open her mouth. "No, Lucy, I want to know. Di, when did you last see Julie?"

"Oh, God." Diana thought. "Christmas, maybe?"

And they stood now in the middle of June. Almost six months. She thought of going six months, six weeks, without seeing Meg. She wasn't doing well after little more than six days.

"Do you really want to see her, Di? I mean, for her sake, not just for yours?"

"Laurie." Lucy sounded pained. "Don't push this. You don't want to get involved, believe me. This isn't a good thing to get in the middle of."

She ignored that. "Di?"

But Diana had drifted out of hearing.

Surely Diana could stay on the straight and narrow long enough to keep her daughter for a few days. And if Julie herself balked – well, Richard must know that no teenage girl was mature enough to realize how much, someday, she would regret spurning her mother.

Cam would have torn me apart if I ever kept Meg from him.

She looked at Diana, fumbling for her keys in the moonlight, and she said softly, "You'll see your daughter, Di. I'll make sure of that."

Tom Maitland showed his steel the next day.

"I'm sorry to bring this up," he said, after a few preliminary thank-yous for dinner. "I overheard you talking to Diana last night. Laura, you need to stay out of this."

She'd had the night to rethink her words. It had struck her that, if Cam had indulged in recreational drugs instead of recreational women, she would not have been generous in sharing custody. As Lucy had said, Richard was well within his rights; he'd no doubt resent her interference, and rightly so.

"I'm sorry, Tom," she apologized. "I know it's none of my business—"

"No," and she understood then what made Tom Maitland a fine lawyer. "It's not. I know you're new back in the family, and I realize you don't understand what's been going on. I'll tell you now, and I expect you to do as I tell you. Don't interfere in this. Richard will cut you to ribbons, and he'll have my wholehearted support. Diana is trying to provoke a fight with him, and she is using Julie because she knows damn well that Julie is the most precious thing in the world to him and he'll do anything and make any concessions to keep her safe."

No one had spoken to Cat Courtney like that in years, and Laura St. Bride knew perfectly well she deserved it. She said softly, "I understand, Tom. I have a daughter of my own."

"I know you do." Tom was unrelenting. "Be very clear on one

thing, Laura. You're important to us, but Richard and Julie are family, and you're an outsider. This family will survive this only if we mind our own business."

Laura was grateful that he couldn't see the burning in her cheeks. "Okay."

"Good." Tom obviously had no intention of letting up on her. "I like you, Laura. I always thought I would, from hearing about you all these years, and I'm happy to see you home—"

"Thank you—"

"But get in the way of my client," said Tom relentlessly, "and – fair warning – I'll mow you down. I may be your brother-in-law, but I am also Richard Ashmore's lawyer, and my client comes first."

She couldn't wait to hang up.

Laura spent the rest of the week alone, exploring her new home, switching bedrooms after one night in an exceedingly uncomfortable horsehair bed. Lucy took her to lunch Thursday to show her off to a client who had agreed to underwrite the concert, and Diana called once just to chat. Neither of them mentioned Julie.

She loved being alone, but Meg's absence left a hole in her heart.

The loneliness of not being part of Meg's everyday life hit worst in the evenings. She had never felt so emotionally severed from her daughter. Even the nightly calls didn't diminish her sense of isolation. Meg belonged to Laura St. Bride, and more and more Laura St. Bride was vanishing into the past, more and more Laura Abbott became the present.

Her sense of distance didn't carry over the line. Meg chattered on as she always had, supremely confident that her mother wanted to know every detail of every day. She did, she did, and she didn't even mind that the price to pay for sharing Meg's day long distance lay in Mark's attempts, even now, to help her run her life. He quizzed her mercilessly. What security did she have at Edwards Lake, what was she thinking, doing a benefit concert while she was supposed to be on vacation, had she seen *that man* yet?

She lied.

Edwards Lake was a showcase. Even the virtual tour on the web site had not shown the full beauty of the polished Chippendale staircase, the etched glass half-lights over the doors, the soft lushness of the bedroom she finally chose. She found Richard's restoration notes in the house guidebook and saw his touch in every corner. Absent he might be, but his work surrounded her. When Mark asked the inevitable question, she considered telling him: *I live in a house he restored, I sleep in a sensuous bedroom he calls his favorite, I cook in a replica of the kitchen at Ashmore Magna, where Peggy taught me to make cookies for him. And he lives only four miles from me. He haunts me, just as Cam always feared he did. But, no, I haven't seen him since last week. Satisfied?*

Friday, she buckled down to work. The drawing room held the grand piano she had requested, an exquisitely tuned Steinway, and she spent the morning losing herself in her classical heritage. The romance of *Sleeping Beauty*, the drama of the *Polovetsian Dances*, the mathematical beauty of Bach…. No flat neighbor complained; no Meg interrupted. Eventually, she slipped into contemporary favorites, adding her considerable projection to a makeshift medley to warm up her voice after ten days away from practice.

The exercise of playing jarred loose a tune from her subconscious, and she switched on her digital recorder and laptop. She played for hours, pausing occasionally to scribble down an idea in her music journal and just as often to throw the wadded page to the floor. Max, coming in to remind her about dinner, allowed her to distract him temporarily by running to catch the paper balls she threw across the room. The tune was trash, of course. She had learned over the years that she always produced a certain amount of drivel before her subconscious would allow her to get serious.

But at least she was writing again! She felt back on track, words and emotions flowing through her like a stream.

Max tolerated another hour of "Just a sec" and "I know, I know" and absent-minded pats on the head. Then, as the shadows in the room deepened and she showed no signs of moving towards the kitchen, he took drastic action and rubbed his cold, wet nose across the back of her legs.

That got results.

"Ugh!" Laura pushed him away, but he had her attention now, and he repeated his cold sweep across her skin. She forestalled a third go-round by picking him up and ruffling his mane. "Okay, okay, you've heard enough, haven't you, baby? Ready for dinner?"

Max nipped at her shoulder.

"I get it." She put him down and followed him through the long hall that connected the kitchen annex to the main house. *The first step to updating Edwards Lake lay in connecting the heart of the modern family home to its living area*, per the architect; the second had obviously lain in the recreation of the kitchen where he and she had spent some of their happiest hours.

She dished out tuna and eggs for Max, cheered on by loud purrs and tail rubs against her ankles. She managed to get chicken seasoned and under the broiler for her own supper before he lifted his attention from his bowl. Then, when he raised his face after a minute, he showed none of his usual interest in her food. His nose twitched reflexively – no use letting those smells go to waste – he froze suspiciously; his ears flattened. Probably some bird noises that she couldn't hear, she figured, and she paid only scant attention. He looked around, then jumped up on the table by the large picture window and brushed aside the curtains.

"Get down, Max." She couldn't risk claw marks on the old trestle table.

His tail waved in response.

"*Down!*" She put down the paring knife and approached the window.

Then she heard it too, very faintly in the distance, the sound of horses' hooves beating against the earth, coming through the back fields. She forgot dinner, she forgot the tune still working itself through her mind, she forgot Diana and Julie, she forgot that she never wanted to see him again. The back fields, and Ashmore Park bordered Edwards Lake…. She fumbled at the latch on the door.

The fence to the stable yard lay a hundred yards beyond the pool, but she had a clear view as he jumped the fence on an enormous gray hunter. She stood still as he cantered to a post and dismounted gracefully. He had ridden all his life, with a landed Virginian's inbred love of horseflesh; he had seated her on her first horse and patiently transformed her into a credible rider.

You're here, you came back.

She brushed her hands on her capris and felt every nerve ending against the cool cotton. Her heart had picked up speed; she was acutely aware of the flush spreading through her body. *You're here, you're here* – and for all that she despised him, for all that she would never forgive him, the sight of him woke her from the protective slumber of eleven years.

He had seen her now and lifted a hand in greeting. She scooped up Max before he made a break for it, and strolled over to the stable yard while Richard filled a water bucket. Max had never seen a horse before and betrayed his cowardly self by clinging to her with all claws.

"Hi," she said into the quiet, and cuddled Max for armor.

"Hi yourself," he threw over his shoulder. His hands were busy running a quick brush over the hunter. A stretch of silence followed his clipped greeting, only a minute or so, a long unfriendly space to drown in.

She offered, "You still keep horses."

"A few." His tone gentled. He reached up into the hunter's mane. "Not as many as when Dad was alive. I don't have the time for a full stable anymore. I'll get a mount here for you this weekend."

"That's okay." Laura relaxed. "I don't ride."

That arrested Richard's attention. "What do you mean, you don't ride? Don't they have horses in Texas? Or the UK?"

"I don't ride." She hadn't mounted a horse since the time she had fallen off in front of Cam and Emma, and they had doubled up in laughter. "Keep the horse over there. I don't want the responsibility."

He might have said more; in fact, he looked as if a whole raft of questions waited on his tongue, but Max rescued her. Securely nestled in her arms, her cat surveyed the tall stranger and the monstrous beast beyond, judged his chances of coming out alive, and hissed.

Twice.

"Good Lord." Richard looked down at Max in amusement and extended a finger to be sniffed. "This one never misses a meal, does he? Where'd he come from?"

"He's mine. I flew him in from home." She caught his eye. "Don't say it. I'm not supposed to have a pet here, but I missed him. I couldn't have him in London because of the quarantine laws, so this is the first time in a year he's lived with me. He's good company when I'm working."

"Is he now?" He slid a finger under Max's chin and rubbed, and her treacherous animal sighed in ecstasy. She tried not to react to the heat of his hand so close to her breast. "How've you been this week, Laurie? Sorry I haven't been in touch. I've been in Charleston."

"I've been settling in. Relaxing. Working some." His hand, as he smoothed back the fur on Max's head, accidentally brushed against her breast, and she moved away hastily. "How's Julie? I heard she's down with a cold."

"Yes, I've got her at home in bed. She was very disappointed not to see you." He withdrew his hand. "I don't know if the agents told you, I generally come over once a week to check things out. If you want to make other arrangements, just let them know."

She resisted his formality; she resisted even more the notion that she deserved it. "I don't want to get in the way. Go right ahead with anything you need to do."

"It shouldn't take long."

Then he would be on his way. Once, he would have stayed – but once they had been friends, no blood, no betrayal, no secret love affair between them. She remembered her chicken broiling away and flipped mentally through her culinary repertoire for an enticement to make him stay. Purely, she thought, because Edwards Lake was so isolated. She wanted company.

"Come on up when you're finished." She saw a faint surprise on his face, a mute echo of her accusation the week before.

"Some other time —"

"I'll fix you some iced tea." He was tempted, she could tell, and she baited the trap. "I bought mixings for cookies."

He laughed. "I surrender, Laurie! Knock off the bribery. I surrender."

She walked him to the pool and then left him to his task. He watched her lure her fluffy feline up the path to the kitchen annex, and his eyes lingered on her for academic reasons. Even a brother-in-law was permitted to admire long legs and a pretty backside shown to advantage by perky capris; he might be forgiven for resting his eyes on the gentle bounce of her blouse as she turned at the door and waved; he certainly had no business wondering how the skin at her throat would taste —

He yanked his unruly thoughts back into line and hoped to God that the rest of him would follow.

The walkaround of the grounds took longer than it should have, considering their immaculate condition. He dragged it out as long as he thought he could; the sky had darkened by the time he locked up the small pool cabana. The lights were shining through the annex windows, and the teal of her blouse let him follow her movements. He really should beg off – Julie needed him, he had work to do, his house demanded his attention. All true. The real reason, of course, was that he was a prudent man, and he knew that it was the worst folly, in his present loneliness, to spend time with a lovely woman who wore her attraction to him on her sleeve.

Such folly, in fact, that he wasn't going to yield to temptation. He was going home to his daughter and a week's worth of mail from his office, and the next time he saw Laura Abbott, he intended to be in the middle of a large crowd. A crowd so large, he hoped, that he would not easily remember the brush of her breast beneath his hand.

He knocked briefly on the back door and let himself into the kitchen. She had her back to him, talking into a headset, telling someone in no uncertain terms to buckle down to her homework and not bring home any more D's. He tried to be quiet as he crossed the room, but she heard him, and she turned to give him a smile and wave a mixing spoon towards the trestle table.

He was not prepared for the feelings that flooded him at that moment: the sharp awareness that the girl to whom she spoke (in a "Mom" voice) was his own flesh and blood; the sense that he had recreated his mother's kitchen so that someday Laura Abbott could stand here; the thought that, had Diana ever once appeared thus, laughing, admonishing, happy to be a mother to his daughter, he might have forgiven her anything.

His daughter. Tom had warned him that an original birth certificate was difficult to come by after an adoption, but the St. Bride divorce petition and Cameron St. Bride's will, both on file in Collin County, Texas, and open to all and sundry, had supplied all the information he needed. He had stared down at the date of Meg's birth, which seemed bewilderingly early but was still – barely – within the range of possibility. Too many pieces had fallen into place to dismiss his suspicions out of hand: Francie's pallor the day he broke off with her; Laura's marriage four months after Meg's birth; her long, unbroken silence. It explained everything except how Francie had legally given Meg away without his consent. Tom thought that she had probably claimed the father as unknown.

Francie had signed away his rights.

Damn her anyway. If she'd played straight…. But Francie never played straight, and he'd known that all along. She'd given him the benefit of her considerable sexual enthusiasm because she wanted to show her sister up, and he'd enjoyed what she offered because he could no longer endure the emotional wasteland of his marriage. He could scarcely complain, all these years after the fact, if Francie had refused to be stuck with the consequences.

But he could wonder. Wonder only, too. He might be unnatural, but he felt nothing more than a reasonable curiosity about Meg St. Bride. He had helped put her on this earth, but he had no ties to her, no bonds born of long years of raising her and disciplining her and loving her. He did not know this accidental child. She might be the fruit of his body, but she was not the child of his heart.

She was not Julie.

Still, he wondered. And here – right here – stood the only mother Meg had ever known.

He decided to stay after all.

Laura bid her daughter goodbye, but she did not hang up, and her voice changed. He poked around the foodstuffs she had assembled on the island, helping himself to a handful of chocolate chips and pretending not to see the stern look she gave him. Her conversation consisted mostly of "All right" and "I'll be there" and "You said that already," finishing up with an indignant "I'll do it myself!"

"Trouble?" he asked lightly, when she disconnected.

She laid down the spoon and checked the oven. Something wonderful floated out into the room, and he resisted the urge to peek. "Another minute or so." She closed the oven door. "No, no trouble, not really. Meg's schooling got messed up from living in London. She got a D on an algebra test in summer school, and Mark's upset, although it really is none of his business."

Julie never brought home anything less than a B. "Didn't she study?"

Laura laughed. "You sound just like Mark. Of course she didn't study, that's the point." She started dumping cookie ingredients into a large mixing bowl. "Meg claims that she's genetically programmed not to understand anything with numbers except her allowance."

So much for heredity; he had minored in math with honors. He was in her way, so he took the bag of chocolate chips and leaned against the counter across from the island, where he had the best view of her. "Another genius like her mother."

She rapped his knuckles lightly as his hand snaked into the bag. "Out! And I wasn't so dumb. I studied."

He watched the overhead light dance off her hair, and for a moment he forgot Meg, forgot his entire purpose for accepting her invitation. Dear heaven, how lovely she looked. She had been sweet as a young girl, alluring and mysterious as Cat Courtney; he saw her now as she must appear in her other life, casual, relaxed, domestic. Why had Cameron St. Bride ever thought to let this woman go? Why hadn't he fought harder to keep her?

"Of course," Laura added, and dragged him back to reality, where a mere brother-in-law was not entitled to dwell on what it must be like to come home to a woman like this, "you helped. I never would have passed trig without you. I was sunk before that."

"So was Francie," he said. "Didn't you take a test for her, Laura Rose?"

She paused in the act of removing a dish from the oven. "Good Lord, I'd forgotten all about that! I can't believe you remember."

He was sorry he had. A fragment of memory coalesced into Francie, hair framed against a pillow, laughing – *Oh, no one will miss me! Laurie's taking a math test for me. My alibi's good for the afternoon.* He hoped to God that Meg didn't owe her existence to Francie's inattention in trig class.

She busied herself setting the casserole on a cooling rack, and she looked no more ready than he was to discuss Francie. He cast around for another topic, any topic, to remove that tension from her eyes. "What's this about being there? Homesick already?"

"For Meg," Laura admitted. "I have to fly down there for a couple of days. Mark wants to hire a tutor for her, and that's really my responsibility. Plus—"

"Plus you miss her."

"Every minute." She took out flatware and dishes. "Silly, isn't it? Here I am, the first time in th – years and years that I've had the luxury of not being a mother first and foremost, and I can't stand it." She stopped in the midst of setting the table, troubled. "Cam used to say that I'd made her too dependent on me, but I'm just as dependent on *her*."

Not politically correct to think ill of the dead, but he was beginning to dislike Cameron St. Bride heartily. "It's easy to get dependent," he said easily, and came over to help her. "Julie went to music camp last summer, and for an hour or two I actually enjoyed myself. For the first time in my life, I had no one to answer to. After two days, I was ready to drive up to the mountains and bring her back."

They settled down with a meal that she described as chicken fajita pizza, and she put the cookies on hold. He complimented her on her cooking and teased her when she blushed. It had been too long since he had enjoyed a meal cooked for him by a lovely woman, too long since he had basked in the feelings she wore for him in her eyes. Then, mindful that he was there to learn about Meg, not to savor the attraction of a woman strictly off-limits, he turned the conversation to his own purposes.

"What grade is Meg in?"

"What?" Laura looked up at him warily. "Oh, she's in sixth."

Algebra in sixth grade? He dug into his dinner and carefully did not look at her. "You never did tell me. How old is she?"

"Twelve," said Laura without a pause.

Oh, you're good, sweetheart. What does it take to rattle you? "She looks mature for twelve. Julie still looked like a little girl at that age."

"How do you know what Meg looks like?" she asked sharply.

"I saw the picture in your room the other night."

"Oh, that's right. I forgot." Only a flicker of her lashes betrayed her thoughts. "She is pretty, isn't she? Don't you think she looks a lot like Lucy?"

Well done, princess! "No, not much," he said. "She doesn't look like you either. Does she take after her father's side?"

"The spitting image," said Laura decisively.

Nothing like lying by telling the literal truth.

"Tell me about her," he said. "What is she like?"

Ah, the heart of the matter. He watched her relax and tried not to hope for too much from her answer. So this question didn't threaten her? And what, he thought, did he expect to hear anyway? The usual rhapsodies of a mother separated from her only child? A pæan to ensure that he knew just what he had lost? Did he really want to hear that Meg was a paragon among daughters?

She's clearly undisciplined. She can't be too perfect.

Laura smiled, and her smile was a warning.

"Meg," she said, "has ruled with an iron fist since the day she was born. She knows exactly who she is and where she's going, and woe be unto anyone who gets in her way. I've fought a battle of wills with her every day of her life, from nursing" (how cleverly she slipped that in!) "to bedtime to homework to household chores. Believe me, Attila the Hun could teach that kid *nothing*."

He deserved that shock.

Had the gods been kind, giving him the rose and Laura the thorn?

"But we don't have to spend all this time talking about Meg," Laura continued cheerfully. "Let's talk about you."

Hoist with his own petard. And the damnable thing was, at any other time he might have enjoyed the chance. If he hadn't seen that photograph…. He squashed the temptation to go with the flow.

She beamed across the table at him, but her body had begun to betray her. He saw the tension in her hands around her cutlery, the tightness of her shoulders beneath the cotton blouse, the desperation in her jaw. *Do I have you on the run now, princess?* And to give her credit, she tried. She asked about his business, his house, his horses. She even did what Lucy never dared and asked him if he was seeing anyone.

Of course, she turned bright red the second after the words were out of her mouth. "Never mind," she said hurriedly. "It's none of my business."

"No, it isn't," he agreed affably, and ruthlessly cut back to his quest. "And, no, I'm not. And you aren't either, you said. Meg takes up most of your free time?"

"Oh, yes. With her school and her ballet—"

"I imagine you've had trouble not spoiling her."

"What?" Laura looked not a little irritated. "Oh, she's spoiled, all right. Cam would never discipline her, and I always ended up playing the heavy. It's sort of hard—"

She stopped. He wondered why.

"It's easy to spoil an only child," he said carefully. "Especially when you're a single parent. I've had to watch myself with Julie."

Why didn't you have any kids of your own?

"She wasn't an only child by our choice." Laura refilled his plate. "But I wonder sometimes if Meg really wanted a brother or sister as much as she said she did."

What a pity Meg St. Bride had never met her cousin. The rivalry might have done her good. "Bring her up so she can spend some time with Julie. She might enjoy being with someone close to her own age."

"Maybe," said Laura briefly, cooling rapidly, as if the idea of the cousins meeting was so bizarre as to be impossible.

Ah, Laurie, you're a window.

He thought he had tapped the limit of her willingness to talk about Meg, at least for one evening. Gradually, he steered her towards the topic of her singing, hoping to drift into a discussion of her marriage. *What went wrong? Tell me there were some happy moments for you. I don't want to know that Meg was all that held you with him.* She accepted the switch of subject and told her about her plans for her next album, the change in direction that she envisioned after the liberating effect of the London show, and he noticed how animated she looked, her hands flying to make her point. She met his eye now. Her childhood shyness had often been so painful that she could never quite look anyone in the eye, and if St. Bride had cured her of that, then it was all to the man's credit.

They finished dinner, and he insisted that she sit while he washed the dishes. She obeyed for a couple of minutes and then hopped up, offering to dry. They worked side by side, and only then did he discover how she had fooled him so completely all those years ago.

"You've grown."

"What?" She looked up, startled.

"You're taller. You used not to come to my shoulder, but now—" He caught himself, and his tone changed swiftly to teasing. "I'm surprised I didn't see it the other night, but you were wearing heels." They both glanced down at her feet. "What happened, Laurie Abbott, you take growth pills?"

She had finally caught up to Francie's height, sometime between her disappearance and that afternoon three years later. The stress of her new life, or had she just been a late bloomer? "Herbal tea, four cups a day." She couldn't know how obviously she was searching her memory to see how her extra inches might have betrayed her. "I gained a few pounds too."

"It suits you," he said gently, and resolutely did not look where those few pounds had landed.

She relaxed again, and he finished off the washing, heartily disgusted with himself. Unfair to tease her, he thought. She was honoring their relationship in its old ease, like the younger sister he'd always considered her. Not like Francie, who from age ten on had hung all over him, flirting, auditioning her budding sexual powers. He had long ago accepted that he must have been aware of Francie on some basic level long before that New Year's Eve, but he had never once thought of Laura as more than vaguely female until the afternoon she had slammed it in his face.

Why did you do it? Why didn't you speak up, tell me the truth, end it then and there?

She had moved away from him towards the kitchen island, hands hovering over her abandoned cookie ingredients, and he stopped her abruptly. "If you don't mind, some other time."

When I can keep you in focus as Diana's sister....

"Oh, sure, this'll keep." Laura covered the bowl and placed it with the dinner leftovers in the refrigerator. "If you like, I'll make up a batch tomorrow and bring it by for Julie, although—" and she glanced at him brightly, no longer Diana's younger sister, "I know who'll scarf them all down. Is Julie a chocoholic like her old man?"

"Worse." *Diana,* he thought, *Diana.* "I talked to Lucy today—"

"Really? So did I." Laura straightened the utensils on the island. "She's been so sick, poor thing. I keep telling her that's a good sign, although it's hard to believe it when you feel as sick as she does."

Diana. "She said that you saw Diana Saturday."

The mood changed in the merest brush of an instant. Her hands stilled, and he saw her fingers stiffen around a spatula. She was still turned away from him, but the easy set of her shoulders hardened, and before his eyes, pretty, confiding Laura Abbott became the cool, accusing stranger of Friday night.

Francie he could understand, but what about Diana upset her so?

"Lucy says that Saturday was not one of Diana's good days." In fact, his wife had apparently drunk her way through the reunion. "Laura, I want you to know—"

She found her voice, quiet, deadly. "It takes a long time to reach that plateau of never being sober. She must be a very experienced drinker."

He was surprised at the insight, disturbed by that cool voice. "Was that all she was? Just drunk?"

"No." Laura turned around, and her eyes chilled him. "She was stoned on something, I'd guess cocaine. I didn't figure it out for a while. She even sniffed it in front of me. She kept dabbing at her nose with a handkerchief, as if she had a cold, and all of a sudden she was alive and animated. It was quite a transformation."

"I'm sure it was." He had seen Diana change many nights, swiftly and terribly, long ago when she still lived with him. He felt weary, drained, all the magic tension of Laura's presence wiped out. He said flatly, "If she used cocaine, it was one of her better days. I thought she exhausted its possibilities years ago. Ecstasy seems to be more her drug of choice these days."

"Ecstasy!" Her cool front shattered. She looked at him in horror. "My God, that could kill her! Why haven't you stopped her?"

Did she think it was that easy?

"I've tried," he said. "Lucy's tried. But Diana doesn't want to stop. I don't think you'll succeed with her either. She'll tell you that she's in control, she can stop whenever she wants, all the excuses we've heard. She doesn't want to give it up."

"But there's professional help…." Her voice trailed off.

"Honestly, Laurie, don't you think we've tried everything?" He did not try to curb the sharpness of his tone. "She won't cooperate. I've told her over and over that, if she will make the effort to lick this, she can have Julie stay over with her again. That doesn't motivate her."

"But she's going to kill herself," Laura repeated, as if he had never thought of that. She bit her lip. "Richard, I know what I'm talking about, really. One of the first musicians I ever worked with died from X, when I lived in San Francisco. It scared me so badly I never even smoked pot. I've never met anyone who can handle it, and Di – she seems really whacked out—"

He reached out and took the spatula from her, just for something to do. "I agree. But we've tried everything we can think of. I hoped when she started the club that it would give her something to do, but it's just turned into a good place to meet dealers."

"If she's drinking heavily too—"

"I know," he said quietly, tiredly. "And she knows too."

She seemed to find nothing to say to that. He turned away from her, back to the counter, seeking some small task to deaden the silence. At that moment, he wanted nothing so much as the solitary comfort of his own home, away from the pain of her eyes. Not surprising, given her career, that she had run into drug users; she had apparently stayed clear herself. He was glad for that, really he was, but he wanted to leave this abruptly unfriendly room.

"She wants to die."

A blunt, bald way to put it – and her voice, calm, indifferent, shocked him.

"That's one way of looking—"

She sliced across his words. "Convenient for you," she said. "You'll get rid of her yet."

Her words hit him in a sharp, brutal blow. He felt their force smashing through his limbs, and for a moment, their blackness echoed in his ears and masked anything else she might have said. *Convenient for you* – He shook his head to clear the sound.

"What did you say?"

She said nothing. She lifted her hand as he turned around, as if she wanted to catch physically at her words. The shock of seeing that defensive gesture cleared the mists from his mind. He watched her swallow convulsively once, twice, and something that might have been fear and might have been regret flashed across her face.

He repeated, softly, "What did you say?"

She closed her eyes, her only refuge.

Her silence stretched between them, and he thought she must now realize that she had gone too far. He might have forgiven her the vicious remark of the week before – he already had, his own guilt demanded it – but this time, he thought, she had crossed a line she had not intended. She had intruded into his marriage, and that sea of anguish and desire was all his own and Diana's.

He looked at her, and he knew that nothing could now be fixed between them.

He said quietly, "Answer me, God damn you."

"Di—" She opened her eyes, and they were wet. He did not care. "Di doesn't have a reason to fight for her life, Richard. You've taken that from her."

He drew in a sharp breath. "Oh? The answer, just like that? I've ruined Diana's life, so she's trying to kill herself?"

Her face relaxed fractionally, and his mind seized upon that inexplicable relief.

"You've taken Julie from her," she said. "You've taken yourself. I've been in her place. I know what it's like to be alone while my husband is out chasing another woman. I was stronger, I survived. But it still hurt. It still robbed me of my confidence. And I had Meg. No matter how Cam and I fell out, he never once threatened to take Meg away. How do you think you've made Di feel?"

Her eyes darkened as she spoke. Her voice ran down, as though her words had only so much momentum, and he thought, *You're scared. Good. Don't you presume to lecture me after what you did, you little bitch.*

Something in his thoughts must have shown in his face, for she started to move away. He reached out and tightened his fingers around her arm to pull her back.

"I'm sorry your husband cheated on you," he said, "but it has nothing to do with me. To answer your question, what I *think* you were asking, no, I'm not hoping that Diana kills herself, and I resent that coming from someone who cared so little about her family that she let them swelter in guilt for fourteen years! My God, you have a hell of a nerve! Diana is my *wife*. I don't love her anymore, and I will never live with her again, but I don't want her to die. I don't need my freedom. I will *never* marry again. After eighteen years of hell, I've had enough of marriage to last a lifetime."

She tried to pull away, but his hand held her. "Then why all the women? Lucy made it pretty clear that you haven't been lonely."

Richard said flatly, "Go to hell."

She flinched. She hadn't been expecting that.

"You're damn right I see other women." Better not to explain; he owed her nothing. She had her own sins to answer for. "I've been separated from my wife for over a decade. In those ten years, I've been with a grand total of three women. I don't feel guilty, and I won't apologize, except that I regret that I didn't feel more for any of them. They were all nice, affectionate women who gave me far more than I gave them in return. I'm grateful to them. I'd have gone mad without them."

She struck back. "Then why don't you get a divorce? Let her go?"

"Go to hell," he said again, and to give her credit, this time she did not react. She merely stood there still and absorbed his anger in her own. "I don't want a divorce, Laura, and neither does Diana. She has the best of both worlds. I'm a very accommodating husband, or haven't you heard? I give her money when she needs it, I lend her a shoulder to cry on when some man dumps her, and I never say a word about her periodic disappearances or the abortions or the times she's tried to dry out and failed."

Her jaw dropped. She backed up a step. "I don't believe you."

"Fine. Don't believe me. Ask Lucy. Ask her about the times we've had to drag Diana out of the most unspeakable dives. We're near a port, remember, there are all kinds of places that you can't begin to imagine. Do you know why she doesn't see Julie? *And,* by the way, that's not my choice anymore, it's Julie's. She doesn't want to see her mother, and I won't force her. Once, years ago, I made the mistake of taking her to stay with Diana for a weekend, and at two in the morning, the police called me to come get my little girl. They found her crying outside Diana's apartment because Diana had passed out cold and Julie was afraid that her mother was dead. She was six at the time."

She had gone completely pale, and he saw the sledgehammer effect of his words on her. He didn't let up on her. She had asked for every bit of this, and he intended her to hear it all.

"There are a few other things you can ask Lucy. I don't know if she'll tell you. She still feels a certain loyalty. Ask her how many abortions Diana's had. I've lost count. The first, not that it matters now, was my child, a year after we were married. Ask her about the parade through Diana's bedroom. I went over there last week to tell her you were back, and I couldn't find her because she had spent the night with someone."

He walked over to the table and slung his jacket over his shoulder. Then he came back, and for a moment he felt sorry for her. She looked shell-shocked. He had grown used to Diana's devastation; he had lived with it for the whole of his marriage. He had not thought how it would affect a sister for whom Diana was still a stranger.

"Be thankful," he said, "that your husband was a decent man, even if he played around. You and he must have still gotten along well enough that he flew across the ocean to celebrate your birthday. I wish to God that Julie would see her mother occasionally. She needs a mother desperately. And I need relief from the burden of being a constant combination of mother and father. If I'm successful at all, it's only because Julie is a sweet and loving girl."

She looked down at the ground, and he caught only a glimpse of the glistening on her lashes.

He added, "Julie is hoping you'll have time to see her. I've no objection, and she will be thrilled. *But,*" his voice held a warning, "that's only if you agree to the ground rule that she doesn't have any contact with Diana that lasts longer than the time it takes to say hello and goodbye. If I find out that you've gone behind my back on that, I'll cut you off from her so fast your head will spin."

He watched her intently until she managed to nod an agreement.

"One other thing," he added. "Your opinion of me seems to be at rock bottom. I'm sorry about that, I'm damnably sorry, because we were the best of friends. But I warn you, Laura, when you're with Julie, keep your opinions to yourself. My daughter loves me, and she needs to respect me. I'm all she has. You are not to interfere with that. You are not to intimate to her that I'm waiting with bated breath for Diana to kill herself off or that I sleep with every woman I meet, and, for God's sake, do not mention Francie. Julie *never* needs to know what a fool I was."

She forced out through bloodless lips, "Of course not. I'd never say anything."

"I hope I can believe that," he said, "but, frankly, Laura, I'm astounded at just what you *will* say." He moved towards the back door. "I need to get back. Good night."

But she followed him anyway, out onto the path to the stables. He stopped several yards down the path, impatient now with her, wanting to get away, back to the safety and warmth of his home.

"Richard—"

"What?"

But, unbelievably, she hadn't finished.

"Please," she said. "I just need to understand." And then she hesitated, and he watched her coolly, his body tensing for the blow he sensed coming, while she bit her lip and rummaged for the words.

"This thing between you and Francie – it wasn't just sex, was it?" Now that she'd started, her speed picked up; the words tumbled out over each other. "Something else was going on, I always felt it, I just couldn't see you and Francie together. Just tell me, please. I want to stop wondering. Something went wrong between you and Di, it must have, you wouldn't have turned to Francie otherwise—"

Her voice, her eyes pleaded with him, but the truth of her words hit him a glancing blow, not enough to wound, but enough to warn. He cut her off immediately.

"That's none of your business."

But, damn her, she would not stop. She was crying again, great tears welling up in her eyes, but she soldiered on. She had more gall – or more courage – than any other woman he'd ever met. "I know, I know it's not, but I have to know."

She'd pushed too hard. He said between his teeth, "You want to know what went wrong? Fine! I adored your sister, I loved her desperately. I married her because she meant everything in the world to me. And she took all that and ground it to dust beneath her heel. You're right about Francie, you're absolutely right. It wasn't just about sex. I wanted to bring Diana down, and, by God, Francie worked."

He walked away into the dusk.

Laura could not remember ever feeling so conscience-stricken, or so helpless to make amends.

She tried all Saturday to reach Richard. First, she reached his voice mail, but, reluctant to apologize where Julie might hear, she hung up. The second time she called, she left a message inquiring about Julie's cold. The third time, the phone rang and rang. Served her right, she thought. She had not answered his calls before.

She spent the rest of the day baking and needlepointing, waiting for him to call. Meg called once to get her flight time; Mark took the phone and offered to send up the corporate jet. She got out of that by reminding him that she could scarcely leave Max to his own devices for three days, and he knew how allergic he was to cat fur. Did he want it all over his plane?

"Just leave him there with some food. It's only a few days."

"*Mark!*"

"All right," he said. "See you when you get here."

She kept her hands busy. She baked the cookie dough – if Richard didn't want it, then Julie might – and when she finished, she made up a recipe for oat bread that Peggy had taught her. Making bread was great therapy. She could pound and knead and exorcise all her demons on the hapless dough, waiting for the phone to ring.

He wouldn't call.

And why should he? She had been crueler to him in a week's time than she had been to anyone else in her life. She had been unable to fire a musician months after it had become obvious that he could not function up to her standards, solely because she didn't want to hurt his feelings, but she had savagely – twice! – attacked a man who had shown her only affection and kindness.

Not that day, he didn't….

No, no, there be dragons….

She concentrated on remembering Francie, Francie who had indicted Richard through her own words. Francie, whose childish plans to win his hand had ended in her own blood shed. She threw more flour and began to knead it in. Francie, whom Richard had scarcely mentioned, and then in the most neutral of tones. Francie, whose revenge on Diana had backfired so terribly.

Francie, who hadn't mattered—

She stopped as the tears blinded her contacts.

Francie, who had died while Diana and Richard lived on.

A tear splashed down onto the flour. She lifted her dusty-white hand to her mouth and bit her fingers against the onslaught of grief and rage.

Rage that he had lived. There, she'd admitted it. He'd partnered Francie in her monstrous scheme, but he had not suffered from its failure. He had gone on with his life, he'd made a home and a family with Julie, he enjoyed all that Francie had lost. He might still be tied to his unwanted wife, but he had not been lonely.

She had to agree with Lucy that there was no reason for him to have lived like a monk; she could hardly object that he'd known other women (but she did mind, terribly). But, damn it, did he have to seem so *content?* So sure in the life he had chosen?

Actually, he didn't seem that content. His voice had echoed of remembered pain, pain so sharp that he'd vowed never to risk it again. He'd learned to tamp down his emotions; she'd had the feeling, from moment to moment, that he kept a tight rein on himself. But nothing she'd seen in his eyes compared to the darkness in Diana.

She wondered what Dominic had thought of Diana's decline.

Had he blamed Richard? She hoped so, not out of meanness – Richard had never cared what Dominic thought – but because he could shoulder the blame so much more easily than Diana. It did not require much imagination to know the scathing criticism Dominic had heaped upon Diana's frail psyche.

She wondered when Diana had started sliding.

Lucy would know.

In all their conversations, hours spent catching up, Lucy had not wanted to talk about Diana. She had admitted her relief at Dominic's death ("I felt like the lowest scum on earth – but honestly, all I could think was, *I never have to talk to him again*"), her grief for Peggy and Philip ("Every good thing in my life started with them"). She had merrily dissected Laura's marriage and gently guided her through the inevitable talk about 9/11. But Diana she had left alone.

"Not now. Maybe when I feel better," she'd begged off, and who could blame her? For all Diana's downward spiral, Lucy had a greater responsibility.

Lucy knew. *He threw her out… he was right to do it.* She and Richard had grown up as sister and brother; they had been good friends all their lives. Laura remembered Lucy advising Richard on his delicate teenage girlfriend – *give her some space, she's stressed out about school* – so surely he had confided in her when his marriage disintegrated.

But Lucy did not know the truth about Francie, or she would never have accepted the story of the crash in the Panhandle.

Laura stared hard at her fingers and thought. She thought for a long time, going about her baking, playing the piano while the loaves rose, writing emails to Roger and Terry, uploading her digital recordings to the servers in Plano, petting Max on the back terrace as the shadows of the evening stretched across them. She thought of her own guilt in her twin's death, and for a second, the pain of that thought tightened her hand on Max, until he howled in protest.

And if she suffered such guilt, what did Diana feel? Such anguish that it could only be extinguished in the seductive oblivion of wine and cocaine?

You didn't deserve that, Di. I'm guiltier of your crimes than you ever were.

She picked up her cell phone and called Lucy.

"I've got to go home for a few days," she said, and winced at her sister's protest. "I'm coming back, really! I'll call every day, I promise. And when I get back – how do I get in touch with Di? I'd really like to talk to her."

I owe you that much, Richard. I owe Diana.

"Fine," said Lucy grimly. "But I want to talk to you first. Richard called me."

11

Diana, Not in Love

So why did I marry Richard?

I look back across time, and I haven't a clue. Of course, we had that dreadful scare freshman year at UVA. It wasn't the first time I'd sweated it out, but three weeks can be a long time in a teenager's life, and right before finals. Richard's grades didn't suffer, because he hadn't left all his studying to the last minute, but mine were terrible for a first semester. And, of course, my period started right after the last exam was over.

So we decided over Christmas that we should get married. Or did *we* decide? Richard came by to pick me up for an afternoon movie, and instead we ended up making love and getting engaged. I think the two were related, really. We'd been so scared that the only way we could justify sex was to say we were getting married.

But I can't shake the feeling that Richard proposed, and I ended up married to him because I couldn't find the courage to say no.

Of course, we'd been going together forever.

I met Richard when I was seven and he was eight. Daddy had just been acquitted of my mother's murder in Dublin, and he had lost no time in reclaiming the three of us from foster care and leaving the emerald shores behind him for good. From the time we left Ireland, we were little American girls; he put away our Irish passports, stamped out any hint of Irish accents, and generally wiped Mama out of our lives. He even changed our name. I'd been Diana Renée Dane-Abbott in Ireland – and with the trial going on, believe you me, you did not want to have that name. Once we moved to America, I became just Diana Abbott.

Sometimes I think how strange it is that Daddy's wife, whose name I can't even remember (Sharon? Siobhan? something like that), changed my life. If she hadn't run off from Daddy, undoubtedly for good reason, and taken refuge with her cousin Peggy until she had Lucy, he might not have tried to get Mama back, and so Francie and Laurie would never have existed. Mama might not have died. We might never have come to Virginia. I certainly would never have met Richard, and who knows how my life would have turned out.

But she did run away, and Mama did come back, and Mama did die, and Daddy did barely escape the noose. And then he left Ireland for good. I don't think you "shake off the dust" of Ireland, but for all practical purposes, that's what he did.

It always was Daddy's goal to restore his life, rescue his reputation, and reconstitute his family, and high on his list was getting his other daughter back.

Lucy had lived with the Ashmores after her mother abandoned her – just up and left in the middle of the night, leaving Lucy in her bassinet with a note pinned to her blanket, "Take care of my baby" – and Peggy and Philip were raising her as their own daughter. Daddy tried to put an end to that – she was an Abbott, after all, and the only legitimate one of us – but Peggy refused to let her go.

Daddy tried everything, short of going to court. I guess he had seen enough of courtrooms to last him a lifetime. He tried charm and persuasion; he tried invoking their common Irish heritage; he tried an appeal to Peggy's priest. He tried waxing lyrically about the ties of parenthood. No dice. Peggy didn't budge. Lucy was hers.

So Dr. Ashmore stepped in with a compromise. He had a rental house out on the James – small, ramshackle, needed a lot of repairs. He had picked it up at a foreclosure auction, he told Daddy apologetically, so he'd sell it to Daddy cheap. That way, we would be living only a couple of miles away from Lucy. It wasn't fair, he persuaded Daddy, to part Lucy from the only parents she'd ever known, plus at Ashmore Park she had a big brother and a horse and a bedroom fit for a princess, and they were more than happy to keep on paying for her upkeep and tuition and braces….

Knowing Philip and his tact, I'm sure he never came right out and made Daddy face up to the truth, which was that, even with Mama's small estate, Daddy was going to be hard-pressed to bring up three kids, much less four. Philip felt that, with cooperation, Lucy could be part of both families. He even arranged for me, and later Francie and Laurie, to attend private school with Richard and Lucy, and I've always wondered about the financial aid that seemed to come out of the blue. Compared to the other students, we were definitely the charity cases. Philip talked Peggy into agreeing that, if Lucy showed any musical aptitude, Daddy would be allowed to train her (except she didn't so he never bothered). We got her on alternate weekends – like visitation, now that I look back on it.

So, anyway, back to Richard. So we came to meet, and no cymbals clashed, no stars fell from the sky. Nothing. We were only kids. I was so curious to meet this half-sister who was eleven months to the day younger than me that I didn't notice the Celtic knight in training who hovered protectively around "his" little sister. Actually, Francie paid more attention to him, and Laurie, just a baby, hung back and gazed adoringly at him. Richard was into model airplanes and science fiction, I was into Mick Jagger worship (to Daddy's horror). He scarcely seemed aware that I existed, although he was very kind to Laurie. I hardly noticed him, until, during a weekend a few years later, Lucy told me that he liked me.

"He thinks you're beautiful," she whispered. "I saw him drawing your face for his pictures."

"What kind of picture?" I asked in alarm. In creative writing class, Richard had been working on a sci-fi fantasy story involving an underground kingdom populated by mutants repelled by the society above. (I'm not making this up.)

"Duchess Julia." The heroine, with long flowing locks, etc. The inspiration of the hero of these stories, who just happened to be a Celtic knight.

Even at ten, I knew that meant something. Over the next few weeks, I kept a covert eye on this boy with his secret crush on me. If he had been the usual run-of-the-mill boy, I probably would have gone out of my way to snub him. But gradually it dawned on me that Richard Ashmore was no ordinary boy and maybe I ought to give him the time of day. First, all the girls in my class thought he was the cutest thing alive. Second, he was smart. Richard knew a lot about a lot of things, and he read all the time to learn more. Third – well, third, Francie had been batting her eyes at him since the day we first met him, and maybe I liked knowing that Francie could have all the crushes in the world on him, but he liked *me*.

So I smiled at him one day. I asked how his sci-fi story was going. I said how wonderful it must be to learn to fly. I let him walk me to my door when we got off the bus one day, which meant that, afterwards, he had a *long* walk back to Ashmore Park.

Francie seethed.

My classmates gazed at me with envy.

Daddy made me practice double time to punish me for straying from my art.

And my Celtic knight, mind stuffed with Irish romanticism by his mother, decided that the future was settled, all tied up with a bow.

Let's see, a few highlights of my life as Richard Ashmore's girlfriend:

His mother never approved of me. Why, I wasn't sure, until it dawned on me that she had someone else picked out for her son. I didn't catch on until the day I heard Richard thanking Laurie for making his favorite cookies. Then I started to notice how Peggy had Laurie over there every weekend, teaching her to cook and sew and – oh, she wasn't even subtle about it after a time – run Ashmore Park. She mostly ignored me, except to tell me that my skirts were too short or my jeans too tight or I really needed to wear a bra. She never once took me under her wing and tried to teach me anything. No wonder I'm a terrible cook.

It never occurred to me to be jealous of Laurie.

I knew something Peggy didn't want to know.

I knew Richard was so crazy in love with me, he'd never give Laurie the time of day.

Another memory. Our first kiss. I was thirteen, and he was fourteen, and we were at a carefully chaperoned mixer at school. But the chaperones couldn't be everywhere, and we found a dark stairwell, and that's when I found out that Richard Ashmore was not only the best-looking guy in school, he was a great kisser. He wasn't one of those god-awful sloppy kissers, and he didn't make a meal of it, and he had this thing with the upper lip…. Now that I've kissed a great many men, I can honestly say that he ranks up there in the top two or three.

The first time he told me he loved me. I don't even remember how old we were or where we were, although for some strange reason I remember that he was wearing a blue shirt that brought out the color of his eyes. I can still hear his exact words: "Don't say anything, Di, I just want you to know. I think I'm in love with you." And he followed it up with a deep, intimate kiss, so I guess we must have been in that transition time between early adolescent kissing and his sixteenth birthday – fifteen or so.

A good thing he told me not to say anything, because the other thing I remember is a quick, panicky feeling of being trapped. For the first time, I realized that he was serious about me, and, by that time, I knew what Richard Ashmore wanted, Richard Ashmore pursued with a single-minded determination. I'd seen it when he had gone out for track, constantly trying to top his personal best. I'd seen it in his studies; he was determined to be first in his class, and he achieved it early and never let it go. I'd seen it when he set out to tame a hunter Philip had bought; Richard had that horse broken in no time.

I imagined his list of goals, and at the top: *DIANA*. With a ten-point plan to achieve me.

The idea terrified me.

Maybe, I thought, I ought to date around, hint that he should wait for Laurie to grow up….

And I might have, I really might have, except for the night he turned sixteen, six months ahead of me. He came over to take me out to a fancy dinner with his newly minted driver's license – I remember him in his dark suit, and I had my hair up and I was wearing one of Mama's dresses that I'd taken down from the attic. I remember Francie sidling into my bedroom while I put on mascara, hopping around, giving me her malicious little look.

"It's smudged," she said, and she sounded gleeful. "You look like a raccoon."

I applied lipstick that I intended Richard to kiss off me later. "Don't you have homework to do?"

"Field trip tomorrow, dumbo." Then Francie leaned in and whispered, "Do you hear that?"

"What?" I stopped and listened. I vaguely heard Daddy downstairs in the music room, talking to – well, it had to be Laurie. I couldn't make out his words. I shrugged and turned back to my dressing mirror. "What's the deal?"

Francie was still whispering. "You know those kittens Laurie found?"

Oh, I knew those kittens, all right. I'd spent a week trying to keep out of their way. I've always had this deep-seated aversion to cats, a visceral reaction that I can't explain – and, yes, I know the irony, since my sister is now Cat Courtney. Over Daddy's vociferous objections, Laurie had dragged them home after she found them abandoned on the side of the road, and she'd been feeding the smallest one with an eyedropper with more patience than I could have ever mustered.

I picked up my blusher and dusted my bosom lightly. With any luck, that, too, Richard would kiss off in the course of the evening. "What happened?"

"The black one got loose and scratched the piano."

Oh, boy. Now I could more clearly make out Daddy downstairs – not the words, but the deep, biting tone. Poor Laurie. She was really in for it now.

But it was not my problem. I was not getting involved. In that household, you learned early not to get between Daddy and the designated victim *du jour*. Laurie would just have to cope, and it wasn't like it was the first time she'd been on the wrong end of a lecture.

I picked up my evening bag, said a meaningful "*Bye*" to Francie's "Your lipstick's smeared," and went downstairs just as Richard rang the doorbell.

From the music room, I made out some of what Daddy was saying: "Irresponsible, Laura Rose – head in the clouds – disobedient – disgraceful – look at me when I'm talking to you—"

Richard looked so tall and handsome in his suit, and I have to admit, even now I remember how fast my heart beat when I saw him. I was so lucky, but I also *so* did not need Daddy, in that mood, to lay eyes on him. From the moment Richard and I had become an item, he had hated Richard with an unreasoning passion, calling him *that Ashmore boy*, or, when he was really pissed off, *that godless Ashmore boy*. I whispered to Richard, "Quick. He's in one of his moods."

Richard gave me a look that conveyed his understanding. We had spent many, many hours talking about what a strange bird Daddy was. "What's the problem now?"

"Oh, Laurie upset him—" and I pushed open the screen door to leave.

But then we both heard it. "Words don't appear to mean anything to you, Laura Rose. Perhaps this will persuade you—"

And we heard the first swish of the belt through the air, and a small, immediately silenced sound.

I'd never heard Richard swear before, and it shocked me. I didn't even know he used that word. Maybe he felt free to say it now that he was sixteen. But my shock went quickly by the wayside, as he yanked the screen door wide open and brushed right by me.

He strode right into the music room, normally a room he never went into because he disliked Daddy as much as Daddy disliked him. After my initial surprise, I started in after him, and from the corner of my eye, I saw Francie, slinking down the stairs, freeze in place.

The scene in front of us appeared surreal. Daddy, in a rage, his belt wrapped around his hand, the better to swing with. Laurie, little Laurie, only ten years old, standing still, a welt on her arm, her face and eyes blank, gone away inside. And Richard – my wonderful Celtic knight, already well over six feet tall, his face hard, putting out a hand to grasp Daddy's wrist.

"You hit her again," he said, "I hit you. Then I call the police."

Daddy said between clenched teeth, "Get out of here, boyo. This is not your concern."

Richard did not back down. "If it takes a man to beat a defense-less girl, I'll be a boy, thank you. I am not joking, Dominic. I will turn you in."

That was the first time he called Daddy by his first name. I saw Daddy's eyes darken. The insult was not lost on him. Neither was the threat.

"And after I call the police," Richard added coolly, "I will call my mother."

I almost clapped my hands, just barely restrained myself. Brilliant. My boyfriend was brilliant. Because if Daddy truly feared one person on earth, he feared Peggy.

If Peggy heard about this, Daddy could say goodbye to seeing Lucy.

I looked at Richard there in that room, that night, and I didn't see the boy who routinely let me think I had him just where I wanted him. I saw a young man unafraid to take on a man almost three times his age, standing up for a helpless child who had no one to stand for her. I saw – and should have been warned by – the underlying steel of his character. I saw him pit his will against Daddy's, and win.

I *really* should have been paying attention to that.

But I was as starry-eyed as Francie, gazing at him from the stairs. To me, that night, he truly became my Celtic knight.

I don't think I ever came closer to loving him. And when we finally left, after he told Laurie to go upstairs and directed Francie to take care of her – Daddy disappeared into the back of the house to sulk – I knew that my virginity and his wouldn't last the night.

And it didn't. That night, Richard became my first lover. I became his. He'd spent the early morning getting his driver's license; he'd spent the afternoon soloing and getting the license that meant more to him – his pilot's license. We instantly put it to good use. We skipped the fancy dinner, picked up some Mickey D's, and flew out to Ash Marine. The entire flight, our bodies hummed with anticipation, both of us telling each other in look and touch what lay ahead that night.

For several months, we had been going steadily further and further, hormones egging us on, but we'd always pulled back. Not this night. Once we were there on that lonely island, with only time and tide to keep us company, we walked down to the cove, ate our moonlit meal, and surrendered to the inevitable.

How much resulted from my sudden hero worship, inspired by the sight of Richard standing up to Daddy, and how much was the idea forming in the back of my mind that here was my savior, I don't know. How much on his part was passion and how much was sheer adrenaline, I don't know. I only know what happened.

It was a lovely, lovely night, full of passion and awkwardness and tenderness. No matter how angry Richard has gotten with me in the years since, I'm sure he still looks back fondly on his sixteenth birthday.

He turned out to be, with a little bit of practice, a very good lover. He wasn't selfish, he worked hard to make sure that I enjoyed myself – I came to see the Standing Stone of Ireland, as we dubbed it, as much an instrument for my pleasure as for his – and he took care of the birth control.

He also took good care of me. He taught me to drive. He looked over my chem and trig assignments and kept me from flunking my junior year. He wrote the essay on my college applications for me. He did my Christmas shopping for me when I got sick.

Every girl in my class envied me my perfect boyfriend. Gorgeous, smart, courteous, caring – hell, if I hadn't had to put up with him, *I* would have envied me.

But, you see, I didn't want to be taken care of. I wanted to be saved, yes, because those hours of practice never stopped, nor the constant reminder of my destiny to replace my mother. But I didn't want someone making decisions for me, knowing what was best for me, telling me what to do! That was the problem! I had enough of that with Daddy. But try telling that to Richard.

As I said, Richard took care of the birth control. With one horrible exception, he did the perfect job there that he did everywhere else.

I know that he insisted on protecting me because he wanted to protect himself, and who could blame him? He didn't want to ruin his future, mapped out in his precise way in his cradle. Architecture at UVA. Master's. A few years apprenticeship in a commercial firm. Then concentrate on doing what he loved best: preserving the architectural heritage of Virginia. How many times I heard it all! And, of course, rebuild that awful Folly, which never looked like much to me. (Of course, I *was* wrong. The damn thing is a palace now. How was I to know he would somehow find 10,000 square feet in there?)

The last thing he needed was a fertile girlfriend.

That's why, when I proved to be a little too fertile my senior year in high school, the weekend he came home from UVA to take me to the Valentine's Day dance, I took care of it.

I didn't tell him. I didn't tell anyone. I couldn't believe it when I was late; I could set my watch by my period, and Richard was nothing if not careful. All I could think was, *It can't be, it can't be,* because Richard Ashmore did not make mistakes like that. The Standing Stone of Ireland couldn't have done this to me. But when he came home the first weekend in March and we went out to a movie, and I nearly tossed my cookies at the smell of popcorn, and then I fell asleep on him halfway through the film, I had to face the fact that IT had happened.

I couldn't even call it anything but IT.

I couldn't bring myself to tell him. I *did* almost succumb to temptation a few days later when he called me from UVA. We talked several nights a week, and that night he asked me if I was still feeling rundown. I said no, which was a lie, because I could barely keep my eyes open and my breasts hurt so bad I could barely stand to wear a bra, and I just felt *weird*. Then he started talking about his biology class – I remember that he was reading Darwin – and I wanted so much to say, "Speaking of biology, Richard – guess what." But I didn't. I couldn't.

Because I knew what would happen.

He'd stand by me. He'd insist on us getting married.

But I didn't want to get married. Not then. Not when I was still a senior in high school. Not when I was on the verge of getting away from Daddy. Not ever if I had to live at Ashmore Park and become a clone of Peggy Ashmore.

I wanted to go to college. I wanted the freedom of living on campus. I wanted to study music, not the music Daddy drummed into me, but *my* music, jazz piano. I wanted (truth!) to date other boys, to see if I was missing anything by tying myself down. I wanted the right to tell both Richard and Daddy to go to hell.

And how could I do that if I was blown up like a whale?

And how could I turn myself into a jazz pianist if I had a baby?

And how could I live out my secret dream, enjoy a bohemian life in Paris in my wild and crazy twenties, hang out at cafés, eke out a precarious existence as a pianist in sleazy night clubs, drink cheap wine and have meaningless flings with bad boys, if I became Mrs. Richard Ashmore?

I'd do the Mrs. Richard Ashmore thing after I'd *lived*.

When I was officially two weeks late, I went across the river to buy a couple of tests because I wouldn't run into anyone I knew there. I got up first thing the next morning and did the test, and the ten minutes of waiting for the result – God, I can't even bear to remember the agony of wondering and waiting. I nearly ran back into the bathroom to look at the test after five minutes. But, no, I followed the directions, I waited ten, and I went back to look at it, and it was bright *fucking* blue.

Blue. Positive. What the hell was so positive about blue?

I remember saying, "Oh no, oh no, oh no, no, no." Just babbling. Looking at myself in the mirror, seeing all the color drain from my face. Taking the test again and getting the same result. Moving in shock, carefully repackaging the tests so that I could throw them away where Daddy wouldn't see them in the trash and that little snoop Francie couldn't "find" them. Sitting huddled in the shower with my face against my knees, feeling the water wash away the tears that I couldn't stop crying. Knowing that, for this moment in time, I was seventeen and I was the future Callas and I was actually a *mother*. And Richard, the future Frank Lloyd Wright, all unknowing up there at UVA, was a *father*. We were – oh, God, how had this happened – *parents*.

How could we be parents! We were kids!

Knowing that I couldn't ruin his life or mine by letting IT happen. Knowing I had to erase IT out of existence. Knowing, because I'd been a good little girl and listened to Monsignor at Mass, that I was going to burn in hell forever.

Not wanting to know that nothing could ever turn back the clock so that IT never happened.

The day my world crashed was March 15. The Ides of March. Every year, I feel a chill when I see that day on the calendar.

I scrounged together most of the money, raided Laurie's secret stash that she thought no one knew about, and stole the rest from Daddy's wallet. Richard was planning to come home for the weekend, so that Friday I signed myself out of school and took a bus to the clinic in Richmond. I sat there by myself but hardly alone – there were other girls my age there, and a lot of older women, and every last one of us carefully didn't look at the others. Nobody talked. We each sat there in our own private purgatories.

I had never seen so much paperwork in my whole life, and I signed it all without reading it. I have no idea what I signed. They called my number and took me in for another test. God didn't listen to me, because it was still positive. I remember thinking that how on earth had I passed this test when I couldn't even pass math unless Richard coached me.

He'd coached me into passing this one, all right.

But I couldn't think about Richard. I couldn't allow him in my mind. I changed him into MY BOYFRIEND, so when the counselor asked me if I had a ride home, I said yes, MY BOYFRIEND was coming to get me. No name, not a person, not half of this equation, certainly not someone who'd have a definite opinion about IT if only he knew. Just MY BOYFRIEND. She asked if I was sure I wanted to go ahead, and I remember just nodding and noticing with mild interest that I felt nothing inside.

I just wanted to get IT over and done with.

Then back to the waiting room. Another hour of being a robot. They called my number, and I followed the nurse into the back. I laid down my money, and I remember that I started to feel guilty, because I had taken Laurie's hard-earned babysitting money – but no, I wasn't going to think that word.

I didn't feel guilty one little bit about stealing the money from Daddy.

I felt nothing about where I was or what I was about to do.

Then *the procedure*. That's what they called it – *the procedure*. Like getting your teeth cleaned or your eyes examined. I didn't have the money for a general anesthesia, so I was awake for the whole *procedure*. That awful sound. The pure indifference of the doctor. An hour in *recovery*. One hour to *recover* from IT in your life, and then you're spic'n'span, good as new.

It was afternoon when I left, and I waited for the bus, sick from relief. IT was over. I had dealt with IT. I didn't have to think about IT anymore, because now I was *recovered*. And then – I saw a Honda Accord drive by, the same color that Richard drove. It wasn't his, of course. The clinic was in south Richmond, and coming from UVA he'd skirt the city on the north. But I saw that car, and I thought how much damage the Standing Stone of Ireland had done to me and how I had to pay for *his* failure. I thought how he hadn't had to deal with IT those last few weeks. I thought about how he had gone to class, done his assignments, driven home for the weekend probably anticipating a roll in the hay – read Charles Darwin, for God's sake – because his devoted girlfriend had taken care of IT for him.

That was the first time I ever wanted to smash his face in.

I wanted to throw up. How could I feel that way about Richard, who was so good to me, who loved me so much, who tried so hard to take care of me?

I couldn't face the long bus ride home. I couldn't face going in the house, seeing Daddy, seeing my sisters, acting like I'd been at school. I couldn't face going out with Richard that night – and, dear God, what would I do if he wanted to make love?

So, finally, I told someone. I called Lucy. She immediately drove the fifty miles to get me, took me home, and tucked me into bed. She listened to me cry when my hormones refused to get the hell out of Dodge. She swatted Francie away from me. She told Laurie to make me some chicken soup. She told Daddy to back off, he had been pushing me too hard. She told Richard I was stressed out over school and to leave me alone for a few weeks.

I owe my sanity to Lucy sometimes.

I still didn't tell him. But it hung over the rest of my senior year, a shadow that never completely left me. Richard knew something was wrong; he could hardly help but know, because for months I burst into tears at the drop of a hat. I was going to hell, and I was so *afraid* of going to hell. It didn't help one little bit when I blurted that out one day and he said that hell didn't exist. It damn well did, whether the great Richard Ashmore thought so or not, because I was getting a pretty good glimpse of it.

He called every night to check on me, he comforted me when I fell from okay to depressed in the blink of an eye, he heeded Lucy when she told him I wasn't feeling well because of problems with my period. He never did pay much attention to my cycle anyway, but that was *brilliant* of Lucy because Richard had the normal male reluctance to inquire deeply into the mysterious world of menstruation. But, at least, for a few months, he never once made a move for sex, and that was just as well, because I think I would have thrown up all over him if he had done anything except kiss me.

He tried his best to take good care of me.

And his best was pretty good. It just hadn't been perfect.

But he couldn't do anything about the nine-month clock that ticked away slowly, slowly in my head. He couldn't do anything, because he didn't know, about the times I sat there in senior English or at the piano and thought, *Three months*, or *Four months*, or *Everyone could tell by now*, or….

He couldn't silence the ghost voice in the night.

After graduation, I felt better about life again. The clock still ticked away, like some invisible metronome, but I was glad to have high school, with the trauma of that year, in the past. I was learning to put all that behind me, as they had advised at the clinic. I buried it under *bad things that happened to me in March*, and since March was dead and gone, I felt stronger and more optimistic. I felt strong enough, in fact, to give Richard his class ring back. Oh, I felt bad about hurting him – but not bad enough to stop myself from doing it. He asked why, of course, because Richard always had to know everything, and he wanted to know what he had done wrong and what he could do to fix it, so I just said something vague about rethinking my goals in life, and yes, we were still friends, and yes, Richard, let's make love, I've missed you....

And all I could think, as we made love, was how terrible the consequences could be.

I didn't enjoy myself at all, and he knew it.

Daddy was thrilled. He offered to pull strings to see if I could still get into Juilliard; he had been livid when I had insisted on UVA. Francie was thrilled; silly little girl, she seriously thought that, at thirteen, she had a shot at Richard. Philip and Peggy were thrilled, because they most certainly didn't want their son throwing himself away on me.

Only Richard wasn't thrilled. And neither was I, to tell the truth.

By mid-summer, I knew that the breakup wasn't working. I alternated between calling Richard to suggest that he take out anyone I thought might need a date for the weekend – and he finally snapped at me to stop trying to fix him up – and suggesting that we go out to a movie. Our dates were fine except for the one time we ended up making love, and I started crying right in the middle of it all.

I couldn't be with him, and I couldn't be without him.

Him, he just preferred to be with me.

So I never mailed the Juilliard papers, and when Daddy kept after me about my audition, I said that my application was still being processed. By the time he figured out what a liar I was, summer was almost over, and it was time for college and real life to start.

So off I went to UVA to join Richard, now in his sophomore year, and immediately I announced my intention to date around. Richard, finally well and truly fed up, told me to suit myself and see if I found anyone else willing to put up with my mood swings. Well, I did. I showed him. I went to my first music theory class, cast my eye around, picked out the least objectionable candidate, and left the guy no choice. He had to ask me out. Once out, he had to kiss me. Once kissed and kissing, he had to....

For two months, the last two of that horrible calendar, I slept with that poor boy, someone with whom I had no history, someone who couldn't know and wouldn't have cared if he did know about the unseen damage I had done. Someone who knew nothing about me....

I don't even remember his name.

But I really missed Richard. I knew that I had hurt him. I knew he wasn't seeing any of the girls I had thrust at him. And whoever that boy was, he wasn't as good as Richard in bed. Richard and I *did* have a history. We knew each other's bodies. We knew how to please each other.

Maybe I was just too lazy to break someone else in.

So, in mid-November, when by nature I was finally free of that calendar, I called Richard. Just to talk. He seemed happy to hear from me. I was happy to hear his voice. He asked me to go have coffee. I accepted. He told me all about his architectural history class. I confessed to having problems in calculus. He offered to come back to my room and look over my assignment. We started off kissing, then got horizontal to kiss some more in comfort, and one thing led naturally to another. He said, "Are you sure you want this, Di?" and I said, "Oh, my God, yes, yes, I do," and we and the Standing Stone of Ireland had a *real* good time, and afterwards he did my homework for me.

And, since neither of us had really thought anything through, of course we used nothing.

This time, I told him I was late. No way in hell was I going through this alone again.

I'll never forget how white his face got when I told him I was late. Or the utter, heartfelt relief in his eyes when my period finally showed up. I knew then that I had done the best thing back in the winter. I was desperately relieved myself. I couldn't have faced another *procedure*. But Richard, certainly, couldn't have faced a baby.

So why then, two weeks later, did he ask me to marry him?

And why, why, *why* did I accept?

12

Said the Spider to the Fly

TOO BAD LUCY DID NO COURTROOM WORK, Laura thought, waiting for her sister to pounce on her. The law had missed a great prosecutor.

She'd worried the entire weekend. The strain of wondering what Richard had told Lucy had shown so obviously in her face that Meg and Mark had noticed and seized on it. "Let me go back with you, Mom," said Meg, sure that Laura was lonely and loath to let any opportunity slide by. "I told you this wasn't a good idea," said her brother-in-law, and added that people who stirred up old wasp nests often got stung.

"Meet me at my office," invited the chief wasp. "Noon sharp. I'll order in lunch."

Ah, Lucy, who knew all about softening up her victim for the sting! "Let's not talk about unpleasant things right now," she said in easy greeting. "I haven't seen you in days! Let's visit first."

And visit she did, with a vengeance, inquiring about Laura's weekend, admiring Meg's baby pictures, showing off her African violets, dissolving over an antique baby quilt that Laura had brought back from Texas.

"Look at this stitching," she marveled. "It's so fine – oh, Laura, this is just lovely." Her fingers caressed it, skimming over its surface, as she might have caressed the child she had borne and buried. She had scarcely mentioned the child she now carried, perhaps because hope so often proved a double-edged blade. "Did you use this for Meg?"

"No. I found it a few years later."

"So you never got to use it." Lucy sent her a sidelong glance. "I'm surprised you stopped at one. Didn't you want any more?"

"Sure, I did." She shut off the hurt, only a small ping now. "It just didn't happen. But I like babies. You'd better make me godmother. I'll spoil that kid rotten."

"Oh, please do! You're the only one so far who welcomes this baby." Lucy's dark hair dipped over the star design. "No one else understands. Oh, Tom was upset, he truly mourned for John, but he was more upset about me. Di said that it was better that it happened before I could get attached, as if I didn't get attached the moment I found out I was pregnant. I felt him move, Laurie, he kept me awake nights, and he wasn't even born yet."

Laura watched her rubbing the quilt, and her throat tightened. Lucy looked so alone, wrapping the quilt around her shoulders, pulling the ruffles down her arms, as if she were already swaddling her child in its warmth.

"Di thinks I'm crazy, you know." Lucy cocked her head and looked at her. "She thinks I shouldn't go through with this."

"*What!*" No need to think through this reaction. "That's outrageous! Just because she's not the mother type—"

"Oh, that's an understatement." Lucy didn't appear upset by the suggestion. "But don't tear into her, Laurie, you have to understand where she's coming from. Di never wanted kids, and she'll tell you that Julie ruined her marriage. She keeps asking why I want to destroy a perfectly good marriage by having a baby."

Laura hesitated (how far to stretch the great lie?) and then said deliberately, "Meg didn't destroy mine. She was the best part of it."

"But Di doesn't know that. What she knows is that Dominic killed your mother after one child too many." That the "one too many" sat across from her didn't seem to enter her mind. "What she knows is that Richard fell in love with Julie after she was born and lost all interest in patching things up. What she knows is that children often drive a wedge between their parents."

So Julie's birth had not initially divided Richard and Diana; something had happened even before that, something so terrible that even the birth of a child had not prompted reconciliation.

Laura asked softly, "What happened between Richard and Di?"

And Lucy said quietly, "Is that what you asked him?"

She shouldn't have reminded Lucy. She really didn't want to talk of this; she wanted no more of the dark unhappiness that had descended on the Ashmore marriage. She wanted the sunlight; she wanted tea and gentle conversation between sisters. She wanted to talk of hope and birth, not of a sister determined to destroy herself and a man who plainly despised her.

She said, "Exactly what did he say?"

"That's the rub." Lucy clasped her hands on the Queen Anne desk in front of her, and fixed her prisoner with a stern look worthy of a Lord High Executioner. The baby quilt still hugged her shoulders. "He didn't say. I asked him when he and Julie could join us for dinner, and he said – I believe this is an accurate quote – 'I'll eat dinner with her the day she learns to keep her god-damned nose out of my marriage.'"

"Oh." Laura winced.

"One other thing." Lucy studiously rearranged several folders, and the quilt started to slip. "As an afterthought, he asked me just what I'd said to make you think that he'd slept with every woman on the East Coast. Well, maybe that's an exaggeration, but you get the general idea."

Silence was the better part of valor. She said nothing.

"Laurie? What happened?"

Nothing could whitewash her cruelty, and she knew it. "I'm worried about Di. I wanted to know what he was doing about her."

A pause. Then, "You're lying. If Richard didn't have the patience of Job, Di would be six feet under. And he's always liked you, so you must have really crossed the line. In fact, Di is the only other person I know who has ever made him swear. So what happened?"

She answered, "Why is Di trying to kill herself?"

She didn't know what she expected – to be told again to mind her own business, to be fobbed off again with an excuse. The burden of Diana's addictions must have fallen mostly upon Lucy. If Diana had already been committed for treatment, then Lucy must have been at her side, loving her through failure and despair. Maybe Lucy now resented explaining all that to someone who had not been there to share the burden.

Lucy examined her nails, as if marshaling her thoughts for a closing argument. "You're perceptive," she said finally. "I can't tell you why. She's been in and out of detox centers for years. She's also seeing a therapist, but I haven't seen any progress."

"Richard said you had tried everything." She was glad that Lucy had decided to acknowledge the truth. If Diana were to be salvaged, no one must discount the damage already done.

"Oh, we have! Dominic even came up with the money for Betty Ford, and she went, and for a few months she improved, she really did. She came back sober and clean, and she seemed to have gotten her life back together. She talked about going back for a master's in composition, and Richard said he'd pay for it if she'd stick with it.

She lived with Dominic then, and he could always shame her into putting on a good appearance, so I don't know how sincere she was, but then—"

She fell silent. Laura prompted, "And then?"

"Then something happened between her and Richard." Lucy sighed and leaned back in her chair. "Those two have the most complicated relationship. I don't know that either one really understands it. This was – oh, last year, right after Mom and Dad were killed." Her voice caught, and then she swallowed and regained her composure. "Richard and Julie were devastated, we all were. Dad was more my father than Dominic ever was. Well, Di went out there to see Richard the night before the funeral, and I don't fault her for doing it. Her intentions were noble. The upshot was – and please understand that I heard this only from Di, who was in hysterics – she offered to comfort him as only a wife really can, and he turned her down flat with the remark that she was years too late."

"Oh, no." Irresistibly, she pictured the scene in her mind, Richard sitting in his father's study, face drawn with grief, Diana standing before him, offering and yielding. She understood Diana, all right. (She'd never come closer to loving Cam than the night after his mother died, when he'd reached out for her, the prince needing Cinderella for the first time.) But she understood Richard too, aching with loss, needing nothing so much as solitude to mourn, recoiling from marital intimacy resurrected too little, too late.

"Di couldn't handle it. So she undid all her hard work with one real bender, and she got picked up for DUI. That really nailed it with Richard, after the way Mom and Dad were killed. He took Julie to England to get away, and Di's hardly seen him since."

"And she doesn't see Julie at all." That still bothered her. "Don't you think that's part of the problem? Maybe if she had Julie to clean up for, she would?"

"Do you think she really wants to see Julie? Have you *seen* Julie yet? She's sixteen and she's beautiful – I mean really beautiful. No wonder Richard goes into a cold sweat when she goes out on a date. I'm sure he remembers what he and Di were doing at that age. And, to top it all off, Julie is very talented. She could rival Di at her best if she wants to pursue her music. Frankly, I don't think Di wants to be reminded of all that." Lucy refilled her cup from the teapot. "Also, if she sees Julie, she'll have to see Richard. *That*, they'll both go a long way to avoid."

The perfect opening. She drew a breath and seized the moment.

"Okay, what happened? And I don't mean then, I mean before." She shook her head impatiently at the obvious answer forming on Lucy's lips. "Not Francie, either. She was a symptom, nothing more. Why her at all? Why did he turn away from Di?"

Lucy's response came too easily. She must have seen this coming. "Why did he marry her, period! I never saw two less compatible people. It was a matter of time before one of them strayed and a matter of opportunity as to who strayed first." She settled back against the quilt, again secure in her dominance. "Don't look so shocked. Do you still see them as Sleeping Beauty and Prince Charming?"

So Lucy had decided to lend Richard her protective silence. Laura didn't doubt that her sister knew exactly what she so neatly evaded telling. "No, I don't believe in fairy tales. But they'd been together for years. My God, they couldn't stay apart for more than a day—"

"Oh, really." Lucy looked at Laura in disgust. "Is that what you think marriage is all about? No wonder you had problems. Tom and I've got a good marriage, and I'll tell you, it's *work* – hard work – but we both understood that going in. I think Di made a big mistake getting married. She and Richard were way too young, and neither one of them knew what they were getting into. Di never got to see a real marriage, and Richard saw an unusually tranquil one because Mom and Dad never argued in front of us. Plus, Mom loved being a homemaker. Richard grew up in a picture-perfect home and assumed that his own would automatically turn out the same way."

"I see." She didn't want to admit that she'd been just as shocked at the reality of marriage, and for the same reasons. It had taken time and experience to learn that one quarrel did not a marriage unmake. The Ashmores' happy home had done a world of disservice.

"Richard, for all his virtues, is not the most flexible of men. He got married with this perfect little idea of 'wife' and expected Di to fit herself right in. Of course, she didn't. Di is the least domestic woman I've ever known. She never intended to live that life. She only got married to get away from Dominic."

That surprised her. "Get away?" But Diana had been Dominic's golden girl, defying him only when it came to Richard. "She was Daddy's pet—"

"Pets run away all the time." Lucy shrugged. "Let's not hash that one out now. Dominic and Di defy analysis. To answer your question – I don't know what happened between Richard and Di. She thought Richard studied too much, and he thought she and Dominic were too close – I imagine our esteemed father, feeling as he did about

Richard, seized every opportunity to interfere. I can tell you that she moved out after their first anniversary—"

That was news. "I don't remember that." Laura tried to think back. When had Dominic started the endless drills, the increased hours of practice? She'd had little time to focus on anything other than music and school. "No one said anything."

"They kept it on the QT. You think Mom wanted to admit that her son's marriage was falling apart after only a year? Even though she never wanted him to marry Di in the first place."

"I guess not." She remembered Peggy's tight lips at the wedding. "Did Daddy know?"

Lucy nodded. "He came up to see her once. She was staying with me – remember that little place I had? He told me to make myself scarce for a couple of days so he could talk some sense into her, so I stayed with Richard. Oh, and Mom went up there too. Not that she liked Di, but she and Dad didn't want Richard to have to deal with a broken marriage while he was still in college."

"So Di went back after that?"

"She found out she was pregnant." Lucy paused. "There was no way she was going to cope with that on her own. So Richard told her to come back and they'd try to make a go of it—" She lifted her hands. "That's when everything *really* went south. I hated to go over there, frankly. I don't think they ever talked to each other except when someone was around. Di said once that the silence broke her."

"My lord." A memory nudged at her – that last Christmas, the contempt in his eyes when he looked at his wife. "But they stayed together—"

Lucy said softly, "Until Julie was five. Those two lived in the same house – maybe shared the same bed, who knows – and *they hardly ever spoke*. Sick, isn't it?"

"Definitely." Obsessed, actually. Terrible that neither Diana nor Richard, in the face of such silent wreckage, had let go. Thank heavens Cam had known when to admit failure. "Why didn't they get divorced? Why don't they now? They're obviously never going to reconcile."

"Di doesn't want a divorce."

"Well, what about him? He can't like living like that, can he?"

"Who knows? He won't tell you. More tea?" Lucy pushed the teapot towards her. "Everyone has a different theory, and not one of us has the nerve to ask, because—"

Laura chimed in, "Richard won't talk," and Lucy laughed.

"See? You've caught on already. His marriage is off limits. Okay, here goes." Lucy leaned her head back against the chair, settling in for a long cozy gossip. "Tom is his closest friend. I know Richard talks to him, because Tom sometimes does work for him that I'm not allowed to see. Tom's theory is – ready for this? – that Richard won't divorce Di because he feels sorry for her."

"No." The man who had so decisively taken her apart in her kitchen had not spared any sympathy for a wife whose sickness was completely self-inflicted.

"Agree," said Lucy. "Tom doesn't like Di, but *he* feels sorry for her, so he's probably projecting his own feelings. But it does make sense, if you remember that Di's crazy. You saw her the other night at dinner. Did she act like a normal human being? I wasn't sure she was even here on earth."

Laura said bluntly, "She was stoned to the gills."

"And you know why? She's a failure. She's failed at marriage, she's failed at motherhood, she's failed at any kind of career. Oh, you know how talented she was, what a beautiful voice she had! She's wasted it all. Her voice is shot now – all those damn drugs, Dominic railed at her to take better care, and she ignored him." Lucy drummed her fingers on the desk. "I can't think of anything that Di has ever accomplished, except give birth to Julie. Richard knows that. He knows what a low opinion of herself she has. He knows that the one thing she clings to, like a badge of honor, is that she is still married."

"I don't buy it." But – *Diana is my wife*. Maybe he clung to that badge too.

"Okay," said Lucy. "Try Di's theory. She thinks Richard likes the status quo. It renders him unattainable. He doesn't have the hassle of a wife, but he has the perfect excuse to hand any woman who might expect him to cough up a wedding ring."

"Surely not." Laura didn't like that any better. "He's not that cold-blooded."

"Oh?" Lucy raised an eyebrow. "His own wife believes it of him, and you don't? Don't want to admit your hero isn't perfect in every way?"

"His wife, to quote you, is crazy. And don't twist my words."

"I don't have to. You do that all on your own." Lucy's eyes rested on her speculatively. "It might surprise you that Julie's theory is pretty much the same, except that, of course, she puts a more charitable spin on it. Julie's daddy does no wrong in Julie's eyes. She thinks

Richard is holding on to Diana for his own sake, to keep himself from caring about a woman again."

"That *is* a daddy's girl speaking." Laura relaxed and reached for her tea. "In other words, Julie doesn't want a rival for her father's affections."

"Maybe." Lucy grabbed at the blanket as it went drifting to the floor. "She definitely has an advanced case of hero worship. I blame Richard. He's created a world where his frailties are never spotlighted, so of course she thinks he slays dragons."

Richard, fiercely protective of Julie's right to an unblemished father.... The stark poignancy of that had escaped her until now. "So what do *you* think?"

"I have two theories." The sunlight through the window glinted off Lucy's hair, creating an undeserved halo effect. "I think Richard will file for divorce in two years, when Julie turns eighteen."

"No way." Laura shook her head. "Once you decide, waiting is intolerable. I *know*. And why then?"

Lucy said softly, "It was intolerable for you because you had nothing to gain by waiting. Put yourself in the position of a man who has already survived a bloody custody battle. On her eighteenth birthday, custody disappears forever. Oh, he'd win if he filed today, no doubt about it. He's done a wonderful job with Julie, she adores him, she scarcely knows Di, and what she knows she doesn't like. But custody would still be an *issue*, don't you see? And Richard will never run that risk again."

Richard, smiling at Julie, as if all his world stood there in his arms. And Francie saying, *he just wants to keep Julie, or else he'd get rid of Di.*

Lucy steepled her hands under her chin. "How about you? Got any ideas?"

Bizarre, and not very generous, to sit here in this sunny office, dissecting that very private man for their personal amusement. Laura shook her head. "No. I'm not like you, Lucy. You should have been a psychiatrist, not a lawyer. Have you been analyzing me all these years from my lyrics?"

"Of course." Lucy didn't miss a beat or blink an eye. "Sexually repressed, a virgin when you married, a faithful wife with no imagination. I got all that from *Waterfalls*. Tom disagreed about your virginity, Di said you're into bondage, and Richard thought you might have strayed once or twice. How far off the mark were we?"

"Oh, Lord." She had to laugh. Served her right. "Wait. Why did Richard think I cheated on Cam?"

"Ask him," suggested Lucy sweetly. "Trade him that for info on his women."

"What about them anyway?" She grabbed at the topic. Better Richard's sex life than her own. "*Does* he get involved there?"

"I don't know."

She thought that not knowing must just kill Lucy. "Come on, you must know *something*. I can't believe you haven't asked."

"I have a spy in his household." Lucy's eyes gleamed. "Unfortunately, she knows next to nothing because Richard doesn't bring his lady friends home to meet his daughter. Tom knows, but you know that male bonding. They must swear an oath of silence."

"He's not seeing anyone right now."

"How do you know?"

"I asked."

"And he didn't take your head off?" Lucy looked impressed. "Normally, I can only tell when he becomes unavailable for dinner on Saturday nights." She half-closed her eyes and surveyed Laura. "I'm afraid the only one we know about is—"

"Francie." She still wished that she hadn't betrayed Francie. "Is she the reason he won't get involved? Did she burn him that badly?"

"Heavens, no." Lucy shook her head. "Don't make the mistake of thinking that Richard loved Francie. He's loved only one woman in his life. He *liked* Francie, and she made herself very convenient. She wanted him, she was willing to break the rules for him, and that must have appealed to him."

"Lucy…." But her sister wasn't done.

"Sometimes," and Lucy casually picked up a paper clip and began to unfold it, "the most attractive thing a man sees in a woman is the way she feels about him. Let's say, she has a crush on him, and they're apart for a long time, so she never grows out of it. Then they meet again, and he's lonely, and she's all grown up now – sparks fly between them – sparks that normally lead straight to bed, but they know better, they see the dangers, so they deal with all that tension by fighting all the time—"

Laura's mouth dropped open in horror.

And Lucy said softly, "I thought so."

Too late. She'd fallen into the trap. Oh, clever Lucy, baiting her, outlining her pet theories, goading her to his defense. She'd not seen the steel jaws closing in on her. And how did Lucy know about that first night! Surely, Richard hadn't admitted how she had curled into him like a kitten seeking warmth, how instinctively he had wrapped himself around her.

But Lucy had guessed.

"Richard refused to talk about the evening he found you." To give her credit, Lucy masked her triumph; compassion and regret laced her voice. "I figured out right away that something had happened, because he didn't want to be around you, and he gave Julie the same impression. Then when he made that comment about you interfering in his marriage, and he got after me for telling you that he's been seeing others – well, I thought, what is the one subject that Richard never talks about? We're very close, Laurie. I know how much he made last year, I know his cholesterol level, for heavens' sake. So what, I thought, can he be concealing from me?"

She wanted to find the nearest hole and crawl into it. But she couldn't move. She could only sit there, prisoner in a comfortable leather chair, and listen to her sister autopsy her innermost thoughts under the cold harsh light of insight.

"And then I remembered how you used to feel about him. We teased you about it. Even Di used to laugh about sleeping late on weekends, because you'd stand in if he wanted to go fishing or riding." Maybe Lucy didn't see the pain she was inflicting, or maybe she did. Maybe the pain was necessary, Laura thought, even as she scrambled to remortar the wall around her heart. "Your crush was very safe, because – face it – you were a quiet, mousy child who never spoke unless spoken to, and Richard was never going to give you the time of day anyway. But you're not that child anymore. You're a successful woman who has made more money than the rest of us ever dreamed about, you've been through a marriage and you've raised a child, you're a beautiful woman now."

"Lucy—"

"A beautiful, *single* woman, living dangerously close to a man you still want. A man who thinks he has reason to avoid you. A man who isn't involved with anyone else, putting him in a lonely and vulnerable position – and how do we know this? Because you asked him. You asked him enough about his marriage to make him very angry. And you took him to task about the other women in his life."

Laura sat perfectly still, hoping that Lucy had finished so that she could slink away and disappear. She willed it with such passion that it surprised her when Lucy merely left her perch behind the desk and came around to take her hand.

"Laurie," no resisting now the gentle timber of Lucy's voice, with all its rich history of healing ancient hurts and dispensing unwanted wisdom, "you must stay away from Richard."

"According to you, Richard won't give me the chance to do anything else." She heard her voice from far away, brittle, falsely upbeat, denying the truth of every word her sister said.

"Actually," said Lucy, and stroked her hand, "I'm not worried about Richard, at least not as much as I am about you and Di. I care about this family, Laurie. Someone needs to. I foresee a disaster if you can't get your feelings for him under control. You'll hurt yourself and him both, and I shudder to think how it might affect Di."

She saw the lifeline of her control floating away downstream; she grabbed and just barely caught it. "You exaggerate, Lucy. Just because I used to hero worship him—"

"Then what happened when you came home?"

Of course, she couldn't answer. That moment of their bodies' recognition, that language of hand against back, of cheek against shoulder, of lip against hair – oh, she refused to share that. She yanked her hand back and walked over to the window, touching Lucy's antiques, picking up the fallen quilt. Lucy watched her, letting the silence ride out, probably (Laura thought, stopping before a pretty framed pencil sketch of Diana that gave no hint of her demons) letting her imagine that she might avoid an answer.

Lucy and her damned power struggles. Whoever spoke first lost.

Lucy waited her out.

She was well-schooled in silence. She waited Lucy out.

"Don't get me wrong," Lucy said eventually. "If things were different, I'd encourage this. I think you're lonely. You've no man in your life, your marriage was unhappy, it ended horribly – you're entitled to one hell of a fling, and I hope you have it soon."

"Thank you," Laura snapped. "But I'm not in the market."

Lucy ignored that. "You will be. Give them a signal, guys will be lining up."

"Oh, my *God*, Lucy!"

She might as well not have protested, as far as Lucy was concerned. "As for Richard, I'd prefer that he see someone who gets him and that whole Ashmore Park mystique instead of some little girl who just sees that face and that house and decides that she wants to play lady of the manor. I worry about him. He's a good man, and he's so lonely, rattling around out there in the country with only Julie. He needs someone else to love, he needs a woman who will shake him up and bring him alive again. I watched him once at a fundraiser, talking to a woman he left with later, and he was smiling, laughing, but somehow," and Lucy paused, "he didn't seem quite real, like he was playing a part. And I thought, how sad, he's let Di and Francie bring him to this."

Laura scarcely had time to picture the scene – Richard standing close to the woman, talking, smiling, admiring her with his eyes (the way he had looked at her) and the woman (young, pretty, soft-voiced) brushing an imaginary speck of dust off his jacket – before Lucy thrust her rapier home.

"So – don't push your feelings for him into an already bad situation. Leave him alone. He's not your romantic hero anymore. He's a man struggling to balance his own needs with the welfare of his wife and daughter. He doesn't need you. If he wants a woman, he'll find one. But not you, Laurie. You stay away from him."

The words neatly found their target, stabbed her, and ran her clean through. In a few words, Lucy had done what no one else ever had. She had explored Laura, filleted her, and laid her most precious thoughts open to view.

I will not let her do this to me.

Please, no tears. She dared not betray any weakness now. She said merely, and marveled at her pleasant boredom, "I'm not interested. Richard is quite safe from me."

"Then why doesn't he think so?"

She managed a shrug, a tolerant movement to convey bewilderment. "We don't see eye to eye about Di, that's all. I – I didn't expect their marriage to be in such disarray, and I'm shocked at how far she's fallen. Naturally, I was concerned that he wasn't doing all he could to help her."

Quiet. Then Lucy smiled, a smile of respect. "You're good, you really are. You may get rattled, but you recover quickly. You're entitled to your shock. You're entitled to talk to Di about it; in fact, I encourage you to. God knows we've talked until we're blue in the face! Make her sing for you. It'll do her good to embarrass herself in front of Cat Courtney. Just don't talk to her about Richard. Stay out of that marriage, and keep away from him. Please."

She made her voice light, and, dear Lord, what it took out of her to say the words. She felt all the exhaustion of a swimmer, drowning, finding the last vital energy to swim for shore. "Because I remind him of Francie?"

She managed to throw Lucy there. "No! Why do you think that?"

One afternoon, when I was young, and blood and tide ran high….

"Don't I remind him of his great lost love?"

No answer behind her. She couldn't stand it; she turned around, away from Diana's picture, and she saw that Lucy had risen, come to stand behind her so that, when she turned, she looked straight into her sister's eyes.

"Oh, yes," said Lucy softly, "you remind him. Remember I had one more theory? Richard won't divorce Diana because he can't let her go. After all this, Francie, lovers, other women – he still loves her. Oh, you remind him, Laurie – of Diana."

Through a night of precious little sleep, as she sat on the window seat overlooking the pool, her face buried in a compliant Max's fur, Laura St. Bride looked deep into herself.

She wanted to hate Lucy. Damn Lucy anyway, for that X-ray vision, for those soft words with their knife-sharp edges, for the glistening tears that had nearly called Laura back before she had walked out. Damn Lucy for calling later, on a pretext, reaching out in reconciliation; damn her own inability to slam down the phone.

Damn Lucy for reminding her that forever and ever Richard belonged to Diana.

Damn Lucy for being right.

She faced facts. All right, she was infatuated with Richard Ashmore. Childish, mortifying – she passed over all that with scarcely a thought. Not too surprising, actually, that she'd fallen straight back into the old emotional patterns with him; she'd never had a chance to grow out of them. Look how quickly she'd reverted to being Lucy's little sister.

But Lucy had forgotten, Laura thought, enjoying the steady throbbing of Max's purring against her breast, that Richard had been her friend. She'd gone fishing with him those early Saturday mornings, helped him cart his RC models to meets, baked endless batches of cookies for him, because she liked him. Oh, yes, she'd dreamed of him, hung on his every word, even written a secret poem to him. (Had she destroyed it? She hoped so.) He'd been her hero, but he had also been her best friend.

And their friendship lay broken now, casualty of his pride and her loss.

She pondered leaving it that way.

If she did, refusing to mend matters between them, she'd please no one. She and Richard would meet rarely, and when they did, they'd speak briefly and coolly, separating as soon as courtesy permitted. She'd never get to know Julie; Richard would see to that. The coolness would spread. Everyone would soon know not to invite her to any function that Richard wanted to attend. She didn't doubt that Richard would hold everyone's loyalty; he'd been here, part of the family, during all the years of her exile.

She'd crack the family in two and force Lucy and Tom to take sides. And she didn't want that. She liked Tom, she wanted his good opinion, and she was sure to lose that if Tom's best friend refused to break bread with her.

And, sooner or later, Diana would find out.

She began to understand, dimly, the core of Lucy's concern.

Richard held all the winning cards. She'd leave in a matter of weeks; she had only this short time to rebuild her relationships with her family. One thing she'd learned with Cam was that an estrangement, once begun, had a life of its own. She couldn't rely on Richard to cauterize the wounds their words had inflicted on each other, because he had too much to gain. He needed protection against the attraction shimmering between them, far more than she, and time was on his side. All he had to do was wait her out, and he could go back to the life he'd built, safe from her, from the dangers she'd brought with her.

She reminded him. Of Diana. Of Francie.

And like them, she wanted him.

She closed her eyes.

It lay there, a darkness in her heart. No longer the shining, romantic infatuation of young Laura, dazzled by the laughing young man who'd taught her to dance one long-ago summer. Ah, Richard of the charming smile, the easy word, the kind gesture to heal a hurt young girl's heart!

And now Richard, quiet, cold, devastated by the mysterious rift in his marriage.

And Laura St. Bride, not a shy teenager any longer, but a woman responding to the man he had become, dancing in his arms and dreaming of the touch of his hands.

A sudden thought slammed into her, and Max yowled in protest as she straightened.

The night she'd come back, Richard had seemed genuinely happy to see her. He had comforted her, teased her, brought her up to date – and all the while, he'd scarcely mentioned Diana. She remembered her impression that he was a widower at heart, that Diana no longer claimed him.

But all that ease had vanished as soon as he asked her to dance and she stepped into his arms.

As soon as they stepped from old friends to man and woman.

A shield, Laura thought in wonder. *He's using Diana as a shield.*

And had Lucy sensed that? Lucy, who knew Richard so well. Now, alone, in the middle of the night, she read Lucy's mind as she had not earlier: that a one-sided infatuation held no inherent dangers, but this attraction lay on both sides.

But of course he wanted her, Lucy had said. She reminded him of Diana.

Laura stared down at her hands, her left curled around her cat, her right stroking his fur, and concentrated her choices. The left – safety, her sisters' goodwill, Tom's approval, a chance to heal the wounds of her disappearance. A return to Laura Abbott. And the right – and she allowed herself to savor the lush fullness of Max's fur against her fingers – on the right, beckoning, the unknown darkness of Richard Ashmore, and a memory of her body against the heart of a man who wanted her and rejected the wanting.

Either/or. Lucy had made it plain that she could not have both.

She smiled down through the night at her cat, and continued to run her right hand along his spine.

Laura planned her approach carefully. Twelve years of living with Cameron St. Bride had taught her the value of strategic planning.

Her timing should be well nigh impeccable. Unless Richard's habits had changed as much as his personality, he was still an early riser, and she remembered enough of country living to know that he'd have chores around the estate before he left for his office. The presence of his Lexus, standing in the circular drive in front of the Folly, proved her right; she backed in smoothly and blocked his way out.

She smoothed her hair down as she approached the door. She'd taken special care with her appearance that morning. Richard had relaxed around her when she appeared the most like Laura Abbott, the least like Cat Courtney, so maybe he'd respond to the jeans and camp shirt and Alice in Wonderland hair band.

Or maybe he'd kick her right off Ashmore Park the moment he realized she'd hacked the code for the security gates.

Laura breathed in deeply, squared her shoulders, and lifted her hand to the door knocker.

He opened the door before she had to knock twice, and for a second she simply stared at him. The doorstep sat below the threshold, so that he loomed over her and knocked all her purpose clean out of her mind. She thought, with the part of her mind that wasn't scrambling to remember why she'd come, that he looked tired and ill. His eyes were creased with exhaustion, the silver glints at his temples picked up by the blossoming morning sun. He looked remote and not at all happy to see her.

He broke her paralysis with a sneeze.

"Laura." Even the sound of her name gave him away; his voice held the faint nasal tone of a cold that refused to give up and go away. "What are you doing here?"

Unwelcoming, but she'd expected it. "I came to talk to you," she said over the punctuation of another sneeze. She felt her confidence rising. She'd cared for Cam when he was ill, and even if Richard matched him in sheer bloody-minded irritability, he couldn't possibly be a bigger baby. "May I come in?"

"What? Oh, of course. Sorry." He stood aside as she entered but made no move to shut the door behind her. He continued to stare at her; maybe she'd overdone it with the Alice hair band. "How did you get in? I didn't hear you buzz from the gate."

She laughed to put herself at ease. "I hacked your password, that's how. Your birthday? Piece of cake."

Reluctant admiration flitted across his face. "It used to be Julie's," he admitted. "I suppose this comes from being married to a computer guru? Did he hack his way into the Pentagon?" He heard his words. "Sorry. I didn't mean that."

"No." She was careful not to let her relief show. "He was too conservative for that." She slipped her shoulder bag strap down her arm and let her purse drop on a small Chippendale table beneath a hall mirror. "How is Julie? Did you catch her cold?"

"She's fine, and yes, I did." He didn't shift his eyes from her, even as she placed her keys on the table beside her purse, taking care not to mar the polished surface of the old wood. She used the mirror to adjust the hair band, putting off the confrontation for another minute.

He appeared in the mirror behind her, and their images, hers superimposed over his, carved away at Laura's resolve. Oh, God, it stretched there again between them, that taut, vibrating string of attraction. She didn't want to see it, not after a sleepless night of coming to terms with herself. Richard's eyes met hers in the mirror, and she saw the embers of anger still burning beneath the surface politeness.

Lucy had been right. In fury too often bloomed the seeds of desire.

Laura said quickly, "Are you okay?"

"No." His honesty surprised her. "My head is splitting. I've got a presentation in Charleston tomorrow, so I'm eating aspirin and working at home to get over this." He waved a hand out towards the main part of the house. "Is there something I can do for you, Laura?"

The moment of truth. And how like Richard to maintain those cool, exquisite manners, when he so clearly wanted her out of his house and out of his sight. She turned around to face him, as she would have faced a hostile critic, and found that he stood close to her, violating her space.

Deliberately, too. She saw that in his face.

"Yes," she said clearly. "You can let me apologize."

He'd braced for another frontal attack, she saw, and her words had ambushed him from the rear. Try as he might, he couldn't disguise his surprise.

Swiftly, Laura moved to press home her advantage.

"I don't want us to be enemies, Richard." Now that she'd started, she felt confident. He was just another audience, after all, the most important she ever remembered, but to be wooed and won like any other. "I pushed too hard last week, and I apologize. I said—" and here she let her voice falter, ever so slightly, to convey vulnerability, "I said some unforgivable things, and I'm sorry—"

"In other words," said Richard bluntly, staring her straight down, "Lucy's talked to you."

"Yes, she did." So, blast him, he *was* going to be stubborn and bloody-minded, holding her off with every resource he possessed. She must pose more of a threat than she had dreamed. "You don't know me very well, Richard, or you'd know that Lucy's influence goes only so far. I don't roll over and play dead for anyone." *Oh,*

please, that's all you do. "But I see her point. We have to get along because—"

"Because otherwise Lucy can't have her grand family reunion
dinner," interrupted Richard again, and folded his arms with an air
of real impatience.

Where had his famous manners gone? He'd come too close now;
she fought off the intimidation of his height. A dozen retorts flooded
into her mind, a dozen light-hearted threats to carry out if he didn't
stop interrupting her, but she stopped before they ever reached her
lips. He wanted that, he wanted her to laugh, make him laugh; he
wanted a superficial end to their quarrel, so they could retreat forever to their old relationship.

The last thing in the world he wanted between them was honesty.

She said softly, "No, not for that. I've no desire to cause one of
those Southern feuds that go on for generations, and I'll do what I
have to do to patch this up. But not because it spoils Lucy's seating
arrangements for family dinners. My reasons are much more selfish
than that."

She'd caught his attention now; she held the string of desire in her
hands, drawing it into a cat's cradle. He was paying attention to her;
he couldn't divine her intentions. She saw the recognition of that in
his face, and a cautious respect.

Good. You're finally listening to me.

"First," said Laura before the steady gaze of his eyes robbed her
of her resolve, "I want to see my niece. I'll behave myself, Richard,
you needn't worry about that. I won't say a word about you and Di,
and I won't talk about Francie. I won't promise never to mention her,
she was important to me, but you can rest assured I won't discuss
your relationship with her."

Richard settled back, seemingly to relax, but they both read it for
the partial concession it was. He said mildly, "I don't mind you seeing Julie. I've said that all along. She wants to meet you – in fact, she
should be in from the stables any minute now, if you care to wait."
He inclined his head towards the next room. "Shall we go have a seat
while you set forth the rest of the terms of my surrender?"

With that one decisive stroke, he stripped her of her advantage.
She cursed herself even as she stared at him.

He said gently, "That's what this is all about, isn't it? You came
back to Virginia to settle things, and I stand in your way. Very well,
Laura, I don't think you'll be denied. What else do you want?"

Oh, Richard, you stand there, so confident that I'll never bring it out in the open between us. You know me of old, you know I'd rather die than tell you how I feel about you. And you'll never speak, because I'm too dangerous. I'm the one woman in the world you mustn't feel anything for.

He had gone ahead of her, stepping down into the living area, so confident that she would follow his lead that he could comfortably turn his back on her.

She held caution in her hands, a fragile vessel of old, and in one second she dashed it to the ground and shattered it into a thousand glittering pieces.

She smiled at his back and pitched her voice low and husky. "You're right, Richard. I came back to settle unfinished business." She counted off two beats. "Like you."

He stopped then, and slowly, very slowly, he turned around.

She stopped then. The wariness of his face warned her away, warned her that she'd gone too far again. She saw that he wanted nothing to do with her, that given his choice he'd rip apart the gossamer attraction shimmering between them. In her direction lay all the perils of desire, all the threat of pain.

She saw, too, that he would do nothing to stop her.

For that one moment, he stood open to her.

You remind him of Diana.

She couldn't do it to him. This man needed badly to be brought to his knees, but she had lost the heart to do it. She wanted him, and he wanted her (or the ghost he saw in her), but she had loved him too much to use it against him.

She gave up.

"I want to stop fighting with you." To her ears, she sounded subdued and defeated. "We used to be friends, Richard. Can't we be again?"

"Of course."

His voice had lightened in his triumph; he was a kind victor. And why shouldn't he be gracious, crossing the entry way to her, reaching out for her hands? He'd won. She had defeated herself; he knew she'd never approach him again.

Numbly, she accepted the tender of peace on his terms.

"Apology accepted," he said. "And I apologize too, Laura. Diana's your sister, and you're right to care about her, and equally right to blame me. God knows, if anything had happened to you, I certainly would have held your husband accountable." He still held her hands, lightly, impersonally, too much the friendly brother. "Let's put this behind us."

No, Laura thought resentfully, letting him guide her down into the main living area, *let's not. And I thought Lucy was manipulative.*

One last skirmish before she surrendered. She had strength enough to last her for that.

She said pleasantly, "Tell me, Richard. Do women always fall into line so easily? Or am I just a special case?" She tasted satisfaction as he turned around sharply. "I'm properly penitent, and frankly I plan to stay that way. Lucy's made it clear that I have a lot to lose if I don't. That works out well for you, doesn't it?"

For a moment, his mask dropped. She saw a flare in his eyes, not quite anger – in the old days, even two weeks ago, she might have thought it a certain rueful admiration.

For a moment, they stood as equals.

"Yes," he said, "it does. Be very clear in your mind, Laura. I will do whatever it takes to protect my daughter and myself from the past. And you, darling," he touched her cheek, "you're the past."

And with that, he broke her.

13

Girl, Eavesdropping

RICHARD INVITED HER TO WAIT FOR JULIE, but her niece did not appear as expected. Laura spent a few fruitless minutes alone in the enormous great room, flipping blindly through a magazine, while Richard retreated to his office in the corner and rang the line out in the stables.

"She must have taken one of the horses out," he said. "She often rides in the morning. Do you want to go out there? You know the way, or I can take you."

"No, thank you." Not even to escape Richard was she going to exile herself out to the stables. "I know you've got work to do. Why don't I just explore on my own, and you get on with what you need to do? I haven't seen the house yet."

She expected him to forestall her – surely, after all that had passed between them, he did not want her roaming through his house – but to her surprise, he merely nodded, sat down at a massive desk, and turned to his computer.

Why shouldn't he trust her, though? Laura Abbott had proved tractable enough. He knew he could control her.

As soon as Richard looked sufficiently engrossed in his work, Laura rose to explore his fortress.

She went first to the music room, separated from the great room by the etched glass wall that she had glimpsed the night she had sat by the trees and watched them. *Be honest, stalked them.* Julie's baby grand sat in the middle of the room, its black lacquer gleaming in the light from the atrium doors. In the corner of the room stood a concert harp. Laura raised her eyebrows. That was a new instrument for the Abbotts.

The music room connected through French doors to a huge library with a staircase leading to the second floor, through another set of French doors to the entrance hall, and across that to a formal dining room. As soon as she saw it, Laura knew instantly where her call had ended up on Christmas Day. This, not the dining room at the old house, must have been the scene for the traditional Christmas dinner. What a gorgeous room – a *trompe l'oeil* mural on the one long wall, opposite a panoramic window, gleaming formal table, the old Ashmore china and crystal in the china cabinet. The chandelier spilled light over the center of the table, perfectly situated to catch the reflection from the marble fireplace on the far wall.

She'd loved her dining room in Plano, but this cast it into the shade.

Still, it seemed very formal for a single father and his daughter. Maybe he entertained a lot.

She stepped through the doorway into the kitchen, and now she was frankly envious. This was the kitchen she'd wanted in her house, and Cam had kept promising that they would get around to remodeling, but they never had. Terry would consider that he'd died and gone to heaven. Huge, with beautiful gray cabinetry, lighter gray granite tops, gleaming copper pots and pans hung on racks above a stove, an enormous island, all the built-ins, including a subzero large enough to live in, a butler's pantry that went on forever, a staircase that led to the second floor, a long oak table and chairs – when she bought a house, she was going to have a kitchen just like this, even if she had to tear down the rest of the house to get it. She'd have to steal Richard's plans.

Maybe she should hire him to design it for her.

No wonder he had girlfriends. Any woman who saw this would fall in love just for the kitchen. But no, Lucy had said that he never brought his lady friends to the house.

Even the utility room – this was a room designed around what it actually took to run a home. She'd never been able to get Cam to understand why she wanted a mud room, or a separate area for laying out sweaters so that they could dry flat. But this house had it all.

The solarium, though – she wondered if Richard had built the room and then not known what to do with it. It was too large to be so bland; it ought to be a haven of peace and quiet, filled with plants and music and comfortable, overstuffed furniture, instead of this rather unengaging room. A pity, because it looked out into the green fields of Ashmore Park, a view of utter privacy and security, and a terrace leading down to the pool. If this was her house, she would make this her sanctuary. She would relax with her books and listen to music and dream the hours away.

She wandered out into the great room and started up the flying staircase. From the landing, she looked down over the railing. Below, the enormous room lay spread out before her, a map of the inner landscape of the man who'd designed it. He worked at his desk, oblivious to the woman overhead, to her eyes sweeping the room in a search for a key to the map.

A cocoon, she thought, a retreat. She wondered why he had not chosen a private study for himself, but she could see that, from his desk, tucked into an alcove set off by columns that rose to the ceiling, Richard ensured both privacy and access to his domain. The supporting columns that held up the massive high ceiling (now, thankfully, devoid of the hideous baroque gods and goddesses of the old Gilded Age ceiling) divided the room into sections – a living area centered in a half-moon in front of an enormous stone fireplace, a second library area papered with bookcases, volumes stacked lovingly, their bindings indiscriminate dashes of color. The immense western window with its myriad lights shone on Julie's music room and his work area. In the living area, a recliner sat slightly apart. She had a sudden, strong vision of Richard sitting in the dark, listening to music.

This house had been built for more than a man and his daughter. He should not have time to sit in that recliner very often.

He lifted his head unexpectedly, and their eyes met.

"Well?"

Laura drew in a breath and swept her hand out over the expanse of space below. "Wonderful! I'm moving in. I am in lust with your kitchen."

He laughed, and did she imagine it or did a shadow leave his face? "So is Lucy. She wants me to move out so she can have it."

"I have to get a house. Will you design one for me?"

"Gladly. And since you're rich as Croesus, I'll raise my fee accordingly. You don't have a house?"

"Not like this, that's for sure." She leaned forward on the railing. "I never bought one after – after I left Cam's. The brownstone in New York is a prewar double – it has great ceilings and all this incredible molding, but it needs a lot of work. I have an Edwardian flat in Knightsbridge – actually, it belonged to Cam's mother, and she left it to me. She had this thing for fireplaces, which is great because the heating is definitely Edwardian. Meg and I spent the winter bundled up in blankets. Our house in Plano was fake French chateau, okay, I guess, but *this*—"

"Beaux Arts original." The phone on his desk rang, and his hand hovered over it. "I had a lot of fun with the upstairs. Tell me what you think."

He answered the call, and she wandered away from the railing. The landing extended around three sides of the house, with a second stairway leading up from the kitchen area, leaving the western wall free for that unbelievable window. She started along the hallway on the south and opened the first door to find a two-bedroom suite, obviously not in use. Another door produced an enormous game room, with a big-screen TV that rivaled the media screen in the St. Bride house.

She peered over the railing. Richard was still on the phone, staring out the great western window, his back to her.

The first door on the eastern end gave her a more fruitful yield. She stepped into a veritable princess's bower, a gorgeous suite of antique lace and bleached oak and peach moiré-covered walls. A loving father had not forgotten a single detail, from the window seat to the old silver dresser set to the corner sewing nook.

Rows of dolls peeked at her from one wall, and Laura was startled to recognize a few familiar faces. She had not thought to wonder what had happened to the dolls Dominic had brought her from his European forays. Francie had deemed herself too old to share her room with a collection of dolls and had banished them to the attic in their early teens. Someone – Diana? more likely Lucy – must have unearthed them and given them a good home.

The room was neat, Julie's clothes all hung away, but still the girl's spirit lingered in the room. Not only the dolls – and the fancy, high-end Cat Courtney bear sold at all the concerts – but pictures, framed in silver and wood, scattered around the room, all gave testament to the world of Julia Ashmore. Laura wandered from one to the next: Lucy and a much younger Julie in front of a Christmas tree, Peggy and Philip (her breath caught in remembered love), Richard astride a magnificent horse with a little Julie in front of him, Richard and a grade-school Julie in front of the castle at the Magic Kingdom, Richard and a teenage Julie in a sailboat. Even Cat Courtney, a magazine picture carefully cut out and framed.

No picture of Diana.

She backed out, aware of a sudden sense of intrusion into a world she had no invitation to enter.

The next door reverted to type, another two-bedroom suite for visitors. Laura closed the door, just in time to hear Richard embark on a sneezing fit. His voice drifted up, "Didn't my mother give you a sure fix for a cold? I'm giving a three-hour presentation tomorrow."

He sounded just as pitiful as Cam when he felt sick, and Laura felt just as sorry for him. "Eat some jalapeños," she said heartlessly, and opened the first door on the northern wall.

She stopped, stunned.

Who could mistake the purpose of this room? In the corner, the old wooden cradle where generations of Ashmores had rocked gave it straight away. This room had been designed as a nursery, although – Laura drew a test finger across the wooden saddle of an antique rocking horse – no one had entered this room in a long, long time.

Along the wall, a connecting door.

She, who had never entered this house before, knew where it led. She stepped through it into the master bedroom, and stepped further into Richard Ashmore's universe.

His suite was even larger than Julie's. The opposite wall held doorways into other rooms: a bathroom, a dressing room, a small study and workroom, a staircase spiraling down to the library below. She recognized the antique furniture from Ashmore Magna, and a couple of paintings seemed familiar. The king-size bed went on for-ever, a vast field covered by the quilt she and Peggy Ashmore had sewn for a wedding present. She wandered over to the bed, her hand outstretched; she could not resist touching the square she had worked the spring before Richard married Diana.

She'd designed it herself, and Diana had obligingly posed for her one afternoon so that Laura could cut an exact silhouette. She traced her finger along the black line of the carefree hair, the lovely profile of Richard's intended bride sewn into posterity with love and despair.

Tiny stitches, Peggy said lovingly across the years. *Take your time, Laurie. You're doing such a pretty job. Richard will be so pleased that you made this specially for him.*

Her hand dropped.

She turned around, and then she saw the painting. It hung oppo-site the bed, and she knew that this painting had never hung on the walls of Ashmore Magna. Peggy would never have allowed it. A woman stood in a room at dusk, turned away from the artist just enough so that the painting gave a hint of her dreaming profile and the curve of her breast. Her arms rose to unpin her hair so that it tumbled onto her bare shoulders. She wore a backless white gown that scooped down low, and what held it up, Laura couldn't tell. The artist hadn't worried with that small detail. He was more interested in the exquisite lines of her back.

It was, without a doubt, the most sensuous painting she had ever seen in her life. Every line in the woman's body spoke of love and longing, of anticipation of the hour ahead, and Richard saw this first thing every morning and last thing every night. It could have been Diana if she had ever worn her hair that long. It could have been Francie if she had parted her hair on the side instead of in the middle.

It could have been her if she had ever figured in this man's life.

She wrenched her attention away from the painting, her heart accelerating.

This was definitely a man's room. For all the colors of the quilt and the paintings, the room seemed somber in the northern light. No woman had ever shared this room. A woman would have added hairbrushes, plants, lace pillows. A woman would have moved that painting so that she didn't have to compete with it.

But he had built this room, this house, with all its abundant space, for a reason.

I'll never marry again, he'd said. *I don't want a divorce.* But Lucy, who knew Richard so well, who had seen this house many times in the past, Lucy thought he was only biding his time.

All those rooms, and that nursery.... She sat down on the quilt and spread her fingers along Diana's silhouette again.

It served her right. She'd sought a blueprint to his thinking, and she'd found it. Maybe Richard had lied to her, maybe he didn't realize himself the future he'd designed, or maybe he considered his plans none of her business. She trusted the signs. He had every intention of divorcing Diana. He fully meant to marry again and start another family, once his first marriage was dissolved and his first family raised.

She looked around the room again, her eyes alighting on items she hadn't noticed before: a couple of books lying on the night stand, a ship model on a chest of drawers, the telescope standing ready near the northern window. Through one of the doors on the opposite wall, she saw into the workroom: model planes suspended from the ceiling, a couple of models in various stages of construction, a computer on a desktop.

A man with too much time on his hands, a man on whom the late hours of night weighed heavily.

"Damn you, Richard." She didn't fear that he heard her whisper;

she didn't fear that he might appear in the doorway to interpret the tears spilling down her cheeks.

Damn you! You should have divorced her, if there was no hope. You should have married again, so that when I came here, you'd be happily ensconced with a loving wife, maybe sons and daughters you could love as much as you love Julie. It wouldn't hurt so much then. I could have buried Francie forever, and I would have forgiven you for taking the second chance life offered you.

Oh, Richard, if only you had…. You could have invited me to meet your wife and children, and I'd have been everything you'd want in a sister-in-law. I'd have stopped loving you then, because you would have been happy and I wouldn't hear my heart saying, if only, if only….

Damn you, Richard! You should have been happy.

Two years. In two years he would divorce Diana.

In two years she'd be close to having Meg raised. In two years she would still not even be thirty-five. She might want to marry again, try again to have a family….

Dear God! What was she thinking?

Lucy had been right to worry. She'd detected the dark loneliness in Richard, the answering shadows in Laura that knew only desire and forgot all conscience. *He doesn't need you.*

She looked around the room once more, imagining her Tiffany lamp brightening that table, her antique dressing table in that corner, her prettiest silk nightgown lying tossed on the end of the bed, a child sleeping in the cradle they'd brought in from the next room….

Imagining getting ready for bed, her back to him as he waited, letting her hair tumble down.

Not for you, Laurie. Not ever for you.

Into her misery intruded a young, fresh voice, high-pitched in excitement. "She's *here!* Where is she? Why didn't you call me?" And she heard the eager sound of feet running up the stairs and around the landing.

Laura brushed her tears from her eyes, left her dreams crumbling at the foot of Richard's bed, and went out into the hall to meet her niece.

She had the eerie feeling of looking into a long-gone mirror. The same long-legged, coltish walk, the mark of a girl not yet used to her height; the same green eyes squinting to bring her into focus; the same long, wild autumn hair that she'd never managed to tame. But Laura Abbott had never possessed the sheer, stunning, drop-dead-in-your-tracks beauty of Julia Ashmore.

No, only Diana had been that beautiful. But cool, sophisticated Diana had surely never shrieked with joy and flung herself into a mere aunt's arms.

"Aunt Laura! I can't believe I'm finally meeting you!" Julie gave her a second, impetuous hug that knocked the breath out of her. "I'm so glad you're here! Can you stay? I'll start breakfast, if you can just wait a minute while I clean up – I was out riding, I'd never have gone if I'd known—"

"Julie." Laura succumbed to laughter herself. Impossible not to catch the delight shining on the girl's face and bubbling in her voice. "Give me a second to catch my breath! One question at a time! And none of this Aunt Laura stuff, either, you're making me feel ancient!"

Ah, she's Diana all over again. The way she tilts her head, that smile – my God, that smile, it must have broken his heart the first time she turned it on him.

"If Dad says it's okay," said Julie. "I'm not supposed to call grown-ups by their first names."

That artless statement had the salutary effect of making Laura feel every one of her years. "Well, I'm different. I wasn't even your age now when you were born. We could have been sisters."

Julie giggled. "Sisters! I've always wanted a sister. I used to pester Dad to get married again so I could have a younger sister." Laura heard Richard choke, and not from his cold. Served him right for eavesdropping. "I hear I have a cousin who's practically my age."

"Not quite." Laura let her niece draw her along the landing towards her room and threw a bright smile at Richard, who had given into his curiosity and come up the stairs to meet them. Let him wonder what she was going to say! "She's twelve."

"What's her voice? Or does she play?" Words of a true Abbott.

"No, she's a dancer. She started in ballet when she was four."

"Ballet!" Julie breathed. "How fantastic! I wanted to take lessons when I was little, but I couldn't even manage tap. I'm not very graceful. But I love the ballet. I remember once, a long time ago, Dad took me to New York, and we saw Baryshnikov dance." She threw a look at her father as he approached. "Remember, Dad? I couldn't sleep that night!"

"Or the night before." Richard smiled at his daughter, and Laura noticed the gentleness of his voice, the easiness of his manner. "The best night of your life, you said."

"Oh, no," said Julie, and bestowed such a dazzling smile on her aunt that Laura was nearly floored. "Second best. The best was when we saw you in London. You looked so beautiful! Didn't you sketch her on the flight back, Dad, because we couldn't find our programs? We left them in the cab."

"I'd be interested to see that," Laura said. "I'm afraid my concerts all run together in my mind." She couldn't remember what she had worn during that concert; she only remembered the jeans and sweater when Cam had taken her to dinner afterwards and told her he wanted a divorce.

"I've got it in my portfolio." He opened Julie's bedroom door for her. "Go clean up, kitten. We'll wait downstairs for you."

"Okay." Julie hesitated in her doorway, then leaned over and gave Laura an impulsive kiss on the cheek. "Do wait for me, please. Maybe we could go around together for the day, if you're not busy? I know all kinds of places to hang out. Do you like antiques? I know this market outside town."

"Sure." She'd never get to know Julie under Richard's eye. "Hurry down."

Julie vanished into her room, and Laura had no choice now but to turn around and face Richard. She was surprised to see that he had not retreated back into his emotional fortress; either he'd decided to tolerate her or she was reaping the benefit of Julie's presence. She was even more surprised to hear, "Well? Look familiar?"

She understood at once, and laughed. "I never looked like that! Heavens, Richard, I'm surprised you haven't gone gray, with a daughter that gorgeous!"

"I'm getting there." He escorted her companionably down the stairs. "She doesn't date much yet, thank the Lord, but even so – I remember myself at that age. I know what those boys are thinking."

"Poetic justice," said Laura sweetly.

Overhead, the sound of running shower water signaled that Julie was now out of earshot. "I'll show you the sketch," he said. "And we need to talk."

She said warily, "What now?"

"Julie," he said. "I don't want you alone with her. Sorry, Laura, I just don't trust you."

In her sixteen years, Julie Ashmore had learned the value of listening.

She'd discovered early on that a quiet child became an invisible child. So quiet, so invisible, that the adults forgot her presence and discussed matters they never meant her to hear.

Her father and grandfather, working to clean up the destruction in the garage. Her grandfather, "This can't go on, son." And her father, "I've reached the end. She's not coming back."

Her grandfather, in the kitchen one afternoon, unaware that Julie was playing on the porch outside, "Of course he's unhappy. He married the wrong girl." And her grandmother in reply, "Oh, I wish he'd waited for Laura. She was perfect for him, she adored him, and he never realized how much he depended on that. Now he's tied to that stupid girl." Pure dislike in Peggy Ashmore's usually gentle voice. "Dear heavens, men are such fools for a beautiful face!"

Lucy, when Julie spent the night, confiding on the telephone, "No, I don't know who he's with, Di! He just said he'd pick Julie up tomorrow afternoon."

A sweet voice on the telephone, "Hi, this is Jennifer, may I speak to your father?" And her father swiftly taking the telephone, his voice dropping. In his quiet laughter and intimate tones were distilled all the mysteries of men and women. Julie wasn't surprised when he took her over to Lucy's for another weekend sleepover.

Richard one Christmas Eve, "No, not until you sober up. I can't risk you taking her anywhere."

Lucy, sobbing helplessly against Richard's shoulder, "All these years, and no word – tell me, please, I won't pry, I just need to know. You've never heard from Francie?" And, in the firelight, Richard's distant eyes, even as he touched Lucy's cheek and said gently, "Not a word."

Richard, a year ago, eluding Lucy with amusement, "I haven't had a date in years. Tell Diana, okay?"

Richard calling Tom Maitland late at night, "Margaret St. Bride. Probably born in San Francisco in late 1988, early 1989. February at the outset. Keep this between us. I don't want Lucy in on this."

Last week, a famous voice on voice mail, unsure and nervous, "Richard, how's Julie? I hope she's doing better. Maybe I can see her after she's over her cold. I'll be back from Texas on Tuesday." The speed with which Julie's father hit the erase button became one more thread to weave into an increasingly bewildering tapestry.

And now, Julie thought, wrapping her bathrobe around her,

Laura emerging from his bedroom with tear-heavy eyes, and he watching them as if – well, almost as if he feared something terrible happening.

And who could miss the way they refused to look at each other!

Richard Ashmore's little girl smiled to herself and let the shower water continue to run.

They had their backs to her as she stole quietly out of her room and pulled the door shut. She knew all the creaking boards to avoid; she'd had plenty of practice in the past, creeping over to watch her father as he worked at his desk. Plenty of long-ago nights when he thought he'd put her to bed, she'd hidden out at the end of the landing behind the enormous plant and read in the faint light from his desk. She hugged the wall and reached the sheltering shadows of the dieffenbachia.

Not that either her father or her aunt were likely to hear her. They were standing near the great desk, Laura flipping energetically through Richard's portfolio and clearly upset with the man looking over her shoulder. Julie, veteran of many a lecture, knew what his folded arms meant.

"Look, damn it, I gave you my word. I said I wouldn't say anything, and I meant it." Laura paused at one page, and her voice altered. "Oh, that's wonderful, Richard. You should frame it. How old was she then?"

"Three or so. The date's on the back." The deceptive mildness of Richard's voice warned Julie. "My favorite's later, with Julie and Mom. What are you planning to tell her when she asks why you left?"

"You said she wouldn't."

I don't have to, thought Julie. *I can count. If Meg was born when Dad told Tom she was, then she's no twelve years old, dear Aunt Laura. So you had a boyfriend they didn't know about, did you?*

"I have no idea what she'll do. But if I'd heard my family speculating all my life, I'd ask."

Laura turned over a page. "I'll tell her what I told Meg. I'll say that I didn't get along with my father and I left to get away from him. Richard, these are terrific. Do you still paint?"

"Weekend dabbler." Julie drew back into the shadows as Richard's arms unfolded and he leaned in near Laura, and his voice lowered. She strained to hear him. "And what are you planning to say about Francie? She knows damn well that Francie and Dominic got along. That story won't wash."

Silence.

Julie's heart was beating loudly; she held her breath so that she wouldn't miss a word.

Francie. The great unknown. She'd never heard her father say her name before.

Below her, Laura's hand shook as she turned to another page, but no one would have thought that she turned a hair as she said lightly, "Oh, that's easy. I'll just say that you and Francie had a mad, passionate affair, and she ran away to heal her broken heart after you broke up with her."

Julie couldn't stop her gasp, even as her hand came up to her mouth, and for one terrible second she feared that her father might have heard. Richard's voice cut savagely across that possibility. "That isn't even remotely funny, Laura."

"Well, that's what you're afraid of, isn't it?" Laura returned savagery for savagery, and as her voice rose, she turned her head and her eyes searched out Julie's closed door. Julie released out the breath she hadn't even known she was holding. "My *God*, Richard, you are paranoid! I *told* you, damn it, I told you I wouldn't give you away! I'll say that Francie and I were too close to leave each other, which, no thanks to you, happens to be the truth—"

Richard's voice whipped out. Julie had never heard him use such a tone before.

"And she'll ask, and you'll just blurt out something like that? The hell you will, Laura, you won't get the chance! You're not going anywhere with my daughter."

"Go to hell." Laura threw a furious look over her shoulder. "For God's sake, Richard, I'm a mother! I have a daughter who was crazy about her father, I know all about girls who worship their fathers. I just didn't happen to be one." Cat Courtney's famous projection carried the low vibration of the words straight to Julie's ears. "In case you've forgotten, Julie's my sister's daughter, *my* flesh and blood! Do you honestly believe I'd hurt her just to get back at you?"

He said flatly, "I don't know what to believe of you."

Neither do I, thought Julie in a daze.

With a few brutal words, Laura Abbott had sewn together the loose threads in Julie's memory: half-forgotten conversations, casual references made to the long-gone Francesca, quick glances thrown in

Richard's direction at the mention of her name. And, through all the tapestry of Julie's life, the monolith of his silence on the disappearance of Julie's two young aunts.

A monolith Laura had broken in a few cruel seconds.

They act like they hate each other.

But he's always said how he missed her. And everyone said she loved him.

*And look how close they're standing. Dad doesn't do that. He's always so good about giving people space from his height, making them comfortable. She's not moving away, either. It's like – it's like they **want** to be close, it's like they're—*

It's like they're lovers.

Laura had not bothered to reply to Richard's last caustic observation. Julie peered out from the shadows and saw that her aunt had turned back to the portfolio. Richard had walked over to the great expanse of the western window and was staring out, his shoulders taut and his hands stuck in his pockets.

I'd better get her out of here before she makes him mad again. He doesn't need that. He's got to rest, get over that cold and get ready for his presentation tomorrow....

Julie flattened herself against the wall and inched back towards the curve in the landing fifty feet away. She had moved only a foot or two when she heard a small gasp in the stillness of the room.

And then Laura, dryly, "You shouldn't worry about me giving you away, Richard. You've done it all by yourself."

"What?" Impatiently, Richard reeled around.

"*This*, that's what. If Julie hasn't asked about this, you're luckier than you deserve. What did you do, sketch Francie in some motel room? She looks like she just got out of bed!"

"What are you talking about?" He vanished briefly out of Julie's line of sight. She heard him approach the desk from the other side. Through the thick leaves, she watched him reach out for the portfolio and turn it around so that the sketches faced him. He stood still for a moment, while Laura stared at him and Julie held her breath.

Her father had shown her his portfolio dozens, hundreds of times, identifying people and places she'd been too young to remember, events that had happened before she was born. For the life of her, Julie couldn't remember ever seeing a sketch of Francie.

But Laura had seen it. Laura, who was closer to Francie than anyone else in the world, who had known her best, Laura had seen a sketch of Francie.

It must have lain there all this time, mute testimony to the great rumor.

Julie thought sickly, *I guess it wasn't a lie after all.*

Then, astonishingly, Richard laughed.

"So, Cat Courtney," and his voice had turned light, teasing, "you don't recognize yourself?"

Cat Courtney! Julie leaned over as far as she could.

"What!" Laura sounded shocked down to her core. Julie saw her aunt snatch the book away from Richard and lean over for a closer examination. After a moment, she straightened, and even through the leaves, the squaring of her shoulders and the shake of her head for bravado signaled, unmistakably, that Laura Abbott alias Cat Courtney had been badly shaken up.

"You have quite an imagination, Richard."

Julie's father was relaxing now, his long range easy, as though he'd just vanquished an enemy. "Oh, really? Take a look at your album covers, princess."

"They don't look like that." But Laura sounded less than certain.

"Don't they?" Richard's voice dropped into those tones Julie remembered vaguely from his long-ago conversations with Jennifer, edged with a touch of – well, if she didn't adore her father, she might have called it malice. "You forget, I'm your target audience, Cat Courtney, I'm exactly the demographic those covers are aimed at. The bedroom hair, those glazed eyes, that mouth that just went through the wars—"

"Oh, shut up!" Laura slammed the book shut. "There's no need to taunt me."

And then, the most mysterious thing of all. Richard leaned across the desk towards Laura, his hands supporting him, his eyes drawing her to him, his voice, gentle now on the surface, but with a fine hard edge.

"*Quid pro quo*, princess. Not much fun to be on the receiving end, is it?"

It took Laura ten minutes to figure out that her niece – charming, sweet, innocent Julie – hid the soul of an accomplished con artist.

Oh, Julie was clever. Somewhere in her sixteen years, she had learned all the right buttons to push. On the surface, she exhibited all the exquisite manners that her father turned on and off at will. She asked politely after Laura's family, she carefully ascertained Laura's interests and devised an itinerary for the day (insisting that nothing could give her more pleasure than to accompany Laura wherever she wished), and she carried on polite conversation that would have done most adults proud.

No teenage girl could be that perfect.

Maybe, Laura thought, she was imagining the cutting edge to the artless questions Julie threw out. Julie asked permission to email Meg so that "we won't be strangers when she comes up here to see you." An innocent, friendly request on the surface, so why did she get the impression that Julie knew perfectly well that she would never lay eyes on Meg in this lifetime? Another guileless comment, "I guess you and Dad are pretty good friends from way back, aren't you?" and Laura fought the irrational notion that Julie divined the sexual warfare she and Richard had turned on each other.

No, no, no. But still – Julie seemed perfect. Too perfect.

The mask slipped occasionally. When they left the Folly, Laura casually held out the Jaguar keys to her niece, for the sheer pleasure of watching Richard's face blanch as his daughter gunned the $100,000 car out of the driveway like the proverbial bat out of hell. Julie's laughter sounded genuine, a rebellious teenager testing her limits, but she calmed down before she reached the first crossroads.

She forgot herself again, briefly, when they stopped in at Edwards Lake, and Max came running into the front hall to greet them. Laura watched in amusement as her dignified niece scooped up the cat in her arms and gave him the petting of his life. Max, lovesick, trailed upstairs after them up, waving his fluffy tail against Julie in a transparent demand for more attention.

"Gosh," sighed Julie from the depths of Max's fur, "he's so sweet. I wish I had a cat."

"Why don't you?" The humidity of the day had begun to wax strong, and Laura's jeans were sticking to her. She searched in her wardrobe for a sundress. "You live in the country. You could keep a cat outside if your father doesn't want one indoors."

"Dad says it's not possible because he has to travel so much and I have to stay with other people when he's gone."

Something in Julie's voice – a keen, bright edge beneath a mild obedience – seized Laura's wary attention. She glanced at her niece, and caught Julie before she completely recovered herself. One second, flashing eyes and a *moue* that expressed her utter discontent; the next, wide eyes and a look of serene acceptance.

Laura's instincts went on alert.

No, this she hadn't imagined. She'd done it herself, this very morning, assuming a sweet, submissive persona for Richard's benefit. She knew about the effect of widened eyes, the shy duck of the head, the quivering of the lips.

What on earth was Julie up to?

"We could always present him with a *fait accompli*." Richard would damn her to hell for interfering between him and his child. "He won't make the cat hit the road, I promise. Did he ever tell you about the kitten he found for me when I was five?"

For a moment, she almost had Julie. Temptation warred behind those eyes, but the girl's better side won. "I don't want to go against my father's wishes."

This girl was a teenager?

Sweet, said Lucy. *A sweet, darling girl*. And Lucy, as she'd proved amply the day before, was nobody's fool.

Hard to believe that anyone could fool Lucy.

So Julie must be very, very good indeed.

"Would you like to go shopping?" Laura zipped up her favorite cotton sundress. "I have fourteen years of Christmases and birthdays to make up for! Is there anything you have your heart set on that you didn't get for your birthday?" She paused deliberately to bait the trap. "Something you don't want to ask your father for?"

Julie appeared to consider this; Meg would have had ready and waiting a list as long as her arm. "No, ma'am. But if you'd like to go shopping, I know some neat outlet malls – oh," she flushed, "I guess you don't shop at those, probably."

For a split second, Laura wondered if Richard had warned his daughter against falling prey to her rich aunt's pocketbook. But why on earth would he object to her spending money on her niece? Did he think she was going to attempt to buy Julie's trust?

"I shop anywhere," she said calmly. "What would you like for your birthday?"

Julie said shyly, "I really have everything I need. But thank you."

The perfect daughter.

She leaned towards the mirror to check her makeup, and let the silence stretch out between them. She knew how to handle silence, how to use it to her advantage, but Julie hadn't yet the experience to match that. She sensed her niece's eyes on her, even as Julie stroked Max's furry back and murmured love words into his adoring ears.

If she hadn't known better, she would have thought that Julie was trying to scam Richard. And Lucy. And her.

Julie is nowhere near as innocent as everyone thinks. She hadn't wondered till this moment why Diana had said such a thing.

Oh, surely not. Julie was a beloved daughter and niece, maybe too sheltered, maybe overly protected, maybe too early separated from a mother with vacant eyes and desperate heart. The product (Laura reminded herself) of a bitterly broken home. And Diana was certainly no expert on her daughter or anyone else.

Still, she trusted her instincts. The girl possessed a superb smoothness, the hallmark of long practice and polished skill. Behind those wide eyes, Laura sensed a first-class mind working away in furious intensity.

Okay, my girl, Laura thought, following Julie down the stairs. *I'll play along. Just remember, I've got fifteen years on you, and a thousand audiences more.*

Julie bore up well under scrutiny throughout the morning. She was the perfect companion, polite, sweet, enthusiastic, even deferential without being too obvious. No stomping on the gas pedal after Laura tempted her again with the car keys. No disappointed face when Laura inserted a classical guitar CD. No flirting with the good-looking young man who pulled up beside them at a stop sign and threw an admiring glance their way.

"I think he recognizes you, Laura."

Laura turned skeptical shade-framed eyes on her. "I doubt he even saw me."

"Sure he did." Julie accelerated smoothly, with all the daring of a little old lady. Maybe she thought better of her absolute denial, because she added, "Oh, I know we look alike. Everyone's always told me that, and it's not surprising, is it, since we're related? Who do we take after, do you know?"

"My great-grandmother." Giannetta Montini had died decades before, but Laura had seen the unsigned painting *Idol of Perversity* that had shown Giannetta in all her natural splendor in *fin-de-siècle* Paris. "Except none of us got her figure."

Julie giggled. "Dad says I'll improve with age. He thinks maybe I'm just a late bloomer. So unfair, don't you think, Lucy says my mother didn't have that problem." Laura intercepted the sidelong glance sent her way and wondered what she was in for now. "You and my mother really do look a lot alike, don't you? Almost like twins. That's what my father used to say—"

Great. So even Richard admitted that she reminded him of Diana.

"Except," finished Julie, "you're much younger and prettier than she is."

Laura stopped breathing for a second or two, long enough to absorb the sheer brutality of those words. When she looked at Julie again, she saw the hint of satisfaction playing around the girl's mouth, the knowledge that she'd struck home magnificently.

Good God, had Julie ever talked to Diana like this?

Well, she didn't have to tolerate this from someone half her age. She opened her mouth to give Julie a setdown she'd never forget.

Maybe Julie sensed she had gone too far. A certain haste shook her voice as she cut across the words on Laura's lips. "My mother was beautiful when she was young, though, wasn't she? Lucy showed me the wedding pictures." Laura saw the girl bite her lip and steal a sidelong glance. "My father must have been very proud of her."

Proud? She wouldn't have used that word to describe the remembered awe on his face, the look of a young man violently in love.

"So," fished Julie, "I guess they were mad for each other."

By now, she ought to be getting used to Julie's hidden agenda. "Yes," she said to nothing in particular, and waited for the next bombshell.

Silence for a few minutes. The Virginia countryside flew past them, the highway lined with the sentinel trees blending into the lush greenness of summer. Julie accelerated slightly over the speed limit, with another sidelong glance, and Laura dug in her mental heels and refused the admonition that the girl obviously wanted.

All those remarks about Richard and Diana…. She surveyed Julie from the corner of her eye. Maybe the girl really didn't know anything. As close-mouthed and private as Richard had proved to be, maybe his daughter had no idea why the marriage had broken up. Maybe he had never told her about the springs of their courtship, the night he had brought over her engagement ring, the day he had danced with his bride in his arms.

Meg had often begged for details of her parents' courtship. Had Julie shown the same curiosity and met Richard's stonewall?

"Did my mother date much when she was my age?" Julie's question, when it finally came, cemented Laura's suspicion. "I mean, besides my father? I've heard how they met in grade school and hardly had eyes for anyone else, but – I mean, what if he hadn't been around? Did other guys ask her out?"

Laura took a minute to sort out her thoughts. She didn't doubt that an entire history lay behind the question, but what it might contain, she couldn't hazard a guess. Unless Julie had somehow heard about Diana's men – but surely that wouldn't shock the girl. She knew her father dated. Wouldn't she expect her mother to enjoy the same liberties?

"I don't remember," Laura said. "Your mom and dad were always together. I don't remember her dating anyone else."

"Are you sure?" Julie sounded intense. "Didn't anyone else ever ask her out?"

Laura shot her a quick look and registered it all at once: the tension of Julie's hand on the steering wheel, the quick rise and fall of her young breasts, the rapid blinking of her eyes. Now what was Julie up to?

But wait…. Lucy had said something…. And Richard: *Julie doesn't have much of a social life… Julie doesn't date much yet.* Julie, with that incredible face, ought to be beating the boys off with a stick.

Laura took a breath and gambled. "Do you have a boyfriend, Julie?"

Bingo! The girl's eyes widened, and her hands trembled. Laura leaned over and steadied the wheel, thankful that the roads were free of traffic.

"Pull off on the access road ahead."

Without a word, the girl obeyed. She regained control of herself quickly; she must have the iron will of the Abbotts. She slowed the car down on the shoulder, staring straight ahead, and if her chin quivered, it was only for a second.

"Cut the motor," Laura said.

Julie did as she was told.

"Now," said Laura, "look at me."

The girl hesitated, grasping for that last one second of independence, but a lifetime of obedience forced her to turn slowly in her seat. Laura stared deep into mirror-green eyes fighting back the threat of tears and reminded herself that, for all that crafty intelligence, behind those eyes lived a daughter sheltered and protected from the adult realities of her world.

Still, she couldn't allow Julie to run circles around her anymore.

"You don't date very much, do you?"

"No, ma'am," Julie whispered, and a stray tear – Laura would swear it was genuine – slipped out of one eye.

"Why?"

She could barely hear her niece. "No one asks me."

Oh, Lord! *Why* was written all over Julie's face. No teenage boy was going to risk rejection by asking the most beautiful girl in the class for a date. She felt a spurt of irritation for Richard; he should have dealt with this, not left his daughter to wonder if she was her mother reborn. "Have you talked to your dad about this?"

Julie's answer surprised her. "Yes. We – he wanted to know how come I didn't go to the prom a few weeks ago. I guess I must have talked about it some, that I wanted to go. Anyway," she swallowed, "he asked if I needed money for a dress, and I had to tell him that I wasn't going. He asked how come."

Score one for Richard. At least, his daughter felt that she could confide in him. "What did you say?"

"The truth." Julie's hand lifted to the tear. "No one asked me. Not even one of the geeks. There's a guy I like, he's sort of quiet—" she looked defiantly at her aunt, as though Laura might despise such a choice— "he studies a lot, he's real smart, and I thought he might ask me because we worked together on a history project and we got along real well. But he didn't."

"Of course he didn't," Laura said gently. She touched her niece's hair experimentally, wondering if the girl would accept her comfort. "He's got an ego as fragile as glass, and he wasn't about to ask you out and have you turn him down."

"That's what Dad said." Laura gave Richard points. "He said maybe Mike figured I'd already been asked. He said the guys in my class are too young to appreciate me, but in a few years it'll get better." Julie wiped her hand across her eyes. "But what am I supposed to do until then? A guy at church asked me out, and he's in college, and—"

She fell silent. Laura prompted, "And?"

Julie said reluctantly, "And Dad said no, he's too old for me. He's twenty."

Laura rolled her eyes and then hoped that Julie hadn't seen. Too bad she couldn't tell Julie the reason for Richard's fear, that at seventeen he'd been climbing a tree into Diana's bedroom. "Fathers are like that, Julie. Your dad's no different. Meg's dad worried just as much about her. His greatest fear was that she might get pregnant before she got out of school."

Julie's eyes widened at that. "No one has to worry about me."

"I'm sure they don't."

A few seconds of silence. Then Julie said unexpectedly, "How about you? Did you date much when you were young?"

Leave it to the truly young to wound with a mere word; she didn't think Julie even realized what she had said. "No, I didn't. Not much, anyway. I only had one boyfriend."

"Why? Were guys scared of you?"

She hadn't the faintest idea what to answer. "I don't think so. I was pretty shy. Besides, my father didn't allow me to date until I was almost seventeen, and I went and got a job in a bookstore after school at the start of my senior year, so I really didn't have the time."

"You had a job? Really?" Julie's interest perked. "I'm going to work for Lucy this summer when I get back from music camp. I want to buy a car. I don't like driving Grandma's car."

"I had a car." Laura pondered briefly the wisdom of telling the truth. "I needed the money."

Maybe her tone warned Julie. She saw a curious light come into her niece's eyes. "You did? Why? Were you saving for college?"

"No. I was saving up to run away."

Her words hit Julie hard. The girl's eyes snapped open abruptly; the lock of hair she had twisted around a finger jerked taut. The silence of a few seconds stretched out into a long string, vibrating with Julie's shock.

"But you were still seventeen when you left."

Whatever she'd expected, it wasn't this *non sequitur*. She gave Julie a quick glance and saw the wheels turning in that active mind. "Right. I left in June, right after I graduated—"

"But," said Julie slowly, "you got a job a – a whole year before then—" She turned and faced Laura. "You planned it," she whispered. "You *planned* it. You *knew* for a whole year ahead of time that you were going to run away."

For all the questions her sisters had asked, for that terrible scene ringing with accusations her first evening back, no one had fingered the core of her disappearance. Lucy had asked; Richard had assumed he knew; Diana had only wanted to know about Francie. No one had realized the true architect of the day she and Francie had walked out the door forever.

Until now. Julie, a toddler at the time, whose memories of her must have come from hearing the rest of the family talk – Julie had looked straight into the heart of the past and seen the truth.

It should not come as such a shock that Julie read her so well. Hadn't she looked at Julie earlier today, in that first moment of meeting, and recognized herself?

She met Julie's eyes. "You're right. I planned it."

"For a *year*," Julie whispered. "Why?"

"I needed the time. I had to graduate from high school."

"But I don't understand. *Why?* What was so terrible that you knew for a *year*—"

She had never told anyone, not Francie, not Cam. Perhaps here, in this car, on this morning, it was time to finally admit what Dominic Abbott had done to her.

She had to go easy. She reminded herself that Julie was a child, and then just as quickly rejected that thought forever. She had been Julie's age when she had made an adult decision to grab the reins of her life.

If Julie wanted to know, then she could deal with the truth.

"The summer after my junior year, I dated a boy named Neil Redmond. He was cute, just a really nice guy. Very shy, like me—"

"I've heard of him," Julie broke in. "My dad knows him, I think."

"I'm not surprised," Laura said. "Neil's mother was a friend of your grandmother – they fixed us up. Anyway, Neil and I dated all summer – we went to movies, and he took me to the July 4th celebration down near the old city, and we just hung out together – he was a very restful person for me, and I think I was the same for him."

She stopped. Just how much could she tell Julie? But, even if Richard was bent on keeping his daughter pure and unsullied, surely Lucy had clued her in. Surely Julie knew *something*.

"I don't think we were in love – he was seventeen, and I was still sixteen, but—"

Julie solved her dilemma. "You had sex?"

Richard's little girl was a lot savvier than he thought she was.

"No," Laura said definitely. She could do her auntly duty and deliver a little morality lesson. "I never had sex until I met my husband, and that's really a good life plan to follow, Julie." *Even if he picked me up in a night club and I went with him because he had a lot of money in his wallet.* "But we were teenagers, so we fooled around some. And then my father found out."

"Really?" The girl sounded startled and a little worried. "You can tell by just looking?"

Interesting. So Julie had done some experimenting of her own. "No. He found out because Neil wanted to discern if he had a vocation to the priesthood and he went to talk to my father because Daddy had been a priest, and Daddy asked him about his experience, and I guess Neil didn't deny it fast enough. Daddy told him to stay away from me, and then he ordered me not to see Neil again be-cause—" Dominic's order still rankled after all these years. She said flatly, "Because he was concerned that I would divert Neil from God. That's what my mother had done to him."

Julie stared at her.

"Something else happened – oh, I think it was a few months earli-er, maybe in late spring. My father was pretty tough on me during voice lessons. He did train me – in fact, he spent quite a lot of time working with me, but I'm a mezzo soprano, and I guess I wasn't enough of a challenge for him." She was surprised when Julie nod-ded – had she already heard this? "We were listening to the opera – the Met used to broadcast on Sunday afternoon – and I was notating the music because I liked the arrangement, and Daddy looked at my music notebook and realized I was notating everything perfectly."

She saw the moment when Julie caught on. "You're kidding! You have perfect pitch?"

"Yes," said Laura. "I'm the only one in the family, unless—?" Julie shook her head. "It's very useful when you write music, believe me. I can hear music and tell you exactly what key it's in – I can tell you all the chords, I can even hear parts in a choral piece and write them down correctly. I can sight-read anything, and I rarely sing pitchy. I can sing *a cappella* without hearing a note, and – this is really useful – I can anticipate the next note based on the key and the chords. If I hear a motif I like, I can remember it to write it down later. Of course, Daddy realized right away what I had and that he could use that. So," she drew a breath, "right after he finished telling me that I couldn't see Neil anymore, he said that Francie could go ahead with her plans for Juilliard, but he needed me to stay here and go to school at William and Mary so that I could work for him."

Julie looked bewildered. "So what was so terrible about that? He was a great musician."

"No." Laura made her voice forceful. "He wasn't. He was a good conductor, but his compositions – don't buy too far into that myth about the misunderstood genius, Julie. There's a reason his work never caught on. He was – well, he was Salieri, just without the fame." Julie looked shocked. She probably couldn't comprehend that a daughter could say such terrible things about her father. "But that's not why I decided to run away – and that's when I made the deci-sion. I stood there, listening to him lay out my future, and I knew I had to get away."

"I don't get it."

"I was the sacrificial lamb," Laura explained. "He was determined to keep one of us by his side – I don't know why, maybe he was still obsessed with my mother. He needed one of us to be his muse. It was supposed to be your mother, but she escaped when she and your dad got married. He never did get his hooks into Lucy because she didn't live with us. And Francie—" She hesitated. It still felt disloyal to tell the truth about Francie's voice. "Francie didn't have a professional voice, her tone wasn't quite there, it was a little muddy. That's why he was willing to let her go away. But I did have a professional voice, and I had the pitch, and that's why he said I had to stay there with him. He said – he said I owed him."

Silence. She closed her eyes and leaned back against the seat.

"So – you decided to run away because your father wanted you to work for him, but you couldn't leave because of school?"

Laura nodded. "I had to make money so I could leave. It took a long time to build up a nest egg. I figured I needed five thousand dollars, and I didn't make much working after school and babysitting."

"Five thousand?" Julie sounded fascinated. "What did you do?"

"I took my mother's jewelry." Julie's eyes flared in acknowledgment, and Laura smiled. So her theft had finally been discovered. How long had it taken Dominic to find out – five years, ten? She held out her hand and twisted the emerald ring on her finger. "See this? It's the only piece I ever tracked down later. At the time, it brought me okay money. She had an incredible jewelry collection from the earl, and she took it when she left him for good. And Daddy had bought me some savings bonds that I cashed in. I had about four thousand, when I finally left, so that's what I lived on. The jewelry was for reserve."

And it would never have been needed, if Francie hadn't given birth prematurely.

"I don't know how you did it." Julie reached out for her hand and angled the ring to catch the sunlight. It glowed, green fire, throwing stars against the leather of the car. "How could you live like that, for a year, *for a whole year*, knowing you were going to walk out? Didn't it bother you? Didn't you feel guilty when someone would talk about the future, or make plans, and you knew you weren't going to be there?"

She cast back in time to that last year, that last Christmas, when she had celebrated with her father and sisters, and each present opened, each carol sung, each cookie baked, had reminded her that she would never celebrate with them again. *Never again, never again*, had echoed in the Alleluia she had sung at midnight Mass. That last Easter, she had sat at the Ashmores' kitchen table, listening to Richard explain tangents and cosines, and she had watched the pencil in his hand drawing his incomprehensible axes. The overhead light had glinted off his hair and shadowed his eyes, and a strange despairing relief had spread through her. Despair that she would never see him again, that he would never again say patiently, "Laurie, stop daydreaming, you have to pass this test." Relief that she was leaving them all. Relief that she would never again suffer the reality of her own flaws, flaws so great that her father wanted only to exploit her and the love of her life preferred her sister.

"No," she said, "I didn't feel guilty."

"But you were lying to them," and the shocked accusation in Julie's voice reminded Laura all over again of the duality in the girl. The princess of Ashmore Park hadn't learned yet that even idols sometimes did what they must to survive. "You didn't even tell anyone what was wrong. You didn't give anyone a chance to make it up. You – you—" she hunted for the right word. "You *deceived* them."

Ah, the idealism of youth.

Laura said gently, "Do you ever deceive anyone, Julie?"

"Of course not! I would never!"

Then Julie stopped, now beyond that first instinct to deny. Laura watched in interest as Julie's hot rebuttal failed on her lips and a quick light of knowledge flashed across the girl's face, and waited, ready to knock her niece swiftly and decisively off her high horse.

But Julie, she saw, Julie with that first-class Ashmore mind, Julie ticked off her options in lightning order and realized that the game was up.

Julie changed then, as the mask shattered and fell away. The too-wide eyes of innocence became older eyes, quick and rich with knowledge; her hands, frozen in flight, relaxed and fell into her lap.

She said directly, "How did you know?"

An honest response. Laura didn't think she could have admitted such a thing herself. "It takes one to know one."

Julie nodded.

"Besides," Laura added for good measure, "you use a lot of my techniques. I'll bet you've watched the video for 'Midnight.' You've got my mannerisms down pat."

Julie sounded a shade rueful. "I guess I should have known better."

"You probably couldn't help it." She could have added that, after a while, playacting became living, and reality and fantasy blurred into one. "It becomes second nature. You don't even have to think about it, do you, when you're with your father or Lucy. You just wear it like a skin."

"I never thought about it that way."

"Well, think."

A small respite. Julie sank into thought, and Laura left her alone. There was no point in pushing the girl. She'd just endured an unmasking with good grace and little hint of the pain that must have come with the ripping away of her veil.

Maybe she might even equate this moment with the humiliation of not going to the prom. A sensitive, intelligent young man might have divined that Julie Ashmore was, at heart, a fraud.

"You know," Julie said into the sunlit silence, "they like me this way."

"They don't know you any other way."

"Oh, come off it!" Julie's eyes flashed. "You haven't been around. You don't know what's going on. Dad likes me like this. He has this idea of a perfect little miss, and if that's what he wants, then that's what I'll be. He's a great dad and he deserves to have his daughter the way he wants. And Tom and Lucy – well, you ask them, they'll tell you I'm the perfect niece. I'm polite, and I listen to my elders and I do exactly what they want, and they *like* me."

Laura sat stone still.

"Tell me, *dear* Aunt Laura, you played such a great part, you were so sweet and meek and mild, did they *like* you for it? I've heard them talking about you for years. I remember when your first album came out, and Lucy and I saw it in the record store, and do you know what she thought at first when she saw your poster?" Julie stopped for breath. "Do you *know?*"

She sensed the volcano of emotion beneath Julie's anger. Unknowingly, she had tapped into some deep vein of feeling that the girl had gone to great lengths to bury.

"I imagine," she said quietly, to neutralize her words, "that she thought I was Francie."

"They all did!" Julie burst out. "That's how much you fooled them! Lucy – she bought your album, and I remember her playing it over and over that afternoon, and she looked like death. She played that song 'Francie,' and she couldn't stop crying, because she said she'd never known you had such feeling in you, because you'd never shown any to her."

"Oh, no." She saw the picture Julie had so brutally drawn: Lucy sitting cross-legged on the floor, tears streaming down her face, mourning the sister who had hidden herself away.

"And my grandfather!" Julie hadn't finished. "I'll never forget how he looked!"

"Philip?" That dismayed her.

"Not *him!* Your father! Lucy made everyone get together for dinner. My father even came, even though he and my grandfather never got along. And no one could figure out what was going on. Lucy made me keep quiet, she said it was a surprise—"

"Oh, no." She felt what was coming.

"Then after dinner, she put your CD on, 'Francie.' And I remember my mother, she started off looking sick, but then she just went blank, and she said something like, 'Wait a minute, that's not Francie, that's not her *tessitura.*' And Dad, he just looked tired and sad, and I could tell he wanted to leave. But he didn't, he was going to stick it out as long as everyone else—"

She had heard enough. "Stop."

"And then my grandfather." Did Julie even realize that she was sobbing? "He yelled at Lucy, he told her to stop that song and take the CD and – and break it into a million pieces. And then he slammed out of the room. I don't really remember what he said, I just remember his face and his yelling—"

"Julie." She saw the horror of memory descend upon the girl's shoulders, and she reached out for her. And Julie, after a second of hesitation, leaned against her and wept in wild fury and remembrance.

"His face. I never saw anyone look like that, not ever."

"I can imagine." She soothed back a strand of autumn hair.

"I saw him," Julie wept. "Dad said that he'd had enough, and he told me to get my coat. So I did. And I saw him then. I saw him, Laura, your father that you tricked and deceived, that you wouldn't even stay and help, that you hated so much you ran away from him and never even spoke to him again!"

"*Stop.*" She put all the authority of her years into her voice.

"I won't stop! You listen to me! He was standing out in Lucy's garden, next to her roses, and I heard him humming under his breath, and his hands were moving like the orchestra was playing—"

"Oh, God—"

" 'Francie,' that's what he was humming. And he turned around and he saw me, and he beckoned to me to come closer, and do you know what he said? Do you *know*? He said—"

"No—"

"He said, 'Laurie wrote that song when she was a little older than you are now, Julie. She wrote it all down in her journal. She must still have that journal.' And then my father came and – and I had to go with him. But I looked back at my grandfather one more time, I looked at him there, standing in the rose garden, and he had tears in his eyes."

At midnight, Julie Ashmore looked into the mirror while she was brushing her hair, and realized that her mask had shattered forever.

She had scrambled wildly to cover herself at dinner with her father. He had asked casually if she'd enjoyed her day with her famous aunt, and he had nearly dropped his coffee when Julie had said without thinking first, "Well, she's the most brutally honest person I ever met, that's for sure."

She had caught herself, as her father's eyes darkened, and tried desperately to repair the damage. Before he could demand an explanation, she had blurted out the story of Laura's last year at home, her short romance with Neil Redmond, Dominic's decree about her future, her job at the bookstore, her theft of Renée Dane's jewelry. Nothing had worked; Richard's face had steadily hardened as she talked.

"Are you upset she told me all that?" Julie asked finally. Better he blame Laura than her for talking out of turn.

"No," said Richard slowly, and Julie watched something flicker behind his eyes. "No, I'm upset that she didn't say anything to the rest of us."

She tried hard, all evening, to recapture the sweet, innocent Julie Ashmore who had gone out merrily for a day with Cat Courtney. She tried all the sweet-Julie things that had served her so well for so long. She made her father his favorite cookies. She called Lucy to see how her aunt was feeling. She composed an email to Meg St. Bride, introducing herself, describing her life in the most Pollyannish of terms, spilling sweetness and light onto the screen until she reread it and wanted to throw up.

My God, she thought frantically. *What's happened to me?*

Laura Abbott had happened to her.

Damn! She'd done just what the rest of them had always done; she'd underestimated Laura. She should have known better. Hadn't she always felt, right from the beginning, that anyone who could execute such a disappearance must be smarter and stronger than anyone had ever guessed?

Strength. And Laura saying, with a touch of humor, *It takes one to know one.*

Julie stared into the etched mirror above her dressing table. She didn't look different; she was still the same flat-chested, too-tall girl who'd walked out the front door that morning. But inside, she felt light, a weight lifting that she'd never even suspected was there.

Someone had finally seen through the mask, and hadn't rejected her.

She went to bed. But, at dawn, she awoke with a single thought.

The sketch. Cat Courtney. Laura for Francie.

She opened her door and peered around the landing towards her father's room, but his door still remained shut. He was a heavy sleeper; she knew from past experience that he wasn't likely to wake up until his alarm rang. Still, he was due to fly to Charleston early; he might be up at any minute.

Not a second to waste, then.

She found his portfolio still lying on the edge of the desk where Laura had shoved it almost a full day before. Cat Courtney, he'd said, and Julie knew that her father always arranged his work in chronological order, so that he could track the evolution of his ability in time and space. He signed and dated every drawing, so that there could never be any question where it belonged.

Cat Courtney's first album had gone out six years before, so she knew where to start.

But Cat wasn't there. Julie flipped through the pages and found nothing except the sketch he had done of Cat's concert. There it was, nestled between Westminster Abbey and the Crescent at Bath; she recognized the dress Cat Courtney had worn.

By no stretch of the imagination could anyone call this sketch sensuous – at least, not enough to upset Laura. Of the two outfits Cat Courtney had worn that night, Richard Ashmore had chosen to sketch the golden ball gown, not even the very little black dress that Julie remembered so vividly from the second half of the concert.

So what had Laura seen?

She thought back to the previous morning, to the two combatants standing so close together, so that anyone not listening might have thought that they were lovers savoring each other. *How old was she then?* Laura had asked, and her father had said she was three.

And then he'd said something about another picture soon after, of Julie and her grandmother.

Fine. She knew which picture he meant; it was one of her favorites too. So the picture of Cat Courtney must be sadly out of order. Maybe it had fallen out at some point, and he had stuck it back in without checking to see where it went.

She found it easily enough, right after a sketch of the July 4th when she and her father had gone to Washington. She remembered that trip in every detail, from tagging along in boredom at the Air and Space Museum, to insisting that they climb the Washington Monument and tiring out halfway through. She had been five years old, and her mother had just left them.

And right after that, Cat Courtney in glowing detail.

She carried the sketch over to the western window.

Oh, now she saw. No wonder Laura had been so stunned. *What did you do, sketch Francie in some motel room?* (Francie and her father in a motel. She'd think about that later.) The woman in the picture indeed looked as if she'd just awakened from a wonderful nap, all heavy eyes and tousled hair and (even in pencil) flushed cheeks. Dreaming eyes that looked upon a lover. And, even though he had drawn only the hint of her shoulders, Julie had the feeling that this woman had lifted welcoming arms towards the man who watched her.

Vivid imagination, indeed.

But still, in space and time, out of place.

Julie turned the picture over, and her heart stopped.

Laura. Ash Marine. 8/6/91.

He had seen Laura then, he must have, to draw her so, looking back at her lover....

But, by then, Laura had been gone for three years.

14

Ancient Crimes

IN THE SPACE OF TWO DAYS, Lucy had dissected her, Richard had ambushed her, and Julie had held up an unsparing mirror.

The last thing in the world Laura wanted to do, when she awoke the next morning, was carry out her unspoken promise to Diana.

"I'd love to see you, Laurie! I'll be at Daddy's. Come right over."

So Laura went back to that house she had hoped never again to enter. Diana's Mercedes sat in the parkway; the front door stood open onto the veranda; Stravinsky floated through the air. No ghosts greeted her as she approached, no phantoms of green-eyed sisters or the thin, austere man who'd ruled them all, only the *Firebird* and a strong atmosphere of old history too long packed away.

"Di?" she called cautiously into the house. "Di, you here?"

Footsteps moved overhead, and she ventured in.

"Up here."

She mounted the stairs reluctantly, still unsure how to say what she had to say. And then she stopped, stunned.

Diana had changed again.

Laura had braced herself so fiercely for the worst that the best left her speechless. The sunlight from the window on the landing caught Diana's hair like flame; she had tied it back at the nape with a gold clip, and in her plaid blouse and jeans, she looked much younger. Not sick, sad, alternatively giddy and depressed, but friendly, smiling, her complexion clear and lightly blushed—

And holding a broom in her hand.

Diana? Doing housework? Diana, who'd never lifted a finger in all the years they'd lived under the same roof?

How could she discuss Francie's death with someone cleaning house?

"I'm so glad you came!" Diana exclaimed, apparently unaware that her sister had been struck dumb. She waved a hand towards the master bedroom. "I've been cleaning out Daddy's closet, sorting through clothes, and it's such boring work."

Laura recovered herself. "What can I do to help?"

She followed Diana obediently into Dominic's bedroom, and it struck her again how much her father had clung to the past. If Diana's room had retained its regal silk, and her own had never been purged of Francie's country cuteness, Dominic had never bothered to soften the monasticism he'd known before he left the priesthood to run off with his star. No soft blankets, no comfortable reading chair, just drab white sheets and the silver crucifix that had hung on the wall as long as she remembered.

It popped into her head, irreverently, that Dominic must never have entertained here. The bed was too narrow and the atmosphere too conducive to guilt.

"How do you like Edwards Lake?" Diana was energetically dumping Dominic's clothes into large plastic bags. "I don't think I'd care to be so far from civilization."

Lucky her, then, that she didn't live at Ashmore Park.

"Actually, I'm enjoying the peace and quiet." Laura picked up a shirt to fold. "I don't mind, honestly. You can't believe how often I've wanted to be all by myself."

"Country life!" Diana pretended a shudder and reached up onto a shelf. "Not for me, thanks! Oh, Laurie, could you give me a hand – this box must weigh a ton—"

The box had been lodged at the back of the closet, just high enough out of reach to cause the sacrifice of a fingernail each by the time they tore it free from its perch and wrestled it, raining old checks and letters, to the floor. The exertion became Diana; she looked disheveled, less than model-perfect, and utterly lovely as she ruefully examined the remains of her nails. Laura knew perfectly well that she looked like an urchin.

"Have you ever seen so much dust!" Diana sneezed dramatically to make her point. "Lucy'll be proud of me. She's been looking high and low for these checks, so she can do the final papers."

"What papers?"

"On the estate. Oh, speaking of that, she found a bunch of stuff, your birth and baptismal certificates and your old Irish passport in his desk. He had it all with his will. We didn't find Francie's, but yours were right there."

Funny, Laura noted, crawling around on hands and knees picking up stray papers, how even Diana showed no grief for their father. She'd asked the week before why Laura had not come to the funeral and had seemed satisfied with the excuse that she couldn't get away from rehearsals. Apparently Lucy and Diana had not expected her to pretend sorrow.

"He left a will?" she asked casually, as she sorted out the papers.

Diana's head jerked up. "Yes, he did. Why do you want to know?"

She hadn't considered the threat her return might pose to her sisters' inheritance. "Oh, no reason," she said hastily. "I know he didn't leave me anything, Di, don't think I'm asking for that, please. I just wondered."

Diana's suspicions weren't so easily allayed. "Are you going to make a claim?"

"No." She wanted nothing of Dominic's. "Don't give that another thought."

She might have added more, but her thoughts, her rush to reassure Diana, died as soon as she looked at the check stub in her hand.

SBFA, read the logo, with an address at the St. Bride Building in Plano, and a phone number she knew as well as her own. St. Bride Family Administration, the group of accountants and assistants who existed to make the St. Brides' lives easier. They paid Emma's bills, administered Cam's estate, addressed Mark's Christmas cards, and prepared Cat Courtney's income tax return. They sent reminders for dental appointments, made travel arrangements, and renewed license plates. She forgot Diana, chattering away, only so much noise in the background.

"I'm glad you feel that way. Daddy left me most everything, and to be honest, I need it more than you do—"

Payable to Dominic Abbott on April 1, 1995, for five thousand dollars.

"I've got the house, and Lucy got his royalties, such as they are. We've been trying to figure out his accounts since he died. He has the strangest royalties. They're every month, even amounts, not like any royalties I've ever seen—"

Not so strange. Authorized by CDSB. Cameron David St. Bride. Charged to his account.

"But, Laurie," Diana's voice turned warm, impossible to resist even as the check trembled in Laura's hand, "I don't want you to feel left out. Look, there's a ton of old clothes in the attic—"

And in the memo field, the notation *monthly stipend: Dominic Abbott*.

"—And some of them must be Mama's. If you see something you want—"

Signed by Mark St. Bride, Comptroller.

And the stub underneath, from SBFA, dated a month later. And the next stub, the next month—

"Laurie?" Diana's fingers snapped in front of her eyes.

"Sorry." She scarcely knew what she was apologizing for. She bent over quickly to hide the shock in her eyes before Diana noticed anything amiss, and tucked the stubs into the middle of the papers in the box. "So there's still stuff in the attic?"

"Probably some of your old stuff too," offered Diana.

She followed her sister, moving through the motions of pulling down the steps from the attic, steadying the stairs as Diana's thin body disappeared into the dark hole. A splinter speared her finger, drawing forth the merest pinprick of blood; she stared at the red drop as if it had nothing to do with her. The first shock was washing away. She tested her mental temperature and found herself cool, calm, ready to rip the dead Cam – and the living Mark – apart.

So he – Cam – had given her father money? After all his fine talk about protecting Meg, he had contacted her father. That money apparently had stretched over a long period of time, and he'd never told her, never so much as hinted at it. So much for his accusation, the night he asked for the divorce, that she had cut him out of her heart. He couldn't keep his women a secret, but he had concealed his dealings with her family?

And the terrible corollary: that Dominic had known where she was, all these years.

She put her pricked finger to her mouth.

Diana's head poked back through the hole. "You won't believe what's up here. Come on up."

"Okay." No one to steady the steps for her. She stomped up the rickety steps, pretending that each step was one of Mark's limbs – in the hereafter, Cam should be heaving a sigh of relief that he was beyond her reach – and Diana reached out to haul her in at the top. "What did you find?"

"Look," was all Diana said, and Laura turned and fell silent.

Dresses carelessly piled up, silks upon satins upon velvets, once rich in color and tone, now rich in dust. The clothes of a woman long vanished from their lives, a woman who had gone sailing in a storm one day and never returned. The love of Dominic's life. His muse.

One dress, heirloomed in plastic, she recognized as Diana's wedding gown. She shoved the checks to the back of her mind – time enough to deal with Mark later – and pulled a long lacy concoction out from under a burgundy velvet robe into the light. "Incredible!" She held the dress against her. "Look, my bridesmaid dress. Was I really that short?" She lifted one dress, then another, shaking the dust, smoothing down torn laces and matted velvets. "I can't believe this! He threw out her pictures, and he kept all this…."

"And look at this." Diana gently eased a black Schiaparelli, fragile with age and use, out from under a discarded prom dress. "Daddy bought this for Mama to wear in Milan, when he conducted *Aida*. Gosh, Laurie, she was pregnant with you right then. I remember, she came and kissed me in bed before she left, and she looked so radiant, like a queen. She was wearing a tiara—"

"The beading!" She ran reverent fingers over the dress. "Will you look at this! That must have cost a fortune—"

"All hand done," said Diana matter-of-factly, but her eyes were sparkling. "These must be worth a lot of money. Antique clothes are all the rage now, I'll bet some museum would be interested—"

"Oh, Di, no." She was entranced by this glimpse into her mother's history. "If money's a consideration, I'll take them! Maybe I can wear these in concert. In fact," she shook out the black silk again and held it out for critical examination, "this might work for the concert, don't you think? That is, if you don't mind—"

She'd seen that immediate stiffening; she saw Diana now relax. Her permission asked, Diana nodded graciously. "No, it's okay. She was your mother too! But that dress has to be repaired."

"Maybe with some of the beading replaced and the shoulder lowered – where's a mirror, I need to try it on—"

They retrieved their treasures from the attic stronghold, Laura standing at the bottom of the steps and catching all that Diana carefully handed down to her. The hallway filled up rapidly with a cascade of falling material and rising dust. Some of the clothes were ruined, stained and eaten by animal and time; a cigarette burn in one bodice probably rendered the dress beyond repair. Dominic had not cared for this sliver of his past.

But his daughters reveled in it. Laura dragged the clothes into Diana's room in the front, and Diana whipped the cover off an old standing mirror. "Try the black on," she urged, and her hands went to the buttons of her own blouse. "And this gold silk – they said Grandma wore this when she sang in Paris the night she died—"

They shucked their jeans and blouses eagerly. They caught each other in surreptitious survey of the other's body (had Cat Courtney had any breast work done? what havoc had gravity and childbirth wreaked on Diana?) and laughed at the obligatory nature of it all. "Sisters," explained Diana with a shrug, and Laura mourned her lack of curves.

"Face it," said Diana, "we're not Lucy, damn her sex-goddess self."

The black silk shimmied around Laura, lush and cool against her body as Diana helped her pull it on and zipped up the side under the arm. Generous in the bosom, Laura noted; it needed Lucy to do it justice. A little short – she must be taller than Renée Dane, but the beaded black fringe off one of the ruined dresses would take care of that. Full through the waist, to accommodate a pregnancy. (And she had caused that; for her, Renée Dane had put away the stunning slim-waisted dresses Diana rummaged through.) One shoulder sloped – she pulled it up, then down, and frowned.

The dress was gorgeous. She took stock of herself in the mirror, noting that the dress set off her hair and eyes but faded her skin into ghostly paste. She'd need a good makeup job to wear this in concert.

"Doesn't quite work," Diana said, and to her credit, she sounded only vaguely malicious. "Not quite Cat Courtney, I'm afraid."

"Oh, yes, it is," said Laura, closed her eyes, and concentrated.

She thought herself into the wings of the stage, waiting to go on, waiting for the fantasy to claim her. She'd learned this trick long ago, to escape Dominic's cold rages by becoming a fairy princess, adored by her father, beloved of Prince Charming. She dipped her head and shook her hair out, then rose up and met Diana's eyes in the mirror.

Not Laura Abbott now, not even that demure matron Laura St. Bride. The woman in the mirror looked mysteriously like a cat now, with a narrowed, intense face and an adventurous mouth and eyes that glowed come-hither. Her posture had altered, just enough that the bodice filled out better, and the recalcitrant shoulder now slipped down and exposed an interesting amount of bosom.

"Wow!" Diana looked impressed, despite herself. "I've heard about this – how do you do it?"

Laura shrugged Cat Courtney away. "I psych myself into it. I used to be afraid that I'd vamp across the stage, and people would laugh. But now—" she stepped back from the mirror, and cocked her head, "I think this will work, don't you?"

"Definitely." Diana unzipped her. "The dress needs altering, but I know someone who's very good and not very expensive. Not that you need to count pennies." She held out the gold dress. "My turn. Who knows? Maybe I'll wear this when I play for you. The gold and black will make a great contrast."

They tried on dress after dress, giggling like two little girls playing dress-up. She had missed this, Laura thought, zipping Diana into yet another gown. She had missed this sharing, this laughter; she couldn't remember ever feeling this close to her sister in her life. And strange, too, that she felt so at ease with Diana, who had thrown away so much that she herself would have cherished.

"Do you think Lucy will want any of these?" she asked, as they carried the last load to her car.

"They're not Lucy's to take," said Diana. "She's not Mama's daughter. And, as she keeps reminding us, she won't be able to fit into them soon."

There it was again, that strange antagonism. She thought she could risk asking. "Di, what *is* it about this baby of hers? Why are you so upset?"

For a moment, she thought Diana might refuse to answer. Her sister paused in the doorway of the house, her face hidden in the shadows.

"She nearly died," Diana said finally, and Laura felt her heart drop. "She didn't tell you that, did she? She nearly bled to death. Her doctor was very firm with her, told her not to attempt another pregnancy for a while. So what did she do at the first opportunity? Get pregnant again, and hemorrhage again, and then get pregnant *again* so she can keep on risking her life! I can't lose her. You probably think I'm selfish, and, so what, I admit it. I don't have my husband, and I don't have my daughter, and my father's dead. Lucy is all I have. I'm damned if I'm losing her too."

She turned on her heel and marched inside. Laura caught up with her in the music room and stopped her with a touch of the hand.

"You have me, Di."

She meant it. She'd never meant it more.

"Do I?" Diana rotated slowly, deliberately. "Do I really? I don't know you. I don't think I ever did. Cat Courtney – what I saw upstairs – didn't exist in the sister I knew. Maybe I was blind. I'll plead guilty to that, I was never very good at figuring people out. But Daddy didn't see it either—"

She couldn't let that pass. "Oh, yes, he did."

Diana considered that. "All right, maybe he did. I never understood why he was so harsh with you, unless you threatened him. Should I feel threatened too? You're a big star. You've got millions of dollars. I don't know why you came home, and I don't trust you to stay."

"I'm staying." She found confidence in the strength of her voice. "You're right to keep me at arm's length until I prove myself. I had to stay away, I had good solid reasons I'll defend to my death. But I came back for you and Lucy. I *am* your sister, Di."

Diana said softly, "Not as much as you are hers."

Francie's ghost beckoned, pleaded, insisted, Francie, her entire purpose for coming here this day, to this house, to confront this woman. How could she have forgotten Francie.... But somehow, faced with a living, breathing sister whose hurt shone through her eyes, she could not hold onto Francie, slipping away into memory. Diana was here and now, and Francie, vengeful Francie, dead-eyed Francie, had lost her power to divide sister from sister.

She'd never thought of her sisters in that light before, that Francie and Diana had fought each other over more than Richard. She and Lucy had been spoils of war too, in the duel over the great unattainable prize of Dominic Abbott. Lucy had belonged to Diana, she to Francie, each a tool useful for bringing a sister down. Rivals from Francie's birth, rivals to Francie's death.

But not rivals over her. Not anymore.

She saw her choices laid out clearly before her, Lucy and Diana, flawed but alive, against dead, missed Francie. And she chose.

She whispered, "Play for me, Di."

Oh, a good move, that. Diana couldn't resist; too much of the performer still lived inside. Maybe the same memories flooded into her: the few happy times in this room, Diana's younger sisters gathered around the piano while she played and Dominic, audience of one, listened and critiqued. The wariness faded from her eyes; she moved towards the piano. "What would you like to hear?"

"Something Rachmaninoff?"

"Oh, you romantic you!" But, for all her mocking, Diana sat down to play.

Of all Dominic's daughters, she had been the most proficient pianist. Laura sat down beside her on the bench, but there was no music to turn, nothing to do but listen to the richness of Diana's great talent. And such richness! Diana was a master. She coaxed, she flirted, she commanded; her fingers flew and attacked, then alighted and soothed, stroked and caressed. Notes of longing, of love forgotten on the shores of another sea, of hearts that should never have broken over loves that should never have bloomed.

But the longer she listened, the more she heard the hollowness. Something atonal, something echoed, she heard shining technique without feeling, notes shallow and dead at their source. No vast landscape of longing and desire, no mountains and valleys and geysers of the heart, only empty plains of ice, frozen in time and space, a static, unforgiving terrain with no promise of fire and life.

Notes. Dots and lines on paper. Finger striking key. No mood, no longing, no warmth. No music.

Laura listened, her eyes closed, chilled to her core.

How could Diana survive in such barrenness? And how had Richard lived with it? Maybe Francie had offered not revenge but warmth and life; maybe he had reached out to warm himself in her laughter after enduring the desolation of Diana's heart.

"Well," Diana swept the concerto to a close, "what do you think? Will I do?"

"You're brilliant, Di." A brilliant technician, yes. She'd have to sing over the music, supply the warmth for them both. "I brought some octavos over. How about a Cat Courtney song?"

"In this room?" Diana winked at her.

Laura laughed. "Do you think his ghost will rise up and smite us?"

"Let's chance it." Diana was a quick study; she started to play, and Laura put her surroundings out of mind and sang along. Not a very polished performance – Diana misread a measure she'd scribbled on the plane, and she disgraced herself by forgetting to switch keys. They ran through the song again and ended up with a mutual look of amused disgust.

"We'll make it," Laura said. "Di, you have *got* it. Are you still studying voice?"

Make her sing for you.

"I don't sing anymore," Diana said, and slammed the keyboard down. Laura jerked her hands out of the way to keep her fingers from being smashed. "And don't tell me Lucy didn't put you up to that, either."

That startled her; Diana was nowhere as oblivious as Lucy would have her believe. "Yes, as a matter of fact, but forget that. Why don't you sing anymore? You had a beautiful voice."

"And it's not beautiful now." Diana stared out the window. "Do you remember the day you came back, and I asked why you didn't do opera, and you said that only Daddy ever thought you were opera material?" She didn't wait for Laura's nod. "Daddy always pushed me on my voice. I mean, *pushed* me, I couldn't have cared less. I *hated* all those hours, day and night and day again, doing those damn scales and working on my breath control and projection – Christ! It was misery! *This*—" She ran her hands lightly over the keys. "This is what I wanted, and he wouldn't leave me alone."

Laura said slowly, "I thought you loved him."

"Loved him?" Diana looked at her, surprised. "Love didn't enter into it. He was a genius, no one saw it but me, he was brilliant, his mind moved like fire – but, hell, Laurie, you know he was a lousy teacher. He had his agenda – it didn't matter what I wanted, or you – we had to do it his way. He decided early on to make me a star, his captive soprano, and be damned to me if I wanted something else. And I *did!* But he wouldn't listen."

"I've wondered – maybe he didn't want us to succeed." She couldn't help the sense of disloyalty, even now, saying the words in this room. It had taken so many years to see Dominic without the prism of fear. "He'd failed – so we had to fail. And he stacked the deck against us. It's been so hard—" Laura felt the flickering of pain behind her eyes and shoved it away. She hadn't the time for a headache, not now. "So hard to get his voice out of my head. I can do it most of the time, but – there are times – I can hear him still – hold that E! Get on top of that note! Enunciate! Breathe! Don't breathe! Posture! Pro*ject*!"

She heard the rising pitch of her voice, and clamped her mouth shut.

Diana was staring at her, and for a moment, only shocked silence lay between them.

She didn't know where all that had come from. Remembering for Julie how Dominic had planned her future for her? Coming back to this house, sitting at this piano, with the shadows of those long-ago lessons too close at hand? Dead or not, Dominic Abbott still dominated the room. She could feel his spirit at her shoulder, as if, even in death, he reached out to hold her down at the piano when she would have escaped, because she hadn't held the note long enough and he still wasn't satisfied.

The memory of those eyes, as he told her to try again, and then again, chilled her skin.

She shuddered, and looked down at her hands, lying in her lap.

"Oh, my God," whispered Diana, "it's like listening to him. Did he do it to you too?"

Laura said wearily, "You got away, Di. What do you think happened after you got married?"

Something strange flickered in Diana's eyes. "You think marriage saved me? Think again." She straightened the octavos. "So what happened? Francie became the next Tebaldi?"

Laura shook her head. "He didn't go after her. He went after me."

She folded her arms against her chest to keep warm.

"You know why, don't you?" Diana considered her. "You *do*, don't you?"

She said nothing. She should have eaten some breakfast; she was starting to feel sick.

"I'll tell you why." Diana's voice did not sound pretty now. "For the same reason he went after me. For the same reason he left Lucy alone. It wasn't just Peggy and Philip protecting her – he wasn't that interested in her ever. How much time did he spend with Francie compared to you?"

Oh, God, Diana had known. She had known, and she had done nothing. Laura drew a breath. "About half as much. He said I needed it more than she did."

"You probably did," said Diana flatly. "Francie had a pleasant little voice. She'd have done real well in a church choir. He wasn't going to waste his time on her."

It had been one thing to say it to Julie. Her niece hadn't known Francie, hadn't hated her. It was something else to hear Francie's enemy – she with blood on her hands – utter the thoughts that had surely never been said aloud before: that Dominic was too much the professional musician not to have known who in the family had it and who did not.

And, with all the ruthlessness and efficiency he had shown for so long, he had channeled his resources where time and effort might pay off.

But he had turned his sights on Laura only because Diana had escaped him.

She gathered her strength. "It doesn't matter about me. You still *sang*, Di, even away from him. I remember your concert, you were – oh, my God, you were incredible. Why give that up?"

She caught sight of Diana's face, hard and withdrawn, and thought that she had never seen anyone so bleak.

"It was yours, it wasn't his. He had no claim over you anymore. He couldn't do anything to you. Richard wouldn't have let him." She felt a terrible pressure in her lungs, as if she were caught underwater, desperate for air. "Why did you throw it away?"

Why did you throw Richard away? Or Julie?

"Why?" Diana's voice echoed eerily in the room. "I'll tell you why. Because it wasn't mine, not really. It was hers. He saw her in me." She gave Laura a hard look. "And I guarantee you that he had plans for me that he never had for you. Do you know what he said one night? *Do you know?*"

Surely Diana could hear the pounding of her heart.

"One night," Diana stopped and considered, her eyes staring beyond Laura, "one night, the year before Julie was born, he said that eventually I'd take her place. I'd—" She turned her head away, and Laura heard a hard intake of breath. "I'd sing Medea. That was her great role, you know, Daddy said at her best she could rival Callas. He wanted his Medea back. He intended," and she stopped and looked down, "to get her back through me."

In her voice, flat and unmelodious, lurked a despairing darkness. The absence of life, love, laughter. Laura couldn't remember ever hearing such hatred in her life. If she had ever any doubts about the pathology of her sister's heart, she had lost them now.

"I will never," said Diana, "sing in public again. He'll never have that from me. And now, if you don't mind, I'm going to make some tea. Want some?"

Tea did not help the sickness. That glimpse into her sister's darkness haunted Laura. She moved around the kitchen next to her sister, brewing tea, fixing toast, and nothing helped. Diana seemed not to notice.

In the few minutes before Laura had joined her in the kitchen – minutes that Laura had spent in the powder room, staring at her colorless face in the mirror, summoning up her courage to go back and confront her sister – Diana had helped herself to one of her stimulants of choice. She seemed revitalized, wound up tight, giddy to the point of absurdity. She started talking, and for a long time, she did not stop. She chattered gaily about clothes, about the concert, about her dream vacation driving around Europe – hopping from topic to topic, talking faster and faster. Her words filled the room – empty, nonstop words, spoken for noise, to banish the silent brutal mirror she could not face.

Maybe those volumes of words kept her demons at bay.

Laura tried to listen but slowly tuned out. She'd left Lucy's office two days before, vulnerable and dissected; now she longed for Lucy's blunt honesty. She knew where she stood with Lucy. Maybe Lucy did not approve of her, maybe that X-ray vision probed into thoughts and longings best kept hidden, but she spoke her mind. No darkness lingered in Lucy; she was sunlight and health. She was one of the living still, rock-solid, not a ghost trapped in this terrible room.

"One thing, Laurie." She became aware that Diana was demanding her attention. "You mentioned paying me for the clothes—"

"Right." Laura shook herself into alertness and glanced around for her purse. "I'll get my checkbook. How much do you want?"

"No, no." Diana shook her head for emphasis. "Not money. I'm not that desperate. But you do have something, if you don't mind – you never went there, it can't mean anything to you—"

"What?" She looked at Diana in consternation. "What are you talking about?"

"The cottage," said Diana. "You know, Ash Marine? Daddy's cottage?"

"What about it?"

"The cottage," Diana said patiently. "I want it."

She said slowly, "Why ask me? Didn't Daddy leave it—" And then, fresh horror flooding through her, "Oh, God, no, tell me he didn't leave it to me."

"Are you saying you didn't know?" Diana didn't bother to hide her skepticism. "I thought that's why you came back."

He had known. Somehow – how? – he had known.

Across the years, Dominic Abbott saluted her mockingly. *Darling girl, of course I knew what the cottage meant to you! Take it, acushla, you earned it, my token of appreciation for nearly destroying Richard Ashmore.*

And if you destroyed yourself too – ah, you learn to live without a soul, don't you now?

Pain burst behind her eyes.

Diana was looking at her curiously. Laura said, "Did he give a reason why? He hadn't seen me for years – he didn't know where I was—" *Oh, yes, he did. Cam was paying you off. Was that it, Daddy? Did Cam strike some kind of deal with you?*

"How would I know?" said Diana. "He didn't say anything to me."

If Daddy knew, did Cam know? How in the name of God did Cam find out?

She forced herself to speak. "Did he leave Francie anything?"

Diana shook her head. "Not that I know of. Nothing that's mentioned in the will."

So Dominic had known that Francie was dead. He had preserved documents for Laura, because he had known definitively that she was still alive. But Francie's birth certificate, her passport – all that was gone. He had discarded those; he had known they would never be needed again.

Laura stared down at her jeans, her ring finger worrying a frayed thread. "I don't want the cottage, Di. It's yours. What do I need to sign? Should I talk to Lucy?"

"I don't think it's that simple." Diana's curiosity had retreated. She poured herself another cup of tea into their grandmother's old Limoges china. "I think there's something about if you don't want it, it goes to your children. I remember Lucy saying that we couldn't just file abandonment papers, because you might have kids."

Under the nausea, she felt consumed with fury. Had Cam told Dominic about Meg, or had that just been a lucky shot in the dark? "I'll talk to Meg's trustee." *And if I find out Cam told Daddy about Meg, I will go spit on that memorial stone. Both of them.* "I'm sure we can decline the cottage for Meg."

"Great." Diana's face brightened. "I've always liked the place. Very private and peaceful." She arched an eyebrow. "Let's just say I've got a lot of sentimental attachment. When Richard turned sixteen—" She stopped. "Never mind. That was a magical night. I'll never forget it, and I bet he won't either."

I'll just bet. She stared hard into her tea cup, fixing on an errant tea leaf, focusing all her anger into that floating little speck. The nausea had receded, the anger had flooded back, recalled by Diana's light tone and fond memories of sexual surrender to a young man her sister would have killed for.

Had tried to kill for.

As quickly as that, she felt something go cold and still inside. The memories of the house vanished into the ether, and she remembered why she had come.

She put her tea cup down and looked Diana straight in the eye.

"How can you possibly talk like that? Aren't you sorry at all about Francie?"

"Francie?" Diana's face altered, shadowed, darkened. She too put her cup down, and Laura noticed, with a clarity born of rage, that the cup rattled as she set it into its saucer. "What's she to do with this? And why are you bringing her up, anyway? You know I don't like to talk about her."

"Oh, I know you don't." The tide of rage began to ebb in its turn, leaving the sands of her emotions cool and open. She felt very much in control. "Too bad, Di. Maybe you don't remember, God knows what you've been putting in your system, but Francie *died* out there. And you feel a sentimental attachment to the cottage? How can you feel *sentimental?* Don't you feel any guilt at *all?*"

Diana had gone pale under the force of attack, her eyes sunk back, her lips open with no words, no defense. Her voice was the merest breath. "I don't understand – Francie *died* out there – how—"

"Oh, don't lie, please!" She was fed to the teeth with lies. "I know what happened."

For eleven years, she had waited to see the guilt on Diana's face. That late afternoon, Francie and Diana had met on the shore of the Chesapeake, and the wrong sister had lived. Francie's killer sat there now, her face still seized with shock, and Laura felt the first breath of doubt. She saw no guilt, only Diana pulling herself together after the surprise attack, a straightening of the shoulders, a forcing of dignity to her lips as she said, "What are you talking about? Lucy said she died in some plane crash in Texas."

"My *mother-in-law* died in that crash, not Francie." The doubts rose up now in siege. "The call, Di. Francie called you from the cottage. August, eleven years ago."

Francie had made the call in front of her, claiming that she wanted a witness, coaxing Diana to meet her at the cottage, a meeting of reconciliation. A meeting that she did not intend Diana to survive…. All the time Francie had talked, she had fingered the handbag where she kept her small automatic, the gun Cam had taught her to use because she lived alone….

"She wanted you to meet her out at the Ashmore cottage. You were supposed to meet at two, I think, to talk things out so she could come home."

Her eyes flickered. "So you must have been there."

"She wanted me there when she made the call."

Diana made a motion towards her cup, blindly, as if she couldn't see it. "Of course I remember that. I was stunned when she called out of the blue like that – she didn't say you were with her."

"I wasn't going to meet with you." Francie had "repented" of her plan to kill Diana after Laura had threatened to go to Cam. *Okay, you don't trust me, come with me! Of course I won't do anything to her. I'm not a monster….* And when Laura dragged her feet about the trip, hoping Francie would change her mind: *I need you, Laurie, you're my balance, my conscience….* But that morning, Francie had firmly nixed her offer to mediate with Diana. *I'll go by myself…. No, don't come with me. We'll discuss Richard. You'll like him better if you don't hear what I have to say. Just wait for me here…. I'm just going to talk to her. Honestly, Laurie, I promise! Would I have asked you along if I was planning anything? Look, have some tea, I'll be back soon….*

"I didn't see her." Diana's lips were barely moving; Laura had to lean in close to hear her. "I – I had an appointment that morning, and then I went looking for Richard—"

"She went out to meet you—"

"Then – when I couldn't find him – well, I thought, maybe she called him too, maybe he went out there to her—"

"No, he wasn't there, she never called him, I'd have known—"

"I have the worst luck with cars – I had a flat tire, and I didn't know how to fix it, and you know there's not much traffic out there. I had to walk a couple of miles in the hot sun to find a phone to call the auto club." Her mouth trembled. "You don't believe me, do you? I can see it on your face, you don't believe me—"

"She never came back, Di! She went out to meet you, try to make up—"

"She never came back?"

"It got late in the afternoon. I needed her." The fever rising, the sun sliding down towards the horizon, the shadows elongating into the worst nightmares, the wind rising through the shattered windows, the baby dying in her womb. "I finally went looking for her, and I found her in the cove."

She lay, half-turned on her back, her right arm flung out with her head resting on it. From a distance, she looked like a sunbather in a painting, but Francie would never again turn to greet her, never again smile lazily and pat the sands invitingly. That sundress might once have been white, those arms might once have lifted towards a young man in ecstasy. But not ever again. Francie had fought hard for her life, and she had lost.

"The cove!" Diana finally heard her. "Good God, did she drown?"

"No," said Laura. "Someone cut her throat."

The shadows touched this room, this room cleansed bright only a few minutes before by camaraderie and music. Horror brushed them now, horror lived with for eleven years in remembered moments, in dreams, in all the lies Laura had told her husband. It swept over Diana, and the darkness covered her, claimed her like a bride.

"You think I did that."

"Yes," Laura said, "I do. Who else?"

"You think – you think I *killed* her. You think—" and Diana breathed in hard, even as her eyes died— "you sit there, right across from me—"

"Di." She could barely speak.

"You think—" and Diana swallowed for control, and her voice escalated— "you think I went out there prepared, with a knife—"

"No, she had the knife, she must have—"

"And she turned her back on me, or I came up behind her, and I grabbed her by the hair so she couldn't move, and even with her screaming and fighting, I slit her throat – oh, God, all that blood, the jugular is full of blood – and you think I killed her—"

"I did think it, Di." She managed only a whisper. "Tell me I'm wrong."

She had never seen eyes like that, remote, washed clean of all light and life. Diana moved, jerkily, like someone rediscovering how to walk; the movement pulled her up and across the room, back into the realm of the living. Laura dug her fingernails into the leather arm of Dominic's chair and watched Diana standing over the piano, staring at the keys, her hands flitting across their ivory gloss in search of memory and remorse.

Diana's fingers slashed across the keys in a jarring cacophony of tangled chords.

"I didn't kill her." Diana spoke to the keys. "I never saw her that day."

"You're lying." Laura forced the words out. "You just stood there and described what you did."

"*Electra.*" Laura saw the scene then on her mind's stage. "Strauss. Orestes nearly decapitates Clytemnestra while Electra watches. Daddy directed up in Canada a few years ago, and I worked in production. We had to stage it like that. You can't cut someone's throat any other way."

"You're lying." But her mind raced into new corridors: *who else? who else?*

Diana turned her head and looked straight at Laura.

"Who are you?" she said, and now her voice seemed stronger. "What kind of person are you if you believe I did that to her? How can you be in the same room with me, and believe that I could do that to my own sister?"

"You're my sister." Laura's turn to whisper. "And – to be honest – it's very tough."

Diana gave a short, mirthless laugh, and sat down at the piano. Her hands brushed the keys again and swept into a strange, atonal melody, one of Dominic's. The music took her over like a master: unearthly, as empty of feeling as Diana herself, sparkling with all the cold inhumanity of a jewel.

My God, maybe she didn't. But the way she talked—

And above her thoughts, rising and falling with the notes, Diana's voice, saying, "Tell me what happened."

"I saw Francie lying in the cove." The music helped her, removed her from the immediacy of this room, this scene. Memory glistened like a painting she had once seen, long ago, in a far-off museum. "I wasn't seeing straight, I felt faint and strange – she drugged me, you see, she didn't want me coming after her to stop her—"

"Stop her from what?" Diana ran her fingers up an arpeggio.

"Don't you *know?*"

Are you telling the truth and you weren't there – or don't you remember? Have you blown your mind so completely?

Are you mad, Diana?

"Laurie?" Diana had stopped playing; her hand whipped around to grasp Laura's arm with unexpected strength. "Stop her from what?"

She said nothing.

"Laurie!" Diana's hand had started to shake. "Tell me! You know. I can see it in your face. She wanted to meet me. What was she planning, why did you need to stop her—"

And she saw the truth then.

Diana whispered, "You said she had a knife."

She felt fragile and unreal in Laura's arms, as though the slightest touch might cause her to crumble into dust. She did not cry. She did not break down the way a sane woman might have, faced with the knowledge that her own sister had intended her death.

Then, somehow, she managed to pull away. "Then what happened?"

My God, I am cold, I am so cold. There's nothing in you, Di, only brittle ice. No wonder Richard left you – but you, my poor sister, you can't leave.

"I tried to get to her." Laura found herself shaking, and her voice shook with her. "I kept hoping – I couldn't believe my eyes – and then I got closer, and I knew she was dead…."

"And you didn't call for help?"

Oh, cool, cool Diana. Nothing touched her, did it? "I didn't – touch her, I don't think I did, nobody could be alive after that. Her dress looked like she was in a slaughterhouse. All that blood—"

Diana said bloodlessly, "That must be a terrible memory."

She swerved on her sister then. "I don't *have* a memory. I talked to a doctor about it, because I only remember bits and pieces. She drugged me so badly, Francie did, to keep me from interfering, she gave me some sort of hallucinogen, I started to miscarry, my skin felt so hot." Her throat closed up. "Nothing's ever come back—"

And in the midst of dimming memory, Diana asked, "So how did you get away?"

Here, finally, the dark center of the horror. If Diana had held the knife, she herself had surely plunged it in. The void of her heart lay gaping open now, the wound made by her guilt, weary from the denial of eleven years.

"I left her there." And now her voice didn't tremble; her hands didn't shake. She took vague pride that her composure matched Diana's. "I don't know how I got off Ash Marine, I don't remember leaving, but I did. I didn't take our car, I must have walked – the state patrol found me, and I was bleeding so badly they airlifted me out to a hospital. I left her there, I never even touched her to see if maybe she was still alive, *I left her there to die—*"

In a spiraling delirium, she had walked away, leaving her earliest and closest fellow traveler to come to the end of her journey. She'd lost child, sister, hero, lover; she'd nearly lost her life. *For God's sake, stop crying! I have to think what to do…. She's bleeding so badly.* Old remembrance, barely dreamed, barely known, and the hysterical cry: *Oh, what have I done, what have I done….* Later, the blood she found on her sweater, blood mingled with her own, but not her own.

"So," said Diana softly, "you killed Francie too."

And looked Laura straight in the eye, and never blinked.

She'd never heard the words before, but once spoken, they became true. She felt tears falling on her hands, and she looked at them in surprise, astonished that she noticed them in the rapier pain of her heart.

Diana said coolly, "So you saw her and you left and you blacked out. Not surprising. You were in shock. Forget it, I'd have done it too. Did anyone else know?"

Her heart threatened to stop. "What?"

"Think." Diana prosecuted her case with a cold verve that Lucy might envy. "Someone helped Francie. She couldn't plan her way out of a paper sack. She simply wasn't that organized." She bent her head over the keyboard. "Plus, if you two had a car, someone gave you the keys to the bridge. You couldn't have gotten to Ash Marine without them."

She marveled through her grief. She'd never doubt Diana's intelligence again. In all these years, she had never once thought of the bridge keys that Francie had magically produced, not even when she herself had stolen them from Dominic's desk the week before. She reached into her pocket slowly and pulled out the keys. "These?"

Diana's mouth curled. "Nice try, Laurie. When did you get those?"

"Last week. I found them in Daddy's desk."

Diana held out her hand. "As far as I know," musing lazily, as though she were discussing something inconsequential, something that she really didn't care about, "only three people had keys. I always had to borrow Daddy's."

She spoke slowly, trying to fit the pieces together, "Then how were you planning to get in to meet Francie?"

"I stopped by Ashmore Park when I was looking for Richard, and I took his."

"But Philip had keys too—"

And Laura stopped. *There's no help in truth.* If Diana were telling the truth – and was she? could she trust that Diana wasn't lying, hadn't gone mad? – she certainly was not going to tell her that the keys filched from Ashmore Park all those years ago must have belonged to Philip Ashmore. Richard had taken his keys with him. She remembered – oh, the little things she remembered – the *clink* of his watch and keys on the old piano bench there in the cottage.

And she completed, because she had to, "But Philip would never give his keys to Francie. He'd have told Daddy she was there—"

She stopped, because she saw it too.

Richard. Francie. Philip now, a new wild card. And—

"Exactly." The first crack in Diana's composure appeared, the first fissure in her glacial calm. Her hands, still clenched around the keys, were shaking. "And Philip probably did want me dead – he and Peggy wanted me out of Richard's life—" More cracks now. Francie's death had started to touch Diana; her eyes were dark now, dark with pain and terror eleven years after the fact. "But Philip was getting rid of me. Richard and I were through – I was giving up, so, oh God, oh God, *Daddy* had keys! Francie had *Daddy's* keys! It was Daddy, wasn't it, it was, he knew I'd told Richard, he knew Richard wouldn't protect him—"

"Di, oh, Christ, Di, no, *listen* – Francie said—"

"Daddy," sobbed Diana. "Oh, God, *Daddy*—"

He'd come back now, filling the room, Dominic Abbott, failed composer, master conductor, deserted lover, acquitted killer, son-of-a-bitch father, with his narrow face and his quiet, icy rage. She saw him there, his long, thin fingers touching Diana's shining hair, caressing Francie's uplifted cheek, beating out the time like a metronome while Laura struggled to reach that high E.

"My God," and Laura heard him break the heart of his most trusting victim, "he hated me that much – I gave up Richard for him, and he still hated me—"

"*Di*—"

Diana jumped up then, and the keyboard cover smashed down, a loud blasphemy against her sobbing as she shoved Laura back from her. Laura stumbled and lost precious seconds as she fell against Dominic's desk, seconds long enough for Diana to elude her. Seconds behind her sister up the stairs; seconds late before the door to Diana's bedroom slammed in her face.

"Di! Don't shut—"

The crash a brutal slash across her words. She threw the door open, and before her lay all that she'd feared.

The mirror smashed to pieces. Diana weeping, tears, blood, every breath a sob. The light carpet beneath already a splotched painting. She stopped Diana before she could rip her other wrist apart.

Laura's mind shut down.

She reached for the mirror shard, tried to force it from Diana's hand. Diana resisted, backing off, and the jagged edge slipped across her hand and ripped into Laura's palm and fingers.

Their blood mingled, spilled, streaking the gold silk of the ball gown swept to the floor by their struggle. The history of their parents' love affair lay there, a canvas for a bloody battleground.

Laura couldn't think; the agony of the slash on her hand drove all consideration from her mind. Diana hung on to her bloody dagger, fighting, sobbing, maniacal in her grief, unreasonable in her pain.

She raised it above her other wrist, and Laura screamed.

"Di! *No!*"

Diana, distracted, stopped and stared at her.

"Di?" She had to make her voice steady. "*Put it down.*"

Diana stared at her blankly, then looked at her bloody wrist, then looked at her again, and then looked at the shard.

"Di?"

No reaction. Not a flicker of recognition where they were, what she held in her hand.

Laura had never seen eyes so empty – so crazy.

She had to act. She didn't stop to think; she went on instinct. She clenched her bloody fist, hauled back, and threw all her strength into a punch that landed squarely on Diana's jaw.

Diana went down immediately, falling limp and docile against the footboard of the bed, her legs bending askew, a puppet whose strings had been brutally cut. The shard fell aside, now harmless.

"Keep your hand up!"

"I can't – let me just *go* —"

"Squeeze! Damn it, *squeeze!*"

The first aid training necessary to raise a rambunctious child hadn't allowed for a suicide attempt. She forced herself into calm. If she let herself react, she'd yield to hysteria or – at the very least – to the stinging burn on her palm. She swallowed her panic and ran into the bathroom for a towel.

Diana pre-empted her and proceeded to have the hysterics for both of them.

"How could you say that, Daddy loved me best —"

"He did, Di, he did. Hold still, okay?"

"Not Daddy, he wouldn't have done that to me —"

"Keep your arm *up*, Di, I don't want this to fall off."

"Why didn't Francie just leave me alone, stupid bitch, Daddy knew I wasn't coming back, she should have gone after you—"

"Because Daddy loved you best and she couldn't deal with it."

"And Richard threw me out, that can't be it, but he didn't want her, not really, he only used her to get back at me because of Julie—"

"Hold your arm up, and squeeze! Can you get your other arm around my neck?"

The room looked like the scene of a massacre. Diana had already lost a lot of blood, and the first towel soaked through in seconds. Laura swallowed hard at the sight. She needed help. She needed Cat Courtney's cool, Lucy's unflinching balance, Richard's quiet strength, but she was only Laura Abbott, trying to deal with the worst emergency of her life, terrified that her sister would bleed to death on her before help could arrive.

If help could get there in time.

"Come on! *Now!*" And she yanked Diana to her feet and pushed her into the hall and to the top of the stairs.

Diana didn't move.

"Go! *Go!*" And she pressed against her sister's back.

Diana stirred, and went, slowly. Blood tracked them all the way down the stairs; the carpet would never be the same again.

Her bloody wrist dripped a trail out onto the veranda.

The Jaguar was piled high with clothes. Laura ran back in the house and scooped up her purse and Diana's car keys.

The sight of the keys woke Diana up. "Not my car! I don't want blood on the seats."

Laura stared at her in disbelief. "It's your blood."

"*No—*"

"Oh, my God." She shoved Diana into the front seat, ruined her blouse as she buckled Diana in, and ground the gears as she roared the Mercedes out of the driveway.

"Where's the nearest hospital?" she asked, and ground the gears again as she attempted in vain to obey a stop sign.

"I don't know," murmured Diana, and fainted.

Oh, dear Lord, Diana was going to die on her. She swallowed the terror rising in her throat, shifted awkwardly (she should have let Cam teach her to drive a stick shift), and floored the accelerator down the country road back towards Jamestown.

She hadn't paid any attention to the roadside before. She'd been more intent on her destination, and she paid for it now. She hadn't a clue where to find help. Oh, she could phone, ask for help, but she was running out of time. Diana was slumped over, her breathing shallow, her face sheet-rock white, the crimson of her wrist a slash against her pale skin.

Damn! Her cell phone battery flickered out.

Salvation, when it came, appeared in the form of the patrolman who flashed her to the side of the road a mile up. His lecture about her erratic driving and the expired license plates died on her lips when he saw her hand and looked at Diana. He knew first aid, thank God. He rewrapped the tourniquet, gave Diana a fresh handkerchief to staunch the bleeding, and gave them an escort to the ER entrance of a small local hospital.

Then he gave her a ticket for the expired license plates.

"Fine," said Laura, and threw the ticket on the dashboard. Diana could jolly well take care of it later.

Inside, Diana was already sitting in a glassed-in cubicle, offering her bloodied wrist to the nurse. "What happened?" he asked, briskly unwrapping the makeshift tourniquet. "You've got quite a scratch there."

"I broke a mirror," Diana whispered.

"An accident," Laura said, and refused to flinch at his knowing expression. "We were moving furniture, and it fell on her."

"*Right*," he said. "Better get those hands looked at."

She'd forgotten the slashes on her own hands. She stared down at them, and on cue they burned.

Somehow, she and Diana weathered the hospital. The doctor quizzed them about the injuries to Diana's wrist and didn't pretend to believe Laura. "Frankly, Ms. St. Bride," she said finally, "you can lie your way to kingdom come and back again, and I don't care, but your sister needs to be watched carefully. She didn't do a particularly skillful job of this, so I don't think she seriously set out to kill herself, but you know she's done this before, don't you? She's got scars. Don't leave her alone tonight."

The admitting nurse proved another stumbling block. "Next of kin, please."

"Lucy Maitland," said Diana.

"No." Laura thought of Lucy, stroking the antique folds of the baby blanket; she and her baby shouldn't deal with this. "Richard Ashmore."

Diana showed the first sign of life since she had disappeared upstairs. "No! Don't tell him, please! I don't want him to know!"

No doubting her real alarm; no ignoring her real pain. "Laura St. Bride," said Laura to the nurse. "I'm her next of kin. I'll take care of the bill."

Miracle of miracles, no one looked at her – covered with blood, hair wrecked, hands torn up – and recognized Cat Courtney behind Laura St. Bride. Not, she thought wearily, traipsing down to the business office, that she really cared, but she hadn't the strength left to deal with the inevitable publicity. The doctor and nurses might dubiously accept her stupid cover story. No self-respecting tabloid would make the same mistake.

Diana said nothing until Laura had checked her out and bundled her back into the Mercedes. She sat quietly in the early afternoon sun, holding her wrist stiffly in her lap, her head tilted against the car window, and winced only slightly when Laura again ground the gears trying to shift out of first. The trauma of the last few hours had barely touched her face, Laura thought, stealing a glance from the corner of her eye; Diana looked frail and unearthly and utterly lovely.

She waited until she'd successfully maneuvered the Mercedes onto the interstate to Hampton before she interrupted her sister's reverie.

"Your prescription, Di." The doctor had prescribed a tranquilizer and bed rest once she got home. "Does your pharmacy deliver?" No answer. Ahead loomed the exit ramp for the exclusive riverfront community where Diana lived. She remembered just in time to hit the clutch before she attempted to downshift. "Di?"

Diana said in a small voice, "Why'd you lie for me?"

She wasn't sure why. Maybe the desire to shield Lucy; maybe the fear of telling Richard. She didn't doubt for an instant that he was going to blame all of this on her. *And don't you deserve it? Didn't you push her, because you can't let Francie go?*

She said, "You're my sister. I love you, Di. You may choose not to believe that, but it's true and I do. Sometimes there are laws about doctors having to report suicide attempts. I don't know if that's true here, but I didn't want to chance it."

"Oh." Still the little girl's voice. A moment of silence, while Diana fiddled with the bandage. "Do you think Daddy wanted to kill me?"

"No, I don't." Surely, the most bizarre conversation she could ever remember having. The sun beat down around them; they rode in well-sprung luxury on the Virginia roads, talking of lost blood and ancient rage. "I swear it couldn't have been Daddy. Francie said—"

Francie had said, unequivocally, that Richard wanted his wife dead.

Not that Francie had ever been noteworthy for telling the truth.

She said carefully, slowing the car down for the turnoff to Diana's condo, "You don't mention Richard. They say the husband is always the first one the police look at."

"Richard? Oh, heavens, no!" And Diana actually laughed. "No one could seriously think *Richard* would hurt me! He'd never jeopardize Julie. Besides, he loves me."

She hadn't a clue what to answer in the face of that confident declaration. And if this wasn't interfering in their marriage, what was? "But if you were separated, and he wanted a divorce, and you wouldn't give him one—"

"If he really wanted a divorce, he could get one." Diana picked again at her bandage, and Laura snapped at her to leave it alone. "I can't stop him, I don't have grounds. Unless," she glanced sidelong, "you'd like to give me an affidavit on Francie?"

"Forget it."

"Francie doesn't matter anyway. He's found someone else."

Instinctively, Laura resisted. "Di, you don't have to tell me—"

"Oh, not just a one-night stand," said Diana, "though I'm sure he's had plenty of those. I mean, I have, I can hardly get mad at him if he hooks up, can I? But Lucy thinks he's interested in some woman in London."

"London!" Her breath caught.

"It's his ring." Diana ducked her head. "He went to London last year, and Lucy thinks he met someone there because he stopped wearing his ring. He hasn't been back, though, so I don't know if there's any truth to it, unless," and she raised her head again, "she's come here, and I don't know."

Laura stared at the unforgiving plane of that bandaged wrist.

Diana whispered, "He doesn't want me, you know. For a long time, he still loved me, but it's all different now. It changed after his parents died, and I kept wondering: is this the day? Will he tell me that he wants a divorce? Sometimes he'd call, and I'd be terrified, because I knew the time had come…. But he never did, and it's been a year now. Maybe Richard still feels that we're mated for life."

London. *Julie and I saw you in London….*

She'd sung to him, part of that great dark, glistening audience, and as he'd listened to her, some other woman had captured his lonely heart. She'd sung to him, and he'd already been lost to her, snatched again out of her reach by the spinning wheels of fortune.

She'd missed him for the third time.

His parents had just died. He'd rejected Diana. For the first time ever, he had stood alone, save for Julie, and he'd been in a mood to fall in love.

And I never saw him.

She stared ahead, she who had never won him, and said soothingly to she who had won and lost, "You have nothing to worry about, Di. No woman will ever take Richard away."

She coped, as she'd learned the September before that she could. She hustled Diana upstairs and into bed, in a pale blue bedroom fit for a fairy-tale princess. The parade of visitors Richard had described hadn't left a mark in this room, as they had not on Diana, the Lady of Shallot floating on bluebell gossamer. Diana had no spirit left in her. She lifted her arms docilely so that Laura could remove her ruined blouse; she stepped out of her jeans, one leg at a time, using her hand on Laura's shoulder for balance; she held her wrist carefully out of the bath in deference to Laura's reminder. And she nodded as though she agreed when Laura told her not to call Lucy.

"She doesn't need this right now, Di."

"But I want to talk to her," said Diana, half-heartedly, and then sighed. "Oh, I know, I know. That damn baby. Like if I call her, she'll lose it?"

She said through her teeth, "Stay off the phone, Di, or I'll rip it out of the wall."

"All *right!*" Diana stomped over to the bed and made a big production of climbing under the whisper-light comforter. "Have it your way."

"Damn straight."

She held up, long enough to call for Diana's sedative, long enough to sit with her sister until Diana stopped fighting the medicine and fell asleep. Long enough to take stock in the mirror and recoil from her blood-stained image (no wonder the pharmacy delivery man had left before she could tip him). Long enough to step into the shower under hot, soothing water and wash her sister's blood down the drain.

Long enough to open a drawer in the vanity, searching for a comb, and find instead a veritable pharmacy. Mostly prescription – she read label after label, her alarm growing – some not – and she dragged a plastic bag filled with grass out of the back of a deep drawer. She opened another drawer and pulled out paraphernalia that she hadn't seen since her late teens: water pipe, roach clip, paper for rolling your own.

She stared at the means of Diana's destruction. Then she met her own reflection in the mirror, and even Dominic would have recognized Cat Courtney now, of the borrowed bathrobe and the towel twisted around her head, in the utter determination in that tilted chin and those flashing eyes.

It took her over an hour. She found a large trash bag in the kitchen, and she searched the apartment thoroughly while Diana slept in blissful ignorance. Everything went into the bag, pills, bottles, plastic bags, syringes, a king's ransom in white powder. She overlooked nothing, and she spared nothing; she ransacked the dresser drawers, the desk, inside the flower vases, even under the bed, Diana sleeping inches away.

Let Diana hate her when she awoke. She didn't care.

She left nothing to chance. She paged through Diana's address book, looking for strange entries, and found a card listing a liquor store that delivered. After she tore it up, she poured the contents of every bottle in the wet bar down the drain. The empty battles vanished into her sack, and that she took with great ceremony and destroyed in the trash compactor.

Every time Richard came to mind, she drove him out.

Until she found the folder.

It lay in the large drawer of Diana's desk, right next to a silver flask, and Laura knew instantly what she'd found. Manila, worn – it had borne handling over the years – and someone had once written on its tab, in now-faded ink, *Divorce.*

She stared at it for a long moment, her instinct at war with her conscience. *Read it, read it,* urged one, against the whisper that to open the folder might answer questions best left unasked forever.

But she had already asked.

She reached for the folder and hesitated for one last moment.

You'll like him better if….

Her heart beat painfully; her breath hurt her throat. She took the folder to the sofa and laid it down.

And there it sat for a while. She put off reading it as long as she could stand it. She checked on Diana, she made herself a cup of tea, she called her voice mail for her messages. She made herself a second cup of tea.

And it beckoned, lured, offering knowledge and secrets, the key to the great rift in Diana's life.

As Richard had so decisively said, it was nothing to do with her.

Or it might be everything.

She resisted no longer. She picked it up and opened it.

A letter from an unknown attorney: *This letter serves as notification that Mr. Ashmore intends to seek a full separation and will petition the Court for custody of Julia Ashmore.*

A letter from Philip Ashmore to Diana: *I beg you to reconsider. Don't fight him on this. Julie is happy with Richard. He adores her. They're good together. Don't persist in breaking two hearts.*

A petition for custody filed by Richard Ashmore: *Defendant has repeatedly demonstrated a predilection for abuse of alcohol and controlled or illegal substances. Defendant's violent behavior on the occasions detailed in the attached affidavit raises questions as to her ability to serve as the custodial parent of Julia Ashmore and the advisability of prolonged unsupervised visitation.*

Diana's counterclaim: *Complainant has shown a flagrant disregard for the sanctity of the marriage bond by engaging in an adulterous relationship with Defendant's sister, Francesca Mariah Abbott.*

Laura stared at the paper for a long time. With no proof, with nothing but his silence and her own suspicions, Diana had accused Richard publicly.

How had he felt, having such damaging truth brought to light? Richard, private, proud, bruised survivor of the bleak wilderness of his marriage?

But he had struck back, and swiftly. The next court document bore a filing stamp the day after Diana's accusation: *Complainant and Defendant must agree that the issue of adultery by either party has been waived by subsequent cohabitation. No independent evidence exists to support Defendant's allegation that Complainant engaged in a sexual relationship with Defendant's sister. The young woman in question has been missing from her home for three years, and her whereabouts remain unknown. She is not available to testify.*

Three years? She looked again at the dates, and her skin turned cold.

The summer of Francie's murderous plans. While Francie had planned and plotted in Texas, Richard and Diana had engaged in combat for the soul of their daughter.

And while coincidence existed in everyday life, surely this could not be.

You knew where she was, Richard.

Laura swallowed hard, and turned to the next page.

Richard to Diana, in a letter fraught with crossed-out words: *Julie is having nightmares again. I think she is picking up on my tension. For God's sake, let's work something out. I can't stand to see her in such terror.* And a photocopy of Diana's return volley: *You're so concerned about Julie. How well do you think she slept three years ago? Maybe she's afraid you'll throw her out just as you did me.*

Richard: *Try remembering why I asked you to leave.*

Diana: *Try remembering what you said to me that night. Or are you just too damn holy these days to remember?*

No wonder they refused to see each other now. Even after eleven years, who could forgive this?

A child psychologist's report: *Observation of the child interacting with her parents leaves little doubt in my mind that her father should retain custody. Mr. Ashmore is a devoted parent and takes great pride in Julie. Mrs. Ashmore appears tentative and distant with Julie, and Julie refuses to go to her mother even when directed to do so. My opinion of Mrs. Ashmore is that she has not bonded with her husband or her child. Her statements indicate an unhealthy dependence on her father and warrant further investigation, but she refuses to cooperate.*

Laura's hand shook as she turned the report face down.

Dominic must have been furious to read that.

A court order, entitled "Interlocutory Judgment," giving custody of Julie to Richard, with supervised visitation privileges granted to Diana, conditioned upon her seeking treatment for her addictions.

Signed two weeks before that afternoon on Ash Marine.

Not coincidence, no, it couldn't be. Diana at the center of this horror, while her rival planned out her murder? Surely not. But Richard might not have known, or cared if he did. This war he had clearly been winning.

It might have made more sense if Diana had tried to kill him.

A motion entitled "Intervenor's Motion to Request Paternity Test" with a note dated the day after the Interlocutory Judgment, in handwriting she remembered all too well: *I will file this if you do not cease and desist. Dominic.* She looked at the motion, unmarred by any court stamps: *Comes now Dominic Abbott, Intervenor, and requests permission of the Court to intervene in this custody action between Complainant Richard Ashmore and Defendant Diana Abbott Ashmore…. Intervenor asserts, on information and belief, that Complainant did not have access to Defendant when the minor child was conceived because Complainant and Defendant were living apart.*

She heard herself gasp in the stillness of the apartment, her breath a sword cutting through the quiet.

The paper started to slide from her fingers. She put it down on her lap and smoothed it out.

Dates cited, bald dates spelling out the disintegration of Richard and Diana's marriage. Dominic's own words, in all their sparkling malice, in the attached affidavit: *My daughter admitted that she does not know the identity of her child's biological father, but she is certain that her child could not have been fathered by her husband, Richard Ashmore.*

And Lucy, recounting that long-ago time: *She moved out for a while after their first anniversary… He told me to make myself scarce for a couple of days so he could talk some sense into her… she found out she was pregnant… Richard told her to come back… everything really went south.*

Richard, in weary, age-old bitterness: *Ask how many abortions… the first was my child, a year after we were married.*

Richard, seen through the glass, smiling at the most important person in the world.

She stared into space and felt the tumblers click softly into place.

Dear God, what a burden he had carried. How had he managed? Where had he found the strength to love Julie, this biological stranger foisted on him after the destruction of his own child? How had he kept her, loved her, sheltered her, built that wonderful home for her?

How had he not killed Diana?

Maybe he tried. Or maybe Francie suggested it, and he hated Diana just enough not to stop her.

The final order granting custody, signed by Richard and Diana. She read through it quickly and then read it again, mystified. Three pages long, spelling out visitation and financial arrangements, with no mention of everything that had gone before. Signed one week after Ash Marine.

What had happened, between Dominic's annihilating motion and this quiet, antiseptic document, to drive underground the bitterness and hatred raging between Julie Ashmore's parents?

Laura saw the answer as she sat there, a vision shimmering in the western light: an afternoon shining on the Chesapeake, a beseeching telephone call made, a treacherous cup of tea brewed, a young woman silenced forever on the sands.

But, while these papers laid bare all the reasons in the world for Richard and Diana to kill each other, Francie had died.

And Diana had instinctively accused Dominic.

She held her breath and turned over to the last document.

Another legal document, again smooth and white, without the usual court date stamp. Clipped at the top, a note, in handwriting Laura knew without question, taut with fury and despair: *Call off your father, or I swear I'll file this and fight you to hell and beyond.*

"Complainant's Counter-Request for Paternity Test": *Now comes Complainant, Richard Ashmore.... Complainant regrets the necessity of this distasteful accusation.... Defendant Diana Ashmore admitted the truth of Julia Ashmore's paternity to Complainant six months before the birth.... On information and belief, the sexual relationship between Defendant and Intervenor Dominic Abbott predates the marriage of Complainant and Defendant.... Clearly, neither Defendant nor Intervenor is a proper party for custody of the child.*

And Julie – with those green eyes, that unquestionable talent, and that Machiavellian mind – was all Abbott.

She was surprised, moments later, to come back to herself and find that the room sang of silence. The late afternoon had scattered shadows and sun dust in the air, a gentle, giving warmth; she lifted her hand in the eastern light and noticed, quite curiously, that it remained steady and that the light sparkling off her mother's ring did not shake down a shower of stars.

The screaming had echoed all within her head.

The papers on her lap were only papers, with marks and stamps; they held no real power. This all lay in the past, new only to her. The battle had finished, decisively, with two signatures on a paper. Diana had crept away in defeat to drink away her wounds; Richard had retreated into his controlled world and shut out any chance of further pain. Francie had washed away into the night; Julie had grown up a willing prisoner to her father's anguish.

And Dominic Abbott, composer of this twisted symphony, had walked away from the destruction he had wrought until one day a person unknown had meted out long-overdue justice.

Damn you, Daddy. May you rot in hell forever.

And if you weren't there already, I swear I'd send you on your way. I'd cut your throat, poison you, drive a stake through your heart.

Across the years, she heard Dominic laughing.

15

Diana, Mrs. Ashmore

SO I MARRIED RICHARD. Was he the problem?

Probably not.

I just didn't like being married.

I think engagements must be a trick. You're supposed to spend the time contemplating marriage, discussing your hopes and dreams for the future… all that. I read all the manuals. What no one tells you is the dirty little truth: that you're so damn busy running around planning the wedding and discussing all those earthshaking details like flowers and should the maid of honor have a different dress and what to do with your spoiled brat sister that you really don't want in the wedding – not to mention, of course, that I was in school, and so was Richard, and we were a hundred miles away from where the wedding was being held, so we had to run down there every week-end – and anyway, with all that, who has time to sleep, let alone reflect upon the gravity of the step you are about to take?

And everything provoked a fight, either between Richard and me, or between me and someone else. I told Daddy I refused to be married in the Church – I was still afraid of going to hell – but of course, I couldn't tell him why. Then he refused to walk me down the aisle if we got married in the Episcopal church where Richard had been baptized. So finally I announced that I wanted a garden wedding at Ashmore Park, which let me out of the Catholic ceremony altogether, and Peggy came to my rescue and suggested the municipal judge husband of one of her garden club buddies. That certainly solved my problem, and since Richard was the next thing to a complete agnostic, he didn't care. Amazingly, Daddy agreed to that, and it was years before I figured out why he and Peggy, both of them more Catholic than the Pope, encouraged a civil ceremony that they knew damn well was not valid in the Church. I was just glad not to have to face the crucifix on my wedding day.

And that was just *one* of the headaches I faced on my way to the altar.

I was so tired by the time we got married. I remember standing there in front of the judge, and Richard said his vows clearly, confidently, with no hesitation that he was doing exactly the right thing in life. And then the judge turned to me, and I could barely even listen to him to repeat the vows correctly. Of course, everyone attributed it, charmingly, to my being nervous. Nervous? I'd known him forever. I'd been sleeping with him since I was fifteen. What was to be nervous about?

And the only thing I remember about the reception was Francie sulking. Stupid little girl – what did she expect? She was fourteen. Did she think he was going to wait for her to grow up?

I heard that Laurie cried. I don't remember that. I don't remember a lot about Laurie.

I do remember one other thing about the reception. I remember dancing with Daddy, who had surprisingly kept his mouth shut all spring once he compromised on the ceremony. He paid the bills and was semi-courteous to Richard. He even walked me down the aisle and gave me away without protest. But he did claim his dance with me. And just when I thought I was finally getting away forever:

"Diana, this won't last. It can't." Now, I ask you, who says that to a bride?

I mumbled something like, "Daddy, I love him," or maybe I said, "Can I get some sleep now?" since that was certainly what I was thinking.

"You aren't cut out for the life he wants. You're like your mother." *Oh, right, Daddy, push those buttons again.* "And that boy is Shilleen all over again. Conscious of his place in that dynasty, bound up in his land, everything else taking second place, and she couldn't take it, she couldn't breathe, she was suffocating...."

Yes, yes, yes, Daddy, tell me that story again, about that night when she replaced your first-choice soprano in rehearsal, and she never went home, because (apparently) there was something irresistible about a man who was supposed to go home himself to a monastery that night.

"Just remember, Diana, you can always come back." *Sure, every new bride needs an escape hatch.* "I don't think your young man, as strait-laced as he is, will satisfy you for long."

No, Daddy, he's just been doing a pretty good job since he was sixteen.

But Richard didn't get the chance that night. I drank so much champagne that I instantly got the fiercest headache. I didn't wake up until noon the next day in our hotel room, and Richard, of course, had been up for hours. He was kind about it. Richard was always kind. He even joked that it wasn't as if we didn't know what a wedding night was supposed to be like.

I remember looking at him and thinking, *Oh, my God, has he always been this nice?*

It was not a happy thought.

Well, I asked for it. Marriage, in all its splendor.

I was so bored! In the few moments I'd had to think straight during our engagement, I'd figured life would be perfect once we were married – no more sex in the reclining bucket seats, no more pooling our money to rent an occasional room, no more sneaking back into the dorm because I'd stayed out past curfew! No one making any more impossible demands on me.

Freedom. Space and breathing room to be who I wanted to be, on my own timetable.

A buffer between me and Daddy.

Now we had a *fabulous* honeymoon. Mr. and Mrs. Richard Ashmore flew to Paris first-class, gift from the older Ashmores, and, for two wonderful weeks, we lived my dream. We stayed up late, slept late, and played hard. We strolled along the Left Bank, danced in night clubs, hung out at cafés and piano bars, browsed bookstores, toured Versailles, drank gallons of cheap wine, and ate lots of great French food. Richard sketched the architecture; I window-shopped the great couture houses. I even got to play one night at a jazz club! (Even though I didn't follow it up with a meaningless fling with a bad boy – I went back every night to a nice hotel room with my very conservative but exceedingly horny husband.)

Mr. and Mrs. Richard Ashmore had a *real* good time, and so did the Standing Stone of Ireland. I swear we hit the mattress at least ten times a day.

Then home we went, back to real life. And, truly, our first summer wasn't too bad. We both had jobs, and Richard had made the decision earlier to skip summer school, so we actually lived something resembling a real life for three months. We fixed up our apartment and entertained our families. We had Laurie and Francie up to stay with us, and Richard taught them to dance. I sang "Nessum Dorma" in concert for Daddy, and Richard praised me as if I had outsung

Sutherland. I kept house and managed a credible dinner for his parents, Richard and Daddy refrained from killing each other, and all my sisters seemed suitably impressed with my new status as a married adult. *Even* that wretched brat Francie, who, of course, hung all over Richard. (Looking back, why I didn't see it coming....)

But Richard changed. In the space of a summer, my devoted boyfriend who'd sent me flowers for no reason at all started talking about budgets and saving. He got testy when I forgot to mail the payment for the phone bill. And once, after I forgot to start dinner because I was working on a new jazz piece, he got more than a little sharp about my cooking, my housekeeping, and my general all-around sloth. I asked him rather nastily if he would like to wear his dinner, and then we ended up going at each other instead of eating. I believe we ordered in a pizza.

But the next morning he asked why I never made the bed when I got up. After all, his mother always had. I said (quite reasonably, I thought) what was the point, since we were going to be back there in no time at all, and he gave me one of those patented Ashmore *I don't believe I heard that correctly Diana* looks.

Over breakfast that morning, I imagined him wearing his oatmeal.

He decided that we should start off right, be independent of our families. The Ashmores paid his tuition, and Mama's estate paid mine, but he wanted us to be responsible for all the rest of it. Fine, I said, thinking that if Daddy didn't pay my way through life, he couldn't dictate it, either. The piano lessons I had been giving in my desultory fashion for fun money became a matter of financial necessity, and I found myself back in church on Sunday mornings, playing the piano and organ for a local Baptist church. Richard found a job doing freelance drafting, which paid pretty well for a college student. We didn't live half badly, considering how unbearably poor our fellow married students were, but the downside of not starving was that we saw less and less of each other. Once school started, Richard took his usual full class load in addition to his job, and I had to scramble to make up the hours I had sloughed off the year before.

Suddenly, we had less time for each other. And when we were home, Richard studied. I'd never realized how much he studied. My studies, except for composition and theory, were all done in lab, but Richard couldn't concentrate if I watched TV, so I ended up staring out the window. I've never been the reader Richard is.

One evening, he finally looked up from his calculations, and I guess I looked lonely. "What about that group you told me about?"

I had been asked to join a jazz group earlier that month. I didn't think he had even heard me when I told him about the invitation. I hesitated, because I knew other music students who were in groups, and they all worked their asses off. But to get out of the house…!

"Sure you don't mind?"

"Of course not." He rose from his desk and came over to put his arms around me. "Di," he said, "I know how dull it is for you here in the evenings. Get out some, okay? This is going to be a tough year for me. I'd feel better if I knew I wasn't boring you to death."

He was so sweet, and I had been so bitchy… and as I hugged him and one thing led to another (as it usually did with us – all that about the first year of marriage and sex is true), I didn't even think my usual thought: *Why is he so damned nice?*

So I joined the group, and I loved the music, the forerunner of New Age, and I loved my new friends, and – after a few sessions in which I took their measure and they took mine – I enjoyed the talk and the companionship and the various other experiments that went on after the instruments were put away and the keyboard covered. I must be a natural addict, just as Richard has said for years, because I adapted to my new-found stimulants of choice very easily. I started seeing the world through a pink-colored haze, filled with dreams, that chased away the chill of Richard's preoccupation and Daddy's nagging and my fear that, sooner or later, Richard would find out.

Which, of course, he did. "Christ, Diana, what are you doing?" I spun him the usual excuses (I learned they were usual at Betty Ford), and he paid not one whit of attention to them.

I'm just having fun, Richard.

I can stop whenever I want to, Richard.

(Never spoken) *Go to hell, Richard.*

He brought home pamphlets from the university health clinic. He made a point of reading aloud every negative newspaper item he found on marijuana. He complained that my car reeked of pot. The more he talked, the madder I got. And then, oh, yes, then he picked what I'm sure he thought was the most convincing argument of them all.

"Think of the future. Who knows what effect this might have on our kids?"

Children! The very thought terrified me. Richard had never made any secret that he wanted children after we got out of school and got established, and, yes, once we laughingly picked out names... but that had been in play. I was absolutely convinced that, if anyone could ever prove why my mother went into the sea that day, the motive would turn out to be too many children in too little time with too little money. My mother, they said, had been a comet, a meteor across the opera stage, one of the great Medeas in history, brought down low by her wretched fertility and her apparent inability (and my father's, as well) to learn anything remotely useful about birth control. Well, I wasn't going to make that mistake.

IT wasn't going to happen again.

I was only nineteen, for God's sake, and Richard was only twenty. Why we even had to think about kids at that stage was beyond me. Maybe in ten years, when he had his career established and I had *lived* – maybe then I would think about it, but not till then.

I thought about it long and hard and told Richard that I was taking over the birth control.

Not that I had to worry about it that much! The boy who could barely keep his hands off me in high school had metamorphosed into a young man who, half the time, merely kissed me good night and fell into bed. Our sex life slid into a frightful routine – not totally unexpected, I guess now (who could sustain that level of activity?), but it certainly was a disappointment the first time I tried to interest him and he begged off from exhaustion.

I tried the pill, but it made me sick and depressed, and Richard told me to stop taking it before my mood deteriorated. He even had the nerve to suggest that the pill and certain illegal substances were not a good chemical mix. I told him to stop nagging me, since after all I had joined the group at his suggestion, and he said – well, who remembers what he said? It escalated until we were smack in the middle of our first major married fight, which ended when he took his books and went to the library to study. I started imagining him with his face smashed in, but by that time he had left, so I calmed myself down by crying, eating a pint of ice cream, and smoking a joint.

When he came home, I pretended to be asleep, and I sprawled across our bed so that there was no room for him. He slept on the sofa, and that weekend he went down to see his parents, alone.

I had the weekend to think through my sins. I decided I was being a bad wife – but then I realized, for the first time, how thoroughly I hated that word. I *hated* being Richard's wife. I hated that I had to account to him. I hated that he expected me to live up to whatever Peggy Ashmore fantasy wife standards he had in his mind.

And mostly, I hated being by myself. I missed him. So, when he returned, I was properly penitent. I cooked him a nice dinner. I put on his favorite music. And, since he readily admitted that he had missed me terribly, we made up beautifully.

That took care of that week, at least.

Then there was Daddy.

With the jazz group activities, both during and after rehearsals, I had – cardinal sin of sins! – neglected my voice, and when Daddy found out, he was merciless in his criticism. I got so I was afraid to hear the phone ring. After a few weeks of making Richard answer the phone, I wasn't surprised when Daddy drove up to find out just what I was hiding.

Oh, my God, I will never forget the humiliation when he made me sing for him! Of course, every skipped day of practice showed; it always did with me. He demanded that I give the group up, and for once, Richard, that treacherous bastard, instead of standing up for me and telling Daddy where to go, agreed with him. I remember standing there, listening to them, and imagining them both with their faces shoved into concrete.

Well, I resisted. I had fun in the group, I was accepted; there I was just Diana. I wasn't a wife or a daughter or a potential star, I just *was*. And we had a gig coming up at a jazz festival, and I wasn't about to miss that.

So Daddy left, muttering dark imprecations about withdrawing my tuition. But he didn't know when to quit, and he kept after me long distance, to the point where I not only avoided the telephone, I smoked dope in the apartment to calm myself down. Richard, in self-defense, took up cigarettes and studied more and more at the library. We fought about the dope, we fought about his smoking, we fought about the brand of cereal I bought. We fought about everything, and less and less did we make up with the Standing Stone of Ireland.

By the time our first anniversary rolled around, my grades were down, my voice was shot, he was smoking a pack a day, and sex happened once a week, in good weeks.

And Daddy continued to breathe down my neck.

I was so nervous and on edge that the inevitable happened. I lost track of three weeks on, one week off, and forgot my pills for two whole weeks, and that damned fertility kicked in, right on schedule.

I knew, right away. I woke up feeling very strange and knew, with the most sinking feeling in the world, that I had felt this way before.

Okay, I'm going to talk about this calmly and rationally.

I've read a lot about abortion, trying to come to terms with IT. Well, I have news for any man who excoriates a woman for exercising her right to choose. No man on earth, and that includes Mr. Bloody Perfect Richard Ashmore, can possibly understand what it is like to look at the blue tip of a pregnancy test wand and know that your entire world has crashed.

And mine had just crashed *for the second time in two years.*

Even smoking a joint didn't calm me down.

It was too much! I'd lost my right to my own space, my right to determine how I wanted to live my life (and, I faced the truth now, the *only* reason I got married), and now I had completely lost control over even my own body. I was well and truly trapped, trapped by the role marriage had thrust upon me, trapped between Richard's expectations and Daddy's demands, and now trapped by this growing thing inside that was going to expect me to grow up and get my act together and be a *mother.*

Mother? How could I be a mother? My two role models, Peggy and Mama, were polar opposites. Supermom and Medea. Great.

I looked into the future, as I stared at that wretched blue stick. I saw myself in ten years, standing in the doorway waving my rising young professional husband off to work, with two or three perfect little Ashmores waiting for their bloody little breakfasts and another perfect little Ashmore undoubtedly ruining whatever figure I had managed to preserve to that point. I thought about the wine bars of Paris and how they did not come equipped with kiddie menus and crayons. I thought of Richard, able to determine his own life as he saw fit, and I thought of me, trapped by biology and a family history of untimely fertility and the title of Mrs. Richard Ashmore.

And then I looked into the past.

The thought of another *procedure* – I thought back two years, I remembered lying there on that table, looking at the ceiling, while the clock tried to run backward in time. I remembered that sound. I remembered how empty I felt. And mostly I remembered how much I cried afterwards.

I thought of the voice I still heard in the night.

Past and future. Both just as unbearable as the present.

So I decided to run away.

I needed time to think, I decided feverishly as I threw clothes into a suitcase. I needed time to plan. I needed time to – and I never really got the chance to figure out what I needed. Richard came home from class, tired, stressed out from carrying twenty-one hours, and, unfortunately for the rest of our lives together, he did not read my mind. Instead, he nearly fell over the suitcase by the door as I sat at his desk, trying to pen a note to him.

If he was upset when I announced that I had to get away for a few days, he masked it well. I look back, and I realize that, as things had disintegrated between us, he had learned to shutter his emotions. He wasn't the boy I had married.

And, somehow, that strange calmness of his provoked everything that followed.

I thought that he had no idea that I was pregnant, but he proved me wrong.

"Is running away going to help the baby?" he asked quietly, so quietly that at first I thought I had imagined it.

"What baby?" But I've always been a terrible liar, and I knew the shock of his words showed on my face.

"The baby you bought the pregnancy test for yesterday," he said, and I cursed myself for not hiding that stupid box any better than I had. I should have dumped it at school. "The baby that has you acting like a terrified rabbit. That baby, Diana."

And then I panicked, and I said it. I don't know why I said it. "There isn't a baby, Richard," I said, "not anymore."

He moved so quickly that I didn't see it coming to get out of the way. Not that he hit me, oh, heavens, no, not Richard Ashmore. But within a second, he had me pinned up against the wall, and not because we couldn't make it to the bed fast enough. "What did you do?" he said, and I think he shouted, and I do remember that his hands bit into my shoulders. "God, Diana, what did you do?"

I tried to twist away, but he held me there. And then I exploded.

I don't remember everything I said. The only thing that sticks in my mind is that I said that the whole idea of having a child sickened me, that I couldn't take a child as smug and self-righteous and bloody *perfect* as he was, and that I would never, ever let him get me pregnant again. I truly don't remember anything else. I know I said more, because, more than anything in the world, I wanted to smash that exquisite coolness of his before I completely smashed his face in.

I shocked him. His face went white, whiter than I'd ever seen it, and in his shock, he let me go. I scooped up my suitcase and flew out the door.

And the next morning, after spending the night on the sofa at the clarinetist's, safe from the telephone, I drove myself to the clinic.

I sat in the parking lot for a long time. I don't know how long. Then, finally, I got out of the car, and I went in—

No. Time to hit that button. I can't talk about it.

It took a disaster for me to go back to him.

I blew off school. I drifted for several months into the fall semester, crashing on spare sofas, experimenting with drugs even some of my group members hadn't discovered yet. I managed to make it down to see Daddy once, when the twins were away on a class trip (I made sure of that, because no way was I going to let on to that brat Francie that anything was wrong). I partied, I met men with time and money to spend on me, and I broke my marriage vows, not once but several times, and not twice with the same man. One, I believe, was a professor of mine, but I'd had a lot to drink at that particular party, and I don't really remember.

Peggy tracked me down one day, probably through Lucy, since I hadn't laid eyes on Richard, and, to my admittedly hazy knowledge, he hadn't seen me either. She expressed concern about our separation, and I managed to fob her off. From what she said, Richard hadn't told her about the baby, and that relieved me. I wasn't in a mood to listen to condemnation or get dragged off to confession or have the priest summoned to give me the Last Rites before she burned me at the stake. I said not to worry, Richard and I were just having a few problems, we'd work things out.

Peggy must have called Daddy, because within a few hours he knocked on the door of the sax player's apartment.

He wanted to know the truth. I parried. He opened a bottle of wine, and then another, and then another. We drank. I told him how miserable I was with Richard. He told me about a woman he had been seeing (which surprised the hell out of me). I admitted to him that I had slept around on Richard.

He reminded me that he'd predicted Richard wouldn't satisfy me for long.

I told him how I wanted to go to Paris and live a musician's life.

He said over his dead body.

We opened another bottle of wine.

We talked about Ireland and the old days of vagabonding around Europe, before Mama died.

He told me what he had done that day long ago.

I told him I remembered.

We drank some more.

He confessed the truth about Mama's death.

I confessed that Francie and I had witnessed the whole thing.

He said I must never tell anyone.

I said I'd only told Richard and he would be silent as the grave.

He said he didn't trust Richard an inch.

I said I trusted Richard implicitly, and that surprised me, because I realized I really did.

He said he should have broken Richard and me up back in high school.

I offered him a joint.

We drank some more.

He told me how much I resembled my mother.

I told him I wanted to be known as more than a second-rate soprano and first-rate slut.

He slapped me hard across the face.

Then he broke down in my arms.

I don't want to talk any more about that night.

For months, I paid no attention to anything that was going on. In the world, around me, or inside me.

Then, in the space of one weekend, I couldn't zip my jeans.

I panicked. I cried.

Then I calmed myself down with a joint, and considered my options.

My future was shot. But then, after the way I'd neglected my voice and my studies, it probably was anyway.

Another *procedure* was out of the question. I couldn't face it. I couldn't face that terrible emptiness, those raw scars on the soul. I couldn't face another voice in the night.

And a little voice kept saying, *How bad can one baby be?*

It certainly couldn't be any worse than not having one.

But what could I do? I couldn't go to Daddy, and no one else was likely to want me in the shape I would shortly be in. I knew myself well enough to know that I couldn't cope on my own.

And, damn it, I was married. I wasn't supposed to have to deal with IT alone.

So I went to the law library, looked up the laws on paternity, and made a decision.

I called Richard and asked him to meet me at our favorite restaurant.

I scarcely recognized my ardent young husband when I saw him. He had changed in those months apart; he seemed colder and harder. Although he stood politely for me when I approached the table where he was waiting, he didn't reach for my hand, he didn't take me in his arms… he acted as if I was an old girlfriend to whom common courtesy dictated that he be polite. I had fixed myself up very nicely, but clearly I had wasted my time. He wasn't the least interested in my new hair style, the new fullness of my breasts artfully emphasized by a soft sweater, anything about me.

But he did listen. I told him that I wanted to come home, and I knew that he wanted to believe me. I caught him flicking a look at my breasts, and knew that I still had some power left. I knew him too well; he loved me (still) too much to turn me away. As I talked, as I let a tear slip down my face, I saw him soften, start to forgive, start to tell me that he wanted me home….

But Richard surprised me. He said, very levelly, that we needed to talk about the abortion first.

I had no choice but to tell him about the baby. He was so cold! I trembled the whole time I told him what I had done those months, and I guess, looking back, who could blame him? But, oh, God, if he could have known how I felt – I was falling apart, and I needed him – I needed *someone*—

And, of course, I didn't tell him that. I became defensive, and he got angry, and within the space of a minute, we were fighting again. Quietly, because other people were around, but more viciously than we ever had before. Because now Richard's anger came from that cold spot inside him, and not from the heat he had felt for me. And I – I told him things about himself he had never heard before.

I told him that he was a bloody selfish little brat who had never considered anyone but himself in his entire life. I told him that he wasn't the crown prince of Ashmore Park to me, he was just another stupid, arrogant male who thought he could mount me on the wall like some god-damned trophy. I told him that, compared to the men I'd seen those months, he'd grown careless and lousy in bed because he was so busy studying and being Mr. Perfect, he never had any time for me… oh, who knows what else I said? I spilled years of resentment in those few minutes. I never knew some of the things I said had actually lived in my heart all those years.

Then, before I could finish telling him off, he stood up. "Give me your address, Diana," and it was a command from the arrogant male I had just accused him of being.

"What the hell do you care?" I said, and I didn't bother to keep my voice down. I saw someone look over at me and hoped to God it was no one I had screwed.

"Because," said Richard with his awful courtesy, "I want to know where to serve the divorce papers."

Well, that snapped any anger I felt right in half. When I had considered my options, that had not been one of them. For the first time, I got served notice that he was not going to forgive me, that I might truly be stuck with this. He might actually divorce me. I could be divorced, alone, pregnant, with my future completely ruined, at age twenty.

Faced with him putting on his jacket, preparing to leave as I had left him, I made my only smart move to date. I gambled that Richard, still loving me, no matter that he wished he didn't, would not be proof against the sight of his pregnant wife weeping her eyes out.

I was right, to a point. He left me sitting there sobbing. He told me to let him know if I needed money and, being Richard, couldn't resist adding the parting shot that he hoped that I wasn't stoning my poor baby into oblivion. Through my tears, I pictured him wearing his coffee, but somehow, that day, the vision failed to cheer me up.

Between the door and the parking lot, he had second thoughts. He was waiting for me at my car.

"I doubt we can get a divorce right now. I'll wait until after you have the baby." That didn't sound encouraging, but it was better than having to slink home to Daddy. "You'd better come back, Di. I'll sleep on the sofa. But—"

He asked the one question I didn't want to answer, and I told him so.

"Too bad, Di." And he asked it again.

Fine, I thought, *you bloody, bloody, **bloody** self-righteous bastard.*

So I told him.

16

Knocking on Forbidden Doors

"LAURA."

Richard's voice filtered through her dreams, rich and soothing, irresistible and inviting, a lure towards the world of the real. Against her cheek, his hand brushed her, and in her slumber, she sought that warmth, turning towards it eagerly, reaching out when it slipped away. She sensed him nearby, a rustle of fine wool, a trace of aftershave lingering all these hours, even the disconcerting aroma of a recent cigarette. He sat at the edge of the sofa, bending over her, his breath a mere whisper on her face.

I wish I'd stayed asleep.

She barely opened her eyes, just enough to see him, but Richard caught her. "So you're awake," and she must have imagined the tenderness. "What on earth is going on? Is Diana here?"

She closed her eyes against the barrage. "Richard," she mustered up all the normal irritability of being wrenched from a sound sleep, "if you have to wake me up, let me *wake* up, all right?"

Silence, and then he laughed. "Okay, sleepyhead."

He reached out to haul her upright, brushed her hair out of her eyes, pulled the lapels of the bathrobe together, and tucked the blanket back around her. As if she were five years old! She loved every moment of the warmth of his hands, the brush of his breath. She rearranged the blanket to suit herself and gave him her most Cat Courtney-like look.

He didn't notice.

"All right," he said, settling back against the sofa, "what's going on?"

"Di's sick. We were over at Daddy's, sorting out old clothes—"

"I know," he said surprisingly. "Julie called me in Charleston and said something was wrong at the house. I came back as soon as I could."

"Di got sick, so I ran her to the doctor—"

"Sick?" He looked over at the stairs leading up to Diana's bedroom. "What's wrong with her?"

She picked one of Meg's favorites out of the air. "Female problems."

"Female problems?" Richard sounded amused. He had probably written as many excuses for gym as she had. "Very original, Laura. Now what's going on?"

He waited only seconds for the answer she didn't have. Then he rose, quick, economical movements, and disappeared into the dark of the stairs, leaving her behind, still wrapped up, nervously waiting for the moment when he saw Diana and realized—

But he didn't. She heard the door to Diana's room open softly, but she heard no foot treads across the muffling carpet, no shocked words of discovery. Of course, Diana's room was shrouded in shadows – she'd drawn the draperies earlier – and Diana herself still cocooned under the blankets, her telltale wrist hidden. Diana's secret, and her own, remained safe for the time being.

No sounds, no words, nothing filtered down to her. She couldn't resist the lure of that silence; she kept the blanket around her as she climbed the stairs, warding off imaginary chills and not-so-imaginary alarm, drawn by the mystery of the marriage unfolding above her.

At the top of those stairs, the prince of her childhood had come again to the chamber of his princess.

I'll look at your face. I'll look, and then I'll know. Maybe Francie lied. Maybe it was her idea. Maybe she suggested it, and you were so caught up in your fight with Di that you didn't take her seriously. No one but me ever did.

Maybe, for one instant, you agreed, and you never dreamed she'd follow through. I'll believe that, I will believe anything, and I will forgive anything. Just let me look at your face, and I'll know.

I'll know if you still love Diana.

The door stood ajar, the hallway empty. She halted in the doorway, and looked at him, and knew.

Oh, dear God, she should never have looked into Pandora's Box. She was sick with the answer. He'd moved to the bedside, where Diana slept sprawled out on her stomach, her head turned away from him, her hands mercifully shoved up under her pillows. He didn't touch Diana, reach out his hand to caress her hair, whisper her name; he didn't have to. He merely stood there, watching her sleep in her large bed, his eyes lifting slightly to travel around this room, as if he'd never seen it before.

She felt that she'd come upon them in the privacy of their marriage chamber.

He noticed her there, still absurdly wrapped in her blanket and bathrobe, and smiled at her. That smile did two things: it told her that he'd not yet tumbled to Diana's real sickness, and it broke her heart. But she didn't resist. He beckoned her to his side, and she obeyed, trailing the blanket behind her.

"You're all in, Laura. Go on home." His whisper reached her before she reached him. "Diana looks fine. Don't tire yourself out."

She hadn't expected that. "I can't. The doctor said not to leave her alone."

Damn! That got his attention. He bent over Diana, no doubt looking for traces of the illness that demanded such constant supervision. "What's the matter with her?" And this time, his voice warned, he would not be put off. "What the hell's going on?"

"She got sick...."

"Sick covers a broad range." The no-nonsense came through even in whispers. "What hap – good God!" His hand shot out and seized her wrist. "What did you do to your hands?"

She'd forgotten. She stared down at her hands, with their bandaged cuts. "Oh, Max scratched me."

He took her other wrist and turned both her hands up in his. She couldn't tell what he saw through the shadows of the room; she couldn't read the look in his eyes. He'd bent his head slightly over her hands, and for one absurd moment, she imagined him lifting one poor abused hand to his mouth, healing her with the warmth of his mouth—

Richard and I are mated for life.

He dropped her hands and raised his head. God! She shuttered herself instantly against his stare. No telling what he'd seen, what longing she might have let loose into her eyes.

He said merely, "No tuna for Max tonight, I hope."

"Oh, I forgot, I have to feed Max." She turned towards the bathroom and the clothes she'd left lying in a heap on the floor. "Richard – she can't be left alone, the doctor was very specific—"

"I'll take care of her. Go on home."

"I'll be back soon, I promise." She didn't want him staying here; she couldn't sustain the fiction of Diana's illness for long. "Let me get dressed—"

In her search and seizure, she'd forgotten her clothes. She recoiled at the dampness of her blouse and jeans, still sticky with Diana's blood. Damn it, she should have washed them earlier, and how was she going to get past Richard in blood-stained clothing?

Very quickly, that was how.

He stood by the window when she came out of the dressing room, and for a moment she might have escaped with her secrets intact. But she made the fatal mistake of hesitating.

He stood silhouetted against the dying day, his hands in the pockets of his pants, his head turned away from her so that he stared out through the sheer draperies at the darkening Atlantic. The shadows followed the planes and valleys of his face, so that the light touched only his mouth, his lashes, the tip of his nose. She saw him, for just a moment, not Prince Charming, not her unattainable knight in shining armor, but a man forced into solitude, a stranger in his wife's bedroom.

And she lost her chance.

She must have made some small sound, a movement that attracted his attention, for he turned around and the moment shattered. He smiled at her, and she compounded her error, letting that smile draw her towards him, into the faint light filtering in from the east.

"She's still asleep. Take your time. I'll stay here until – good God!" The shock in his voice pushed her back. "What in the hell – *blood* –"

"Huh?" was all she came up with, even as she backed off, back into the inviting darkness of the room.

But he followed her, overtook her, his hands closing in on her shoulders to immobilize her even as she shrank back away from him.

"It's still damp," and he kept her in place with one hand while his other hand explored the ruined blouse, the soaked jeans. "What happened? And don't lie about your cat. What did she do?"

"It wasn't Di," she managed, too late, as his hands dropped and he walked away.

Diana still slept soundly, so soundly that she never stirred as her husband switched the light on and efficiently swept the covers back from her body. Not the intimacy of a lover, not even the wrath of a justly annoyed husband, but the disinterested movement of a man watching a strange woman in the bed. Diana's body revealed nothing, and he must have seen all that in an instant, must have seen that Diana had fortuitously hidden part of herself away. He reached under her pillow and pulled out the bandaged wrist.

She saw that first betraying, instinctive recoil.

"It was an accident." Oh, God, where she found the wherewithal to lie, she didn't know, somewhere deep inside where she dared not look too closely. "We were moving furniture—"

He turned Diana's wrist over, studying it, a scientist cataloging a particularly unappealing specimen.

"The mirror broke." He hadn't cut in, told her brusquely to stop lying, and he would have, surely, if he hadn't believed her. "The glass cut both of us, but Di got hurt worse – she needed stitches—"

"Go home, Laura."

Diana had chilled her; his voice now stripped her. He finished examining Diana's wrist and laid it down gently; Diana might not have been attached to it, for all that it invaded her slumber. He hesitated a moment before he drew the comforter over her again, maybe studying her with the dispassionate eye of a man finding a strange woman sleeping in his bed, maybe seeing his bride, fragile, lovely, as she had once lain waiting for him.

A bride already destroyed by her own father.

Laura said faintly, "We can't leave her alone."

"I won't." He didn't look at her; his eyes never moved from his wife. "Go home."

She moved vaguely towards the door, the smell of the blood on her blouse assailing her, the means of the escape she had not taken earlier opening up before her. The hallway, the living room, the door beyond, away from this man trapped on an unlovely carousel with his ice princess – and she'd almost made it to freedom at the front door when he said wearily behind her, "We'll talk later, Laura. I'll come as soon as I can find someone to stay with her."

Laura had forgotten, and Richard had not reminded her, that her car was still parked miles away in front of her father's house. The gathering darkness covered her, so that the taxi driver couldn't see that his bedraggled passenger looked like a fugitive from a mass murder. She tipped him liberally to run the meter in front of Dominic's house as she closed it up, and he stayed to help her when she ran back upstairs to fetch the boxes of Dominic's financial papers.

She remained strong until the nightly call came from Texas.

"Mom!" cried Meg in alarm, when Laura reacted to the sound of her voice by bursting into tears. "What's wrong? Are you okay? Mark, come here! Something's wrong with Mom!"

"It's nothing," Laura found herself explaining to Mark, in between sobs. "I felt homesick all of a sudden—"

I almost killed my sister this afternoon.

"I told you so," said Mark briskly. "Let me know when you're packed. I'll send the jet up."

"No." Oh, not tonight of all nights! "I *need* to be here. If I come back now, it'll be like I couldn't handle it, and I can, I can, that's not what—"

"No," he said with no trace of sympathy, "you'll be showing the first sign of good sense in months. Give up, Laura. Nothing good ever comes of stirring up the past. Have you seen that man yet?"

"You know what, Mark?" She couldn't take this anymore. "Not everything that happens around here is Richard's fault! You don't even know him, and you have no call, Mark, no call to say anything. I don't want to hear another word."

I am defending a man I've believed guilty for eleven years.

And if he was guilty, I no longer care.

Only Meg's reappearance on the conference line shelved what promised to devolve into another tense discussion. Mark left mother and daughter alone, and Laura took comfort in Meg's chatter about ballet class and algebra tutoring and her running battle with Emma, who had cracked down on Meg's choice of low-rise jeans. Meg was everyday, real life, sunlight in the darkness Diana had cast, and Laura drew strength from her daughter's laughter and nonstop patter. Max, too, lent comfort. She had thrown her bloodied clothes in the washer and put on her old bathrobe, and he curled up on her terry-clothed lap and purred loudly against her arm.

When Mark finally dragged Meg off the phone, Laura expected him to resume the interrogation, but he surprised her. Maybe the day had worn him down; maybe her show of resistance had knocked the fight out of him. He said merely that he'd check up on her the next day and to call if she got lonely again.

She remembered, too late, that she had questions of her own. He had signed every one of those checks.

She didn't stir from the sofa, not even to switch on a light in the darkness. She couldn't tell the time; she thought from the embers of the sunset that it must be late. Max, snoozing on her lap, seemed in no hurry for dinner, and she slouched down into his fur and let herself retreat into her thoughts.

She wondered if Diana were still asleep.

She hoped so. Diana shouldn't see Richard until she felt stronger. Strange, that she didn't fear for Diana's safety, but he hadn't killed her when she'd made her terrible confession before Julie's birth, when the desire must have ridden well nigh irresistible. And Diana had survived Ash Marine, survived to sign that document handing Julie over a week later.

If Diana had been there at all.

She resisted remembering her words to Diana, words that had put the dagger into Diana's hands. Words that sparkled now before her, in all their malice.

She hadn't considered Diana at all, in that moment when she'd struck back, eleven years too late, to avenge Francie. She considered her now, Diana who might have lied when she'd said she had never seen Francie that day, Diana who might have told the truth about the flat tire and the keys she'd picked up from Ashmore Park.

If Diana had lied – if she'd lied, or blanked the entire memory from her mind – how much must that burden have weighed, all these years? And the memory of Francie coming at her, murder in her eye – had that haunted Diana in her dreams?

Had it driven her mad, driven the memory straight out of her mind?

But if she had not lied, then another person, unseen, had crept up behind Francie.

And if Diana had not killed Francie – if Richard had not lured Francie on – if she, Laura, had blamed them both unjustly for eleven years—

Then she had done her sister and her love a terrible wrong.

And she'd not only finished Francie's murder by abandoning her dying twin, but she'd helped the murderer walk away forever.

An hour passed, maybe more, before Richard came to her.

He forestalled her immediate question with "Any coffee?"

She inspected him from the corner of her eye while she started hot water boiling and set out cream and cookies. He looked tired, withdrawn, as he loosened his tie and draped his suit jacket over the chair. She remembered that he'd been in Charleston on business earlier, before Julie's message summoned him back. "How did your trip go?"

"What?" He looked startled, as if he'd forgotten her presence. "Oh, fine. We're going to contract to restore and expand an old subcathedral. It's diocesan money, and everything has to be approved up the church hierarchy all the way to Rome, but at least it won't fall apart." He accepted the steaming cup she held out to him. "Ah, thank you, Laura."

He'd drained one cup and asked for another by the time her tea steeped properly. She joined him at the table, and fell uneasily into his silence. The coffee apparently wasn't reviving him; he was stirring it endlessly, his hand cradling his temple, exhaustion around his eyes.

She finally asked about Diana.

"She's not alone. I called a nursing service, and they sent someone over."

"Good," Laura said faintly, and tried to repress a shiver of reaction. "Richard, I – I'm sorry about what happened, really I am."

He said quietly, "I didn't know that you had anything to be sorry about."

She hadn't seen that coming. She opened her mouth to speak, then closed it again and took refuge in a swallow of hot tea.

"Diana tried to kill herself about six years ago." His voice held all the interest of yesterday's news, but she knew better now. "We were in the middle of a shouting match about – well, never mind, it's private, but suffice it to say that we were having another interminable discussion about our marriage. It was – ungodly, to say the least. I turned my back and—" He stared into his mug. "What happened today?"

She thought of Diana's blood spilling onto the carpet, splotching the gold dress, and papers coldly spelling out the destruction of a marriage. Diana, sobbing that she had given up this man for her father.

She said faintly, "I can't. Not right now."

Above her bowed head (her turn now to seek sanctuary in the bottom of her cup), he said quietly, "If it helps, I can assure you that Diana was in control today. I looked at her wrist. She slashed herself sideways, didn't she? That's not the way to do it, and she knows it. She demonstrated for me one time, laughing as if it were all a game. She was playing with you, Laura, she wanted attention. Tell me what happened."

She barely managed, "She was *playing*... she bled, she bled all over the place. And you're saying she didn't mean it?"

"No." No resisting the gentleness underlying his firm voice. "Don't torture yourself, Laura. I intend to talk with her when she wakes up, and I promise you she'll admit the truth. But I want to know. What brought this on?"

She swallowed once, hard. "We were talking—"

"What about?" Quiet, inviting, seductive.

"Daddy." She turned her head nervously away. "We tried on some old clothes that belonged to my mother. Daddy's will." She couldn't bring herself to mention the cottage, not to him. "Lucy's baby – Di's mad at her for getting pregnant. Some trip Di wants to take driving around Europe—"

You and how you're mated for life.

"And Francie," he said, "you talked about Francie, didn't you?"

"Yes," she whispered, and looked down at her hands.

He waited her out, his coffee cup hanging forgotten in his hand, the heaviness of his stare on her head. The uncertainty grew, until it was more than she could bear, and she looked up at him, unable to survive the vast silence between them.

He was watching her steadily, with no apology for staring, his eyes cool and unemotional. She deserved this; she and her sisters had brought him to this, killing off the warmth and kindness at this man's core. Betrayed by Diana, used by Francie, nearly destroyed by her – if she chilled under his gaze now, if he lacked the heart to forgive her, she had herself to blame.

He continued to watch her for a minute or so, while he drank down his coffee and refilled it with quick, decisive movements.

Laura could take this no longer. "Richard—"

He held up his hand. "Be quiet."

And she did. They remained there, in the deadening landscape of the kitchen, while her dread and his anger grew. Her tea grew cold, and the cream in his coffee condensed into islands. She couldn't tell what he felt behind his shuttered eyes or what he thought he saw when he looked at her.

When he finally spoke, it was worse than she had ever imagined.

"Did you know that my parents once approached Dominic about raising you? My mother wanted Lucy to have one of her sisters, and she wanted you with us. Dominic wasn't fond of you, even when you were small, and he didn't have the money to train all of you." He stopped and put his hands on the table in front of him, and he studied them because, she thought, he did not want to study her. "But you and Francie were very dependent on each other – she more than you, I recall – and Dominic didn't want to separate you. My father couldn't bring himself to take her too. He watched her once trying to take one of your dolls away – the sort of silly, childish trick that you see on any playground – but there was something about her attitude, he said, that gave him pause."

He looked up, and his gaze took hers, and she could not turn away.

"But you, he thought, you were worth time and attention and love, and it was clear, even then, that you would never get anything in that house. I was ten, eleven, and they sat Lucy and me down one day and talked to us straight about you, asked how we felt about you coming to live with us. Dominic lavished affection on Diana and Francie, so they were all right – or at least, Dad thought so at the time. But you – you were different, Mom said, you needed us."

Somehow, through the crushing regret in her chest, she found her voice. "I would have loved to have been their daughter. I loved them very much."

"And they loved you." How steady he sounded, how remote. "You know, don't you, that Mom was hoping I'd forget Diana and wait for you to grow up. They didn't like her. They never criticized, of course, they trusted me to know my own mind. But they never warmed to her." He shrugged. "Maybe they were right. Maybe I should have waited until you were old enough, maybe we would have suited each other. We'll never know. All I know is my parents loved you, and they were devastated when you left without a word to anyone."

He stood up then, and he walked over to the window overlooking the pool, and he stood there for a while, his back to her, his hands resting in his pockets.

She couldn't speak. *Maybe we would have suited each other.* Peggy and Philip Ashmore had picked *her* for their son. No wonder Peggy had carefully taught young Laura Abbott how to run Ashmore Park, no wonder she had passed along her recipe for his favorite cookies to Laura and not Diana. She had certainly not intended to benefit a computer genius who was allergic to chocolate.

His voice, when he spoke again, was dusty and strained. "They loved you," he said, "so did I. I may have used you like my personal slave – I'm sorry for that now – but I knew, even then, that you were the best of the lot. You were a quiet little kid, I don't remember you ever arguing with a soul, but I used to look at you and wonder what you'd buried behind those eyes. Dad thought the world of you. You had all the courage in the world, he said, all the heart." He stopped, and then he turned around, and he looked straight at her. "It would break his heart to know you now."

His words hit her lungs like a hammer and knocked the air out of her.

He advanced towards her then, and now she saw that he was not merely cool and detached. Below the calm of his face lay a very angry man.

She raised her hand instinctively in defense.

"Your sister is a very disturbed woman," and now there was no mistaking the fury in his words. "It's safe to say that she's not always in her right mind. She's tempted the devil for years, and payment is coming due. I can't really say that she has ever valued either Julie or me. Being a wife and mother never meant much to her. To her, we are not her family, we never took the place of her father and her sisters."

"Oh, please *don't*, Richard. I am so sorry…."

He waved a hand that swept the kitchen. "She came here to dinner, didn't she? Do you know why? Your sister was thrilled to see you again. She was so happy when you came home—"

Diana? Diana, who'd drunk and sniffed her way through the reunion?

"She's very excited about playing for you in this concert you've got going," he said. "She called me about it. She felt honored – that's the word she used – to be accompanying you on stage. She even told me that she was going to make a good-faith effort to stay sober so that she'd be in tip-top shape to appear with you. She won't even make that effort for Julie! But this is different. Diana is going to play for her famous sister, and she wants to make a good impression. She wants her sister's good opinion."

He paused and thrust the knife in.

"And how do you repay all that?" he said. "You deliberately talk to her about the one person Diana needs to forget ever existed. Don't look at me with those great teary wide eyes, Laura. You didn't forget for one minute how badly Francie hurt Diana, and not just over me. And whatever you said – God, I don't even want to know – she had to slash her wrists to stop you."

He still loves her.

"Not Francie, it was Daddy…."

His voice cut through hers, rode above the rising roar in her ears. "You were such a sweet kid. Lord, I used to think that every stray kitten in the county knew to come to you. Look at that gray beast chewing on my tie – I'd lay odds he showed up on your doorstep, and you took him in. But when it comes to your own sister, you are a cruel, judgmental, cold-hearted *bitch*, determined to make everyone suffer for your own pain—"

"No, I'm not!" He'd flicked her right across the heart. "How dare you—"

"I'll tell you how I dare," he interrupted, and he stood over her and held her still with the sheer force of his anger. The heat from his body prickled her skin. "You're living in the past, Laura! You shove Francie down our throats – I hate to break it to you, but we left her behind when she left us! No one thinks about her, she's gone, she's in the past, and, damn it, let her *stay* there—"

Rage, long-buried, white-hot, erupted within her.

"You bastard!" She nearly knocked him off balance as she rose and shoved at him. "What do you mean, you don't think about her?"

"She was a mistake." He caught at her arms, to stop her flailing, and the touch of his hands sent her rage spiraling upward. "A mistake! I let her go because I came to my senses—"

"Francie loved you! You call her a mistake—"

He said very quietly, "Calm down, Laura."

"— My God, you were a disaster for her! She loved you, she ruined her *life* for you—"

"Calm down."

"No, I won't calm down!" She felt consumed by a vast flame born of pain and fury, half a lifetime's worth of anguish and loss, touching the heavens and shaking down the stars. "You son of a bitch, you used her! That was the real war, wasn't it, not Francie and Di fighting over you to get at Daddy, but you using Francie to get revenge on him! He adored Francie, so it was sweet vengeance, oh, wasn't it just, to take Francie because he had ruined Di—"

She'd struck home.

He never moved, but he shut her out. She saw it instantly. She was too much the mistress of other personas not to recognize it in him, and she wasn't having any of it. She grasped his shoulders and shook him as fiercely as her strength allowed.

"Stop that! You can use that trick on everyone else, but I won't stand for it. You *listen* to me!" He came back to life; she saw surprise, suffering, fury take fire on his face, and she gloried in it. She'd dammed up fountains of agony, and he, their architect, had damn well better face his handiwork. "You took my sister from me! She was all I had, she was the only one I could count on, and you stole her from me! All that spring, Richard, I was desperate, I was getting ready to run, I needed her, and where was she? Skipping school to meet you, having me lie for her, take her tests, cover with Daddy—"

"Oh, dear God—" And he reached out for her.

She struck his hand away.

"And for what?" She was light-headed, delirious, from the relief of unleashing emotions too long restrained. "It was all so useless! Francie scarcely made a dent, did she? Oh, Di screamed and carried on and tore into her, but in the end it didn't make a damn bit of difference, did it? It tore her life apart, but, hell, as long as you got away with it, who cared? To you, she was just a regrettable little mistake, a little fall from grace, no big deal, all men do it, just another condom wrapper in the car—"

"That's enough." But, in his voice, she heard dawning realization.

"Don't you tell me it's enough! Maybe she used you, but you used her worse! All these years, I felt sorry for you, Richard, I thought you were a pawn just like me – oh, so much more valuable, of course! What was a sister compared to a lover—"

"Oh, for God's sake, Laura!" Her anger had laid flame to the timber of his own; the fingers holding hers tightened painfully. She refused to back down in the face of his fury – let him raise his voice to her, let him crush the blood from her fingers! She didn't care. "Is that what you're after – to punish us all because you were *jealous?*"

The word hung in the air between them, a living, palpable presence.

In one fell swoop, he had broken the back of her fury. She lifted her hand to her throat, speechless, unable to think in the sheer horror of that one word.

The silence of her shock screamed at him. He moved in quickly for the kill.

"That's what all this is about, isn't it? All this bitterness – that scene yesterday, trying to bring me to my knees because I'm not the boy you remember – and, my God, that filthy lie, Francie bleeding to death—" She recoiled, fighting off the sickness that arose at his words, but he had caught her, and he would not let her go. "Did you think I didn't know? I felt it, I saw it every time I saw you, your eyes accusing me—"

A surge of humiliation swept over her, pulled her under. "*No—*"

"I talked to Francie about it." He caught her chin in his hand and forced her to look at him. She shut her eyes tightly against him. "She said not to worry, you knew nothing, she'd kept you in the dark. I didn't press her about it. I persuaded myself that my conscience was making me hypersensitive. That I was just imagining the fury coming at me in waves." He added, "You were so young, you were such an innocent, I thought, you couldn't know."

She was going to be sick. She could see them still: Richard asking, Francie saying earnestly not to worry, that eventually Laura would grow up.... Talking about her, laughing indulgently at the sweet schoolgirl crush that could never compete with Francie's exuberant sexuality.

"Of course, she had to talk to you," he added, "I see that now. She needed you, she needed that link with reality. She didn't need your sulking. She sure as hell didn't need this kind of rage. I only hope," and she had never dreamed his voice could cut her so into ribbons, "that you didn't treat her to years of this nonsense after you left."

She was bleeding from the thousand thrusts of his words. Jealous. Jealous of Francie. Listening all those nights to Francie, her fingers biting into the pillow to contain her anguish. Later, in San Francisco, in their tiny apartment, watching Francie swell with the child Laura could never bear. For a lifetime, aching with words unspoken and love unwanted.

For fourteen years, she had sheltered behind a great wall, and in one second it came crashing to the ground.

She looked at him, he who had so ruthlessly mocked her defenses, he who had scarcely noticed the lovesick Laura Abbott whose great crime had been to love him, and she remembered that the last thing in the world he wanted was honesty between them.

"Jealous?" she whispered, "oh, yes, I was jealous."

His head snapped up, and his eyes flared in attention.

"Times, that spring, I'd look at you both, and I wanted to tear her heart out—" Her voice faltered, and she pulled herself back together before he could humiliate her further. If he meant to mock her, though, he stayed strangely quiet, with only the rigid set of his shoulders to signal his watchfulness. "But then – I kept thinking, she was just in the right place at the right time—"

"Better to tear my heart out than hers."

"Yours?" she said. "*Why?* You went to *her*—"

And then she stopped, for the startled look in his eyes and the sudden compassion that then softened his mouth warned her that she had spoken in terrible error.

She barely breathed, waiting for him to say something, anything, to break the silence.

He ran his fingers through the silver threads at his temple. "I'm sorry," he said. "I thought – I never meant—" He stopped, and he met her eyes with a touch of chagrin. "I didn't know you felt that way about her. I thought you were angry with me."

She held her breath.

"I thought," he added quietly, "you were jealous of me, for taking her away from you."

She stood dead still then, in the horror of her inadvertent confession. Anger, betrayal, everything dropped away in that second, as her mind pitilessly replayed her words.

He said nothing else. He merely stood there, watching her with wary compassion, waiting for whatever she cared now to say. All pretense had collapsed between them, as she grasped the unbelievable fact that he had never truly known how she felt about him.

She had betrayed everything – or almost everything; he still did not know, and he never would, please God, that his blood lay upon her hands. But he knew the rest of it. He knew now the rage she had nourished in her heart; he knew all the despair and love she had thrust down ruthlessly until she had forgotten that they still lived.

He knew.

He might even understand. Seventeen years ago, when Diana had made her unspeakable confession, he must have swallowed a rage even more overpowering, a love even more unwanted.

She had nothing further to lose.

She said numbly, "I'd lie awake at night, listening to her talk about you. She told me everything, every detail, you wouldn't believe what she told me." He winced, and she noticed it without interest. "I'd listen, and I cursed the day I came down with the flu. It might have been me, if I hadn't gotten sick, I'd have typed your thesis, I'd have stayed home with you that night, you'd have turned to me—"

"Laura—" A new note in his voice. He didn't want to hear this, but, oh, dear God, she would not be denied. Not now. Not when he already knew the truth. Her need to tell him far outweighed his need not to hear her out.

"I'll hate myself in the morning, I know, I know, I don't care. It can't be worse than fourteen years wishing I'd been there instead of her." In the dim light, through the tears, he had blurred and faded, a tall white-shirted presence before her. "I loved you, Richard. I'd loved you forever, I lived for a smile from you, anything, just as long as you noticed me—"

"Damn it, Laura," but anguish had destroyed anger. He spoke in tired sorrow. "Stop this. Now."

"And when you turned to her, and she told me – oh, God, it should've been me, not her—"

"Stop – you don't want to tell me this—"

"At least, I loved you. You weren't the first for her, you weren't even the second." A sob sliced through her words. "She wasn't good for you, any more than Di was. Look what they've done to you, they've robbed you, they've taken all the kindness and goodness – you're so cold now, you keep going away and leaving this shell where you used to be – I wouldn't have done that to you—"

"No," he said wearily, the cracks growing in his emotional fortress, "you wouldn't have. Stop – there's no point to this—"

"Oh, yes, there is – you never saw me, you could have had me and you chose her instead—"

She broke down then, and sank to her knees.

He came down with her, cradled her in his arms, smoothed her hair and her back, whispered to her words that she scarcely heard and could not comprehend. She understood other things: the heat of his hand as he brushed her cheek and her throat, his breath against her temple, the security of his body. He leaned back against the cabinet and brought her up against him so that she wept into his shoulder.

"Cry it out, Laurie." He was rocking her against him. "Don't bottle this up anymore. It's eating you alive."

She had lost all sense of herself, of the years she had held her love inside, hidden, unwanted. Always unwanted. She knew only that he held her, *her*, not his wife sleeping in a dream-filled neverland, not Francie lost these years to the embrace of the sea. She spoke into his collar, afraid to look at him, afraid to lose the wildness that had seized her soul.

"I missed you. I always missed you. You were always out of my reach.... First Di, then Francie.... I was never there, I always reached you too late. It was okay about Di, I knew about that forever, I knew you belonged to her. I wanted you to be happy with her—"

"I know, Laurie. I think you were the only one."

"But Francie – oh, God, Richard, you broke her heart, and I was glad, *glad!* She was hysterical, Di ripped her apart, and I didn't care. I didn't want her to have you—" She turned into the plane of his shoulder. "She trusted me, she didn't know I listened to her at night, talking about you, and I hated her so badly – *I really hated her —*"

"No," he said, "she didn't know."

"I made her leave. I was going away, and I put it straight to her, I said, 'I won't be here, do you want to come or not?' I promised I'd take care of her —"

His hand came up to hers. "To get her away from me? You did the right thing —"

"I saw it all like those spinning wheels, you on the inside, me outside, and when the wheels stopped, I'd always been carried away from you." She became aware that she was gasping for breath, that her heart had started to race, that his matched hers beat for beat. "You spun out of reach with Di, then Francie, then I took myself away, so they would stop spinning —"

"Good," he said, "good. Let it go. Let me go. I'm no good for you, I never have been."

"But they didn't stop!" A last, forgotten sob caught in her throat. "I thought they had, I'd never have come back if I'd thought there was still a chance —"

"It's not a chance you'd want."

"Yes, I would!" She put her heart into her words, beyond pride, beyond caring, beyond any sense of self-preservation. "Don't tell me what's good or proper for me, I don't care! I did the right and good and proper thing, and all I got was twelve years of trying to be someone I wasn't and trying to love someone I couldn't. I'd take the chance, Richard, if you ever wanted me, I'd destroy the world and laugh among the ashes." Her voice sank into a whisper. "If I'd seen you in London – we came so close —"

The word sent a shock racing through him. Lying against him, she felt it sparking along his body; she knew the tightness of his arms, the breath he forgot to take, the painful beat of his heart. Within a second or two, the dark comfort of his arms disappeared. She found herself abruptly upright, abandoned to her grief, and Richard had withdrawn from her, his arms crossed on his chest.

He said coolly, "What are you talking about?"

All at once, a vast exhaustion swept across her, an exhaustion born of Richard's rejection, Lucy's condemnation, Julie's playacting, Diana's blood. She had left her daughter, her West End success, all the safety of fourteen years to come to this moment, sitting on a cold kitchen floor explaining a life's worth of loving despair to a man who had no use for it.

She said wearily, "The woman in London."

Even as he answered, she heard the lie in his flat voice. "There was no woman in London. Lucy dreamed that up. She took the fact that I finally accepted reality and she manufactured an affair that has done nothing but agitate Diana for no good reason."

"But – you stopped wearing your ring, you didn't feel married anymore—"

His fingers caught her chin and forced her to look at him. "Lucy knows nothing! Do you think, do you really think, that I would carry on an affair with someone I'd just met, on what was only a *two-week* vacation, right in front of my daughter? Diana – *and* my marriage – meant more to me than that. I didn't take it off until—"

And then he stopped, and his mouth shut abruptly.

She heard what he'd said at the same moment he did.

All fury, all pain, had drained away, in the face of the truth. She said dully, "Do you know what I thought? This time we'd come so close, we'd come to the same place in our lives.... You were there, and so was I, and you even tried to see me, you said so yourself. And I—" Her shoulders lifted and fell in defeat. She was already beginning to hate herself for confessing all her heart. "I never knew. I missed you again."

Silence. A great, dark moor of silence.

Then, his voice exhausted, a man reaching the end of his emotional tether.

"No, Laura. You didn't miss me."

But even as he said it, the room vanished, and his voice faded down a long tunnel. She stood at his desk again, staring at the sketch of her own hungry reflection, and his words broke and scattered and coalesced again into new, unknown patterns. *You didn't miss me....* His eyes closed against hers, but his hand touched her fingers, played with her ring, twisted it around so that the diamonds caught the overhead light. It came to her then, a slow awakening, that he had taken her hand long minutes ago, through all the accusations and bitterness, and he still held it.

Oh, dear God, how had she not seen it, the ring was just an excuse.... *After Mom and Dad died, he stopped feeling married....* One year, that was all, since Peggy and Philip had died.... *Julie and I saw you in London....* A man watching a woman while she cooked him dinner, like a suitor – the closest he could bring himself to courting a woman he wanted, just to sit and talk.... A man sketching a woman whose desire meant something to him, his voice taut and teasing as he described her back to herself…. *Quid pro quo, princess. Not much fun to be on the receiving end….*

No, you did not miss me in time.

I have lived my life to come to this.

She came back to herself and to him, sitting there on the floor. He studied her ring as if it mattered, and she looked up at him, and met eyes that watched her gravely. Her blood began to race, sparkling through her veins like the finest spirits, and she was helpless to keep her desire from shining back at him.

No clock ticked off the seconds – or minutes – or ages – to measure the length of that silent appraisal. Only the swinging pendulum of her heart kept time, a deliberate metronome with its own inexorable beat. Slowly, slowly, she raised herself to her knees in front of him, she reached out to touch him, and her fingers knew him, fine firm skin, as she drew her finger lightly across his face, over the twitching muscle of his mouth. And then, lightly, she touched her lips to his.

"Laura."

She waited, and never breathed.

"Laura," he said again, and she watched him go to war, judgment against desire, head against heart.

She said nothing, afraid to break the silence of the great battle she saw in his eyes. She watched and waited as the seconds wore on, and she saw Richard Ashmore's eyes change from the eyes of a sinner faced with his greatest temptation to the eyes of a lover faced with his greatest prize.

"Damn you, Laura," he said, and his arms reached for her, "damn you, damn you, damn you."

But she didn't care. His body bearing hers down onto the cold stone floor was a lover's body, his voice a lover's caress. His mouth, warm, alive, moved over hers like fire, across a parched desert of forgotten desire. She welcomed his weight, she welcomed the unyielding hardness of his body above her and of the floor below, and she linked her hands at the base of his neck against his hairline, and surrendered to the sanctuary of the arms that held her against him as though he would never let her go, would, indeed, fight to keep her.

As she would never let him go, as she would fight to keep him.

He explored her, long lean fingers learning her hair, the curve of her neck, the plane of her shoulder, the slope of her breast. She welcomed the swell of pleasure that overcame her, pleasure long lost and now reclaimed, an old familiar friend, and she surrendered into the swell, knowing only the touch of a hand on her breast, and it was Richard Ashmore's hand.

A long time later, he remembered the floor; he lifted himself away from her, and she panicked that he was leaving her. She moaned, a small protest deep in her throat, and held onto him, fingers clutching his shirt. When he rolled onto his back, he took her with him, and she lay across his shoulder, breathing shakily and wincing against the unforgiving light overhead.

He held her head against his heart, and when he spoke, he sounded as if she had knocked the breath out of him.

"A kiss worthy of Cat Courtney," he murmured, and Laura lifted her head lazily to send him a brilliant smile, aware of new and glorious power.

"Anything for an admiring fan, I always say."

"Don't kiss your other fans like that, you'll start a war." He closed his eyes against her, but she refused to lose heart. It was enough, for this moment, that she lay nestled to him, enough that he kept his body against hers. "Lord, Laura, why did you come back, anyway? Why didn't you stay in Texas and leave us all alone?"

In the wonderful euphoria of their uneven heartbeats, she saw no reason not to tell the truth. She lifted herself up on an elbow and bent over him, her free hand touching the fine thickness of his hair, punctuating her words with a string of kisses down the side of his face. "For you," she whispered, and kissed his temple, "I came back for you—"

One second, his hands lay warm against her back; the next, they were setting her firmly away from him to a safe distance. Confused at his move, she swayed back towards him, but he had moved away from her and had risen to his feet.

"Richard—" She looked up at him, bewildered, blinking into the light, as he stood over her.

"No," he said, "no."

He turned towards the counter, away from her, and he put his hands on the edge and leaned against them. She saw the battle he fought to control himself, the rise and painful fall of his shoulders, and she knew that she hadn't yet lost.

He wasn't paying attention to her, busy as he was fighting off his demons, as she rose slowly from the floor. Her robe sagged open, her nightgown had fallen off her shoulder, but she made no move to cover herself as she approached him and laid her hand on his sleeve.

"Richard," she said softly, "Richard." And she leaned in against him searching for warmth, resting her cheek against his back, loving the wall of his wonderful body.

He said, and his voice shook, "Laura, stop this. *Now.*"

She refused to listen. She slid her hand further down his arm, reaching for his fingers.

"No." He stiffened against her, and instinctively she stepped back before he turned back around to face her. "This is as far as it goes."

She shook her head, to clear it of the fog of desire that still whirled around her.

"We can't do this," he said, and all she really understood was the catch of his voice. "Your sister is still my wife. I may not like it, and you may not either, but she is still there, and she is not going away. I made a stupid mistake when I married her and an even stupider one when I slept with Francie, but I am damned if I am making another one with you tonight."

Through the fog, his words scarcely made sense to her. She whispered, "Come upstairs."

"No," Richard said flatly, although he wanted to. She saw that in his eyes. "You are my sister-in-law. I've been down that road once, thank you, I'm not going that way again. I owe Diana more than that."

He walked over to the chair at the table and picked up his jacket. Her eyes pricked her; she watched him through a haze of tears, watching him spin out of reach again.

Diana. Diana, undeserving bride, unloving wife, Diana, always the winner.

Laura, forever losing in the spinning wheels of their fortunes.

But not now, she thought, seeing him shrug on his jacket. Diana had enjoyed a long and lucky winning streak, aided by an unfiled pleading in a lawsuit and his love for the daughter she had thrust upon him. No one had ever called on her to account for her crimes.

Until now. She knew enough now to bring Diana to justice.

She spoke as he turned towards the door, ready to leave her, and fought for him.

"You're not her husband," she said from the desperation of her heart. "Not anymore. I watched you tonight, Richard, you've never seen that room before, have you? She's never invited you there – she shut you out, years ago – you, her husband! And your room, at your house – you've never taken her there, have you?"

He said briefly, "No, I haven't, but it doesn't change anything."

She stepped in front of him, blocking his way out.

"Your marriage is *dead*, Richard!" She put all her strength into the words, hating his shock as he heard his own words echoed back to him. As if her voice made it real…. "Di is *gone*. You haven't let her go, you've spent all these years in limbo waiting for her to straighten up and come back to you, and those years are gone too, she'll never give them back!"

"I can't get them back through you, Laura."

"But you can have all the years ahead!" She thrust her hands towards him, pleading. "For God's sake, don't throw me away! I'm not Francie, Di won't care about me, but I love you, I love you—"

"Oh, my God!" He ripped across her voice in his own shock; his hands grasped her shoulders. He didn't realize his own strength, but, oh, God, she didn't care. She'd take the pain as long as he cared to give it. "Laura, look at me! Is that what you think, that I want you for revenge?"

She whispered, "I don't care."

"Well, I do!" His anger bewildered her, still lost as she was in the pleasure of his tight fingers upon her. "Do you want that – to be taken on a kitchen floor as if you don't matter, all for a misguided in- fatuation from twenty years ago? You're worth more than that, you're worth a man who can come to you honestly and offer you his heart and home."

He stopped, and he took a deep breath.

"All right," he said, "you want the words, I will give them to you. I want you. I want you most damnably. I think of you at night, your hair spread out across a pillow, those great eyes of yours looking up at me – I wonder what it feels like to lose myself in you—" His hand came up, with a will of its own, and touched her hair shining under the light.

"But I am not going to let you do this," he said then, and hope flickered out in her heart. "Laura, you came back because you want- ed something, and no matter what you say, I don't believe it was me. You came back for your sisters. You need them as much as they need you. I came between Diana and her sisters once. I won't do it again."

She said numbly, hopelessly, "You wouldn't."

"Yes, I would." He walked away from her, back into the center of the room. "Sex changes things. A man and a woman change once they sleep together, the way they act, the way they look at each other, the way they *don't* look at each other. They give themselves dead away. Even an outsider can tell."

He shoved his hands into his pockets and turned back to her. "Listen," he said, and his voice dropped, "if I did what I'd like to do – and right now, I'd trade my soul to take you upstairs – we'd never keep it a secret. We could try, but I promise you, Lucy would figure it out in nothing flat. Diana's no slouch herself, if it comes to that. You'd lose everything you came back for, and I – dear God, I have worked hard to put together a decent life for myself and Julie. I won't wreck it for a one-night stand."

But once he had not been so cautious. Once he had nearly destroyed the world for her, but, of course, that had not been the same. Eleven years divided that moment and this, a vast abyss she could no longer lure him across.

And if he knew, he would never cross it for her.

He reached out to her then, and she started to lift her arms to him, but instead he straightened the shoulder of her nightgown and pulled her bathrobe back around her. She stood stock-still under his hands, the part of her mind that still worked noting the impersonal touch of his fingers, the quick movements as he tied her sash.

"I'm going home now," he said gently. "Don't walk me to the door."

He walked through the house then, and he must have known that she trailed behind him. She had gone numb, her heart anesthetized against the coming pain. She knew only that he was leaving her, that she had gambled supremely and lost him for good.

Diana, damn her, always Diana, Diana had won.

At the front door, he hesitated, aware of her shadow behind him, and maybe kindness drove him to it, or some desire still cindered within him. Softly, through the dusk, he said, "Good night, Laurie. And – don't blame yourself. It was a splendid moment."

She stared back at him.

"But the next time I see you," he managed a smile, "we need to be in the middle of a very large crowd."

He hesitated once more, and then, before she knew to react, he enfolded her in his arms; she felt his lips against her hair. She lifted her hand to his face, and he let her touch him for a moment, a light brush across his cheek, a brief moment against the warmth of his mouth. She tried to speak, say his name, and could not manage a word.

"Goodbye, Laurie," he said, and was gone.

She made herself stand by the open door and watch him leave her. He walked away, a man set on his path, not a second thought, not the slightest concession to what he had left behind. This was it, then, Laura Abbott's one great roll of the dice, and she had lost all in the depths of conscience and loyalty.

Not her conscience either, not her loyalty. She'd remember that later, when she could bear to think, one more crime to add to her mounting account.

He reached his car, a dark shadow among many shadows in the dying day, and she watched him stop, reaching into his pocket for his keys.

And then she forgot to breathe, she forgot that every moment of this night would carry him away from her, spinning forever on their separate wheels. For he did not get into his car, start the engine, drive away from her. He merely stood there, staring down at his hand, that hand that had lain moments before on her breast.

She waited in the darkness.

What demons of a relinquished past accosted him, what visions of a hidden future enticed him, what titanic struggle engulfed him, she could not guess.

She knew only that he won, and she lost.

She sank to the floor, and watched as he left her.

17

Here Be Dragons

RICHARD ASHMORE DID NOT ALLOW himself to think. He concentrated on the four-mile trip along the country roads that he had known since childhood, staring hard at each stop sign, pausing at each crossroad like new and mysterious terrain.

He avoided looking at his hands.

Ashmore Park loomed up all too soon. If not for Julie, he might have driven all night. Not with any particular destination in mind, not for any reason except to drive. Driving dulled the mind, exhausted the body, stripped away any real capacity to think.

The night Diana had confessed her great crime, he had gotten into his car and headed off blindly. The hours passing had scarcely registered on his consciousness. He had been stunned the next morning to find himself in Ohio, at the gray shore of Lake Erie. How he had gotten himself there, what part of his mind had sorted out freeways and toll roads and interstates and watched the speed limit, remained forever a mystery to him. He had no memory of stopping to gas up his car, although the gas gauge told him that he had done so, and more than once.

But he had been young then, filled with a pain and rage he could scarcely contain. Now... he locked his car for the night, still carefully not looking at his hand, that hand that had lain across Laura's breast, that had made of her hair a coronation ring.

With that hand, he had reached for and thrust away a woman rare and precious, a woman not likely to offer herself ever again.

And all for Diana, he thought, and watched himself strike the keys on the security pad, Diana, and her mockery of a slashed wrist.

Damnable Diana.

Diana, he discovered as he switched on the light on his desk, who was not quite finished with him that night.

DAD! Julie had left a large message taped to his computer monitor. CALL TOM! SAYS IT'S IMPORTANT! NO MATTER HOW LATE! As an afterthought, *Page him on his cell. Lucy's asleep.*

He glanced at the darkened second story and saw that Julie had closed her door for the night. Not even eleven yet, according to his watch… he had lived a lifetime during the evening.

Tom returned the page immediately. "Julie there?" he asked without preamble.

"She's gone to bed." His alarm rose. "What's up?"

"I'm faxing you something. Diana's latest." In the background, he heard Tom punching the number on the fax machine. "We may have a problem."

Oh, God, what now? He sat down at his desk as his fax rang and engaged. Tom said nothing as the lines of letters began slowly to materialize on his own end of the line. He took the first page off as the second began to appear, and one quick, appalled glance told him that Tom had not been exaggerating.

"Richard? Got it?"

"Got it," he said, and read through it again.

NOTICE OF INTENT TO TAKE DEPOSITION AND SUBPOENA DUCES TECUM, after the pleading heading, directed to… oh, damn, damn, damn… Laura Rose Abbott St. Bride. "Can they do this?" he asked. *Subpoena duces tecum.* Every architect knew those words; producing documents under subpoena was part and parcel of the profession. "*Can* she do this? This isn't even relevant anymore."

Deponent is hereby ordered to produce any and all of the following in her possession, custody, or control… any and all papers and documents, recordings, and photographs… any and all materials which may prove the existence of a sexual relationship between Francesca Mariah Abbott and Richard Patrick Ashmore between the time period of 1987 to 1988… Deponent is required to render an affidavit as to her knowledge of the alleged extramarital relationship….

Tom had shifted into lawyer mode; his normally casual voice was crisp and decisive. "We'll fight this, of course," he said, and Richard heard papers rustling in the background. "It is irrelevant, it's old news, and it has nothing to do with the issues Diana has raised so far. This is intended to apply pressure to you through Laura. If Laura even knew anything," and he paused, "well, of course, she did, she's had Meg St. Bride all these years. She probably knows—"

"She knows everything," Richard said wearily, and stared down at the subpoena again. "I doubt Francie kept anything from her."

She told me everything, every detail, you wouldn't believe what she told me.

"Fine. Doesn't matter. It's hearsay. Did Laura actually witness anything?" Thank God for Tom's ability to shift into the mechanics, away from the sheer immorality of it all. The great thing about having your friend for your lawyer, he thought with the part of his mind that wasn't vivisecting Diana with relish, was that you could confess practically anything to him, and he would start thinking of ways to diminish the impact of even your worst deeds. *Adultery with your sister-in-law? Did anyone see? Well, then, it never happened.*

"No. No one did. Just Diana that last day, and she only saw us talking."

"Good." The clicking of Tom's keyboard as he made notes came through the phone line. "Then Laura has no direct knowledge, and any affidavit she gives is worthless. We'll contest its introduction. Frankly, I'll be surprised if Laura doesn't challenge this subpoena. She won't want to give this deposition any more than we want her to."

That observation struck him forcibly, and he read the document yet again. *Any and all documents....* "Oh, my God," he said, and this time he understood the real danger that Laura faced. "That birth certificate—"

"Forget that," said Tom. "I stand by my theory that Francie didn't name you. I researched the adoption laws in California, and she'd have had a hard time relinquishing the child for adoption if she'd named you. Fathers' rights were in legal force for at least fifteen years before that. I'll tell you what I think: even if there *is* such a birth certificate, Laura doesn't have it. I think Cameron St. Bride retained it and it's still among the papers in his estate. Since she's not his executor, she doesn't have control of it. If you look at their divorce agreement—" a second of silence, and then, "look at page 5. Look at all the restrictions on her use of the stock he'd given her during the marriage. Page 7 – same thing, and this is apparently some foundation she helped set up. He kept her voting proxy on a charitable board, for God's sake! And then page 8 – I can't believe her lawyers didn't stop the inroads on her managing conservatorship of Meg. She must have used his lawyers. I'd never let a client allow a husband to get away with this nonsense. This guy was a control freak. If anyone had that birth certificate, if it even existed, St. Bride had it."

He had followed along in his copy of the pleading with Tom's logic, and relief washed through him at the solidity of the argument. "That makes sense," he said. "I have all the paperwork for Julie. And you're right. From everything Laura has said, he was a control freak."

A control freak who had prevented Laura from seeing him and Julie in London. *I am all the family she needs.* St. Bride had shown a hell of a nerve, keeping Laura's own family from her.

Yet, less than two months later, they had started divorce proceedings. For the first time, the strange timing of that struck Richard. And he saw too, on the first page of the pleading, what he had not noticed before. Laura had not been the one to file; she had been filed against. Cameron St. Bride's desire to control the divorce that his wife wanted? Or had he actually been the one to want out?

"Good," said Tom. "Now let's get down to the rest of this. Please tell me, just so I can file a motion to quash in good conscience, that no docs, photos, etc., exist that show anything between you and Francie. Please tell me that you did not see fit to write her any letters."

Well, that, at least, he could answer without hesitation. "Of course not. I was a fool, but I wasn't that big a fool. The only problem is," and he heard Tom groan, "I haven't a clue as to what Francie wrote. She never wrote me any letters – just some cards and tapes, and I destroyed those. But those girls wrote everything down. Dominic trained them to keep journals for their music from the time they were little. Diana stopped once she went to college, but I remember seeing Laura writing in hers. And she and Francie took those journals with them. That's how we knew right away that they hadn't been abducted."

Tom swore. "Damn that man! No wonder Lucy makes lists of everything. All we can hope is Laura doesn't have any of Francie's stuff left, or maybe Francie had the journal with her when the plane crashed—"

Richard stopped making notes on the fax.

"Plane crash? What are you talking about?"

Silence. He could almost hear Tom's mind racing.

"Laura told Lucy that Francie died in a plane crash." Tom sounded tentative, as though he searched for something. "Lucy didn't want to press Laura for details, so she asked me how we could get more information. Sorry, I thought you knew. Where did I put... oh, here it is." His voice resumed its authority. "I have a coded file on Francie.

Private plane crash, en route from Angelfire to Texas. Laura didn't say when."

The air conditioning must be on high, or else shock was chilling his skin. "That's not what she told me," Richard said, and heard again Laura's words, full of pain and a desire to hurt. *She bled to death. Right here in Virginia.* "Check WESTLAW or LEXIS. The NTSB investigates every private plane crash in this country, and they publish their reports. And – look after August 1991."

His attorney paused for a telling moment. Then Tom said dryly, "Tell me how you know that."

"Because—" What he would have done not to admit this! "—I saw Francie then, and she was far from dead."

At that moment, he benefited from Lucy being asleep in the Maitland house. "God damn it," and Tom's voice did rise, "how many years have I represented you, and you are just now telling me that salient fact? You said that you ended things in June 1988—"

"And I did."

"And now I find out that you had contact with Francie, what, three years later? Where the hell was this, anyway?" He didn't like the sharpness of Tom's voice, but knew he had earned it. "And who got in touch with whom?"

"Francie called me. I saw her on Ash Marine. And," he cut in before Tom could say anything, "there was nothing even remotely sexual about it. I saw her. She saw me. We exchanged a few words."

Don't ask about Laura. Don't ask.

"Hell," said Tom. "Okay, and I need a straight answer on this. Was Laura there? Could she possibly know about this meeting?"

Had Laura been there... he had a vision of bright, passionate eyes, of a body that melted and responded... as, dear God, she had melted and responded beneath him on the floor of her kitchen an hour before, no longer a child, but a woman offering herself heart and soul. *I came back for you. I've loved you my entire life....* And he had thrust her away.

Come upstairs with me.

For Diana. Diana, who sought to strip away the secrets Laura had fought so hard to conceal. Diana who had slashed her wrist, put her sister through a terrifying afternoon, and now was attempting to divide her from the rest of the family by resurrecting old wounds, old feelings, old moments that no longer meant anything.

He had, he thought, truly meant to preserve her relationship with Diana. He had not taken her upstairs, as she had begged him to take her, because he had wanted her still to have her sister. And for what! Diana had already broken her relationship with her younger sister for good, with this damnable piece of paper, threatening the core of Laura's life.

Because he knew how Laura would react to the subpoena. She had to avoid it. To give that deposition, she had to perjure herself, lie through her teeth, anything to keep them from knowing that Meg was not her natural child. Laura deserved Meg. She had married for her, taken her as her own, endured twelve years of Cameron St. Bride for her. He and Francie had accidentally created Meg, but by accident or design, she had ended up with exactly the right mother.

And no one, especially not Diana, was going to interfere with that.

It struck him then that, in the space of a heartbeat, his priorities had shifted, that Diana was no longer his axis.

Your marriage is dead. Diana is gone.

"Richard?" Tom said again, and he sounded suspicious. "Was Laura there?"

He had to shut that avenue off decisively. Only Francie and his father knew, and they were both gone. He said swiftly, "No, she wasn't," and skimmed through the subpoena again. "What's the impact? Bottom line?"

"Bottom line? Zip. Zero. *Nada.* An affair that ended fourteen years ago after Diana had refused you your marital rights for three years? After which time she then lived with you another three years? With no witnesses and no written documents? It doesn't even matter that it produced an illegitimate child." Richard winced. "Let's face it, the child's adoptive mother is never going to divulge that, and Kevin doesn't know to ask the question. Here's what will happen. Laura will be served, she'll notify the St. Bride lawyers immediately because she won't want to testify, and they'll file a motion to quash. I can imagine the firepower St. Bride kept on retainer. Kevin doesn't stand a chance. They'll demand a hearing, and we can sit quietly by as they trot out all the reasons why this is pure harassment. Then, if Laura can't prevail at a hearing, the deposition will get delayed and she'll get a call to return to London. Then she'll get whisked onto a private jet and out of the jurisdiction."

And she would never be able to return.

Richard said bluntly, "She'll lie if she has to testify."

"Yes, I'm afraid she might. And I hope it doesn't come to that, because I'd have to report known perjury to the court." Tom sounded calm. "No, let Laura's attorneys file the motion to quash. I'll hold off on ours, because it'll look better if we act as if we don't mind her testimony. We'll take the position that she is welcome to testify because she knows nothing that hurts our case, and we want to get this whole matter out in the open."

But he didn't, he thought after Tom hung up. All the reasons why he had never told anyone, why he had never confessed his guilt, still held strong. He had never wanted his parents, and now Julie, to know what he had done to his marriage vows. He did not want to risk his stature in their eyes. He did not want them to know that he had failed to meet their high standards.

That he had surrendered to a pair of hungry eyes and a young man's desire too long denied.

But Diana – Diana, whose own sins couldn't bear the light of day – Diana had forced his hand.

And she had forced Laura's as well.

Either Laura lied, and Tom felt himself honor-bound as an officer of the court to report her perjury, or she ran again to avoid testimony.

And if she ran, this time there was no coming home.

Not unless he divorced Diana.

I should have divorced her years ago. Julie would be safe. Laura would be safe. Meg would be safe. I wouldn't have to worry about her hurting Julie. I wouldn't have to worry about her.

I'd be free to build another life. I'd be free to love another woman.

Laura.

He stood again in her kitchen, feeling her body against his back, her hand sliding down his arm, as he fought his arousal and she fought his resistance. He remembered her lovely soft skin underneath his hand, and his pen in his hand trembled in remembrance. His body reacted in memory of hers beneath him, her pale breast lying warm to his hand, her mouth opening to meet and love his in return.

And Laura, as he had left her, stricken with rejection. No matter that he had not rejected her, but rather the situation in which they found themselves. The woman that his parents had thought perfect for him had walked back into his life after all these years, and she had still loved him enough to risk her heart and her pride. Laura, knowing the worst, had still loved him, and he had handed her heart right back to her. She had laid herself wide open, after a lifetime of silence – *I've loved you my whole life, I came back for you* – and he had walked away.

Diana is still my wife. I may not like that fact....

God! What had he done?

You can have all the years ahead with me.

And he had told her that the future didn't matter because the past still lived.

Well, that at least I can change.

By the time Tom called back, thirty minutes later, he had outlined a plan. He glanced down coolly at the legal notepad in front of him, with its columns of pros and cons and numbered items, and the financial spreadsheets that detailed the price of getting rid of the past. This was no more than a business deal, a buyout of a troublesome partner.

"Guess what," Tom said. "I found the NTSB reports—"

It took Richard a few seconds to orient himself. The NTSB reports. The putative plane crash. "Really?" But he didn't care. Laura had lied for her own reasons, and he'd find those out in good time. "So did you find anything?"

"Sure did," said Tom. "There was a plane crash, all right. A Kate St. Bride, resident of Plano, Texas, who just happened to be St. Bride's mother, was a passenger on a private plane that went down in the Texas Panhandle five years ago, killing all aboard. But no Francesca. I ran every name variation I could think of, and there are no matches on any private plane crashes in the last fourteen years. I did get a hit on a Francesca on an international crash a few years ago, but I don't think it's worth pursuing."

"I agree." No, Laura had lied classically; she had woven facts from something she knew and gambled that no one would ever find out. Who knew how Francie really had died... and heaven help poor little Francie, the truth might be so much worse than a plane crash. But time for that in the future. He drew the pad closer to him. "Back to Diana. Here's what I want to do."

Tom was silent.

"Monday morning," Richard said, "file for divorce. I want this clean and simple. We haven't lived together for over ten years, and that should be reason enough. I want Julie, I want my company, and

I want my separate property. Specifically, I want the Park and all the belongings. She keeps her separate property, she relinquishes any claim to my mother's jewelry, and she drops any custody threat. In return—" He consulted his notes. "I'll pay her a generous allowance until Julie turns twenty-one, and I'll give her Ash Marine, my father's cottage and all the land in a trust, to be turned over to her unconditionally at that time. It'll be worth a fortune in another year or so. I've already been approached by developers who want to build a resort."

Dead silence at the other end. He could imagine Tom's surprise.

"There are two nonnegotiable conditions," he added. "I'll waive any claims of adultery against her, if she'll do the same for me. And she has to drop the subpoena against Laura immediately. I will not have Laura harassed by her sister."

More silence.

"Well? What do you think?"

He heard Tom suppress laughter. "What do you expect me to say? High time? Good riddance?" He sobered down. "That sounds comprehensive. Do you really want to give up Ash Marine?"

"Yes. We'll have to find somewhere else to fly RC." He rubbed his eyes. "This way, I won't have to worry about her. She'll have enough money to live on the rest of her life if she's careful. And she gets it only if she behaves herself. She welshes on any part of this deal, and it stays mine."

"Fax your notes over," Tom said. "I'll start drawing up papers. Do you want me to approach Kevin with this first?"

"File," he said. "Have her served. I know Diana. That will scare the hell out of her. She'll be much more amenable to an offer then." Cold, ruthless way to talk, he thought wearily, the way he might talk about an enemy, not a woman he had adored. "And, before I pay her a cent, she drops that subpoena and signs a custody agreement."

He added, as he put his notes into the fax machine, "Oh, and one more thing, Tom. Write this in. No more fake suicide attempts."

For a man who had just tossed away a potential fortune, he felt curiously light of heart. In one evening, a marriage of eighteen years – half his life! – ended; in one evening, his daughter's emotional safety secured; in one evening, the long-planned restoration of Ashmore Magna postponed for the foreseeable future, the money now to be given to the woman he had once promised to cherish for life. In one evening, his future returned to him....

You can have all the years ahead with me.

No. No, better not to think of Laura, not to think of that silky pale skin beneath his hand, better not to feel that sudden splendid rush of longing. *Come upstairs.* Better not to think that, if not for Diana, by now he would have explored her, tasted her, met her desire for desire. Better not to think of her at all.

Come upstairs, come upstairs, come upstairs....

He dressed in jeans and polo shirt, comfortable clothes for doing paperwork, but he was loath to return downstairs to his desk. He lay on his bed in the dark, hands clasped behind his head, and thought longingly of a cigarette. For once, he was tempted to break his own rule and smoke in the house, as if the simple mindless pleasure of nicotine could chase Laura's specter away into the night.

His shoulder ached of an old wound.

But not as lethal as the wound he had dealt Laura all those years before.

You might have turned to me.

She was right. Had she not come down with the flu, she would have been there with him that New Year's Eve night. Oh, Laura would never have thought, as Francie had, to bring a bottle of her father's finest champagne, so something else would have loosened the bitterness he felt welling up as Diana danced out the door on her way to her overnight trip to Washington. He might still have voiced his deep, biting suspicion that Diana did not intend to spend the night alone, the first crack in his monolithic silence about the disintegration of his marriage. And Laura, a warm, lovely young woman, witnessing the despair and pain he could no longer conceal, might have put her arms around him to comfort him.

It might have begun as innocently as that, as it had with Francie (and hadn't it? *hadn't it?*), and lost all innocence as he saw in her lovely upturned face the ghost of Diana past. And when he lowered his head to kiss her – *face it, damn it, you did!* – she would have opened her mouth for him.

And he might have fallen into that sweltering morass of desire and guilt with her instead.

But he had chosen Francie instead, simply because Francie was there.

You never saw me. And she was right about that. He never had.

The temptation was too great. He lit a cigarette, drew on it too deeply, and coughed.

I saw you there on Ash Marine. My God, you made sure of that.

But impossible to dwell on that terrible afternoon, impossible to avoid the memory of Laura under the kitchen lights an hour ago, defiant, lashing out in pain and anguish. Crumbling beneath the weight of a lifetime of unspoken longing, sinking to the floor in his arms, touching his face, finally recognizing in him what he had so long refused to recognize in himself. Laura....

And Laura there, as he left her, stricken again, as he walked off in the self-righteous certainty that he had done the right thing, and when, he asked himself savagely, when had he ever done the right thing for her? All those years before, when he had let Francie blind him to her desperation? *I was getting ready to run.* She had planned her departure for over a year, according to Julie, but in all that time, he had seen nothing wrong. Had he done the right thing by drawing Francie away, causing heaven knew what hatred and unspoken jealousy between the sisters, and then throwing the intolerable burden of her sister's pregnancy on a seventeen-year-old girl? Had he done the right thing in London, accepting St. Bride's harsh rebuff without protest when she might have needed him? Had he done the right thing since the night she had come home, holding himself aloof, rejecting her, letting the chasm of the past yawn between them?

And tonight… he had left her there, alone as usual, to face the emotional wreckage of his rejection, just one more piece of debris of his damnable marriage. He had left her there.

He had a sudden mental image… not even a memory… of standing at his car and glancing back through the night. She had stood in the doorway of the old house, and slowly, slowly, she had slid down the door frame.

He swung his legs to the floor in one movement, stubbing out his smoldering cigarette.

She lay there for minutes; she lay there for hours. She no longer knew. Her mind had emptied of all thought, all feeling, when he had left her. Better to empty than to feel the great onslaught of pain that surely waited if she remembered any part of him.

She was aware of the chill coming in from the starlight outside the open door.

The part of her mind that still thought, but could not feel, knew the beginning of shock, but it could not rouse her from the fugue that had trapped her. He had left her. He had wanted her, he had rejected her, and then he had left her. Across the years, across her life, he had occupied the greatest part of her heart, and in one hour that corner of the universe had crashed down into dust.

She did not think she could ever get up again.

It seemed to her finally that he came back to her. The door, half open, he flung wide, and the long tall silhouette stood there for a moment against the night. He called her name, first quietly, then in urgency. He even knelt there beside her on the floor, displacing Max, and his voice as he spoke to her was urgent and worried. She heard a frantic element in his voice that she had heard only once before, and maybe she heard something new, something that might have been precious but now could only be unbearable for what it wasn't. She imagined his hands running over her, smoothing her hair, touching her face, calling her name again and again. *You wake up now, Laurie. Wake up, wake up!* She even imagined that eventually she opened her eyes and saw him through the light in her mind.

She thought she said his name once, "Richard," and she dreamed that he lifted her up against him, that he pulled her against his body and enfolded his arms around her.

That he said, in a voice shaking with some unfathomable emotion, "Oh, my dear Lord."

But this really wasn't happening. She had so disconnected that she only imagined his hand against her back, his heart beating hard against hers, his arms trembling because – because why? Why? He didn't ache for her; his heart didn't beat for her; his arms didn't tremble to hold her.

This couldn't be real.

"Richard." Did she really whisper? Did he hear?

"Laurie," he whispered back in her mind, "oh, my God, Laurie." She filtered his words into the meaningless void of her pain, vaguely aware that if she woke up and remembered any of this, she might want to seize upon those words, ponder them, tuck them away in her heart.

Perhaps then she imagined him forcing her to stand up in his arms, coaxing her up the Chippendale staircase, step by step by step. *Come on, Laurie, keep walking, don't you stop....* Maybe she dreamed the warmth of his arms holding her, beside her that long journey down the hall to the room she had chosen for her own. She had gone so far into insanity that she dreamed the sight of him pushing that door open, guiding her through the door to that bed overlooking the pool. But, in a dream, she wouldn't have winced against the light he turned on by the bed, her arm coming up instinctively to shield her eyes.

"No." She even sounded normal.

Surely a dream figure would not have turned off the light at her protest. In the soft light from the window he stood there, a tall dark ghost against the darker wall. She knew that dark shade, she had dreamed it through the years, she had glimpsed it from the corner of her eye, felt its presence behind her wherever she had walked in the time of her exile. But she had never known him in the night, in her bedroom, the two of them alone in a room that now had become the entire world.

And she had never conjured up the reality of him stepping forward into the starlight, flipping back the comforter and blankets on her bed.

He came to her and led her to the bed.

"Get into bed, Laurie," and his touch felt real and warm against her cheek. "You'll be more comfortable."

She stared at him.

He drew in a ragged breath in the darkness of the room. "Laurie," he said, "stop looking like that, are you in shock—" and she felt his hand along her face again. "Come on, get into bed."

She obeyed the pressure of his hands on her shoulders, and sank down onto the side of the bed. And she heard him sigh, perhaps in relief, as if – as if some burden had just lifted from him.

He moved away from her then, towards the chair, as he had moved away earlier that night. She watched him widen the distance between them, once more putting time and space between them, and a terrible rage bubbled up through her. She hadn't even known it lay there within her, a vast unknown magma chamber of fury, until the moment it erupted, burning its way up through the layers of shock and despair into her heart and mind and soul.

She screamed, and he swung around at the sound.

"No! No, no, no, *no*—"

Terror, fury, rage propelled her then towards him, across time and space, towards that tall ghostly silhouette, and she reached for him, reached before he could vanish.

"You left me!"

He stood stock-still, as if her scream had stabbed him clean to the heart. She felt only his reaction, as his hands reached out to hold her.

"You left me! Oh, my God, you left me," she cried, as her mind shattered and the anguish she had tamped down flooded into her heart, and she pushed against him even as he tried to hold her, and her panic escalated. "You left me—"

His voice, shaking, the words torn from deep within.

"I came back."

The words hung there between them like a talisman.

Who moved first remained forever unknown. They met in the center, body to body, mouth to mouth. Neither offered restraint or gentleness; neither accepted it from the other. "Laurie," he whispered, and "Richard," she whispered back, and their whispers set fire to the smoldering embers and all that remained unspoken and unresolved between them roared up in flames, and he kissed her again, a second, harder kiss that drove them back against the wall.

Somewhere I will always taste you....

And he tasted like – he tasted like Richard.

His mouth, warm and living against her throat, made a hungry exploration, learning the feel and flavor of her. She caught her breath as he tasted the curve of her neck into her shoulder, and she leaned forward to bury herself in the spring freshness of his silver-tipped temple. The thick feel of his hair against her fingers, the summer smell of his skin – how had she forgotten, how had she not remembered – oh, but she had, she had....

His hand against her back, too, now a voyager, ventured down her spine, and his other hand trembled, fingers shaking as he freed the sash of her robe. She felt it swing free against her legs, and then she paid no more attention, for those slim fingers now worked the top buttons of her gown, and his mouth followed the trail they blazed across her flesh.

She closed her eyes against the rush of feeling that surged inside her, savoring every second of the lovely feathering of his lashes across her breast, the warm breeze of his breath against her skin, the heated imprint of his body against hers. She felt him bringing her back to life. She touched the crown of his thick hair, her hand skimming through the fine strands until her fingers reached his ear and journeyed from the temple down along the jaw line. She leaned over his bent head, and tasted the subtle valleys and hills of his skin.

She felt herself bringing him back to life.

"Laura...."

In eleven years, her body had never forgotten. She remembered now: for this she would have destroyed the world, for this she would have laughed among the ashes.

Slowly, slowly, he raised his head.

"Laura, listen," he said, and she heard the breath that she'd knocked out of him, she felt his heartbeat against hers. "God help me, I *have* lost my mind – listen—"

She moved against him, and loved the catch in his throat.

"No," he said, and with some last resistance, he held her an inch or two away, enough to break the current that ran through them both. She obeyed the demand of the hand that forced her chin up; she met his gaze with glazed eyes that saw only him, and knew only the bed behind them. "Listen! I want you, I want you badly, but – this is it, there's no going back – Laura, are you listening, do you even understand what I'm saying—"

Oh, yes, she understood. She understood that, in that moment, she stood at the brink of joy and catastrophe, and if she jumped, she risked it all.

She moved back against him.

"Laura?" She would remember his voice all her life, low and warm and promising against her temple. "Do you want this?"

"I want *you*," she whispered, and this was not a dream.

His fingers moved against her breast, and she closed her eyes and stepped into the abyss.

She did not recognize the disaster until they had gone too far.

She turned away towards the bed. She knew she must move first, so that he knew her willingness to roll the dice. Once there, she turned and held out her hand. He crossed the room to her, knowing her acceptance, signaling his own, and she saw him coming towards her, stranger, friend, lover, as he had once come towards her….

She stood somewhere far off and watched him as he knocked on the door.

She'd been shocked to see him there, standing against the afternoon glare of the sun. He looked different, older, eyes full of shock and wonder. "Richard," she said, with the trace of her newly acquired alto huskiness. When he stepped inside, something possessed her, she didn't know what, and she reached for him. Oh, he looked so good to her, no matter what he'd done, no matter what he and Francie planned. He resisted her there, just for a moment, and then he kissed her as only Cam ever had. He didn't realize, he thought she was....

But hadn't Francie told him? her mind screamed, as her mouth opened for him, didn't he know where Francie was? Had he no idea—

"My God," he whispered in a trail down her throat to her breast, "you taste even lovelier than I remembered—"

Possessed of an old passion, caught up in an old dream, she reached for the buttons of his shirt, and almost came back to herself with the shock of his warm skin against her fingertips and the fresh scent of his hair in her lungs.

He was here; he was real; he was Richard.

He said nothing but "Fran" several times, between deep, hungry kisses. She made no effort to stop him. It made no sense, his showing up like this, murmuring into her hair that he was so glad to see her, she looked so pretty, where had she been, why had she left, why had she come back....

In the twilight, she saw his eyes close as she drew her mouth down his chest, her tongue following behind her fingers working the buttons of his shirt. She felt his fingers tangle in her hair. "Don't stop – oh, dear God, that feels so good—"

He was hers to touch, now, finally.

Not Diana's husband.

Not Francie's lover.

Gradually, it seemed to her that Francie must have decided to kill Diana without him. Something had gone wrong with her thinking; she knew that in the midst of her fever, but every logical thought drifted elusively just out of reach. Better if he went on thinking she was Francie, she decided hazily, even as he pushed her gently towards the unmade bed where she had

napped. She couldn't bear the humiliation if he realized that he'd kissed Laura, invisible Laura, with all the passion reserved for her sisters.

She managed a smile when he said, "Sit down, Fran, you look all in," and she promised to behave and tell all if he'd sit down with her. "All right," he'd said, once they were settled in against the headboard, "now where have you been? And where's Laurie?" And she'd cuddled up against his shoulder and conjured up tears in her eyes and said that she couldn't talk about Laurie, not right now, it was too hard, she was too overcome. This, she thought, this would give him an alibi, and she pressed herself right over him. His hands hovered reluctantly over her back for a second, maybe two or three, and then they closed around her. He kissed her then deeply, thoroughly, a parched man drinking at an oasis.

"My God," a silk whisper in her hair, "it feels so good to touch a woman again."

She forgot, as he stretched out beside her and gathered her back into his arms, that she had already seen to it that no alibi would be necessary.

He wove his fingers into her hair, lifting it, stroking it, making a fine veil over her forehead. Through the night, she saw his face, serious, intent on the study of the intricate strands spread across his palm, and she regretted then that she hadn't Cat Courtney's mane. Now she could not weave it into a shimmering mesh to bind him to her heart.

"My God," he whispered, "it feels so good to touch you."

She spared a small, delirious thought that later he would surely find out who she really was, how she'd thwarted their plans, but she'd be back in Texas with her husband and her daughter and her baby, and she wouldn't ever have to face him again, or Francie either, for that matter....

But did he have to know now? Just once in her life, couldn't she take what she wanted?

"Laura," he breathed, in a voice sinking lower and lower into the warm southern velvet of the night, "wait – I want to see you—" And his hands made short work of her nightgown.

Even though she expected it, even though she wanted it, the shock of being held once again against a man's warm, willing body sent Laura's mind spinning.

Heat and power and magic, and her own eager journey down his body. Oh, she had forgotten this, the superb pleasure of being a woman in a man's arms.

And not just any man. Not Cam, receding into dim memory.

Richard.

Diana's husband.

Francie's lover.

She called on every memory of her twin's whispered confidences. She used everything she knew about him to convince him that she was Francie come back to him, and she succeeded beyond her wildest dreams. She flirted with him, she played silly lovers' games, she told him in teasing detail what she wanted to do to him and what she wanted him to do in return.

Her performance would have astonished her husband.

Especially when she stopped performing.

"Take me," she whispered against his temple. "I'm dying for you."

"Not so fast," he whispered back, rocking her against him, a man partnering a dancer, a lover savoring a woman. "We'll take our time. There's no rush. I want to enjoy you—"

And he suited action to word, his mouth moving across her, his hands molding and shaping her into his own landscape of desire. And when he eased her down onto the lush quilt, she melted beneath him, warm and liquid and open. In the languor of lazy arousal, she ignored the first frisson of desperation that crossed her heart.

Almost.

She experienced not a twinge of uneasiness when he took off his shirt, and she halted his hand at his belt by unbuckling it herself. Thank God Cam had taught her about sex, she thought as she turned her back on him to wriggle out of her jeans, which were getting tighter and tighter. And thank God she

didn't show much yet. Not even Cam knew. Of course, given the state of their life together, she had made no effort to tell him either.

"Am I okay?" she asked him, lying anxiously under the slow inspection of his hands, warm and sensitive against her screaming skin. "I mean, is there anything you want me to do?"

His lips lingered against her abdomen, while his clever fingers drew circles on the tender skin of her inner thigh. "I want you to relax."

"But—" She couldn't keep all the fear out of her voice. Too much history, too much remembrance of never measuring up. She swallowed hard and whispered, "I guess I'm just nervous."

She felt his breath on her skin. "It's just me, Laurie, you're not bidding a project." He paused. "Or, in your world, auditioning for a part."

That made her laugh, and that small insistent whisper of dread fell silent for the moment. "Oh, is this a casting couch? Do I have a shot at the lead?"

She felt the exploration of his tongue on her left breast in response, and heard him laugh briefly under his breath. "Depends on the script," he said in that voice that turned her liquid against his hand, and then, "Laurie – oh, God, I can't believe it's really you—"

She watched him, memorizing him, all the time he made love to her, and never once remembered her husband. How could she, when she had wanted Richard Ashmore back beyond her early memories? This was how he kissed her, his lips moving slowly across her throat, laying down a lovely necklace of desire; this now was the tip of his ring finger, outlining her, caressing her, summoning a response she had never surrendered to Cam. This was how his eyes darkened and hardened and his breath caught when she leaned over him, her hair brushing his chest, and claimed the same freedom to learn him.

The feverish darkness descended upon her. She watched her young phantom in his arms, lingered on that moment of enclosure and possession, raced through driving thrusts of passion and whispered words of lust and longing, went into reverse at the culmination that touched her memory as, eleven years later, Richard drew her over him.

She knew a moment of the darkest panic, the worst stage fright in her history. She stared down at him in the night, at those lashes covering his wonderful eyes, at his firm mouth, and it came to her then, in horror, that the curtain was opening on the part she had wanted and fought for all her life, and she had forgotten her lines.

I can't, I'm not ready, and she opened her mouth frantically to say so, because if she said it, then everything would be all right, Richard would understand, they could take things slower....

And then Cat Courtney, bless her, whispered in her soul, *Step aside. I'll take it from here.*

Then it was all right, for Cat knew how to woo and win an audience.

Later, they lay there drowsily, her long legs wrapped with his, and she heard him sigh in a mixture of release and regret. Perhaps he felt guilty for betraying Diana once more, for falling into bed with Francie all over again. She felt nothing but a hard-won peace. Let me have this, I'll live on it for the rest of my life.... She was too young to realize that she had just destroyed the mental fabric of her marriage. Ahead lay years of comparing her husband to the man who rested against her breast, stroking her hair – a contest that Cameron St. Bride, only a flesh-and-blood man, was destined to lose against the legend Richard Ashmore became in her mind.

Cat took over then, Cat who'd occasionally made a guest appearance in the St. Bride bedroom and delighted and perplexed Cameron St. Bride with a glimpse of what might have been. Cat didn't worry about the size of her breasts or the skill of her hands or the bite of her teeth against his shoulder. Cat wanted only to please and serve. So when he reached back for her, long lean fingers stroking against her, his mouth traveling the curving equator of her thigh, and when he whispered, "How does this feel? Do you like that?" Cat lied in the face of Laura's rising dread.

"Then relax," and his breath blew against her, "you're shaking."

"I'm excited," Cat whispered back, and banished Laura to the sidelines.

Later, later — how many times had he returned to her arms? Surely memory erred. She had sat on the edge of the bed, her back turned to him, pulling her jeans on as he buttoned his shirt behind her. He knelt on the bed to put aside the heavy curtain of hair from the nape of her neck, and then his hand slipped down to caress her breasts.

Her breasts were sensitive, and so she winced. He drew back in surprise, and then his eyes opened and he really looked at her, he looked at those tell-tale blue veins and that bulky waistline, and then, worst of all, his eye fell on the wedding ring she had forgotten to draw from her left hand. Passion no longer blinded him. "What the devil is going on?" he demanded, and she could only hold onto the notion that he still didn't know who she was, and he mustn't find out until she could get away. Let Francie explain, let Francie dig herself out of this, let Francie hate her, if she wanted, but, dear God, let her get away first.

"Not the best time to ask," his voice, edged with rue, brushed her in the darkness, "but do I need to use anything?"

Cat shook her head, Cat who understood Laura's internal calendar, and Laura knew a moment of dismay at her cowardice, that she'd let slide such a perfect opportunity to pull them both back from looming disaster.

"Then," he whispered, "invite me in."

"You're pregnant, aren't you?" His voice reverberated in the dream, and she nodded and bent her head. How far along? Was she married? his voice continued to demand, and she replied, trembling, afraid now, because his eyes were burning with fury and contempt and pain. The words he threw at her, the names he called her, made her sick, and she covered her ears defensively, and he leaned over to jerk her hands down so that she had to listen.

He must have known right away that it had been a long time for her, because her body tensed and she resisted him, for just a second, when he sought entrance. It might even have been Cam who whispered, "Put your arms around me." And Cat, ever obedient, ever responsive to the mood of her audience, clasped her hands around his neck.

And Laura looked into his eyes and saw, in shock, that he stared down at her. The thought hit her, sickeningly, that he was staring straight through time.

Well, maybe she was a whore, she admitted painfully to herself, but then what was he? He wore a wedding ring too! How dare he treat her this way, when she was a perfectly respectable married woman carrying a child conceived within the confines of her marriage bed? No matter that she had just disregarded those marriage vows as if they were as flimsy as tissue, how dare he force her back onto the bed and say contemptuously that she hadn't changed, that he supposed he ought to consider himself lucky that he had found out just how despicable she really was, she always had been a world-class liar, did her husband know what sort of deceitful bitch he had married, or was that baby even her husband's? How dare he taunt her with the threat that her husband ought to know how lightly she took her marriage vows? How dare he tangle his fingers painfully in her long hair, trembling as if he still wanted her, and accuse her of being unworthy to be a mother, that perhaps she might find herself fighting to keep her child when her husband learned what had happened? How dare he hold her shoulders so tightly, accusing her of coming back to ruin his life, and he wouldn't stand for it, he'd see her in hell first before she destroyed anything else? How dare he tell her that he had enjoyed the show, she had become quite the actress, and thank God he saw right through her, not like that poor bastard she was married to?

A long time later to him, even longer to her, Laura knew in despair that all her fine desire had fled in the face of memory. Francie, Diana, Cam.... He worked hard over her, his mouth and hands moving lyrically across her, and nothing helped. He tried, oh, God, how he tried, but her mind had left her body. She found herself watching dispassionately as he tried to bring her back to him, wishing he would just hurry up and get it the hell over with.

When she heard the strain in his voice and touched the sweat on his face as he whispered he couldn't hold out much longer, she took the only humane course open.

She resorted to fraud. She did what she had seldom had to do even with Cam, even in the last days of their dying marriage; she called on all her skills as an actress, and she faked it.

He, of course, did not.

Later, of course, she saw those words for just what they were, the expression of a pain and betrayal rocking him to his very core, but maddened with the ferocity of his attack, she was filled with a furious terror that he might make good on his threat to tell Cam… she might lose… everything. She might lose… Meg. She couldn't focus clearly for the toxins pouring into her blood. He paused in the open door to demand one last answer, fling one last insult, what it was she didn't hear, and her hand trailed along the floor, and her fingers closed around the cold metal of the gun she had hidden from Francie earlier. She didn't stop to think or even feel. She pulled the gun up in one fluid motion, and she shot him.

He did not leave her after he left her body. He did not even fall asleep, as Cam usually had. She lay on her side, her back to him, and he held her against him and stroked her hair and shoulder. They did not speak; he told her musingly that he wanted to enjoy the quiet, and she stared out into the vastness of the night sky and the bleakness of her own heart.

How many times she fired, she couldn't remember later.

The memory played over and over in her mind, he staring at her in a sort of stunned horror, clasping his hand to a rapidly spreading patch of red on his shoulder, she breathing harder and feeling sicker as Francie's poisons spread through her blood. The baby, having made only a few tentative motions in the course of its short existence, lay quiet and dying in her womb.

Without another word, he walked away and left her.

After a while, he shifted against her, and she knew a moment of aching despair that he wanted to make love to her again. Not that, please, anything but that, she didn't think she could endure another failure…. But when he spoke, he said merely, "Do you know one of my great fantasies?"

His voice was low and affectionate, and she thought in relief that she must have brought it off, after all. She whispered back, "You want to tie me up and play pirate?"

Ah, Cat, what a godsend she was.

A pleasant, tired laugh. "Another time, perhaps. I'm not into bondage tonight. No," and he dropped a kiss on her shoulder, "a lot of nights I turn off the lights and listen to your music. I use the time to recharge my creative batteries. I've solved a lot of engineering problems, sitting there, listening to you in the dark." His hand traveled slowly down the side of her body, into the curve of her waist and up again onto the slope of her hip.

She tensed, wondering what he wanted, afraid to hear any more musing confidences. She didn't want to know what lay in his heart, what he thought about her lying there in his arms, his wife's sister, his mistress's twin. Or, God forbid, the woman of eleven long-ago Chesapeake summers.

"Sing for me."

A request from the audience, an encore after the curtain call. She relaxed.

"What do you want to hear?"

"Anything," he said, "your choice."

She sang. She sang her heart out. A new song, one she had written in those last London afternoons of searching through the depths of her memory for traces of the Laura Abbott who had once lived in her father's house and loved her sister's husband. She had thought it a painful song and left it rough and unfinished, determined never to record it. She heard it now, her voice echoing against the southern pine of the walls, and thought it only melancholy.

When she finished, he said only, "Ah, Cat. Another lovely performance."

Act Three:

Remnants of a Late Afternoon

But love is blind, and lovers cannot see
The pretty follies that themselves commit

(The Merchant of Venice, Act Two, Scene Six)

18

Falling Off the Edge

W<small>HEN</small> L<small>AURA</small> <small>AWOKE</small>, she was alone.

She blinked against the early morning light tiptoeing in through the window, and her arm reached out towards the other side of the bed. The sheets felt cool and vacant. Only her body bore mute witness to the man who had occupied both the night before.

And occupy her he had, twice, a second time at dawn when her eyes had fluttered open to meet his watchful gaze.

And now – now he was gone.

She bolted upright in bed, and she knew that she hadn't dreamed the night before. Her nightgown lay discarded on the floor, the other pillow still bore the imprint of his head, and his leather jacket hung neatly on the back of her dressing table chair. And her body remembered his very real presence.

She lifted her hand to her face, and smelled their mingled scents.

Mingled… oh, God, mingled scents, shared mouths and bodies. No turning back, he had said, and she had agreed and led him to the bed. *Do you want this?*

Richard had become her lover. She had become his.

She started to sink back against her pillow, until she heard the unmistakable closing of the front door downstairs. Was he coming or going – but then she heard the faint purr of his car, and the opening of the gates. She squinted at the clock on her nightstand and saw that it was only seven.

What if he decided not to come back?

What if he did?

Laura took one look in the mirror and recoiled. The emotional storm of the evening before still haunted her face; she had cried so hard that her eyes were still swollen and red. She had the faintest red marks across her jaw; she touched them and realized that they were whisker burns, and that she had matching sets on both her breasts. She could see the marks on her shoulders where he had held her tightly and she had gloried in the pain.

She had gloried in it all, she thought deliberately, and held a cold cloth to her eyes. Heaven only knew he had given her plenty of chances to back out, but she hadn't. She had wanted him from her earliest memory, and last night he had finally become hers.

And she had failed, at the very moment when she had gained all she had ever wanted.

She distanced herself in the shower, smoothing the soap over her shoulders, letting the soothing water wash away the emotional damage to her face. Okay, so she had failed. It wasn't the end of the world. It wasn't even the end of them. She had started off badly with Cam, and they had managed to make a marriage from it—

Not a good comparison. He paid you. You sold yourself. You took two hundred dollars for sex with him.

And you never once faked anything with Cam. There was always honesty there, at least.

Richard obviously hadn't been too upset at her emotional disconnection at the critical moment. When she awoke at first dawn, she had turned towards him, following his breathing in the still of the night. She had thought he had been sleeping too, and maybe he had, but she focused on him through the night and saw him watching her steadily. She hadn't stopped to think. She had leaned over and kissed him, and slowly, Cat Courtney had started to make love to him.

Surely, he wouldn't have urged her to put her hands on him, or let her take the lead, if he hadn't wanted her or—

If he had looked into her eyes and seen the woman who had lain beneath him at Ash Marine, the woman who had teased him and loved him and—

Her mind skittered away from the thought.

The woman who had pointed a gun at him and pulled the trigger.

It lay there then, in front of her, the ending of the nightmare that she had never quite relived, the moment she had managed never to remember. For one terrible moment, she knew the heaviness of the gun in her hand, felt the tension in her finger as she pulled back on the trigger, watched the blood spread on his shoulder.

Oh, God! She reached out to brace herself against the shower wall.

Her hands still ached from the cuts Diana had inflicted.

Diana! How could she face Diana today? How could she face her ever?

Richard and I are mated for life.

How could she ever face him?

He came back. As she toweled off, she heard his car. As she rummaged for something to wear, the front door opened. As she covered up the last ravages of the night, she heard him moving around the kitchen downstairs.

She selected a pretty floral sundress from her wardrobe, all white roses and violets on a shimmery green background, and laid it carefully on the bed. Downstairs, she heard him talking. Max, that traitor, must have run downstairs to hang out for a while with another male. She wondered how long she could linger in the room, but nothing, after all, could keep him from coming upstairs to find her there hiding from him.

And she *was* hiding. *I don't know how to face him. I don't know how to act the morning after. I don't know what he wants or expects….*

I don't even know what I want.

Oh, but she did know. She wanted to turn back time and tide, to make the great sea of their adult lives still uncharted before them. Passion and blood, rage and adultery and the most terrible of betrayals, all still ahead, and this time the iceberg seen in time to prevent the tragedy….

She wanted to wipe the slate clean, and her hands with it.

You will not find absolution in this room.

She stiffened then, and marched back to her dressing table. Her eyes looked better now, not so stretched-out. She said aloud, "All right now," straightened her shoulders, and walked downstairs to meet her lover.

He'd gone out to get breakfast. A box of bagels lay open on the island counter, and he'd left a cup of fast-food orange juice for her beside a container of cream cheese. But the room, and the house, had an empty stillness. Not even the ghosts of last evening lingered.

Through the picture window, she saw an unexpected movement

of a blue sleeve out near the pool.

For a second, she felt disconnected from all her knowledge of him, as if time had indeed run backwards on her. He appeared as a stranger. He had a book open on the table, and the sun glinted softly off his dark hair as he lost himself in his reading. One hand absently crumbled a bagel. He seemed alone, self-contained, as if he had nothing to do with a common past, a shared afternoon of blood and lust, a past night of anguish and discovery.

This was probably how he appeared to the rest of the world.

Then he turned a page, and that gesture summoned up a small memory, tucked away all these years.

It might have been long ago, a Saturday morning when she joined him for fishing or flying models, and they ate a light breakfast first to satisfy Peggy. So many times she had come across him like this, reading, lost in his own world, relaxed and peaceful. So many times he had looked up with an offhand smile and a "Good morning, Laurie." Casual and careless always, dispensing the minimal attention due a bit player in his life.

But it wasn't all those years ago, and he wasn't her secret crush anymore, and he wasn't a boy with all his life and loves before him. And she was no longer a girl content to settle for a careless smile and the honor of cleaning his catches or watching him crash a model into the lake.

The world had changed.

Hands shaking, she fixed a bagel and brewed a cup of tea. He lifted his head when she opened the door, and his eyes met hers as she came down the terrace stairs and across the flagstones to the table.

He rose immediately, silently, his book forgotten. In the morning light, she saw further evidence that he was no longer a boy. She saw the remnants of their broken sleep around his eyes, she saw his eyes flare with an awareness she didn't dare consider, and….

And the world shifted again. He stood there before her, no longer Diana's boy knight or Francie's young demon lover. In the darkness, this man had met her equal to equal on the vast plain of desire.

His voice, low, husky, "Good morning, Laurie." And he took the bagel and tea from her, placed them on the table, and turned back to enclose her in his arms.

I have wanted you across these years, I have waited to step into your arms. Now you're here, and you're mine, and what do I feel? What do I say?

His hand rested warmly against the small of her back, stroking her, comforting her. That lovely, reassuring gesture melted her body into his. She lifted her face to kiss him, and with that he too relaxed. Perhaps he had wondered too about this first meeting, perhaps for him also the world had shifted on its axis. She tasted coffee on his mouth; she felt the warmth of his body along hers, and a sudden glorious certainty glowed luminous in her blood.

"Good morning to you too," she murmured against his shirt.

He smiled down at her. "I thought I was going to have to drag you out of bed. Did you get enough sleep?"

"No," she admitted, and then it was all right. He guided her to the table with his hand still warm against her back, and she knew in relief that he didn't know, the nightmare ending hadn't happened after all. "But I got more than you did. Richard – you look so tired."

He caught her gaze and held it as he sat down opposite her, an aware, knowing look that told her he well remembered the feeling of her body against his. "I'll pay for it later," he said, "but it was worth it, by God, it was worth it indeed."

She felt the blush creeping up into her face at the frank look in his eyes, and she wanted to drop her gaze. But no, that was the reaction of a girl, and she had been a woman now in this man's arms. She had told this man that she loved him, she had confessed her heart to him, she had welcomed him into her body. And in the light of day, face to face with him, she was not sorry.

She sipped her tea steadily. "Maybe you should grab a nap later."

"Or an early night," he returned, equally steadily. Oh, what a wonderful idea... an early night together, and forget her failure of the night before. She'd make it up to him tonight. "Actually, I wanted to talk to you about that. We need to talk, Laurie."

We need to talk.... No, no, no....

Dear God, was he going to tell her it had all been a horrible mistake, he'd changed his mind, had second thoughts.... Let her down easy, because she was still the friend of his youth? But he was still looking at her gently, openly. *It was worth it, indeed.* He had meant that. He had kissed her this morning in welcome, and not as a friend.

She was not going to panic.

She made herself keep looking at him. "I'm here, Richard."

Now it was his turn for silence. She watched as he bought himself time and space by pushing his book away, tasting his coffee, brushing aside bagel crumbs. What was he composing in his mind as he leaned forward, shifting ever so slightly to get the sun out of his eyes?

"There was—" he began, and paused. "When I came back here

last night, I didn't intend," he gestured, "what happened. That wasn't my intention at all. I shouldn't have left you, Laurie. No matter what had happened between us, I shouldn't have left you alone, not after what you went through yesterday. I realized that once I got home. I just left you here, part of the debris of – this whole damnable mess, and I couldn't let you face that by yourself."

He stopped and waited for her. She had to say something. And the honesty in him demanded the same of her. "I thought," she moistened her lips, "I thought – when you left – I thought that was the end."

"And it nearly was," he said. "I realized that, if I didn't come back, we were finished. We'd never survive the way we left things."

She saw the truth of that. She'd laid too heavy a burden on him, she saw now, with that desperate confession. She had made it impossible for them ever to meet again, except....

Her heart was beating fast now. She took all her courage in hand. "Richard—"

He looked at her, and waited.

She gestured blindly, and to her horror she felt the burning of tears in her eyes. "But you came back. And you – you said that there was no going back. That sex changes things." Oh, God, she was not going to cry! She was going to face this squarely. After everything else she'd endured, she *would* face this. She said desperately, "Has everything changed?"

Silence. She blinked away the sting in her eyes and stared hard at him, across the table, across the whole of their lives, and waited for the answer she could not read in his eyes.

He said quietly, "That's up to you."

She drew a painful breath.

Richard's hands closed around hers, and she surrendered to the warm, firm touch of his fingers on hers. "I was wrong last night," he said, "wrong for more years than I want to think. You were right, I never saw you. But I do know I'm doing the right thing, Laura, when I tell you that you can decide that last night changed nothing. If you want to write off last night as an experiment—"

"No—"

"We can, you know." He overrode her words, ignoring the way her fingernails were digging into his hands. "We can decide that last night we laid some old ghosts, satisfied some old curiosity. We grew up together, and it's only natural that, after all these years apart, our friendship has turned into attraction. But we can take care of that.

We can sit here rationally and decide that last night changed nothing, and we put it aside and go on from there. And, I promise you, we can make that work."

Her heart sank.

"Or," he continued, "we can decide that there's no going back, last night changed everything. We can go forward, see what we have to give to each other. Laura," and his voice made her look at him, "it is up to you."

She wanted to look away, but couldn't. She whispered, "What do you want to do?"

"What I want," Richard said, "is to do what you want."

"I don't—" and now she had to look away. She couldn't stand to keep looking at his unflinching gaze. "I don't want last night to have been – some kind of casual sex – it wasn't, was it?"

"No," said Richard above her bowed head. "I've never had casual sex. I've never made love with a woman I didn't care about, and last night was no exception. Laura. Look up at me, Laura. It wasn't casual."

She regained her voice. She *had* to say it; she couldn't let it languish unspoken between them. "Last night – last night I told you I loved you."

The gift so long unclaimed… and did he claim it now? Or ever?

He took a deep breath, and his eyes turned grave and distant. "I know," he said, "and of all the gifts you've given me, that one I deserve the least. I've abused your feelings for me for longer than I want to remember. But, after all that, you still love me. And – and of course you want it returned, don't you? I wish I could say it, Laurie. But I can't. I just don't have it in me anymore."

The morning stood still. She didn't breathe.

"I was in love once," he said, "you know that. I've been in love with one woman in my life, and what a disaster that turned out to be. I don't trust being in love. I don't trust feeling that the world is well lost for love, because I nearly lost the world for it, and it wasn't worth it. Still—"

He lifted a hand and touched her hair. She lifted her free hand and held it to his, and she felt the lifeblood in his wrist against her face.

"It felt very right waking up beside you this morning." And now the distance had dropped away from his eyes. "The world has felt very right for the last couple of weeks, ever since you came home. Dear God, Laurie, I never realized how much I missed you, what a hole you left in my life. Maybe I'll never be in love with you, maybe I'll never be able to give you all that you want and deserve, but I do love you, you're part of me and part of my life, the best part too. When I think back to the best moments of my life, you were always a part of those, you're as interwoven into my life as the air and the sun here in Virginia, and that's worth a lot to me, and we can build from there – if you want to."

So it was up to her, as he had said. She thought, a wisp of a thought to tuck away and take out later to ponder, that he had laid his heart in her hands, no matter that he thought he hadn't a heart to lay.

She didn't trust her voice. She nodded vigorously, and held on hard to his hands.

"Then," and she heard him controlling his voice, "we certainly owe ourselves a chance."

Joy sparkled in her blood.

She wasn't aware of her movement, that she stood up or that he pulled her towards him, but somehow she ended up in a rush in his arms, on his lap, her arms around his neck, her cheek against his hair, his head resting warmly against her breast. And for all that he could never love her – he held her tightly against him, as if he could never let her go.

"All right," Richard said presently, when they came back to themselves and reality, and she was warmly tucked in at his side, "let's get busy. What are your plans for today?"

He sounded so businesslike that Laura decided to have some fun. She had precious little experience in flirting with him, anyway. "To see if you can repeat your performance a third time in twenty-four hours."

He had been pulling out his Blackberry, so her words caught him off guard. She watched with interest as a dull color hit his cheekbones. "I said today, not tonight," but his mouth was twitching in laughter. "Any plans?"

She helped herself to the remains of his bagel. "Nothing that can't wait. Why?"

"I thought we might get out of here for the weekend." He was consulting his Blackberry. Oh, heavens, so he was as gadget-happy as Cam... she had much to learn about this man. "Julie said you like antiques. There's an antique fair up near Gettysburg and another at Charlottesville. We could go up to Pennsylvania first and then come back down this afternoon and stop in at the other one."

She didn't need time to think. "I'd love to. Are you going to fly us?"

"Yes. We can stay in Charlottesville tonight – I know a great B&B, and then—" he gave her a smile, "I made you a promise years ago that I didn't keep, that I would show you Monticello. I'd like to take you there. Next to Ashmore Park, it's my favorite place in the world."

A romantic weekend away… and more of his heart. "Give me ten minutes."

It took thirty minutes, though, to pack, set out food and water for Max, and leave word that she would be gone. Laura pondered the wording of her email to Meg and Mark – how much truth to include? – but then wrote tersely that she was going for a long drive in the mountains and not to call her unless there was an emergency. She'd hear from one or the other soon enough.

Oh, and wasn't *that* going to be a pleasant conversation… *I'm going away with my lover, no one you've met, but he has been the defining arc over my life…*

She spared a moment for a practical matter. A quick glance at a private calendar on her computer confirmed that last night was safe; she had nothing to consider for another few days, long enough certainly to get through the weekend. But by the end of the week she was going to need that diaphragm tucked in the upper right drawer of her dresser in the London flat. She wrote a quick email to Terry, who had an extra key.

Laura clicked *Send* and had a sudden mental image of Terry's face when he received the message. No doubt he and Roger would fire back emails demanding details after they sent her package on the next plane. She powered down her computer and looked across the room at Richard, pacing around while he called for a reservation for the night.

All this technology, she thought. Two hundred years ago, she might have written a quick letter and run off with her lover on horseback, turning their backs on a world that would have roundly condemned their liaison. Now… cell phones and call forwarding to shield their location from discovery, and emails to summon birth control on the next transatlantic flight – all the trappings of a modern couple, and yet here they were in this old-fashioned room, engaging in a timeless lovers' gamble. *Will I win your heart? Will you love me?*

Richard finished his call. "We're in luck. One of my professors and his wife run a B&B in Charlottesville, and they've got their best room open."

She wondered if the professor had ever met Diana, and immediately shut away the thought. *He's mine now. She doesn't count anymore. Not after what she did to him.*

"Just one more call," he said. "I need to send Julie over to Lucy's for the weekend. She wasn't awake when I went home this morning."

For most of the night, Julie Ashmore had sat waiting, arms wrapped around her knees, listening for her father's return.

Something terrible was happening. She could feel it.

It had happened at her grandfather's house earlier that day. The sight of Laura's car outside the house had surprised her, at first, as she drove past, and only when she slowed down did she notice the front door standing open.

And, when she'd parked next to the Jaguar, she'd seen the splashes of red on the veranda.

She'd stood outside, screaming for Laura, for ages. Her throat still hurt. But no one had been in the house, no one alive at least, and all the time she screamed with answer only from the birds, she had remembered the last time blood had stained this house.

Finally, because she had to know, she'd taken the only weapon in the trunk, a lug wrench. Heart beating so hard that it hurt, that she could scarcely breathe, she had entered the house. Eyes darting constantly, making sure that her back was covered – she hadn't watched hours of television drama for nothing – she'd searched through the house.

Her mother's tote bag lying carelessly in the music room had brought fear high into her throat. And the room itself – she'd seen right away that things were slightly out of place, sheet music in disarray, the piano bench pulled out, the metronome no longer front and center. She'd dropped the lug wrench in favor of the metronome, because those ugly spikes could inflict far more deadly damage, and she'd crept upstairs in search of Diana and Laura.

Diana and Laura. Two sisters. One not quite right in the head – she knew that, no matter how it hurt to think that about the woman who had given her birth – and the other still a stranger, subtly mysterious, subtly dangerous in her secrets. What had happened between them that blood stained the house and her mother's car was missing?

Then, in Diana's room, she'd found a horror beyond imagination. Even a body, she thought now, rocking herself in the heart of the night, would have been less terrifying. At least she would have *known*. But no fallen sister had haunted the room. Only a shattered mirror, shards of glass lying on the floor, and a gold silk ball gown damaged forever by bloodshed.

Had Diana turned on Laura, or Laura on Diana? And why?

She'd torn downstairs and called her father in Charleston. He'd been mildly irritated at first at being called out of his meeting; his irritation had turned to alarm as soon as she'd stammered out what she had found. "Get out of there!" he'd snapped. "Now!" And she'd dropped the phone and run to the car, conscious now of her stupidity in entering a deserted house where horror hung in the air.

And then – silence. She'd driven home as fast as she could, car doors locked, and run into the house as if all the furies pursued her. And there, protected by the fortress of land and security gates and passworded keypads, she'd waited in silence for word.

Surely her father would return soon.

Tom's phone call mid-evening had broken the silence, but despite the urgency in his voice, he told her nothing. "Tell him to page me. Doesn't matter how late. I have to talk to him ASAP." And she'd dutifully written the note for her father, and worried what was keeping him.

The house was still. She didn't mind being alone. Now that she had her license, Richard no longer obsessed about leaving her by herself if he had to work late. Normally, she welcomed the solitude; she could play her CDs as loud as she wanted, dance around the living room, and watch junk movies on the satellite TV. She could play the piano in the conservatory and shake the rafters. She could call anyone she wanted for as long as she wanted. She could chat on the Internet without her father asking her what she was doing.

She found solace this evening at her piano. She hadn't practiced in a couple of days – not since Laura had ripped off good-Julie's mask – and she had a lesson the next day. Out came Tchaikovsky, and for two hours she immersed herself in notes and arpeggios and pathos.

When the bulb in the lamp burned out and thrust her into the twilight of a darkened room, she ignored it and kept on playing.

She kept part of her mind disengaged, listening for the faint hum of Richard's car.

Then – late, later than she would have ever thought – she heard him pull up in front of the house. She traced his footsteps up the steps to the door; she heard the front door open. And, in the light filtering in from the great room, she saw him toss his suit jacket down on the back of the sofa.

Any thought she had of coming out into the light, asking what had happened, vanished. She had never seen her father look that way before. He looked exhausted; he looked, beneath the grimness, strangely vulnerable, and she thought that, maybe, something terrible had happened to him too.

He looked – he looked as if he had lost something precious.

Diana? Was she dead? Oh, God, no....

He crossed the floor to his office area. He always checked his messages when he came in; he'd log in and read his email, and of course he'd see the sign taped on his monitor. Trapped in the darkness, she huddled as he called Tom, and gradually she realized that, whatever had happened earlier, that wasn't the urgent matter that had so alarmed Tom.

And what she heard, she tucked away.

That birth certificate... Plane crash? What plane crash? That's not what she told me... I saw Francie then... She'll lie if she has to testify.... Richard hanging up, covering his face in his hands, and after a while, pulling a notepad towards him. The second phone call. *File for divorce... she drops any threat of custody... I'll waive any claims of adultery against her, if she'll do the same for me... will not have Laura harassed... Have her served. It will scare the hell out of her... No fake suicide attempts.*

Fake suicide attempt. Julie, sitting at her piano, felt sick.

And divorce. He was actually doing it. He was divorcing Diana.

Whatever had happened today, Diana had finally pushed him too far.

Had she tried to kill herself? Had she tried to kill Laura?

Was she all right? Was she dead? *Well, of course, she isn't. He wouldn't be filing for divorce if she'd killed herself.*

When he rose from his desk and went upstairs, she seized the moment. The moment his door closed, she sprinted into the kitchen and ran up the kitchen stairs to the landing. Ten short steps, and she was in her bedroom, breathless, heart pounding, tears streaming down her face.

She flung herself down on her bed and cried.

During the firestorm – grief at the end of the whole sorry saga of her parents' marriage, heartbreak at the death of any hope for a fairy-tale resolution – she had barely registered the sounds in the house. She heard the shower running, heard her father moving around in his room. Later, as her sobs faded and she buried her hot face in the cool pillows, she heard him going back down the stairs.

And then – shock – the front door closed, and the Lexus purred as it left the driveway.

Julie kept vigil, but her father did not return all night.

She fell asleep finally, so his early morning return caught her off guard. She scarcely had time to dive under the covers before he knocked lightly and opened her door. She pretended to sleep through his low "Julie?" and held her breath until he closed the door again, gently.

Dawn was filtering in through the blinds. Julie squinted at the clock. 7:05. Where had he been all night?

An unpleasant thought intruded, and she shoved it away.

It came back again.

He'd spent the night somewhere else, and now a divorce – oh, no. Another woman?

Richard Ashmore hadn't had a relationship with a woman in over three years. For a few years before that – Julie thought maybe since she was about ten – he'd dated that rare book dealer who kept sending home Judy Bolton and Nancy Drew volumes, so that Julie ended up with an impressive set of out-of-print girl sleuth books. Judging from the number of times he whistled that annoying song "Jennifer Juniper," her name was Jennifer; judging from the rare times that Julie answered her phone calls, Jennifer had a sweet disposition and a great deal of patience. Judging from the conversations she'd overheard as the relationship wore on, Jennifer had eventually run out of patience and presented her lover with an ultimatum.

Julie thought he'd taken the breakup hard. For several months, he'd seemed at loose ends. If he'd liked Jennifer that much, why hadn't he divorced Diana and married her?

"Because like isn't love," Lucy had said. "I'm not sure he'll ever divorce your mother. If he does, then someone important has happened to him."

I have to tell Lucy about this.

No problem with calling Lucy in private, though. Within half an hour, Richard left again. This time, his daughter observed from a window, with an overnight bag in his hand.

The summery hills of Virginia stretched out below them like a verdant tapestry. Woods guarded the ribbons of highway running through the Peninsula; small neighborhoods broke up the landscape; an occasional great house stretched before an expanse of land running down to the James. From the air, it looked like a grassy quilt laid on the earth.

Air space over much of the Peninsula was restricted, Richard had explained. They'd fly a zigzag course along the Peninsula to avoid the military bases until they drew closer to Richmond, and then they would turn north. "You're going to think we're flying too low," he'd added, "unless you're used to flying in private aircraft. Don't worry."

Laura nodded; she'd flown with Cam numerous times back in their early marriage. Even so, she discovered once they were airborne and climbing in the Bonanza, she'd forgotten how truly close to the ground they seemed, compared to the distance seen outside an airliner window. They swooped first over Edwards Lake and then Ashmore Park. From the air, the Folly seemed like a model; Ashmore Minor looked like a dollhouse in the morning sunlight. She saw the gardens and the steps leading up to Ashmore Magna, the enormous stable block, the back gardens stretching out for acres, the family graveyard next to the old slave chapel with the oddly slanting roof.

Richard spoke into the headset. "We've got an hour of flying time ahead of us. Try to get some rest before we get there."

Her throat still ached and her hand still stung from the day before, so she nodded. Richard gave her a slow smile before turning his attention back to the instrument panel. Laura donned her sunglasses to block out the glare and settled back in her seat.

But she couldn't sleep. She'd never been able to sleep on an airliner or a private jet; her manager had learned never to book her on a flight the day before a show. The Bonanza was smaller, noisier. She was closer to the vibrations of the engines now than she ever was in first class. Still, the warm sun spilling in through the windshield lulled her into a quiet dreaming wakefulness.

Her body felt more alive than it had in years. The warmth of the sunlight touched her lightly, as he had touched her. She felt the light cotton of her dress lying on her body, across the breasts he had kissed, across the thighs he had explored.

She wondered if he felt the same acute awareness this morning. His hands, now competently guiding their plane through the skies, had known her skin as the sun now knew it. His lips, now set in concentration on his flying, had drawn down her spine. His body, now decorously hidden in the weekend wear of the suburban professional, had pressed her into the featherbed.

She let her fingers trail towards her locket, in remembrance of his fingers trailing across her, and felt a moment of pure joy, in remembrance of his head against her breast that morning.

Tentatively, exploring her new rights, she touched his sleeve. His quizzical glance softened and warmed as she stroked him through the sleeve and then leaned over to kiss the spot she had stroked.

She felt his lips against her hair, and then he returned to flying, and she settled back.

But sleep was still an impossibility, so she turned her face towards him and watched him through her lashes. Unexpectedly, she felt the dissonance she had felt earlier, that a stranger had stepped from behind the familiar mask. She had accused him of never seeing her, Laura thought, was she herself guilty of never truly seeing him? Had she always seen him through the prism of Diana and Francie?

But, of course, he was now hers as he had never been Diana's or Francie's. She had her own acknowledged claim on him, and not only from the language of passion of the night just past. *The best moments of my life… the air and the sun.* Moments of innocent friendship, and to this man, so terribly betrayed by the woman he loved, friendship had become more important than love. Still, the best moments? Shouldn't his best moment be like hers, the moment he first held his child?

Richard's hand moved the stick lightly, and the airplane began to bank.

But Julie was not his child.

Laura felt a mental jolt at the thought.

And, then, from the past, she remembered that moment in time.

Diana was coming home from the hospital with her baby. Peggy had gone up to Charlottesville the day before, so Laura and Francie had ridden up with Philip and Dominic. Francie had spent the entire ride buried in a book. "Aren't you excited?" Laura had asked, and Francie had shaken her head sharply.

Okay, so Francie wanted to sulk. Fine. She was thrilled. She was now a bona fide aunt, and no longer the youngest one in the family. And a girl! Just as well. Diana, intensely feminine, wouldn't know what to do with a son, and Richard would adore a daughter. She couldn't wait to babysit her niece.

Everyone went to the hospital to visit before Diana was discharged, and strangely, Richard had not been in the room with his wife. Laura went in search of him, and some instinct drew her to the nursery window. He'd been standing there alone, hands jammed in his pockets, staring through the glass. The spinning wheels of fortune had carried him farther away from her than ever. Her Prince Charming was now not only a husband; he was the father of his very own little princess. His world now only tangentially intersected with hers.

But she'd never expected anything else.

"Richard," she'd whispered, touching his arm, and in the second before he turned to face her, she'd realized that he wanted to be alone.

"Laurie," he'd said quietly, and gave her a half-smile. "Great to see you." And he'd meant it. Whatever solitude he'd sought, he seemed eager to cast it away. "Where's everyone?"

"They're in Di's room." They stood companionably side by side, and she looked for a bundle tagged "Ashmore." "Which one is she?"

"Second from the right, last row." He pointed. "Can't see very much of her from here."

She'd pressed close to the glass, trying to see this small scrap of life that was, amazingly, her own sister's baby, and she was only vaguely aware that Richard had stepped back. She had the most discomforting feeling then, almost a disappointment in him, because surely he ought to seem happier or more interested in his own child, and he certainly shouldn't have left his wife alone in her hospital room. Was he upset because Julie was a girl? Maybe he'd wanted an heir for Ashmore Park, and Diana had failed to deliver the goods.

The notion of Richard as Henry VIII in modern dress made her giggle, and she turned around to share the joke with him. He'd laugh and tell her what a silly goose she was, and the tension she'd felt would vanish. Instead, her sense of unease increased as the three grandparents came walking down the hall and Richard moved to greet them, with that grave expression still on his face. Peggy and Philip made a beeline for the window, but Dominic stopped in front of his son-in-law and held out his hand.

And Richard pointedly ignored the gesture and walked past him.

Later, at the small apartment Richard and Diana called home, she found time to talk to him again. Most of the family gathered around Diana and the baby, leaving him apart and alone. Diana seemed in high spirits, not at all exhausted from childbirth, and more than willing for everyone to take turns holding her baby. She held court on the sofa, letting Peggy tuck a blanket around her, accepting Lucy's offer of a cup of tea, and apparently not minding at all that her husband was sitting alone across the room. Unable to compete with Diana's undeniable triumph, Francie spoke briefly to her and retired to her book, so Laura went to sit by Richard while Lucy and Peggy argued over who got to hold Julie next.

"What's it like?" she asked. "You know, to be a dad?"

Richard gave her a curious look. "I don't know yet," he said slowly. "I'm still getting used to it." As if he hadn't had nine months warning. "Why do you ask?"

She said honestly, "Because it must be the most tremendous feeling, to know there's this little person and you're the center of the universe to her. I envy you and Di."

"You've never talked like this before, Laurie." Richard seemed more relaxed now, not so stiff and distant. "Don't tell me you're going to chuck your great operatic career for kids. I thought you were going to set the world on fire, not tie yourself down," and his voice sounded strained, "to motherhood."

That last phrase told her a great deal. Diana must have complained that a baby might thwart her career plans. She said quickly, "So who says I can't do both? Have kids and set the world on fire? Women can do it all these days."

"I'd better not hear of you having kids any time soon." This from the college senior who had just become a father. "And you watch those boys in your class, Laurie. Not a one's good enough—"

Peggy came over to them, Julie nestled in her arms, and sat down. That stopped his warning dead in its tracks, thankfully before she had to admit that she was still too young to date. He must have forgotten that she wasn't even sixteen yet. And she forgot him, as Peggy put Julie in her arms.

She gazed down into Julie's tiny pink face and fell in love. Not only was this little creature Richard and Diana's offering to the future, this was her own flesh and blood. And how lovely and natural it felt to hold Julie against *her. She knew she was glowing as she never did, she knew that Francie might mock her later for her sentimentality, but she didn't care. She loved holding her niece, and someday, she was going to hold her own child just so.*

She turned to Richard eagerly. "Oh, she's just perfect!"

He had been sitting companionably beside her, shoulder to shoulder, as they used to sit on their Saturday mornings at the lake. But then his shoulder was no longer touching hers, and she saw in bewilderment the bleak look on his face. She couldn't fathom what flashed across his face for a moment, but was it – resentment? Good heavens, was Richard jealous? Of his own daughter?

Certainly not because he had to worry that Diana was going to love Julie more than she loved him. Diana hadn't looked over once to see where Julie was. Poor little scrap, her mother was totally self-absorbed and her father had withdrawn into himself. Or, Laura thought, trying to excuse his mood, maybe he was just apprehensive. He had never been around babies, and he probably didn't know what to do. So she said softly, "Richard, why don't you hold her for a while? We've all monopolized her."

She saw his deep in-drawn breath, his search for words. "I'd better not," he said. "I might drop her. She's pretty fragile, isn't she?"

So he was nervous. Laura drew on her years of babysitting and said gently, "Oh, you do it like this," and she laid Julie in his resisting arms.

For a moment, she was afraid that he would indeed drop Julie, but instinct came to the surface, and he caught the baby as she started to descend to his lap. Laura showed him how to support that tiny head, and it came to her then that this was really, truly, the first time Richard had held his child in his arms.

She leaned towards him to arrange Julie's receiving blanket. And so Peggy caught them on film forever, Richard making his first acquaintance with his daughter, and Laura by his side in loving support.

Julie had always enjoyed the contrast between her Aunt Lucy's public and private faces. In public, Lucy always appeared the consummate corporate attorney, in her correct navy blue suits and polished professional demeanor. How could anyone facing her in contract negotiations ever know that her favorite room in the house was her little study, with its feminine wallpaper and lush fabrics and African violets? And that the formidable Ms. Maitland became this comfortable woman in her drawstring pants and lacy camisole top and bare feet?

Julie wasn't sure if she felt closer to Lucy than to her father, but she did know that, with Lucy, she didn't have to be quite so perfect all the time. They could curl up in this gorgeous room with hot tea and cookies and gossip the day away. Lucy could lounge on the sofa with her feet propped up, and Julie could sit sideways in a big easy chair, her legs dangling over one arm, while they talked about anything and everything. Lucy could tell her about sex frankly and realistically, and she could ask the questions she wouldn't dream of asking her father. She could tell Lucy about making out with the one boy she had dated more than once, and Lucy wouldn't immediately ponder locking her up until she was thirty.

Today, they were discussing the unexpected turn in Richard's love life.

"All night. Hmmm." Lucy stirred her tea. "Well, that's very interesting. And he hadn't mentioned this antique fair till this morning?"

"No," said Julie. "And I can't believe he's left for the whole weekend. I'm going to music camp next Sunday, and you know what he was like last year. He stuck to me like glue that whole week before I left, and now he doesn't even care that this is his last chance to go riding with me for two weeks?"

Lucy leaned her head back against a pillow and closed her eyes to think. "Well, well," she said finally, "and to think I was worried – never mind. I wonder where he met this newest one. Has he bought any books recently?"

"Books?" Sometimes Julie had trouble following her aunt's thinking. "Well, he goes to the bookstore a lot, but I haven't seen him bring home anything new for the last couple of weeks."

"I say that," said Lucy, eyes still closed, "because they always seem to be connected with books, and you know how he loves to read. I think that's how he meets them. There was Jennifer with the rare books – and I'll lay you money he met her at one of those antique fairs! – and the librarian he met at the library fundraiser – that's the one I saw, wasn't it? – and didn't we figure out that the other one worked in the bookstore at the visitors center? So this one is probably a writer or something."

"Wow." Maybe going to law school taught you to look for connections like that. Or maybe Lucy was just thinking out loud. "This has come up so suddenly, though. Do you think he just met her?"

"Who knows." Lucy stretched out. "But this is very good news."

Oh, really? Just wait. You won't like this at all. "But he must be really serious about her. To meet her this fast, and go off for the weekend, and file for divorce?"

Lucy's eyes flew open. "What?"

"Didn't you hear?" Julie said innocently. "I thought you knew already, since you're Dad's lawyer. He told Tom to go ahead and start divorce proceedings."

"He's filing for real? And when did you plan to tell me?"

It was one of the rare moments when Lucy wished she had never given up her safe corporate position in the law firm to go into practice with her husband. She had wished more often that she had never agreed to do any of Richard's legal work. She should have seen this coming, she thought as she drove at high speed to their offices, she should have known that inevitably Richard and Diana's tangled personal lives would force her to choose one over the other.

Tom was no help. He had his priorities straight. He was Richard's lawyer, and it was Richard's lawyer who surveyed her calmly and told her to sit down and catch her breath.

"All right." Lucy dropped into the chair closest to his desk. "Okay. I'm catching my breath." She laid her hands on the desk. "Tom, how could you not tell me? You knew I had to find out!"

Tom leaned back in his leather chair and looked at her steadily. Oh, she hated that look, she knew what was coming, and she resented Richard putting her in the position where she was going to have to hear this. "How'd you find out about this? He hasn't told anyone except me, as far as I know. Did Julie hear something she wasn't supposed to?"

"Never mind." She had to protect her niece. "Why didn't you tell me?"

"Lucy," her husband said patiently, "there's hardly been time to tell you. He decided late last night, after you went to bed. You were still asleep this morning when I came in to draft the petition. I had every intention of showing it to you this afternoon—"

"I hear he's filing Monday morning. Why the rush?"

Tom paused a moment, and an alarm rang in her mind. She watched as he opened a manila folder and slid a document across the desk to her. "Here," he said. "Read that, and then you tell me."

Lucy took the subpoena and started to read, and her heart sank. "Oh, no," she murmured, and she looked up at him. "Oh, *no*. I don't believe this. Why didn't you tell me as soon as this got filed?"

"Because," Tom said flatly, "my policy is that you don't get upset, Lucy. Not while you're pregnant. I'm fed up with you rushing off to rescue Diana all the time."

Lucy swallowed hard. There was some truth to his comment. She seemed to spend a lot of time trying to put Diana back together. "I'm feeling fine, really I am. Tom, I don't understand this. What makes her think Laurie will cooperate? And what documentation does she have? Don't tell me Richard sent Francie love letters?"

Tom avoided answering that question. "Richard mentioned some music journals. Any chance that's what Diana is after?"

Lucy was reading through the deposition notice again, but she shook her head. "No way. Dominic read those journals. Francie couldn't have been stupid enough to write down details where he could read it whenever he wanted." She reached for a pad of paper. "Laurie must not have seen this yet, or she'd be calling me. Look, Tom, I know Richard must be furious, but let me try to reason with Di. I can. She won't pursue this if I tell her to back off—"

Tom was already shaking his head. "No, Lucy. You can't. You can't even talk to her about this. You're part of this firm, and we're about to sue her for divorce on behalf of our client. Richard has the right to expect our complete support, and that includes you not running off to mop up her tears."

There was no answer to that. He was right. Lucy swallowed hard and handed the folder back to him. "What about talking to Laurie? What's our position on her?"

"Well, as far as I know," Tom said, "she doesn't know yet. Once she's served, she'll want her own attorneys representing her. Now, technically, we should deal with them, but—" he shrugged, "she's your sister, and she's not an adversarial party. *Yet.* That may change."

"Oh, Lord." What a mess. She wondered, not for the first time, why Diana had chosen this spring of all springs to challenge Richard again. Diana ought to be thanking her lucky stars she wasn't facing trial for murder instead of pursuing legal actions that she wasn't going to win. "So what's the game plan, or can I know that? Are we just going to file, or do we make an offer?"

"Of course you can know." He picked up a pen and started to balance it between two fingers. "Neither Richard nor I want to keep you in the dark. We know that you're going to bear the brunt of Diana's reaction. We're going to file first, then let them approach us for an offer."

"Richard already knows what he wants to do, I suppose." She

hadn't dealt with her foster brother all these years for nothing. She came around Tom's desk and stood behind him as he pulled up the petition on his monitor. "Okay, that's fine… sort of mild, I guess, I expected something stronger than irreconcilable differences… property division looks okay. Custody looks standard. I don't know if we can get the good-behavior clause past the judge, though. Won't that be considered restraint of action?"

Tom seemed more relaxed now that the threat of emotional disruption seemed past. "Well, look at the compensation she's getting in return for behaving for five years."

"Yes, but whose definition of behaving? Richard's? Di will contest that. She'll say that an ex-husband doesn't have the right to set her standards of behavior."

"He faxed over a three million dollar appraisal for Ash Marine. Surely even Diana can keep from getting arrested or slicing up her wrists for that kind of money."

"That's his biggest disposable asset. And he could use the money. I wonder why he isn't stopping her allowance when Julie turns eighteen." Lucy bit her lip. "Slicing her wrists? Isn't that a little strong? That was years ago."

"That's his condition. He specifically mentioned it." Tom moved his shoulder to give her access to Richard's faxed notes. "He had a couple of ancillary demands – drop the subpoena against Laura – here it is. No fake suicide attempts. Those are his words."

"I wonder why." Lucy wandered over to the window and leaned against the sill. Her husband turned his head to look at her. "Tom, is something going on here that I need to know about?"

He settled back in his chair. "What do you mean?"

Oh, she hated that, answering her question with another, and meaningless, question. "I mean that this is out of the blue. Why now? All he has to do is wait two years, and he's home free on custody, and he can get out without paying Di a thin dime." She gestured towards his desk. "That offer feels like a man trying to buy a quick divorce. Richard needs that money for other things. What's the urgency? Does he have a girlfriend applying pressure? Is there some female he doesn't want brought to Di's attention?"

That last was a shot in the dark, but she caught the flicker of Tom's eyes and knew she had scored. Her instincts went on alert. "Look, I know he's seeing someone new. He's been traveling a lot this spring – lots of trips to Raleigh and Charleston on business. Maybe he's met someone down south? Or maybe it's the woman from London that he claims is such a figment of my imagination."

Tom said nothing, but then he wouldn't. It didn't matter. She knew she was on the right track. It was just a matter of thinking out loud until she found the answer.

"Okay, he's got a new girlfriend. And now he wants a quick, quiet divorce. He wants a worthless subpoena withdrawn, he doesn't want Laura testifying, and he's willing to throw a lot of money at Di to make her go away fast. Either Richard's trying to cover up something, and I don't mean Francie, or – he's protecting someone."

"Julie?" Tom suggested, and Lucy shook her head.

"No. Julie's safe. She's sixteen. No judge is going to go make her live with Di at this late date. You know," she twisted a lock of hair around her finger absently, "I can't see how Laura is threatened by this subpoena. It's going to be quashed anyway, so even the harassment is minimal. Her knowledge of Francie is all hearsay. She never witnessed anything, as far as we know. I just don't see," and she hesitated, feeling her way through her thoughts, "how it can be Laura that Richard's protecting."

"Why would you think it was?" Tom seemed too casual, and Lucy mentally smiled. Oh, darling Tom, he still hadn't comprehended, after eight years of marriage, the depths of her circuitous mind. "Laura is a bit player in all this."

"I say Laura," and she matched his casual tone, "because Richard and Laura are madly attracted to each other and are fighting it tooth and nail." He turned startled eyes on her. So he hadn't figured that out yet! "But I put the fear of God into her a few days ago, and I don't think Richard has lost his mind yet. Laura's too dangerous for him. It can't be her."

"I sincerely hope not," said Tom, and he sounded sincere too. "That's all we need, a relationship between our client and the witness who's been subpoenaed against him."

"*Cherchez la femme*," murmured Lucy. "A woman's behind all this. But why does a man blow the discretion of over ten years of waiting to get the divorce he can waltz into in two years?" She smiled and leaned across the desk towards him. "I'll tell you. *Cherchez l'enfant.* There's a child mixed up in this. Does Richard not only have a girlfriend, but a pregnant girlfriend to boot?"

Dead silence for a second. Then Tom laughed.

"Oh, Lucy." He was shaking his head indulgently. "Only you. He's going to love this. First you make up a love affair in London, and now an illegitimate child—" He stacked the folders up near his computer. "Look, I know the guy, and he *wishes* he had the time and energy for all the activity you ascribe to him."

"He had the time to spend last night away from home," Lucy said flatly. "He had the energy to go jaunting off for the weekend. And I find your use of the word illegitimate interesting, because that's not the first thought that came to my mind. If a girlfriend of his did turn up pregnant—"

"He's a little old for that, don't you think?"

"Well, it happens. Remember, the Jamisons got married in a hurry last year. Richard would want to put things right. He'd at least make sure Di couldn't make hay of it. After all," she stared him straight in the eye, "the thing we know about him, first and foremost, is that he will protect a child of his."

Tom stared her back, but it was too late to stop her. She was right. She felt it in her blood.

"That's it," Lucy said. "There is a child, isn't there? And I suspect this one is already born, because," she was thinking her way through this, "you used that word as if it had some meaning, and a child isn't technically illegitimate until it's born. And for some reason, Richard thinks Di may find out – in fact, he's acting as if he just found out himself—"

A horrible thought struck her.

"Oh, no," she said. "That subpoena. Maybe it isn't worthless after all—"

"Lucy," her husband said, and she knew then.

Francie, and the disappearance that had never made any sense.

Laura, and all those stubborn years of silence.

Diana, with this dangerous subpoena, forming the third angle of the triangle of sisters.

A child with dark hair, whose mother had inexplicably left her behind on this journey home.

Cat Courtney, and the elaborate identity shell game.

Of course. Not to keep out the world, not to protect a singer, but to shelter a child from discovery.

"That's it." Her hand covered her mouth in shock. She felt great tears welling up in her eyes. "That's why Richard wants this divorce so fast. He doesn't want Di finding out about Meg."

Tom rose and put his arms around her, and that one gesture of comfort confirmed everything. She clung to him, her steady rock in the turmoil of her family; he pressed her to him, warm and secure. And for a very small time, the world steadied.

"That's why Francie left, isn't it? She was pregnant. Did he know?" She looked up at him. "Tom, you must tell me. *Did he know?*"

Tom was silent for a moment, as if he intended to deny it, and then gave up and shook his head. "No," he said, "he didn't find out until Laura came back."

"Well, he should have known!" She felt suddenly, deeply angry with her foster brother. Forget that they'd grown up together; forget that they'd been each other's closest friends during their adult lives. "It's bad enough that he got involved with Francie, but couldn't he at least have been more careful!"

"Didn't you just say these things happen?" Tom was trying to be reasonable, and that made her madder. "You weren't this indignant a few minutes ago."

How would he like it if someone had gotten *his* sister pregnant? "It wasn't my sister then. It wasn't my niece. I know he was young, and sure he was miserable – but Francie was younger – she was eighteen, Laurie wasn't even that, and they were all alone, dealing with this—"

She drew a breath. Tom, wisely, didn't interrupt her.

"And none of us *knew*. I would have helped. They could have come to me. If I'd had a clue, I would have done anything to help—"

"I haven't gone into detail on this with Richard," Tom said carefully, "but you know him, and I know him, and we both know he never would have thrown Francie to the wolves. We don't have a copy of the birth certificate, but it's a dead certainty that Francie didn't name him."

"She probably didn't. Laurie must have adopted Meg. Tom, you tell him, he'd better not get any ideas about challenging Laurie for custody, or, client or not, I *will* fight him—"

"Calm down. He's not challenging her for his rights. He hasn't even told her that he knows. He hasn't indicated in any way that he intends to interfere."

"Well, that at least explains why Laurie married that man. This must have been the only way she could take care of Meg." So many pieces were falling into place.

"Possibly. She married when Meg was four months old. Lucy," he leaned back against his desk, "you *cannot* meddle in this. You know how he feels about his privacy, and he'll shut you out if you confront him. This is delicate stuff here—"

"I know." Lucy swallowed her anger. As much as Richard deserved it, she had to rally around and help. And she did feel a little sorry for him. He must feel terrible, knowing that he had fathered a child he could never claim. "But I can't help him protect them unless I know the truth. Is that why he's paying Di to behave for five years? Meg has to be thirteen, not twelve. It's not Julie's twenty-first birthday he's concerned about. It's Meg's eighteenth."

"I guess. I didn't ask him." Tom fell quiet in thought. "Now that I know about him and Laura —"

Lucy interrupted, "There is no him and Laura. They're just attracted to each other, that's all. And it's more her than him."

"Sure about that? She's legally his daughter's mother, and we know how he feels about Julie. If Diana weren't such a damn fool, he'd take her back in a heartbeat just to give Julie a mother. That's why he stayed with her as long as he did." That insight startled her. "In my opinion, Laura can be one ruthless character, and if she wants to play the motherhood card —"

"No." Lucy sighed against his shoulder. She was beginning to find her equilibrium again. The world had shifted, but she was learning this altered family landscape. "She won't. Now I am amazed that Francie didn't try to use Meg to her advantage."

And there was a thought to ponder later: Why *hadn't* Francie used Meg to win her way back into Richard's life? It wasn't like her not to use such an obvious trump card over Diana.

She said finally, "The one thing we can be sure of is that Laura won't use Meg."

"I hope you're right about that."

"I am," Lucy said with certainty. "Laura stayed away to keep Meg a secret. She's gone to great lengths to make sure we believe Meg is her child. I know my sister. Subpoena or not, she will never admit that Richard is Meg's real father, because that's tantamount to saying that she isn't Meg's mother."

"Well," said Tom, "for his sake, and for an easy resolution of this divorce, I hope they stay away from each other. The last thing he needs right now is to get involved with another one of your sisters."

Out in their small reception area, Julie stood stock-still.

19

Diana, Treading Water

So I moved back with Richard, and it was like going to prison!

For a man only biding his time until he could get a divorce, he behaved as if he actually had a stake in this child. The first night I was back, he ferreted out my stash of weed and made a big production of pouring our small wine cellar down the drain. Despite my protests, he insisted on going with me to the OB, although I refused to let him hear a single detail of what the doctor and I discussed. I was past the stage of feeling sick (actually, I'd hardly felt that way; for someone who hates pregnancy as much as I do, it doesn't bother me one iota), but I started showing almost right away. When I complained about not having anything to wear, he handed over our one credit card without any of the usual caveats about a budget.

On the surface, Richard was the perfect husband for a pregnant college student.

He even spent one whole weekend painting the spare bedroom in our little apartment, and he took it upon himself to scour the garage sales for a crib. I was shocked when he brought it in, actually; I'd forgotten that eventually this child was going to need somewhere besides me to sleep.

But – he never really looked at me, at least not below my head (well, being Richard, occasionally he looked at my breasts), he told me nothing of what was going on in his mind and his life (and I missed that, I truly missed hearing all his plans and dreams), and he never touched me.

Two months before the baby was due, he grew even quieter, and I noticed that he avoided looking at me altogether. Okay, I looked terrible, I knew that, I had eyes, but I'd looked terrible for months. So I snooped around his desk and found the letter from the lawyer at Student Aid advising that a divorce would be difficult to get. He had made the unpardonable error, in the eyes of the law, of letting me move back. (I could have told him that, from my research.) Even worse, he could not keep his name off the birth certificate; we were married, he'd had access to me around the time of conception.... ("Had access"! What a way to put it! But a few times, lying there in the dark by myself in our old bed, I wished he would abandon the too-short sofa, come back in there with me, and let the Standing Stone of Ireland take access again.)

He was at an engineering seminar when I went into labor, so he wasn't present at Julie's birth, but then I tried not to be, either. None of that earth mother, back-to-nature, drug-free martyrdom nonsense for me! I'd told my doctor that from the very beginning. Like everything else about pregnancy for me (unlike poor Lucy – what irony, when she wants a baby worse than anything), labor was not a big deal. I delivered Julie easily and in short order. By the time Richard found my message – *Gone to hospital to have baby, see you later, Di* – and came to the hospital, I was in recovery, looking down at Julie and wondering just who this stranger was in my arms.

I can't imagine what the recovery room nurses thought of our conversation.

Richard, stilted, awkward: "How are you feeling?"

Me, sore and just relieved it was over: "Have you called the family yet?"

One of the nurses, bustling over to scoop Julie up and hold her out for Richard's inspection: "So, Dad, do you want to hold your little girl?"

Richard, backing away, for once at a loss for words: "No!" And then, when he heard himself, covering up with "I don't want to drop her."

Well, to be honest, I didn't blame him. I didn't know what to do with Julie, either! Who in the world ever said motherhood comes naturally must have been a man. At first, I was so thankful not to be pregnant anymore that Julie held no reality for me. But then that blasted lactation consultant put Julie into my arms, and the poor child tried to nurse, and it was a disaster. I never could get her to latch on, and she cried non-stop. I gave up and went to the bottle right away. I'd failed my first task as a mother, and Julie and I both knew it. She seemed no happier to have me as a mother than I was to have a helpless infant on my hands.

Her name was another problem. The one thing Richard told me before he left the hospital that day sticks forever in my mind. "I don't care what you call her – just don't use my mother's name."

As it happened, I didn't care for Margaret Ashmore, the name or the person. "Fine," I said, and cast my mind back to the fabled Great Lakes shipping heiress. "How about Julia?"

He opened his mouth to protest; I could see it coming. "Hey," I said sharply, before it became necessary to remind him just who had given birth that day and who had been goofing off in an engineering seminar, "you said I could name her what I want. I want Julia."

That round went to me.

I could sleep on my stomach again, and when I wasn't sleeping, I entertained my visitors and enjoyed the limelight of new motherhood. I even had my own labor war story to tell now. The families, of course, all gathered around. Philip and Peggy adored Julie on sight and even went so far as to tell me what a good job I had done. Daddy said he was proud of me; at long last, I had done something right. Lucy begged to be named godmother. Laurie, poor, sad little Laurie who hardly ever smiled, turned into a different person when she picked Julie up. Even Francie seemed to accept this decisive defeat, although, as usual, stupid bitch, she couldn't resist getting her dig in: "Doesn't look much like Richard, does she?"

But *everyone* noticed that the new father was less than deliriously happy.

They made excuses, of course. They put it down to his sobering new responsibilities and his crushing class load, and even Daddy forgot he hated Richard long enough to offer him a congratulatory cigar. For a moment, I thought Richard was going to stub it out in his face. Julie and I came home from the hospital, with all the clan in attendance, and the only time I saw him smile was when Laurie talked to him. She even brought Julie to him, and he couldn't pull that afraid-to-hold-the-baby nonsense with the family's veteran babysitter. She just said, "Oh, you do it like this," and, lo and behold, he was holding the baby I knew he'd sworn never to touch. And everyone oohed and aahed.

Only Francie had the nerve to say, "Well, I guess he hasn't had much of a wife for the last few months."

I couldn't let that pass, even if it was true. "Francie," I said in my most cheerful, adult tone, "don't you know better than that? Don't they teach you anything in sex ed?"

"You can't have sex when you're pregnant," said Francie, fount of all wisdom. "It's disgusting."

"*Au contraire,*" I couldn't resist bursting her balloon, even if I had to lie through my teeth, "what do you think made labor start?"

She looked at me and then at Richard, and the sheer horror on her face was worth the lie.

I turned down Peggy's offer to stay for a few weeks and help with Julie. No way could I endure having her around, cuddling Julie, cooking for Richard, showing me up for the bad wife I'd turned out to be! I felt fine, I said, everything was under control, and I really appreciated her offer, but....

She looked dubious. "Richard says you're not nursing."

That bastard! My little sister had to shame him into holding Julie, and he had the nerve to criticize me to his mother for not being a lunch counter! But I'd never get away with losing my temper in front of Peggy. So I said sweetly, sadly, "I know. I was so looking forward to that. But," and I sighed, "I just couldn't get Julie to latch on."

Peggy instantly became sympathetic; she even gave me a quick, commiserating hug. "That's such a shame," she said. "Maybe with the next one, it will be easier. It's the most wonderful experience you can have with your baby. Nursing Richard was one of the highlights of my life."

I looked at my nice, meddling, Irish mother-in-law, and two thoughts came immediately to mind:

One, it would be a cold day in hell before I had another baby.

Two, no wonder her precious son had turned into such a devout breast man.

Well, *three* thoughts. The third was that I couldn't get my house, my body, and my life back to myself fast enough.

Everyone finally left.

That evening, after a few hours of peace and quiet, Richard came into the bedroom where I was giving Julie a bottle. I didn't have a light on, so the room was full of shadows. I wish the light had been on. I look back on that moment, and I know now what I was too busy to know then: it was another turning point in our marriage of turning points.

"Di," he said, with no preamble, "what do you want to do?"

What I wanted! What I wanted, more than anything else in the world, was to go back two years and erase the entire marriage. I wanted to be a kid again. But then Julie gurgled, and I looked at her, and it hit me then: this was real, this was permanent, there was no turning back the clock. This was real life.

"I don't know," I said. "Do I have to make up my mind this instant?"

"Of course not." He paused, and we had another awkward silence. "Do you want me to leave?"

Through the shadows, he could not see me panicking. Alone… with a baby… even as good a baby as Julie was turning out to be….

"Suit yourself," I said.

Another awkward pause. Then he said quietly, "I'll wait until you're back on your feet. I want to make sure—" Yet another pause. "I want to know that you and Julie are all right."

He never left.

For the first few weeks, he never approached Julie, never looked at her, never held her. I kept her in the bedroom, far out of his sight. Of course, given that finals were right around the corner, he was deep in his books, but he didn't even go to the library to study, as I might have expected. (He also curtailed his smoking in the house.) When I tentatively mentioned having Julie baptized, because both Daddy and the Ashmores were calling me up hounding me about it, he looked up from his drafting long enough to say "Fine," and he left all the details up to me. The families all came up again for the big day. Daddy took rolls of pictures, and, to this day, I hate looking at them. Not because of how I looked, because actually I didn't look half bad, but because Richard seemed bent on playing the invisible man.

And, then, the ultimate insult.

Julie liked him better. Richard's voice combines Philip's Virginia drawl and Peggy's Irish lilt, and it appealed to her. By the time she was just a few weeks old, she was starting to listen for him. The few times he reluctantly helped me out (although he always made himself scarce when it was time to change a diaper), she took her bottle better and fell asleep faster, lulled by that voice. I could see that he liked her. Maybe it was that protective streak, maybe it was just that Richard has always been a sucker for the weak and helpless, but he couldn't help himself. He liked Julie.

The great thaw began.

But not towards me. Here, I worked like a fiend to get my figure back, and everyone said I looked better than ever, but my husband didn't notice I was alive. He never talked to me. He scarcely even looked at me. Most of the time, I might as well not have been in the house.

I took that for a couple of months, and then I rebelled. I had cabin fever. I was tired of being in the house all day with a baby, and when my group called and asked when I was coming back, I said, "To-night." Then I called Lucy and said, "Let's go out to dinner."

Richard walked in the door, and I said directly, "I'm going out with Lucy. Watch Julie."

He startled me by saying, "Sure. Take your time, Di."

"And, by the way," I said sweetly, pausing at the door, "she needs to be changed." And I ran.

Lucy and I had a great dinner. Then I went to group and stayed late, I admit out of pure meanness. But, when I let myself in, bracing for whatever cold aspersions he could cast on me, my character, and my total lack of motherhood instinct, I found him stretched out on the sofa, Julie cuddled on his chest.

I looked down at them, contentedly asleep, oblivious to my pres-ence, and I felt an uneasiness crawling down my neck.

He and Julie were a twosome, from then on, and I was odd man out. Richard became human again, no longer the ice man, and grad-ually he remembered to smile at me occasionally. It didn't matter even when he did. I no longer mattered. He'd come in the door from class, and he'd head right for Julie's playpen. I'd hear his "How's my girl?" and I knew that I wasn't, not anymore.

I had created my own rival.

Francie kindly pointed it out for me, just in case I hadn't noticed, when we took Julie back home for a visit. "Looks like Richard's in love, Di."

Trust that bitch to rub it in! I fought the temptation to pinch her – after all, we weren't children anymore, at least I wasn't – and settled for an airy "Yes, Richard adores Julie. Isn't that wonderful?"

"I meant," said Francie, matching me sweetness for sweetness, "that he doesn't seem to pay attention to you anymore."

I started to snap back that everything was fine, and realized just in time that Francie was watching me oddly. There was something… calculating, assessing, in the way she watched me. She wasn't just angling for the usual jab.

So I took refuge in silence. I decided to show her that her remark meant nothing to me, that it hadn't landed its mark….

But it had. I could feel the weight of all those months of Richard's silence and coldness in my own refusal to answer Francie, and I felt, eerily enough, that she could too.

She watched me the rest of the day, always that strange, appraising look, and gradually I could feel my own anger rising. Bad enough that Peggy was monopolizing Julie, bad enough that I had scarcely seen my own child the entire day… bad enough that Daddy had started on my case about going back to voice… bad enough that all I heard from the Ashmores was how much Julie reminded them of Richard when he was a baby… but to have to tolerate Francie and those all-too-knowing eyes (and she was sixteen now, old enough to sense, old enough to *see*)… that was too much. I sat through the most interminable dinner, listening to everyone, knowing that Francie was staring, knowing that even Laurie was beginning to wonder.

Then Richard did the unforgivable. I don't even think anyone else heard him.

He asked Francie about her latest boyfriend. And that little tramp stopped staring at me long enough to say, "I'm still waiting for you, Richard. When are you going to wise up and dump Di?"

She meant it, too.

And, instead of being smart and saying, "You can rot in hell waiting for that, sweetheart," Richard merely laughed.

And then, *then*, that idiot said, "Good to know I'm still someone's standard."

And he winked at her.

And Francie aimed at me the most blood-curdling smirk.

And then she smiled at him and said, "Oh, please, Richard. Like you don't *define* perfection."

And he laughed again. And then he turned and started talking to Philip about a horse, and Francie lowered her eyes.

Mr. Perfect himself. Mr. Perfect Richard Ashmore.

I wanted to tear her heart out. And him…. I couldn't think of anything terrible enough to smash his face into. I couldn't think of anything harder than concrete, and by that time, concrete was an old, familiar image.

Peggy had given us his old room. For the first time in over a year, we going to have to share a room. We didn't even have Julie to buffer us; Peggy had snatched her away for the night, claiming grandmother's privilege. The nightgown Peggy had bought for me, long and silky and slinky ("When you're a new mother, sometimes you have to remember you're still a wife"), should have encouraged me. Instead, it galled me, as I got ready for bed, because I had actually thought… and Richard himself didn't seem to mind. He seemed relaxed; he started to talk about that damned stupid Folly and how

Philip was going to sign over the title to him…. I don't think he had really talked to me like that for ages.

And then his voice changed, got even deeper… I knew that tone. I'd heard that tone, in his car, at the cottage on Ash Marine, in my bedroom after he'd climbed the tree and I had locked my door against Daddy, in my college room when he had come in to help me with my math… I had heard that tone murmuring my name, while his mouth moved all over me, while he moved inside me… and then, *then*, he came over behind me and put his hands on my shoulders.

"My God, Di," I remember every word, every syllable, "you are so beautiful." And he dropped a kiss on my shoulder.

I thought of Francie and her staring, Francie and her barbed words, Francie and that triumphant smirk… And Richard, not having the good sense to keep his winks to himself.

I said immediately, "Get your hands off me."

We weren't standing near a mirror, so I couldn't see him behind me. But his hands dropped instantly.

He said nothing. The silence started off with a second, and then it grew and grew and grew…. I picked up a brush and started to pull it through my hair, and I felt my hand shaking.

I was schooled in silence, but even so, I had to turn around. He hadn't moved. He was staring at me, his hands hanging by his side, his eyes going blank before me, as they swallowed his desire for me and buried it forever underground.

He never approached me again.

That was sixteen years ago, and I know now what I didn't know then, because I focused so on Francie. I didn't understand him that night. He handed me the perfect chance to reclaim it all, to make good the past between us, and I – I threw it all away in a fit of temper at a malicious remark by a jealous teenager and a wink by a man who meant nothing by it at all.

If I could have one moment back in my life, that one is it.

I was very stupid when I was a young woman.

In the months and years after that, I often thought that I would do anything to break down the wall of politeness between us. There were no more fights. No more nasty comments. We went out of our way to be considerate of each other. Richard stopped smoking cigarettes around me; I stopped smoking dope around him. We did small things for each other occasionally. I ran errands for him, when he barely had time to raise his head from his books. I cheered for him when he graduated with top honors. He attended my senior recital the next year, Julie in tow, and stood by my side at the reception that followed. He helped me write my resume so that I could get a teaching job to tide us over the remaining year of his master's program.

We were a perfect couple, beautiful, considerate of each other, devoted to our child.

We had no heat, no passion, nothing at all between us.

Richard assumed that I was content with the status quo, so he went on with his life, which had nothing to do with me. He slept on the sofa. I slept in the bedroom. We made sure that we were always fully dressed in front of each other. We never brushed by each other in the hall. Neither of us ever walked into the bathroom on the other. And sometimes I woke up in the middle of the night to find my face wet with tears, wondering if this was all I had to look forward to for the rest of my life.

I didn't stray. I didn't dare.

I was afraid that, if I did, and we split up, Julie would want to go with him instead of me.

No one will ever believe this, but I loved my daughter. She was such a little sweetheart. She slept through the night; she didn't make a fuss when she got dragged out on errands; she sat there patiently, playing with her toys, during all the endless hours of my practices. On the nights when Richard had evening classes and couldn't usurp me, I bathed her and put her to bed, and some nights I just lay down with her and held that warm little body against me. On those nights, the little ghost voice fell silent.

But I got to love Julie only when Richard wasn't around. In typical Ashmore fashion, Richard had turned into the perfect father.

Oh, he scrupulously consulted me about Julie, but he clearly considered himself the primary parent. After the first time I said no to one of his ideas and had to endure an hour of explanation about why he was right and I was wrong, I didn't bother to second-guess him again. Julie needed a yard to play in? We moved to a rental house, and Philip and Richard spent an entire weekend building her a swing set. He didn't want Julie in day care? He and Lucy coordinated their class schedules so that Julie wouldn't have to stay with a babysitter; I, of course, got summers, holidays, and weekends. Julie had the sniffles? Simple, Diana, call in sick and stay home and take care of your poor sick child. Julie gave you a rip-roaring cold, Diana?

Well, you'd better go in and teach anyway, because you need to save your sick leave for Julie. You're tired and you don't feel like getting out of bed this morning, Diana? What the hell kind of mother are you anyway, what kind of example is that to set for your child?

I was too weary – and too intimidated – most of the time to resist.

But except for his ideas on raising the perfect little Ashmore child (instead of letting Julie grow up to be whatever she might like), I had no idea what was going on in his head, because he never talked to me, and he didn't seem to care what was going on in mine.

Talk about a deafening silence! I lived with such a silence until I couldn't stand it, and I fled back to my music group. To hell with my voice, to hell with Richard, to hell with my baby! I needed to be me again. No one in the group demanded anything of me except that I play like an angel during rehearsal and like the very devil afterwards. I didn't care anymore, and apparently Richard didn't either. The first time I came in stoned, his eyes narrowed, but all he said was that I'd better keep my god-damned drugs away from *his* daughter.

His daughter. Apparently my twenty-three chromosomes, nine endless months of pregnancy, and five hours of labor counted for nothing.

He scarcely spoke to me at all, the fall of his last year in graduate school. I was desperate for company in that silent house. Even Lucy wasn't around as much, because she had started law school and was studying almost as much as Richard. "Sorry, Di," she said after Christmas dinner, while we were washing dishes for Peggy, "I've got cases due. I've got to live at the library. Why don't you take Laurie back with you? She's good company. Besides, poor kid, she could use the break from Dominic."

Laurie! What a splendid idea! The more I thought about it, the better it sounded. Laurie was a virtual unknown to me, but what I did know was that she was nothing like Francie. She was quiet, sweet, and a good babysitter. She didn't spend all her time batting her eyes at my husband.

It occurred to me that I really ought to know my last sister a lot better than I did.

"Do you think she'll come?"

Lucy dried a dish, and she did it so deliberately that I knew, knowing Lucy as I did, that she had a purpose.

"I can't put my finger on it, Di," she said at last. "Something is badly wrong with Laurie."

"Oh?" She had piqued my curiosity now. "What do you mean?"

"She's changed," said Lucy. "Oh, she's always been such a little sober sides, but this last year… did you know she works every day after school in a bookstore at the mall? And Francie says she's out babysitting every weekend."

I thought that the answer was perfectly obvious. "She's trying to make money."

"Well, of course she is," said Lucy, and she sounded annoyed, so she must have thought it was obvious too, "but what for? Dominic bought her and Francie a car. Your mother's estate will pay for college. She's going to live at home. What does Laurie need so much money for?"

Well, I thought to myself, the winter of my senior year in high school, I'd had to blow every cent I had on *the procedure*, but I couldn't imagine Laurie in that fix. She'd been dating some boy during the summer, but that was over. Lucy had a point.

Well, if I hadn't spent it all on rescuing my future (and a great job I'd done of that), why would I have wanted a lot of money?

An irresistible picture came into my head: a wonderful little *pied-à-terre* in Paris, my piano for company, an occasional bad boy to fall asleep with. Free from Daddy and Richard and their oppressive desire to run my life.

The frisson of an idea drifted through my head.

Quiet little Laurie doing something radical like—

Like what? Making a break for it?

The thought seemed so alien that I shook it away. That was me, not Laurie. Still….

I went out to the Ashmores' great room to find this suddenly interesting sister and found that, once again, Richard had trumped me. He needed someone to do some heavy-duty typing on his thesis, and Laurie, eyes unusually bright, had just agreed to come back to Charlottesville and spend her Christmas vacation working for him.

(Honestly, what was it about Richard that we stupid Abbott girls always fell over ourselves to do his bidding?)

"If that's all right with you, Diana," Richard said courteously, apparently realizing that I was nominally the hostess of the household and might not appreciate an uninvited guest. But I was long past the stage of wanting to bury him in something hard and cold just because he had nice manners.

"That's great," I said, and I really looked at Laurie for the first time. Lucy was right! My withdrawn little sister seemed different, and not just because her hero had shanghaied her into doing slave labor for him. "We'll have fun, Laurie. I'll take you out and show you around when you're not trying to read his handwriting."

"I want to go to Monticello," said Laurie, and sneezed. "I want to see Sally's staircase."

"They've closed it off, but we'll go there anyway," said Richard immediately, but he didn't see what I saw, that Laurie looked different because she was flushed with fever. What maternal instinct I had came to the surface, and I laid my hand on her forehead. She was burning up. Within minutes, Richard had carried her upstairs to one of the guest rooms, Peggy had her tucked in, mothering and comforting her, and Philip was giving her an antibiotic shot, while Laurie protested that she couldn't be sick, Richard needed her to type his thesis.

"Why don't you do it, Di?" said Francie, hovering around Laurie with blankets and wet cloths, and looking genuinely worried. (I will give Francie credit for this. If she cared about anyone besides her own precious self, she cared about Laurie.)

"Because I can't type." Several sets of incredulous eyes swung my way. But what did they expect? I was a pianist and, reluctantly, a high school music teacher. I wasn't a secretary. I hadn't sworn to love, honor, and type his damn papers for the rest of my life.

"Really?" said Francie, as if she had never heard of a female who couldn't type. "I can. I'll do it for you, Richard."

And, all at once—

Me: "Oh, no—"

Richard: "Fran, are you sure you want to give up your vacation for this?"

Francie: "I'd *love* to help you out, Richard."

And Laurie, poor little Laurie, innocent catalyst of the disaster, sneezing again.

In that sneeze lay the end of our marriage.

20

Nocturne

DIANA ESCAPED SATURDAY NIGHT.

She'd waited all day for her chance. She'd awakened late morning to find a total stranger sitting beside her bed, reading a paperback, and that had upset her. She didn't like strangers in her bedroom. It was her refuge, her place of safety. No matter what her husband thought, she'd never entertained a lover there. She often shared someone else's bed, but she never permitted anyone access to her own. She'd waited too long, endured too much, to let another human being intrude on her in her bluebell solitude.

And this intruder was no lover, either. As became increasingly clear throughout the day and a shift change of nurses, the intruders were there to make sure she got some rest, change the bandages on her wrist, and keep an eye on her.

"Did my sister put you up to this?" she demanded of the evening nurse, after the woman marched her through a bath with all the delicacy of a drill sergeant.

"I don't know who called the agency," said the woman, probably a very fine nurse when her patience wasn't being tested as far as it could go. Diana knew she was being a bitch, but she was too mad to care. "Come on, let's get this done, and then back into bed. I think you're ready for another tranquilizer."

And me for a drink, the woman's expression plainly said. Lord, Diana hated nurses. Every nurse she'd ever met had seen her at some nadir – enduring the throes of labor, recovering from a particularly hideous hangover, shaking from withdrawal, or bleeding from an ill-advised swipe at her wrists. And every single nurse reminded her of the one she'd hated most, her blasted mother-in-law.

The thought of Peggy Ashmore stiffened her resolve.

"No." Diana wrenched her wrist, in the process of rebandaging, away from the nurse and back behind her back. "This is my *home*," she said in her most imperious tones. She'd gained something from all those years of Dominic's coaching; she could play the ice queen figure to the hilt. "You are here without my permission. Get that? *Without my permission*. Now who the hell authorized this invasion of my privacy?"

The answer, when it came, was worse than she'd imagined. Laura or Lucy were one thing; she could reason with them or at least scream at them without any real consequences. She could overturn their actions because neither had any legal rights concerning her. But the villain turned out to be Mr. Perfect, and he, damn it, had plenty of rights.

Even if he only exercised them when it was most inconvenient.

"Richard!" Diana sat down hard on the bed. "How the hell did he find out about this?"

"I don't," said the nurse coldly, "have the faintest idea. Time for your pill."

She wanted to wipe the smug look right off the woman's face. Judging from her tone, the feeling was mutual. But then she got a whiff of something… a trace of tobacco clinging to the woman's uniform, and an idea bloomed.

"Well," making her tone haughty, "I *am* rather tired." Too much docility after all the bitchiness might tip the woman off. She took the pill and pretended to swallow; the pill went immediately under her tongue. She climbed back into bed and switched the light off before the nurse could reach it. In the abrupt darkness, she spat the pill out into her hand before the woman's eyes could adjust to the sudden change of light. "I'll deal with all this in the morning."

"Fine," said the battle-ax, turning towards the door. "You can let the next shift notify Mr. Ashmore."

"Sure," said Diana, sounding more cooperative. And then, after a deliberate pause, "Oh, by the way – do you smoke?"

She saw the hesitation of the woman's silhouette, already at the top stair, and then the nurse came back into the doorway. "Yes," she said, "I do. Do you want me to go outside to smoke?"

"Yes, if you don't mind." Diana tried to sound helpful. "There's a balcony off the living room. Just unlock the French doors."

"Thanks." And the woman went downstairs.

Now she just had to wait. She calculated that, after their confrontation, the woman would need a smoke *tout de suite*, and she'd hear the French doors open. A cigarette should last ten minutes, going by what she remembered of Richard's smoking, time enough to dress.

She was in luck. The nurse turned out to be a chain-smoker. That not only gave her time to throw on shorts and shirt, but also time to fix her hair in her bathroom and transfer some grass to her purse so that she could light up later on. She opened the drawer where she kept her stash, and discovered that Laura had cleaned her out.

For a moment, she saw red. Damn that interfering –! Or maybe Laura wanted it for herself. Hmmm, now there was a thought. Maybe Miss Goody Two-Shoes didn't mind an occasional joint herself.

Except that even a joint-smoking Laura was unlikely to have helped herself to the bag of cocaine she'd hidden in a pair of shoes. Diana's mouth dropped open as she searched through her hiding places and found them empty of the drugs she had assembled painstakingly – and expensively! Did Laura have any idea what this stuff cost! – so that she could hold reality at bay whenever it got a little too insistent.

Well, that settled the question of where she was going when she broke out. She had a *major* bone to pick with her interfering little sister. Hell! Laura was an even bigger pest than Lucy.

While she fumed, the nurse had come back inside. She heard the French doors close, and she switched off her bathroom light and dove under the covers seconds before the woman looked in on her from the doorway. She made her breathing even and shallow.

It was another full hour before the French doors opened again. This time she wasted no time. She stole down the stairs, handbag and sandals in hand, and peered around into the living room from the foot of the stairs. Now to hope that Laura had left the Mercedes keys somewhere accessible – yes! Over there on her desk. She crept across the room, praying that the woman kept looking out over the Atlantic as she puffed away, back turned to the shadow stealing over to the desk.

The keys lay on top of a manila folder on the blotter. Diana's hand reached out for the keys, touched the largest key, and carefully lifted up the key chain. She dangled the keys in the air, pulling them towards herself soundlessly until her hand clutched them against her blouse. She slid them down her body and into her pocket.

One mission accomplished.

Her recorder lay there on the desk. She hadn't recorded anything in a couple of days, and she was keyed up and mad enough at Mr. Perfect to do some reminiscing tonight. This might be a good time to vent some spleen about Francie. She picked up the recorder and—

Damn! She must have made some noise. The woman stirred out there on the balcony. Diana melted back into the shadows under the stairwell and prayed that the woman didn't come back in. If she did – well, the game was up. There was no way she could miss her.

She saw the nurse's uniform in the glass through the French door panels, and her heart started pounding in her chest. Just when she thought she was getting away! But then the tip of another cigarette glowed in the dark. So Nurse Ratchet was still craving nicotine – really, the weakness of some addicts. Maybe she'd stay out there long enough to finish….

After a few seconds, the woman decided that all was well. The uniform vanished out of Diana's line of sight, and the cigarette tip waved back and forth amid the smoke.

She didn't waste any more time. She dropped the recorder into her bag, slipped her sandals on, and unlocked and ran out the front door as if the hounds of hell were biting at her ankles. Down the steps, into the parking lot... damn, where *had* Laura screeched the Mercedes to a halt? (*The brakes are probably shot, thanks again, little sister, learn to drive, why don't you?*) She fumbled for the keys and clicked the remote, and the lights of her car flashed on.

Ten seconds, and she was turning the key in the ignition, just as the nurse came running out onto her front doorstep. Diana didn't spare her a glance as she roared out of the parking lot.

Another minute, and the Mercedes blended smoothly into the highway traffic. Diana glanced in the rear-view mirror, but there was no one following her. No one! She was free. She heard herself laughing in delight, an unfamiliar, long-lost sound.

Delight. She hadn't felt that in a long, long time.

She headed up towards the interstate. By now, the woman was probably phoning the agency, and the agency would burn up the lines notifying Richard that his errant wife had slipped the leash. And, bloody hell, how had he found out, anyway? She had specifically told Laura that she didn't want him to know.

So she had *another* bone to pick with her younger sister. Diana settled back against the leather seat. Too bad if Laura had already gone to bed. It was high time she paid Miss Cat Courtney a visit.

And maybe she'd get her stash back.

Except Laura wasn't at Edwards Lake.

Her car was there. Her cat, peering out the window, was there. But, Diana discovered after a half hour of ringing her number, breaking in through the gates, circling the house, and throwing pebbles at the upper windows, Laura herself was not there.

Which brought up the interesting question of where Laura, minus cat and car, was spending her Saturday night. So she had a gentleman friend, did she? But she'd have to come home sooner or later to feed that stupid cat.

Diana settled down on a chaise lounge by the pool, stretched out under the starlight, and prepared to wait.

And while she was waiting, she might as well revisit that time when Mr. Perfect had not been so perfect. She fumbled in her bag for her recorder and flask, leaned back and looked out into the night sky, and pressed *Record*.

"Was I, the wife, the last to know?"

"We need to be at Monticello early," Richard said. "The tourists won't be out until late morning."

Laura sat on the side of the sleigh bed and watched him unpack his duffel bag, laying out a shirt for the next day. She kicked off her shoes and luxuriated in the feeling of free toes. After all the walking they'd done that day, it was sheer bliss to enjoy cool air on bare feet. "We don't qualify as tourists?"

He gave her a quick grin. "Not me. I'm a son of the Old Dominion. Now you, on the other hand – Irish immigrant or Texas matron or whatever you are – you're a tourist. You can gawk and take all the pictures you want." He put the duffel bag down on the floor beside an elaborately carved desk. "Do you want the bathroom first? I need to check messages and call Julie."

She fell back on the bed and stretched out her arms against the chenille spread. "I'd love a bath."

"Go ahead. I'll shower down the hall."

By the time she had soaked in an old-fashioned tub with gorgeous brass claw feet, deliberated between the short peach silk slip packed at the last moment (too obvious?) and the long cotton T-shirt she usually wore (too boring?), and examined her face in the mirror to make sure that the redness around her eyes had subsided, Richard had finished his phone calls. She tried on the peach slip and then changed her mind and donned the T-shirt when he called out, "Have you drowned in there?"

"Coming right out." Off went the T-shirt. On went the silk slip again. She drew in a deep breath and reached for the bathroom light.

Most women her age, she thought, were more experienced, that is, if they hadn't spent their sexual lives to date with a husband married very young. Marriage, even a marriage that worked superficially, offered a comforting familiarity. The routines of intimacy were established, the awkwardness of learning another's patterns over and done with. Sharing a bed was taken for granted. Coordinating baths and showers was second nature. A wife didn't have to worry about making the first move or learning a new rhythm of desire.

Without Cam, she would have had at least one love affair by now; she would have gone away with a man for the weekend before this. A shared room for the night in a charming B&B would not be a new setting for her. She wouldn't hesitate, wondering if she should just turn out the light and get into bed and take her nightgown off in unspoken acknowledgment of the night ahead. Or get into bed and wait for him to take her clothes off. Or walk right out there and take *his* clothes off—

Good heavens! That was what she got for marrying too young. She had no idea how to act with a man who wasn't a comfortable old shoe husband.

And the sad thing was, the world expected that Cat Courtney was exactly the sort of woman to walk out self-confidently, in eager anticipation of the night. She'd played Jane Eyre for months, and even Jane would run joyfully to Rochester's arms. Jane would never cower in the bathroom like the limp reality who lived behind Cat Courtney.

"Laura?" An edge to Richard's voice. "Are you all right?"

"Coming." She snapped off the light.

But then, Cat might have missed the heart-stopping sight of her lover sitting against the headboard, hair still damp from his shower, jeans unbelted, blue shirt hanging open, bare feet reaching almost to the end of the double bed.

Cat might not feel struck by a sudden, delightful feeling of pure lust down to her very fingertips.

He looked relaxed and younger than his years, and very masculine as he cycled through the channels with the remote. For the moment, he hadn't a care in the world. She forgot her trepidation and laughed as she climbed onto the bed beside him. "What is it with guys and remotes? Is it encoded on the Y chromosome?"

"You bet," said Richard, and settled on CNN. "We can't control the universe, but, by heaven, we will control our TV sets. And our women." He clicked the remote at her. "Come over here. You're too far away."

She scooted over and settled in against him. The headboard and pillows at their backs, two pairs of long legs reaching to the end of the bed. It would be a tight fit tonight, two tall people in this small, old-fashioned bed. They'd have to sleep very close together—

She breathed in deeply and leaned her head against his shoulder. The denim of his jeans lay warmly against her thigh; she felt the seams through the silk. "Did you reach Julie?"

"Yes." Richard sounded less than happy. "I sure did. And I forgot about her going to music camp next weekend. She was very understanding about it—"

Not too difficult to imagine Julie's sweet, wistful, deliberate thrust into his heart.

"—And she was planning to get new clothes for camp this weekend, and I forgot to leave her a credit card. So we'll have to get her kitted out this week." Oh, Julie was playing his heartstrings and wallet like a pro. "I should have remembered, put this weekend off until she leaves, but—" He gave her a sidelong glance and put his arm around her shoulders. "I'm glad we came. I'm enjoying this."

"So am I." Even though he'd ruthlessly marched her through two enormous convention halls of antiques till her feet ached, they'd had a good time. There had been no sexual tension, no thought of the tangled lives left behind them in the Tidewater. They'd companionably held hands, looked at old silver and Victorian fabrics and rare pocket watches, argued over the authenticity of a Tiffany lamp, disagreed vociferously about the attraction of a folk art cistern (she loved it, he thought it was a piece of junk), and relaxed over surf 'n' turf after their flight into Charlottesville. Both of them had turned off their cell phones. "So how many calls were Lucy?"

"Five," said Richard. His fingers rubbed absently along her shoulder. "Julie must have let something slip about my being away last night. Miss Infernal Busybody wants to know where I am and what I'm doing and, of course, she really wants to know who I'm with." He stretched out his legs. "She should be grateful I don't call her back and tell her."

Lucy. Laura tried to ignore the slight uneasiness that drew a finger along her spine. Thinking about Lucy led to inevitable thoughts of her other sister, who had no doubt awakened from her drugged sleep this morning to discover the ransacking of her cocaine stash. Diana, who'd said, *Richard and I are mated for life*. She couldn't bear to think of Diana, not now while she curled up next to Richard in bed.

She hesitated and then laid her arm across his chest, and was rewarded by his sudden stillness. "Lucy warned me off you."

"Did she now?" Richard clicked the TV off. "When was this?"

"Right after I got back from Texas this last week." His fingers moved on her shoulder, exploring the tie that held up the gown. Laura's heart started to beat faster. "We argued over it."

He turned to her, and now he wasn't the companionable man who had bought her the Art Deco pin she liked even though he thought it was a fake, or the laughing man who had dared her to order a large steak and then finished it off for her. She saw a purposeful look in his eyes, the look of a man who saw something he wanted and intended to go after it without wasting any more time. "Did you tell her what she could do with her meddling?"

"She thinks we're dangerous for each other." That didn't come out the way she intended, probably because her voice caught as she tilted her head to allow him access to her throat.

"She's right there." His voice dropped, and she felt his tongue trace the edge of her nightgown. "Hard to think of two people more dangerous for each other – I like this on you, very pretty, like the wrapping on a present – no, keep your hand there, I like you touching me—"

The lamp shedding a gentle glow on the room came within her reach as he guided her down across the bed. "Should I turn this off?"

"No." Richard put her hand above her head, away from the switch. "No, I want to see you." He brushed a stray strand of hair from her face. "Does the light bother you?"

She shook her head. Nothing bothered her right now, except the hand that was slowly, slowly untying the bow at her shoulder and drawing the silk down to uncover her breasts. He had closed out the rest of the world to her, his body leaning over hers to block out all other realities. His eyes were in shadow, lashes covering his thoughts, as his hand traveled down from her hair to the soft mound of her breast. She felt the tip harden as his fingers brushed over it, and desire shot through her all the way to her toes.

She couldn't stop the soft sigh in the back of her throat.

"Do you like that?" His voice had dropped even lower, lazy and knowing.

She liked it, of course she did, and he knew it. But maybe he wanted to hear it, and so she whispered, "Yes."

"You are so lovely – so soft and warm—" His fingers were gently shaping and massaging her flesh. He gave her a grin. "You've grown up nicely, Laura Rose."

Impossible to hang on to shyness in the face of his frank delight in her. "You told me once they were smaller than mosquito bites."

"Did I?" He tweaked her nipple lightly and studied its reaction. "When did I see—"

"I was eleven. We were fishing and I fell in the lake and lost my top. You said not to worry, no one would notice."

He laughed. "How ungallant of me. But – in my defense – you probably scared the fish off."

"Yes, you said that. But you let me wear your shirt till we got home."

"Oh, Lord. My careless youth comes back to haunt me." His lips traveled to the soft flesh on the undercurve. "Well, you can wear my shirts any time. Now – about your breasts – from a structural point of view—"

She was laughing now. "Structural? Are you planning to build yourself a woman?"

He shook his head. "Can't. Ask any architect. You can't improve on the female breast. It's nature's perfect structure."

Oh, she loved this silly, sexy pillow talk, and she loved the way he traced lazy circles on her sensitive skin. Who knew that Prince Charming could flirt so outrageously in bed? She stretched out luxuriously and rubbed her foot along his denim-clad leg. "I thought you guys worshiped skyscrapers. Bigger is better, or – um, something like that." Her hand traveled down his chest to the waistband of his unbuttoned jeans. "Speaking of which—"

She received a look of mock sternness, but he leaned into her hand. "Skyscrapers do not occur in nature."

"Oh, my mistake. I thought they did. Like this one."

"Besides," his voice caught for a second, as her fingers came trailing down his zipper, "do you have any idea how much trouble a skyscraper is to erect? You can only build on certain types of land – yes, like that – the permits are hell to obtain, half the time you have to resort to bribery—"

She whispered, "I'm easy to bribe."

Another indrawn breath. "I thought you might be – Laura, take it a little slower there—" He shifted against her hand. "And a skyscraper, once built, still has to make a respectable return on investment." She giggled. "Now the breast, on the other hand, has none of those disadvantages."

She kissed his chest. "Oh, you think so, Master Architect?"

He leaned over her again. "Well, let's examine the evidence objectively." His fingers molded and lifted her left breast. "Focal point equidistant from all points on the perimeter, so we have precise concentricity – perfect load-bearing weight distribution—"

"Not anymore. Gravity is already doing its evil work, I'm afraid."

He quieted her with a kiss. "Aesthetically pleasing from all angles. That's of paramount importance. Then, of course, it fulfills architecture's driving principle—"

"What's that?"

"Form follows function." And Richard lowered his mouth to her.

The rhythm was different tonight, they were different, relaxed from their day together. No frantic reaching out to claim each other before it was too late, no jumping off an emotional point of no return. Last night's storm had played itself out. Tonight was gentle, leisurely, fun. She could wriggle out of the silk gown, putting on a show like the most exotic of fan dancers, with an audience whose eyes glowed at the sight of her. She could insist then on wearing his shirt, which he surrendered to her on the laughing condition that she not button it up. He could lie on his back and let her draw his jeans down with excruciating, teasing slowness. He could reward her by covering her body with his own, kissing her long and deep, so deep that she felt touched by the sun all the way to her core.

And, in all those long moments of his discovery of her, she could explore him. He was an unknown continent to her, a beloved friend, now become a stranger, now become her lover. Her hands could run along his back, feeling those long muscles that gave him that incredible height. Her skin, against his, could feel the different textures between them – where she was soft and delicate, he was hard and masculine, where she was round and pliable, he was straight and unyielding. She learned that he loved her hands against the back of his neck – that he delighted in the flushed skin and shallow breathing of her own arousal – that he had a hidden weakness for the sound of her whisper in his ear, telling him what she felt and what she wanted him to do to her next.

She drifted into the later stages of lazy desire, warm and liquid and secure, and when he entered her, she enclosed him like a river. Her body surrounded him, her arms encircled his shoulders, her hands held his head to her. They rested there together, melded as one, in no hurry to accelerate into a great culmination. He seemed content to enjoy the ebbing and flowing thrust of the tide of desire, content to let her mouth trace along his shoulder—

She tasted him, and unexpectedly, her lips found a change in the texture of his skin. No longer the warm smoothness of masculine flesh covering broad shoulders, but something different, out of the ordinary. A strange roughness, a spot where the skin pulled together oddly, as if a wound had never quite healed right—

Her eyes snapped open.

Lost in the pleasure of their union, he didn't see her dawning horror as she looked at the wound on his right shoulder. A sudden, hideous flashback to a moment of blood and rage, a flash of light, a loud retort – his hand clapping to his shoulder—

She stiffened involuntarily, but he took that as her coming joy, and he surrendered to his own climax. Her mind froze, and then, without a second of hesitation, Cat Courtney stepped in and shut Laura down and took over. It was Cat, blameless that long-ago afternoon, who let herself flow into the swell of fulfillment. It was Cat, unburdened by destructive conscience, who snuggled against him in afterglow. It was Cat who kissed him good night and told him that she loved him.

It was Cat whose face he touched tenderly in response.

Laura found herself watching them both, her mind detached from what was going on inside and outside her body.

Afterwards, they fell asleep, two tall people wrapped together in a small bed. He slept first, exhausted from the day, his arm thrown over her to keep her close. She slept later, much later, and all night long she felt the remnants of his wound against her back.

"War."

Diana stopped.

She was out of breath, out of voice, out of memory on the digital recorder, and, she discovered, out of whiskey.

Maybe this made a good place to stop for the night. Obviously, her self-righteous little sister was off enjoying the fleshpots; repeated calls showed that Laura still hadn't come home. She didn't know what time it was – past midnight, if she read the time on her cell correctly – and she was getting cold.

She rubbed her arms for warmth.

Kevin had said to take the memory card out of the recorder when the red light started blinking, indicating that it was 90% full. She fumbled in her bag for the case, found the other memory card, and switched the two. Too bad Francie hadn't used this kind of recorder when she had made that purple prose tape for Richard – she wouldn't have known how to destroy a memory card, and then she would have had her evidence.

She picked up her flask, dropped the recorder in her bag, and rose unsteadily to her feet.

She couldn't go back to her condo; the Gorgon was probably still there, waiting for her errant charge to come dragging home. Lucy's house was closest – well, not as close as Ashmore Park, but Richard had told her flatly the year before to stop treating Ashmore Minor as her personal flophouse. The problem with crashing at Lucy's at this time of night was that she wouldn't be able to avoid Tom, and he'd rat her out to Richard.

So she'd have to go to Dominic's and brave the sight of the smashed mirror and the ruined ball gown in her room. She could always sleep in the twins' old room.

She started off across the flagstone terrace, heading for the gate at the side of the house, when she saw two eyes watching her from one of the back windows. Two small, glowing, unblinking green eyes with a strange transparency… she felt a frisson of fear across her skin. If someone had broken into the house… maybe something was wrong with Laura, maybe that was why she hadn't answered, someone had broken in and hurt her… she reached in her bag for her cell when the eyes turned away, and she saw the flick of a tail.

That stupid cat!

She caught her heel on an uneven stone, and she went sprawling across the terrace.

The fall knocked the breath out of her. She lay there, motionless, for a moment, before she began to hurt all over her body. Her knees, her hands, her elbows, her breasts… all had slammed into the unforgiving surface. She gingerly dragged herself to her knees and tried to force air into her lungs, but the deeper she breathed, the more she hurt.

"Damn cat," she said aloud. Just like Laura to have a cat to scare the hell out of you so that you didn't watch where you were going.

She'd spilled the contents of her bag. Through the night, she could see dark objects against the lighter-colored stones, and she crawled around scooping them up. Her brush, her cell phone, her recorder, a lipstick… she threw everything into her bag and rose painfully to her feet.

"Screw you," she said to the cat in the window, and limped over to the gate.

I'll get you, my pretty, interfering sister.
And your stupid cat too.

21

Diana, Discovering

WAS I, THE WIFE, THE LAST TO KNOW?

Probably. Of everyone who knew or suspected, I was certainly the last.

I have thought and thought about this over the years, and it must have started over Christmas vacation, when Francie volunteered to type Richard's thesis. I don't remember that much about that week, truly, and why should I? At the time, I never thought it meant anything. I never dreamed that I would spend years, going back over and over it in memory, searching for clues.

I thought of it as just a week to get through with Francie.

I don't remember smoldering looks or strange silences or anything at all.

What I do remember is that, for the first time in our lives, Francie was pleasant to me. That, of course, should have tipped me off, because that girl never did anything unless there was something in it for her, but maybe I was so sick of the silences with Richard, I was willing to take her at face value.

No smart-ass remarks. No rotten little digs. No batting her eyes at Richard. When he practically fell all over himself the first night back in Charlottesville, volunteering to take the sofa so that "you girls can stay up all night talking" (and who was he kidding? he knew better), Francie didn't raise an eyebrow or make one nasty comment when he went right to the closet and dug out the blankets and pillows with long-practiced familiarity. She even talked to me a little before we fell asleep, admitting that she was worried sick about Laurie.

"It's just flu," I said sleepily. "She'll be better in a few days."

"But she seemed so sick," said Francie, on the verge of tears. "Laurie's never sick. She's always so strong."

She sounded so concerned that I turned on the light and handed her the telephone. "Here," I said, "call Peggy. See how she's doing."

And, of course, Peggy said that Laurie was on the mend but was sleeping and couldn't be disturbed. Still, Francie seemed relieved, and I figured that, if it kept her in a good mood and off my back, it was worth the long distance phone call.

She worked hard too. Philip had bought a new PC for Richard for Christmas, and of course it wasn't like the computers now. It was bulky and slow, but Francie sat down gamely and went to work. It would have been my idea of hell, reading and typing all those engineering notations in that precise dissertation style, formatting all those footnotes and equations, but she did it, and she didn't utter a single complaint. I kept Julie in the bedroom, playing and watching videos, so that we wouldn't disturb them, and the few times I ventured out, I saw nothing suspicious. Richard wasn't even there half the time; he kept running out to the library or the architectural school to check citations, or going to the firm where he worked to get some drafting done.

I didn't have time to think about either of them, really. My group had been hired to play at a New Year's Eve dance in Washington, so I was tied up in rehearsals. Did anything strike me as odd when I came home? Not at all. No guilty looks, no springing apart… nothing at all. The only mental image I have is of Francie, typing away industriously at Richard's desk, and Richard usually across the room, working at our dining room table, books piled out around him, calculator at his fingertips.

If it started that week, it must have been during one of my rehearsals… or maybe it was on New Year's Eve. I don't know. We played at the party that evening, my group and I, and then, since we didn't intend to drive back until morning, we all got thoroughly bombed. One of the guys even came on to me, but I turned him down flat (that I do remember). I had no birth control with me, and he didn't either, and I wasn't about to get caught again – or hand Richard another bullet engraved with my name.

When we got back to Charlottesville the next morning, I found Richard, Francie, and Julie all having breakfast. And this is why I never suspected anything: Richard was hung over. Yes, it's true, Mr. Perfect had also gotten bombed the night before (on Daddy's champagne… Francie had bootlegged a bottle and then didn't like the taste and gave it to Richard to finish off), and since he wasn't an experienced drinker, he had not held it well.

He looked terrible. All dark circles under his eyes, and his face drawn and tight, his shoulders hunched beneath his sweater, not at all like a man who'd had sex the night before… and Francie was bubbling around, playing with Julie, who was twenty months by then and well into the "no" stage. That's what I remember of that breakfast, the next to last time that Richard and Francie and I were ever together. Richard sitting in morose silence, Julie saying "no" to everything, and Francie saying teasingly, "No! Gosh, you're all Abbott, aren't you, Julie? That's our favorite word. No-no-no-no-no. Bet you say that all the time."

And Richard, straightening up, and looking at me with chilled eyes.

So did it start then? It must have… but how could it?

I didn't see the other signs.

Richard, who really didn't know how to conduct a clandestine affair, practically advertised it in neon lights, and I was so used to him being perfect that I didn't see a thing.

Early that spring, he decided that he wanted his plane up there in Charlottesville with him. I remember my surprise… he'd always said that it cost too much to keep it there at college, but he just shrugged and said he missed his flying, and now that his thesis was in the hands of his advisor and he was doing his last seminars, he had time to fly again. Besides, he said, his internship required that he go to Richmond periodically. Why anyone would fly to Richmond, less than one hundred miles away, was beyond me, but I knew how much he loved his plane, and I figured that he was just grabbing at an excuse to fly it.

He also decided that Julie could go to a playgroup once in a while. I had been pushing for that for a long time, because I thought she was terribly isolated and I wanted her to be around other kids, so I didn't contest that. I even said, innocently enough, that putting her in the playgroup freed him up from having to rush home and relieve Lucy from babysitting.

How could I have been so stupid! Cell phones were too expensive back then, or I'm sure he'd have had one of those too! (Not that I ever saw the phone bill. After that time when I forgot to mail it, Richard had never entrusted it to me again.) All the earmarks of a man needing rapid transportation, with a gas gauge I could never check, and ensuring himself some unaccounted-for time. I never saw it.

I didn't even suspect a thing the day I was driving home from work, and I passed a car that looked a lot like the twins' car, with a driver who looked a lot like the twins, turning onto I-64. I said something to Richard that evening, and he said (feigning concern, the bastard) that Laurie had taken the day off, and he had taken her up to Monticello, since she had missed it at Christmas. And then he cautioned me not to say anything to Daddy, because Laurie had skipped school to do it.

(And I swallowed that! I was so dumb! As if Laurie would skip school to go traipsing up the mountain with Richard to commune with his architectural god! But, on second thought, she would have. That's why I believed him.)

So we drifted through that rest of that spring, and I taught school, and Richard went flying every Saturday, and Julie, my sweet, sunny-natured Julie, started having nightmares. (Did she know? Did she sense his distraction? Did she know, in her baby heart, that her father had disengaged mentally, emotionally, physically, from her mother?) We took her to the doctor, who could find nothing wrong with her, and he suggested that she might be suffering separation anxiety because she had a working mother.

Not because she had a cheating father.

Oh, no, of course not. It had to be *my* damn fault.

I did wonder, from time to time, as I made lesson plans and drilled the worst high school band ever put together, what lay ahead of us, once we left the cocoon of college. Thesis completed, Richard started entertaining offers from several architectural firms, and I had an opportunity for a composition seminar at UVA during the first summer term. He decided to accept a position doing commercial and public buildings, with a base near Williamsburg, and told the firm that he would report the middle of July. I saw that as a huge concession to me, so I could attend the seminar, and it touched me. It had been so long since he had acknowledged me as anything more than an inconvenient roommate that I even thought (in the dark hours of the night, in my lonely bed) that we might make another start once college was behind us.

How was I supposed to know!

It's hard to believe, even now. Richard, my straight arrow knight, hooking up with my slut of a sister. Other than the obvious signs that he practically hit me over the head with, he didn't seem different. I'd have thought that a man in the middle of an affair would seem happy or relaxed or at least looser, not so tightly controlled. Still….

He was a man, after all, not a boy anymore, and heaven knows, he liked sex, and he had gone without for longer than I cared to remember.

I can just imagine the web Francie spun around him.

Francie made herself scarce at Easter, when we went home to look at houses. I wanted something nice and modern that could take care of itself, but of course, the worst possible home buyer is an architect. Nothing measured up to Richard's idea of what he wanted; he didn't like the ceilings, or he hated the layout, or he found the property lacking in some way. So he and Philip made a deal about Ashmore Minor, and before I knew it, I found to my horror that I was going to be living a stone's throw (OK, half a mile) from my in-laws.

"This way, we won't need a mortgage," said my pinch-penny husband, and ignored my glare.

He went out alone a lot, so maybe he met Francie then. All I remember is, I hardly saw her, and when I did, she seemed smug, but then she always did. She had been accepted at Juilliard and took every opportunity to rub it in. I made sure she knew that I hadn't bothered to send in my papers.

Laurie was actually the one I was interested in, at that time.

She was so keyed up…. I couldn't understand why only Lucy and I saw it. I thought sometimes, if I said the wrong thing to her, she'd come apart, she was that tightly wound up. But I also noticed something else, something perplexing. Richard helped her with her math, and instead of falling all over herself to please him, or just soaking up his exalted presence as she usually did, she seemed to shrink from him. She wouldn't even look at him.

Even weirder, he gave her some searching glances, but, at least in my hearing, he didn't ask her if anything was wrong.

Like maybe he knew.

I wondered if they had quarreled.

Then I wondered how the hell she ever got up the nerve to quarrel with him.

"Did you like Monticello?" I asked her casually, making sure that Daddy was out of earshot.

So an easy question, you'd think. She nearly jumped.

Deer in the headlights – no, more like *Danger! Danger! Danger!* She looked so scared that you'd think I'd asked how she liked robbing that bank. *More* weirdness.

"Oh, I loved it," she said after a moment or so, and she wasn't the actress that she is now. "The dome room was great. That was wonderful of Richard to take me up there and show me around."

"No, it wasn't," I said idly, already starting to lose interest. "He just wanted another acolyte to worship at the shrine of Thomas Jefferson. I hope he didn't bore you."

Something bugged me about that conversation… and then later, I remembered. Tourists aren't allowed in the dome room; the fire marshal won't even let you go upstairs because of those cramped staircases. Richard and I, as young engaged lovers, had often teased each other about sneaking in and making love at night under the dome so that the stars could shine down on us, but, of course, we never did.

Richard graduated with his M.Arch. I finished my one and only year of teaching and started my seminar in composition. Lucy finished her first year of law school, thankful that the worst was over, and volunteered to watch Julie for us all summer. Francie and Laurie graduated from high school, and Laurie took a summer job as a typist, in addition to her job at the bookstore.

I wondered when she was planning to make her break.

Then, on June 11, the blinders came off.

I was packing for the move home, and I had told Richard that morning, before he left for a meeting in Richmond, that I would tackle his desk. He never blinked, so clearly he thought nothing of it.

That's because he thought like an Ashmore, not an Abbott.

He had his cassette tapes stacked up all around the desk, hundreds and hundreds of them, and that's where I found it. Boïto's *Nerone*, one of the most obscure operas ever written, and a 1949 performance at La Scala, at that. Daddy had picked up a pirated copy in Italy several years before; it had never been released in this country. So what was Richard doing with a copy—?

(And why on earth would he want one? Why would *anyone*, except Daddy?)

And a tape with Daddy's handwriting all over it?

So I popped it in the cassette player.

Francie's voice. "Oh, my darling, how I wept to leave you. What a wonderful day this was, it will live forever in my memory, I will remember it as I lie dying…."

What idiotic drivel was this?

"I loved that we were there alone at Monticello, Richard, no one else around. I felt so close to you, as if we had stepped back in time before Diana ever was…."

"Oh, Richard, when you kissed me in the dome room, I knew I was yours forever…."

"Darling, you *are* like Jefferson, after all. Wasn't Sally his sister-in-law, too?"

"How did you even know to do that to me in the forest, Richard, who would ever think that you knew how to use your tongue like that…."

"Your body was a warm blanket, I can still feel you over me…."

"My breasts are still tingling and sore…."

I let it play all the way to the end.

I was in shock. My skin was cold; my ears were humming.

I played it again.

And then – I ripped it out of the machine. I ripped it out so hard that the tape snapped. Stupid me, I didn't think. I didn't tell myself that this was the best evidence that was ever going to come my way. I didn't see that now, after all these years, Richard and I were on a level playing field. I didn't think at all, I just reacted. I yanked the tape out of the cassette, grabbed a lighter off his desk, and held the flame to the tape.

No wonder he no longer looked at me as if he'd been locked out of heaven! No wonder he brought his damn plane up to Charlottesville! No wonder that bitch looked so smug at spring break! No wonder Laurie acted as if he had the plague. And where the hell was that bastard anyway!

He had left the number of the Richmond conference hall where he was attending a seminar, in case I needed him for Julie. I called, of course, and discovered that the seminar had let out at noon, not six as he had told me. So I called Daddy's house, and Laurie answered.

And no human being ever sounded guiltier than she did.

"Where is she?"

"Who?" Laurie was stammering, clearly playing for time while she thought. "You mean Francie?"

"Yes, I mean Francie," I said nastily. "Or Richard. Either one. I assume they're together."

"I – I don't know—"

"The hell you don't," I said, and slammed the phone down across her anguished "Di! Wait! Don't—"

And that was the last time I talked to Laurie for fourteen years.

I picked Julie up from day care, buckled her into her car seat, and made record time to Richmond. As I drove, I cursed and screamed and cried. I cried more than I had in years. And when I ran out of tears, I rummaged around in the glove compartment and found a joint I hadn't quite finished.

I knew his favorite haunts in Richmond, I knew that park where we had gone as teenagers, I remembered that little meadow where an amorous couple could find privacy. I parked in close, because I certainly didn't intend to drag Julie around – who knew what I might find! – but no sooner did I pull up than I saw them, my husband and my sister, standing under a tree, not touching, but for all the world like lovers in their own little world.

I saw them, and I knew.

Francie was crying quietly, and he laid his hand alongside her face, the sort of tender gesture he had not given me in three years. She was staring down, and his back was to me, so neither one saw me until I tapped him on the shoulder. The shock on his face and the guilt on Francie's confirmed anything and everything I could ever have suspected.

Richard's hand dropped immediately, but I didn't care.

The blackest fury I'd ever known seized me.

I scarcely even saw him. I looked at her, and I saw Daddy's little flirt, the tormentor of my early years. I saw she who had made so much of my childhood a hellish competition.

I saw my sister, who had slept with my husband, who knew my husband's body, who enjoyed the kisses I no longer knew.

Whose breasts tingled because my husband had enjoyed them.

And I blew up.

I don't remember what I said, but it surpassed even my two major explosions years before. I screamed. I threatened to kill Francie. I threatened to castrate Richard. And I did it at the top of my lungs. I truly don't know all what I said. It's hard, all these years later, to recapture the depth and heat of the rage inside me. Richard told me (years later, when I was trying to pry a confession out of him) that I sounded like a madwoman.

Lucy asked me once, when I was replaying what I remembered of the scene, why I got so mad at Francie, who after all just moved into a void, instead of raging at Richard, who had broken his vows to me. Answer: I had it coming. I had insulted him, cheated on him, kicked him out of bed, and that's the fastest way to make a man fall out of love with you. I guess I deserved anything I got with him. Hell, I don't know if I ever expected Richard to remain faithful forever, it seems like most men cheat sooner or later, but at least you should always be able to count on your family.

But Francie! We had the same parents. We had the same heritage. But it didn't matter to her. That bitch had it in for me from the time she could talk. I never did anything to deserve it. She had no excuse! Did she think I didn't know what she was doing? Did she think I didn't know she planned it all?

She was just using him to get back at me.

So I screamed, and then Francie started screaming back, and that's when, without another thought, I reached right past Richard and smashed my fist into her face. She staggered back, and I pushed her. Hard. Right down into the dirt. Just like we were kids again.

Managing to knock her head against the tree for good measure as she went down.

And two things happened, simultaneously.

Richard grabbed me, hard, around the wrist, and swung me away, I guess before I could reach Francie again. That's the only time he ever hurt me.

And, back at the car, Julie started screaming.

In an instant, Richard changed from the guilty confronted husband to a raging protective father.

"Julie's here? You brought Julie?" And he shook me hard enough to make my teeth hurt. "God damn you, you left my daughter alone in the car—"

"She's my daughter, you bastard!" I screamed, but he had already tuned me out, and was helping Francie up. She was clinging to him, her face pasty with shock.

"Are you all right?" he said in a low, urgent voice. "You hit your head."

She swayed for a second, trying to focus on him, and then she caught sight of me. Her look became sharp.

She was going to have a *wonderful* bruise on her face.

"I'm okay," she whispered, and started to lean towards him. He was holding my wrist so tightly I was afraid to move for fear he'd break it. A pianist can't afford a broken wrist.

"Go home, Fran," he said, and with his other hand smoothed her hair back. "Call me when you get home, or do you want to call Laurie to come get you?"

She looked alarmed, and shook her head. "Please, Richard—"

I said nastily, "He's not going to help you. He's just interested in saving his own ass."

Dead silence among us.

Richard said very quietly, "Fran, would you please go watch Julie for a moment? I want to talk to my *wife*."

I can't even describe how he said that word. He made it sound as terrible as it had been to me for years, and that's when I knew he truly hated me.

She walked away, stumbling, heading towards the car, where Julie was yelling her head off. She didn't want to go, you could tell by the slumped shoulders and the sobbing under her breath, but she went, because the great god Richard Ashmore had told her to.

"By the way," I yelled after her, "you need to go on a diet. You're getting *fat!*"

She didn't even look back at me.

Before I knew it, he had me backed up against the tree, in the same position Francie had been in a few minutes before. But he had no tenderness as he looked at me, he didn't touch my face gently, and his eyes were cold and hard.

I wished – how I wished – that I'd had time to smash his face in too.

"You listen to me, Diana, and you listen up good," he said, and his voice chilled me. "You don't know what you saw here today, and before you go screaming or flinging accusations around, you get a few things straight. I'm not beholden to you, wife. I don't owe you a god-damned thing. *You* left *me*, remember? And then you compounded it by doing about the worst thing a human being can do. Every time I've reached out to you, you've made it abundantly clear that you want nothing to do with me. So don't ever try to hold me or Francie accountable to you." He paused. "Not unless you want a divorce."

"Yes," I said without missing a beat, "I do."

"Fine," he said, and he never hesitated either, "I'll make it easy for you. Just give me Julie, and you can do what you want."

I drew in my breath. "Julie? What do you mean, Julie?"

His eyes, those eyes that had caressed and loved me, that had glowed when he saw me, burned right through me then, the way ice burns through skin.

"I mean," he said, "that Julie is my daughter. By your own choice, she's mine. I've raised her, I've been ten times the parent you've been. You're not taking my daughter away from me."

His words hit me physically, and broke my fury right in half.

"You can't," I whispered, because the fear in my throat kept me from talking any louder. "You wouldn't."

"Oh, wouldn't I?" He looked at me contemptuously. "My God, Diana, you reek of pot. You drove down here with her, all the way from Charlottesville, and you must have toked up the entire way. Is that your idea of taking good care of her – getting stoned in front of her?"

"Is that your idea of taking good care of her," I said, "fucking my sister?"

He straightened then, and I breathed easier. Just for a second.

"Whatever I've done," he said flatly, "I haven't involved Julie. And you don't know, do you, Diana? You really don't know."

Fourteen years began of the unfaithful husband's credo: *deny, deny, deny.* I didn't know that this moment, when he was emotionally off-balance from the shock of discovery, was the closest he would ever come to a confession, or I would certainly have pressed him harder. But even in his shock, Richard, clever Richard, had outmaneuvered me.

"I know," I said. "You fucked your own sister-in-law."

"Prove it," he said.

In my mind's eyes, I saw a tape, disintegrating in flames. I knew then, sick at heart, that my only evidence was gone, destroyed by my own hand, and nothing else was out there. Richard was always too damn clever for me.

"I drove down," he said, "so I'll take Julie back with me. Get yourself under control before you come home. I don't want Julie upset again."

And then that bastard, that utter hypocrite, turned and walked away from me.

I saw him stop and say something to Francie, slumped against the side of my car. Whatever it was, she grabbed his hand and held it hard. He touched her hair, just once.

And I never saw Francie again.

I was so shaken from my explosion and Richard's threat, I wasn't fit to drive, and I managed to rack up a speeding ticket before I made it back to Charlottesville. Thank God the cop didn't pay attention to the joint smoldering in my ashtray, or all Richard's dreams would have come true. Me, busted for drugs, him proved once again to be the long-suffering, superior husband. I sat in the driveway, terrified to go in. What if he really divorced me? What if – and the idea made me ill – he really wanted Francie? What if he inflicted the ultimate humiliation on me and left me for my sister?

What if he took Julie away from me?

I stayed out there in the car most of the night, smoking dope and sitting in frozen fear.

By the time he finally came out and told me to come inside, I was out of my mind, and I stayed that way. Richard didn't speak to me again. I overheard him once on the phone, canceling a planned weekend home, telling Peggy that we were too busy to come down.

Not a word passed between us.

I don't remember anything else until Daddy called ten days later.

I didn't answer the phone, Richard did. And for a minute, his voice was clipped and short. He wasn't even trying to hide his contempt for Daddy or me.

Then, in the space of a few seconds, he changed. He said, "Hold on, Dominic," and he said to me, "Have you heard from Laurie?"

I was stunned to hear his voice, and even more stunned to hear his words. "Laurie?" I said, "no, why?"

"Your father seems to think she's staying with us." He turned back to the phone. "No, she's not here. Diana hasn't heard from her… no, I saw Lucy yesterday, and she didn't say anything… what does Francie say?"

My mind flashed to Laurie, and her taut, secretive face.

"She *what?*" Now Richard looked really alarmed. "No, we haven't seen her… Baltimore? Good God, Dominic, have you called the police?"

The police! I grabbed the phone from Richard.

Six days before, Laurie had told Daddy that she was driving up to help us pack. Francie had decided to visit some friends in Baltimore. They had left on what should have been, at most, a two-hour drive up to UVA to drop Laurie off, and they had disappeared off the face of the earth.

Then, earlier that day, the Baltimore police had called Daddy. They had found the abandoned car, stripped, in a parking lot. Daddy called Francie's friends and discovered that they knew nothing about the proposed visit. Then he called us.

Then, at Richard's insistence, he finally called the police. And he called Lucy.

Lucy came slamming into our duplex within ten minutes, and

that's when I discovered that the one person on earth I still trusted had betrayed me too.

She stormed in, went straight over to him, and smacked him full in the face. "This is your fault, you son of a bitch! What were you thinking?" And then she turned on me. "What's the matter with you? Either sleep with your husband, or get a divorce!" And then she broke down. "They're so young – my sisters—"

Richard, ashen-faced, picked up his keys and walked out.

Where he went, I can only guess. But he and Francie must have been meeting somewhere all those months, and I think he went there to look for her, hoping against hope that she had gone to earth after that fight in Richmond, taking Laurie with her to mop up her tears. I think – I *think* – he flew to Ash Marine, to the cottage. He called several hours later from Ashmore Park, where he had flown after his search, and Laurie and Francie were still missing.

After he left, I was left with Lucy.

"You knew," I said without preamble.

Lucy was crying, great, huge tears running down her face. "Of course I knew," she managed between sobs, and she didn't look at me. "God, Di, how could you be so blind?"

I didn't care about her tears. I'd had enough of all the subterfuge. All I knew was that Lucy, the one person I'd thought I could still trust, had known that my husband was having sex with our sister, and she hadn't told me. She'd let me skate along in innocence. She'd set me up for that terrible day in Richmond. I grabbed her arm and held it tightly until she glared up at me in pain. "You knew," I repeated through my teeth, "how did you know? Did you see them together? Was he touching her?"

"Oh, shut up!" Lucy wrenched her arm away. "Is this all you can think about? I *saw* them. I saw them at Easter dinner. They weren't touching, they weren't even looking at each other. But I could tell. The air was practically vibrating between them."

I was so angry with her, I could have spit nails. "You should have told me," and I'm sure I was shouting. "What kind of sister are you, anyway?"

"I'll tell you what kind," said Lucy, and I remember her shoulders shuddering with her sobs. "You're my sister, Di, but I'm his, too. I grew up with him. And I've seen how miserable he is." Her voice rose. "You think I don't know what goes on in this house? How you never speak to each other? How you never sleep together? Are you crazy, Di, did you think he was going to live that way forever?" She wiped her eyes with the back of her hand. "He's so damn lonely, and the only time he's even looked alive was in the past few months."

That flicked me right across the heart, and I reacted in the worst way possible. "Get out," I said, "get out of here right now."

"Di—"

"*Get out!*" I couldn't bear her in my sight one second longer. She'd known. *The only time he's looked alive....*

Lucy studied me for a long, cool moment, a harbinger of many to come. I swear, that girl was born a lawyer. "Fine," she said, and her voice was cold. "In case you've forgotten, Di, our sisters have disappeared into thin air. You might try thinking where they could be. And I," she paused at the door, "I'm going home. Maybe Dad has some ideas."

She slammed out.

I was left there, alone, no husband, no sisters.

The fear that they had fallen into the hands of some psychopath hovered throughout that day. Richard, when he called, said that the police were proceeding on the theory that the girls had been abducted, because of the state of their car. "Do you think that's what happened?" I asked, because in the back of my mind, I still saw that strange determination in Laurie all those months.

He said wearily, "I don't know, Di, I hope not. But—" only the slightest pause in his voice, "this isn't like Francie. She wouldn't leave without a word."

Daddy said the same thing.

So did Philip and Peggy, who were even more upset than Daddy.

Sad – that Laurie would leave without a word, everyone took for granted.

But the abduction theory was laid to rest forever the next day. The police learned that, the day before she disappeared, Laurie had withdrawn over four thousand dollars from her bank account. In fact, she had left a total balance of a dollar, just to keep the account open. The bank teller said that Laurie was alone, in good spirits, and not under any duress. Everyone but Lucy and me was stunned to find out that she had that much money.

Daddy, prompted by the police, discovered that Mama's jewelry was missing.

Francie's winter coat had been removed from storage.

Laurie's journal and current piece of needlework were gone from her room, along with every piece of music she had ever written.

A clerk at Williamsburg remembered selling tickets to Francie and Laurie.

A waitress remembered serving them lunch.

By that time, two days passed, and the police told Daddy that they couldn't put more time into it. Francie was eighteen and a legal adult, and she had the right to go where she wanted. True, Laurie was underage and a technical runaway, but she was with Francie, she obviously had enough money with her, and (no one said, but everyone thought) she appeared to be the brains of the entire escape plan.

They were gone. Four sisters, cut down to two.

And Lucy and I weren't speaking.

Nor was she speaking to Richard.

However, Philip had plenty to say.

Philip had always intimidated me, mostly because he didn't like me and he didn't think I was good enough or smart enough for his precious son. But we all knew that he had genuinely loved Laurie, and it was no secret to me that he and Peggy had been praying that Richard would come to his senses, ditch me, and wait for Laurie to grow up. As soon as the police proved that Laurie and Francie had not fallen prey to a serial killer, Philip drove up to Charlottesville to see us.

He told Richard that he wanted to speak to him privately, and Richard never uttered a word of protest. They went into the back yard and stayed there quite a long time. I peeked out the window a couple of times and saw Philip talking, Richard forcing himself to look at his father. He looked even more taut and drawn than he had before. He had taken the twins' disappearance hard. I think he blamed himself for not seeing that Laurie had been planning this for a long time.

I didn't feel sorry for him. Laurie had given him a lifetime of loyalty and devotion, and he had let Francie and lust blind him to the turmoil that had ripped her apart. I truly believe that, if Richard hadn't been so caught up with Francie that spring, he might have noticed something was wrong, or Laurie might have confided in him, and I'm certain Richard feels that way too.

And he took the estrangement from Lucy hard. They had grown up together, and now his best friend wasn't speaking to him.

Who knows what Philip said, though. Richard never told me.

Then Philip summoned me. "Diana, I want to talk to you."

That whole interview with Philip was so terrible, I've blocked most of it from my memory. Suffice it to say that Richard came by his self-righteousness and, worse, his bloody awful *niceness* honestly. Actually, it was worse talking to Philip, because at least I could tell Richard to go to hell.

Philip was older than Daddy. I had to be polite to him.

But Philip made his living as a pediatrician, and so I had to listen to what he said about Julie. He and Peggy were worried sick about her, he said, she seemed timid and subdued these days, and he worried that she was badly affected by the strain between Richard and me. He felt that we needed to make a fresh start in our marriage (so I knew Richard hadn't told him the truth about Francie, because no one could seriously suggest I forgive him for that), and perhaps we could make that start now that we were both out of school, and "real life" could begin.

He suggested, too, that I not get a job right away, take some time to be a wife and mother. After all, Richard would be making enough; it was no longer up to me to bring home the bacon. It was tough, he said, being in college all those years, with a young child, working hard to make ends meet, and now Richard and I could relax and enjoy our lives and each other and Julie and any other children that came along.

I remember sitting there, listening to Philip's calm, reasonable voice, looking down at my hands, and wondering how much time I'd do if I pushed his face into concrete and killed him.

But he meant the best, and I knew it. I had to remember that he and Peggy loved Julie and had a right to be concerned about their only grandchild, and I knew that he was right about college being an artificial environment for a marriage. Richard and I had been married for four years, and, after our first summer, we had never lived a normal married life.

Maybe he was right. I didn't see that I had a choice. I had to stay with Richard in order to stay with Julie.

Because I knew, I knew even then, that Julie was Richard's, more than she had ever been mine. I had lost her to him. And the only way to be with her was to stay with that self-righteous, cheating bastard.

If I'd known what hell the next three years would be, I'd have left him on the spot.

22

Sex, Lies, and Thomas Jefferson

FROM THE PAST, FRANCIE SAT ON HER BED after her trip to Monticello and made her tape: *I can't believe how passionate you are about Monticello, Richard. It's like you built it yourself. Do you think you're Jefferson reincarnated, lover?*

"Is everything all right?" said Richard. "You're very quiet this morning."

Laura turned her head to look at him as he walked beside her on the roundabout circling the great house. He looked relaxed, hands in his pockets, not at all out of breath from the climb up the mountain. His voice was casual; his gaze upon her was not.

"I'm fine. Just a little winded. I'm not used to climbing a mountain." She touched his arm; she had discovered that he liked her doing that, touches that told him how much she enjoyed being with him. "I guess we got here just in time. Look at all those people."

"Well," said Richard, "we could have come earlier, but—" His grin at her was a shared memory of waking up at dawn together. "We're not on a schedule. We'll explore the grounds until the tour."

She nodded. The silence lay there between them, not yet uncomfortable, but nevertheless a presence that she couldn't shake. Two nights of failure, two dawns of Cat taking over her mind and body… two mornings of having to regain Laura and act as if she were the same woman he'd made love with, whose bed he had shared.

Two mornings of waking up and finding herself alone. He had gone out again while she slept, leaving only a cryptic note – *Back soon, R.* He hadn't gone out running; he'd returned, not dripping from a hard workout, but neatly dressed in polo shirt and jeans. He'd sat casually in the bedroom's one chair, watching her pack her bag, talking about his occasional lectures in historical preservation at the architectural school. He'd offered no explanation of his absence.

She couldn't ask, *Where did you go this morning?* He might have replied, *Where did you go last night?*

They walked around to the terrace, a long L-wing on the northern end of the house, and mounted the stairs at its midpoint. Richard put his hand on her waist to guide her away from the house into the bend of the wing – how quickly they were becoming used to each other's touch. "Here." He halted her at the end of the terrace and turned her away from the house. "See through the trees there?"

The warm wind was gently tossing the tree branches that obscured their view, so it took her a few seconds of peering intently in the direction of his pointing hand before she saw the rotunda of the University of Virginia. "Oh, I see it!" Her cheek brushed the hand resting now on her shoulder as she turned to look at him. "Jefferson really liked domes, didn't he? Is that the Palladian influence?"

He sounded surprised. "Yes, it is, as a matter of fact, but how do you know about that?"

"I read it in your book."

"You read the book? Laura, you amaze me. When was this?"

"I found it on the Internet last winter." She let herself lean back against his shoulder. "In fact, if you saw a spike in your sales in one day – that was me. I bought ten copies."

"Ten? That was excessive. I would have given you one."

"I wanted to boost your royalties."

He laid his hand against her hair, and she thought that nothing in her life had ever felt as warm and secure as Richard resting his hand like that against her. "You probably doubled the sales for the month. Julie's college fund thanks you." They heard a group of tourists approaching, and he put his arm loosely around her shoulders and guided her over to the stairs leading down to the dependencies. "So what do you plan to do with all your copies?"

Laura pretended to give it some serious thought. "Hmmm. I don't know. Give them out as Christmas gifts to my friends."

"I'm sure they'll appreciate that. You'll probably get them back next year." A burst of laughter came from above them. Monticello was beginning to fill up. "Sales are going okay. A lot of universities and libraries have picked it up, what we expected when we planned the project. University press books don't hit the bestseller list."

"Cat Courtney could help boost sales," said Laura, tongue-in-cheek. "I'm on tour this fall – we could buy up the remainder and give it out at the champagne receptions. Sort of a gift with purchase, like at the cosmetics counter. They can choose between it and the DVD and screen saver."

Pause. "That's unusual sarcasm from you, Laura Rose. You *are* kidding, aren't you?"

She grinned back at him. "My manager would never allow it. Cat merchandise only. Sorry."

His voice dropped into a lazy intimate tone. "I'd like a copy of that screen saver."

"I'll email you a copy when we get home."

They had reached the ground floor now, and now they met more people. The mountain that had seemed so empty when they had walked up – but, of course, everyone else had taken the bus ride – seemed to be getting crowded. In unspoken agreement, Richard and Laura turned away from the dependencies and walked out on the roundabout that encircled the great western lawn.

I loved that we were there alone at Monticello, Richard, no one else around. I felt so close to you, as if we had stepped back in time before Diana ever was….

They walked along the herringbone path, close but not touching now. Peggy must have loved the riot of flowers in these gardens; she had taken such pride in restoring the gardens at Ashmore Park to the glory days of the Great Lakes shipping heiress. Laura had planted a flower garden a few years before, but she'd missed the prime plant- ing season when walking pneumonia had felled first Meg and then Cam, and only a few sections had bloomed properly. All for naught, she thought, the garden was Emma's now. Maybe if she bought a house, she could plant another garden.

"Last time I came up here," Richard said, "one of those singers was here – I don't know her name, she's the one who prances around the stage mostly undressed—"

His out-of-the-blue comment was so welcome that she forgot her depressing lack of a garden and the even more depressing thought of the night before. "Which one? They all prance around undressed."

He laughed. "You have a point. She was blonde and built and looked barely out of high school, that's all I remember. I think Julie listens to her. But the girl had this unbelievable entourage – at least thirty people, and not one of them knew who Jefferson was except the head on the nickel. A sad commentary on modern American ed- ucation."

"I can do a little better than that," said Laura. "He's the face on the two-dollar bill, right?" She laughed at his expression. "I know who he was. I'm not a complete ignoramus."

"I would hope not. You had a good education. I'm paying through the nose for Julie to go there." He leaned to pick a blade of grass and started to bend it around his fingers. "So where's your entourage, Cat Courtney?"

"No thanks." She pretended to shudder. "I couldn't stand to be surrounded night and day."

He turned to her. "You've not very diva-like, are you? No stories of you throwing a fit because someone forgot to get you the right kind of bottled water. You fly under the radar, don't you?"

She felt on familiar ground now. "When I first signed with the label, Cam hired a manager for me. He knew before I did that Cat Courtney was going to be bigger than – than just me writing songs at night. So I've got this manager, Dell Barnes – he'd handled some other singers, and right off the bat Dell told me that I could be a diva or I could be an artist but practically no one gets away with being both."

"And, being Dominic's daughter, you'd choose to be an artist."

"We weren't brought up to be divas."

"No." Richard threw the blade of grass into the breeze. "I'll give Dominic that. He had enough temperament for all of you, but he didn't tolerate it in you girls."

"Yes." They had reached the apogee of the roundabout, and with a quick touch on her upper arm – that unspoken language of hand caressing her skin! If only it meant that he could love her – he turned her to look back at the great western front. "I'd never seen myself as a star. I always thought I'd just keep on writing songs and poems and stories, put them away, and maybe someday I'd get to make an album to prove that I could sing. Dell and Cam saw much more, and Dell said that I needed a persona to back up my music. No one was going to suspend belief for all that pathos coming from a mom with a grade-schooler. I'd used the name Cat Colby in San Francisco, and Dell took that and helped me create Cat Courtney. She's as much his creation as mine."

He didn't speak for a moment. "I thought – we all thought that Cat Courtney was just a way to keep us from finding you."

Laura heard a quizzical tone in his voice. "Well – I won't say that wasn't part of it. It was. But I really liked being able to go to the grocery store, or drive Meg to school, or go shopping without people knowing who I was, and we saw all those tabloid stories about the royals and Hollywood, and I didn't want any part of that. I didn't want an entourage or a bodyguard, or to be at the mercy of the pa-parazzi. So Dell mapped out a strategy to promote me in Europe, so I mostly work over there, and then the rest of the time—" she shrugged— "I can just be myself here at home."

He said musingly, and ripped comfortable ground out from under her, "I have to wonder how you get away with it, going out in public, and not being seen for Cat Courtney. I *look* at you, and I see it so clearly." Oh, she did not like the direction of this at all. "I suspect people recognize you more than you think."

She shook her head.

"Then how do you pull the wool over everyone's eyes?"

Her heart was beating hard. "Richard, you've seen how I live. I don't go to parties, I don't give interviews, I don't go to openings or fashion shows – I lead a very quiet life. Besides, you know me. If you didn't, you wouldn't see Cat Courtney." She stopped to catch her breath. "My fans are older. They're not the kind to mob me. They're the kind to line up politely and pay big money for the champagne receptions so that they can say they've met me."

"Speaking as a specimen of the group, I imagine you sell pretty well to middle-aged men," said Richard. "And, may I say, Miss Courtney—" he raised an eyebrow at her— "you're not exactly covered head to toe on stage yourself. That concert we saw – I held my breath waiting for that dress to fall down."

"Haute couture. It only looks as if it's going to fall down." She tried to sound light. "Believe me, I'm pinned and boned within an inch of my life. Those dresses wouldn't fall off in a hurricane."

The silence returned between them and stretched into an almost tangible being. She found her fingers shaking and deliberately pressed them against her side. Uncanny, his questions about Cat Courtney, as if he knew – Had he seen a hint of Cat, had he seen the echo of that woman on Ash Marine? Was she turning into as big a fraud as Julie?

I have to do better than this. This is my love. I can't be afraid to be with him.

The sun had risen high enough in the sky that the light now flooded the western lawn and made the dome gleam white in the light. Other tourists crossed their line of sight, but the grounds absorbed the sound, and in the silence, they might as well have been alone on the lawn. His arm rested around her shoulders, and she felt the heat from his skin sink into her body, and she relaxed. If they could keep it like this, if she didn't freeze up at the thought of Ash Marine... *dragons*... maybe she could keep Cat Courtney at bay when he made love to her.

"I'm Laura, you know, not Cat." The words came out of her mouth before she stopped to think. "Cat Courtney is just a job."

He said nothing.

In for a penny.... "This—" she gestured at herself. "This is the reality, Richard, what you see right here. No haute couture, no wig. This is it. Gap jeans and – and no makeup and—"

"And a silver Jaguar," he said unexpectedly.

That stopped her for a moment, until she remembered his terse words to Diana on the voice mail. "Okay. All right. A silver Jaguar. Cam gave me that for my birthday." A guilt present to talk her back into their bedroom. "It's extravagant, I know, but it's not even two years old, and I've hardly driven it since I moved to London—"

"Hold it," Richard interrupted, and held up his hand. "Don't apologize. Drive whatever you like."

"Anyway," she persevered, "I want you to know that I know the difference between Laura and Cat. Cat's a costume I put on to perform, but – she's not really me. I'm still Laura."

She made herself look at him and was disconcerted to see that he was giving her the same appraising look he'd given Diana Friday night.

"What?" The word came out before she could think to stop herself. "What is it?"

He said slowly, as if reasoning through disparate thoughts, "You said it yourself, Cat is a creation. A job." Her heart dropped. "My God, when I saw you on that stage, I thought you looked like a goddess. Golden, very untouchable and not accessible by us mere mortals, and I have to say that was only reinforced when we were turned away backstage."

"Oh, I am so sorry—"

He overrode her. "Until we saw you that night, I didn't realize how much you had changed – at least on the surface. You weren't the Laura who used to go fishing with me on Saturdays. I get the feeling that you think being Laura isn't good enough for us – that we're holding you up against Cat and finding something missing in you."

She had to head this off at the pass. "You have to admit that Cat makes a bigger splash."

Oh, stop, stop, stop, what are you doing… don't explain, don't excuse, change the subject….

"You may not believe this," he said, "but you are so much more than Cat. She's mist and smoke, like a will-o'-the-wisp dream that you forget as soon as you wake up. I'd much rather have you here in your jeans and that little shirt of yours, the wind blowing your hair around." He stopped, and then his voice lowered into the bedroom voice that had melted her the night before. "I'd much rather wake up next to Laura."

Oh, please, he mustn't feel the catch in her throat at his words. If ever a man had fired a warning shot across the bow…. She felt raw and exposed, and more than a little afraid.

"Believe me," his hand gently swept the hair off her neck, and she felt his fingers in that sensitive area right below her hairline, "you do just fine."

She tilted her head to glance back at him, and if that happened to give him greater access to her neck so that she could melt right down into the ground, it was just a bonus. "Richard, what are you doing?" Her protest didn't sound very convincing. "There are people around."

He looked down at her, laughing. "Definitely Laura and not Cat. And what is it I'm doing?"

"Something you shouldn't be doing in public," she said primly, which earned her another laugh. She didn't resist when he pulled her back against him. She could feel his heart against her back, his breath against the crown of her head, and she could definitely feel the effects of his voice and mouth. Her toes hadn't curled like that in a long time. "That dome seems so strange to see on the back of the house. Every picture you ever see of Monticello shows the dome – I thought it was in the front."

"It is in the front." Richard sounded normal, unaffected by the closeness of their bodies. "There's no rear to the house. Jefferson considered that the house had two fronts, east and west."

"Have you ever been up to the dome?"

Oh, Richard, when you kissed me in the dome room, I knew that I was yours forever.

"Sure." He held up his wrist in front of her so that they could see the time. "Damn. We need to get in line. Let's go."

He grabbed her hand and took off across the lawn, and she had to scramble to keep up with him and his long legs. As tall as she was, she couldn't cover the same ground as quickly as he could. Maybe he didn't realize how easily he outpaced her, or – she couldn't shake the suspicion that, deep down, he divined the fraud she'd put over on him the night before, or the night before that, or eleven years ago. Maybe he didn't know it consciously yet, but he knew it in his bones, and it disturbed him.

Might her playacting – her fleeing into Cat at the first sign of trouble – rip the fragile fabric of the world they were beginning to weave for each other? This man had just told her plainly that he would never want Cat Courtney; he would never want the sham mystery and glamor of the golden goddess. He'd had enough of darkness and mystery and love that drifted away like smoke.

He wanted an ordinary woman of sunlight. The woman she might have been if she'd never sold herself to Cameron St. Bride for two hundred dollars. The woman she might have been if she had never reached for him that afternoon at Ash Marine.

I wonder if I can ever go back.

I wonder if I can give Cat up.

They waited for thirty minutes in line. While they waited and the sun grew hotter, Richard kept in neutral mode, as if they had come too close to matters best left untouched. Or, Laura thought, he imagined he was being neutral. Perhaps he didn't realize how much of his mind he was sharing with her.

When he had talked about architecture when they were young, she hadn't really understood; her job had been to nod and adore. But now she listened and understood, and he showed her how one man could take theory and possibilities from the air and translate it into a solid building that people could see and touch. He unfolded her guide map showing the layout of the house and the gardens, and with a few pencil strokes, he showed her how Palladian theory translated into an American treasure. He did this too, he took ideas and he made them into reality, into homes where families could thrive, museums that could store priceless treasures, churches where worshipers could touch God. He was, she thought, a man of imagination and vision.

She knew that already. He'd shown imagination and vision with her the night before.

How did you even know to do that to me in the forest, Richard, who would ever think that you knew how to use your tongue like that….

She ventured, "It's like writing a song."

"Exactly," said Richard. "You start off with a finite number of notes and a finite number of keys, you have an infinite number of ways to combine the notes and keys. Same principle here. You have certain human functions that you have to build around, and you have only so many workable shapes – you can't construct an inverted pyramid, for instance, not if you want it to stand in a wind – and you have certain immutable laws about materials and their behavior, but you have untold ways to combine any of these into an original structure. And this one," he nodded at the house, "is an original."

A couple ahead of them in line had shamelessly eavesdropped as he talked, and now they turned around and asked questions. Two women from New Jersey joined in, and others started listening, and before they knew it, they had an audience.

Richard had an audience. He told them what an extravagance the dome room was – accessible only by a small staircase, useless as living space. He told them the purpose of the Venetian portico on the southern side of the house; Jefferson had built it for privacy so that no one could look in his bedroom windows. He answered questions easily, and as he did, she saw the attention people were paying to him. This was how he appeared to others – a confident, engaging expert in his field.

Laura watched in amusement as two almost twenty-something girls managed to sidle up to his side and look on – oh, so innocently! – as he sketched a Doric column on her map. They couldn't have cared less who Palladio was. They were more interested in 6′5″ of Black Irish splendor landed improbably in a waiting line.

"How did you learn all this?" One had a Bostonian accent and the hint of a rose tattoo showing over the low bust line of her tank top. "Wow, you're like an expert."

"I'm an architect in historic preservation," said Richard with a shrug, and Laura wondered if he noticed the girl thrusting her considerable charms at him. "I did my master's at UVA, and Monticello is a lab for preservationists." As if the girl had the slightest interest in historic preservation other than her own, eventually. But then a professional-looking couple in their forties asked him about the dependencies, and the nymphet's face fell when he turned to talk to them. The New Jersey women asked him about the layout of the gardens, and a man whose *Trust Me I'm a Doctor* T-shirt announced his profession started an impromptu consultation about a house that he was renovating, and business cards started changing hands.

By the time the tour started, Richard had educated his new fan club about everything they needed to know to take a knowledgeable tour, and the fact that the docent greeted him cemented his status as a Monticello expert. Unfortunately, it also gave everyone his name, and then it was *Richard this* and *Richard that* and *Richard what's a good source for antique glass.* Enough people were talking to him, as they trooped into the main hall, that the two Boston girls managed to separate him from Laura. That he and she had been standing together didn't discourage them at all. Maybe Laura Abbott was so ordinary that a female more than ten years younger didn't consider her serious competition. Maybe they thought she was his sister.

She worked her way back to his side.

"Oooh, look at all these books!" Boston A said, and Laura missed the last part of the docent's comments about the library. Something about the Library of Congress, and bankruptcy – she'd have to read the guidebook later on to see what she was missing in all the post-teen pheromones floating around. "Do you think he read them all?"

Maybe she should come to his rescue. *Sorry, girls, I know he looks like a Celtic god, but he's twice your age. Besides, he's taken, and I am not giving him back.*

Richard was a grown man. He could get himself out of this.

She stole a look at him. He wasn't even paying attention to Boston A and Boston B, despite Boston A being snuggled up close enough for her rose-tattooed breast to brush his sleeve. He was listening to the professional couple about fireplaces, and the doctor was impatiently trying to tell him about some staircase he had seen at an auction. She wished he would forget the others. She wanted to ask him: *Is this where you got the idea for your bedroom suite? Did you create it as your personal men's club as he did? That workroom of yours – do you dream and invent and explore there as he did here in his cabinet? He left no room for a woman in his room – is there room for me in yours?* In this ancient house lay a fundamental key to Richard Ashmore, and she couldn't ask him because a gaggle of silly girls and some people looking for free professional advice wouldn't leave him alone.

Jefferson's bedroom was the worst. They stood beside the alcove bed under the skylights and listened to the docent, and over the giggling of the fan club, Francie's voice came back. *When you pulled me down in front of the fireplace under the skylights, I rejoiced to feel your long body over me, around me, in me....* She touched her forehead as pain flickered behind her eyes. Bad enough that she had to listen to post-adolescent nonsense behind her; to have it echo from the past was too much.

"Are you all right?" Richard said from behind her.

Laura glanced up at him and saw his genuine concern, and she nodded. "It's nothing," she whispered, and in that moment, she wondered if he really didn't see what was going on. He'd certainly been oblivious to his effect on women when he was a young man. Francie had flirted with him, she'd had a crush on him, and a couple of Diana's classmates had tried to get his attention, all to no avail. Maybe he had considered himself off the market for so long that he truly had his blinders on.

In those ten years, I've been with a grand total of three women. She hadn't even thought before that three relationships in ten years didn't sound like very much for a mostly single man. Cam had probably had twice as many in the same time, not counting the wife who was living with him.

"Oooh, do you think they did it in that bed? It's so short." That must be Boston B. She pronounced *short* as *shawrt*.

The docent said diplomatically, "It only looks short in the alcove. It is actually Jefferson's height. He died in that bed on the Fourth of July in 1826, the fiftieth anniversary of the signing of the Declaration of Independence. Ironically, later the same day, John Adams died in Braintree, Massachusetts, and his last words were—"

Laura missed John Adams' farewell to the world, as the Boston duo giggled something about tall men and big feet. She wasn't the only one growing more irritated by the minute; a few other people in the group were starting to give the girls pointed looks. She would kill Meg if she ever caught her behaving this boorishly in public.

Boston A said, "So do you think they did it on the floor? The slave girl, the one with the DNA thingie – what's her name, Sally something—"

She heard a muffled snort behind her – the doctor, perhaps – and Richard hissed in her ear, "How the hell do you shut those girls up?"

He was the father of a teenage girl, didn't he know? But then Julie would make sure that he never had to tell her to mind her manners. This was a woman's job. With a sigh, she turned around and fixed the girls in her sight.

She made sure that they saw Cat Courtney's gaze upon them: firm, unfriendly, and unavoidable. She held silence for a measure of four beats, long enough to fix the post-teen deer in the headlights.

"Her name was Sally Hemings," she said pleasantly. "She was his wife's half-sister. She was also his mistress for over thirty years, and they had several children together. Now – would you girls *mind*? I can't hear anything. You are ruining my tour."

"His sister-in-law? *Gross*—" said one.

The other said, "Hey, we paid to be here, same as you. Don't tell us to be quiet. *You* be quiet."

And the other chimed back in, "What are you, anyway, the Sally expert or something?"

"No, I'm not the Sally expert," said Laura, and then her mind disconnected from her mouth, and the words came, from nowhere, words that would haunt her for the rest of her life. "I'm the Richard expert, I'm *his* mistress, we *were* having a nice quiet weekend together, and I would very much appreciate it if *you* would leave *him* alone so *we* can continue *our* tour."

Her words fell into an appalling well of silence, a black hole absorbing all other sound. Everyone heard her, there was no doubt, not from their faces, and, in that second, she finally heard her words, staking a devastating claim to the man standing in shock beside her.

It was the voice cracking before an audience, the heel coming off a shoe during an entrance, the sneeze during a soliloquy picked up by an open mike. It was every embarrassing moment she'd ever imagined, rolled into one.

She reacted on instinct, fight-or-flight adrenaline overtaking that first wave of leaden horror. She had one thought, to live through the next minute, the next hour. Not to stand there, rooted in icy horror, unable to move, unable to speak, unable to muster a covering laugh that would say, *I'm joking, I'm joking! Of course, I'm not his mistress!*

But of course, she said nothing. Laura St. Bride, having said it all, had nothing to say.

And then, salvation.

Not missing a beat, Cat stepped in, Cat who could outstare, outwit, outlast anyone. Cat, who would always survive. Cat, who had the courage – or the nerve – to give the entourage a blinding smile and take her speechless lover's arm.

"Let's go, Richard, I don't want to miss the rest of the tour."

Cat, who practically dragged him out of the bedroom.

Her bravado lasted most of the way through the parlor tour. She was aware of Richard standing silently beside her, of the attention from his newfound friends: speculation from the doctor, unwelcome interest from the professional man, comrade-in-arms respect from the wife, disapproval from the New Jersey women, who, she now noticed, wore crosses and probably couldn't wait to report to their Bible study group that they had met Jezebel in the flesh. On the plus side, the Boston girls scurried to the other side of the group after she glared at them.

She'd been a mother for thirteen years. She'd perfected the art of the quelling glare.

It took a few minutes of standing in the sunny room, with its gorgeous view of the western lawn where they had so recently stood, half-listening to the discussion about the artwork and the original panes of glass in the windows, before the adrenaline flood began to recede and reality began to wash in on her, and the full weight of what she had done in Jefferson's bedroom fell on her.

I'm his mistress.

Oh, dear God, had she really said something that crude? She hadn't, she couldn't have. Those words, that scene – that wasn't her. That wasn't Laura Abbott, who gave new meaning to holding up the wall. That wasn't Laura St. Bride, who never caused a moment's unease to anyone.

Those immortal words.

I'm his mistress.

Not *girlfriend*, with its innocuous claim of ownership, unlikely to cause anyone discomfort. Not that quasi-legal term, *partner*, meaning anything. Not *wife*, the ultimate keep-your-hands-off.

Mistress.

A story in one word: *This man is married. I am not his wife. I sleep with him.*

Mistress. Richard probably thought she had lost her mind. Crown princes had mistresses. Presidents had mistresses. CEOs of Internet companies had mistresses. An architect in Virginia who treasured his privacy did not have a mistress.

Oh, Richard, if we could live up there alone, on the mountain… I would be your truest mistress till the day I died….

No, she couldn't be remembering that correctly. It didn't even sound like Francie.

She had embarrassed him, Laura thought numbly, as they followed the docent into the dining room. The doctor was a potential client, and Richard was in business for himself, surviving on commissions and referrals from clients. Not that the doctor looked as if he might not enjoy a mistress himself – she'd seen him look at Boston A's half-hidden rose tattoo – and not that Richard hadn't established himself firmly as a restoration expert par excellence. Still, it couldn't do him any good to be viewed as a man with an unstable personal life.

I have worked hard to put together a decent life. I won't wreck it for a one-night stand.

No, just let me wreck it for you.

Oh, why, why, *why* had she let two silly girls get to her?

Laura tried to keep her distance from the rest of the tour in the dining room and the adjacent tea room. She loved rooms like this; Peggy had taught her how to set a gracious table long before anyone had ever heard of Martha Stewart, and she had taken pleasure in creating beautiful dinners in Cam's home. She loved the fireplace, with its Wedgwood inserts; she loved the tea service; she loved the walls with their robin's-egg blue contrasted against the white crown moldings. She hated the island of silence that had surrounded her ever since she had opened her mouth.

She stood in front of the fireplace and stared at the Wedgwood inserts. Maybe she could find something like that for her fireplace in London. She'd seen a gift shop down near the waiting line; maybe she could buy a replica of the mantel clock or the mirror and have it shipped to the flat. Maybe she could forget that she had ever in her whole life heard of a place called Monticello.

She heard people talking behind her, laughing, admiring. The women particularly liked these rooms. Good old Martha, she'd made homemaking chic again.

Richard had come to stand beside her. They stood there without speaking; she stared at the mantel carvings until the silence grew more than she could bear. She opened her mouth to say something, anything, to break the stillness between them, and out came, "Cam would never let me paint the walls."

What a stupid thing to say, as if Cameron St. Bride's preference for boring eggshell walls was even worth thinking about.

"I wanted to paint a mural in our dining room, and he said no, he didn't like *trompe d'oeil*, if you want something on a wall you should just hang a picture. Then I wanted a faux finish in our bathroom, and he said it was impractical and we should get hand-painted back-splashes instead."

It took a moment – long enough for him to think *Who took Laura away and left this crazy woman?* – before he said carefully, "You can paint anything you want now."

"No, I can't," she said. "It's not my house anymore."

The rest of the tour was leaving the dining room now, going back towards the front of the house. She slipped past Richard and the other people in their subgroup, who had been openly eavesdropping on this first post-mistress exchange. Even the New Jersey ladies looked sorry for Richard; his mistress had gone completely around the bend, crying about not being able to paint her walls.

The tour of the house finished on a flat note in the northeast bedroom. It should have ended back in that spectacular front entrance, or Jefferson's greenhouse, or the tea room, anything except this bland bedroom with the flowered wallpaper. The room was small and stuffy, and she felt a touch of claustrophobia. She couldn't wait to file out the door to the terrace where she and Richard had begun their exploration of Monticello.

Maybe they could leave now.

But, oh no, now Richard's groupies were asking him to take them through the underground dependencies, not part of the regular tour. She saw him pause and look over at her with reservation, and she saw that he wanted to do it. Well, why not? The man was an expert; he'd written the thesis that she hadn't typed on the structural engineering of the dependencies.

Laura said, "That sounds like fun," and the rest of the group relaxed. She hated that everyone was tiptoeing around her. She'd spent a lifetime accommodating other people, but let one ill-advised word escape her mouth, and people treated her like a volcano that might blow at any moment.

Richard led the group around the terrace and down the same stairs they had descended an hour before, before he'd told her he did not want Cat Courtney in his bed. She thought of that uneasily as they circled around to the ice house. She'd told him that Cat was just a job, she was still his true-blue Laura, but he had then seen – as had everyone else – Cat Courtney demolishing two silly little girls, overkill for a minor *faux pas*.

Not two silly little girls. Francie.

Oh, dear Lord.

Had she been striking out at Francie? Had she looked at two rude but harmless twinkies trying to catch Richard Ashmore's attention and seen Francie resurrected, Francie moving in to type his thesis, Francie coming up the mountain with Richard, Francie trailing off into the forest with him?

Francie winning once again?

She hadn't even fought fair in Jefferson's bedroom. No twinkie could hope to compete against a grown woman who'd made a man moan in ecstasy a few hours before.

She saw Boston A and Boston B gazing at Richard flirtatiously, two children who had no idea who they were up against, doubtless thinking that any man with a cranky mistress might be interested in trading her in for a newer model. And suddenly she was sick of the whole thing.

She waited until Richard had finished talking about the ice house – who knew there was so much to say about an ice house? Before the group moved on to the next room, she hurried over to his side and touched his arm. He looked down at her, and she saw in relief that he wasn't angry. On the other hand, she didn't see the man who had touched her like a precious treasure the night before. He showed no emotion as he looked at her.

"If you don't mind," Laura said softly, "I need some sun. I'll meet you down at the gift shop when you're done, if that's okay." Without waiting for his answer, she turned to the others, smiled a Cat Courtney smile – no sense in not making that work for her right now – and said, "It was lovely meeting you all. Enjoy the rest of your tour. And do have Richard tell you about his book. It's wonderful."

Her good deed for the day, to add to Julie's college fund.

It was a relief to walk across the lawn down to the gift shop, away from the press of people around them. The sun was high in the sky now – noon, she saw with a glance at her watch – and a huge line waited for the next several tours. They had indeed just beaten the heavy crowds.

Maybe she ought to set up a trust fund for Julie for college. She didn't know what architects earned, but surely keeping up Ashmore Park, a stable of horses, and an airplane and then adding college and possibly graduate school in music to the mix was going to be a financial burden. She'd already told Lucy not ever to worry about the cost of schooling for her child.

If Richard would even let her help out. *I'm his mistress.* She already knew his answer.

She had plenty of time to shop in the gift store. The shop didn't stock the mantel clock, and the mirror was a special order, but the staff was more than happy to help out someone who seemed determined to buy out the store, assuring her that they could ship whatever she wanted wherever she wanted. She browsed around, glancing up nervously every time the door opened, and the longer he delayed, the faster her heart beat, the more anxious she became.

By the time Richard came to her, she had been staring at a blown glass ornament for ten minutes, unable to decide if she wanted a miniature Monticello to hang on her tree to remind her of this day.

"Are you going to get that?" His voice was calm, the voice of a man talking to an acquaintance.

Laura carefully did not look at him. "I might. I collect blown glass for my Christmas tree."

"Then you should get it as a souvenir of your first trip to Monticello." First trip – there wouldn't be a second; she was never showing her face here again. "There are some other ornaments over there – oh," he saw the pile already waiting at the counter, "I see you found them. Ready?"

Laura had just signed the receipt for a truly frightening amount and was replacing her card in her wallet when a thought struck her. All the St. Brides, even Meg, carried a corporate credit card; it simplified the St. Bride Family Administration's bookkeeping, and she had never given it a second thought. But that meant that Mark probably saw her account activity. He could tell where she had been and what she had been doing from her purchases. He'd see the fabric she had bought in Gettysburg, the purchases at Monticello. He'd see that she hadn't once paid to put gas in her car, even though she had supposedly driven all over the state. He'd see that she had not paid for any meals or a hotel room.

Damn! So much for thinking that a cell phone covered her tracks.

She and Richard had walked halfway down the dirt and gravel path past Mulberry Row, past the slave quarters, before he said, "Well? Are you going to tell me what's wrong?"

"What?" She needed to get her own American Express card. She would have her cell phone bill redirected – no, she was on the corporate account, and Mark could see the bills. He could probably tell where she was from the cell tower listing for each call. He could tell who she called, who called her.

She needed a new cell phone.

She needed independence from the St. Bride cocoon, no matter how convenient it was to have someone take care of the little details of life for her. Her checking account wasn't even private. The personal assistant assigned to her and Emma had access so that she could balance the account every month and file the checks away.

She needed a new bank account.

She used the St. Bride email server, and every single employee of the St. Bride companies knew that emails were subject to corporate scrutiny. No one in the family had paid attention to the warning; no one would ever dare read their emails – except the CEO, if he became curious about her activities. He could read her email to Terry, asking him to send her diaphragm to her.

She needed a new email account.

"It's obvious," said Richard evenly, "that you are upset about something. I want to know what's wrong. If my mistress is going to blow hot and cold all morning and then top it off by announcing to the world that we are sharing a bed, I think I am entitled to know what is going through her mind."

"Oh, Richard." She stopped, genuinely contrite. She had bigger problems than Mark's access to her personal affairs. How could she have overlooked the effect of her moodiness on Richard? She hadn't thought that he might wonder what he had done or even care that she was unhappy. She bit her lip and looked up at him. "I'm so sorry. That was inexcusable of me."

"Not good enough, Laura Rose." Richard's voice was firm, giving no quarter, and that startled her. "I lived with the queen of mood swings for seven years, and I won't play guessing games. What's going on?"

"Nothing, really—"

"Laura."

Oh, no, she was going to have to tell him. Most women wanted men attuned to their moods, she thought ruefully, and it was just her luck to actually have one.

"I got tired of the Boston bimbettes hanging all over you." It sounded ridiculous when she said it aloud, and it wasn't even half the truth. The girls she could have handled, maybe even the others who had taken his attention. Their monopoly of him paled in comparison to Francie's voice from the past echoing in her head, reminding her that he had brought her twin up here on a snowy day and made love to her.

"Don't be absurd," he said brusquely, and she flinched. She'd hate to be on the receiving end of that tone very often. "Those girls are practically Julie's age, for God's sake. You can't think that I'd have the slightest interest in a pop-tart, especially one with a—" He broke off impatiently. "Never mind. Don't you think you went a little overboard? You flattened the hell out of them."

"Good." His sharp tone had gotten to Laura. She was tired of feeling tense and remorseful. *She* hadn't chattered like a demented magpie. *She* hadn't hung around thrusting her bosom in his face. "They were rude. I couldn't hear, and neither could other people. You know all this stuff, Richard, it's old hat to you, but it wasn't to me, and I wanted to hear what the guide was saying. *And*," she emphasized, "I didn't notice the rest of your groupies doing anything, and you did ask how to shut them up."

"You still went overboard." He stopped, then said slowly, "But that wasn't it, was it? You were all over the map before we ever got in line. What's bothering you?"

"Nothing, it's just—"

"What's bothering you?" He stood over her, staring down at her hard, and his eyes were dark with suspicion. He wasn't going to let her slide without an answer.

She waited a long moment, her heart beating fast, while he continued to stare down at her. She was going to have to tell him the truth; he wasn't backing down.

"You brought Francie here."

The words hung in the heated summer air between them, and the silence stretched out beyond reason. She couldn't look at him. She was more tired than she could remember being in months. She was tired of Francie, tired of hearing her twin's voice in her head. She was sick to death of Richard's past with Francie. She wanted to go home to her flat in London, crawl into her solitary bed, and sleep until she forgot that Francie had ever existed.

"That's right," said Richard flatly. "I brought Francie here. Now I've brought you. I've also brought my aunts from Ireland, my mother's garden club, and, on one particularly hideous trip, Julie's Brownie Scout troop. I've brought lots of people. So I brought Francie. What of it?"

She stared off along the path, anything to keep from looking at him. Her voice was low and miserable. "Well, I doubt those other trips were quite the same."

"And what," Richard's voice sounded dangerous, "is that supposed to mean?"

She said nothing. She'd said far too much already.

He was furious now, every inch of his long body rigid with anger. He had folded his arms across his chest, glaring down at her, and for all her own height, she was at a disadvantage. She should have never said anything, she thought unhappily. She should have squashed down her jealousy – yes, it had been jealousy, she was still jealous of Francie, because Francie's feelings for him had at least been honest. She hadn't had the guilt of his blood on her hands.

"All right," Richard said, "I've had it. I am not putting up with this. We're going to fight about Francie sooner or later, so let's get it over with. Come on. We'll have some privacy down here unless the – what did you call them? – the bimbettes find us."

He didn't wait for her. He veered off the roundabout, went down a set of wooden stairs from the higher ground on Mulberry Row, and strode down a path through the vegetable garden. In the middle of the garden, some hundred feet out, a small garden pavilion stood, overlooking the orchard and vineyard. It looked for all the world like a miniature house, and, as Laura saw when she followed Richard inside, it was indeed private. Sunlight washed in through the double-sash windows, with the instant effect of shutting them off from the rest of Monticello.

She sank down on a chair against one of the walls. He took up a spot against the opposite wall, and the couple of minutes of walking hadn't made a dent in his anger. His body language announced that they were teetering on the brink of explosion. All 6'5" shimmered with tension.

"Speak," he said abruptly. "You have known about my trip up here with Francie for fourteen years. You covered for her at school that day. Why – when we have had such an enjoyable weekend – are you dragging that up now?"

She tried to concentrate. Her thoughts were skittering all over; she couldn't keep them in order.

"You might as well tell me," Richard said. "We are not going anywhere until you do."

And he crossed his arms and prepared to wait.

She said, "I know what happened that day. I remembered, and I'm sorry, it bothered me."

"And what," he said, "do you think happened?"

She looked away, deeply humiliated. He wasn't going to rest until she exposed every bit of her stupid, childish jealousy over a past he could do nothing to erase. "Oh, God, Richard, do we have to go through it all? I know what happened, okay? I know you can't do anything about it. It's my problem to deal with. I'm just going to have to learn to—"

"What is it that you think happened?" Deceptively soft, uncompromising.

"Okay." Laura looked at him bleakly. "You and Francie came up here. It was snowing – she had trouble getting here because some parts of I-64 still weren't clear. No one was around, and you—" No, she couldn't tell him that Francie had detailed their lovemaking in front of the fireplace in Jefferson's bedroom. Now that she had seen the room for herself, she wasn't sure she remembered that correctly. They wouldn't have had the necessary time or privacy. "You went upstairs to the dome room, and it was empty, and you – oh, for God's sake, Richard, you know what happened."

"No," said Richard. "I don't, because Francie and I did not go up to the dome room."

That statement hung in the air. "I remember that pretty clearly."

"I don't care what you remember. Tourists aren't allowed in the dome room. The only times I've ever been up there have been on research trips through UVA." He settled back against the wall, and she was too miserable to enjoy the splendid picture he made. "Is that it?"

"You went down into the dependencies, and Francie said you pulled her into the wine cellar."

"Which then – as now, as you'd have seen if you'd come down there with me – has a locked gate door."

She couldn't quell her uneasiness. Either Richard was a smoother liar than she had ever imagined, or her memory was badly off – but he was genuinely angry. She didn't think he was lying.

"And then what?" said Richard. "Mad passion in the parking lot? I'll stop you right now. I drove a Honda back then, and you girls had a Toyota. I couldn't fit in the back of either with my height."

"No." She drew a breath. "Not there. Before. You walked down the mountain, and there's a forest or a grove or something."

"That's right. You'll see it in a few minutes."

She stared down at the wooden floor. "You pulled her back into the trees, and—" She remembered Francie talking dreamily, her eyes closed in remembrance, the smile playing around her lips. She remembered methodically shredding a tissue into a snowstorm of specks as she listened. It was the first time she'd known men could do that to women; Peggy had left out this part of the birds-and-bees talk. "You had oral sex."

She didn't dare look up. And if he touched her – she was going to fly apart.

His voice sounded strangled. "Who was the lucky recipient?"

"Francie." This had to be the single most humiliating moment of her life. "You did it to her."

Dead silence. And then he started laughing.

Laura looked up, incredulous, as he collapsed back against the wall, and she drew back. She knew men had a different perspective about sex – how many times had Cam joked that women needed a reason, men just needed a place – but she had never seen a man laugh so hard about it.

Richard's laughter ended in a coughing fit. He took a deep breath and sank into the chair opposite her, leaning back and stretching out his long legs. "I'll make you a deal, my love," and he swallowed another laugh. "I'll bring you up here next February – when it is usually snowing, and the average temperature is thirty degrees, as you'd remember if you hadn't been living in Texas all these years – and we'll go out in the forest, and then let's see how interested *you* are in sex, oral or otherwise."

"Oh, my God." Laura stared at him, and the world turned upside down. "It didn't happen."

"Of course it didn't happen. I remember that day. It wasn't only snowing, the road coming up the mountain had patches of ice. I damn near spun out of control a couple of times, but, oh no, Francie was determined that she was going to do what Diana refused to do, she was going to share my interest in Monticello, she was going to learn all about Palladian architecture. Then when we got up here, it was almost deserted – she got that right – because most people had the good sense not to drive up a mountain in that kind of weather." He stopped, and shook his head. "We did walk down the mountain, true, and I won't say that there wasn't a kiss or two, but mostly she bitched about how cold she was."

"Richard – she made this tape." She had to work out the memory. Had she dreamed it all? "She came back that night, and she sat on her bed right across from me, and she told me everything. She was wearing the nightgown Lucy gave me for Christmas, I can see it now, and we were drinking lemon tea. She swiped one of Daddy's tapes and taped over it. She described everything – I mean, some of it embarrassed me half to death, I didn't even know men did that to women. And you're telling me *she made it all up?*"

"Oh, those tapes!" Richard dismissed it out of hand, as if the tape was hardly worth remembering. "Francie made four or five tapes. I don't recall that specific one, but she was always sending me stuff at the school – books, cookies, tapes, cards. I told her she had a promising future ahead of her, writing erotica."

"Why – why did she make the tapes?" Laura asked in bewilderment.

"Because I liked them." He shrugged. "They were fun, and Francie had a clever way with words. I'm a normal heterosexual male, Laura, even if I live a life of depressing celibacy. I like sex. I like reading about it. I like hearing about it, even if—" and he laughed again— "it's in the realm of fantasy. Oh, my God, in the snow!"

She was stunned. She thought of all Francie's confidences about him in the dark of night, Francie describing what he had said, what he had done, how he had touched her. For fourteen years, she'd brooded over Francie's words, letting them poison her thoughts and feelings – and now he sat there, telling her that none of it was real.

What else did she believe that hadn't really happened?

She said cautiously, "You – you and Francie did, you know, have sex, didn't you?"

You are Meg's father, aren't you?

"Yes, as much as I wish we didn't, we did," Richard said, and his voice was rueful. "You know about New Year's Eve, although I'm not sure I want to hear what she said about that. I'd been drinking, and I'm not at my best when I've had too much to drink. A handful of other times." He looked at her straight, and she trusted his words. "For all the trouble it caused – not an affair for the ages."

A handful of other times. But Francie had said— "Richard," Laura stopped to put together her thoughts, "you saw each other every weekend. You flew down to pick her up at that airfield – I know, because she'd drop me off at the bookstore, and then she'd take the car and leave it at the airfield while you flew off to Ash Marine." She hated even mentioning the island. "I always had to wait at the mall after I was off work until she came to pick me up. Richard – that was practically every Saturday."

Richard regarded her curiously. "Didn't you know?"

"Know what?"

"I was teaching her to fly," he said. "I'd gotten my instructor's rating at Christmas. I had some idea about making extra money giving flying lessons, and she had asked me to teach her before – well, before anything ever started. I arranged for the insurance, and Francie sweet-talked your father into paying for the fuel. Sure, we went out to the island. It has that flat plain for landing, and it was the only place I knew where no one would see us." He shrugged. "I wasn't crazy about the idea at first, but she made an ideal student to practice on. She did what I told her to do."

Laura stared at him in shock.

His eyes were speculative upon her. "You really didn't know, did you? She thought it was more fun to spin all these great sex tales and let you believe that she was living the great romance."

Laura shifted abruptly, hugging her knees to her chest, burying her face against her crossed arms. She felt numb. All these years, she'd believed a lie – and Francie had known, she had to have known, the effect of her words. Impossible that she hadn't known, as she played make-believe, that every mention of Richard had driven a dagger straight into Laura's heart.

What had she done to Francie to deserve that?

"Now that's out of the way," Richard said, "can we have a rational discussion about her?"

She lifted her head wearily. "Do we have to? I – I am tired of Francie."

He nodded. "Yes, we do. She's there. In her own way, she's a greater barrier than Diana."

Diana. At the moment, she scarcely remembered that Diana was actually his wife. She managed to nod, and waited for him to begin.

He was silent for a moment or so, marshaling his thoughts. Laura watched him, and it occurred to her that they were back on her terrace the morning before, a man and a woman meeting honestly to lay out their hearts. This was even more important, she sensed, their entire future lay here in this small garden pavilion. Their words here would determine what was to come.

"A couple of nights ago, I told you that I wanted Francie to stay in the past." Richard leaned back and clasped his hands around one bent leg. "I know it bothers you when I say I don't think about her, but I don't. That's the truth. Francie is part of my life, but she's in the past. She reminds me of a painful time in my life, and – just as I'm sure you have painful times that you don't like to think about – I don't spend much time dwelling on my relationship with her."

She nodded nervously.

"I don't know," he said, "if you've ever done something that you are so ashamed of that you would do anything to keep it a secret. That's Francie to me, Laura. To me, she represents – well, a lot of things, but mostly, she represents the time when I discovered that I am not exactly the upright and honorable man I thought I was."

Laura's breath caught.

"All my life," Richard continued evenly, "I had this image of myself. We all do, we all think we are much better than we really are. Few of us look in the mirror and see our inner flaws. No one ever says, 'I'm weak' or 'I'm dishonest' or 'I can't be trusted worth a damn.' I never saw myself as a man who would cheat on the woman he had sworn to love and cherish his entire life."

He leaned over towards her, and his gaze took hers and held it.

"Francie was only the second woman I'd touched in my life," he said. "Up till that time, even before we were married, I was completely faithful to Diana. I don't know if you know how unusual that was, you were pretty sheltered, but trust me, I was an anomaly among my peers. I never dated around, never went out behind her back. Diana was all I wanted, and I swear to you, Laura, it never once crossed my mind that I would not be a faithful husband to her. And then – well, I won't go into specifics, but you've already guessed that things went badly wrong between us."

She scarcely breathed, not waiting to miss even a second.

"Even then—" Richard shook his head. "I was convinced that everything was Diana's fault, that I was blameless. After all, when I looked in the mirror, I saw a man of integrity and loyalty and steadfastness – I saw myself as everything my father was. God knows, he was the most uxorious of men, he was as deeply in love with my mother on the day he died as he was when they got married. I'll admit too – I made life miserable for Diana, sitting on my moral high horse, looking down on her laziness and her addictions – and then one night I drank too much champagne, and I kissed Diana's sister who looked so much like her, and I found out that I was not such a saint after all."

He walked over to the open wall of the pavilion, his back to her. She couldn't tear her eyes away from him.

"I might have excused that in myself," he said. "I wasn't so naïve as not to know that Francie was culpable too. But then Diana returned the next morning, and Francie made a comment that reminded me of all that had gone wrong, and I looked at my dear wife, and I remembered what a true deceitful bitch she could be, and I deliberately embarked on an affair with my nineteen-year-old sister-in-law."

Laura whispered, "Eighteen."

"What?" He looked over his shoulder at her.

"She was eighteen."

"Oh, Christ." Richard sounded appalled. "Well, at least she still wasn't jailbait. And the next time you start wishing you'd been there instead of her, you need to remember that you *were* jailbait, and it would have been a criminal act for me to touch you." He looked at her gravely. "God, this feels strange. I have never talked about this before."

"Not even your father?" How isolated he must have felt, as isolated as she had felt about Ash Marine... *something that you are so ashamed of... you would do anything to keep it a secret....*

"No. Lucy guessed some of it that spring. You know how she is – I'd feel those X-ray eyes on me, and I knew she was trying to figure out what was going on. Francie and I were particularly careful when I was home for exactly that reason. I didn't care, Laura. I knew I was doing something as dishonorable as it could be, and honest to God, I – did – not – care."

She thought he had cared, very much.

"Besides – and this excuses nothing – I liked Francie. Oh, she was a world-class liar, and she never missed a chance to take a swipe at Diana, but I didn't care. She was warm and funny, and she was always laughing. Diana and I lived in such an armed camp that it was a relief to be with someone who smiled, who put herself out to please me, who was glad to see me, for God's sake. It was a relief to make love with a woman again, even if it violated every principle I held. When you live with a woman who wants nothing to do with you, you lose confidence in yourself as a man. Francie restored that, and for that, I will always be grateful to her."

She swallowed hard and nodded, even though he didn't see her. He was still staring into the distance.

"Finally, though," Richard made a gesture, "it was time to cool off. We were moving back home, Francie was going off to college – I knew it was time to end it. So I met her to tell her we needed to stop, and somehow, I have never figured out how, Diana found out and tracked us down. And that was such a disaster – I had sweating dreams about it for a couple of years afterwards. I woke up then, believe me, I saw what a hash I had made of things, and the first thought that went through my mind was that I was going to lose my daughter."

"Oh, no."

"Oh, yes." He turned around. "I'm not the first man to have risked my child for a few afternoons with a pretty girl, but I can tell you I was the sorriest in a hurry. And then – then Dominic called a few days later and said that you and Francie were missing, and I knew I had driven her away, and I looked in the mirror and all I saw was a faithless bastard."

She felt tears welling up in her eyes. Her heart ached for him. He'd been only twenty-three, after all, and it was easy to sit in judgment from the thirties and forget that he'd been a young man, with all the maturing and tempering of adult life still ahead of him.

"Here I was, finally out of grad school, finally ready to get started on the career I'd wanted all my life, but I had wrecked my personal life beyond repair. There was no hope for Diana and me – there hadn't been for years, and it's not all her fault. She doesn't bear all of the blame. I didn't know what to do, except go back home, and start working, and try to rebuild myself into the man I had hoped I was." He fell quiet. "And the one thing I was determined was that no one would ever know. My father suspected, and Lucy outright accused me, and by that time I figured you had to know. Diana thought she had the whole picture. But the only two people who knew for sure were Francie and me, and I wanted to keep it that way."

Laura thought of her ill-advised remark to Diana and Lucy.

"It's an old joke about unfaithful men. Deny, deny, deny. I didn't even do that. I just never spoke of it. And gradually – as time went on, I gained some perspective. Part of it was work; I'm damn good at what I do, and people knew it. I worked hard at being a good father, and you can't feel like a complete failure when your little girl thinks you hung the moon. I reached out to Lucy, who took her time forgiving me, and I worked to get my father's respect back." He stopped and then said slowly, "I worked harder at relationships with other people in those years after than I had worked at anything in my life."

She wanted to put her arms around him, tell him that he had succeeded, become the man he wanted to see in the mirror – but somehow he divined her intention, and he put up a warning hand.

"Something else about that time, Laura. I'd been an agnostic for years. I got fed up with my mother's piety in my teens. I'd see her with her rosary and her novenas, going to confession every Saturday afternoon, and it all seemed like so much claptrap to me, it seemed absurd that someone as good as she was had to worry all the time about her salvation. I remember one time I lectured you about how you couldn't prove that God was even there, and you just blinked at me, because you were like her, you never lacked faith. Well—" he gave a short laugh— "God might have gone on vacation, but when I needed help, He came back fast enough. That's when I learned what true charity was – that gift of mercy, wiping the slate clean, no matter what you've done, it's not irretrievable. You're not irretrievable. And

I found out – it took a while – if you truly believe that God has forgiven you, you'd better learn to forgive yourself."

Laura stared at him. "You went to church this morning," she whispered.

He gave her a smile. "I went to Eucharist. I go every week. I never miss."

Her hand went to her mouth. She couldn't stop staring at him.

"I guess years of listening to Mom worry about my going to hell rubbed off. I started going to church with my father, and I joined a men's study group – that's where I met Tom – and I found—" He paused. "Truth. Answers. Peace. All the things that a rationalist can find once you lay down pride at the foot of the cross. All the things that came so naturally to you and Mom. It took the worst moral failure of my life for me to get past my empiricism."

That boy, so sure of himself and his intellect. It must have indeed come as a shock to him, this crisis of self and identity and faith. He had never doubted himself before.

"One day – I looked in the mirror, and I had a sense of integrity back. I felt better – I'd flunked the big test in life, but I'd pulled myself back together, and I was," he sounded ironic, "pretty damn proud of myself. And Diana was sliding badly, she was drinking heavily, and we were so alienated from each other, I wasn't even interested in helping her. I just wanted her out of my life. I didn't want any reminders of what had happened. She tried once to patch things up, and I rejected her out of hand. I was back on my moral high horse, because at least I'd faced my demons, but she hadn't undergone the spiritual transformation I had. I told myself I'd forgiven her, but I felt justified in never trusting her again. I wasn't about to wipe the slate clean for *her.*"

She wanted to tell him that he hadn't flunked the test, that the real test was how he had dealt with failure – but he wasn't finished.

"Sorry, I know I am going on too long, but you need to know this. You have a decision to make after I finish, so you need to hear it all. About three years later, Diana and I had one last huge blowup – an appalling scene, you cannot believe, I don't think either of us ever behaved so badly in our lives – and I threw her out. I was full of righteousness at that point; she'd strayed off the straight and narrow, while I had remained faithful, and I didn't consider that she deserved any of the forgiveness I'd claimed for myself – anyway, we separated, and I filed for legal custody of Julie."

Was he going to tell her about the custody fight? Tell her the truth about Julie?

"Then Francie came back," and she stiffened in shock. "I know you know, Laura, you said as much the night you came back. She called me from Ash Marine, and I went running out there to tell her as gently as possible to stay the hell out of my life. I had left her behind, it was time for her to move on and forget me – oh, I had a whole speech to give her. I was on my high horse about her too. This time, I was going to do the honest and decent thing. And I saw her, and – well, suffice it to say within minutes we were going at each other."

She couldn't breathe. Tight bands had wrapped around her lungs.

"I hadn't been with a woman in three years. I was starved for physical love – I have no idea if you know what that feels like, Lucy says women have the same hungers men do, they just don't dwell on them as much. That may be true, I don't know. I was in my mid twenties, and in seven years of marriage, I'd had one good year with my wife and six years of near-total abstinence. I have a normal sexual appetite. I touched Francie, and it was like going up in flames." He heard his own words and winced. "Not the best way to put it. I'm sorry."

She shook her head. She couldn't speak. *He still thought he'd seen Francie on the island.*

"It's hard to know what metaphors I can use with you, although," he showed a gleam of humor, "I noticed you teased me about skyscrapers last night, and it didn't seem to bother you. You'll have to tell me if I say something that upsets you."

She forced out, "Don't worry about that."

He resumed his story. "So we were together, and then afterwards it turned – never mind, suffice it to say that the row I had with her cast the time in the park with Diana in the shade. I lost my temper, and Francie lost hers, and we behaved unforgivably towards each other."

He wasn't going to tell her. She wasn't to know that he had goaded *Francie* with the threat of losing her child. She wasn't to know that *Francie*, in retaliation, had picked up a gun and shot him.

"That's the last time I ever saw her. But – it didn't take long for all the guilt and self-loathing to descend again. I'd fallen off my pedestal again, and this time I had hurt a young woman that I cared about deeply. It wasn't like hurting Diana, who gave just as good as she got. Francie was so much more vulnerable, and I had been cruel be-yond belief to her. I had driven her flat crazy. So now I had to look in the mirror and square that in myself."

She felt sick. She'd spent so many years trying not to remember Ash Marine – *there be dragons* – that she had never thought beyond the physical damage she had inflicted. She had never thought that he might struggle with guilt about the way he had behaved towards her – because she had never realized that he might feel guilty over Francie. She had loved Richard Ashmore, and she hadn't known him at all.

"How long did it take that time to come back?" she asked.

He smiled at her; he knew she understood what he had been trying to tell her. "Not as long this time – a year or so. I had a lot to keep myself busy. I was a single father, I'd gotten my license as a reg-istered architect so I got assigned more challenging projects, I started working on the Folly – and I kept going to church. I learned to accept myself as a flawed individual who was going to fall, and I learned to repent and ask for forgiveness and start anew." He stopped. "At some point," he said, "you know you're going to make it."

She watched him with wet eyes as he came back and sat down op-posite her.

"That's it for Francie," he said. "I never saw her again. But I had finally learned one thing, and it's that I am a fool when it comes to women. I had made three monumental mistakes, and I had screwed up any hope I had of a normal life. And, honestly, that's all I ever wanted. I never wanted to sow my wild oats, sampling women like a buffet; I didn't consider that part of being a man. I wanted to be like my father. By the time I was twenty-six, that was all gone."

"Oh, Richard." She looked away, blinking away tears. "You should have had what you wanted."

"Instead," said Richard, and his voice had started to strain from talking, "I knew that I was going to be by myself until Julie was old enough that Diana couldn't take her. I'm sure," he cocked an eye-brow at her, "you've heard Lucy's theories about why we never di-vorced, and it's true that I didn't want to risk another down-and-dirty custody fight. So you can see my dilemma – how to build a de-cent life as Julie's father and balance that with my own needs. I need-ed to matter in a woman's life, and have her matter in mine, and when you have to tell a woman up front that you are not getting a di-vorce, that is not easy. Most women aren't interested."

She said hoarsely, "But some were."

He nodded. "Three, after Diana left. Two were shorter relationships – very nice women, both of them were getting over bad marriages, and I made a pleasant stopgap. I treated them well, and they treated me well. I made it crystal clear from the beginning that there was no hope of anything else, and everything ended gracefully and with no recriminations on either side."

He paused. "The third – well, Jennifer was a different story. I met her when Julie was ten. It lasted three years, and that was the only time that I seriously considered divorce. She wanted me to, Lord knows we talked the subject to death. I put all my usual restrictions on her – she was part of my private life, and that meant no meeting Julie or my parents, no coming to the house, no socializing near home. She lived in Richmond then, and we saw each other there most weekends. After a year or so, she was chafing at that. She wanted to be an official part of my life. She wanted us to get married and have children and be a family, and I don't blame her for that." He ruminated. "By year two, we were in trouble. I had to weigh my genuine affection for Jennifer against the need to keep Julie safe, and the problem was – that's all it was, genuine affection. It simply wasn't enough to outweigh the risk to my daughter."

He lifted his hands briefly. "So we limped along for another year, and she grew increasingly impatient, and I grew increasingly tired of being on the defensive, and we enjoyed being together less and less. Then came the ultimatum, and I told her no. She went off with a girlfriend on a cruise, and when she came back, she told me it was over. She'd met someone else. She married him two months later."

"Oh, Richard." Her natural compassion bubbled up. No matter how glad she was that Jennifer was out of his life, she ached for him. "I am so glad she was there for you."

He leaned back against the rough wall, and now his gaze was level upon her.

"Your turn, Laura. You have a decision to make. I've told you everything, I've told you things I planned to take to my grave with me – this is who I am now. Francie is part of my life, she is part of who I was and who I've become. I failed with her, she was a terrible mistake, but – strange to say, she ended up making me a better man. I cannot go back and undo the past, so – Laura—" And his voice was straight and uncompromising, and she could not look away from him.

"Yes?" Her voice was shaking.

"You have to decide if you can live with that. You have to decide if you can accept me for who and what I am, even though that includes Francie. You have to decide if you can forgive me for her."

His gaze bored in on her.

"I am not going to put up with your jealousy. I can't deal with you still mourning that she was there that night and you weren't. If you are going to let Francie eat at you, then let's call it quits right now and go our separate ways." In her horror, she saw a muscle pull at his mouth. He said quietly, "I can't deal with another scene like to-day. It's up to you."

She sat there rigid, unable to move, her heart beating painfully within her. He was watching her carefully, intensely, waiting for her answer; he was no longer the man whose eyes had glowed at the sight of her the night before. She had come up against a wall.

She had wrecked it all because she, not he, was still stuck in the past.

She had thought she would destroy the world for him, and in-stead, she had destroyed the promise that lay between them. It might not have been love – he might never have fallen in love with her – but, she thought numbly, he had seen in her his last best hope for the life he'd wanted and been denied.

She didn't have to ask if he had ever told Jennifer about Francie. She knew he had remained silent. He had kept Francie between him-self and God.

But, in one morning, he had laid himself right out for her. This man who kept his inner self private and isolated had trusted her enough to let her in.

And she was going to destroy it all because she still had Francie's voice in her head.

"Well," he said briskly, "I guess that's that." He started to rise. "Are you ready to go?"

Laura found her voice, shaking, rough. "Sit *down*, Richard, don't – you – dare – move."

He stilled and watched her warily.

She rose and crossed the pavilion, and sank to her knees before him. She took his hand, tightly clenched on the arm of the chair, she coaxed his fingers open so that they touched palm to palm, and she kissed his fingertips. The floor was brutal against her knees, every muscle was going to ache later, and she didn't care. That didn't mat-ter.

She made herself meet his eyes, and maybe he saw the desperation in her face. She felt like a swimmer drowning, with no strength left, turning to try to make it to shore.

"I'm still seventeen inside," she said. "I know that's stupid, I know I've gone beyond that. But still – I feel like that girl. I know it's a cliché, but that girl was always on the outside, looking in, pressing her nose against the bakery window, and honestly – I still feel like that."

She looked down, and drew in a long painful breath.

"That's how I felt about you and Francie. I was outside looking in at you both. For fourteen years, I've been that girl. I've been the loser. That's how I always saw myself. The loser. I think – sometimes I think that I made up Cat Courtney because she was a winner like Francie, she had all Francie's passion and fire, and at least when I was Cat, I could be that girl with you."

She caught the bare shake of his head. "No," he said. "I never saw Cat in Francie, not once."

"You should have," her voice was high-pitched and frightened. "You made love with Cat the last two nights. I faked it, Richard, I was a fraud. You thought you were with me – and you wanted to be, didn't you, you said so – and instead," her voice caught in a sob, "that was Cat – I was failing again, and Cat wouldn't fail, she never fails, she wins, and I – I just stepped right out of myself and she took over."

"So that's it." She heard an element of interest in his voice, but she couldn't see him. Her eyes were awash with unspilled tears.

"And you know why?" she demanded. "It's because I'm still *seventeen!* I'm still trying to get your attention from when I was *seventeen!* I'm still trying to win that boy you used to be. And that's so stupid, I'm so stupid, I'm a grown woman, and I don't even *like* boys anymore. That girl and that boy – and Francie – they don't matter, they no longer exist."

She looked at him, and now she felt no fear. She was rolling the dice, and maybe she was going to lose everything. Maybe he was going to walk away from her, and this time he would not come back. She trusted herself. She had never done anything so right in her life.

"I'm a woman now. I'm not a girl," she said clearly, "and I don't want that boy. He is not enough for me anymore. I want – I want *you,* Richard, I want the man you are now, nicks on his soul, banged-up heart, and all. I want the man who can admit he was dead wrong. I want the man who's failed and fallen and screwed up, who knows how to pick up again and go on living, because he can forgive me if I fail and fall and screw up. And if Francie helped make you that way, well, then," her voice shook with tears, "I guess I am in her debt."

She scrambled to her feet and looked down at him. "Back there at the house," she said, "I saw those silly girls making up to you, and I saw myself trying to get your attention all over again and failing, and I saw Francie again, winning. I was irritated with the others talking to you, and that was selfish, I know, but the girls – they got to me. They got to that girl who's still inside me. So I did just what you said I did, I flattened them, and it wasn't a fair fight."

"Not even close. They were outclassed, and you let everyone know it."

"And if Francie had been there, hanging all over you," Laura said, "you know what?" She stared down at him, her breath rising and falling hard. "I would have flattened her too."

He looked at her silently for a long moment, and then he rose, and his arms went around her very gently. "Francie," he said, "wouldn't have known what hit her."

She breathed a sigh of relief, tension spilling from her, and her arms went around his waist, but her voice was fierce. "You're mine," she said. "Don't you forget it, Richard Ashmore. Diana may have been dumb enough to blow it with you, and Jennifer settled for second best, and Francie gave up without a fight, but I won't. I am serving notice on you and any woman who looks at you and thinks, 'Hmmm, I'd like that' – I will sweep her out of the way, I will fight for you, I will not let you go, *I will not lose.*"

He framed her face in his hands, his long fingers warm against her temples, and he kissed her then, and this was not the lover's kiss of the night before. His kiss did not seduce, did not explore. He kissed her, fellow survivor of a life-and-death battle, he kissed her, banged-up heart to banged-up heart, and she kissed him right back.

When they parted, they stared at each other for a long time. Her face was heated, she could feel it, and her heart beat so hard so that she was sure he could hear it. Underneath his tan, she saw a flush on his cheekbones, and he was breathing as hard as she was.

She saw in him the same recognition she felt, that they had breached a point of no return. There was no going back now.

"My God – you have the heart of a warrior," and his eyes were alight. "If we had a door—"

"I don't mind," said Laura immediately, before her nerve started to fade. "No one's around."

"Three people came by a while ago and left when they saw us in here. Besides, that's a hard floor, and you bruise too easily." He leaned against the wall, and pulled her close against him. "Come here, my lady. We need to cool down. I can't go out in public right now."

She laughed up at him, giddy with relief. "And standing like this is going to help?"

"No, but it doesn't hurt either." He looked down at her. "How, Laura, how did you ever hide this from us – this lioness?"

"No one looked."

"I never saw," he said, almost to himself. "All those years – I never saw. I will not make that mistake with you ever again." He looked out at the fields for a moment and then back at her. "We're well and truly caught. You know that, don't you?"

She nodded and whispered, "What – what do we do?"

"I don't know," Richard said. "This is a royal mess. I have no idea what we do or where we go from here. But—" he lifted her chin to look at her squarely— "whatever happens, we stand together."

She nodded again, and he pulled her tight against him, and she pulled him tight against her, and they kissed each other. Not a kiss of passion, she scrambled to think, with the small part of her mind that even *could* think, but a pledge, a promise, a vow. A seal to a covenant, truer than those vows they'd each made, long ago, to other people.

They ran out of breath, and he settled her back against him, his hand against her back.

We stand together. She was not alone anymore. And he no longer stood alone, as he had for so many years, fighting his way through the consequences of his disastrous marriage. He had been in exile for even longer than she had – a silent, self-imposed exile, but no less solitary. But no more. Their cold years of exile had come to an end in this quiet pavilion.

She pressed her cheek to his shoulder.

"Listen, Laura, about what you said." She looked up. "About faking it."

So much for her high. She slid right back down to earth.

"Now don't start apologizing," he said. "It took a lot of courage to admit that." He brushed her hair from her face. "I knew something was wrong Friday night. You were there with me – then you weren't. I know women can fake it to get it over with, and we men don't always see it – you have the advantage of us there. Did I pressure you, Laura? Did you feel you had to pretend to satisfy me?"

She bit her lip. She couldn't tell him the truth, that she, not Francie, had pushed him off his moral high plane on the island. He'd made it clear that he thought he'd been with Francie that day. How could she explain what had happened to her when he had moved inside her and it had all come back?

I put a bullet in you.

No. New reality. Francie did.

She made herself look at him. "I was having trouble – you know, getting to—"

"Did you have problems with your husband? Did you feel you had to please him?"

She wasn't sure of the protocol, discussing one lover's performance with another. "Not after a while, after we got used to each other. It took a few months before – well, I got into the swing of things."

"That makes sense." He sounded matter-of-fact.

It seemed very strange to be talking like this, when he was leaning against the wall and she was practically lying on top of him. "What does?"

He lifted her chin with his hand. "Good sex takes time. You've had – what, I'm guessing the one sexual partner before this? And you were very young when you married. There's a learning curve. We have to learn each other, see what we enjoy together, find our own rhythm. But that's not going to happen if you think you have to pretend in order to please me."

She felt herself turning bright red. "Friday – it wasn't going to happen for me. I tried to concentrate, I really did, but – I just lost it."

"Not surprising, after the traumatic day you had – Lord, you scared me when I saw you lying on the floor. It would have been a miracle if you'd been able to relax." He brushed her mouth lightly. "Lighten up, Laura. It's supposed to be fun. The only one you have to please is yourself. And if I'm not doing something you want me to do, tell me. I'm not a mind reader."

She kissed the shoulder she had wounded. "Okay. I'll tell you what to do every minute."

He laughed. "Thanks, *Lucy.* Now – last night – I have to say it wasn't obvious. You seemed very much with me. What happened?"

She stared at his shirt. "I froze at the last moment. It was easier to let Cat take over." She winced. "Boy, that sounds crazy, doesn't it? It was easier to put on the Cat mindset."

"Don't," and she heard the firm note in his voice. "You're cheating us both if you do. I told you, I don't want Cat between us. She is smoke and illusion, and I want—" He grinned down at her. "I want my mistress."

She glanced up at him through her lashes. "You're not going to let me forget that, are you?"

"Hell, no. I'm going to hold it over your head for the next fifty years."

"I was afraid of that."

"Mistresses," Richard said, "have one well-defined duty. If you're going to talk the talk—"

Laura kissed him, loving the touch of him, the taste of him, the feel of him against her body. She felt ready to slay dragons. "Take me home."

They talked about it halfway down the mountain. They talked about it in the car in the parking lot. They talked about it in the plane. They eyed his car on the ground, but they were so close. They could wait another few minutes.

They made it as far as the drawing room at Edwards Lake. And the only cat present waited patiently, meowed once at his oblivious owner sprawled in exhaustion across her equally exhausted lover, and went off in search of his food bowl.

23

Diana, Smashing

I THOUGHT RICHARD WOULD DIVORCE ME. For months after the girls disappeared, I waited for him to speak… but he never did.

Home we went, back to Williamsburg, back to Ashmore Park and the old bachelor quarters, Ashmore Minor, that turned out to be a rather nice house to live in. Richard settled into his architectural career, and I found to my horror that I really was expected to settle into being a wife and mother. I wasn't a student or a teacher anymore, and away from my group and on the days when I could avoid Daddy, I wasn't much of a musician. I was a child care giver, but a toddler is sufficient company for only so much of the day.

And I certainly had no company at night.

I had to do something with myself. I spent a couple of weeks staring glumly at the house, listening to Julie and her little songs, flipping through magazines. I'm not a reader. But I am a looker, and one day some of those pictures in *Architectural Digest* made an impression on me.

And maybe years of listening to Richard praise the glories of Monticello had rubbed off.

So I turned into an interior decorator. For months, I ran around with fabric swatches and measuring tapes, picking out tiles and colors and paints. I rearranged. I painted. I varnished. I replastered. I installed crown molding. I scoured antique stores for the right finishing touches. I even installed a new dishwasher.

I spent Richard's paycheck with a vengeance, and he never uttered a word.

With nothing else to do, I finished the house in record time. So, in true Jeffersonian fashion, I started all over again. And I finished that.

I thought about getting a job, but the problem with being a pianist is that the only real-world job out there is teaching, and teaching high-school music ranked way below digging ditches. I'd hated every minute of it. I talked about doing some part-time consulting with some of the builders in the area, but Richard said that consulting involved too much time and travel, and he didn't want Julie in day care again anyway. (Bloody hypocrite. When he needed free time, day care was fine, but when I needed to save my sanity, I wasn't being a good mother.) I volunteered my time at Williamsburg, but that lasted only during tourist season. The rest of the time, they didn't need me.

Most of my friends from high school had scattered to the winds. The few who had returned were in graduate school or pursuing their careers, like most of the architectural wives. I might have found someone to pal around with among the other stay-at-home moms, except that they were in full reproductive mode, engaged in *What to Expect When You're Expecting*. After the third "When are you going to have another one, Diana?" I closed the door to anything beyond a nodding acquaintance.

I didn't even have Peggy to talk to. She and Philip were sensitive to our problems, so they left us alone, and that turned out to be even worse than if they'd interfered. Sometimes I'd see my nice Irish mother-in-law, who probably could have given me pointers on being married to a workaholic if I'd asked her, and she'd be working out in her gardens or dashing off to her volunteer work. She always had enough to do. The hours of the day didn't weigh heavily on her hands.

They weighed on me so heavily that one day, while grocery shopping, I bought a bottle of wine. It lasted three days. I bought another, and it lasted two.

The third one went in an evening.

After a month when I became the Wine Cellar's best customer, I tried some Scotch. It felt like fire going down my throat, but it did make the long evenings after I put Julie to bed easier to take.

Sometimes I'd lie on the sofa at night before Richard came in, drinking my libation of choice, staring at the ceiling and wondering if I wanted to paint a mural à *la Michelangelo* or just splash some paint à *la Pollock*, and wonder what Laurie and Francie were doing.

Francie, I speculated, was in dire straits, waitressing or working a blackjack table (I always saw her in Vegas). She went home to her cold garret every night and wept in remorse for her sins against me, or maybe – and I liked this even better – she was so hardened that she went to bars and let men pick her up for money.

Laurie I saw in a quiet New England college town, wearing a twin set and Mama's pearls and working as an *au pair* while she studied music. Despite her perfidy in not telling me what Francie and Richard had been up to, I couldn't really stay mad at Laurie. (Of course, now we know she married some zillionaire, or he wasn't yet, but he was going to be, and she was writing songs, well on her way to becoming Cat Courtney. But she was still probably wearing a twin set, even in Texas.)

It says volumes about the mind-numbing sameness of my life that I envied Francie turning tricks or Laurie taking care of someone's brats, because at least they were doing *something* with their lives.

I didn't even have my music. We couldn't afford a grand piano, and I was too stubborn to settle for a studio piano when Richard still had his blasted plane and we were paying hangar rent every month. Daddy tried to bribe me back to voice by offering to buy me a piano, using the money he wasn't spending on the twins' tuition, and I wanted one so bad I almost said yes. But I had nowhere to put it. The one room that would have been appropriate for a music room, an insulated room off our garage, Richard had taken as a workroom so that he could work on his stupid model airplanes.

Besides, if Daddy bought me a piano, I'd have to go back to voice. He'd control me again.

So I lay on the sofa, stared at the ceiling, drank whiskey, and thought of what I'd wanted to do with my life. And the only time I got to play was when Daddy was out of town, which thank God was a lot, and I could go over to the house and use his piano.

I was so damn lonely! Richard worked late, came home and worked some more, and rarely talked to me. Even with the recession, building was on an upswing, and even though he didn't have his license yet, he was seen as such a comer that he got picked for the plum projects. He spent several months on the road one year, working on a museum building project in upstate New York, living there during the week and flying home every weekend. He spent those weekends catching up on his work, doing whatever chores needed doing, seeing his parents, and being with Julie.

Me, I certainly came too far down on his list to get around to.

One thing I couldn't hang on him: he didn't neglect Julie as his career blossomed. When he called every night from New York, it was to talk to Julie. I existed only as a receptionist. He spun her a never-ending story about Duchess Julia and her talking cat, and Julie looked forward eagerly to each new episode. My few feeble attempts to read Dr. Seuss to her flopped; she wanted Richard to read to her. So they read Dr. Seuss together over the phone, each with a book, while I sat nearby, seething, wondering how on earth I had given birth to such a daddy's girl.

To Julie, I was good only for the mechanics of life, and even those she mastered early on. It became obvious that she didn't need me, and didn't even really want me around, unless it was to fix her hot dogs and get her drinks of water or put new videos into the VCR. Laughably (or sadly), she perceived me as a rival for her father's affections. One cold rainy weekend, Richard and I spent a rare evening together watching a pay-per-view concert in our den, and because his recliner was out being reupholstered, we had to share the sofa, stretched out at opposite ends under a large afghan. I put my feet alongside his leg to keep them warm, and, after a moment, he put his alongside me. I think it was the first time in years that he had touched me. Julie, bored with her toys, wandered in, spied her parents behaving like real married people for a change, and immediately plunked herself right down between us.

I told her to move. She refused. Richard told her to move. She started whining for him to read to her. When he told her no (because he really wanted to see the concert), she burst into tears and sobbed so noisily that he finally gave up and carted her off to her bedroom. I watched the two of them as they left the room, and over Richard's shoulder, Julie, still sobbing her heart out, gave me such a feline smile that I swear I could see the canary feathers sticking out of her mouth.

Julie was smart, and by the time she was four, she knew the lay of the land. Her Barbie and Ken had separate bedrooms. Barbie kept her dream house, and Ken left for work. Barbie watched a lot of television and drank "grape juice," and Ken worked late every night. Barbie and Ken never kissed. She made that abundantly clear when Lucy brought a boyfriend home to meet the Ashmores, and Julie saw Lucy give him a quick kiss after a get-to-know-you family dinner. "Why'd you do that?" she asked.

Lucy laughed. "Because I like him."

The men seemed not to be paying attention, but Peggy had come up, and of course my dear mother-in-law had to throw in her two cents' worth. "It's a grown-up thing, Julie. Ladies and gentlemen kiss each other when they're in love."

"They do?" said Julie, and her childish voice fell into one of those moments when it seems that all conversation has stopped and everyone is listening. "How come you don't kiss Daddy, Mommy?"

Not, of course, *Why don't you kiss Mommy, Daddy?* Her voice had an uncanny echo of the past, as if Francie had come back to mock me. That moment of hearing my hated sister in my daughter was so traumatic that I don't even remember what transpired to smooth over the horrible awkwardness of the silence. I remember being in shock, so much so that later that evening I consumed an entire bottle of Jack Daniels before I calmed down enough to go to sleep.

It took longer than a drunken night to forgive my daughter. I never was quite convinced that she hadn't meant to needle me.

During the week, she pestered me so much— "Where's Daddy? When's he coming home? I want Daddy to call me. I want Daddy to tuck me in. I want Daddy to kiss me good night —" that it was a relief, even the way things were, when he walked in the door each Friday evening.

She was his problem until Sunday evening.

But then... he started disappearing for hours on the weekends. And when I called him in the evenings in New York, to tell him an estimate on the car or find out where he had put something, often I couldn't find him in. During the weeks when he was back home, working from his office, he often called to say that he would be home late – but he was not working late at his office.

This time, I was not stupid. This time, I kept notes of dates, times, excuses. It didn't take long for the pattern to emerge... Sunday mornings when he said he was going to church with his father (as if!), Wednesday evenings until ten. I wondered if she was married too, but I didn't care. I didn't care at all about the other woman, who she was, why she felt it necessary to sleep with my husband.

All I cared about was that this time I wasn't going to burn the evidence up. I was going to wait until I had enough, pack Julie up, and leave that perfect Ashmore atmosphere forever.

No way was Richard stopping me this time.

I bided my time, kept my suspicions to myself, kept out of his way... and then, two weeks before Christmas, it all collapsed. It took only that one phone message, and someone who forgot to call him at the office.

"Richard," a deep male voice, and one that might have seemed attractive to me if I hadn't taken a vow of chastity, "group's off tonight. I've got a patient who looks like she'll go into the evening, and Tom is tied up in court. I'll try to reach the others about next week, but with the holidays, who knows. Give me a call at the hospital, though, we have to talk about the Luke study. It's your turn to lead."

I must have played that message twenty times, trying to make some sense of it. Whatever "group" was, it accounted for those Wednesday nights (I sadly waved goodbye to my fantasies of charging Richard with adultery). So he was meeting with some men to study something? Why had he been so mysterious about it? And who or what was Luke?

I spent hours that day searching his desk there at the house, scrutinizing his address book, rummaging through his room. Other than an old box of condoms (unopened), I found nothing of interest. I even managed to bring up a schedule on his computer, but he had no suspicious entries. All the while I searched, I kept turning that name over and over in my mind: Luke. Luke. *Luke*....

And then it hit me, all in a flash.

Matthew, Mark, Luke, John.

Bible study?

And those Sunday mornings …was he going to *church*?

Now Richard had never been religious; in fact, he had always said that, if God existed at all, He had long since walked away and left the universe to run on its own. Peggy was a devout Catholic, and Philip was a devout Episcopalian, but Richard had been even less interested in organized religion than I was. Daddy, the fanatic ex-priest, had resigned himself to my permanent fallen-away status, and he had hardly squawked when I had Julie baptized as an Episcopalian. (Which I did because the Catholics made the parents show up for classes before they'd allow a baptism, and the Episcopalians were, like, whatever.) Richard hadn't been interested in her baptism at all. So why was he now studying the Bible?

I said nothing to him when he came home that evening, other than to tell him that he'd had a call that his meeting was off. He registered no guilt, no surprise, and he said nothing about the fact that his desk was in disarray. But he didn't tell me about the Bible study either. However, a couple of days later, I noticed a study outline on his desk blotter… a subtle way of telling me to mind my own business.

"So what's the deal, do you think?" I asked Lucy at our Saturday lunch. She had graduated and come back to Williamsburg as an associate in a law firm. It had taken us a year after the twins ran off, but we had finally made up and things were good between us again. I knew that she talked to Richard far more than I did… she had dinner with him at least once a week. She was his best friend, and she was mine. She was the only one in the world I could ask.

"Why don't you ask him?" she suggested. "Going to church is not exactly a social disease. He's not ashamed of it."

"Then why won't he tell me himself?" I fiddled around with my fork. "I mean… why was he so secretive about it?"

"Maybe," said Lucy more gently than usual, "because it's very personal to him. Think about it. Why do most people turn to God?" And when I didn't answer, because I couldn't think of a single reason why I should turn to God after the mess He'd let me make of my life, "Richard knows he let everyone down, Di. He let himself down. He's been wracked with guilt over Francie and over you, too. I think he went looking for forgiveness, and he found peace."

I seized on the only part of that I could face. "He admitted it? About Francie?"

"No." Lucy took a deliberate sip of her tea. "But I know him. Stop waiting for him to confess, he's never going to do that. But—" she studied me for just a moment, "maybe it's time you forgave him. I think – if you did," and now she hesitated, "he might forgive you too."

That struck me so hard that for a second I thought I might pass out. Surely Richard had never told her… but of course, he hadn't. He would never tell anyone. I looked at her, and I saw those eyes, just like Daddy's, just like mine, studying me intently. Oh, of course, typical Lucy, she was trying to read my mind, figure out why I was reacting so…. I tried to look nonchalant, and not as if Richard had anything to forgive me for.

If nothing else, the revelation of Richard's newfound spirituality shook me up. It drove home to me, hard, how little I knew the man whose name and address I shared. True, I knew things the rest of the world didn't know… that he was a fanatic about refolding the newspaper after reading it, that he misplaced his pager at least once a week, that he was one of the few men alive who didn't worship the Three Stooges… but I really didn't know the man anymore.

For Richard had become a man. In fact, I thought ruefully to myself one night, having a last shot of whiskey before bed, as he worked late at his desk only a room away but a universe distant, he had grown into the sort of man who would have been my downfall if I hadn't lived up close and personal with him all these years. Although he told me next to nothing about his work, I knew from the responsibility he was given that his superiors at the firm thought highly of him. I knew from his paycheck that they were rewarding him in the best possible way. I listened to him talking to the contractors who were doing work on the stable block, and it was obvious from the authority in his voice that he knew exactly what he was talking about and they knew it too. When he and Philip got together, in the few times I saw the senior Ashmores, I saw that Philip now regarded his son as an equal.

And women found him attractive. At a command performance at the firm Christmas party, to which Richard took me because he couldn't think of a good excuse not to, I saw more than one woman appraising him. A couple looked at me in consternation (yes, ladies, a wife really *did* go with that wedding ring), and one tried outrageously to flirt with him, gauging just how far she could go before I reasserted my ownership.

I couldn't tell, as a couple of his fellow architects sized me up, if Richard experienced the same awakening about me. For the first time in years, I realized that I was still an attractive woman. I was polished, sophisticated, and educated. I dressed nicely, I had a pretty face and a good figure, and I was a good conversationalist. Men actually desired me.

Except, of course, for the man who took me home that night, thanked me politely for accompanying him, and then went into the spare bedroom he used as his own and shut the door.

"I had more sex than this when I was single!" I wailed to Lucy at lunch.

"Stop talking about sex so much," said Lucy shortly. "I haven't had a date in months." The boyfriend hadn't lasted too long. Partly, it was her schedule. Sixty-hour weeks had become the norm for her, just as they were for Richard. "I don't know. Buy yourself some lingerie and seduce him. He's not made of stone."

I said bitterly, "This is Richard Ashmore we are talking about, isn't it? Yes, he is."

Lucy steepled her hands under her chin. "Di, you know what Mr. Spencer told me before the Berenson trial? There are no unwinnable cases. Sometimes, you have really stupid juries, but that just means you have to work harder. Same principle here. There are no unseducible men. You have a stubborn one, but you just are going to have to work at it a little harder. I mean," she thought about it a moment, "look at Dominic. Here's a monk, sworn to chastity, devoted to God, and it took your mother one evening and all she had to do was flutter her eyes at him and off he went. Richard can't possibly be as tough as that."

"I don't know," I said dubiously.

"Give it a try," Lucy urged. "Really, Di, just do it. Just show your husband…" and now she hesitated. "Show your husband you love him."

We looked at each other in a moment of perfect understanding, because, after all, we both knew the problem with that.

"One other thing," said Lucy, after the silence grew too long, "knock off the booze. You aren't fooling me, and I'm not breaking any confidences when I tell you that you aren't fooling him, either. He worries about you being alone with Julie all day. He doesn't like you driving Julie around."

I blew up at her. "How dare you! Julie is perfectly safe with me!"

We didn't speak for a couple of weeks, but I did try to cut down.

Something had to give. I had to act. We had existed three long years since Francie, six long years since our estrangement, and we couldn't live the rest of our lives this way.

The direction I took amazed even me, at first.

Richard came home one Friday evening – a couple of days before our seventh anniversary – and I had made his favorite meal. I had foisted Julie on Lucy for the night, and I had prepared the scene with music and strategically lit candles. I had gone to the spa that day for a manicure, pedicure, and excruciatingly painful bikini wax. I had taken a long, luxurious bath. After college I had started wearing my hair in a French twist, but that evening I took it down and let it brush around my face and neck. I dressed in one of the outfits he used to like me in: simple knit shirt with no bra, filmy black skirt that floated around my legs, ankle bracelet, bare feet. Underneath, the skimpiest thong Victoria's Secret had to offer. I looked *hot*.

I put new Egyptian cotton sheets on my bed and fluffed up the pillows.

Richard seemed taken aback. "What's the occasion?" he asked.

"No occasion," I said merrily. Maybe he'd forgotten; we hadn't celebrated an anniversary since our first. "I just felt like it. Go put that briefcase down and get comfy. Dinner will be ready in a couple of minutes."

He looked at me as if I had lost my mind, but maybe he was tired of the silence too. He did exactly as I asked him – placed his briefcase on the desk he kept in the alcove of our family room, went to his room and changed from his oxford shirt and khakis and loafers (what a yuppie he had turned into – but he'd always been one, I just hadn't wanted to see it). In a few minutes, he came back into the kitchen, in jeans and polo shirt, his eyebrows knit together warily. I forestalled his question by handing him a Merlot that one of his fellow architects had given us for Christmas.

He took it with an I-don't-know-what-you're-doing-but-I'll-go-along-with-it-for-now look.

"Dinner's ready," I said gaily, Miss Suzy Homemaker, and set in front of him a freshly tossed salad with a homemade vinaigrette, *coq au vin*, vegetables from Peggy's garden, and just-baked rolls.

I drank ginger ale, which I loathed, and I was dying for something stronger. But I needed all my wits around me, and I knew he was still a little upset about the dent I had put on the side of the car a couple of days earlier when I had misjudged the distance between the edge of the road and the Ashmore Park mailbox. I had to ignore the siren call of that whiskey bottle in my bedroom. *No unseducible men*, I thought. *Hold on to that thought. Remember that he used to be so hot for you he couldn't keep his hands off you. Remember that sex with him was better than any shot of whiskey ever was.*

He enjoyed the dinner and wine, and, after a couple of minutes when I knew he was trying to figure out what I was up to, he even talked to me a bit about his current project. I asked his opinion about the aftermath of the Gulf War – like I cared – and we gossiped about the senior partner of Lucy's law firm, who had left his wife for one of Lucy's fellow baby lawyers, a former Miss Roanoke. We talked about the pros and cons of starting Julie on swimming lessons during the summer. He even – gasp! – asked me what kind of cabinetry we should look at for the kitchen in the remodeled Folly.

I felt a pang. This was real married conversation. Husbands and wives were supposed to talk to each other like this. Seven years of marriage, and I couldn't remember the last time we'd really talked.

I cleared the table, and he shocked me by saying, "Relax, Di. You worked hard over dinner. I'll take care of the dishes." And he did – rinsed them off, put them in the dishwasher, and scrubbed the pots and pans. When he finished, I told him firmly that he could just leave his stupid computer alone for one night, and he said, "Sounds like a plan." He followed me out to the just-repainted family room, settled down with his Merlot on the newly-covered sofa, and even smiled at me.

Good enough. Time to drop the bomb.

"I want to have another baby."

I had thought it through carefully. Julie would start kindergarten in the fall, and if I knew one thing, it was child care. Peggy had hinted broadly that Julie needed a sibling, and it had occurred to me that, not only would it be a good thing for her, but it would benefit Richard and me, as well. After all, having a baby required some basic preliminary bedroom activity, and the physical intimacy might lead to communication beyond "Please pass the butter" elsewhere in the house.

Plus, I'd gone almost six years without sex, and Richard, I was now certain, hadn't been with anyone since Francie. He had to be going as crazy as I was.

If pregnancy was the price I had to pay, so be it.

Well, I took him by surprise, that was for sure.

He put his wine glass down in a very measured way, the kind of precision that may make for great architecture but makes a wife want to knock his head in.

"Diana," he said, and I could tell that I had thrown him for a loop, he was trying to marshal his thoughts, "Diana, are you pregnant?"

I had anticipated that question, and I knew I deserved it. Still, I felt myself flushing. "No," I said, "no, I'm not. But I'd like to be."

He stared at me blankly. "Why?"

Why? I had rehearsed this. So I gave my little speech. How Julie needed a brother or sister, how I thought he might enjoy a son, how I was more mature now and ready to handle motherhood. How a baby might bring our family together. I recited it all, in my brave confronting-Richard voice, and all the time he stared at me as if I were some stranger asking him for a sperm sample.

And while I talked, his mind raced. I knew that lightning fast Ashmore mind, I'd been its captive for too long. I knew that he was combing through all the implications, twisting each one inside out and examining the impact on the balance of power in our marriage. It must have occurred to him that he stood on shaky ground. Up till now, he'd held me by his threat of claiming custody of Julie, and because he had covered his tracks on Francie.

But this wasn't about Julie now, or about Francie. This was about us. A wife was asking her husband, very reasonably, to make love to her. On no grounds, moral, legal, or human, could Richard turn me down.

So he stalled. He pointed out, equally reasonably, that Julie was about to start kindergarten, and I was about to be free of constant child care. Perhaps we could consider my getting a job, or I could go back to school, or I could join Peggy in her volunteer work....

I interrupted what promised to be another endless discussion of why he was right and I was wrong. "Richard, I want another child."

"Diana," Richard said, the man of intellect and rationalism, anything to keep from being the self-righteous bastard who wouldn't take care of his wife's sexual needs, "you hated being pregnant. You hated every minute of it. You hated the way you looked, the way you felt—"

"Oh, that." I waved my hand airily. "I was twenty years old, what did you expect, earth mother stuff?" Yes, that was exactly what he had expected – someone like his damn mother, thrilled speechless to be reproducing. "I'm older now. Sure, I hated it, who wouldn't? But it's not forever, and look at the prize you get at the end. Besides—" and before he knew what I was doing, I slipped onto his lap, straddling him, "getting there," I purred, "is all the fun."

Before he could think of one more stall tactic or say one more reasonable word, I put my arms around his neck and I kissed him.

And, before his brain could remind his body how despicable and deceitful and all-around unworthy I was to be an Ashmore wife, his mouth kissed me back, one hand covered my breast, the other pulled me closer, and the Standing Stone of Ireland sprang immediately to life beneath the thong.

Well, some things hadn't changed. He was still, hands down, the best kisser I'd ever known, and I was swept away with nostalgia and even – hallelujah! – hormones. Oh, it felt so good to be in a man's arms again – and this was a man now, with a man's body and a man's confidence and authority – it felt so good to have a man's tongue in my mouth again, tasting me as if I were the most precious elixir – and I could taste the Merlot – it felt so good to feel his fingers on my breast, tweaking my nipple.

I never knew what "swoon" meant before then, but I wanted to swoon from the feelings that came flooding back. I wasn't a girl now. I was a woman, with a woman's body and a woman's desire, and I wanted a man to touch my body, to feel warm skin to skin, to feel him sliding into me, filling me. I'd forgotten how damn good his hair felt beneath my fingers, and I thought I'd forgotten, but I hadn't, how much he liked it when I licked his ear and kissed my way down the side of his neck. He was breathing harder than when he came in from an evening jog, and beneath me, he was hard and heavy, hot right through his jeans.

Oh, God, it was going to happen. He was going to take me, and the long empty years would end, he'd look at me again with desire and love, we'd have life and laughter and fun in the house again….

And if it meant that I had to give up my body's sovereignty to grow a perfect little Ashmore, that in nine months' time I had to lie in a delivery room, pushing nine pounds of a perfect little Ashmore out into the world, well, I'd take it. Maybe this time he'd show up and hold my hand.

I pulled back for a moment, and I don't know if I started to take off my knit shirt, or if he did, but somehow both of us were pushing it over my head, and it floated back down in front of the sofa. He put one hand warmly on my back, and he leaned forward and suckled a nipple into his mouth – there was my devout breast man again, and I wondered if he noticed that they were a little larger than the last time he'd seen them, before Julie – and I thought I would melt right down into him, because his mouth was tugging on all my senses right down to my womb, and whole *galaxies* were cart wheeling behind my eyes, and I thought I was going to come, right then, right there.

He was about to bust the zipper on his jeans.

This was going to be a *great* night.

He switched breasts, and his other hand slid gently up my leg and under my filmy skirt to the thong, and I sighed in happiness, because his mouth felt so warm and exciting, and his fingers felt incredible, and I felt so alive, and the nightmare was about to end. And then I said it. God knows why I said it.

"Take me, Richard," I whispered. "Take me, it will be so wonderful, it will be like it always was, think of how you liked to be inside me, you always said it was the most welcoming place in the world, think of us making a son, it'll be like the night we made Julie—"

He went completely still – his mouth, his hands, the Standing Stone of Ireland.

I froze.

He sat up so fast that I toppled off him sideways onto the sofa and then onto the floor. I landed hard on my butt, and for a second I could hardly believe what had happened, what I had said. I glanced up, not even wanting to breathe, afraid to say one more word, and he was leaning forward, breathing hard, staring down at the ground, his hands clasped together, his knuckles white.

This had to be fixable. *No unseducible men.* Lucy had been right. We were too close to finding each other again; we couldn't screw this up, not now, not when the end of all the loneliness and coldness and silence was so close....

"Richard...." I said softly, and I knelt there on my knees before him, bare breasts and all – and oh, how they tingled, how alive they felt – and I let my hand trail up his blue-jeaned thigh to his crotch.

He lifted his gaze from the floor, and I couldn't help it. I recoiled at the sheer fury in his eyes. He rose to his feet, and I swallowed hard, my heart beating so fast that I thought he had to notice.

He picked up my shirt and dropped it on my still outstretched hand. "Put that on."

The flatness of his voice said that he would not brook any defiance. The shirt was inside-out. I straightened it, my fingers shaking, and pulled it hastily over my head. As soft as the cotton was, it scraped over my well-used nipples, still erect from the pull of his mouth, and I thought I was going to jump out of my skin.

He watched me as I smoothed the shirt down. I remained kneeling; I couldn't have stood up if my life depended on it.

"Richard," I whispered. "Richard, please."

Oh, God, it had come down to this. I was going to have to beg. This was his revenge for what I'd done. Francie hadn't been the ultimate humiliation, after all. He was going to make me beg for him.

But all wasn't lost yet. I could see that he was still aroused. The Standing Stone of Ireland hadn't gotten the message that I was toast.

"What are you up to, Diana?" he said, and his voice sounded strange. He was having to fight all his instincts, which were telling him to lay me right down, strip everything off my body, and make love to me until we forgot everything that had happened.

"I told you," I said. "I want us to have a baby. I want us—" I had to swallow hard. "I want us to be married again."

"This isn't a marriage," Richard said roughly. "A child deserves better than that – to be brought into the world under circumstances like these."

Oh, God, was he going to go all idealistic on me? "Richard," I said, and I tried to sound sweet and reasonable, "the circumstances could be better, but don't you see? Making love will help make them better! If we wait for the perfect time, it'll never get here."

I put my hand on the sofa and bore down hard on the cushion to help myself stand up. I felt wobbly and shaky. He was standing absolutely still, watching me as if I were a dangerous chemical that might blow up in his face at any second.

I reached out for his arm and stopped, stunned, at the look in his eyes that said that it wasn't worth my life to touch him.

"This is what you wanted," I said, and my voice was starting to sound desperate. All I could see were more years of lonely days and empty nights ahead of me. "When we were growing up, when we were dating, that's what I always heard from you, how someday we'd live here at Ashmore Park, and you'd be an architect, and I'd be your wife, and we'd have children. We'd be a family. You've got it, Richard. You wanted me to be your wife, the mother of your children. Well, now I want that too."

He said nothing, but he never took his eyes from me.

"I'll do whatever you want," I said. "You want children, I'll spend the next ten years barefoot and pregnant." What a hideous thought. I noticed that his eyes immediately dropped to my bare feet and the little gold chain gleaming seductively around my ankle. "You want me to play the part of Mrs. Richard Ashmore, I'll play it to the hilt, I'll be the best architect's wife you ever saw. You want me—" I had a sudden inspired idea— "you want me to forgive you for Francie, I forgive you. That's all in the past, it's all behind us. I just want the future with you."

There. That ought to appeal to him. Lucy said he was all into forgiveness these days.

"Well, well, what a generous offer," my husband said softly. "You'll forgive me. You'll play the part of Mrs. Richard Ashmore – leaving aside the fact that it isn't a part, you *are* Mrs. Richard Ashmore, you've had seven years to get used to that. And, in the spirit of this newfound resolve of yours, you'll let me take you to bed and get you with child – do I have that right?"

I heard the stiletto in his voice, but he had me pinned to the spot with his gaze. I nodded slowly, and I can't remember when I have ever been so afraid. Even finding Daddy dying at the piano doesn't compare to that moment.

"And how long will your resolve last, Diana?" he said. "Till your father comes home and crooks his little finger? How long would it take you then to scrape my child away?"

Oh God, oh God, *oh God*. I felt as if he had landed a chop right across my throat. "I wouldn't," I whispered, "I wouldn't—"

"Sure you would, Diana," he said, "it'll be even easier the second time around."

So much noise was crowding my mind, I had to grope for words. "I wouldn't – I *couldn't* – believe me, Richard, once was enough, I wouldn't—"

"You know what I've always wondered? Why didn't you get rid of Julie too? Maybe you were so stoned that year, you didn't pay attention to anything that was going on, even if it was inside you – I'm betting you lost count of the weeks, and then it was too late. So you ran home to me, hoping I'd get you out of the mess you'd gotten yourself into."

That was so close to the truth that I couldn't clear the noise to answer him.

"I'm grateful," he said, "that you can't count. Julie is the treasure of my heart, and God knows she deserves better than the mother she got. She deserves better than someone who sleeps away half the day because she's hung over from the night before."

His voice was so brutal that I was starting to get mad.

"I don't trust you, I won't trust you again. You yelled at me once that you hated the idea of having a child with me, that you'd never let me get you pregnant again. And you know what, Diana? I believe you. Oh, you might sing a brave song right now, you'd go to bed with me tonight, and I'm sure it would be spectacular, because you were always spectacular in bed. But I also believe that, in a few months, when Dominic comes back and you're feeling sick and out of sorts and you're not liking what pregnancy is doing to your pretty body, you'll abort this child just as easily as you did the first one."

His eyes rested on me with a cool hardness.

"So I'm declining your offer. To put it in words that you'll understand, I do not wish to have a child with you. I won't take the chance that I will ever get you pregnant again. I want children, true. But I'll pick a mother for them who wants them too, and not just as an excuse to get laid."

And he turned on his heel, and walked over to his desk.

I stood there, utterly humiliated, feeling sicker than I had felt in my whole life. I saw him turn his briefcase towards him, saw him popping the locks with those long fingers that had explored me so gently just a few minutes before, saw him reach for a couple of folders. I didn't even feel my feet moving, my mind didn't say to my legs to walk over to him, to fight for him, but somehow I crossed the room.

I stood beside him, and he glanced over at me impatiently, because the great Richard Ashmore had said his piece, he'd put me once again in my place in the dust, and to him, that was that. I had no rights. I had no claim on a happy life. I was – I was nothing to him.

"I thought you were all into God these days," I said. "All into being a good Christian and grace and mercy and all that. Doesn't the Bible say—" I groped for a hazy memory of a long-ago Gospel reading at Mass, do unto others, seventy times seven, whatever— "aren't you supposed to forgive others if you want to be forgiven yourself?"

He didn't like that one bit, I could tell, although a sanctimonious soul like his should have loved being able to dispense forgiveness to his harlot wife.

"It also says something about not sleeping with your father," said Richard, and deliberately started reading the paper in his hand.

I slapped it out of his hand.

"It only happened that once, you self-righteous bastard, so don't you get on your high horse with me! If you'd paid any attention to me, maybe nothing would have ever happened. I got drunk, I made a mistake. It's not like I went out of my way to be with him. You don't do one damn thing to be a decent husband. If you're so into your Bible these days, then maybe you'll remember that you are bound by God to act like a husband, and that includes that thing Peter said about it's better not to burn—"

"Paul."

"Whatever! And while we're on the subject of incest, let's see what it says about fucking your wife's sister—"

"It just says not to marry her while you're alive."

I saw it in his eyes. *Don't tempt me.*

"Well, I'll bet it says plenty about adultery, Richard Ashmore! As I recall, David paid through the nose for fooling around with his little floozy, and I could take you to the cleaners and take Julie with me! After all, you really don't have any claim on her at all! You're damn lucky I haven't told your parents the truth about Francie—"

"And you're damn lucky I don't make a bigger deal out of your drinking," Richard interrupted. "You're damn lucky I haven't taken your car keys away from you, although I'm about to, because I do not want you driving Julie anywhere. Our insurance is going through the roof. Let's see, that latest dent makes how many in the last three months? Boy, you are shaking, aren't you, Diana? You must need a drink pretty damn bad right now. You're well on your way to becoming a raging alcoholic, darling. Better watch out – you'll ruin your looks if you aren't careful." He looked at my face with a careful, examining contempt. "It's already starting to show – you're getting hard lines around the mouth, Diana, you're going to start looking a hell of a lot older soon, you'll be able to play Medea—"

I smashed his face in.

He moved in that last microsecond, so my fist plowed up across his jaw into his cheekbone instead of his nose. I caught the edge of his glasses and shattered them, and my engagement ring sliced across his jaw line and cut his face open.

We stood there for a couple of disoriented seconds – I don't know who was more shocked, him or me. He had a look in his eyes of horror, and I think it was horror at how far he had gone, horror that he had goaded me into this. I don't know what was on my face. I hope to God it wasn't a smile.

Slowly, he took off his shattered glasses and put them down carefully on his desk. He put his hand to his face where I had cut him, and looked at the blood that came away on his fingers. Moving like someone in a dream, he reached over to a box of tissues, pulled one out, and lifted it to the cut.

He was going to have a hell of a bruise, maybe even worse than Francie's. I'd always regretted that I didn't get to see the bruise grow nice and dark on her face.

He said quietly, "Don't ever do that again, Diana."

I stepped up to him deliberately, and now I did smile. I felt what an evil smile it was.

And I spat right in his face.

He stared at me hard, not moving, and I felt my smile fade. I felt the adrenaline that had so wildly pumped through me start to drain, leaving me sick and afraid. I saw my dreams and my future, the hopes I'd had, all in tatters.

He wiped the spittle from his face and said, "What an unspeakable bitch you are."

Then he walked past me over to the staircase. A few seconds later, I heard his bedroom door shut upstairs, and I heard running water.

I stood by his desk, I don't know how long I stood there. Except for the sounds coming from his room, the house was completely silent. No Julie singing her little songs, no Richard playing a CD while he worked, nothing. It was like my life stretched all out before me, devoid of music and laughter, devoid of happiness.

I looked around the room I had worked on so carefully. I saw the walls I had painted, the crown moldings I had installed, the furniture I had rescued and made lovely and comfortable. I had worked so hard on this house, and for all my effort, I had failed to make a home. I had failed to make a family.

Without any hurry, I walked over to the hall mirror and took stock. I was mussed up – his hands had made short work of my hair earlier, there on the sofa. My lips still had that kissed look to them; my cheeks were bright red. And – I was imagining things – I saw a couple of tight lines down around my mouth.

I rubbed at a small crease and deliberately relaxed my mouth until the line faded into nothingness. Then I went back to his desk, picked up his unfinished Merlot, and upended it in his briefcase.

I went to my bedroom and pulled the bag of weed from underneath the bras in my lingerie drawer. I found the three-quarters full bottle of Jack Daniels that I had stashed under the bed. I helped myself to a couple of lines from the bag in my jewelry case. Then I picked up my shoulder bag and my keys. I was not going to spend the night in my lonely bed, not tonight.

Still no Richard downstairs. I went over to his desk to survey the damage and saw, to my satisfaction, that the Merlot had soaked into the leather and completely ruined the contents. The bruise on his face would heal, but this damage was permanent – like the damage he'd done to me the weekend of the Valentine's Day dance, like the damage I'd done a month later at the clinic. Like the damage that had started the day I'd lied to him, told him I'd been with Daddy, told him that Julie was not his child.

God, what a relief it is, to finally say it. I can't even keep my lies straight anymore. I'm surprised I ever could.

The truth is a lot easier.

I remember standing there, looking down at his ruined briefcase, listening for – what? Did I hope that he would come out, confront me once again? But he wouldn't. Richard had gone too far, and I suspected maliciously that he was confronting himself about that right then. I suspected that he had shaken himself down to his sinless soul.

I'd finally smashed his face in. I wished I found it more satisfying.

The Merlot had soaked into a pack of cigarettes in the briefcase. I picked the pack up, shook off the excess drops, and dropped it and his engraved lighter into my shoulder bag. I'd given him that lighter for Christmas the year before. Well, I was taking it back. I was taking everything back.

I went out through the kitchen through the utility room, and opened the door to the garage. I was just opening the door to my car when I looked across, and I saw the room on the other side of the garage, the room that would have made such a perfect music room for me, the room that he had taken over for his stupid model airplanes.

In the years we'd been back in Williamsburg, he had never asked me if I missed my piano.

I went into the room. I hadn't been in there in years; I usually passed by without a second thought as I brought groceries in the house. But now I entered, and I looked. Where I would have hung delicate, feminine artwork, he had tacked schematics. When I would have placed flower arrangements, he had put workbenches that held model airplanes in all stages of construction. A laptop computer sat open on the nearest workbench, its screen dark. And, in the middle of the room, where my piano should have been, stood a doll house.

Except that it wasn't a doll house. It was a model of the remodeled Folly that opened from the front – very clever – and showed the interior that he had designed. I looked at it, and around it, and in it. It was very grand – more than we could afford, but perhaps Philip was going to dispense money from the Great Lakes shipping trust. The whole house wrapped around a great room that opened up three stories. It had rooms labeled *dining room, kitchen, Julie's room, master suite, nursery.*

Nothing for *Diana's room.*

I wasn't to occupy that master suite. I wasn't to help fill that nursery.

He must have been working on this at night. He must not be able to sleep any more than I could.

I don't know how long I stared at it.

Then I saw a toolkit lying beside the model, the toolkit that he had used to assemble this little masterpiece.

I picked up a hammer.

I smashed the computer screen. I smashed every one of the model airplanes, from the little biplane that he had built as a flight-dazzled six-year-old to the five-foot wing he was currently constructing. And then I smashed the model to bits. That took the longest, and made the most noise, and brought him out to the garage just as I had reduced it to rubble.

I threw the hammer to the ground and walked past him as he stood there, frozen in shock.

I don't know what I intended when I left Ashmore Park, but I was on a high. I felt alive again; I felt more like Diana than I had felt in years.

I drove over to Virginia Beach because it was sufficiently far away from Williamsburg that I wouldn't see anyone I knew. I found a club, thought it was too tame, and found another. This time, I had a blast.

I was twenty-five years old, in my prime, and I'd never looked better in my life. I met a lot of men willing to buy me drinks. I met even more who asked me outside to roll a few and lie on the beach and sink into the oblivion of the night. I found one who gave me what I hadn't known with my husband for six long years... that surfeit of sensation and relaxation that came with a really good orgasm.

What happened, and how many times it happened, I don't really know. I was stoned and drunk, and I did not care.

I sobered up on Sunday afternoon, and I went home to confront my destiny.

My head ached, and I felt drained, and I was busy counting days because I suspected, uneasily, that I'd had a lot of sex at the wrong time of the month. (That, of course, being the reason I'd picked then to make my approach to Richard.)

I tried to unlock the front door, and my keys didn't work. I scarcely had time to work it out in my head – he'd changed the locks – when who should open the door, but Mr. Perfect himself.

"You're not coming in, Diana," he said, and came outside, closing the door behind him. He had one hell of a bruise and stitches on his face where I'd cut him.

I had no idea what to say to him. I had no idea where to start apologizing for my appalling behavior, and I couldn't believe he'd actually locked me out of my own home.

At least, he hadn't thrown all my stuff out on the lawn.

As it turned out, I didn't have to worry about apologizing.

Where the hell have you been....

Back at your old game again, I see....

My God, Diana, you reek of sex....

The most miserable excuse for a mother I've ever seen....
You're a menace to Julie and a menace to yourself....
Someday you're going to wrap yourself around a tree....
You don't live here anymore....

I really didn't want to fight, I hadn't the energy, but I was damned if he was going to accuse me after what he'd done. And what he had manifestly refused to do.

So I ripped back at him.

You never talk to me....
What am I supposed to do with myself all day....
I'm going crazy here....
I worked damned hard on this house, what do you mean, I don't live here anymore....
How dare you call me a bad mother....
You self-righteous bastard, you don't know the first thing about forgiveness....
You won't make love to me, I'm too young to give that up....

One moment there, when I said that, I saw something flash through his eyes, a startled recognition that we both felt the same horror at our actions, the same hunger for each other, but then it died, and we never had another chance.

He said slowly, "Who was he?"

"I don't know," I said wearily, "I don't think he told me his name."

A long, long silence.

"Next time," said Richard politely, with that terrible courtesy, "get his name. I'm not accepting paternity for any more bastards you accumulate."

That shocked me down to my toes. "Is that what you think of Julie?"

"No," he said, "Julie's mine. I made her mine. But I don't have it in me to do it again, Diana."

I counted again fast in my mind, felt a little better about my numbers this time, and my mouth, totally disconnected from my brain, said, "Fine. You don't have to. I'm going home to Daddy."

Another long, dreadful silence.

And then—

"How very convenient," said my husband, and packed my car in record time.

I spent Sunday night back in my old bed, back under Daddy's roof, where Richard and I had made love when we and the world were young.

Daddy, flying home from another tour, was ecstatic to have me home again, and started talking about training my voice again.

I felt relieved to be away from Richard's presence (although I did miss Julie). I'd been released from the prison of marriage, and I was determined never to go back, not even if he broke down and begged.

Richard, it turned out, had no intention of begging.

Two weeks after he threw me out, he sued me for permanent custody of Julie.

I cried for days.

Then I got tired of crying, and I stewed.

Then I got mad.

Then I got a lawyer.

You want war, Mr. Perfect?

Fine.

War.

24

Eyes Only

ENTER USER NAME:
    CDSB
    Enter password:
    Aural13Gem$

Meg St. Bride knew all about computers.

Her earliest memory was of cuddling against her dad while he programmed around her. He didn't like people coming in to disturb him while he worked, but he hadn't minded her, as long as she didn't talk his ear off. She'd climb up on his lap, or he'd lift her up, and she'd snuggle against his chest and watch him writing *open loop* and *end case*.

Even before she could read, she was playing games on the computer. Later, he'd shown her how to download music (*Don't tell your mother*) and how to burn her own CDs.

She'd been only six when he presented her with her own laptop. Of course, he had put every parental restriction possible on it, and her Internet time was strictly monitored, and she wasn't ever supposed to IM with anyone she didn't know personally, blah, blah, blah….

She didn't mind the restrictions, at least not for a few years. She'd really liked having a bond with her father that no one else in the family shared. He'd taught her some basic programming (*Hello, world!*), and he'd shown her some of the cooler things a daring hacker could get away with in cyberspace.

With the caveat, of course: *Don't get caught*. And then, mindful that he was her father and was supposed to set a good example: *In fact, don't do it at all*.

Wink, wink.

She'd been his star student. So, to reward her, every year he had up-graded her to a new laptop for Christmas.

But not the Christmas *after.*

Not ever again.

So now her laptop, bought for her that last Christmas, the last good Christmas ever, was hopelessly obsolete. Slow, slow, slow… fit for the junkyard, really.

She didn't want to ask her mother. The less anyone or anything re-minded Laura of *the day,* the better. She didn't want to bring on one of those headaches that made her mother's eyes go dark with grief and drained the color from her face.

Not that *the day* ever strayed far from her mother's thoughts. Or hers.

She'd nearly asked right before her mother left on that cross-coun-try trip to see her family. Laura had been so worried, so full of guilt about leaving her, that she could have played on that guilt and asked for anything, with a high probability of success.

But she hadn't.

Because, two nights before Laura left, Mark had brought home a familiar briefcase. The briefcase that Cameron St. Bride had handed to his corporate counsel before he waved away that last elevator. The briefcase that had made it down all those flights of stairs and out of the tower to safety.

The briefcase holding her father's laptop.

One of the last things he had ever touched.

Do you want it? Mark had asked her mother, and Laura, pale, with those tightened eyes, had shaken her head.

I do! I do!

But Meg had absorbed more from her father than world-class hacking skills. She had learned to bide her time, to watch, to wait for the opportune moment. So she said nothing after her mother left for Virginia. She left the briefcase languish, seemingly forgotten, for an-other week, in the corner of Mark's office. Then one evening, she sur-prised her uncle with some fresh-baked cookies while he worked on financials, and, on her way out to the family room to watch some TV, she adopted an off-handed tone. "Hey, Mark, can I use that?"

"Use what?" He sounded irritated.

Meg swallowed and bit her lip, and said nothing.

Predictably, her uncle looked up and noticed her distress. "What's wrong?"

"Well, it's just – Dad—" and she swallowed again. Okay, no point in being *too* obvious. "He used to – you know – upgrade me, for Christmas, you know—"

Mark came over to her, numbers momentarily forgotten. She felt his arm go around her shoulders, and he looked at her with concern that she knew she didn't deserve.

His voice was reassuring, comforting. "I'll have one of the IT guys get it ready for you. Can you wait a couple of days?"

Meg nodded. True to his word, Mark took the laptop to St. Bride Data to get it backed up and scoured of all business data and any – *inappropriate* files that his brother might have left on the hard drive that his daughter shouldn't view.

And then he kept forgetting to bring it home.

Only after the night of the alarming phone call from Laura, when Meg had heard her reserved mother fall apart without warning, did Mark finally remember. He pulled the briefcase from the trunk of his car, and then – Mark being Mark – he made a big production out of handing Cameron St. Bride's laptop over to her.

Like it held the meaning of life, or something.

Throwing a "Thanks, Mark!" over her shoulder, Meg raced upstairs to her room, settled the laptop on her desk, and looked over her new toy. It wasn't *new* new, of course; her father had bought it just a few weeks before – well, *before*, and it had been top-of-the-line then. Of course, it too was obsolete now, surpassed by ever-evolving technology, but still it had all the bells and whistles that her father had put on it *before*.

It would do. For the time being.

She spent several hours setting everything up. Email, IM, Degas' *Green Dancer* as her wallpaper, her screen saver of family photos – and then she had to transfer all her games and files from her old computer.

It took *forever*.

Finally she had it just the way she liked it, just in time for Emma to call her down to dinner. She had to endure almost an hour of polite conversation over one of her aunt's gourmet meals, since Emma insisted on dining like they were royals, but finally she was excused, and she raced back up to her room.

Time to go exploring. See what treasures her father had left that Mark hadn't deleted.

An hour later, Meg looked around her room, a stranger in her own home, her world, her identity, everything she knew about herself tumbled into the abyss.

Gone forever, like the tower that had entombed her father.

A letter written to Mark in the late hours of September 10, over the ocean en route to New York. Saved in a hidden folder, overlooked by the tech who had cleaned off the machine for her use. She'd seen the date stamp and opened it, and read it, and the world had changed.

She might live to ninety, but she would never forget those words.

This man has cast a long shadow over my marriage. His name is Richard Ashmore, and he is an architect in Williamsburg, VA. He is married to Laura's sister Diana, and he is Meg's biological father.

Shock. Horror. Disbelief. And, in the midst of her instinctive protest – not true, not true, *not true!* – the thought that why would her father have written this to his brother if it wasn't true?

And the realization that, if he *had* told the truth to his brother —

Then her mother had lied to her.

Do not immediately assume the worst about Laura. She did not trick me or cheat on me, and she did not betray her sister. She is not Meg's biological mother.

Her mother had lied to her.

You're in shock. Close your mouth, get some coffee, and keep reading.

He'd meant those words for Mark. Meg closed her mouth and kept on reading.

She needed our marriage because she needed money. I knew, and I didn't care. I knew, the night I met her, that she was the finest woman I would ever meet, and I was willing to take her any way I could get her. I've never changed my mind. I'd do it again.

Her mother had lied to her.

Francesca got some kind of infection and went into premature labor. By "premature," I mean that Meg was three months early, weighed only two pounds, and had very little chance to live. She was immediately put into intensive care with round-the-clock monitoring.

Her mother had lied to her.

But no, not her mother.

When she wasn't singing, she was sitting at Meg's side in the nursery, willing the baby to survive. I asked her why, when it wasn't even her child, and all she said was "I had to." It never occurred to her to leave and get on with her own life.

The B, Francesca – she'd come out of her. Laura St. Bride, the woman she'd always called Mommy, who kissed her and grounded her and rocked her through illness and grief – not her mother, not really. She hadn't grown inside the young Laura, who had gotten pregnant and run away with her boyfriend, who had refused to get married because marriage was only a piece of paper.

Francesca did not want to admit she even had a child. She seemed to think she could wish the child away if she never saw her. It fell to Laura to bring Meg home and give her a name.

Her mother had lied to her.

And, she realized with a sickening crash, so had her father.

She told me that she was planning to take the child and leave. She has never gone into detail, but I sensed she felt Francesca was a danger to Meg.

Danger? What danger could a mother be to her baby?

But then – that lady down in Houston, the year before, who had drowned her kids. All of Texas was still reeling from that.

I asked how much money she had, and she said, with a defiance that showed just how young she was, that she had $33 but she'd survive.

She'd heard Mark and Emma downstairs, arguing about remodeling the kitchen. Who cared about a kitchen? Who cared about anything at all?

Dr. Ashmore was a true gentleman – polished, urbane, and not above blasting me to bits about my behavior. Like an idiot, Francesca had blabbed everything to him, and he gave me a dressing down that, believe me, put Dad's lectures in the shade. He told me that I was a damn fool if I couldn't tell the difference between a girl like Laura and a girl like Francesca. He also warned me that, if he ever heard of anyone in the family mistreating Laura or Meg, he would tell his son about Meg and force a paternity test.

Dr. Ashmore? It had dawned on her, only gradually, that this must be her grandfather.

No, not her grandfather. She knew her grandpa. His name was Matthew St. Bride and he rode a motorcycle and owned a bank and slipped her money for candy whenever he saw him. And she was the apple of his eye. She had cried and cried when he died in his sleep. She still missed him.

I didn't doubt him for a second. Something about him made you believe every word he said. He said that he did not want to hurt Laura or disrupt Meg's family life unless it became necessary, but he left no doubt in my mind about the alternative. I promised to mend my ways and take better care of Laura, and I meant it. I did not want my marriage to fail over Francesca.

WTF? Her dad and Francesca?

I could not pretend that Laura had nowhere else to go – Dr. Ashmore told me flat out that he and his wife would take her and Meg to live with them if I didn't shape up.

She had a grandmother too. Not Kate St. Bride, who took her to tea like a real lady and set her up with an easel in the studio. She had splashed watercolors all over a canvas and all over herself, having a hugely good time while Kate painted a real painting beside her.

Richard Ashmore never gave up his paternal rights because he never knew he had any. He could invalidate the adoption and sever my rights. Given my track record, I won't father a living child. Even if I did, Meg is mine. I don't give a damn about his rights. He will never get his hands on my daughter.

Her family wasn't really her family, after all. She'd grown up, the center of the universe, the darling of their hearts, and never questioned her place in this Viking brood. *I'd never miss your recital, Emma* had said after flying in from New York. *How could I forget my best girl?* Mark had said, and brought her back a present from a business trip. *You're the best thing I've ever done,* her father had said, and twirled her around.

You are the light of my life, her mother had whispered, tucking her in bed.

Lies, all of it, and liars, all of them. She wasn't one of them. They were all strangers to her.

Well, all but one of them. She had a connection to one. She was the niece of the girl who had sat at her side and willed her to live. Who had tried to save her from unknown danger on $33, who had married her father so that she could keep her.

And she was connected to this unknown man in Virginia, this Richard Ashmore.

She had decided, right then and there, to confront Mark. He'd tell her the truth. Or he'd lie so badly that she'd know anyway. He wasn't a great liar.

Not like her mother and her father.

But when she charged downstairs, ready to break up that stupid argument about the kitchen, she heard words even more shocking. Even more world-shattering.

Why her mother sometimes had that other-life look in her eyes.

Why her mother cared about her father, but never seemed to be *with* him.

Why she had never met her mother's sisters, or her father, or this cousin she already couldn't stand.

She didn't bother to confront Mark, who would probably just get mad at her for reading a private letter written for his eyes only. She'd get nothing out of him.

Nothing more.

She crept back upstairs and sat on her bed, lights off, thinking.

Through the night, she sat there.

Mourning the loss of her old world, her old life.

Trying not to think about *him*.

Trying not to imagine her mother with *him*.

Unable to escape that indisputable truth.

Her mother had lied to her.

At dawn, she pulled her laptop to her.

Her father – her *real* father, the man who had swung her up on his shoulders, laughed at her knock-knock jokes, taught her how to hack into every computer but his own – her father had also taught her how to get the jump on any opponent.

Do your research.

Gather your intelligence.

Know your enemy.

She opened the search engine and typed her search term.
Richard Ashmore.

End of Ashmore's Folly Trilogy: Book One

To be continued in:

All That Lies Broken
Ashmore's Folly Trilogy: Book Two

Et Cetera

Historical and Architectural Note

Acknowledgments

About Lindsey Forrest

Historical and Architectural Note

On September 11, 2001, the company I worked for lost 16 people: 15 in the Twin Towers and one on American 11. Like so many of us, I found myself haunted for years by the recurring specter of the falling towers, and eventually I found myself integrating the events of that day into a rewrite of a novel I had been working on for many years.

When I decided to write about that September morning, I determined up front that I would not alter history and I would not take anything from those who died that day. So where to place Cameron St. Bride in his final hour?

- Not in the Pentagon where, despite the horrendous damage, only (*only!*) 120 people died on the ground. I felt that, given his business interests, I could have made a believable case for his presence, but I did not want to alter history by adding a victim or dishonor someone by having my fictional character take his place.
- Not on United 93 – he would not replace one of those 39 brave passengers who saved so many more with their sacrifice.
- Not on any of the other three planes, since the passenger lists encompassed a finite group of people. Besides, someone like Cam St. Bride would certainly not be traveling commercially if he could help it, and I knew that the presence of a private corporate jet would come in handy later on. (Plus, I work across the street from the airport where St. Bride Data keeps its jet!)

So that left the Twin Towers. *Which* tower became a matter of character, because Cam would have assessed the situation and gotten the hell out of Dodge (the South Tower) as soon as he saw the smoke pouring from the North Tower. Most people in the South Tower did not know that a plane had hit the other tower, since the damage occurred on the side of the building away from them, but they certainly saw the smoke and knew that *something* had happened. In fact, even in the North Tower, many people did not know that a plane had hit the tower; they thought a bomb had gone off.

Those who had worked in the World Trade Center in 1993 remembered the earlier bombing, and many people chose to leave as a precaution. Although the occupants of the South Tower didn't know what was coming at 9:03 a.m., and in spite of the building announcement that everything was under control, many decided to evacuate and thus survived. Because of this precaution, the South Tower saw far fewer casualties, even though the strike zone in the South Tower was lower and the hit destabilized the building more severely (which is why it fell first). The cool and rational Cam would have disregarded the announcement, factored in the disruption to his travel plans of the emergency vehicles already gathering on the streets, and left the building as quickly as he could.

Then I learned about the restaurant at the top of the North Tower. No one in the restaurant at 8:46 a.m. had a chance once the hijackers rammed the 767 into the building. All the stairwells were blocked, and the elevator shafts were either damaged or completely destroyed, so no one above the 91st floor made it out alive. Add in that the Windows on the World restaurant was exactly the sort of place where Cam St. Bride might conduct a breakfast business meeting, and his final destination was decided.

Remember that, even though there is an *official* total number of victims from the towers, no one really knows how many souls were actually trapped there, because very few bodies were recovered intact and many, many remain unidentified to this day. So Cam St. Bride does not replace anyone.

The one liberty I took was the timing of the last elevator. It actually left at 8:40 a.m. that morning, six minutes before AA 11 struck. I placed the last elevator at 8:43 a.m. so that Cam might reasonably still be on the phone with his brother, but gave his corporate counsel and the briefcase time to escape.

There are so many references on 9/11 that it is hard to single one out. I have included a brief bibliography at the end of this note.

✑

On a happier note, I have also included a bibliography for anyone wishing to learn more about Thomas Jefferson, Monticello, and his influence on Virginia architecture. I have always had a passion for old houses, and in writing this had the fun of creating not one but *four* houses.

Ashmore Magna and Ashmore Minor are both based on James River plantations; the "minor" house, once owned by the Colonial

Williamsburg Foundation but sold to a private investor after 9/11, is close to the old city, while the other, privately owned by the same family since its building, sits in lordly splendor in Fluvanna County. Both are beautiful homes. The interiors are my own invention and come from a plethora of sources. The Folly is based on one of the smaller Newport summer cottages (smaller being relative, as these cottages were magnificent mansions). I based Richard Ashmore's renovations, which remove the worst of the Gilded Age excesses, on numerous different houses.

There are so many books on Jefferson's architecture, Monticello, and Virginia plantation homes that, again, I have listed only a smattering. I have focused the Jeffersonian bibliography on his relationship with Sally Hemings, as that has the most relevance to the story of Richard Ashmore and Laura St. Bride.

Several years ago, the original photographs for the Guinness/Sadler book, *Mr. Jefferson, Architect*, taken by Desmond Guinness, went up for auction on Ebay. Guess who was the lucky winner?

Lindsey Forrest

9/11 Bibliography

Botte, John. *Aftermath: Unseen 9/11 Photos by a New York City Cop*. Collins Design, 2006.

Brill, Steven. *After: How America Confronted the September 12 Era*. Simon & Schuster, 2003.

Carter, Abigail. *The Alchemy of Loss: A Young Widow's Transformation*. HCI Book, 2008.

Der Spiegel. *Inside 9-11: What Really Happened*. St. Martin's Press, 2010.

DiMarco, Damon. *Tower Stories: An Oral History of 9/11*. Santa Monica Press, 2004.

Dwyer, Jim and Flynn, Kevin. *102 Minutes: The Unforgettable Story of the Fight to Survive Inside the Twin Towers*. Times Books, 2011.

Frankel, Max. *September 11, 2001*. Andrews McMeel Publishing, 2001.

Glanz, James, and Eric Lipton. *City in the Sky: The Rise and Fall of the World Trade Center.* Times Books, 2003.

Meyerowitz, Joel. *Aftermath: World Trade Center Archive.* Phaidon Press, 2006.

Murphy, Dean. *September 11: An Oral History.* Doubleday, 2002.

National Commission on Terrorist Attacks. *The 9/11 Commission Report: Final Report of the National Commission on Terrorist Attacks Upon the United States.* W. W. Norton & Company, 2004.

Photographers of the New York City Police Department (Author), Christopher Sweet (Author), David Fitzpatrick (Author), Gregory Semendinger (Author). *Above Hallowed Ground: A Photographic Record of September 11, 2001.* Studio, 2002.

Torres, Francesc. *Memory Remains: 9/11 Artifacts at Hangar 17.* National Geographic, 2011.

Jeffersonian Bibliography

Brodie, Fawn. *Thomas Jefferson: An Intimate Biography.* W. W. Norton & Company, 1974.

Gordon-Reed, Annette. *The Hemingses of Monticello: An American Family.* W. W. Norton & Company, 2008.

---. *Thomas Jefferson and Sally Hemings: An American Controversy.* University of Virginia Press, 1997.

Monticello Bibliography

Adams, William Howard. *Jefferson's Monticello.* Abbeville Press, 1983.

Beiswanger, William L. *Monticello in Measured Drawings: Drawings by the Historic American Buildings Survey / Historic American Engineering Record, National Park Service.* University of Virginia Press, 2001.

Beiswanger, William L., Peter J. Hatch, Lucia C. Stanton and Susan R. Stein. *Thomas Jefferson's Monticello.* University of Virginia Press, 2001.

Frary, I.T. *Thomas Jefferson, Architect and Builder.* Garrett and Massie, 1950.

Giordano, Ralph G. *The Architectural Ideology of Thomas Jefferson.* McFarland, 2012.

Guinness, Desmond, and Julius Trousdale Sadler, Jr. *Mr. Jefferson, Architect*. Viking Press, 1974.

Howard, Hugh. *Houses of the Founding Fathers*. Artisan, 2007.

---. *Thomas Jefferson: Architect*. Rizzoli, 2003.

Lautman, Robert. *Thomas Jefferson's Monticello: A Photographic Portrait*. Monacelli Press, 1997.

Lay, K. Edward. *The Architecture of Jefferson Country: Charlottesville and Albemarle County, Virginia*. University of Virginia Press, 2000.

Leepson, Marc. *Saving Monticello: The Levy Family's Epic Quest to Rescue the House that Jefferson Built*. University of Virginia Press, 2003.

McLaughlin, Jack. *Jefferson and Monticello: The Biography of a Builder*. Holt, 1998.

Nichols, Frederick Doveton. *Thomas Jefferson's Architectural Drawings: With Commentary and a Check List*. University of Virginia Press, 2011.

Stein, Susan R. *The Worlds of Thomas Jefferson at Monticello*. Harry N. Abrams, 1993.

Wills, Chuck. *Thomas Jefferson: Architect: The Interactive Portfolio*. Running Press, 2008.

Virginia Plantation Homes Bibliography

Blackley, Pat. *Virginia's Historic Homes and Gardens*. Voyageur Press, 2009.

Brodie, Steven, Leroy Phillips, James Waite, and Richard Yen. *Carter's Grove Drawings*. The Historic Buildings Survey, U.S. National Park Service, United States Department of the Interior, 2007.

Carson, Cary, and Carl R. Lounsbery. *The Chesapeake House: Architectural Investigation by Colonial Williamsburg*. University of North Carolina Press, 2013.

Edwards Betsy Wells. *Virginia Country: Inside the Private Historic Homes of the Old Dominion*. Simon & Schuster, Inc., 1998.

Gleason, David King. *Virginia Plantation Homes*. Louisiana State University Press, 1989.

---. *Plantation Homes of Virginia*. Portfolio XVII. Private commission of limited edition photographic prints. No. 914 of 1100 copies. (Author's personal collection)

Green, Bryan Clark, Carter Loth, and William M.S. Rasmussen. *Lost Virginia: Vanished Architecture of the Old Dominion*. Howell Press, 2001.

Masson, Kathryn. *Historic Houses of Virginia*. Rizzoli, 2006.

Roberts, Bruce. *Plantation Homes of the James River*. University of North Carolina Press, 1990.

Wenger, Mark R. *Carter's Grove: The Story of a Virginia Plantation*. Colonial Williamsburg Foundation, 1994.

Acknowledgments

Even though writing is a solitary activity, no one writes a novel in a vacuum. I have been blessed with the support of my husband and family as I prepared to publish this story.

For everyone who supported and encouraged me, I thank you all! Especially:

- my editorial team: Diane Mumpower, Pam Murphy, Marianna Stone
- my mentor: Patricia Burroughs (who told me long ago that she really liked it and had only one teeny suggestion -- rewrite a first-person narrative into third person! Much easier said than done! But it made all the difference.)
- my web team: Ricardo Nunez of TailoredWP.com, who set up two of the web sites, and Jeev Sen who set up the other and launched me on my way with WordPress
- my web logo designer, Christie Gucker of Provoke Something LLC
- my cover designer, Robin Ludwig of Robin Ludwig Design, who guided this newbie through the procedure of designing the perfect cover
- my tax advisor, Erik Kinard
- my dearest friend John Cope (1953-1994), who came to the rescue when I said that I needed the most obscure opera ever written (and who actually had the referenced recording in his own collection!)
- my parents and siblings, who supported me in my writing, and especially my sister, who was always only a phone call away with love and encouragement
- and, of course, my husband and daughter, who knew that seeing my story in print was my deepest desire.

Lindsey Forrest

About Lindsey Forrest

Lindsey Forrest began her career as a famous novelist in fourth grade, entertaining her classmates at recess with short stories about her favorite TV shows. A few years later, she discovered Georgette Heyer, Mary Stewart, Victoria Holt, and other romantic suspense/Gothic authors, and angsty heroes (who might or might not be cold-blooded murderers) replaced her first imaginary friends. In eighth grade, she wrote her first five novels, full of shameless references to *Gone with the Wind* and replete with kidnappings, ladies in peril, heroines who took no prisoners, and the original Richard Ashmore*.

And UST?** Oh, yes. Even though, at her tender age, she had no idea what that meant.

After college, she sadly realized that she needed real money to pay the rent and buy food, so she went to work as a lead writer/editor for an international information company. She now spends her days writing about the scintillating world of income tax, saving her energy at night for a world where everyone has more important things to think about.

When she isn't daydreaming at work about her next chapter, she is reading on her e-reader (never leave home without it!), stitching her way through her never-ending stash of needlepoint canvases, and collecting shoes, handbags, dolls… you name it.

For outtakes, news about future projects, pictures of her cat Max, and anything else she can think of to throw out there on the Internet, visit Lindsey at her web site: www.lindseyforrest.com.

* These will never see the light of day. They are locked away in a trunk for all eternity.

** Unresolved Sexual Tension, for the uninitiated.

Book Club Questions

Book Club Questions

1. The title of the book is *All Who Are Lost*. In what way does this apply to the living as well as the dead? Who among the living characters can be described as "lost"?

2. The author states on her web site that the chapter titles often carry secondary meanings. Pick a chapter title, and describe its hidden meaning.

3. Richard and Laura have different ideas about what really transpired at Ash Marine eleven years before. What do you think, and whose perceptions come closer to reality?

4. Diana was the only witness to her mother's death off the Irish coast in 1970. She has told only Richard, and he has sworn to keep the secret. What do you think happened? Did Dominic really kill the girls' mother?

5. The first thing Diana says about herself is that she is "no good with the truth." What is Diana lying about? Can we believe anything Diana says, or is she an unreliable narrator?

6. Richard resurrected and rebuilt the Folly at Ashmore Park. In what way does this mirror the rebuilding of his life after his own great folly?

7. What do you think lies beyond Julie's playacting?

8. The author has stated her interest in the Myers-Briggs classification of personalities and discusses the character types of the main characters on www.ashmoresfolly.com. Richard (INTP) and Laura (INFJ) are very compatible, where Richard and Diana (ISFP) are not, even though they too share only two of the four major characteristics. Based on MBTI classification alone, why is Laura better suited to Richard than Diana?

9. Richard and Lucy seem to be exact opposites, and Richard finds Lucy's tendency to meddle irksome, to the point where he describes her as "Miss Infernal Busybody." Why do you think they remain so close when they have such different personalities?

10. Richard's hero is Thomas Jefferson, and he shares many of the same characteristics, tastes, and flaws. Like Jefferson, Richard is a religious skeptic. How does the crisis precipitated after his great failure change him?

Coming Soon

Spring 2015

LINDSEY FORREST

All That Lies Broken

Ashmore's Folly Trilogy: Book Two

*Laura and Richard now stand face to face, equals,
at the same place in their lives,
living in their own world, safe from past and present.*

*But the world is not so easily forgotten.
Even as Richard begins to dismantle
the past that blocks the future,
he struggles to open his heart to
the last love of his life.*

*Laura finds herself chafing against
her place on the edge of her lover's life,
wanting so much more,
no longer willing to settle for less.*

*An estranged wife will not give up her desire to smash
the man she hates so fiercely.
A younger brother will not relinquish
the rage against the man who bested him
in life and in death.*

*Secrets unravel. An identity is uncovered.
A world begins to shatter
when a reporter stumbles across Laura's secret.
Then a sliver of bone resurfaces in
a place of great sorrow
and a ghost of a girl rises from the past....*